[ JYZE OF THE HEAVENLY YEAR ]

Annals of The Jyze Age
________________

Jyzeburst

Jyzemelt

Jyze and Jyze Alone

Jyze in Love

Deep Jyze

The Jyze Millennium

Jyze of the Heavenly Year

Scat Jyze


Also by G.P. Sandefjord
________________

Have Mercy (a novel)

# Jyze of the Heavenly Year

G.P. Sandefjord

Annal Seven of The Jyze Age

Draft printings 2020, 2022, 2023




Cover art by GPS
Published by House of Jyze
ISBN 978-0-9964173-8-9
Library of Congress CIP Pending
www.HouseOfJyze.com


The War Memorial inscription quoted on
page 145 was written by Archibald MacLeish.

For Ticiang D. and Zoelie B.

-- The three of us, we're inseparable!

    There comes a time when you
realize that everything is a dream,
and only those things preserved in
jyze have any possibility of being
real.

                    -- James Salter
                    [but he said "writing"
                     for "jyze"]

# BOOK A

# [ Jyze of the Black Horse ]

-----

1

-----


    Jyze comes shivering back at the Heavenly moment.
Or almost -- within a minute or two.
    Freezing my ass off on the cement steps of a bank.
Twenty minutes to midnight, maybe closer to fifteen.
Gazing out at a spot on the eastern horizon.  An
extremely skinny sliver of new moon should be rising
there, in theory.  So skinny it'll almost certainly be,
or maybe already is, what's known as a "dark moon."  The
sky's clear and a few stars are visible -- despite all
the city lights -- but no moon's in sight.  And that
will likely remain the case for another day or two.  But
-- no matter.  I'm here welcoming it.  The Year of the
Horse is officially about to begin.  My Heavenly Year.
    Temperature's right around freezing.  That's one
reason this old J-stick is sputtering a bit.  Another is
that it's rusty -- hasn't been used for some thirteen
months.  Needs a good internal cleansing with warm
water.  As it is I have to shake it every couple of
sentences to start the flow again.
    Got a good spot here, though.  Also in view about
half a mile to the east and slightly to the south, the
north end of south hill.  The big former marine hospital
riding the prow of the hill some four hundred feet up is
ablaze with historical-landmark floodlights.  "The DC
castle."  A couple of blocks behind that the Z-spouse
sleeps, presumably, in our same old apartment 203.
    -- Strings of firecrackers crackling and cherry
bombs booming.  It must be midnight.  Directly across
the street lies the parking lot for A-mart, the big
Japanese department store that dominates the area.  The

store's closed for the night, but strings of red holiday
lights are still shining and a Year of the Horse banner
is gently rippling outside the main entrance.  To the
east and north of the store the streets of the Asian
quarter are a good deal livelier than usual for this
hour on a Monday night.  Yet they're still not all that
lively.  Most folks who celebrate this occasion -- it's
the start of the year 4700 by Chinese count -- are
probably doing it at home.

Me, I'm still this dubious Cawk guy in worn jeans
and cheap sneaks.  Also for this special occasion I'm
wearing a scruffy tan winter jacket with a hood, a bulky
sweatshirt beneath that, other layers -- and a long
ponytail too, though it's entirely hidden by the raised
hood.  I'm huddled up against a big column.  Jyzing
away.  Thrilled, just wanna say, to be back at it.

No one's walking by.  A lone worker is visible
through the front window of A-mart, pushing a mop in the
produce section.  The in-store restaurant's yellow neon
sign is glowing, but the joint itself, like the rest of
the store, is closed for the evening.

And I'll soon be shutting down myself.  For the
night, I mean, and also for this first entry of the
first jyze cluster.  As for my life as a whole, I've
decided I might as well act as if I have one more full
cycle of the Chinese zodiac left in me, which is to say:
sixty more years.  Why not?  The wisdom of the day says
the current maximum length of a human life span is
roughly two such zodiac cycles.  I'll hope for the max
and try to be prepared for whatever's in fact to be.  An
actuarial chart I saw a few months back gave me
somewhere between eighteen and twenty-four more years.

But this year is the one.  I won't try to explain
why now, but this year I get to hang loose.  Be crazy.
Not worry too much about consequences.  Be grateful for
my good fortune in lasting this long, yes, and be
suitably humble, but primarily wig out in jyzical
fashion.  Because this is my year of celebration.  (As a
guard walks by quietly behind me, paying me no attention
and giving me no grief.)

[ Jyze of the Heavenly Year : Black Horse ]

*

(Or no, I spoke too soon.  Had to talk him out of moving me along.  It's his job to make sure no one "loafs around on the site."  To my surprise he said I could go ahead and finish up whatever the heck it is I'm doing here but then I should scram.  And I can say right now I'll be doing just that, scramming, very soon.  Because I'm freezing to the bone, that's what.)

-- But first I want to note that a few changes have gone down since "The Jyze Millennium" gasped its last, which was about four hundred days ago.  A small band of foreign terrorists, mostly Saudi religious fanatics of highly reactionary stripe -- but certainly not lacking in extreme provocation by us -- launched a spectacular suicide attack involving hijacked airliners crashing into large and fully occupied buildings on the USAn far coast.  Security's still tight everywhere, right down to this second-tier regional bank outside of which I sit (but the building itself is owned by our local plutocrat #2, currently the world's third-richest person, so he's got lots else to worry about protecting).  The globe's heating up, yes it is.  And in more ways than one. "Interesting times."  Crucial times.

And changes have occurred in my personal life as well.  The important pieces are still in place, or at least seem to be, by which I refer to love, job, health, and jyze itself.  Some of the lesser ones no longer in place I'll get to, I expect, later.  Or won't.  For, to repeat, this year jyze doesn't have to worry about being too scrupulous about such things.  It happens or it doesn't; it makes it into the J-book or it doesn't.

(Steamy breath too.  Right from the start I've viewed these pages and everything else through pulsing mists or I could say through vital chi energy that powers my very own jyze cloud-making machine.)

*          *

Roughly twenty-two hours on and I should be a lot warmer here.  And safer too -- maybe.  At this moment two young guys are being arrested about twenty feet to my right.  But they're sitting on the outdoor front steps of the hideaway building and I'm sitting on a chair just inside the lobby.  And between us stands a set of locked glass doors and a pull-across iron-grillwork gate.  ("If you fail to show up in court," I overhear, "you'll be"  -- and then the grim details.)

Behind this arrest scene, the Mardi Gras crowd streams by beneath the totem pole and in the gaze (plenty stony) of the great chief whose name was bestowed upon this city a century and a half back.  (In these pages, however, I'll continue calling it Jyze City or, for short, J-town.  No diss of the chief is intended!  -- And I'll be abiding by the same jyze rules as in previous volumes.)

A year ago tonight a riot took place out there. "Roving black gangs beating up whites."  One white death.  Outraged media (white).  Police (mostly white) supposedly did nothing to stop the carnage.  Vows by the authorities (mostly white) that it wouldn't happen again this year.  Reams of self-defeating publicity about all this.  But the police presence out there right now is massive.  And has been since last Friday.  Cops on bicycles, horses, vans, rooftops.

As is only apt in the new USA.  Today's big headline: FBI warns a new terrorist attack is imminent -- might even happen today -- maybe even at the hyper-securitized Winter Olympics currently taking place some seven hundred miles southeast of here (but, from a world perspective, just a quick hop over the mountains) (and this afternoon the small portion of those mountains visible from south hill was gorgeous, as was the range to the west, vivid, massively snow-covered in surprising new ways after a series of storms over the past week).

But today's not just Mardi Gras, it's also, still, Chinese New Year's Day.  It's approaching the end of the same day that began a few minutes after the "dark moon" viewing last night.  And it's the second day of the Mardi Gras-associated Feast of Fools in certain parts of Europe.  And we're in the first full year of the Gregorian twenty-first century, or so lots of people are saying.  By their lights the new century didn't begin until the 9/11 attack last fall.

Here at the hideaway building a few people are coming in and out via the side entrance. No one I've recognized so far. And yes, I'm still "officing" in my same old ninety-square-foot room ("Jyzer Ink World Headquarters") up on the second floor. And pinned to the flap on my shirt pocket is a button showing the Chinese character that literally means "word temple" but denotes "poetry." I'm hoping maybe a little of this button's magic will rub off on these pages.

Warm in here, cold out there. Unlike every other Mardi Gras I've attended in this city, not much female flesh is showing. Few recognizable costumes. Special beads and necklaces seem to be the main celebratory accoutrements. Lotsa macho dudes in shorts and short sleeves and goosebumps. Whoops and laffs and police whistles. Sirens. Horns. Persistent beer whiff despite the cold. Last time I peeked out the side door -- about seventy feet down the L-shaped hallway -- four TV trucks were parked in a row nearby, their extendable towers erect and throbbing some four stories up.

-- The Asian quarter (AQ) was fairly quiet when I walked through it on my way down. No lions dancing, darn it anyway. (A janitor just appeared and asked in hostile tones, "You work here?" The guy's seen me numerous times before but he's usually been zonked out of his mind. -- Here in J-town's historic quarter, HQ. Ground zero of city history, of the Great Fire, of the salvaged "old town" of cobblestone square -- also known as "the stone" -- and home of more than a few stoners. And in the darkened nineteenth-century city entombed a story below street level in much of the quarter, the ghosts must be stirring on a night like this.)

And so a night for celebration -- let's do it! We fools! -- And we newly one more year aged. Which would be all of us, and officially so, given the right officials and the right administrative zone. For that's how it is the Chinese lunar way: everyone becomes one year older on New Year's Day (or technically six days afterwards). Not only is spring starting right in the middle of what we USAns in general know as winter but it's your birthday and everyone else's.  So let's party!

Z-wiff did some of that last night.  Her book group met at our apartment and the theme was Chinese New Year. Takeout food and such.  I contributed red good-luck "Lai See" envelopes, each containing a "rare coin" as is traditional, more or less.  The coins in this case were cheapo Mardi Gras medallions from the party store; I doctored them up with "Lucky Horse Year" on the front side and, on the back, blue cartoon bubbles with pithy sayings similar to the ones found on old-time Valentine's candy: "Let's Hoss around" and "Neighsayers rule" and like that.  And: making this a truly exceptional week for celebrating, Valentine's Day itself is day after tomorrow.  (And I'm only marginally ready for it.  Could be in big trouble if I can't conjure up something good real quick.)

-- But jyze comes first this year, it's just gotta. And even more so here at the start.  Hopefully I've adequately prepared Z for this.

"No standing -- just keep walking."  No standing? It's the newly enhanced national security state!  (That was a cop on horseback, which is to say my kind of cop in this Horse Year.  -- My particular Horse, I should note, is the Water Horse, also known as the Black Horse, representing year nineteen in the sixty-year cycle. It's also called by at least one astrological commentator of the lunar variety "The Horse in the Army."  And for me that's both ironic -- since I've never been in the army -- and apt.  But I'll save the story on that for another occasion.

A few more words about today.  A brief chronology. Up at the first alarm at one p.m., breakfast and newspaper at home as almost always.  Then a drive to the far side of east hill to watch "niece" Kat's hoops team take on a local private school.  I had trouble finding the place -- arrived shortly before halftime.  The Katgrrrl broke a nail early in the third quarter so I saw her in action for all of maybe two minutes. Afterwards she and her mom Betty dropped by our place to

deliver a delayed Christmas present.  Kat stretched out
on the couch with her hand in an icepack, reminding Z of
a certain scene in the movie "Cleopatra."  I gave Kat
and Betty their Lai See envelopes.  And for Kat alone --
she being a fellow Horse person but a Metal one, color
White, born twelve years ago this month -- a special
Horse Year poster.  And then we all slurped on New
Year's noodles, always a must for the occasion.

   -- People running out there now, sirens, flashing
lights, screams.  Another riot breaking out?  Quite
possibly.  Crowd whooping.  Perhaps a baring of breasts
in exchange for beads -- it's becoming a beloved local
Mardi Gras tradition.  Bass lines booming from nearby
clubs rattle the windows here.  (And up pulls a "black
Mariah."  It's met with loud jeers and cries of "Fuck
you!"  But this is the year of venerated law-enforcement
officers.  "Heroes."  Could it be that for this Mardi
Gras J-town style not even "heroes" can be heroes?)

   Clip clop -- six horseback cops in a row.  Crowd's
becoming bigger and rowdier.  Right here behind the
locked gate is a good place to be, yes it is.  Ancient
wood, marble -- the original elevators still in place
and working fine at age one century and one decade.
(Big animalistic roars out there now.  No heavy action
in sight but things are sounding raucous and righteous.)

   -- And it's almost time to venture out that way
myself.  See if I can steer clear of major trouble.
Hike two blocks up the hill and catch a bus home.  Last
one of the night for my route, just as nearly always.
(It's still the case that I usually walk in from the
hilltop but rarely walk home.  It's a kind of de facto
self-prescribed eldercare, could say.  But even if I
were a twenty-something I wouldn't be walking home.
Especially not on a night like this.)


[+2]


   -- In the black armchair for follow-up with a
couple of days' perspective (thus the "+2" up there).

[ Jyze of the Heavenly Year : Black Horse ]

The black armchair where I spend roughly a quarter of my
waking life (and a much smaller but still not negligible
slice of the sleeping part).  In place of springs it now
boasts a stack of newspapers; in place of a seat cushion
it sports several towels.  Yet somehow it's shaping up
into the most comfortable chair I've ever come across
anywhere.  It even looks somewhat presentable.

    A hard worknight -- I'm too tired to rustle up a
full serving of jyze.  But then again this is how it
spoze to be.  So herewith half a portion maybe.

    And I can now say I've caught my first glimpse of
the new Horse Year moon.  Lovely.  Low in the western
sky when that sky was still indigo blue roughly an hour
after sunset (to the east all was black) and just to the
right of, and slightly lower than, the clock-faced top
of the campanile at the west train terminal.  And those
round clock faces were illumined moonlike as well, and
perspectively about the right size to be surrogates or
clones of an authentic full moon.  Cheshire-smile moon,
though, the real one up in the sky was, with the rest of
the cat face of course missing.  Seen as I walked the Z-
woman to the bus stop after our "Valentine's tea" at our
favorite Japanese teahouse in the AQ.

    Just want to say right here I consider myself --
still! -- a very lucky fellow to have such a wife as
this Zoelie B.  Cradling a bouquet of hubby-bestowed
Valentine's gladiolus in her arms and looking oh so very
fine.  So full of life and charm and wit and spunk.  It
was just five years ago this week that the heavens
finally carried out the final steps of their elaborate
long-term plan for bringing us together.  And the
meeting late this afternoon brought on some of the
heightened awkwardness of that very first one -- or
better to call it excitement.  "Strange charm."  By gum
it's still happening for us!

    She'll be away for a training session the next two
days.  Meanwhile I have plans.  Intriguing days they
just might turn out to be.

    Headline story in one of the English-language AQ
weeklies says we Horses face a "challenging" year -- and

especially the males among us.  Turbulent and fast-
paced.  "Avoid dangerous activities" -- if you can!
(Kind of tricky, though, I'd say, since avoidance itself
sometimes turns out to be a rather dangerous activity.
As in, just to cite an instance, avoiding the draft back
in the day.  Not meaning to imply I faced anything much
in the way of that kind of danger myself.)
    I think I managed okay with the Valentine's stuff
for Z.  Yesterday's return visit to the edgeville party
store yielded six usable items, including a campy
spring-action bug-antenna headpiece with a big sparkly
red heart quivering at the end of each antenna.  I even
wore this today -- though not for long -- at the
teahouse.  And Z did marvelously by me as always: a loaf
of strawberry passion bread, a yin-yang card, a nifty
miniature hand-held pinball game.  Also we turned the
fan up on last year's Valentine's display of dangling
red paper hearts attached by strings to the bedroom
ceiling, setting them once again to rapturous swooping
and spinning.  So corny, true.  But the thrill is still
hard to beat when you're both palpitating right there.
    I should mention that the annual Chinese New Year's
card came in yesterday from Evan W., who's employed in
the A-mart produce department across from the bank where
I was sitting on opening night.  And it's a fine piece
of work: a cutting from one of his watercolors.  The
other day Z ran into his wife, Moeko, and she told Z
Evan "liked very much" the card I made for them this
year: a hand-painted "perennial Christmas card" made of
balsawood.  (And I'll just note here that in several
cases card recipients have informed me the post office
sliced open the envelope containing the card, presumably
because to an inspector the short length of pipecleaner
it enclosed (for hanging purposes) suggested a potential
bomb mechanism.  This is also the year of anthrax in the
mails.  Irradiation.  Orange alerts.  Gunboats escorting
our J. City ferries.)
    Some new things around here since jyze last went
down in this room.  Mainly two big acrylic paintings
(canvases thirty by forty inches) I did for Z as gifts

for her own Heavenly Year -- last year -- and one is a
portrait of the woman herself which is hanging on the
wall a few feet behind my right shoulder.  Also creamy
new runner rugs spread atop the same old gray carpets.
Much plant growth and proliferation.  And mostly new
neighbors living above, below, and to the sides, with
only two of the eight other units besides ours occupied
by the same tenants as a year ago.  Among those who've
left are the owner/landlords, Dana and Raphael, along
with their nine-year-old daughter Bethany.  They now
live in a fancier place (which they also own) on east
hill.  And yet they're still our landlords.

One big loss: Z's half-sister Camilla died this
past December.  Camilla was sixteen years older than Z
and the two of them lived together only very briefly and
when Z was an infant, but the shock for Z was still
great.  I met Camilla just once, for an hour or so
during Z's and my Centropolis trip more than three years
ago.  Didn't know quite what to make of her -- a
technofreak of sorts -- at her age! -- and a raving
political libertarian whose favorite book was "Atlas
Shrugged."  Yet she was also warm, friendly, a pleasure
to look at in a Eurasian way (clearly related to Z) and
mondo sparky to talk with, also much like Z.

And ripples of this death.  It happened suddenly,
as with their father twenty years ago, and again before
Z could fly back to Centropolis for a last visit.  As a
result she decided to press her mother, now eighty-six,
to move somewhere near us so we could keep an eye on
her.  And her mother -- still "Mama E" to me -- was
likewise frightened enough by what happened with Camilla
(who was her stepdaughter but again only briefly raised
by her) to agree to do it.  So in September we'll be
returning to Centropolis to transport Mama E out here,
the three of us driving back to J-town in a rental van
which will likely contain most or all of Mama E's
worldly possessions.

Clocks ticking.  Deep of the night.  Soft jazz
playing on my chairside radio for a while, but when the
DJ started yakking too much I flipped it off.  On the

[ Jyze of the Heavenly Year : Black Horse ]

coffee table stands a big brown vase displaying those
same Valentine's gladiolus(es).  Next to them lies an
origami heart Z made for me, some very loving and
seductive words handwritten on it.  I don't even care
how much I undermine anything serious-minded here in
this jyze (huh?  like what?) with displays of my ongoing
sappiness over her.  Must sound like self-congratulation
or smugness or worse as I keep repeating myself on this
over the months and years.  Don't care.  Am fiercely
cleaving to this woman and this life with her.  "New
lease on" -- whoa, gross understatement!
     And before calling it a night I should at least
mention what was going down in the first Black Horse
Year of my life a mere five "great years" ago.  Namely,
I was going down, that's what, down down down the mama-
chute, and emerging into a world at war that bore more
than a passing resemblance to today's.  Not that I'm
saying I was up to noticing this back then.  But at the
moment of my emergence my father was overseas fighting
in that war.  And, as noted in previous jyze annals, I'd
been conceived the standard nine months earlier, more or
less, just hours after the shocking Pearl Harbor attack
-- surely every bit as shocking then as 9/11 was just
five months ago now.  And so for me I expect that in
some sense this second coming of the Black Horse Year
will be a year of very deep -- at times no doubt to the
point of inarticulacy and way beyond -- deja vu.
     -- And one final note.  Two nights ago it was
indeed the riot squad moving in outside the hideaway
building, though nothing much came of it.  And despite a
little tiff at the bus stop between two guys fighting
over a joint of the cannabis type, I made it home
without incident.  And the new terrorist attack warned
about in screaming headlines across the country hasn't
happened either -- but there's still plenty of time for
that.  When people start tiring of the cry-wolf warnings
(as they easily could before much longer) it might even
behoove the managers of USAn internal security to stage
a little incident or two just to keep things hopping.
(Keep things real?  More like unreal, I'd say.)

-----

2

-----

Up on the third floor of the hideaway building.  In
a chair pulled close to the balcony railing in such a
way that I can look down at an angle into my own office
windows giving on the second-floor hallway.  A gap
between the bottom of the half-raised blinds and the top
of a bookcase inside No. 225 allows me to see the brown
armchair where I'm usually sitting if I'm not at the
desk.  The floor lamp to the side of the armchair is
glowing warmly.  I feel a bizarre sense of affection for
the ghostly occupier of that chair, who I imagine is
diligently jyzing away.
     -- It's been a crowded three days.  I'd like to
jyze it all up right now, but that just won't be
possible.  A few strokes for this, a few strokes for
that, and it'll already be time to head on out.
     Very first stroke, today by the Chinese calendar is
what it calls the "Birthday of Humanity."  On this day,
as mentioned earlier, we all become a year older.  Which
means this in at least one sense is my true Heavenly
birthday.  But several other senses of it will be coming
along before the year's over -- equally official and
true in every case but by other measures perhaps more
relevant to this jyze account.
     Meanwhile lots of news.  A massive national energy-
peddling scandal, for instance, is keeping the media
jumping.  "Enron."  Has the corruption of our USAn
corporate system ever been revealed more starkly?  More
juicily?  And our country's supreme leader is off
whomping the war drums in the Far East: Japan now, then
China and South Korea.  A key stretch of geography for

the world as a whole and also, as it happens, for my personal life and for these pages.  And today is Presidents Day so I ought to at least mention what our current officeholder's doing.  -- And now having done that, enough said.  (A jyze-rules exception, or JRX, on naming the energy company up there.  I just couldn't resist.)

Quiet building.  Rainy night.  I'm still damp after walking down from the scope office where I had about thirty minutes' work to do (I'm once again in danger of going broke if the current slowdown lasts much longer).  Before that I was out in the Yuke (UQ, university quarter) watching the masterful and grimly upsetting French flick "The Town Is Quiet."  It's about the early stages of the global-roasting crisis which I figure is now close to passing the point of no return.  (Z-spouse wasn't able to join me; for only the second or third time in our years together I saw a movie alone.)

And I say to all this, yee-ha!  Or better, "Wu ha!" -- "Wu" being the name in Chinese of the "Heavenly Branch" of the Horse Year.  I, for example, was born in the "Jen Wu" year -- "Jen" being my "Heavenly Stem" or "element": Water.

Earlier this afternoon I went out for breakfast with my main informant on things Celestial: June Q.  Her middle name is Kung, same as Confucius, and her family on the maternal side traces straight back across scores of generations to the Sage himself.  So she knows.  But then again she's been in this country more than thirty-five years, so she's sometimes a bit fuzzy on the old-country details.

Yesterday a good time with the high-spirited Kat. Two hours of coaching her in hoops at a high-school gym as Z looked on.  Then a stop for salmonburgers at the usual drive-in overlooking our central J-town urban lake.  Then a viewing of "Miracle at Morgan's Creek" up at the cine-cafe theater in the Yuke -- the oldest movie Kat's ever seen (it came out two years after the previous Year of the Black Horse) and the tiniest movie theater she's ever been in.  Z had to bribe her into going by promising to take her to another movie today, "Crossroads," starring the latest teen sensation, who's actually already post-teen and post-nubile at least to my eye but apparently still highly bankable.

Kat's mom, Betty, is meanwhile off visiting her friend Wanda who's just gotten married. The ceremony was moved up several months because Wanda's been diagnosed with terminal lung cancer: the docs are giving her two years at most. Death's rattling around in our lives more and more these days, it seems -- and it seems that way because that's exactly how it is.

Then Saturday. First, the Chinese New Year festivities at the east station. I wrenched myself out of bed ninety minutes early to be able to attend the last couple of hours. A big crowd including even a fair sprinkling of other Cawks or, as I actually heard a Eurusan man say, "Occidentals." A stage with taiko drumming, Filipino singers, Korean martial artists: a lively cross-section. Saw maybe a dozen friends and acquaintances. Bought a number of low-cost novelty items. Best of all, Joey J., who owns a dry-goods shop in the AQ, recognized me (I often walk by his shop and we wave or nod if he happens to be looking out) and he did a special "Heavenly Year" wall hanging just for me, black Chinese calligraphy on diamond-shaped red paper -- as a gift! It's now taped above my desk in 225.

And finally the meeting with recently discovered second cousins Ron and Karl H. at a restaurant in their hotel near the airport. "The lost branch." Brother Rob, who was also present, had met them twice before during Mentoka trips but this was my first time. Said Ron as he embraced me, winning my undying clan-based allegiance: "So at last we meet Mr. Charisma!" (It seems he got this dubious chunk of hype from brother Jeff last summer.) Several hours of story-swapping followed. Ron's brother Karl would like us all to collaborate on a book about celebrated murders in our ancestral Wachute area, with a crucial chapter of course devoted to our own notorious great-uncle Roar. I found Karl's relish for ghastly crimes a tad excessive --

close to ghoulish -- but probably it's not really that.
A couple of friendly and smart small-town Mentoka guys:
that's what these two were to me.

I passed out Lai See envelopes and also hit the
jackpot: brought along a centennial book about Longdale,
the town near Wachute where Ron and Karl grew up -- and
they'd never seen it before!  Raves over that.  Ron
vowed to conduct some research on the mysterious
Kristian, Roar the murderer's twin brother.  Was he
possibly the one killed in the Philippines during the
Spanish-American War?  Nothing definitive yet.  And he,
Ron, might go up to Turtle Rapids to try to crack the
mystery of exactly what caused the family schism that
kept our branches ignorant of each other's existence for
most of the past century.  The records are all still
there in the former Jondahl store -- it's just that
they're in Norwegian, of which none of us can speak more
than a few words.  (And Ron and Karl regaled us with
tales of their Norway trip.  They're the only two people
we know who've actually visited the tiny burg of
Sandefjords-Stolen in the old Viking fjord country.  In
fact they're the ones who alerted us to its existence.)

They had to fly out early the next morning, meaning
yesterday (Sunday).  Because of the time difference they
both started fading in amusing tandem at about eight-
thirty.  -- But I felt quite comfortable with them.
Liked their humor.  Found them to be less country-boyish
than Rob's descriptions had led me to expect.  Again I'm
thinking this will be just an introduction, with more to
follow in due time about family roots and other matters.
Perhaps, to cite one possible instance, during the
Midwest visit in September to pick up Mama E.

(All this time I've had one foot pressed against
the wrought-iron railing here in the hideaway building
-- pressed lightly against it as I thought, but just
now the nearest post gave an audible little gasp and the
whole railing seemed to wiggle.  I could easily envisage
it crashing down into the atrium lobby.  And all of this
would be captured on security videotape, no doubt, with
me up here probably appearing to give the railing a

shove with my foot.  -- But now I've checked and the
nuts and bolts on the post appear solid.  The railing
shifts about a bit in a certain way when I push against
it but only a few millimeters.  That's not bad for a
building this ancient -- one that just went through a
major earthquake less than a year ago.)
     But still I'll take this boundary jiggling as a
sign it's time to be moving along.  Grab my jacket and
flip off the lamp in the office down there and plunge
back into the rain.


                          [+3]


     -- Three days later, yup, not just the planned two,
but what a day it is.  Talk about auspicious!  At eight
p.m. I stood before one of the two-story-tall flasher
boards at the downtown symphony hall waiting for the big
moment, which was to arrive in two minutes.  I was
optimally positioned as well, with the mist-blurred half
moon weakly shining down in the east-west street
corridor between the hall and the fifty-story bank
building standing across the street to the south.  I saw
the temperature flash up there on the board -- 45
degrees -- and then a series of promos for upcoming
performances, with names and logos of symphony sponsors
intermixed -- and then the temperature again.  No time.
But time was (and is) of the essence.
     In short, today's what I'll dub Grand Palindrome
Day.  And it's gotten some extrajyze notice here and
there, including a box on the front page of today's FAP,
as jyze is still calling it.  (Talking about the former
afternoon paper which switched to morning publication
two years ago; the original morning paper, which also
still exists, is the OMP.)  At two minutes after eight
the time in digitized military fashion would be 20:02
02/20 2002.  Feng-shui enthusiasts say this number is
highly auspicious because of its "significant symmetry."
The last one like it was just over a thousand years ago
and there will never be another, ever, as long as the

[ Jyze of the Heavenly Year : Black Horse ]

Gregorian calendar holds sway (personally I'd give that calendar a century or two tops before it's dumped).

Well, better to miss the big moment anyway, I thought.  The time being military was what put me off. Even for the "Horse in the Army" -- the zodiacal appellation, as noted before, for those born in my year -- things military are looking mighty bad these days. Nor am I saying this is the first such instance.

And now it's three hours after the failed attempt at an "official" -- because electronic and digital -- palindromic sighting.  I'm up in the scope office, the conference room, my scoping work for the night all done. Again it came in at under an hour.  -- But I'll say it's still an auspicious day regardless, and for two completely different reasons, both of which have to do with the lunar calendar.  First, as the traditional stretched-out Chinese New Year's festival continues, it's the lunar birthday of the Jade Emperor, top deity in the Celestial pantheon; and second, since it's the ninth day of the first month, it's also the lunar birthday of the top maternal deity in my personal filial pantheon, which is to say: my mother.  As far as I know, this is the first time anyone ever's observed her lunar birthday.  (How am I celebrating this great day?  This is it right here: the jyze tribute.  -- And in ol' Mom's case I read partway through her babybook and looked searchingly at some photos of her.  My mother was a Metal Monkey Year woman -- probably not an animal she'd yearn to be associated with.  But then that might be the case for most or even all the other zodiacal animals as well.  (And she wrote in my babybook during my second year, "He is truly a wonderful companion."  And in another spot: "He's 25 pounds of TNT!")

So it's the same old scope office, but the security's been beefed up and the place has been redecorated a bit as well.  A truly tacky job, I have to say.  This is perfectly exemplified by what's hanging on the wall about ten feet to my left: a huge silver-framed and black-bordered photo of the major far-coast megalopolis of 9/11 notoriety but with the twin towers

still standing tall at the center.  Black-and-white, a
night view, most of the lights blazing.  "The most
monumental symbols of American capitalism," as I read
somewhere (an idolatrous post-9/11 description in a
mainstream USAn publication).

The new security system in this building here --
alarms on all the doors, a pad into which I must punch
my code when I arrive for work at night or otherwise the
gendarmes will descend in force -- that system, I say,
actually became operative before the twin towers fell.
But the firm's business, and my own as an independent
contractor working solely for one of the firm's members,
has been cut roughly in half by the combined whammy of
the recession and the 9/11 attack fallout.  And the work
I do has been affected even more, because many of the
federal attorneys and agents have turned their attention
to terrorism-related issues (or at least that's how
they're characterized) and are pursuing far fewer normal
grand-jury matters.  Right now most of the federal
agents assigned to this region are off beefing up
security at the Winter Olympics.

So far I've been able to hang on financially, but
I'm down to my last thousand bucks in the bank.  If
things don't change in the next couple of months -- and
it's unlikely they will -- I'll have to either look for
extra work elsewhere or withdraw a good-size chunk from
my "deep reserves," which themselves have already been
reduced by a third owing to the stock-market downturn
after the bursting of the dot-com bubble.

Today our supreme leader delivered a speech in the
far-off land of my only known child's birth.  He called
for "a free, unified Korea," but everyone knows he's
just jiving.  He says he wants good-guy South Korea, our
ally -- my son's homeland and my ex-wife's as well -- to
unify with one of the three lands that constitute what
he himself has dubbed "the Axis of Evil" (Iraq and Iran
being the other two).  Not too likely this will happen
anytime soon.  He's just ducking and weaving a bit to
avoid stirring up too much protest among the good guys
while the cameras are rolling.  Wouldn't want his trip

to look like anything less than a smashing success.

        At home, meanwhile -- our personal one atop south
hill, I'm talking about -- the Z-spouse is becoming a
tad restive.  And understandably so.  The normally quite
sexually attentive G-spouse has been slacking off a bit.
Yet her sense of humor (always splendid except when
suppressed or if her amygdala's working overtime -- viz,
"the mygs are swarming") -- her good humor, I say, is
saving the day.  Last night when I arrived home I found
a "cake" on my chair.  It was made of photocopies on
pink paper of the "Jyzedays of the Heavenly Year"
calendar -- which I made for her last month -- pasted
together into something like a large round layer cake.
And it had written on it in superimposed fashion: "Doan
worry Swede Heart" -- meaning she understands there will
be times when the needs of jyze must come first.  That's
probably the best and certainly the most welcome of five
or six nifty little gifts she's come up with just in the
past week.  -- But then at the WOC earlier tonight --
same old fitness joint in what was once a bank, the
eighty-year-old building only slightly damaged by last
year's quake -- she said I've been acting very odd
lately.  She's wondering if "the deep passion, I mean
the really, really deep passion, is still there."

        No, I don't think it's crunch time yet.  I'm also
not forgetting she knows the jyze eye is trained on her
and she is through and through (as she herself insists)
a diva.  A diva with a heart of gold who is nonetheless,
as she likes to say, "not a good person."  But good copy
she is -- almost always (though of course she also needs
her downtime).  And irrespective of all that, I still
must take care of a number of home things during the
three-day break ahead.

        The blinds are stirring.  Could be it's raining on
the other side of those thick conference-room windows.
Or...now I can hear the building's air-circulation
system whirring, and that's probably causing the blinds
to flutter slightly.  And while looking up at them and
puzzling over the question I also notice it's almost
time for me to hit the road.  A good stopping point!

-----

3

-----

Tonight's jyze goes down in the AQ at the bad old east-depot saloon. Coldest night of the year. Moon two nights short of full -- so two days short of Lantern Festival time -- and sailing over south hill as I came down off it. The DC castle was all aglow with the quake crane hovering above it for just about the last time; today's news says it -- the crane -- will be dismantled this week. Meanwhile I've been thinking about that moon. I figure it's been in the same condition with respect to fullness some sixty thousand times since the Celestial calendar took on its numbering scheme.

This dive. Only when it's about to become a jyze venue do I darken its doorway. So this is my first visit here in at least twenty of those full moons.

The seat's new to me, up in the southwest corner by the bar. Where the pull-tabs pile far deeper on the floor than any snow in these parts in the past five years. (News confirms it: this winter is once again the USA's warmest in all "recorded history," meaning Euro-invader history of course. On the three TV screens floating above the roiling masses in this saloon a hockey game is in progress, U.S. versus Canada for the gold. But hockey appears to be no one's thing in here. Later tonight the Winter Olympics end and we can get back to the kind of games that really matter.

And I'm so grungy tonight. Other potential jyze venues would've shown me the door or wanted to. Lots of sexifying this weekend -- and just in time to ward off those rising wifely grumbles -- and afterwards no shower, no shave.

[ Jyze of the Heavenly Year : Black Horse ]

(Just before starting in here tonight I reloaded
the J-stick on the run for the first time in, again,
probably close to fourteen or even fifteen months.
Buried the trusty nib in the bottle and sucked up liquid
J-ammo.  Same brown backpack here full of same totemic
stuff, and most indispensable of all is the "amusingly
scrotal," as Z-wiff describes it, leather J-ammo pouch.)
     The very corner.  Outside, a green hydrant like a
stubby scarecrow standing spread-armed on the sidewalk
-- I'm innocent!  Frisk me if you want! -- and the long
low Victorian ironwork and glowing globes of the AQ bus
station, bricks of the depot behind it, top of the
cement tunnel beneath it, downtown cityscape rising far
above it on the hill to the north.  At the hill's
western foot the majestic white tower, its pyramidal
topmost portion crowned with a glowing blue beacon.
     Why did we have time for loving?  We got aced out
of Kat's birthday, that's why.  This gripes both of us
but so it goes.  Today's the solar version of her big
day.  Instead we'll be taking our bag of gifts (which I
worked on for much of last night, as Z did for days
prior to that) -- be taking them over, I say, to her and
Betty's place next weekend.  We were planning to stop by
briefly on the way down there today at the south-end
community college's Lantern Festival, but that got
scratched too.  It's the wrong day for it anyway.
Tuesday's the official one.
     Also today is Gregorian Calendar Day.  I'm trying
to pay as little attention as possible to that calendar
but still: this is an important occasion.  On this date
the thirteenth of the popes named Gregory said let the
hoary old Julian calendar jump ahead ten days and it
did.  Let New Year's be celebrated on January 1, he also
said, instead of March 25 (or March 1 in some cases),
and so it was, and still is, at least among the
nonheathen.  But "The Jyze Millennium" laid all that out
in detail, so no need to go into it any further now.
     And that had better be it for today.  Time to pack
up and head for the beckoning blue light.  And then
onward, because tonight I actually have some work to do.

[ Jyze of the Heavenly Year : Black Horse ]


[+2]

    As fitting a spot as any to bring the long Heavenly
birthday celebration -- enhanced and expanded part,
first round -- to a close.  Sitting outdoors on a bench
by the splendid stone lantern at the hilltop garden
terrace park, also known as the "peace park."  Facing
south, with a view through crooked junipers (and one
cherry or cherrylike tree, already flowering) of the
mountain range to the east and also the mountain range
to the west and also, straight ahead across the valley,
south hill, its northern prow prominently featuring the
craggy old landmark DC castle.  All this ablaze with
late sunlight so intense it caused me to stop,
unshoulder my pack, and break out my shades as I hiked
across the high bridge headed this way.
    Any minute now the full moon will start its rise
over the mountains to the east and the Festival of
Lanterns can launch.  As far as I know, this right here,
inside and adjacent to the J-book, is it, the only such
festival in town today.  Nothing about any others in
either OMP or FAP.  But I imagine there will be private
ceremonies scattered all over the area.  And I like
doing that imagining.  I picture hundreds of lanterns,
winding processions, shining happy faces.  (The
lanternlike pole lamps lining the serpentine paths of
the hillside park here as well as those of the extensive
terraced gardens down below, they just flicked on.
Nearby a jogger is doing statuesque stretches and two
young women in jeans and black leather jackets are
chirping away in Japanese as their almost identical
white poodles excitedly sniff each other.)
    We have no lanterns in the apartment or I would've
brought one along today to light at the first sighting
of the moon (I stand up and scan the horizon for it --
the orb -- but again, just as on opening night, see no
trace).  A dozen or more kerosene lanterns sit in my old
storage unit across the sound, though, so maybe next
time I go over there I'll fire up a belated private

ceremony of my own.  What else is this year for if not
finding ever more excuses to be festive?
    -- Also on the way over here, just after passing
the bridge, I ran into the Z-woman on the street as she
headed home, pulling her little backpack cart, her
flamboyant chartreuse quilted jacket hard to miss.
First, though, she had to chase after me as I split down
a side street by the Natusan center.  I'm not supposed
to do that -- so as to optimize the chances of our
meeting, we long ago agreed to walk the same streets at
or around this hour on our respective ways home and to
work -- but today I unilaterally asserted an exemption
in my haste to get over here to start in on the jyze.
"You're bad, bad, bad!"  -- But she forgave me.  And
handed me her work-issued bus pass so I won't have to
pay when I catch the last coach home tonight.
    Still no visible moon.  But the air's hazy over the
eastern mountains.  And the quadrant of sky I can see
may not be the right one for this moonrise.  Fifteenth
day of the Tiger moon.  Also the Jewish holiday Purim,
celebrating a victory several millennia back in another
struggle between monotheisms -- or no, that's wrong,
because of course in those days Persia was still many,
many centuries short of being an evil Islamic land.
    Sun's starting to set and the park's getting
chillier and the pole-top lanterns are looking better
and better as they become more visible through the trees
along those winding hillside paths -- like a torchlight
procession stop-framed -- and still no moon.  In all
directions the horizon's going rosy (except behind me to
the east, where, through a fairly dense screen of trees,
Jyze City's major north-south freeway roars and blares
relentlessly, flashing occasional enigmatic chrome-
reflected signals this way through small needly gaps in
the greenery).
    And it's almost night now.  Sky's still blue but no
sign of sun rays remains anywhere except on the upper
reaches of the DC castle.  I got work, work, work to do.
Grand jury today, another full day of it tomorrow.  This
means with luck my income for the month ending two days

from now -- Gregorian-type month I'm talking about --
will reach two-thirds of what it needs to be for me to
be able to keep on scraping by.
One last look.

*

No moon.  It's got to be there somewhere but even
when I stand on the stone wall here I can't see it.  So
I'll finish up by citing a great Sufi poet's words on
the nature of reality (I just came across them last
night): "It's hidden, and it's hidden, and it's hidden."
I like that.  -- But do I think it adds up to any kind
of truth other than partial?  Certainly not.


[+2]

-- And two days later it's still missing!
Therefore I guess it can't, after all, be my excuse for
kwikjyzing this postscript.  No snap-shut closure here.
But then who needs an excuse anyway, other than to say
today's yet another special day.  The official
celebration's over but from time to time -- until the
next official one comes down -- the ad-hoc type will
suffice.  And the whole year's a celebration anyway, as
noted a number of times already, so we're just talking
levels of intensity here.  (And then we'll have the
celebration spoilers.  Misfortune.  World news.  Bad
moods.  Screwups.  But today's not an active day, it
seems, at least so far, for any of those.)
But today is the one-year anniversary of the big J-
town quake.  It's also my very own mother's solar
birthday (she'd be eighty-two) and my very own son's
lunar birthday (he's turning thirty by lunar count, and
last week he turned twenty-nine by solar count).  And
it's a great French essayist's 469th birthday by solar
count once all the necessary Gregorian adjustments have
been made.  This is not the day, though, for a paragraph
or two on the essayist, much as I wish it were.
Hopefully sometime later during a slow spell maybe.
Jyze going down in an indie coffee shop this time,

a table by the window looking out on the SQ redbrick triangle park and six sun-incandesced flags friskily flapping: five for the Nordic lands and then of course the USAn imperial.  (SQ, that's the Scandi quarter.) Also a big mural out there showing scenes from the nearest big city a couple of fjords down from Sandefjords-Stolen mixed with views of the sister city right here, this chunk up in its northwestern quadrant, the former shingletown, longtime home of an imposing fishing fleet.  A Norwegian king traveled thousands of miles to dedicate that mural.  Two or three times a year I get up here and prostrate myself before it and the other atavistic bell-ringers in the hood -- not failing to include the statue of the continent's very first known pink invader, also a Norski.

Seven or eight blocks to the southeast the Z-mobile's being lubed.  The garage closes at five-thirty and I must show up down there before then and it's probably past four by now, so I won't be at this for too long.

Today's mail clears up a mystery.  Cousin Kar is moving to the U.S. southwest to take a new job -- that's why we haven't heard from him for so long.  He'll be running a large environmental organization (a different one), and that sounds very good.  It'll even allow him and Kerani to work out of Jyze City in the summers, he writes, meaning he'll probably be showing up in these pages in person, or rather by direct physical contact with myself, Jyzer G, later on.  And I'm sure we'll both do our best to make that get-together well worth taking jyze note of.

A year ago today I was awakened by my old red windup alarm clock bonking my skull just above my left ear (as a guy right now strides by with forearm extended, a handsome red-and-green parrot clamped to his left wrist).  This bonking happened a few minutes before eleven a.m.  The room was rocking, books were tumbling from the high bookcases along the north and east walls. I leapt up and more or less instinctively assumed a judolike alert position, totally naked, legs spread,

knees bent, in the space at the foot of the bed
(reminding myself even as I did so of the Pink Panther
thinking he's about to be attacked by the flagrantly
racially stereotyped Kato in the movie).

Other than fallen books all over the place, the
only damage done was a small lump on my head and a
shattered chicken pitcher -- the one I'd given Mother
for her birthday back in the late eighties and retrieved
at her death.  That pitcher now stands in partially
mended condition atop a cabinet in the dining area of
unit 203 as our "Great Mother's-Birthday Quake"
memorial.  The joke at the time was that she, ol' Mom,
felt we hadn't done a good enough job at keeping her
memory alive and kicking and so she had the chicken put
up a squawk for her.  (Presumably unaware that in doing
so it would lose its head.)

When I came home later that same night a voicemail
from Elgie was awaiting me.  Had I survived?  (This
quake was big news around the world, although it turned
out not to be so newsworthy: a paltry billion or two in
damage, mostly to the old brick buildings in the part of
town where I usually hang out -- the HQ and the AQ and
atop our hill -- and no deaths and few injuries.)  But
then Elgie answered his own question, saying the message
(the one Z put on the voicemail he'd just heard) said we
had survived, yes, and all was well.  "That's the
important thing," he observed.

This was the first time I'd heard from him directly
(except that we didn't connect) in many months.  Maybe
it was the first time he'd ever taken the initiative --
although I figured his mother, Lady S, had probably put
him up to it.  So I wrote him back -- snail mail, yes --
suggesting, as I had also done the year before, we start
up a correspondence.  And again he didn't reply.  Then
not too long after Father's Day a curious gift came in,
a stainless-steel mug inscribed with "Happy Father's
Day" and no further message included in the box.  Again
at Lady S's urging, I figured, but I wrote back -- to
both of them -- and repeated my suggestion about a
correspondence.  Again no reply.  (I did deploy the mug

as a pen/pencil cup on my hideaway desk and it remains
there today, right beneath the new Heavenly Year wall
hanging, black on red, with calligraphy by Joey J.)

Earlier, about a year and a half ago, Lady S had
called asking for my help regarding applications Elgie
wanted to make to graduate schools of business (all
highly ranked).  I asked her to send up the papers so I
could provide the information she needed.  They never
arrived.  My guess is she'd been angling for an offer of
financial help from me, though that might be wrong, and
in any case the notion of my making such an offer is,
for me, absurd and impossible.  And that communication
was the only other one from her except for a brief reply
to my Father's Day thank-you in which she said she
hadn't sent me the application papers because to her
mind I hadn't seemed "serious" about them.

At this I just shook my head, and still do, in the
same old dismay.  Helplessly.  So far as I know there's
nothing I can do to change this sort of reception from
the two of them.  I've tried many times before.  And
I'll try again if either of them gives me any hope of a
different reception the next time.  But I'm expecting
nothing.

Quake damage.  One year later on my usual route
into town I pass several buildings which remain cordoned
off and "red-tagged," meaning no one can enter.  They're
all fronted or flanked by big piles of fallen bricks.
Otherwise I see little sign of the quake.  Nonetheless
it's still the case that one major branch of the J-town
fault line (fortunately not involved in last year's
quake) runs directly under our house.

-- And so here's the real end of the lunar New
Year's celebration.  (Last night the "Grooveyard" jock
did say the full moon was sensational and I expect it
will be much the same tonight with the sky so clear.)
Party's over, candles on cake blown out and though
they're still smoking, I can tamp down the embers with
my fingers.  And must go now because the guys at the
garage won't wait.

So let the real Heavenly Year begin.

[ Jyze of the Heavenly Year : Black Horse ]


-----

4

-----


    Unexpectedly I get to address the jyze gods from my
favorite podium.  And at the same time stake a claim for
formal parallelism, since this is the same spot where I
started and finished -- except for codas -- the TJM
annal.  Therefore I'll call this the start of the
enhanced profane main body of the Heavenly Year annal.
    Upper left-hand corner of the country as defined by
the freeway system.  Upper end of the high bridge.  The
big-time view: AQ in the valley, downtown skyline
marching across and down east hill on the far side of
the valley; and, to the west, the bay, the sound, the
islands, the coastal mountains.  On a day that's not
rainy, contrary to the forecast, but brilliantly blue
except at the western horizon, where the blue bleaches
gradually downward into a white mist which veils the
mountains so they become a one-dimensional dark gray
silhouette like a stage backdrop.  And spread out at a
level a hundred or more feet below me here and to the
west, the multilayered maze where the east-west and
north-south freeways meet, the northern-border ribbon
tying into the western-coast ribbon along with numerous
lesser ribbons in a vast loose multibowed horizontal
knot.  And if I follow the line of the bridge railing,
it points directly at the spot above the terrace gardens
where I was jyzing at the start of the last cluster.
    So March doesn't exactly come roaring in like a --
well, like a Tiger I guess it should be, since this is
still the lunar Tiger Month.  (And I've gotten more than
my fill of slightly gibbous moon the past couple of
nights.)

[ Jyze of the Heavenly Year : Black Horse ]


     But Tiger Month, Rooster entry.  Wood Rooster, also
known as -- sounds like a tavern in ribald Olde England
-- the Blue Cock.  Speaking of which, this bridge, known
to many as Ho Bridge, still boasts a complement of hos,
more properly described these days as sex workers, who
show up from time to time, though none appear to be in
view today.  Most of these sex workers seem to be
Eurusans from southern states and many work out of vans.
And I should note the bridge is again being lit up at
night.  After only a few months of operation the mayor's
millennial bridge-lighting program (which to my
knowledge never did light up any other bridge in this
town) had to be shut down last year because of the
electricity shortage.  Now the mayor's gone, run out of
office as a result of the various crises of the past two
years -- WTO, Mardi Gras, electricity, dot-com -- but
the lights here are back on at night.  Why that is I
don't know.  But Z probably would, so I'll ask her.
     Meanwhile, what news?  A U.S. shadow government is
revealed to be in place and ready to take over in case
the bad guys try again to take out the capital.  U.S.
troops are preparing to enter more nations as our
modern-day crusade continues to crank up.  (We're
hunting terrorists, don't ya know.  At this point
anybody who opposes anything we do is considered a
terrorist or a coddler of terrorists; terrorists are
evil, so coddlers of them are evil as well; and we've
publicly pledged to eradicate evil from the face of the
earth.  No shit, we really have!)
     In other news, the EPA caves on more enforcement
issues.  The congressional out-party manages a squeak of
protest against the neocons' slow-motion coup -- though
for sure the outs don't call it that; rather they call
it, sensibly enough, "the stolen election" -- and
they're jumped on as traitors.  Oh these are sad sad
days.  But fascinating and exciting if you're among the
privileged.  And we here in J. City surely are, unless
we squeak too much.  (Can this mouse do that?  This
Black Horse?  He's trying!  Let the buck start here!)
     And speaking of shadows: today is Z's "Julian

shadow" birthday, as I'm calling it.  If Pope Gregory
XIII hadn't decreed his calendrical alterations, Z's
birthday would fall today, March 2nd.  (She's up in the
apartment now, awaiting the arrival of her grad-school
friend Lee M.  We'll be meeting at six at the same
Japanese teahouse referred to earlier and then doing
dinner somewhere nearby; and after that we'll be seeing
the late show of the documentary "The Turandot Project."
It's about the recent staging of the opera by that name
in Beijing and is said to feature some extraordinary
diva fits which Z says she hopes to learn from.)  ---
                              *
     -- Well, and I just got grilled by a cop.  A polite
grilling though, seeing as how, like him, I'm a Cawk and
what's more engaged in the act of jyzing.  "When I see
someone standing out here," he said, "I always think the
worst.  So you're okay?  You're not about to jump or
anything?"  (Pretty preposterous.  Over the past four-
plus years I've seen hundreds if not thousands of people
standing at the railing on this bridge for long periods
admiring the view -- some even clicking expensive
cameras set up on tripods.  Maybe he suspected I was
waiting to meet a hooker?  Peddling drugs?  A pimp
maybe, could it possibly be?  Or -- who knows what.)
     (As now just a slight golden arc of sun hangs above
the mountains.  And I'm chilling out.  Those same winds
that got to me at the terrace gardens are getting to me
here as well.  -- But I glance over my shoulder and
upwards and the orange-brick DC castle looks spectacular
seen up close, gotta say, as its upper stories again
seem to go molten in the late rays.)
     -- But I still can't get over the cop.  And:
suddenly it dawns on me he must've suspected I was
dashing off a suicide note.  Unprecedented for this
jyzer or probably any jyzer.  He did ask, after I said
everything was fine the first time, "What're you writing
there?"  "Just a little bit about the view," I said.
"Hard to beat this, wouldn't you agree?"
     Surely one of the early high points of the Heavenly
Year right here.  And as the Land of the Free becomes

more and more a police state, entirely appropriate.  And
yet, just like the bank guard back on opening night,
this guy was not all that bad.  Come to think of it, he
didn't even ask for ID.


[+2]


    Z-geist cafe, still the finest coffee shop in the
HQ.  Only half the tables are occupied at half past five
-- not a good sign.  Two new franchise coffee shops
have opened nearby in the past few months, one across
the street to the east and the other a few doors to the
west.  Can an indie compete? Probably not.  It draws
most of the scruffy local potential customers (a good
many artist types among us) while the franchises skim
off most of the presentables.  Soon the balance tips:
too much scruffiness at the indie shop and all the
presentables go elsewhere.  It's a lot like the old
racial blockbusting.
    As befits a setting with such a name, there's
electrifying news of world-shaking importance.  Or at
least that's how the first news accounts make it sound.
"The biggest battle of the war has erupted in
Afghanistan."  What's more, at least two U.S. soldiers
have lost their lives.  After six months of turkeyshoot
over there come the first confirmed U.S. combat deaths.
    What it really is is a mop-up operation.  The high-
altitude bombers are again doing their thing with their
high-IQ bombs, including some new "thermobarbaric" -- or
no, sorry, that should be "thermobaric" -- devices which
suck the air out of caves and cause any occupants to
suffocate to death.  But this time, because in earlier
killing fields the Afghan mercenaries employed by the
U.S. allowed too many of the evil infidels to slip away,
a thousand or so U.S. and "allied" ground troops are
involved in the encircling operation.  Media rumor has
it that the Al Qaeda supreme leader might be hiding in
one of those caves.  It's the same rumor, pretty much,
we've heard in a number of previous cases, or just say

with just about every cave or nearby dwelling attacked,
but this time the odds are supposedly the highest yet.

Z-geist material.  No end of it in today's OMP and
of course even more of it in the far-coast paper.  But I
don't want to overload any circuits here -- especially
not with the joint closing in less than forty minutes.

On the corner across the street to the north stands
a historical three-story redbrick hotel -- but just
barely stands, with the aid of all sorts of props and
supports.  A year after the quake, two lanes of the
adjacent streets are still blocked off.  The piles of
fallen bricks, however, have recently been removed and
word has it the building will be saved through purchase
by a city historical society.

And located right behind the hotel, to its north,
is an ancient saloon, also red-tagged owing to extensive
quake damage, and perched outside it, on a metal bracket
extending over the sidewalk at second-story level, is a
life-size statue of -- a horse.  If the colors of the
five Horses of the Chinese zodiac -- Black, Green, Red,
Yellow, White -- were mixed together, I figure they'd be
about the color of this statue: a muddy brown.  So in a
way this horse is all the zodiacal Horses in one, could
say.  And therefore I've anointed it as one of my lucky
Horses for this Heavenly Year.  Any time I'm in the area
I stand silently for a moment directly beneath it, stare
up at it, and ask the Taoist deities for help and
guidance.  (They're the ones behind this whole Chinese
zodiac business, see.)  (And yes, I'm very serious about
paying my respects to that Horse and the broader ideas
it represents and to Chinese culture in general.)

So -- three fine days, referring to the weather and
also to ongoing personal relations.  I've just arrived
downtown from Kat's final game of the season, a
maddening 13-12 loss for her previously, and still,
unvictorious team.  Kat's a hoops neophyte but she's
quick, determined, a good defender -- and lots of fun to
watch.  And she's improving her game (though she still
lacks a jump shot).  Because I arrived before Betty did,
I was entrusted with security duties for the grrrl's

watch and her sweatshirt.  And while there I had Kat and
Betty -- this was at halftime -- "brand" the black
wooden Navaho "Laughing Horse" they gave me last night
at our usual spaghetti restaurant (ugh!) as my Heavenly
Year gift.  "B" with a heart, "K" with two hearts:
that's what they chose for their brands.  (I brought
along a special white marker for them to use.)  And
Celine's grandmother was present too, for her first live
basketball game ever, at age eighty-something lithely
maneuvering about the sidelines and stands to snap
photos.  (Celine herself is shooting up -- by which
phrase I refer to her suddenly being almost a head
taller than Kat.  All these Lolita-age girls tearing
each other apart on the court, what a spectacle!)
     Penultimate moments here at the Z-geist.  The PA
just switched over to funky stuff, all by Soul Brother
No. 1.  "Cold Sweat," "Sex Machine," and now the
delicious "Lickin' Stick."  Party time!  Will Z's
favorite, "Popcorn," be next?  Or "Hot Pants"?  -- And
once again I'm the only partier, baristas excepted.
     Saturday night "The Turandot Project" at the cine-
cafe theater.  Marvelous portrayal of East/West cultural
conflict artistically bridged and transcended (though
not entirely cleansed of colonial stereotypes, sorry to
report).  Moved me to tears, it did (regardless!).  And
Z proclaimed the diva fits to be everything she'd hoped
for and more.
     -- Okay, all outdoor tables and chairs are now
stacked in the alcove.  And I'd like to squeeze in a few
more paragraphs.  So, elsewhere for that.

                    *              *

An hour later and I'm roosting on a bench in the
hallway around the corner from the hideaway, out of
sight from it, out of the pathway to it, and hoping no
one will be disturbing me here.  Tonight not being
Friday or Saturday, it's without a musical soundtrack,
loud and dissonant -- dissonant enough on many weekend
nights to make the large plate-glass window a few inches
from my ears rattle in fortissimo resonance.
     I'm almost forgetting why I wanted to come back for

this encore.  But no, not really.  It's just to say a
few words about the weekend with the Z-woman.  Ever
since Camilla died -- only a little over two months ago
now -- Z's been going through mood swings and "labile"
moments, as expected by me and even welcomed by me in a
way -- because I like having the chance to play the
consoling role with her -- and now lately she's been
facing added stress caused by the biennial budget crunch
at work (though this is still in its early stages and
won't top out for months).  Then on Sunday -- not before
but after a very fine full-service roll in the sheets --
she announced she'd had an "aha moment" and now she knew
what was really bothering her: it was anxiety about
moving her mother out here.  And that's still more than
six months away!  But last week Naomi gave me the okay
to take a week of vacation in September, and so Z, great
planner that she is, drew up a detailed schedule for
what needs to be done between now and then and suddenly
the reality of it all hit her square between the eyes
(amygdala territory for sure).

And almost simultaneously she let drop a remark
about my "smothering" her.  Not that I'm doing that,
exactly, she assured me, or at least not so far.  But
she does have concerns.  When she was growing up her
mother had a smothering effect on her, and whenever this
occurred she, Z, would consequently start to feel
everyone else was smothering her too.  She believes this
was a primary reason in later years why none of her
relationships with men lasted very long.  She became
sensitized to suffocation, even the slightest hint.
That's why she lived in the dorm during college even
though home was just a few miles away; took her around-
the-world trip at age twenty-eight; went to grad school
out of town at thirty; and four years later moved to
Jyze City.  -- To escape suffocation, yes.  That's what
she told me.  And: "That's one reason why I thought you
and I could live together -- you were independent
enough, I didn't think you'd be smothering me."

So I stand forewarned.  Clearly she's already
wanting more space than before.  And I'm joking about

it: dubbing myself "Smothers Brother number three,"
answering the phone for one of her presignaled afternoon
calls with "Smother Works, Chloroform Cloth Division --
how may I stifle you?"  But I'm also, I'll admit, a bit
miffed.  Taken aback really.  Me, smother?  This is a
first in my entire full Heavenly cycle -- all sixty
animals -- and by now I'm supposed to have seen it all.

   Speaking of which: this weekend I also caught my
first glimpse of Z's ol' man previous to me -- caught
roughly a dozen of them in fact, in a batch of photos
she discovered she hadn't thrown out after all.  Jerry
II, "Jerry of the Yacht."  Retired early from the fire
department, parlayed his lump-sum retirement and an
inheritance into a fabulous fortune through the stock
market.  I'd always pictured -- oh, I don't know what.
Say an older grayhaired dignified fire-chief type in a
yachtsman's cap.  But no, he's a black-bearded English
Department kind of guy, to my eyes, and in all but a
couple of the photos she showed me he has his hands all
over my future wife!  From our many long talks on the
subject of the men in her life I know she often went for
bearded guys, offbeat ones to be sure, artists and
eggheads and musicians, all races/creeds/colors/sizes/
temperaments.  And a good thing too, because why else
would she think I'm okay?  I, a straightlaced meat-and-
potatoes Cawk boy from the burbs.  She's even said she
never met a guy so plain-vanilla as me.  (Except, that
is, back in high school and college -- and how she loved
to dump on them, not just back then but right up to the
present.  Still cackles over the way I squirm as I try
to describe for her what I was like at that stage.)

   Consequently I was frequently reminding her of the
recent letter from cousin Ron H., each time trying to
slip in one of the adjectives he used.  "Dapper."
"Charismatic."  "Mesmerizing."  (I did confess I
suspected it was all tongue-in-cheek or maybe a typical
instance of Mentoka small-town sass.  But the truth is
I'm not really sure how to think about it.)

   And I'll end with a gratifying moment, with Lee at
the teahouse, when I told him it was his advice to

Zoelie not to yield to my "pressure," which in turn led
her to write me (they were at the mountain resort for
grad-school classes) that she was taking back some of
the encouraging things she'd said about our prospects,
which in turn provoked me into writing her that burning
ten-page declaration of outrage, which in turn caused
her to believe I was for real -- and then motivated her
to stick it out when we had the big fight after she got
back to town.  And now when I told Lee all this, he said
he'd had no idea he played such a key role.  But Z-
spouse, listening as I spoke to him at such length and
with such passion, gave me an adoring look and squeezed
my leg under the table and was very loving for the rest
of the night, including even at the theater when she
knew she was seeing a near look-alike for one of her own
predecessors (Lady S) sensuously hotfooting it up on the
screen as I tried to sit stoically beside her (and on
her other side Lee was leaning forward with eyeballs
bulging going "Wow!  Wow!  Did you see that?!").


-----

5

-----


   The new round (last with a Tiger in its tank)
offers quite the lineup.  Fire and ice just for
starters.  Fish and chips too, coming up any minute.
But also a threat to domestic security.  And a
tantalizing mystery.  A marvel of nature.  Preparations
for a big dance.  And just outside the window here a
sleeping dog I realized right away I couldn't let lie,
in a sense.  I was headed for the firehouse tavern but I
came in here instead -- another HQ saloon, upstairs from
the basement comedy joint.  Halfway between Z-geist and
the hideaway, more or less, a block from my lucky

composite Horse, which is visible from here, and in the
shadow of the great white tower if the moon were low in
the sky north of it.  (Not too likely.)

It's not the Red Dog it should be -- Fire Dog --
but it's sleepy looking all right, and that definitely
chimes with the slogan for 1946 and thus this cluster:
"Sleeping Dog."  Curled around the base of the parking
meter it's leashed to.  Black dog, medium size,
indeterminate breed.  Hound.  Never saw this dog before
and probably never will again -- not that it matters
either way so far as I know.

Friday night, the HQ stirring to life.  A retro
rock band called the Beatniks grinding it out in the
dive right below my office -- I stopped outside to
listen to "Maybelline."  Would the authors of "On the
Road" and "Howl" and the rest of the Beat gang be
pleased to know they live on in this way?  Probably
they'd say no but I say yes.  (JRX on the band's name.)

First the news.  The recession's over in the U.S.
for sure; the chief of the Federal Reserve says so.
Mop-up battles continue in the mountains of Afghanistan
as the first U.S. body bags arrive home.  "Cycle of
violence" escalates in the Middle East as the Saudi
royals nervously float a peace proposal and the U.S.
pays it lip service while preparing to attack Iraq and
various other harborers of "evil" -- but in which order
we'll be taking out those evildoers we haven't yet been
told -- and meanwhile our smart-bomb factories, even
though working around the clock, are falling hopelessly
behind demand.

It's also International Women's Day -- another U.S.
product doing better as an export than it is at home (I
haven't come across a single reference to the occasion
in the U.S. press).

So fire and ice.  Ice first.

(No, black dog rides away first in a yellow cab,
along with his human companion: a very big, full-bearded
Cawk man in orange denim overalls.  -- The juke music in
here so loud I still haven't heard any laughs coming up
from the basement, although I know the crowd down there

is large -- lined up outside too, in fact, foolhardy young'uns machoistically or masochistically (or both, sure, in some cases) wearing no jackets despite the bitter cold, and many women included in that line, usually with arms folded over their chests, stomping for warmth as if putting out endless cigarette butts.)

Winter storm warning -- and for once it panned out. When I left the hideaway last night at seven minutes after one, the usual time for last-bus catching, wow: some crazy picturesque northland urban scene!  Just four or five inches, but fresh and pristine, for the most part, lending the triangle an aura of highly unusual innocence and purity.  The old "middle road" was especially gorgeous, the rows of ginkgos (or some such urban adaptor) looking like rows of cherry trees in rapturous blossom as three-ball street lamps floated amongst them.  Stunning for me, like a certain night snowfall in a Kyoto springtime I can never forget.  (I lived there!  I saw that!)  ( -- And even so must JRX the city name because it's no longer the capital of a country and neither is it fictional.)

Icy underfoot last night with the temp just at freezing, as it still is now, or maybe it's a degree or two above.  The only way I could climb the hill to the bus stop was beneath the roofed sidewalk quake scaffolding at Z's building (just a diagonal block from my own).  And then at the stop, wow again: bus on fire! Flames and black smoke, ubiquitous flashing lights, half a dozen fire trucks, heroic firefighters frantically hosing -- almost like war coverage on the tube.  As the terra-cotta walruses of the city administration building across from my alternative stop a block to the north gaped down in astonishment.  Northbound buses backed up past the courthouse but southbound had just started crunching along again, all fitted out with chains, the trolley antennas kicking up twin roostertails of accumulated snow from the overhead wires.  But my bus didn't appear until forty minutes later -- latest it's ever arrived in all my years of J-town busing.  And then what enchantment riding through the snow-draped HQ and

[ Jyze of the Heavenly Year : Black Horse ]

AQ and grinding across the high bridge beneath the DC
castle, orange-brick-roading it, whooee again as the
view opened up -- a city out there I'd never seen
before.  A slight squinch of the eyes and it was the
preinvasion turf all over again, a century and a half
back -- even all that disguised landfill below might've
been snow-covered tidal mudflats as in the original.

Reminded me of olden days, natch and of course, par
for the new life-flashbacking elder in his Heavenly Year
trance.  Prior strandings in downtown J-town offices, no
possibility of making it home for days.  Valiant hike of
ten miles due north from downtown, another time from
port jingo across the water to our backwoods town --
same distance -- both of these hikes of course in the
Lady U era -- for the second one wearing a Santa Claus
hat and thin-soled low-cut chucks, stopping at every
open bar and store to warm up freezing tootsies, once or
twice using my bare hands after stripping off my socks.

Today, hiking in, the snow was almost all gone.
But the exceptions were glorious enough: banks of spring
flowers back in the shadows on the DC castle grounds,
daffodils and primroses, still snow-shrouded.  "Awww!"
said Z when I told her about all this at the WOC.  And
just two days ago the Chinese calendar hanging on the
wall at the hideaway announced the new fifteen-day
period: "Waking of Insects"!

Meantime I'm excited myself because my Lunar New
Year's gift has finally arrived and I don't know yet
what it is.  I'll find out when I get home tonight.
That's the element of tantalizing suspense announced
earlier.  (And I've given away the last of the Lai See
envelopes -- lucky coins -- including two I sent to
sister Barb and her partner Keith, always the toughest
of my correspondence nuts to crack.  Hopefully that
envelope will fare better with the post office than the
perennial Christmas cards did.)

(This impulsive stop for the Sleeping Dog is
costing me sixteen bucks, two drinks included, tip not.
I nibbled on the fish and chips left-handed.  Now I'm
nursing ice-cube meltwater.  As a couple of bicycle cops

whose helmets flash powerful lights they don't even
bother to shut off -- like miner helmets -- tromp
through just to make their presence known and remind us
what kind of state we really live in if you strip away
the appearances, which of course many of us would rather
not do -- not that by "us" I'm trying to imply I'm one.
But I'll gladly give the appearance of going along if it
means I'll be allowed to keep on jyzing.  After all, the
cops know mere written words will never hurt them, sans
the Hollywoodization.   -- And not to forget either that
I'm the privileged Cawk dude and so accrue endless
benefits of the doubt, as these pages have already
attested.  Along with a few other benefits as well.)
     The threat to domestic security?  A notice taped on
the 203 door: all units between the hours of one and
five on Friday -- that's today -- would be subject to
"structural inspection."  It didn't happen to 203 while
I was there (until four p.m.) but we're assuming the
notice means the building's about to be sold.  That in
turn could lead to a giant rent increase, condoization,
or simply an unceremonious eviction.  Or maybe it's just
a matter of looking for quake damage a little belatedly,
as with virtually all building-maintenance tasks at
1511.  Maybe one chance in ten it's that.
     -- So, would we buy if our place were offered to us
as a condo?  Z asked if I thought we should go for it.
If the price is right, I said, yeah, I think so.  But
can any price be right for us?  Even with the recession
still grinding locally, housing prices are continuing to
skyrocket -- or more like moon-rocket -- and they were
already outrageous several years ago.  And now Z's
mother will be coming to town and needing a place she
almost certainly won't be able to afford by herself.
And the city's looking to cut $30 million to $50 million
from this year's budget and the word is they'll be going
after middle managers and planners who make $70K or more
and that's Z (on the nose at $70K).  She'd have bumping
rights but the move itself would likely be downward.
     So -- more suspense!
     And domestic fun.  Z dreaming of sexy times

featuring coworker Blair A.  She has so many sexual
dreams and loves so much to rile me up with them (as
indeed I enjoy her doing, and I also like to rile right
back myself, even if I sometimes have to fabricate the
dream -- "dream it up").  This week I asked her who's my
Blair A. equivalent in her eyes and she said it's
Estella at the WOC who she's quite sure has a serious
crush on me.  Coincidentally, this week Estella came up
and asked me to join her for drinks some evening soon --
because she'll be moving to the Netherlands this summer
and wants to say goodbye.  So it appears I'll have to
start searching for an understudy just to keep Z on her
toes.  Can't let her be the only one with a Blair A.

The big dance, I might note, should provide more
opportunities for such enjoyments.  It's the twenty-
fifth anniversary of the start of the power utility's
home energy-conservation program, for which Z worked
five years back in the eighties (as did our friend Wei
-- that's how he met wife Alison, having been called in
to provide free advice on how to weatherize her house --
"and he's been giving me," as Alison likes to say, "a
whole lotta free advice ever since!").  A number of the
attendees, Z cheerfully admits -- boasts! -- will be
former Blair A.'s in her life and possibly even more
influential types -- but not types, no.  We're talking
about the studs in the flesh.  And she gets to show me
off as the one she snagged and took the plunge with when
it was widely believed she'd never again, after dumping
Jerry II, get serious about anyone.  And there'll be
dancing so we can show off our best geezer moves, let
them all gasp with -- awe, shock, pity, whatever.

(Joint's hoppin' now.  Cheeks of swaying booties in
black leather all but scraping against my own bristly
facial cheeks.  I'm impervious -- as befits a J-master.
Screechy voices though.  Some open curiosity about what
the hell's going down here in this jyze operation.  But
short attention spans.  Or they're thinking let the
Sleeping Dog lie.)

Last bits.  My storage-unit rent again went up a
"nominal," as the notice said, amount -- ten percent!

[ Jyze of the Heavenly Year : Black Horse ]

I'd like to dump the space but I can't without giving
away a whole lot of stuff I can't bear to admit I no
longer need.  And: I'm using one of my backup J-sticks
right now because the first-stringer leaked badly at the
end of the Rooster round last time -- not only was my
hand Dalmationed with black ink spots but when I got to
the bathroom I discovered my face was too: black eyes,
black cheeks and lips, even tip of nose!

But my trusty pocket watch is telling me I have
twenty minutes to make it over to the office to pick up
my bag and then rush up to the bus stop.  -- And still
not a single yuk from the comedy room down below, not to
mention raucous hilarity or hoots of derision.  It seems
highly unlikely they'd have the place soundproofed....


[+3]


At the ORB cafe, basement of the only real
bookstore.  The cafe itself is now run by the same folks
who do Z-geist.  Otherwise scarcely any change at all
from a year ago or twenty years ago.  Some funkified
seventies soul playing at the moment.  Late in the
dinner hour, quiet, half an hour or more until tonight's
reading begins in the adjoining room, something about a
bible.  Maybe it'll be a big draw with the religious
war on ("Clash of Civilizations") but I doubt it.  Walls
down here lined with old books and old bricks -- from a
distance it's not always easy to tell them apart.

The bricks go back more than a century.  By
stepping through an arched doorway at the far end of the
cafe one could enter an underground pathway (through the
"hidden city") leading to a doorway in the basement of
the hideaway building two blocks to the northeast, then
climb three flights of stairs to Jyze Central.  It's
like a vast sunken palace grounds down here in this part
of town.  And a century and a half ago they were still a
few weeks away from starting work on the first Cawk-
invader cabins in this area.

Anniversaries.  They matter.  Their arbitrariness

is part of why they matter.  It's by Pope Gregory XIII's
calendar as well as by its Julian predecessor that today
can be said to be an anniversary of the 9/11 shocker --
half a year or six months.  And this is regarded as big
news.  Front-page stuff: how we're doing at recovering,
how the world's changed, the country's changed, the
city's changed, individuals have changed.  Last night a
film ran on national TV showing events taking place
inside the twin towers at the time of the attack --
despite some misgivings regarding the highly sensitive,
the nation was deemed ready to see this.  And apparently
it was.  Today it appears the level of traumatization is
no higher than it already was yesterday.

But that's mere appearances.  Because on the
worldwide scale the level's far greater.  A Pentagon
document has been leaked to the media: the U.S., it
says, is changing its nuke-'em policy.  We've now
decided we'll use nukes in first strikes under certain
circumstances, for example if another country launches a
"surprising" kind of military operation or has built
bunkers so far underground they can't be reached by
conventional "bunker-buster" weapons.  Members of our
neocon cabal -- elevated into office by a shameful
Supreme Court decision some fifteen months ago after the
cabal lost the popular election by half a million votes
and was about to lose the electoral decision as well --
are now trying to institute damage control through TV
pundit shows as the first waves of overseas outrage on
the new nuke policy roll in.  (In-country outrage is
minor or nonexistent as far as can be learned from the
corporate-controlled media.  Open expression of such has
become far too dangerous.)

Saturday was another kind of anniversary.  March 9,
1945, was the day U.S. planes firebombed Tokyo, killing
more than eighty thousand people, almost all civilians
and the vast majority women and children and elders.
This shows you can confirm national characteristics by
studying history (as if this is a surprise!).  For
example, extreme hypocrisy.  Terrorist groups with an
agenda attack civilians, three thousand die?  The

perpetrators are evil and inhuman.  Terrorist states
with an agenda attack civilians, millions die?  We're
talking collateral damage.  (See U.S. attacks on North
American indigenes, on Mexico, the Philippines, Germany,
Japan, Iran, Korea, Vietnam, Guatemala, Chile, Iraq --
and many, many more.)
    -- Okay, so enough screed for today, or at least
for the moment.  Yesterday was a different kind of
anniversary: a personal one.  It was First Call Day.
Five Gregorian years ago on the tenth day of March this
jyzer right here first made live contact with Zoelie B.,
albeit only by telephone.  That initial exhilarating and
anxiety-inducing ninety-minute (guessing) talk from
which all else followed.  -- And now with her solar
birthday coming up in just four days a different sort of
anxiety level is rising in me, because I don't have time
to do right by her, especially in comparison with the
way I've feted her on previous birthdays.  And day after
tomorrow is Kat's lunar birthday, and considering all
the ballyhoo I've lavished on the lunar-birthday concept
for the Heavenly Year I'd better come up with something
good for her too or my name will be, as she might put
it, space junk.  So I'm scheming.  And I've got some
ideas and some rudimentary makings.)
    A fine First Call Day.  No time, though, for
loving; we had to make the four o'clock showing of
"Iris" so we could squeeze in our fortnightly Sunday
grocery shopping on north hill before the store's nine
o'clock closing hour.  (Saturday afternoon was for
loving -- third Saturday in a row! -- and lived up to
the billing I would've wanted for it if such intimate
doings were ever to be accorded a billing other than in
jyze: "Hot & Full Plan A Consumm!" -- or some such.)
    "Iris" was a downer for both of us.  Not much
enamored of the woman's novels or philosophy,
nonetheless we both admire her and especially her long-
lasting marriage (we both read her husband's "Elegy for
Iris").  And Z in her college years and twenties -- and
later too -- was wild in much the same way Iris was.
But the inexorability of Alzheimer's as presented in the

film brought back fearsome memories for me (of Nana's
street-wandering ten-year bout with the disease) and
fears of what we might soon be facing with Z's mother
(who just sent us a letter confirming she'll be ready to
move out here in September and listing ten pages of
belongings she wants to bring with her) -- and also, of
course, fears of what we may be facing ourselves
healthwise at some point.  Our jocular declarations of
120-year longevity suddenly looked just as puerile and
foolish as we've always known them to be (including the
earlier period when they declared only 105 years) but
more or less openly agreed not to admit to each other.
A conspiracy of bravado in the face of the ultimate Mr.
Ugly.  For a few hours that mask slipped rather badly.
But better to try to nudge it back into place, we
agreed, and try to keep it there, though clearly this
will become more and more difficult over time.  (That
last clause states the whole problem in a nutshell!)  In
the meantime we'll be going in to do our wills.  Which
was the plan all along, but Z wanted to be sure to light
a fire under it so we'd have it done before the
Centropolis trip.  I felt the heat and agreed.  Besides:
for a year or more I'd been envisioning that trip as one
of the dramatic high points of the Heavenly Year.

*

So then the big dinner/dance.  For the first time
in a while I donned dress pants, white shirt, courtin'/
weddin' shoes, and Z decked herself out in a funky new
silver "Chinesey" jacket and capri jeans -- making me
the overdressed Mr. Vanilla, true, but I didn't mind.
Pavilion Room, Jyze City fairgrounds, the iconic
gigantic golf tee all aglow as the flying-saucer-shaped
restaurant teed up on top rotated slowly almost directly
overhead.  About a hundred fifty people showed up.
Among them were many Z knew (maybe a third of the people
in the room, she guessed, and half the enrollees of her
twenty-five-member training class from exactly twenty
years ago).  I heard many stories and peered at many
photographs but didn't dance a single dance -- the
setting and the band just didn't do it for either of us.

49

[ Jyze of the Heavenly Year : Black Horse ]

Nor was the food much good (and at twenty-five bucks per
person I thought it should've been better; but Z, who
knows about these things from attending dozens if not
scores of similar job-related functions-with-meals every
year, said no).  Still and all we did have fun.

     Sat with several of Z's old pals I'd never met
before.  I was being belatedly "vetted."  Passed all the
tests, Z told me today on the phone after checking her
e-mail from the vetters.  One was the infamous Rhea, Z's
fellow boat-rocking big-city girl from Centropolis.
Rhea told me a number of tales from back in the day,
including one about Bad Arvin R., the man Z came within
a week of marrying (guests were already arriving from
distant cities!) before a priest advised a postponement
in light of her "hysteria" and his own opinion -- this
is the priest talking now, advising her in grave lowered
tones -- that Arvin was a "sociopath."  Rhea told me
this story; Z thought I knew about it already but no,
she never included that delicious detail about a priest
being involved.  Arvin the con man, "independent
business consultant" super charmer.  Z heard a new story
too: a couple of years later Arvin showed up on Rhea's
doorstep pleading homelessness and hung around for close
to a week before she kicked him out.  She kept it from Z
all this time for fear of reopening old wounds.

     During those early years at the power utility Z was
notorious for being outspoken -- "mean and rude
Centropolis style just like me," confided Rhea -- and
also for being highly safety-conscious: she was the
first to insist on wearing masks and rubber gloves when
conducting "free home energy-conservation inspections."
Now that kind of gear is mandatory (though most of the
city's housing stock has already been inspected and so
the gear's rarely used these days).  At the time Z was
also "sort of preoccupied," she said, owing to not only
the Arvin disaster but also her father's death, which
preceded the arrival of Arvin in her life by about a
year and no doubt helped cause her to be susceptible to
his gonzo charms (and she says this herself).

     We ran into several other men who'd made plays for

her over the years, including the amusing Norm W.
Beforehand Z had told me she'd "just laughed
hysterically" when Norm tried to kiss her on their one
date.  At the big dance now he laughed hysterically
himself when she mentioned this.  "I'd had way too many
beers," he said.  "I never drank so many beers in one
night in my life, before or since."  (She often cites
Norm's reaction to her when discussing how Asian men --
he's Japusan -- tend to find her too independent and
aggressive and therefore impossible to get along with.)
    The one former suitor she'd most wanted me to meet,
a purportedly big handsome Cawk dude named Rudy (guess
she thought I'd be impressed or something), didn't show
up for the party.  But she learned a startling new fact
about him: the Filipina he'd wound up marrying (as she
knew already) had come to him from a catalog and was
many years younger.  A "Filipina Dream Girl" (as in the
movie by that name).
    There's much more I'd like to mention, but --
can't.  Except this one note I saved for last.  (And my
timing's not too bad, because just now the cafe's
counter guy came around and said, "We're closing in
fifteen minutes," and sounded regretful.  So I say
myself it's good to see the joint is still jyze-
friendly, unlike a whole lot of other places around here
these days.)  -- I'm talkin' about the suspense item
mentioned earlier, the big Heavenly Year gift I was on
tenterhooks awaiting.  And the gift is -- an authentic
Year of the Horse light-pole banner!  One of the yellow
ones that were flapping on the poles near the east depot
before the New Year's festival!  The ones I gazed at
with rapt admiration and longing -- thinking: if only
such magnificent banners were available to
streetwalking, jyzeslinging AQ interlopers!
    Twenty years with the city paid off.  Also a
quarter century of working with the AQ community.  She
called her friend Ann T. at the AQ community office and
Ann -- needing to hear a bit of explanation first --
"Your husband's what kind of year?" -- allowed as how
it could be done.  And it was.

[ Jyze of the Heavenly Year : Black Horse ]


    It's gorgeous.  About three feet by six, black on
yellow, featuring a huge Chinese ideogram for "Horse."
Almost too big for our apartment -- but that's where
it'll be hanging as soon as we can figure out the best
spot and a good way to mount it.  Because as I reminded
Z, you always want to mount a Black Horse just right.



                        -----


                          6


                        -----



    The waning hours of the day most associated with
the word "beware," as in "the Ides of."  Z's birthday,
that is, except now we're well into what lunar adherents
have for millennia called the fifth watch of the night,
dawn about an hour away, so we'll need to summon the
concept of Glennarian NUT time to keep the celebration
going.  Gregorianly it's been the 16th since midnight
but by Nightscoper Upside-down Time we're still Ides-
ing.  Or as Z might say, Middlemarching.
    I'm squeezed into place at the back end of our
dining table.  Green leaves dangling overhead to both
sides and behind, orange birthday tulips preening
directly ahead, and beyond them the living area, big
cream-colored futon couch hugging the far wall, picture
window above and just behind it looking out on sparkly
black night (but mostly reflecting back the contents in
here of what some call the "great room," including the
jyzer in reverse image in the depths I see now as he
waves a hand to identify himself).  Two reading lamps
glowing.  Books and plants and newspapers.  A string of
silvery birthday pennants cutting across the middle of
the room at just above my head level when I'm standing.
Two of my own big acrylic canvases riding the walls.
    I do love it in here.  Do hope we won't be forced

to give up the apartment, not ever and especially not soon.  (Haven't heard anything more about what might've motivated the inspection.)

World's still spinning.  No new nukes have gone off yet.  "Key battle" is over in Afghanistan: we declare smashing victory even though it appears most of the hostiles have again managed to escape somehow -- perhaps including the arch-villain Al Qaeda leader -- and what's more after we've announced our "iron-ring" encirclement of them.  A story in today's paper from the largest of the far-coast megalopoli -- from now on to be known in jyze for reasons of concision, among others, as FCM #1 -- notes U.S. military spending is greater than that of the next sixteen biggest spenders combined.

This spot right here is where I usually set up for important projects.  The "perennial Xmas card" was the last such effort (some fine photos of the assembly line for those cards just came back, taken by Z unbeknownst to me, when I wasn't home).  And then there was the effort last night.  Thirty-nine more altered cards set in seven large frames -- completing the wedding exhibition from three years ago -- including three new cards, all of which are maulings of works by the great Russian fabulist painter renowned for his wedding scenes.

A lovely day -- gift presentation shortly after I arose at two p.m.  (No birthday whoopee-making this time, though I was rampantly ready, or "ithy" -- she'd just eaten a burger and it was disagreeing with her.)  Then for the rest of the afternoon we played the "Coltrane Live in Europe" boxed set which was my other big present for her, breaking our $25 cost limit by a factor of more than three, and it would've been five if not for brother Rob's employee discount.  And she read "The Beauty of the Husband" in one sitting -- or couch-lying for the most part -- announcing early on that a wacko like the book's eponymous husband never would've lasted long with her but then falling silent on that score, I noticed, as she read on.  In some ways the guy was indeed her kind of crazy -- his retro macho romantic ways mixed with intellectual sensitivity -- just as he was the author's (a woman mostly known for her poetry). But I'm even more Z's kind of crazy and I know it so I can take in stride her fascination with that other guy.

She, Z, had also written a poem and read it to me. It was inspired by something she learned during the birthday call from her mother.  Z had been hoping to pick up an armchair -- "the sedan chair" -- which had been her father's "main place for hanging out" during his hours at home for most of the years she was growing up and then also the years after she left, all the way to his final months.  But lacking room for it in her new apartment, her mother passed it along to her own sister Clara, and today Z learned Clara herself had passed it along to her daughter Marcia who lives on the far coast. So it's gone for good.  And the irony is that Aunt Clara and the rest of her branch of the family -- in fact all of Z's maternal relatives -- would have nothing to do with Vincenzo, Z's father, while he was alive.  Sheer racial prejudice, Z believes.  No other known possible cause for it.  (The famed director of "Last Tango in Paris," by the way, was born one day after Z was.  The only same-dayer she knows of -- and only because I told her -- is a member of a classic fifties surfer singing group, never a favorite of hers.  In fact she didn't recognize the name of the group much less the singer.)

Birthday goodies right after my breakfast.  Carrot cake with frosting: she picked it out herself.  And fruit-juice-sweetened soy vanilla ice cream.  When I walked in to work shortly thereafter I was so swollen I felt perfectly round between shoulders and hips.  And a serendipitous encounter along the way: I took one of the longer routes through the HQ so I could drop by the ORB to pick up a copy of our local radical rag (it offers some of the best political commentary of any periodical I'm familiar with, including the national ones) and just inside the door bumped into a sassy little black-haired browser: Kat!  And Betty was ambling around in back looking for something for Z's birthday.  I hung out with them for a while and escorted them to their car before slogging on up to the scope office.

But that remark about being swollen to roundness, I meant to link it to this cluster's reigning animal spirit.  1947, Year of the Purple Pig.  Perfect, I thought, because this Pig is also known as "Pig Passing the Mountain" and earlier as viewed from the high bridge the mountains were rigged out in unusual splendor with a few wispy black clouds artfully brushstroked above them to frame a sickle of about-to-set new moon -- this indicating today is indeed yet another New Year's Day, 1st of Muharram, the Muslim calendar, year 1423.

Celebrations!  And more ahead!  And with this same moon signaling the start of Rabbit Month we know Easter can't be far away.  And, and, and -- but right now I just want to be recalling this fine day.  All the clocks in our unit (203 I mean) either covered over with paper or turned to face the wall: what Z likes to do for long get-away-from-it-all weekends, as she's penciled this one in to be -- though now last-minute changes are in the works, as so often happens, piling up one after another: exceptions to take in a movie, a gallery opening, maybe a play, and also to visit an art-supply store.  The fridge freezer's so stuffed with birthday bonbons, including many from her party at work, you can't open it without triggering a foodslide.  And stacks abound of the library whodunits Z zips through at such an astounding clip.  And today's mail brought her another batch of birthday cards.

We've known each other just a few days more than five years but because of the coincidental timing of that first meeting this is the sixth birthday I've "been with" her.  Grand old days back then, yes indeed. -- And grand days now!  Damn right!  (Early birds chirping gleefully, this proves it.  Also suggests the fifth watch is over and it's bedtime and I must sleep now, mainly because I slept so little last night, which is to say: this past morning and early afternoon.  But it was worth it, because the wedding card collection looks great and the birthday grrrl loves it.)

[+2]

Now sitting in the brown hideaway chair I imagined seeing myself sitting in from the floor above ours a few clusters back.  Hearing an odd cricketlike sound coming from the heating system, almost as if the windows were open somewhere to a balmy Mentoka summer evening.  And a vacuum cleaner is roaring sporadically down the hall: apparently one of the new janitors is working a swing shift or maybe an early graveyard.

-- And from below, loud rock'n'roll.  Unusual for a Sunday evening but again this is a celebrating kind of day: St. Patrick's.  The green beer's flowing, I know that.  And I have some Scotch-Irish blood myself so maybe I ought to be down there guzzling away.  But I don't much like beer and still less beer-drunk crowds (though even today I suppose I could tolerate both if some good danceable live R&B were playing -- as on, for example, St. Pat's Day thirty-five years ago today (yes, this very day) at Nick's Tavern in Mentoka Falls when I met spouse number one, the half-Irish -- through the paternal line, obviously, as the name gives away if only the jyze rules would permit me to write the whole thing -- though the first name does it well enough all by itself -- Colleen D., also known herein as Lady C.

Today's also the third and final day of the B-day weekend of the current spouse -- to my mind number one of all time without question, as everyone already knows anyway, so no need to be saying it so often.

This afternoon we saw "What Time Is It There?" -- about clocks, mourning, obsession, alienation, culture clash, death.  Too slow and arty for Z -- she was barely able to stay in the theater all the way to the end and then "chaffed" me a bit afterwards for having such weird taste, since I'd chosen it (at her request!).  And she was already a little bit out of sorts to begin with, possibly because she'd tried to read a scatological shrink-inspired manuscript she wrote herself back in her college days, 120-some single-space pages in tiny elite

typeface printed from a nearly depleted ribbon.  This
was her first full rereading of it, she said, since the
year she wrote it.  I've read it twice myself in the
past several years and find it fascinating and touching
and talented.  In her view it's too raw, too revealing,
too close to the bone.  Shows too much of her alienation
from her family, in which she was to all extents and
purposes an only child, and they were living in a small
apartment -- just like the main character in today's
movie.  And the death of the father in the movie (or
seeming death; at the end it appears to be revealed as a
fraud) surely reminded Z of her own father's death and
the bad period she went through immediately afterward,
leading to the Arvin near-marriage fiasco.

So chaff or no, I felt I ought to be cutting her
some slack.  And was able to do so and get away with it
(that is, without being accused of being patronizing or
smarmy or "avuncular").  Dropped her off at 1511 -- our
street address which I'm pretty sure I haven't mentioned
before in this annal -- and drove to work and then,
after pounding away for two hours there, came here.  She
still likes having Sunday evenings alone at home so she
can gather herself for the workweek ahead.  Even if I
have no work to do on Sunday evenings I act as if I do
and head on out.  It's not a deception, the way we both
see it; it's an agreement whose terms we avoid repeating
each time so as to bypass the awkwardness of seeming to
want to be away from each other.

Earlier in the afternoon we stopped by Sybille A.'s
gallery in one of Z's old north-end hoods to see the
"Labor of Hercules" exhibition.  This included life-
size prints of the large murals which the state
legislature commissioned and then rejected once they'd
been hung on the walls there; a posse of right-wingers
detected obscenity and blasphemy in their silhouetted
shapes (a celebrated controversy in these parts, and I
mean both the philistine and the arts-loving parts of
these parts).  Fifteen years on it's harder than ever to
believe anyone could find this work offensive -- but
then in truth it was never really that hard to believe.

[ Jyze of the Heavenly Year : Black Horse ]

It's simple: among the orthodox, if they're feeling
threatened, anything that varies even slightly from
orthodoxy is upsetting, and that which is truly
unorthodox or anti-orthodox is outrageous.  It's just as
true of orthodox Christians as it is of orthodox Jews or
orthodox Muslims or adherents of any other religious
orthodoxy I know of.  In the minds of many observers
(I'm one) this is a big piece of what the current
"terrorism" business is all about.

     On that score I'll also note it's a period of
backing and shuffling by the cabal in the capital.  Our
faux cowboy president runs things up the flagpole, the
world shrieks its dismay, the solemn secretary of state
-- an Afrusan! -- says the president didn't really mean
it.  But the prez just lets it ride, not taking anything
back, and when the uproar's died down he moves on to his
next shocker, leaving the previous one fully in place.
And the media don't nail him for this.

     As I've been saying, the fix is in.  Hard to see it
any other way.  Another war -- or more likely a series
of wars -- coming right up.  I mean, we can't help it,
can we, we USAns?  It's what we do!

     So back to yesterday.  A big birthday-weekend
dinner in the AQ at one of Z's favorite Chinese
restaurants and featuring one of her favorite dishes,
honey walnut prawns -- but it seems the restaurant may
have changed hands since our last visit and in terms of
quality the dish is no longer what it used to be.
Worse, the new owners, if they actually are new, are
less strict about enforcing the no-smoking rule, and
smoke in a restaurant is upsetting to Z.  Complicating
matters, though, the prime offenders in this case -- at
the very next table -- were not only a group of lesbians
but most were Filusan lesbians, a couple of whom Z knew
slightly, and she didn't have the heart to throw a scene
and ruin their evening.  So instead her own was ruined,
or at least seriously diminished.  (Personally I don't
mind smoke too much -- usually -- and enjoyed the lively
setting, not only the raucous lesbians but also two
large family groups of the more traditional kind, one

Chiusan and one Vieusan, and both with several excited
kids.  So it turned out my main job for the evening was
to try to keep Z distracted, and I always like doing
that.  She laughs at my distraction act, I light up.
Still!  And she laughs a lot and often very heartily and
toothily -- though not usually in smoky restaurants.
But this time, except for a few short spells, yes.)
     Then out to the swanky mall near the U so Z could
cash in the gift certificate that Leola gave her for her
birthday.  This was at an outlet of my least favorite
chain bookstore of them all.  The clientele is a mix of
upscale burbish types and smug university students and
it's close to one hundred percent Cawk.  It's an enclave
I can scarcely bear to visit anymore, every bit as bad
for me as smoky restaurants are to Z -- and she doesn't
like this other kind of enclave either.  So we got in
and out as fast as we could.  (I was about ready to kick
and trample my way through a crowd of blase' students in
expensive rags sprawled on the floor in front of the
magazine racks, blocking all access to the mags.  But
then I said to myself what the hell, I was already well
aware this chain carries few of the mags and journals
I'd be interested in, so why work myself into a lather
over such asinine behavior?  Save my outrage for more
important things.  Over and out.)
     So back home and Z was in bed by ten.  For her
that's late -- an hour later than usual.  Most nights
I'm away at work regardless so it doesn't matter too
much that I have a wife who goes to bed eight or nine
hours before I do.  (What does matter is that she
usually wakes up for the day about the time I go to bed
and then we have half an hour to an hour for pillow talk
or horseplay or whatever we want in bed -- and how many
couples can match that?)  Saturday nights I stay in the
bedroom and read, at first in the bed itself until she
dozes off and then in my old green armchair as she
sleeps right in front of me, sometimes with our bare
feet touching as I prop my legs on the bed.  We've done
this almost every Saturday night since we started living
together -- and sometimes even before, because our work

schedules were just as out of sync then -- and it's
become one of my favorite times of the week.  Talk about
mellow!  It's now very hard for me to do anything else
on Saturday nights.


-----

7

-----


     Snow on the first day of spring.  And I'm out in
it.  -- Or anyway in and out of it.  And in fact a few
snowflakes are reaching me here, blowing in from the
west beneath the overpass.  (As now I shift seats on the
bus-stop bench, four feet or so farther east and away
from the flake source.  Some flakes scudded across this
J-book's facing page and stopped, melted, blurring the
jyze a bit in several places.  -- And up on the hill I
was enjoying the way the flakes were landing on my nose
and cheeks and brows and lashes, making lacy white
filters that as they melted briefly deliquesced patches
of an already gorgeous urban scene.
     When what to my wondering eyes!  Huge flakes too,
some close to an inch in diameter.  At the start in
swirly winds it seemed swarms of white moths had been
startled into flight.  Or all the world was a pillow
fight featuring the leaky goosefeather type.  -- And
those same daffodils by the DC castle were dusted again
and then some, many bending to the ground beneath the
wet weight.  And lots of folks cavorting.  Though others
trudging grimly, it's true, especially the upwardbound
slippy-sliding along, several panting and/or grunting
and/or cursing.
     And it's cold.  Can't go very long here.  But lest
such unseasonal coldness be thought to count against
"theories" of global roasting and to discredit notions

of the Century of Ecoclysm, this morning's OMP talks of
the spectacular sudden collapse of a huge ice shelf in
Antarctica.  Stunning images -- an area the size of 13
Jyze Citys.  Scientists say this area hasn't been open
water, as now, since before the previous ice age.  And
yesterday an even huger iceberg "calved off" not far
from the new collapse -- size of 24 Jyze Citys.  (That
may be irrelevant.  But I suspect not.  All things,
famously, and now even more ominously, are connected.)
    Buses rolling by.  Bundled-up people huddling
nearby and at the stop across the street.  Snow still
swirling.  -- And I came here because this is one of my
favorite calendrical spots.  A prime Jyze City founder
(Cawk kind) platted his claim in this area 150 years ago
in such fashion that the streets run due east and west.
If you stand at the far end of the AQ colonnade holding
up the freeway overpass (columns painted Chinese red and
Vietnamese yellow, with spiraling fishes and dragonflies
stenciled thereon) -- if you stand at that point, I say,
just before sunset on the day of an equinox, vernal or
autumnal, the sun rays reach you through the tunnel-like
downhill passage beneath the freeway.  The main drag
down here forms a corridor that leads straight west into
the sunset (including a glimmer of reflected sun on the
water of the bay).  It's a glorious view, exciting,
like, say, Stonehenge in England on the equinoctial
days, and for pretty much the same reason.  Or like
those famous cathedrals with holes cut through the stone
walls so the sun will shine on the enstatued face of
this or that saint only on the saint's holy day.  Here
we occupiers of the bus stops are the saints of the
moment patiently awaiting our beams of illumination.
    A good day for starts and restarts.  This jyze
cluster, by good fortune, is under the sign of the first
animal to make it all the way across the river and thus
to start the Taoist cycle.  It's the Rat, that
auspicious creature, and in this case the Yellow Rat.
(An excellent test animal for probing cultural
differences and the play of signifiers.)  It's also
known as the "Rat in the Warehouse," and so as I was

trudging (delightedly but with cold feet) through the
warehouse district in the upper AQ on my way here I was
keeping my eyes open for lucky rats.  I often see rats
there -- but they're the kind known locally as Norwegian
rats.  Big and aggressive.  (And lots of big and
aggressive shopping-cart vagabonds hang out in the same
area, so best for a trekker on foot to stay alert -- and
if you want to be especially cautious you might cross
the street three or four times in the same block on
certain days in the hope of avoiding confrontations.)
     But this time no rats.
     All right, enough.  Numb fingers.  Feet oh so cold.
Time to shuffle off in a due westerly direction into
what might yet be a sunset.
                         *              *

     -- Now, beneath the picture-window-size photo of
the twin towers before they fell, a kwikjyze follow-up.
     For starters, in two days three cards and letters
have come in: one from Justine, mother-in-law of Z's
nephew Jacob in Centropolis (accompanying another of her
amusing frog cigar-box paintings); one from Jim Q. in
Brazil (at the midpoint of his cruise circumnavigating
South America via the Panama Canal); and one from sister
Barb down in MSM #2 (in reply to my Heavenly Year card).
Barb says the 9/11 aftermath may've placed her job in
jeopardy but she's been able to hang on to it so far,
and the octogenarian owner of the building in which she
lives is now confined to her apartment owing to chronic
illness and Barb fears the rent-control jig may soon be
up (if the owner dies and the building changes hands,
rents could legally revert to market level, which would
probably amount to a doubling or tripling of what Barb
and Keith pay now -- this being the same apartment Barb
"inherited" when Mother died there seven years ago --
and Rikki and her son Mischa are still living
downstairs, and if things had gone a bit differently
between Rikki and me, I might be living there with them
myself -- though it sure is hard to feature that now).
(And I should note "MSM #2" up there follows the same
form as "FCM #1."  It's the second-largest megalopolis

in the megastate to the south.)

As for the Z-spouse, she's been in exceptionally fine fettle the past few days.  Yesterday she received her twenty-year service pin at the city's annual ceremony for such bestowals; her reaction was to raise a fist and cry out "Geezer grrrls rule!" which brought down the house.  Then she came home and threw a seduction at her old G-hub -- that's me! -- that ranks right up there with her best ever (for me, I'm saying; obviously she must've uncorked more than a few other such doozers in the long dark age before we met).  And she's been presenting me with all kinds of cards and little gifts, she's been abrasive at times and restless, she's announced we're in a rut, she's amended that to mean she thinks we ought to be rutting more -- on and on.  Oh, and she's very pleased with a new fridge magnet she found somewhere and placed dead center on the metal hood above the stove.  It shows an inanely smiling stereotypical fifties-type housewife in front of a fully stocked fridge and she's saying "I'm happy...yet aware of the ironic ramifications of my happiness."

Meanwhile another "world's oldest person" has died.  This reigning titleholder made it to 115.  And we've watched with interest as a college classmate of Z's -- "one of those nerdy science guys" -- has been appointed chair of our supreme leader's so-called Council on Bioethics.  He's antiabortion, of course, but may not be quite as hard right as he originally looked.  It turns out he bases his concerns on respect for nature and a well-justified fear of science flying out of control.  And one area in which he believes it's bordering on sheer frenzy already is the quest for immortality and the indefinite prolongation of life spans.  On this I think I may even agree with him.  I'd like to live as long as possible, true, but only by natural means.  Eating right is okay, cloning myself is not.

Also, Z was invited this week to give a speech on recycling in the nation's capital.  She turned it down.  Been there, done that; it's time to focus on the more urgent issue of environmental justice and especially as

it applies to the climate crisis.  How impressed I was
-- and am! -- that she would take that stance.
     One o'clock straight up, time to pack it in.  So
I'll leave any further political talk until day after
tomorrow.  But will say right now the magnificent yellow
"Year of the Horse" banner has gone up on the wall in
the 203 front hallway, just barely fitting into the
space next to the big bookcase across from the entryway
and partly hidden behind the coatrack.  But the most
important parts are all on view.  It's a stunner!


[+2]


     Lazy lazy lazy.  Hunkered over on the white deck
chair tucked back in the corner to evade the cool
breeze.  That breeze causes steam to swirl up from the
jacuzzi and bead the leaves of the artificial palm
(which shake gently and throw off droplets much like a
dog coming in from the rain, except in slow motion) and
the gray steel of the six-foot-high and three-foot-
thick vault door, circular, which is wide open.  But I
feel secure regardless.  Despite the noticeable
earthquake cracks in the tile wall.  As the waterfall
thunders on, spawning just as always an impressive
procession of frothy foambergs that circle the border of
the pool, spinning slowly as they go.
     All alone in here.  Most of the usual soakers
present for the first four evenings of the workweek
apparently have something better to do at eight p.m. on
a Friday.  As I do myself, matter of fact, if making a
few bucks pushing out a deposition transcript would
truly qualify.  And regardless I'll have to do it
anyway.  But it'll wait an hour or two.
     I still do a lot of soaking and mulling in here.
I'm getting a rep for it -- "statue of The Thinker
perched on the edge of the jac."  "Too much jaccing
off."  I'd like to be here at least three evenings a
week for an hour or so.  If I could do that I think I'd
be able to work through all my quandaries, I mean every

last one, and my life would be conflict-free (except, of course, for the new stuff coming in from outside -- or for that matter percolating up from inside).  As it is I usually make it here twice a week, so some things are always left hanging for the next time.  But when I'm not here I generally don't think much about that kind of conflict.  I could almost say this is a place I come to to have troubles.  Except -- when I'm here they don't seem like troubles.  They seem more like puzzles which are a pleasure to try to solve.

Idle rambling.  Well, why not.  If ever there was a place for it, this is it.  (I'm wearing my usual pair of skimpy and ragged black running shorts with a white house towel thrown across my thighs and the J-book resting on top of that.  Two familiar naked pink feet, crossed at the ankles, stick out below, viewed above the top of the J-book.  And here's my furry pink belly at the bottom of the J-book, as in a kind of still (almost) life.  Also a navel for gazing at during the slow spells.  Hairy pink arms and backs of hands.)

(And: scores of inch-square tan tiles laid out down below, or hundreds, even thousands at the right and left visual peripheries.  The thunder of the waterfall is so loud you can rarely hear anything else -- the main exception being the sudden explosively klunky arrival of a soda can at the end of the lower-lobby vending machine's internal chute just around the corner.  Otherwise it's peaceful here in the way white noise is peaceful.  This is the kind of loud peacefulness that I as a night worker am used to sleeping in during the daylight hours.  Real peacefulness tends to make me feel alert and a little wary.)

So this'll be a lazy entry, yes.  I'll be a pack rat but a lackadaisical one, just sort of glance around internally to see what the memory banks have stored away, if anything, since last time.  As the foambergs keep circling and spinning and slowly diminishing with the popping of their tiny bubbles one by one by one.

First, though, before the memories, this is a good place to do a quick personal health check.  Bring the

medical records up to date.  Since the last such jyze
inventory roughly two years ago not a whole lot of note
has happened to me physiologically so far as I know
other than normal wear and tear, and in truth that's
something I usually don't notice too much.  I do try to
keep an eye on all my personal health aspects that are
detectable to me.  Of course most of the inner systems
aren't accessible in that way, and I don't see doctors
either, so basically I'm flying on a wing and a prayer
and a moderately diligent effort to live healthfully.
Eat good, sleep good, walk and exercise a lot, socialize
and laugh a lot, have sex often and lengthily and in
addition do a lot of touching and rubbing and dancing
and licking if possible, and I mean for that "if
possible" to refer to every item on the list.  Also,
take any affordable vites & supps for which some real
evidence of effectiveness at least seems to exist and
also pop half an aspirin and drink a glass of red wine
every day.

And that's pretty much it.  Well, dress warmly in
the cold.  Try not to breathe traffic fumes or a lot of
secondhand smoke.  If sitting for a long spell, remember
to sit ergonomically and jiggle the limbs a bit and
stretch from time to time, and also every fifteen or
twenty minutes take a brief break in place to focus the
eyes on some distant point, well away from the primary
focus of screen or printed material.  Also try to keep
shoelaces tied good and tight so as not to be trippin'
too much, which is to say: to keep the dreamy kind of
trippin' from being interrupted too much.

I did throw out my back last fall, as I may or may
not have mentioned before.  In any case I'm now being
more attentive about back care.  Likewise for knee care
(the twinges of a few weeks ago have stopped, but I
figure a lifetime of highly frequent spates of jumping
-- as in hoops -- must've worn down something or other
in there and they'll only be getting kinkier with time).
Likewise for wrist care in hopes of minimizing the
damage caused by an adult lifetime of keyboard bashing,
which continues even now, despite my fierce efforts to

type more gently.  (Just this week I had to replace
another battered keyboard.)

And yet: as of now, my Heavenly Year, I still have
no aches and pains to speak of.  I can hear, I can see,
I can taste, I can get around -- all as well as ever and
in a few respects even better than ever.  Even for sex
I'm still more or less normally functional, I'd say --
especially compared with the major extended glitch of
some four years ago, which I now consider to have been
symptomatic of a PTSD of sorts caused by the breakup
with Lady U.  (Only this phony palm trunk here looks
woodlike, as far as what's in sight, so I'll knock on it
-- and now dodge the rain of palm-shake droplets.)

Is there a mole somewhere on my body I should be
worried about?  An artery narrowing even as I do my very
best to avoid fried foods and other bloodstream
congesticants?  Colon okay?  Any of those nasty TB germs
I'm exposed to on the bus -- of this I have absolutely
no doubt -- succeeding in wrestling down my immune
system?  Oh the possibilities we all have, always, for
bodily breakdown, how they take on new shades of seeming
omnipresence as we move into our second sixty-year
cycle.

And I do fall victim to more colds and flus now
that I'm with Z.  She works in a public place and is
exposed to a lot of whatever's going around, and soon
we're passing it back and forth between us.  In our five
years together we've had three or four such ping-pong
illnesses lasting up to several months each.  But
lately, since last September, nothing.  It's a good
year, knock knock, shower shower.  (Z did a six-month
course of an experimental drug and it halted her herpes
outbreaks.  It also seemed to disturb her sleep and
cause -- shudder -- considerable flatulence, especially
during the morning hours at work, so she gave it up.
That was four or five months ago and since then she's
experienced no new outbreaks.  And now the flatulence is
at an all-time low because, while on the drug, she
drastically reduced her garlic intake and since then
hasn't reupped to anything like the former level.

[ Jyze of the Heavenly Year : Black Horse ]



    And onward to the news.  Briefly!  Our high USAn
honcho addresses a world conference on poverty and
development and announces a piddling increase in U.S.
foreign aid for the poorest nations, with of course all
kinds of strings attached.  Observes today's below-the-
fold story about this in the far-coast paper, the
headline: "POVERTY BREEDS TERROR, NATIONS SAY."  Well
gee -- really?  And half the world living on less than
two bucks a day and a fifth on less than one buck a day.
A lot of terror ahead, I'd say, if the rich nations
don't wake up.  But then if they took the matter
seriously and tried to do something truly helpful about
it they wouldn't be as rich anymore.  So instead we'll
have more "security," less democracy (it's tempting to
put that in quotes too), more poverty, more pain and
humiliation, more terror, more ecocrisis in the Century
of Ecoclysm (because it's all related!).
    -- End of today's preachy news break.
    A lovely moment in the garage yesterday.  The
Japusan woman living on the first floor -- married to a
Eurusan -- arrived home after picking up their daughter
from school.  I always say hello to them and goof with
the kid a bit and the mother always smiles wanly and
says nothing.  Same this time.  But then, as they
stopped at the mailbox and I by the garage door across
the way to zip up my jacket, I heard the daughter, maybe
five years old, say, "Mama, I like that boy!"  And then
when Mama offered no reply, the daughter repeated it
even louder.  "Mama!  I like that boy!!"  Made my day,
it did.  And I told Z about it and ever since she's been
whispering in my ear at odd moments, including twice in
separate phone calls, "Mama, I like that boy!!"
    A fine closing line for this entry.  But no, even
though I can't hang on here much longer (and another
soaker is present now, eyeing me with entirely
understandable wariness -- what am I doing over here,
she may be wondering, using whirlpool soakers as
involuntary sketch models?) -- even so I want to catch a
little more of what I had in mind for the "all" in this

catchall entry.  And so the double stars, please.
    **  At the hideaway building someone's been
smearing feces on restroom walls, men's and women's,
second through fourth floors on weekend nights.
    **  At the scope office our security system is down
for the third straight week, the building elevators are
being "modernized" (causing night workers all sorts of
entrance/exit grief because the updating's being done at
night); and the lights are no longer left on at night in
the newly remodeled ground-floor lobby, making the way
out a shadowy obstacle course strewn with plants,
chairs, and janitor carts (something must be done!).
    **  At home I'm now the chief waterer of the plants
in the building stairwell landings and lobby, which I
pass through on my way down to pick up the morning
papers before going to bed (but otherwise all seems well
and the pigeons are still perching and fussing about on
the balcony railing, meaning another nesting episode is
probably in the works).
    **  For the first time since age fifteen I'm
wearing chuck high-tops instead of low-cuts.  (I had a
pair of high-tops lying around, plucked from the half-
price shelf at a downtown sports store years ago.  My
low-cuts developed a hole in the sole at a bad time
considering the week's snow and cold.  I didn't want to
break in a new pair of low-cuts under such poor walking
conditions.  Ergo, I'm the "lanky frosh center" all over
again, because that was the last time I wore high-tops,
actually at age fourteen I now realize.)
    **  Also wearing out these days: my brown backpack,
my one pair of jeans that fit right, my tan hooded all-
weather wear-every-day jacket, and these running shorts
I'm wearing right now (the inner lining has developed
holes which my droopily geezerizing genitals like to
peek through and sometimes even dangle out of, and so I
have to wear sweatpants over them and I get too hot
working out and therefore must quit early and come down
here and laze around).
    And that's about it.  Z had another of her "aha"
insights today -- "I realized this is really it, my

cheese is right here!" -- but best at this moment not to
go into the pop-psych system it's based on or the Z-
woman's complicated reasoning behind that realization.


-----

8

-----


Can't let this pass by unjyzed.  A beautiful day
for celebrating if ever there was one.  Sudden
unexpected springtime balminess -- with full sunshine!
And just as inspiring, it's another of those "official"
(at one time and place or another) first days of spring
which is also first day of a new year.
In this instance it's "Old New Year," the English
and North American version, pre-Gregorian.  Up until a
mere quarter of a millennium ago this was it -- strike
up the band, "Should auld acquaintance...."
And thus it's also the anniversary of the last (and
only) millennium celebrated in English-language and
various other Christian lands before the one that took
place two years ago.  Which is to say it's the True
Millennium, a/k/a the Jyze Millennium, plus two.
On that morning two years ago today some fifty to
sixty thousand people, maybe even more, including the
crews of several TV networks, gathered right here in the
hillside strip park and environs to watch the big bang.
Oy vey, the hullabaloo!  Helicopters swooping overhead,
hawkers selling "Domesday 2000" sweatshirts by the
truckload, live feeds to the networks going out from
elevated platforms via satellite trucks with their huge
extendable "War of the Worlds" antenna pods.
Today I'm the only one present in the entire park.
Me and the pigeons and the gulls.  And the view's even
better than it was two years ago because city crews have

cut back some of the hillside greenery and the branches
of the trees bear no people clinging to them like flocks
of massively overgrown starlings.  (And the trees are
only beginning to bud, so no leafy obstructions either.)
     Mountains.  Sound.  Islands.  A ferry crossing the
bay.  The works.  Including the newer of the two new
stadiums, and from where I sit I can see that edifice,
its major parts all in place, a big flag rippling at
just about the spot where the dome's flag once did.
Come football season it'll be ready to go.
     And we're almost to the auspicious days 47 (of year
4700 by the Chinese calendar) and 49 (that important
Buddhist number), it's the Rabbit Month still, the full
moon is coming up again, we're in the cluster of the Ox
-- the Golden Ox -- and this is the "Ox Inside the
Gate" as, I'm just realizing, I'm the Horse inside the
gate of the chain-link fence here at the drop-off -- the
gate leading to a shifting network of steep hillside
paths, sort of like the old Ho Chi Minh Trail (that is,
the cops close down one path, a new one quickly emerges
elsewhere) leading down to the hobo "jungle" or "rez"
(but better JRX that trail name).
     Across the street at my back, the DC castle.  And
this is the park named for the hero of the Philippine
independence movement.  It was just a hundred years ago
this spring that the U.S. was mopping up after
demolishing the last pockets of Filipino resistance
against our invasion -- just as we're supposedly doing
to the Taliban resistance in Afghanistan right now.
     Lovely scene though.  The grass in this long narrow
park hasn't even started growing again after its winter
hibernation but today it's smelling marvelously good.  I
just checked: no palm trees are in sight here.  But this
city does boast a few.  And yesterday was Palm Sunday,
which means we're into another Holy Week.  Today, in
fact, is the Feast of the Annunciation.  On this day the
maiden Mary -- not to speak too formally now -- got
herself knocked up by a total stranger.  Today would
anyone hesitate even a moment to call this act by its
proper name?  Gabriel, the rapist's accomplice, first

whispers in her ear it's about to happen.  Nine months
later, presumably after an uneventful term, the
Christian Age begins.

And this year Annunciation believers have special
reason to celebrate as the current USAn emperor himself
has announced the resumption of the Christian Crusades.
(And as I say this a potential enemy missile roars
overhead -- a 747 -- but apparently it's an unarmed and
maybe even friendly one.  But that might not be true of
the next or the next after that.  And just a few miles
up the road, and also a few miles down the road, our
aerospace/"defense" goliath is cranking out more and
more of these 747s.  So maybe we should send in the
B-52s to bomb the factories that are supplying the enemy
with their main weapons?)


[+3]


Back on with the puddle-hopping high-tops.  No
spring zephyr is forever.  But this is the year the
celebration goes on and on (at various levels and
intensities) and it does that today as well.  Right now.
Right here.

This is the AQ's main park.  The pavilion at its
center.  The green marble chess-playing table at the
center of the pavilion (it's octagonal, surprisingly
enough; I'd expect hexagonal, as in I-Ching hexagons).
A drizzly day, chilly, gloomy at five p.m., but I've got
fresh eyes and a roof, tiled and Asian-eaved, over my
head.  And today's the birthday of an ancient without
whom, I think it can fairly be said, neither jyze nor
this Heavenly Year project would exist.

I'm talking about the author of the "Tao Te Ching."
And to pay my respects and also for dramatic effect a
statue of this worthy is standing here atop a copy of
the book he wrote.  The statue is about two inches tall.
I just bought it at a shop a block up the street for
$1.99 plus tax.  In one hand he's holding up the peach
of immortality -- teasing me with it.  "Keep on jyzing,

[ Jyze of the Heavenly Year : Black Horse ]

Mr. Jyzer G, and you too can live forever."
     Or not.  But I'll keep jyzing anyway.  "Make J-
books.  Keep filling them.  What else is there?"
     -- Well, there are other kinds of love too.  Most
notably for me there's my love for the Z-spouse.  And as
happens now and again on serendipitous days, we just ran
into each other on the street a few blocks from here,
she on her way home and I on my way to work.  Under the
freeway, by the colonnade, within a few steps of where
jyze was going down during the snowstorm last week.
     I didn't recognize her at first from a distance
because she wasn't pulling her rollered backpack with
the extendable handle (she left the pack at the office;
didn't have a big enough load to justify making the long
uphill pull with it).  We stood right by the "No
Hazardous Materials Allowed on the Premises" sign at the
entrance to the parking lot.  "No Hazardous Materials
Allowed": that could almost be her personal slogan.
She's not exactly an expert on them (that's for the
scientists) but she's extremely well informed and one of
the best around at making people aware of their -- the
materials' -- toxic existence and what can be done to
avoid them.
     So she handed over the bus pass and we necked a
little behind the sign.  Nuzzled.  Spoke mush.  Today,
after all, is the day when love is supposed to reign
supreme, sort of the way it did in MSM #2 in the summer
of '67 (when this J-slinger right here moved there as a
newlywed -- though it soon stopped reigning supreme for
him, at least temporarily, and he quickly became a newly
unwed).  Today is, besides Lao Tzu's birthday, Maundy
Thursday.  What's that mean?  It's the day when the
holiest of the Christians advised the gathered throng
we should all love each other!  (And we all know what
happened next.  And the mono Sky Power didn't lift
a finger to stop it.)
     (Hey, very fine, some lights just came on in the
pavilion -- as a group of Taiwanese tourists line up for
a picture in which this jyzer will appear as the oddly
brown-hooded and long-nosed supplicant bent over the

table at the pavilion's center, seemingly bowing to or possibly interviewing a tiny statue.)

And in imagination I have a seder candle burning here too.  As of just moments ago -- probably about when the lights came on -- we're into the first day of Passover.  Earlier in the day a bomb exploded at a seder in Israel -- twenty died, hundreds were injured.  It was a Palestinian bomb, part of the cycle of retribution, also part of the larger North/South battle.  Right now our USAn juggernaut is briefly stalled while our neocon cabal tries to figure out how to ease its way past the Israel/Palestine stumbling block.  Our faithful right-wing Israeli ally is becoming a bit bumptious, seeing fresh opportunity in the uproar over Islamic terrorism following 9/11.  If they keep this up we might find it unpolitic to invade Iraq, as we're currently fixing to do in late summer or fall (it says so right in the current edition of the premier far-coast weekly lit mag, the glossy one with lots of ads for luxury goods).

-- I should note Mr. Tao here was the beneficiary of an origin story every bit as unlikely as that of the Christian immaculate conception.  His mother was said to have been "startled into pregnancy" at the sight of a spectacular celestial event -- and the pregnancy lasted sixty years!  And then the holy Lao Tzu lived on earth for 960 (or some say 360) more years before he officially became immortal, although he also, just like Christianity's top holy man but in somewhat different fashion, remained human.  And pretty soon the missionary work and the institution-building was well underway and eventually those who invoked his name with reverence numbered over a billion, just as with our top western human immortal and also the Islamic one.

But the fact remains: Lao Tzu wrote a pretty damn good book.  Or someone did.  As mystical writing goes it's a lot more in tune with our times -- sez I, yes -- than any old Bible or Koran or any other official holy book I know of.

But -- carumba!  I'm cold!  Dusk has merged into darkness and the cars double-parking in front of the row

of Chinese restaurants while all those people run in to
pick up takeout meals have become legion.

*    *

And here's a little celebratory kwikjyze.  It's now
three a.m. and the fog is lunar-luminously lovely and
the day, by Gregorian count, is the 29th of the month,
which means it's been five full Earth orbits of the sun
(or a tiny fraction of an orbit short of that) since
lightning struck.  It's We Meet! Day.

In acknowledgment of which the Z-wiff has left me
one of her special cards on the green bedroom armchair.
Pop-up/foldout type, hand-drawn by her, with glittery
little hearts floating among these words:
First fold: "5"
Second: "I guess."
Third: "It's sorta"
Fourth (big bright all caps): "A BIG DEAL."
And woven among those large-lettered words these
smaller-lettered ones:

 Dat ol' G magic gots
 Z in his spell
 Dat ol' G magic
 dat he wiles so well

So tomorrow, or later today by Gregorian measure,
we'll return once again to the site of the first
sighting.  Front door, the magazine shop a block from
the drawbridge and ten blocks from Z's apartment.  And
then a few steps around the corner to the meet-day cafe
for the ritual reenactment of her infamous first recoil
at my "casual" touch of her forearm.  As somewhere in
the heavens Comet Haley-Bopp streaked by.

And recoil or no, on that night we both stuck
around long enough.  The rest is history: some 1825 full
spins of the globe (or about 68 full 27-day spins of the
sun), a good many of both of these types of spin quite
giddy.  And the same goes for moon orbits around the
Earth, which now number just slightly over 64.  Or to
put the matter differently, for each year we've lived, Z
and I, we've now been together approximately one month.

To her this is a shocker: it's twice as long as

she's ever been with anyone else.  In a way it's hard
for her to accept.  She'd built up a self-image as the
ramblin' kind -- "No man could satisfy her for long."
It grates on her sometimes, this long-running schmaltz
she and I are engaged in, this togetherness and
coupledness and hitchedness.  But she's vowing anew to
live life, as she put it, "one limerence day at a time."

Me, I just hope I can keep her happy, insipidly or
any other way as long as it works.  And I think I know
how to do this, at least most of the time.  By
miraculous coincidence and lifelong hard labor I just
happen to be something like a natural at it where she's
concerned.  And she with me.  Maybe it wouldn't've been
true for either of us a few turns of the romance mill
back -- or maybe it would've.  -- But regardless we both
know how to let it happen now, and how not to panic if
it momentarily seems not to be happening.

In one's Heavenly Year one gets to wallow in such
syrupy sentimentality just as much as one wants.  But
jyze well knows it should try to limit it in the written
form (and yet somehow forgets to do that or says to heck
with it more than this jyzer right here for one ever
would've figured or allowed to happen in earlier times).

-- Meanwhile, I've gotta say, startling new twists
in the world drama.  The Arab countries, convening a
summit meeting, hang together: they reconcile with the
leader of Iraq and say an attack on that country, or any
other Arab nation, is an attack on them all.  You can
almost hear the anguished cry arising from the USAn
capital: "Coises, foilt agin!"  Well, let's hope so
anyway.  But let's also remember how little power the
Arabs actually have.  And at this very moment Israeli
tanks are breaking up the Palestinian leader's compound
as he awaits them defenselessly inside.

But, yes, teeth are gnashing, I'm sure.  The world
takeover (nothing less!) might turn out to be a shade
more difficult than our cabal's been thinking.  Yet --
they're fools but they're not all that dumb.  They knew
someone might toss a wrench or two into the works from
time to time.  Is the U.S. going to worry overmuch about

flying spanners when we're the ones with the nukes and
the Arabs have none?  (This is why we're not really all
that concerned about terrorists either.  We're just
seizing the opportunity afforded by 9/11 to ratchet up
our world dominance.  Deep down everyone knows this.)

   The article in the weekly far-coast lit mag
mentioned earlier still has me shuddering.  Our plan to
rule the world.  There it is, all laid out and signed by
the planners themselves.  Such hubris!  Such arrogance!
And that's what's really appalling about it.  As the
article itself points out, in its broad strokes the plan
isn't new.  It was first revealed in the press roughly a
decade ago (personally I'd say three decades ago) -- but
then Iraq invaded Kuwait and the general USAn populace
and most of the mainstream media forgot all about the
nefarious plan.  Then the hardcore planners got tossed
out of the capital after the '92 election.  Now they're
all back, with the son of the '88-92 president as the
new president, and this time they're not fooling around.

   will the USAn people be upset to hear about this
plan?  Well, we probably won't hear about it, by and
large.  Wouldn't widespread publicity about it from the
mainstream media -- not to mention criticism of it -- be
considered unpatriotic, even seditious by those who hold
power?  Quite likely.  But if the word does get around,
expect no groundswell of protest.  The public is primed:
it's us or them.  (And of course this could become true
-- self-fulfilling prophecy -- if the plan unfolds much
further.)  Better we rule the world than someone else
does, popular USAn thinking goes, or otherwise no one
rules it and therefore a global form of anarchy reigns.
That could significantly shrink our bottom line.

   And does the public here think the other 95 percent
of the world -- the ruled -- will see things this way
too?  Probably not -- but who cares?  Who has to care?
who's got the power?  Whose military budget exceeds the
next sixteen largest combined and has done so for
decades?  (Or however those numbers go -- they're
lopsided beyond belief.)  The ruled can like it or lump
it.  And eventually we'll send 'em enough of our good

fast-food franchises and Hollywood action flicks that
they'll forget about lumping it.  And besides, it's
obvious: the ones who have anything at all are going to
need us on their side or they'll lose what they do have
to those who have far less.  The white hats and the
desperados, the savages: which side you on?  Us or them?
    -- Another cluster, another rant.  Golden Ox gored?
We should be so lucky.  Rabbit trembling?  You bet.
Black Horse bucking and wild-eyed?  Yeah, true.  How
could it not be when the official Heavenly Year calendar
shows a furiously bucking bronco and the legend below it
(drawn in by me) says, again, "The buck starts here!"
    And, again again, it's We Meet! Day.  A good, good,
good Friday with some good, good, good lovin' comin'
right up -- but first I gotta swab myself down a skosh.


-----

9

-----


    On April Fool's Day I've taken myself out to the
ballpark.  Opening day.  Two-year-old ballpark,
Centropolis versus Jyze City -- my old hometown (one of
'em) versus my current and most likely last hometown.
And though I haven't paid a dime and I don't exactly
have the best view of the field, I'm still right here,
under the sheltering roof, an undeniable part of the
action.
    No April Fool's joke this.  Crack of the bat, roar
of the crowd.  I'm sitting on a concrete block --
antiterrorism block, I'd wager -- just outside the
players' entrance, and a couple of hundred feet up is
the retractable roof, and it's retracted.  At my back,
railroad tracks.  Through the chain-link fence a view
of the field itself -- a patch of vivid grassy green --

by way of an entrance to the center-field bleachers.
Our J-town guys down two to one, top of the seventh.

A sign here says the players will not be signing
any autographs.  Am I a player?  Am I a player?  Well,
on the sidewalk thirty feet west stands a saxophonist
and he's a player.  I mean, he's playing.  And if he's
playing, I'm playing.  Main difference between him and
me, he's got his hat on the sidewalk and it's filling up
with coins.  (I've got my bag at my feet and a few coins
in it but only my own, "emergency stash" for the bus.)

Big roars, whistles, cheers.  As all the
commentators are noting these days (no known
exceptions), this is what we USAns badly need more of
right now.  Escape.  And not just any kind of escape but
one with a strong element of patriotic nostalgia.  It
has that for me too, I can't help myself.  Roughly half
a century ago Dad took me out to my first major-league
ball game, another Centropolis club playing, the one
from the north side of town.  And less than a mile from
that old ballpark, of course unbeknownst to me back
then, one of my future spouses was busily and, from
everything I hear, raucously growing up.  I'm referring,
of course, to the Z-spouse.  (As the railroad gate
behind me lowers with clanging bells and a regional
passenger train rolls clamorously by, thirty feet away.)

-- And now, right on cue, an opera singer doing
"Take me out to..." inside the ballpark: and inspires a
mighty roar with his powerful final high note (though
it's quavery): "...at the old ball GA-A-A-A-ME!!"  (Must
be the seventh-inning stretch.)

I love the walk down.  View of cloud-enshrouded
volcano to the south as well as snowcapped mountain
ranges to the west and, briefly, the east.  Descending
the old Cawk hilltop "pioneer"'s steeply winding cowpath
-- now paved -- through what's called the greenbelt on
the west side of south hill.  You round a bend and soon
reach a bridge angled farther downward over ten lanes of
freeway, with the spectacular cityscape spread out
before you.  A six-block westward hike through an
industrial zone (including big rail yards with lots of

idle passenger cars on view) and then a couple of blocks
north and here you are, the ballpark, at the southern
edge of the HQ and near the western edge of the AQ.
Encountering lots of alkies and drifters along the way,
some headed for the old ball yard just like you.
(Didn't even mention the harbor, the cranes, the massive
stacks of containers so reminiscent of Lego blocks, many
different colors.  -- And JRX that product name.)
    -- Just found a better way to sit, one foot on the
ground and one on the cement block, repurposing right
thigh as jyze platform.  (Another passenger train, local
commuter type, its diesel blast immediately behind my
shoulder almost blew me away, nearly imploding my
eardrums.  Or so it sure did seem.  Clickety-clack, now
blithely rolling down that railroad track, after washing
me in a slight yet still unmistakable Doppler melisma.)
    I can see I'll have to be fighting off the
autograph hounds in a few minutes.  Already a dozen or
so are lurking about.  The two guards are no longer
sitting; they're up and looking huffy and brutal.  The
crowd's starting to drift out of the stadium.  And
here's another train.  Up in the girders a giant Stars
and Stripes is rippling and bristling like, as jyze just
can't stop noticing in this era for so many kinds of
slow rippling, a Siamese fighter fish.  Sidewalk
saxophonist going to town.  Ya gotta love this spot!
    And get this: a new comet has appeared.  Or not
really new; it last came around, according to Chinese
astronomical records, 341 years ago, when the greatest
of the old English protojyzers had just completed his
first yearly volume and the greatest of the old Japanese
haikuists was still in knee pants.
    (Can't prop this leg up here forever.  A strain in
the sacroiliac or some other nearby body part.)
    This is a Tiger cluster, by the way, and I'm
assuming my Tiger aspect to keep the hounds at bay, the
autograph hunters.  -- Cluster of the White Tiger, it
is, officially.  A beast I've actually seen, in zoos
here in J. City and elsewhere.  Yet it's still mythical,
just like the white buffalo (the one born in Mentoka ten

years ago, though it's now turned a brownish tan, is
still drawing pilgrims by the thousands -- because, just
like mythical gods, mythical beasts matter).

From the volume of the roars I can tell some hope
still lives in mythical Mudville, though not much.

Just noticed: from this vantage I can see several
buildings in our block and the next one to the south
atop our mile-distant hill, with the fifteen-story low-
income tower rising high above the rest.

-- Nobody's leaving the ball yard now.  Thunderous
foot-stomping, boos, cheers.  -- And here's the organ
again, wild flourishes.  A pitching change maybe.  A
rally in the bottom of the ninth?  (Must be.)

Nobody's leaving, that is, except me.  Gotta hurry
on to the WOC so I can meet Z at the appointed hour.
Will return to the jyze later with a few tales of the
weekend and other updates including, to be sure, today's
baseball final score.

*          *

Under the blown-up photo of the fallen but
sanctified twin towers.  Scope-office conference room.
And I'll just note turmoil continues at a very high
level in the Mideast.  Palestinian suicide bombers,
Israeli military incursions.  Our USAn cabal appears to
be tilting toward Israel rather than seeking a
negotiated way out.  This is frightening because it
suggests the U.S. might go ahead with its Iraq attack
even in the face of unified Arab opposition.  If so,
it'll be Christians versus Muslims all over again.  Our
cabalian brain trust might be thinking the time is ripe
for civilizational clash on the largest scale and at its
most violent.  Take 'em down for good while they're
still relatively weak.  Just about everyone would oppose
this -- Europe, the UN, the world.  In that sense it'll
be the U.S. against, yes, the world.

Would we be this foolish?  This demented?  We just
might.  Stay tuned.  (Why would we be?  Simple.  The
cabal figures that at crunch time it'll be global North
versus global South.  Better to take them on now while
our military advantage is at its max.  Europe can't stop

us; the UN can't; Russia, China, India can't.  They'll
all stay more or less neutral.  Later Europe will rejoin
us because they'll have nowhere else to go and, in
grossest terms, they're Cawk Christians like us.  Then
we'll pick off the others one at a time, the group that
won't accept our rule, with China probably the first big
target.  Any other terrorist brushfires arising in
desperate regions will then be easily extinguishable or
containable.  It'll be fortress USA controlling the
world.  Massive desperate migrations by land or sea,
caused by global roasting interacting with extreme
poverty, will be turned back by sheer USAn firepower.

     Anyone opposing this course at home will be branded
a terrorist sympathizer.  It's already happening.  And
it'll be getting a lot worse.  But gradually, most
likely.  Step by step by step.  We wouldn't want to look
too eager or too greedy.

     Okay, so that's the world situation in the usual
nutshell.  It's horrendous out there.  Nothing I or
anyone else not already in a position of immense power
can do about it right now, though, other than redouble
efforts to raise the alarm.  It's being raised already,
of course, and loudly, but so far few are listening.

     So instead, for now, more jyze.

*

     Tales of the Z&G weekend.  In which March goes out
not so much like a lamb as like a rabbit -- or better a
pair of rabbits.  Especially Saturday morning and even
more especially Sunday morning, Easter, holiday of the
bunny and also the Scandi fertility goddess Ostra.
Copulations galore!  -- Well, one each morning, or
afternoon by standard time.  But that's plenty for this
old trouper.  (Z-spouse announcing a new "theory":
balling is just more congenial now for me in the NUT
morning after I've had a chance to rest up, and doubly
so if she's done a little stoking of my fires the NUT
night before, or stroking, could say, which seems to act
as a leverager, so to speak, or ithyfier or erotic force
enhancer silently at work during my sleep hours.)

     Three days.  Abbreviated accounts must suffice

82

because the unexpected political rant at the top here
snatched too much time and the last bus will be coming
along all too soon.
     **  Friday.  A lovely ZAG & GAZ return to the meet
spot, doorway of the magazine shop, and then over to the
cafe (whose funk and high spirits are not, sad to say,
what they once were), and then at dusk retracing the
steps of our first walk across the drawbridge, though we
couldn't agree just how far we'd gone along the highway
on the other side and so with that as the topic nearly
reenacted our discordant behavior of the meet-day walk.
(And I sported the same "Waiting 4 Zoelie" button I wore
on that day.  She informed me she no longer has the
outfit she wore then: white top and sexy black tights.
Wore 'em out, she said, because I liked 'em so much.)
     **  Saturday Kat and I worked in delicious
conspiracy on our gift for Z in the 203 bedroom as Z and
Betty hobnobbed in the living room.  Then since Betty
was taking us out for dinner -- her delayed birthday
(solar) present for Z -- we headed down to an AQ
restaurant Z picked out.  By happenstance a Chinese
association was holding their own delayed New Year's
celebration there so we got to witness the festivities,
including some sadly feeble Year of the Horse fireworks
set off outside the main windows and a speech by our
state governor ("the most famous USAn of Chinese
ancestry ever" -- and he happens to be an old commuting
buddy of Z's friend Serafina).  Kat boldly ordered duck
but took only one bite and never did completely unscrew
her face.  Then up to the strip on east hill for
extended browsing at the infamous "320" used bookstore
(where a Hell's Angel whose weight I estimated at that
number of pounds tried to put the moves on Z one night
last year as I uneasily watched from outside unobserved
hoping I wouldn't have to intervene) (and didn't, by the
way; Z coolly finessed the situation) and then back home
for birthday dessert of hand-packed ice cream with a
topping of fresh blueberries and G-sliced strawberries.
     **  Sunday, Z's lunar birthday, she unwrapped her
present from Kat and me -- a hand-painted ceramic Horse

of the rare "Katglen" breed, characterized by a black-and-white checkerboard coat (because Kat's a White Horse and I'm a Black Horse) -- and the paint of our inscriptions was still a little wet and smeared in several places so I had to do a major touchup job on it later.  But Z proclaimed herself thrilled.  And then: a quiet afternoon at home reading the papers.  And in the middle of that a return to bed for some very fine encore side-lying whang-dang-doodle sandwiched between naps.

Also to mention: today's the birthday (solar) of the woman who opened my eyes to a lot of the things I'm seeing these days (and that are carrying me ever Heavenward) and who brought me as much pleasure and heartache as any one person could in that pre-Zoelie era and also very likely combined her alleles with mine so that a genetic copy of some parts of us both will be carried forward in the world, at least for a while.  The splendid Lady S.  Surely the single most influential person of my life after my parents and now Zoelie B.

** And finally, as promised: that was a four-run rally I heard from outside the ballpark, bottom of the eighth actually, not ninth, but it fell one run short and the old home team prevailed over the new, six to five.  Game two of the series tomorrow.


[+3]


Fine spring day.  Warm enough to be sitting outside in the shade with no coat on -- which is what I'm doing. Ideal for Cold Food Days too; and of those, we're now in the middle of the three.  In honor of an uppity scholar burned at the stake by an emperor of long ago we turn off the fires for three days.  No heat, no cooking.  Go ye scholars while ye may!

Not everyone honors this holiday.  J-town's gargantuan international coffeehouse chain certainly doesn't.  A steaming cup of its house brew sits on the table in front of me (as Jay the juggler strides by, presumably on his way to the WOC -- I can see it from

here, a block north on the other side of the street, a
low blockish white-marble building, formerly a bank --
but he doesn't see me).   ---
*

He did see me.  A few minutes' chat and now he's
off to the big lighting shop four blocks to the south,
visible from here straight down the old "middle road,"
in search of new fixtures for his workplace two blocks
west of here -- it's a local business newspaper, but
exactly what he does for them, I'm not sure.  A kind of
handyman who can also run the press, I think maybe.
We're longtime workout buddies, Jay and I, and just
lately it's begun to appear we'll take it a little
further, maybe see a movie or two the spouses aren't
interested in.  "Longtime" meaning about four years.  I
met him when I first started visiting the WOC with Z.
He's five years my junior, just like brother Jeff.  That
means they're both Fire Pigs.
The danger to a J-slinger of knowing too many
people.  Jyzing in public becomes much more difficult.
Kitty-corner from here stands the city office
building where Z works, and visible halfway up the hill
and then up three floors (on the fifth floor by official
count) is the window of the office next to hers.  In
about fifteen minutes she should be emerging from the
big arched entrance down here on my level and walking up
the street to the WOC.  We're due to meet on the
exercise floor at the usual time, about five-fifteen.
I've got my workout bag with me.  (I've also got an odd
little orange hammer made of some kind of hard rubber or
plastic or a combination thereof.  It was sitting here
on my table.  Jay thinks it might hail from the ancient
steam plant across the street from his office.  And
though the heat in the hideaway was off when I stopped
by an hour ago -- the steam plant provides heat for a
lot of the buildings in this area, including my own -- I
doubt the plant is observing Cold Food Days.  In any
case Jay's planning to ask about the hammer over there.
I, however, am claiming it as a Heavenly Year artifact
no matter what.  "If I had a hammer" -- and it's true I

already do have, in fact, several.  But never before one like this.  "Objet trouve.")

The hideaway building occupies the opposing corner, diagonally, of this same block, at my back, meaning to the southwest.

I should also note today's April 4th, 2002.  That's written out numerically, U.S. style, as 4/2/02.  And 4202 (read and spoken the same way as the date: four-two-oh-two) was also the address number for the house in which my mother spent her teen years and most of her college years and which then, after a gap of less than a year, became, as I later thought of it, Nana and Popeye's house, the place where I lived the first couple of years of my life and which I visited frequently for the decade following that and much less frequently for another couple of decades.  That number also served as a metonym for the house itself; that's how we all came to refer to it in letters or on the phone.  And even today to hear 4202 evokes a flood of associations, in the same way those numbered prison jokes evoke a laugh (supposedly).  And the same's true for 2015 and 636 in Gatewood and several other of my lifetime address numbers.  1511 will, if we're lucky, soon be reaching that status for Z and me.  Or maybe it already has.

Meanwhile buses.  Also lots of foot traffic headed for the ferry dock -- you can tell because they tend to move along much faster than everyone else.

On a day like this the walk in -- it's just under two miles, mostly downhill -- is sweet.  The sniff of fresh grass clippings -- three different times.  On the bridge I was briefly halted so that a commercial shoot could proceed: to sell football tickets, the grippe told me, with the new stadium gleaming in the background.

Z-spouse probably slipped out the doorway over there while I had my head down over this jyze.  Don't want to be late today, as I was on Monday.  And today being our lunar We Meet! Day!  No way!

As Passover ends.  As the headline in the box three sidewalk squares east blares: "FIERCE FIGHTING IN MANGER SQUARE."  Crisis -- deepening.

------

10

------

Is this crazy?  To be sure.  But an impulse says it must be done and the rest of me can't say no.

So, deep in the night we find our fleshly correlative parked on a bench in the downtown plaza. The city square, it's called by some, although it's actually, like the park outside the hideaway building in the HQ, a triangle.  A few odd characters are skulking about but the deep of the night is still only just beginning.  A block away at the other end of the plaza, right in front of the sparkly glass arcade building, classical music plays over a PA system -- whose, I don't know -- and it wends its way sinuously through the leafless potted trees and double-back bench clusters to this sacred little spot.  A spill of french fries (not mine) on the tile near the black-and-white low-cuts which carried me here drifts westward awaiting its likely cleanup crew of pigeons or gulls.

Two of the three street clocks within sight say it's early in the third watch and thus still the birthday, at least in this NUT zone, of the great English romantic poet of "emotion recollected in tranquillity" fame.  But the third street clock and the big electronic news-crawl flasher two blocks to the north both insist it's actually late in the third watch and thus we're already, Gregorianly speaking for this zone, forty minutes into Buddha's birthday.

The Z-mobile is parked in front of the scope building, where I just punched in the corrections on a couple of deps and printed the finals.  Rather than go for the sterile conference room with its unsettling

photograph of the ghostly towers as the opening venue
for the cluster of the double Rabbit I decided to wing
it on the streets.  When I reached the sidewalk, the
aforementioned impulse hit me -- stroll north.  Nothing
risked, nothing gained, or at least nothing truly
jyzerly gained.  Two blocks -- or less really; a block
and a half -- and I'm here.

Last entry of the Month of the Rabbit, and also a
Rabbit entry for its 1951 connection -- my tenth year on
the planet, as this is cluster ten of Heavenly Year jyze
-- so I'm just following my nose down the Rabbit hole to
whatever's poppin' down there.  "The Rabbit in the
Burrow" is the official slogan of the day.  But it looks
like Oz is the man.  Or Joz.  Or Jyze.

It's not too warm here.  But bearable even without
a sweatshirt under my jacket.  I'm surprised by the
absence of skateboarders.  (As the classical music hits
a zany crescendo without a soul in sight, not even a bus
or a taxi.)  And the two squad cars I've seen go by
haven't pulled over or even slowed to check me out.  I
guess crime is expected to be elsewhere tonight.

Two and a half years ago, during the Battle of J-
town, for a while a main body of subversives was penned
in right about here, on this spot.  I stood watching
across the street in front of downtown chain books #1, a
very large police horse's haunch intermittently blocking
my view (and several times whacking my shoulder).  But
that wasn't the Year of the Horse.  And this
peacefulness here -- not a piece of litter is stirring
-- is close to Heavenly.

I cross a leg for relief, noticing again the newly-
broken-in chuck low-cuts.  Black-and-white, the ancient
hoops style.  I dug them out from my hoard the other
day.  When the company that made them went broke last
year I panicked and bought half a dozen pairs.  After
wearing these things for roughly six years short of half
a century I figured I might not even be able to walk
without them.  As it turned out, someone else is making
the shoes now and they cost only a little more than they
did a year ago.  But I'm still happy to have the stash.

[ Jyze of the Heavenly Year : Black Horse ]

I feel safe.  I'm good to ramble for quite some time.

The international crisis?  It's continuing.  More bombs in Bethlehem, more mass protests across the Arab world.  Europe isn't happy either.  But the cabal has blinked.  Our supreme leader is now ready to cut a deal with that bloodthirsty terrorist in Palestine.  It seems some "terrorists" aren't quite as evil as others even if they're still on the side of the bad guys.

The hope?  This will be a turning point in popular support for the cabal -- that is, turning away from it, I'm saying.  But whether it actually will be is still far from clear.  The atomic doomsday clock has been moved back a couple of minutes, that's all; instead of three minutes to midnight it's now five to.

God, the violins!  Such rambunctious flurries -- as accompanied posses on the move, for instance, in old westerns.  And my hood's up: the chill's starting to get to me.  A glance around and I see all these shop windows lit up and no one to gaze at the splendors within.  An elephantine garbage truck, red, rumbles by, with dumpster-lifting arms sticking out in front like tusks, moving faster than you'd think it could (just as they say elephants or rhinos or hippos authentically do).

-- And now a comical exchange, at least by my lights.  Afrusan woman in a ragged blue cloth coat wanders by, sez to me, "That Amadeus or Beethoven?"  I say: "Danged if I know."  She: "You don't know?  You're a white boy, you should know, you got a lock on education."  "Yeah, but the sad fact is most of us are still ignoramuses."  "You got that right."

Cackle cackle.  The verdict of the street.  "The USAn street."

In the past several days two "spats" between Z-spouse and me.  I insisted on the term "spat"; she preferred "fight."  But both were tiny, in my view scarcely even mini spats.  Noticeable at all only because so rare for us in recent times, and that fact itself no longer even seems surprising to either of us.  Sometimes she jokes I've "tamed" her or somehow I've got her number.  But the reverse is equally true, or

corollary or whatever it is: she's tamed me and has my
number.  It's just I'm a little more ready to accept my
domestication than she is hers.  Nor am I complaining
about this.  I like it that she brings an abundance of
feist and provocation to the daily slog; always have.
And that's good because she so frequently does.

Yesterday I was touched and impressed by the
birthday doings she worked up for ten-year-old Ben, son
of her six-years-deceased Chiusan friend Julie K.  He
and his father were in town for a visit, staying with
two other close friends of Julie's: Serafina first, then
Aida.  All of us, including four kids in total, met up
at far-north books for a party.  (It remains a favorite
destination for Z and me, a used/new bookstore combined
with a restaurant arcade and a performance venue in one
large ex-supermarket space.)

Today on the way to a movie we drove by the spot on
east hill where Julie used to live -- it's now part of a
city-owned P-patch -- and Z's tears rolled again.  Her
loyalty to, and the depth of her attachment to, her
friends are something to behold.  -- The movie was
"Monsoon Wedding."  It reminded us of our own.  More
tears rolled, including some of mine.

Last night, I should note, the time changed.  It's
two a.m., you think?  Middle of the fourth watch as the
Tang poets and lots of others might say?  No, it's three
a.m., start of the fifth watch.  (Also called the Hour
of the Tiger, I think it is -- although it's actually,
like all traditional Chinese hours, two Gregorian hours
long.)  And by fiat also USAn Daylight Savings Time
arrived.  It fell to me to "spring" all the clocks ahead
an hour, except for the one on the stove whose digital
controls have always mystified me (and Z also).

So in a way this is yet another start of spring.
And the season is visible everywhere now, even, if you
look closely, in all these trees here in the plaza which
at first may seem leafless.  But no, tiny buds
proliferate.  And elsewhere in the city clouds of
blossoms have materialized -- the cherry trees at the U
drawing big crowds, just as they did back in the day

when I could walk over from the house where Lady U and I
lived some six blocks to the west to join those crowds,
and numerous times did -- and tulips blooming by the
millions or even the billions if you include the massive
commercial fields of same two counties to the north.

A final note before my brain shatters from
chattering teeth and cascading shivery spinal arpeggios.
Two days ago, Friday, at the end of Cold Food Days, also
known as Qing Ming, also known as Pure Brightness, was
the day for spring sweeping of the grave where the
revered ancestors lie.  De rigeur, it almost is, to get
out in the country on that day, picnic at graveside,
drink some wine, maybe dash off a poem or two.  Along
about twenty-eight years ago -- exactly one full
Glennarian cycle, I note with surprise -- I myself went
through a family crisis over Qing Ming, just one of many
in that year of major personal culture clash.  Should
the long-nose foreigner be invited to sweep the grave of
his son's distinguished grandfather?  If invited, should
he accept?  Just whose face most needs saving in such a
situation?  And should a daughter of that same
grandfather be allowed to co-sweep, even though
tradition would judge this a no-no simply because she's
female?  (In the end the foreigner stayed home.  Some
thought this move was wise; others thought it was an
across-the-board diss.  It turned out to be just a kind
of entry-level cross-cultural ethics conundrum and soon
was succeeded by others of far greater complexity and
much deeper personal import.  Or call it a precursor.)

This year for Qing Ming I at least did a little
token sweeping at the hideaway.  That's the closest I
can come to fulfilling my filial duties.  No picnic.
And at home we did some vacuuming.

Enlightened One, on your birthday I extend
congrats.  Two and a half millennia on and statues of
you are still being blown up because you failed to be
fanatical enough.  Or is it because all those less
enlightened ones had to go and make you a god, yet
another embodiment of the absolute and therefore
unacceptable to rabid believers in some other absolute?

[ Jyze of the Heavenly Year : Black Horse ]


[+2]

    It's the recently swept set of Jyze Central.  And
here, bending over these pages from a makeshift vase on
the chairside table, a couple of tiger-stripe tulips,
orange on yellow.  When I came in I found them popping
up from the maw of my gym bag, where Z-spouse had
planted them as a surprise.  (It's her first visit to
225 in a while.  I think she stopped coming so often
because she decided I needed my own inviolable space.  I
never said or even hinted I wanted this, but at home I
don't go into her room unless invited and I think she
concluded I'd like her to be the same way about my room
here.  Or it could be she's taking the same lesson from
my infrequent visits to her utility office.  But of
course by the time I'm up and out of the house and have
reached downtown in the late afternoon she's no longer
at that office; and even if she were there, I'd have no
way to get into the building to surprise her.  Once in a
while I'd like to slip in if I could: to leave her a
couple of orange marigolds, for instance, like the ones
that festooned the marriage tent in "Monsoon Wedding."
I might even have tried to do that yesterday.)
    But there's this: the taxes are a wrap.  And it's
not even April 15th yet.  Not even April 10th!  But we
know we're owed a refund of $777, so I managed to
overcome my normal deadline-hugging habit (which I
developed for taxes, aside from my natural tendency to
procrastinate, because that way you're most anonymous
and least likely to be audited).  Of this Z will receive
$437, I $340.  Even though she makes in a week half
again (almost) what I make in a month, that's fair.  Our
being married raises my tax rate considerably and lowers
hers -- and without me she wouldn't even be eligible for
the couple of hundred bucks she'll be receiving as a
rebate of interest on her student loan.  So once again I
may just be a chloroformic old husband but at least in
some ways I'm useful and even profitable to have around.
    She immediately celebrated by going out and buying

a new laptop computer.  She wants it mainly so she can
fire off political missives, which she's forbidden to do
on her computer at work.  And she wants to have it
around for Kat to play with when she visits us.  I,
meanwhile, will inherit her home desktop computer (PC)
which has some sort of glitch that prevents reliable
internet access but doesn't affect steno translation and
word processing, which are the only tasks I ordinarily
use a computer for.  Now I just need to figure out (A) a
way to load my antique software on it and (B) a place to
set it up.  The hideaway desk I'm jyzing at right now is
the logical spot, but I like having it available for
other tasks.  So where then?  I dunno, and I'm not even
going to worry about it until next year.

Tonight I'd been thinking I might focus on
nostalgia.  Three reasons.  First, the roadshow of the
revived musical "Hair" is in town, opening soon at a
downtown theater (whose marquee I can see, through a gap
between skyscrapers, some fifteen stories below and one
block to the east of the scope office; a blotch of
incandescent colors over there often catches my eye when
I'm gazing out the conference-room windows).  Second,
the city's giant golf-tee icon has been repainted its
original colors to mark the fortieth anniversary of its
opening for the 1962 Jyze City World's Fair, and I see
it most nights floating to the north straight up the
"middle road" as I'm walking in -- and forty years ago
this summer I was working in the World's Fair carnival
almost directly beneath the icon (just as thirty-five
years ago I was working on the expanded set,
figuratively speaking, of the production of "Hair"
during the "Summer of Love" in MSM #2) (and never dreamt
a day would come when I'd be swamped with nostalgia-
upwellings precipitated by either of these icons -- at
the time they both seemed to be more or less hokey
tourist attractions).

And third, a very good pianist is opening at the
fanciest of the downtown jazz venues tonight -- about
halfway between the golf-tee icon and the "Hair" theater
-- and she was born just three weeks after my mother

was, as Mom (a big fan of hers in the last decade or two of her, meaning Mom's, life) -- as Mom, I say, several times pointed out to me. Makes me think of the tears welling in old Mom's eyes as she said to me shortly after receiving her lung-cancer death sentence: "I don't mean to sound greedy, but I think seventy-five is way too young for me to die." Her struggle to hold out to at least seventy-six fell about three months short.

    -- But back to the present. Current events. Politics. Everybody's still defying the cabal's orders; fighting rages in Palestine; oil prices appear ready to blow the tops off the pumps. Yet it's still no sure thing our homegrown cabal villains have been foiled, other than temporarily. The Iraq attack might have to be canceled or at least postponed until next year (but that's far from a sure thing). Otherwise the big world-domination power play continues all but unopposed -- or so you'd guess from the media (ours) -- just as does the garrison-state buildup at home.

    And in my own home, it's been a week of never-a-dull-moment Zoelie. The true mark of Zoelie B.! For one thing, it's definite, the H-rag (shorthand for a herpes outbreak) is back. "My poor hubbin." But I can handle it. Just as always we still can go sexual plan B. -- And she's suddenly taken to licking my ear every morning when I come to bed, since that was supposed to be the signal she's interested in getting it on. She decided to subvert it. She's very good at subversion with a smile. She also announced, contradicting former announcements, she now generally prefers genital to nipple "O's," but that this isn't really a change. So I'm confused, but no more so than before -- just differently so. And after you've been with someone for five years it can even be good to have an occasional change of confusions. (She's also had several nightmares related to child abuse, presumably sparked by "Monsoon Wedding.")

    And a final note: June's now taken several additional steps to assure Z -- and me, though me just incidentally -- she's grateful for our help in tutoring

her through law school, of which we gave plenty.  Z
thinks I'm too "nice" in not insisting on more
recognition myself.  Sorry, but it just doesn't matter
that much to me -- probably because I well know how
grateful June is and why matters of face keep her from
expressing it more directly.  I learned this way of
seeing things from the same person who introduced me to
the Water Horse, the Silver Rabbit, the Tiger, the whole
Chinese zodiacal calendar menagerie: Lady S.  As jyze
has noted many times before over the past five years, in
some ways June resembles her quite a bit.

     March went out like a Rabbit, I was saying ten days
ago (it's past midnight).  Now my line -- and it better
be tonight's wrap-up zinger -- is the Rabbit goes out in
a march.  Jyze march.  Around the corner and gone.


------

11

------


     Found me a fine spot for this one.  Children's park
in the AQ.  A cherry tree eye-poppingly abloom at my
back, a new-fangled aluminum-and-glass pavilion rising
overhead, a big dragon humping along horizontally, sea-
serpent-like, in the sandbox.  It's the start of Dragon
Month and this is the Dragon cluster.  Water Dragon, to
be more specific, also known as "Dragon in the Rain."
And that's where this dragon, or let's cap that, Dragon,
in the sandbox is, and I'm almost in there with it.

     A drippy, mizzly Saturday, probably close to six
p.m. by now.  It's Sakura Week at A-mart a couple of
blocks west of here and they're giving away blossom-
laden twigs in the shadow of the big metal Dragon there.
Across the street from that Dragon a dozen other
Dragons, large and small, made of fiberglass, are

bivouacked behind glass in the back room at a bakery/
cafe -- with a show window for gazing both inward and
outward -- as they await city permits for mounting on
lampposts and telephone poles throughout the AQ.  (It's
part of a plan to spruce up the quarter a bit and draw
in more business, of course -- and thereby to keep the
place viable as the ethnic enclave it still mostly is.)
     And if I sight along a straight line directly above
the tail of the Dragon in the sandbox -- a creation of
Z's friend Gilbert S., she'd surely want me to note --
and above the trees on the other side of the park, there
stands the DC castle towering above the greenbelt and
the trees of the hillside strip park.  And located right
behind all that, but not visible from here, is a
residential block where most of the homes bear peace
signs among all the flowering fruit trees and camellias
-- a morale booster for sure in these trigger-happy
times (I walked down that street on my way here today).
     And behind that block, on our street, at 1511, also
not visible from here, and up in unit 203, some big
doings.  It's been a turbulent J-week (also known as a
sixer for this Heavenly annal).  Mama E was hospitalized
in Centropolis and now the rest of the year's looking
much different, for her and for us.  Z's reserved a
Tuesday-morning flight to Centropolis; a week later
she'll be flying back here with Mama (whose goods will
be shipped).  In the meantime I'll be trying to find her
a place to stay temporarily while we line up something
more permanent -- most likely some sort of group-living
arrangement in a private home ("adult family home").
     I can do this but it'll be quite a chore for a
night worker.  I'm way out of sync with the utilitarian
day world of apartment hunting and such.  But I can
adapt for a time.  And jyze can too.  This project right
here -- Heavenly Year -- is going ahead just as planned,
but is prepared to be flexible if necessary -- and it
probably will be necessary.
     Stiff upper lip!  After all, what's this new twist
in our personal lives compared with the current horrific
doings in the life of the world?  For Z and Mama E it's

likely to be very tough at times but I'm mostly just a
helpmate in the matter, resolved to do all I can to ease
their troubles.  And can't help thinking of what people
with ordinary lives more or less like ours are going
through now in, say, Afghanistan and Pakistan and a lot
of other places where bombs are falling and wars raging.
(The outrageous Israeli invasion continues.  The
slightly modified U.S. pro-Israel policy is getting
nowhere.  The danger of an even greater catastrophe
resulting from this invasion remains high.  The whole
world is hanging on its outcome -- it's sort of like the
Cuban missile crisis of forty years ago, a mash-up of
that and the Iranian hostage crisis of '79 and the
crisis surrounding our massive military response to the
Iraqi invasion of Kuwait in '91.)
        -- Crisis everywhere.  A number of homeless men are
regulars at this park; one of them just came up and eyed
me with some hostility, probably because I've grabbed
the only dry seat in the park.  And I intend to hang
onto it.  Any parents wanting to bring kids to this park
I'm sure would perceive me as being a member of this
sorry homeless contingent.  Or not "sorry"; they're too
aggressive and nasty-looking to be perceived that way.
And me too, I suspect.  Big Cawk guys -- why can't we go
hang out in some other hood?  Oh, the contradictions,
the explaining to be done, and how unsatisfactory it all
would be and is.
                            *

(That seat's not so dry after all.  The rain's
increasing and now I'm forced to jyze standing up,
leaning against the aluminum pole at the center of the
pavilion.  Even here there are leaks.  So I'm thinking
I'd better roll out the tarp for a rain delay.  Right
now!  Drops hitting this page like tiny water bombs!)
                      *           *
        -- A little rainstorm melodrama there.  As for
damages, I did get soaked during the uphill walk home,
but otherwise just a few splotches on these pages.  And
I could've taken shelter somewhere.  But I figured Z
would be feeling lonely.  I liked the Z-like idea of

arriving home earlier than expected.  Surprising her!
    Now it's four in the morning and things seem
better, though maybe they shouldn't.  Today, speaking
Gregorianly, could be a real trial as Mama E taxis home
from the hospital two thousand miles east of here,
stopping along the way at an auto dealer (yes!) to pick
up the four hundred bucks Z wired her and then stopping
again at a drugstore for her medication.  Is she capable
of doing this when, at age eighty-six, she's depressed,
near hysterical, and hobbled by severe arthritis?  Her
friend and apparent semi-roomie Tito will be with her,
yes, but he's in bad shape too and one source of her
anxiety is his questionable ability to survive on his
own after she leaves Centropolis.
    Z's spirits are much better, however, at least
temporarily.  As she said soon after I came in, "We've
just got to try to look at this as a big adventure.
It's the only way we can get through it."  And she liked
the thought so much she called Mama E moments later and
urged her to try to see it that way herself.
    And here I sit in the bedroom as she tosses about
before me.  It's our same old Saturday-night tradition.
Just one reading lamp lit, the shade tilted up toward
the wall behind my chair and a cloth draped across the
top of the lamp to cast the rest of the room in shadows.
She always says this is when she sleeps best, in the
shadows on Saturday night as I sit in the room with her.
(Even better when our toes are touching, but right now
hers are a bit out of range.)
    I didn't mention it yet: today's still another New
Year's, this time coming at us from Sri Lanka.  And it's
a kind of second New Year in India, I gather, the solar
version this time after the earlier lunar one.  So
roughly a billion people are celebrating tonight as the
really big shadow sweeps across their part of the globe,
and that doesn't even include anyone who might be doing
so elsewhere for reasons other than the turn of the
year.  So why not celebrate here?
    And we did.  Our original plan for today had been
to see a movie with Wei and Alison (first screening of

an independent depiction of efforts to counter racism in
South Africa) and then, after dinner in the AQ, they
were to accompany us over here for dessert and to view
the new Black Horse banner and the collection of framed
"wedding cards" (which I finally finished mounting on
the hallway walls late last night, pausing between turns
of the screwdriver to keep squeaky noise disruptions
down for any day workers sleeping nearby, e.g. Z).  All
those plans had to be canceled, unfortunately, but since
we'd already laid in a blackberry pie and vanilla ice
cream and tidied up the dining area in anticipation of
W&A's visit we decided we might as well pig out on our
own.  And so did.  And an hour ago I had to chomp down
half a dozen antacid pills (from a new bottle with
tropical flavors) and my stomach's still booming a
madcap soundtrack with bizarre percussion and blaring
trombones and braying whoopee cushions -- perfect for
next year's Oscar winner "A Beautiful Borborygmy."
       Reminding me: what got all this started with Mama E
was, as it was later diagnosed, an "esophageal reflux."
That's sort of like my borborygmy (which is a big word I
recently learned, or actually relearned, for growly
stomach) only much worse.  She, however, at first
thought it might be a heart attack and Tito took her
straight to the emergency room.  For one very long night
Z feared it was the end -- her forebodings worsened by
still-fresh memories of the way her half-sister died
after a similar emergency-room visit less than four
months ago -- but this time the doctor reassured Z by
telephone the next morning, saying Mama E appeared to be
physically fine, all things considered, but she was
emotionally depressed and anxious.  This was owing in
part to Mama E's growing inability to get around and in
part to the fact that her older brother Joe -- he's
ninety and "was once a big guy in her life," Z tells me,
though the two sibs haven't been that close in recent
decades -- Joe was himself near death.  Making matters
worse, Mama E'd stopped taking her antidepressant a
couple of months ago -- thinking she didn't need it
anymore -- but hadn't told anyone, including her doctor.

[ Jyze of the Heavenly Year : Black Horse ]

    For one day we thought we'd be traveling to
Centropolis in June to move her out here.  That is, we
advanced our previous plans by three months.  Then the
doctor said he didn't know if Mama E'd be able to live
on her own for that long, even with Tito's help; the
sooner we could get her out here, he said, the better.
"The more time she has to worry, the worse off she'll
be."  Z decided to bite the bullet immediately.  And to
her surprise, Mama E not only was willing to leave
within a week but also said she'd prefer to fly --
whereas before she'd told Z (or rather Z had interpreted
her unclear statements as meaning) she'd prefer to drive
out.  And this meant my presence in Centropolis became
unnecessary and possibly counterproductive.  Thus we
could save a bundle on airfare, which is shockingly
expensive these days if you must fly on short notice.
    Z will be maxing out her credit cards to make this
trip and set her mother up here.  Even under the most
optimistic scenario Mama E's $1100 monthly Social
Security stipend will almost certainly fall far short of
covering her living expenses in J-town.  So as Z says:
it's time for us to clamp down on spending.  This really
means just her, since I'm already close to the
subsistence minimum.  But we're both prepared for such a
contingency.  We've known the chances were high it would
be coming sooner or later.  In fact that's why we're
still living where we are.  A year ago when several good
housing opportunities presented themselves -- good but
expensive, at least by the standard of the rent we're
paying now, at the very least doubling that amount in
monthly mortgage payments -- we explored the options in
depth and decided to continue renting so long as her
mother's alive, and preferably we'd be staying right
where we were then and still are now.  And this is
looking to have been a wise decision.  It's surely part
of what enabled Z to regroup quickly and say we should
try to think of it all as an adventure.
    But that's the way she is.  She may lose it, melt
down, rant and rave as the mygs swarm, but she catches
herself and tries to make up for it.  This latter

ability of hers is something I can (and not infrequently
do) count on.  The key for me is riding out the rough
hours between meltdown, say, and recovery without
overreacting.  Generally I can do it.  Maybe with
someone else I couldn't.  It's a matter of temperamental
chemistry.  We're good for each other.  (What smarm!  So
smarmy and yet also so prosaic it must be true.)

    And it's good she has her deep-rooted network of
friends for support.  Wei managed to find cheap tickets
(relatively) for her and Mama E, and even though this
will mean flying in and out of a small in-city airport
instead of the huge international one out in the burbs,
and the airline's unknown to us, mother and daughter are
both willing to override their fear of the unfamiliar
and brave it.  Aida, Olwen, June, Betty, and Leola have
all offered succor -- as have many others at the utility
and elsewhere indirectly -- and will also be helping me
in the search for temporary accommodations for Mama E.

    -- This room of the trembling red paper hearts
dangling on strings.  I huff out a couple of big-bad-
wolf puffs and instantly they're all dancing, swooping,
swerving.  The Jyze Gang cowboy sneers restlessly in the
corner in life-size cardboard-cutout form; he's been
deputized to watch over Z-wiff while I'm away and so he
has nothing to do right at this moment.  Bookshelves and
knickknacks galore in here.  Piled in category stacks on
the top two shelves to my right -- off-limits to Z --
are some 700 or so of the existing roughly 850 cards
I've altered for her, with another approximately 150
still to go to meet my thousand-card wedding pledge.
Every day, if I don't have a newly made card ready for
her, I pick out one of these 700 old ones to leave on
her pillow.  And most likely few, if any, new ones will
be appearing before next year.  For this Heavenly Year,
jyze itself will almost surely be it.

    A funny and touching scene yesterday.  Z and I went
down to her credit union -- in the next building uphill
from the WOC -- and she added my name to both of her
accounts, checking and savings.  They're now joint.
After the way former fiance Arvin ripped her off back in

the day this is something she thought she'd never be
doing again.  But it was her idea: she wants me to be
able to pay for things in her absence -- a deposit on an
apartment for her mother, for example -- and she knows I
wouldn't be able to do that out of my own meager
accounts.  And there I was seated at the account rep's
desk, looking the way I usually look -- that is, ready
for the night streets, scraggly, scruffy, in jeans and
chucks and worn hooded jacket -- digging deep in my
funky duct-taped backpack to come up with an ID.  My
state driver's license has expired, my birth certificate
wouldn't do (no picture), and the only other picture ID
available, my 1975 international driver's license --
which I keep around for laughs -- is written entirely in
Japanese.  Z's take on the photo of me on that license,
which she hadn't seen for years: "You look sort of like
the young Jim Morrison on a real bad day."  (In the end
the account rep accepted the totality of all this plus
my bank debit card as proof that I am who I declare
myself to be.)  (And a JRX on the rock star's name; I
just couldn't pass up the chance to slip it in.)
     And I should also mention today's the solar
birthday of my "black magic" lover whom symbolic
structure requires I call Silver Rabbit (or by less
exacting standards the much more appropriate, but still
nowhere near appropriate enough, White Rabbit -- she
having eloped to MSM #2 on her sixteenth birthday at
just about the time when that anthem to hallucinogenic
bliss was topping the charts -- and also at just about
the same time as the newly married Black Horse trotted
into town).  Also aptly, this year's lunisolar birthday
span for Silver Rabbit (or Silver Cat, the even apter
name for Lady V, since it's the Vietnamese version of
Silver Rabbit and half her heritage is Vietnamese/
Chinese) -- this year's lunisolar birthday span for her,
I say, is relatively short -- just a week -- and it
overlaps the much larger lunisolar span for Gray Rooster
(we're currently in the fourteenth day of that).  In
real life my overall relationship span with Silver Cat
was half what it was with Gray Rooster (Lady S),

[ Jyze of the Heavenly Year : Black Horse ]

starting slightly before the latter's halfway mark and
ending just months before its ending: all part of the
final showdown marking the close of the first half of my
life, at least by the standards of "The Inferno" --
whose protagonist is famously thirty-five.

    I'd be amazed if any of the above paragraph were
clear to anyone.  But it's all simple calendrical fact.
("Lunisolar birthday span," it might help to mention,
is the period between one's lunar and solar birthday,
including the birthdays themselves.)

    -- A moment ago one of the Sunday papers arrived
with a big THOMP.  Best that I fetch it right now before
it becomes rain-soaked.  It's still stormy out there.
Whooing wind, rain splatter on the windows and walls in
sudden flurries at times almost like hailstones.  It's
been this way all week with only brief respites.  No
moon viewing, no comet viewing (its prime is already
past and I still haven't seen it and probably won't --
Ikeya-Zhang, I'm talking about, the big astronomical
event, which is to say heavenly event or celestial
event, of my Heavenly Year).  -- And I'm now, as of
yesterday, sixty days deep into my sixtieth year,
lunarly speaking.  For a jyze tale structured on a
sexagesimal system this fact must carry some serious
significance.  If so, let it now make itself felt in
whatever way works for it.  I'm off, barefoot, to
fetch the news and, while at it, water the plants.


[+2]


    Bizarre.  Jyze never did it quite like this before.
At the concert-hall bus stop on the high road downtown,
across the street from the main post office.  Sitting on
a window ledge at mid-building, a little closer to the
cross street to the north than the one to the south, my
chest resting against the back side of the hip-level
aluminum bar, round and shiny, that standing people lean
their asses against while awaiting their buses.
    Odd posture.  Odd perspective.  Jyzing seems to

103

become a whole new kind of act down here.  (You might almost call this an anti-jyze bar.  A long row of them has been installed to prevent people from sitting on the window ledges or, worse, leaning against the big floor-to-ceiling windows.  But from long hours of waiting for buses at this stop -- it's one of my two main downtown boarding points -- I know you can sit back here if you slide in around the end of the bar or sort of limbo in backwards, under and up, which is what I just did.)

A rare night too.  Jittery is the word for it.  The one night in the year the post-office lobby stays open past eight p.m. -- until midnight, in fact.  Right now at about twenty minutes before midnight it's about as crowded as you'll ever see it over there, no matter what time of day.  Long lines of cars are slowly moving toward a group of mail-handlers stationed just around the corner and also toward another group around another corner in front of the scope building -- whose back side, which dominates the view from where I sit, towers above the three-story-tall post office and runs nearly the full length of the block.  All these folks are just-in-timers, also known as JITs, making their last-minute income-tax deliveries.  Jittery JITs, yeah.  And I'm one of them, or rather just moments ago was, though in my case the only form delivered was a quarterly prepayment for the self-employed.

All of us feeding the insatiable maw of our very own world-domination machine.  For people like me the only possible defense is that we're forking it over under extreme duress.  If we don't fork it over, we'll pay much more later, both financially and quite likely in other ways far more unpleasant.

Out in the world the Mideast crisis ratchets down a notch as U.S. pressure gains grudging concessions from Israel and the Palestinians, although the battles continue and the concessions might turn out to mean little or nothing.  The atomic clock moves back one more minute but the likelihood of a U.S. attack on Iraq and other horrors increases.  Then again a seemingly successful right-wing coup in oil-rich Venezuela is quickly reversed by the Venezuelans themselves, leaving the U.S. with egg on its face because we said nothing against the coup attempt even though the country's leader was democratically elected, and we supposedly support democracies. Right?  In the medium run, at least, if not the long run, this reversal could surpass in importance anything happening in the Mideast.

And here at home the Great Adventure, as Z-spouse has christened it, continues.  Tomorrow she flies off to Centropolis.  And by great good fortune we've been able, while she was still here, to come up with acceptable temporary housing for Mama E.  The very first apartment we looked at this afternoon -- after spotting it in the classifieds -- met all the basic criteria: first floor (only three steps up from the courtyard), not too expensive ($510 a month), reasonably safe hood (it's in the hospital district near the southern crest of east hill), conveniently located (just a mile and a half from us -- a few blocks behind the terrace-gardens peace park overlooking the AQ -- and within shouting distance of a small grocery store and several emergency rooms).

This triumph left us enough free time to hunt for furnishings.  But though we came up with two of the requisites -- table and chairs, chest of drawers -- we couldn't find a couch that converts into a bed.  So my major job while Z's away will be to locate and install one of those, as well as to assemble the other pieces, and then to prepare the apartment for occupancy.  This last-named task shouldn't be too tough since I have a good idea now what Z has in mind for it.  I'd've been a lot more stressed trying to come up with an acceptable apartment on my own (for my mother-in-law, no less).

The other good news: Z says Mama E sounded much better on the phone today.  "It's amazing what those antidepressants do for her!"  Z herself has been unable to use her favorite antidote for anxiety, the herbal cava cava, which a recently published study shows can cause severe liver damage for longtime users (and Z is one of those, sporadic but heavy when using it).  And if you ask me she's handling all this turmoil extremely

well while also keeping up with her job duties.  The
frenetic final days and weeks of my own mother's last
year are still fresh enough in my mind that I feel I
have a pretty good idea of what she's going through.

-- The posture I must assume in contorting behind
and under the ass-rail here at the bus stop, I'm finding
out, can cause some discomfort when maintained too long.
Like for instance one's own ass numbs.  I'm perched on a
sharp edge.  without all those years of booty-building
biking I'd've had to limbo back outta here long ago.

The usual drunks, fights, mock fights, boom boxes,
beer bottles, flashing lights, buses rolling in and
roaring away, beeping of handicap ramps being lowered
and raised.  The downtown swing-shift crowd.  A few nods
to familiar faces and so far no major botheration.
Meanwhile the post-office lobby has emptied out.  The
midnight deadline has long since passed.

What other news?  well, if the historians and
scientists are right, today (or possibly yesterday)
should be Christmas.  The latest studies agree the
composite man/deity for whom the holiday is named was
most likely born on April 14th (which happens to be Lady
V's solar birth date), or perhaps the 15th, of the year
5 B.C.E.  And what would all those gubmint-hating, tax-
despising Christian Identity militants of our era do if
it turned out Tax Day was also their Main Dude's true
birthday?

Squally weather continues.  A cold breeze is a-
blowin'.  I hear ropes banging against flagpoles atop
the post office.  Looking up I see my scope-firm floor
-- easily identifiable because the lights always stay on
late in the law-firm office next to ours; and because we
have an internal entrance to that office that's always
open, I'm the one who usually winds up turning those
lights off -- but the windows behind which I would
ordinarily be banging away at a keyboard right now if I
hadn't timed things so I could leave early, they're on
the far side of the building.

-- And with that I gotta go: the next bus could be
mine.

------

12

------


    And now the last spasm of the Black Horse cycle --
a Gray Snake cluster.  As is only appropriate for the
Month of the Dragon as the sun moves into Taurus.
Because this is a happenin' time.  One of my busiest
weeks in years if not (especially if I dare to skip over
wedding month in '99) decades.
    Starting out in an odd place: at a card table in
the apartment that will be Mama E's new home.  Along
with its two matching chairs this is the only piece of
furniture in here.  Or the only whole piece in one
piece, I should say, or rather in three pieces, because
the makings of a chest of drawers are spread out in many
more pieces on the carpet.  I won't be trying to
assemble it until Sunday or Monday, most likely, but I
wanted to see what I'm up against and what tools I'll be
needing.  Yikes!  It's gonna be a test case for
complexity theory!  -- But that's fine.  It'll help me
feel I'm doing my bit.
    Will this Mama E move work out?  Friend June thinks
not.  She's surprisingly vehement about this.  "Plucking
up a flower by the roots."  She thinks Mama E (the
flower) will be causing nonstop disruptions in our
lives, Z's and mine.  I'm hoping, and Z is too, that
Mama E'll adjust and take some pride in not causing
disruptions -- maintain the quirky spirit of
independence she's long shown in Centropolis.
    (It's maybe eleven on a Friday evening and for the
past ten minutes or so a trio of young women have been
talking loudly in the courtyard outside.  Otherwise it's
been quiet.  I lucked out in finding a place to park

where I could unload these furnishings, but Mama E
doesn't drive and Z and I can walk over or take a bus,
so maybe the parking difficulties in this area won't
matter too much.  And she can always turn down her
hearing aid if loud noises are bothering her -- whether
voices or, say, sirens of ambulances bound for nearby
emergency rooms, which I've been hearing quite often
tonight.  And I think she'll like the sofa-bed I bought
from Z's friend Karen K. earlier this afternoon.
Karen's nephew will be hauling it over here tomorrow
night in his truck, and that's good news; I won't have
to be calling on Gerry J. for help after all -- though
he's kindly offered it.  All of Z's friends are coming
through just as we hoped, and expected, they would.)

     Bare walls, floor molding visible all the way
around.  This reminds me a lot of moving into my
edgeville apartment back in '96.  The place where I
thought I'd be living forever.  That move also occurred
mostly at night, incrementally, just like this one.
-- The carpets here are sort of an off maroon, I'm
noticing.  The sofa-bed is olive.  The combination will
make for a subdued Christmasy effect, maybe, a little:
green and red.  Wonder how Z-spouse'll react when I tell
her about all this later tonight.  (I'm calling her
every morning at quarter to five our time, quarter to
seven back there.)

     Her mission seems to be proceeding about as well as
could be expected.  It doesn't take long for Mama E to
get on her nerves and then Z goes off -- loses it, has
to step out.  But this is par for the lifetime course.
After a while she goes back in and another round starts
up.  Some rounds are better than others; the relative
peace lasts longer.  Z well recognizes the broader
family pattern from her growing-up years.  Mama E would
bug her father until he blew up, a tense period would
follow, sometimes including a stomp-out by him lasting
up to several days, and then he'd reappear and normalcy
would gradually resume for a while.  Then repeat.

     Will I become a player in all this?  No doubt.  Z's
already calling on me to try to talk Mama E into things

over the phone when Z's own attempts to do so on the
spot fail.  The stern male.  Supposedly she'll listen to
me.  For now that may be true but probably not for long.
     The drama of our daily lives, such as it is, will
be altering a bit.  Ratcheting up maybe.  So one of my
tasks in the months ahead will be to provide Z with the
kind of support she'll be needing from her husband-
person and another will be trying to calm things down as
much as possible.  The voice of reason and proportion
and patience.  Whoopee!
     But what a sixer it's been.  I'm racing around like
crazy, answering calls, leaving messages, meeting people
hither and yon.  My schedule's quickly reverted to that
of the pre-Z era: I go to bed later, get up later, do
everything later.  Tonight I still must put in about
three hours at the scope office and then make it home in
time to call Z at the appointed hour, so I'll be cutting
it close.  Dinner will be one of the tuna-salad handy-
packs I've stashed in the lockbox on my shelf at the
scope office in case of just such emergencies.
     All kinds of things going on out there, meanwhile,
on the concentrically larger stages.  Dissent's heating
up locally, nationally, internationally.  Our USAn out-
party is actually daring to speak up a bit against the
cabal.  Voce tremolo, yes, but it's better than nothing.
And the pathetic former veep and presidential candidate,
also out-party now, is back from the realm of total
silence.  A group protesting another senseless killing
of a black man by a white cop stopped traffic on the
freeway near here two days ago -- in fact about five
blocks from where I sit.  Amnesty International is in
town for its annual world convention and a number of
demonstrations will be (coincidentally) taking place
during their visit: to protest the "War on Terror," to
continue the anti-WTO campaign, to heighten attention
on environmental issues -- for this is also Earth Day
weekend.  For hard-core right-wingers it's the glorious
anniversary of the Oklahoma City bombing (JRX), the Waco
disaster (JRX), and (for the proliferating cadre of the
truly extreme) Hitler's birthday (JRX!).  The nationwide

scandal involving molestation of kids by Catholic
priests is deepening day by day.  Israeli tanks are
still crushing Palestinian refugee camps despite outrage
everywhere (except among USAn fundamentalists of Jewish
and Christian stripe, the odd-couple alliance of our
era).  Oh such interesting times we live in!
     Last night Aida and I were June's guests at a law-
school "luau" (or should that be "lawu"?).  It was held
in the upper AQ at the same Chinese rec center I walk by
most days on my way in to work.  Poor June was mortified
by the high-schoolish quality of the affair: cheesy
decor, bad music, a small crowd lost in a big gym, and
most of all bad food (none of it Chinese).  I was
reminded yet again of some of the reasons I'm glad I
didn't follow in Dad's footsteps and become a lawyer.
But I like being around June and on this night Aida was
good company too.  She even asked my advice about an
affair of the heart -- should she attempt once more to
make a go of it with Kirk M. (and thus resurrect a major
subplot of the previous jyze annal, TJM)?  He called her
for the first time in months on Valentine's Day and
since then she's bumped into him -- seemingly by
accident -- no fewer than four times.  And she's
realizing she'd like to settle down and he's the only
one who's really done it for her in recent years and she
knows of no other good prospects.  Of course I said she
should ring him up and go for it.  (But personally I
think Kirk's a pompous jerk.  Of course that could just
possibly be because Z was involved with him herself at
one point some two decades back.)
     Also, on Wednesday night I got together with
Malcolm, another friend of Z's from his days working as
a consultant for the city -- and more recently as a
board member at the same leadership group she belongs to
-- and we talked writing.  He's an old newspaper guy --
I hadn't known this before -- and for some years now
he's been trying to write a book about his own
experiences overcoming racism.  Part of the reason he's
been blocked is that he's gay but he doesn't want to be
writing from that perspective, and yet a big part of

"getting it" about racism for him was experiencing discrimination as a gay man.  (He's from an immigrant Italian family, youngest of five siblings, grew up on the far coast, attended four different colleges.)  I thought maybe he'd be inspired to see it's actually possible to crank out pages if you have a structure to work with and so I showed him what I've been doing with this and previous jyze annals.  It's possible I gave him the impression of being just a little obsessive on the subject.  But he's thinking about making a run for city council (just as Aida's mulling a run for Sylva S.'s seat as a state rep since Sylva will almost certainly be giving it up at the end of her current term) and his days are full of phone calls and meetings, so he's just the opposite of obsessive about his writing.  Or better, say he's maximally distracted.

I'd hoped to talk with him a little about my own wrestlings with cross-cultural differences of various kinds but we didn't even get around to that topic.  (At 8:30, after meeting for dinner at the HQ diner at 6:30 and then going up to Jyze Central, he suddenly announced he was late for an eight o'clock appointment and left immediately -- a strangely abrupt departure.)

-- And one last item.  The heavens are putting on another show right now and I wasn't even aware it was coming up.  It's a rare planetary alignment -- another one, great if not quite grand like the ones in 2000 -- and it's of a type not seen since 1940, the year of Z's conception -- and won't be seen again until 2040, the hundredth anniversary of same, yes.  The five brightest planets all in a row, ascending at an angle slightly off ninety degrees above the western horizon shortly after sundown -- and this one I actually saw tonight from the high bridge as I was hiking across.  It's the kind of thing I wouldn't've given a second thought to (or maybe even noticed at all) if not for the fact that this is the year it is -- Heavenly -- and therefore anything celestial is drenched with meaning for me.

What meaning precisely?  They're pointing straight down, those planets, at the yearlong peregrination of

the J-slinger!  What more is needed?  "Following yonder
stars" -- five of 'em.  And so if one star's going in a
direction you don't like, latch onto one of the others.
      Sheez, talk about grandiosity.  It seems!  Because
I'm not saying they're just for me, these planet/stars.
Anybody else can claim them too.  Could anything be more
absurd than trying to restrict the heavens to a single
meaning?  (And yet that's what many religions do.  One
might even say that's a good way to define religion.)
      -- And this last and final note (for sure).  Today
is also the lunar birthday of the mother of my single
known offspring (I do believe he's mine -- because she
said so, Lady S did, and because I was there to do, and
did do, what needed to be done to make it happen,
although someone else was also there with her in the
right time frame, and Lady S acknowledged this but said
nope, I was the one; and the kid does look a whole lot
like me, as everyone has always said).  And Lady S was
the one who started getting me interested in whole
universes of meaning about which I'd previously known
next to nothing.  Opened doors of perception.  Inspired
entrances.  Made a lot of consequential things happen.
Shook up my life for sure.  Thank you very much, Lady S,
and I hope you still think I did some good things for
you too.  I tried oh yes I did.  And: happy birthday!


[+2]


      Just had to put in an appearance here today.  It's
only two in the afternoon so some sacrifices have been
involved and this jyze will be groggy.  Grogjyze!
      It's the J-town fairgrounds, the cavernous indoor
food arcade and event center.  Three big celebrations
are taking place at once: the '62 World Fair's fortieth-
anniversary bash, Earth Day weekend, and the Japanese
Cherry Blossom Festival.  The crowds are immense; I was
lucky to find an empty table in the far northwest corner
in front of the Magic Dragon Chinese eatery, overlooking
the volcano walk of the children's museum, one of whose

live trees extends several welcoming sprigs of leaves
one story up and between the rails of the fence and
right onto the table here.  (JRX on the eatery name,
whose thematic relevance makes it insuppressible.)

All three of these celebrations resonate with me.
Right now on the stage far across the room traditional
Japanese dance is being performed just as the Blue Sheep
used to do it on that same stage twenty years ago.
"Sakura" -- oh I remember it well, the tape playing over
and over in her room at our little rental house, my
being called in to offer critiques: and much of this
during a very rocky period for us when she was
performing in "Indigenes" and I often met her after
rehearsals in this very room where I'm sitting now.

Earth Day -- well, the urgent concerns it
represents have been at the center of my life since
roughly eleven years before the first Earth Day thirty-
two years ago.  Today that's more true than ever.

And then I recall taking many of my meals in this
room during the summer of '62 while working as a
pitchman in the World's Fair carnival just outside,
literally in the shadow of the iconic golf tee in early
afternoon and an hour or two later in the shadow of the
monorail as well.  Today a water ride occupies much of
that carnival space and the three gaudy color panels of
local billionaire #2's rock-music museum loom just yards
away.

"Hot stuff!  Hot stuff!"  You'd hear that
frequently in this area of the arcade back then as
workers cut through the crowds making deliveries to the
food stalls.  And for me that was a hot-stuff summer: my
first, thanks to fellow carnival worker Kristi K., for
all-out bona-fide humping.  She'd grown up as an army
brat in, as it happens, the Philippines (but she was
Cawk).  Before that I'd never gone all the way, to coin
a phrase -- about ninety percent at best, starting my
last year of high school -- but she was the first who
wanted it, liked it, and was willing and even eager, and
also happily knew what she was doing (and eased me along
the path like the raw beginner I was).

[ Jyze of the Heavenly Year : Black Horse ]


     -- As the row of little dancers trips the light
fantastic in their blazing kimonos.  (Now singing.
-- And now big applause.)
     -- The interesting news of the day being that April
20th has passed relatively uneventfully in the U.S.  The
right wing, after all, is in power here; this year they
don't need to be blowing things up domestically to
commemorate earlier domestic bombings by their
compatriots.  Now they have their very own unending "War
on Terror" -- and they even get to define what terror is
and who's perpetrating it and who's behind the
perpetrators.  And all the demos coming from my own side
of the political spectrum seem to have been remarkably
peaceful -- and disappointingly ill-attended.  Yesterday
I caught up with the one here in J-town when it reached
the downtown plaza.  The usual thing: drums pounding,
banners waving, speeches echoing, police glaring,
shoppers scurrying around the outskirts -- but the
protesters numbered probably under a thousand.  In other
cities the turnout was similar.  And the hostility of
the mainstream was palpable.  If Vietnam is the
comparison, this is 1965.  And just as then, the war
rages on regardless.  At least it's apparently quite
clear to just about everyone that the neocon cabal is
handling this little crisis poorly, hoist on its own
petard.  Its self-proclaimed moral blacks and whites are
already smudging to a noxious gray.
     -- And I say goodbye, graceful dancers (as they
leave the stage).  Yes, one did remind me a bit of the
Emerson Street Dancer herself, i.e., the Blue Sheep, at
least in size and looks, but none were anywhere near so
talented.  What a shame the lady's bad back prevented
her from continuing with it.  Though I'm probably
idealizing in a way: I suspect she would've kept losing
interest, as she was already showing signs of doing
before the main injury occurred.  Could even be that's
why the injury occurred, unconsciously, or why it
lingered.  Though on second thought I doubt that.
-- And now it's the grunts and thuds of martial arts up
there, a row of boys in white robes and a teacher who'd

do well at a marines boot camp.  "Warrior spirit."
     While assembling the dresser for Mama E last night
I flashed on my father closed up in his study laboring
away on his own mother-in-law's finances (and I re-
realized what I already well knew but had forgotten,
that she wound up outliving him by several years).  No
doubt it's true some of my motivation for helping out
with Mama E comes from my inability to contribute much
with either of my parents in their end-times: Dad
because he died suddenly at a point when I hadn't been
home for almost four years, and Mother because she had
Barbara living less than a mile away in case of
emergency and in any event didn't want her boys around
too much to witness her deterioration at the end and the
three of us had our own lives and jobs in far-off
cities.  We all had an in-person farewell stay with her
-- mine of several weeks' duration -- but we weren't
part of the long-term grind.  Now with Mama E it appears
my turn to be a major grinder, as it were, is coming.
     So this is how an unexpected development changes
the content of jyze.  When I started thinking about this
project a year ago I figured it would include a trip to
MSM #2 (to visit my old stomping grounds there and pay
my seven-year respects to Mother at the hilltop park
where her ashes were scattered and perhaps to attempt a
Heavenly Year reconciliation with Barbara) and possibly
also to visit MSM #1 (to attempt a Heavenly Year
reconciliation with the offspring).  Then that trip had
to be dropped in favor of a projected Midwest journey in
September to move Mama E out here, and that journey
would've included visits to my raising-up town of
Gatewood and raising-up city of Centropolis (Z's also)
and my birth city of Lahontan (Z's grad-school city) and
the Sandefjord/Fritsch ancestral turf of Wachute and
Mentoka Falls and La Chevalle County in western Mentoka.
Mama E's medical emergency forced a change of that move,
first to June (when it still would've been made by van
or truck on the return, but with the western Mentoka
portion dropped) and then to this coming week (with my
role in it and the van/truck both scratched).

[ Jyze of the Heavenly Year : Black Horse ]

        What happens now?  Maybe the two megastate
components can be resurrected.  Probably not, though.
As it looks at this point, Z-spouse would have to stay
here to watch over her mother; and for me to go down
there on my own, though it's not entirely out of the
question, would probably be too expensive.  And I'd hate
to leave Z behind when she's the one who's been trying
for years to persuade me to make such a trip (among
other reasons, because the most torrid of her exes,
Bradley, himself lives in MSM #2 and she'd love to see
him -- meaning that to keep things in balance I'd almost
have to meet with one or both of my own torrid exes who
both live in MSM #1 five hundred miles to the south of
MSM #2, the Gray Rooster and the Silver Cat).
        -- And WHOOM!  Now it's a squadron of taiko
drummers.  The crowd roars.  The leaves of the tree
branch that's sharing my table tremble impressively.
Quite a show -- I can see the glistening muscular stick-
wielding arms of the drummers rising in unison above the
heads of the crowd.  A fitting climax and ending, I'd
say, for this first Heavenly Great Year cycle.
        Time to bid goodbye to the Black Horse -- but it'll
be back.  That's the whole point here: the cycles will
recycle.  The creature of the birth year becomes the
creature of the sixty-first.  But when that happens this
Heavenly Year will be about to end and this particular
jyze project -- No. 7 -- with it; and also to the junk
heap will go the comforting illusion that all this
cycling and recycling means I too as a living hunk of
flesh can somehow just keep on cycling and recycling
forever.  Or then again maybe I'll just try to hang on
to the illusion anyway.  Or pretend I'm succeeding at
doing so just for laughs if not for comfort.
        Whoom whoom whoom!  Rumble rumble rumble!  The
drums of the Heavenly Year throb on!  (Or -- for comfort
too, I should say.  Some folks built for comfort, some
folks built for speed.  Jyze likes speed but also likes
comfort.  Also likes anguish up to a point.  Certainly
likes laughs, yes.  Likes to throb throb THROB -- and a
big roar in the room right now.  That's it, folks!)

BOOK  B

[ Jyze of the Green Horse ]

------

13

------

How the era of the Green Horse starts: I'm
beseeching the gods for good fortune during the
difficult days ahead.  And asking the moon to bless me
with wisdom.  Here at one of my prime lucky spots at two
a.m.  But it's too cold out there for jyzing.  Instead
I'm sitting in the passenger seat of the Z-mobile and
going at it by street lamp and moonlight.

Down the hill the inky bay, the park bordering the
public market, the scenic overlook, with a jumbo ferry
gliding in toward the dock right now some seven or eight
blocks to the south and the moon hanging directly above
the shoreline across the bay where the original Eurusan
invasion party was packing up for its big move to this
side a mere century and a half ago this month.

And it's also too risky out there in the park.
Loud voices, rowdy drunken horseplay, so to speak.
Mostly Alaska indigenes, I'm guessing, with no place to
stay in this city and excellent reason for showing
hostility to a Eurusan dude wielding a J-stick.  I
ventured out to my usual spot at the north end of the
overlook but stayed there only about five minutes.
Okay, that's it, gods and moon, I'm skedaddling back to
the wheeled sanctum with the lockable doors.

The news is this.  Mama E wasn't permitted to board
the plane in Centropolis.  Because she lacked a proper
piece of government-issued photo ID she was suspected of
being a terrorist.  At age eighty-six, incontinent and
virtually immobile from arthritis and on the verge of
senility (or so she might at least appear), it's obvious
she'd make the perfect suicide bomber.  Who'd ever

suspect her, except for her one slipup of failing to produce the right ID?  And even that might be exactly the kind of gambit a savvy senior terrorist might deploy to win a reprieve from a soft-hearted airport security agent.

Z-spouse was already at her wit's end owing to the longstanding mother/daughter dynamics in her family, not to mention a lengthy series of frustrations accompanying this sudden uprooting of an elderly woman who's lived a very limited life mostly on her own for the past twenty-two years.  My attempts to console and reassure and bolster by phone were having less and less effect.  "You don't understand, Glen!  You didn't grow up in a family like mine!  Why do you think I had to see shrinks in my twenties and move two thousand miles away and not speak to Mama for years after Daddy died?  It's happening again!  She's driving me mad!"  Wailing and moaning, beseeching me to come out and drive them back.

But a couple of flashes of hope about boarding the plane helped her pull herself together.  A relatively brief flight would be so much better than a long drive because then she, Z, would be back home sooner and could find some (well-deserved!) relief.  But the first hope was dashed.  Airport security would suspend the rules for someone obviously incapacitated over the age of eighty -- or so the airline rep assured her on the phone.  After undergoing the ordeal of schlepping two huge suitcases and Mama E herself to the airport gate she found out it wasn't so: you still had to furnish proof you were who your ID said you were.

That's when I agreed this was an emergency and the federal justice system here in Jyze City -- the grand-jury portion of it anyway -- would just have to cool its heels for a week or maybe, if it wouldn't do that, I'd be out of a job.  But Naomi was very understanding: she'd make all the U.S. attorneys wait.  (Right now she's mad at the system anyway because of the way it's dissed her husband, Larry, who's one of those attorneys himself, after his stellar work as acting head attorney responsible for convicting the one Al Qaeda member who's

been talking, the Algerian "Millennium Bomber."  But
apparently Larry is too closely associated with the
previous administration and so the cabal wants him out.)
     There was one other hitch.  Because my driver's
license had expired I too, just like Mama E, lacked the
requisite photo ID for traveling by air.  This morning I
hit the downtown office of the state licensing
department and was able to obtain a renewal on the spot
in less than an hour, but since it hadn't been clear in
advance I'd be able to do that, Z had decided to go
ahead with another scheme she dreamed up overnight
involving Fed-Exing to the far coast for Social Security
papers and also requesting a search in Centropolis city
and county records seeking to confirm Mama E's married
name, which is different from the name on the Social
Security papers.  Trouble is Mama E either can't
remember or doesn't want to remember when she and Z's
father were married, assuming they actually were.  And
even if she could provide a date, would the city or
county be able to come up with the records to confirm it
on such short notice?  Z says she thinks the chances are
one in five.  I say they're one in five thousand.
     Meanwhile the personnel at our local office of the
same airline that previously misled Z about the
satisfactoriness of Mama E's ID have told me my new
license, issued in temporary form but with a photo on it
(and it's a classic), will be sufficient to get me on
the plane as long as I can produce various other forms
of ID, all of which I happen to have.
     I'll be trying my luck at eleven a.m. tomorrow.
Municipal bus downtown, shuttle bus to the airport.
I've already removed everything metallic or even faintly
subversive-looking from my backpack and small leather
suitcase.  But I'm still who I am, "a vigorous male of
dubious intentions," as Z puckishly said, and what's
more one with nonconforming hair, so I know it's no
gimme.
     -- And now everything upside down about my life, as
in NUT time, is suddenly being turned right side up,
which still seems like upside down to me.  Also the

Heavenly Year scheme is undergoing some slight
modifications.  This new J-book and new cluster weren't
even supposed to start until the 25th and here it is the
night of the 23rd, solarly speaking.  And a big road
trip might lie ahead and who knows what could happen
during the course of that.  I'm trying to hold to form
but also to stay flexible.  My idea, if I do manage to
get on the plane, is to stretch out this opening Green
Horse cluster for the length of the trip, maybe an extra
two or three days or whatever it takes, and then to
return to the regular jyze schedule of a new cluster
every sixth day ("On the sixth day he jyzed") with a
follow-up a day or two later.
     Three a.m. -- headline news on the radio.  Car
windows fogging up.  Steep bricky road outside, a
natural amphitheater of sorts where many a political
rally has taken place over the years, though I've rarely
joined them because they're usually held at lunch hour
to attract downtown workers during their lunch break and
I'm almost always asleep then.
     "The Great Adventure."  It might even turn out to
be just that!  And I should mention: Z's friends have
been terrific.  Betty called with medical advice, Olwen
with meditational advice, June with practical help, Aida
with a dinner invite (had to say no), Terri G. all the
way from Lahontan with consoling words for me: "So now
you get to be the white knight!"  If Mama E can survive
all this, yeah, maybe so -- although I'd prefer a
different heroic term, please.  And in any case Z's the
one who truly deserves a major accolade.
     And the apartment on east hill is all set.  Flowers
in place -- they'll wilt, sure, but maybe not too badly
with the heat off.  Balloons floating above the card
table -- they might wither.  Oh well.  The big "Welcome
Elza!" sign with the red heart glowing between the two
words should still be okay.  If the gods are with us,
that is, and the moon (which has now ducked behind a
building) has indeed implanted me with wisdom, or will
do so shortly.  After all it'll be up there for a while,
floating overhead as I return -- maybe for the last time

ever -- to my old raising-up grounds and then as the
three of us journey back here.  And we won't even have a
chance to explore the haunts of my Black Horse and Green
Horse eras -- at best maybe do a drive-by or two.

(Fun scratching this out, sliding the J-book back
and forth to keep it in the narrow patch of light from
the street lamp.  Makes jyze into a moving target.)
                    *              *

The Green Horse, they say, is the "Horse in the
Clouds."  For the past hour I've been exactly that but
suddenly I'm the Horse above the Clouds.  Or at least
sometimes I am, as now I see only white wisps passing
below, above complexly wrinkled shades-of-brown badland.
Dakota territory maybe, since we're probably a bit more
than halfway into our flight.  But definitely I'm at
least above the level of a great many clouds, a whole
horizonful, snowy white with barely off-white tints here
and there and splendid meringuey and mashed-potatoey
upcroppings, all off to the north, my left, as my face,
just inches from the glass, makes for a faint and even
ghostly reflection superimposed on all that.  Also a
circular engine air-intake (cowl?) of this two-jet
plane looms close-by outside, blasting us along our
path.

A vigorous male of dubious intentions I may still
be, relatively, but apparently not vigorous or dubious
enough to trip any terrorist-profile alarms.  (Could
writing the word "terrorist" do the trick all by itself?
Are tiny cameras hidden inside the oxygen valve hissing
above the seat here?)  I saw lots of people being wanded
-- almost as many women as men, and some folks older
than me and one man maybe even slightly more dubious-
looking than me -- but the worst indignity I faced was
removing my shoes for an x-ray check.  The driver's
licenses, the new temporary one and the expired one with
a hole punched through it, worked fine all by
themselves; I never had to produce any of the carefully
gathered auxiliary ID.  The only difference from my last
flight three and a half years ago, which is to say pre-
9/11 and thus pre "the world's changed," was the shoe

removal and a repetition on the IDs -- had to show 'em
twice.  And today's lines were much longer and the
agents much more numerous, most of them youngish men,
one even peeking out from behind a column and fixing me
with what Lady U used to call the stink eye.

But the airlines are still doing badly because of
reduced travel post-9/11 as well as the alleged
recession or economic slowdown, and the one I'm flying
on is no exception.  Our flight took off more than two
hours late and roughly half the passengers are
disgruntled layovers from yesterday's flight, which was
abruptly canceled without explanation.  For economic
reasons maybe?  I don't know, but I wouldn't be
surprised.  And these layover passengers weren't
compensated in any way; they had to find lodging on
their own or stay overnight at the airport.  (One's
sitting right behind me and she's been griping out loud
about this forced bivouacking ever since we boarded.)

One compensation of a sort, at least for me: a red-
haired kid with impish blue eyes strolled around our
concourse waiting area playing classical music on a
violin.  A wandering mini-minstrel.  He was probably
about the age I was during my own brief stint of taking
violin lessons, at eight or nine, but this kid could
play.  Not a single squawk or squeak.  Several people
shoved dollar bills in his pockets.

I'm going on four hours' sleep.  Hoping I'll be
able to snatch some shut-eye right away at the motel --
I'll probably arrive there around ten p.m. local time --
and be all bright and fiery-nostriled to take off in the
rental car in the morning, if that's what we decide to
do.  The other possibility, much less likely, is that
we'll be flying back, either tomorrow or the next day.
But a new health emergency with Mama E (or for that
matter with Z or me) could change things in a hurry.

On the way downtown by bus to catch the airport
shuttle -- on an extremely bright and blue-skied J. City
morning, and seeming doubly so to me because I rarely
see mornings much less blue-sky mornings and that's been
the case for twenty-odd years -- I again bumped into

Adele U., Z's Japusan friend.  It's the third time our paths have crossed like this since the Heavenly Year started up.  It's gotten to the point now where she asks me how the jyze project's going.  To my recollection no one else has done that -- and certainly not by name, that is, "How you doing on your Heavenly Year thing?"

Doing fine, sez I, and I think that's true, as viewed, at least, from my vantage point at the moment again totally immersed in the clouds.  (Interesting how they appear to be flowing by not at five hundred miles an hour but at a very leisurely pace, sort of like the bow wake of a rowboat.  Are they always like this or is it a matter of the jetstream going almost as fast as we are?  And they're getting grayer at a surprisingly rapid clip, like speeded-up film, since we're rushing eastward as the sunset line rushes westward.)  -- As my life itself rushes toward the sunset line, it suddenly occurs to me.  I even sort of like thinking of it that way -- like it better than, say, "The reaper is stalking you."

"Hardball" ending now on the drop-down screen.  Seatbelt signs are back on and we'll soon start descending.  This means the land of my ancestors (at least on my father's side, and of course only the few most recent generations) is invisibly holding steady down below.

I'll be one happy knight of whatever hue to see the Z-spouse again.  She'll be happy too, I don't doubt, but her principal emotion will surely be relief.  A reinforcement has arrived!  And when I'm around, she says, Mama E behaves much better, either because I'm a male of a certain vintage or vigor or heft or dubiousness or simply because I'm a male or because she likes me or because I'm nicer to her than her daughter is -- Z's given me all of these potential reasons and more at various points.  It's a potpourri, I'd say, and it's also just a fact that Z must be tough with her at times in a way I don't.  Hard-ass dude's not really a role I can play with Mama E and feel good about it, at least not yet.  And I suspect things will go generally better if we, meaning Z and I, can keep to this division of labor as much as possible.

     But all the above is really just airy speculation
right now -- as the amount of air between us and the
ground rapidly shrinks -- because in my five years with
Z I've spent no more than five hours total with Mama E,
and all of them were three and a half years ago ---


                          [+1]


     Big prairie moon arisin'.  Big prairie rigs a-
rumblin'.  As Z-spouse watches the late news after
announcing she's spotted a patch of dried spunk on her
inner thigh -- which is to confirm that a couple of
hours ago, after a night's catchup on sleep while bedded
down in the same room with Mama E in a Centropolis motel
and then a full day's drive north and west on the
interstate, we finally got a chance to reacquaint
ourselves carnally in our own private room.
     A small city twenty miles south of the farm where
friend Betty grew up and maybe fifty miles west of the
farm where my own Lady C grew up.  A motel in "the rough
end of town."  At the nearby truck stop where we did
dinner a group of right-wing militia types (I'd wager a
bundle on it) were plotting away a couple of tables
over.  Should I perhaps report them to the authorities?
Or perhaps they are the authorities?  In any case Z and
I fit in quite well, I thought, with the boothfuls of
husband/wife long-haul truckers.  The casino crowd next
door looked a bit more surly and we took a pass on that.
     Mama E, meanwhile, is resting up in the next room.
She's been a trouper all the way.  Not until the very
end of the day, as we sat outside a motel while Z
checked out the prices, did an incontinence emergency
arise, and we managed to deal with it successfully, or
so she informed us later.  (We didn't stay at that
motel, though; Z didn't like the vibes.)
                           *
     -- I've just moved to an armchair out in the hall
near the vending machines.  I'd advised Z I might do so

126

when the news came on.  The story about the local guy
who intentionally infected a woman with HIV was the
tripwire that set me off.  (The grave tones.  The male
anchor's smug sanctimony.  The warning that you might
want to send your children out of the room -- and that
was when I made myself scarce.)

     And here I sit barefooted.  But happy-hearted.  In
my maroon sweatpants with the six-inch split along the
ass crack, but only the chair cushion knows.  And not to
worry: of the four people who've passed by since I sat
down, I'm by far the best-dressed.  At least I'm wearing
a shirt, and it's even one of my proudest henleys (the
blue one that still retains all three buttons).

     A lightning rescue behind enemy lines, that's what
my Centropolis foray amounted to.  A vision of endless
golden grids in changing perspectives, as if being
viewed on a computer screen rotator for architects, as
the plane banked and turned while descending during its
Centropolis approach.  And my formative years were
played out against -- and massively informed by -- those
same grids.  Phone call to Z, a wind-down/get-caught-up
drink with her at a local pickup tavern where the array
of short-haired guys on the make (and Z one of only two
female customers in sight) reminded me way too much of
similar dives infesting those same grids back in the
pre-sixties era, meaning up until about 1967.  -- So up
to the room, hello to Mama E who was already under
covers for the night in one of the double beds --
rasping out heart-rending repetitive apologies "for
putting you to all this trouble" -- and I crashed.
First, though, Mama E's hearing aid, laid out on the
nightstand between our beds, started squeaking and
squawking quite loudly, as if it were an alarm set off
by the presence of a strange man in the room (and in bed
with Mama E's daughter!).  We wound up wrapping it in a
towel and closing it in the bathroom.

     "Continental Breakfast" this a.m. and then we were
off, trunk of the rental car stuffed full and part of
the backseat too, and the rest of the backseat
protected with a rubber sheet under Mama E just in case.

[ Jyze of the Heavenly Year : Green Horse ]

South and west via local freeways to the toll road and
then northwest, outta there, never passing closer than
ten miles to the city hood where Z grew up or the burb
where I grew up.  Soon we were into Mentoka, then past
Lahontan, past Mentoka Falls, past Wachute, with nothing
visible of any of them either -- it was sort of like
flipping through a pile of picture books you'd studied
long ago, recognizing names here and there, contours,
certain roadside scenes, gaining a sense of a
resurfacing whole but then moving on to the next volume
before the whole actually arrived.  And for Mama E,
goodbye to the home city of all but her childhood and
early teen years up to age fifteen or so, almost
certainly never to see it again.  If she was feeling
anything about this, she wasn't letting us know what it
might be.  Her ninety-year-old brother Joe died just
last Thursday.  She's focusing everything on the task at
hand: making it in one piece to J-town.
     Z's saying she'll do anything I want at any time
forever as thanks for my coming.  Truth is we're having
a real good time.  Rarely do we get to be together for
such long stretches, not to mention sleeping whole
nights together, even if her mother's also in the room.
     -- Meanwhile: what's going on here at the motel?
Female sex workers plying their trade in some of the
rooms, no doubt about it.  Drunken guys from the casino
pounding on doors, braying, "Is this the action?"  Door
opens, music and laughter burst out: it is.  Drug deals
going down too.  Scruffy longhairs who would've done
the sixties proud, at least appearancewise, and they're
twenty-somethings.  This is a classical gas.  Everybody
wondering, if only briefly, what the hell the ancient in
the armchair -- me -- is doing.  Now I'm gonna stand up
and show anyone who wants to know where the real bare-
ass action is, as in "Here's to you!").


[+1]

Z-wiff, lover of the dramatic gesture, sprang for a

fancy suite here at a renowned mountain hotel. Jacuzzi, fireplace, kitchenette with two-seater bar, his-and-her bathroom sinks, couch and chair, massive plant exfoliating like a one-piece jungle atop a hip-high Roman column, emperor-size bed, huge bedroom writing table, and this deluxe dining-room table at which the J-slinger's set up to do his thing -- a quick thing for sure on this occasion, like a certain famed swordsman slashing out a few of his signature Z's, and then to bed (on the foldout from the couch; Mama E gets the emperor crib in the adjoining room).

It's Arbor Day and the moon is full and we covered over seven hundred miles in slightly under eight road hours. Averaged over ninety! Barreling down the nearly empty four-lane interstate on a perfect driving day -- sunny, not too warm -- and again with only one emergency cleanup stop for Mama E, who probably should've restricted herself to just one plain fast-food burger with fries at our lunch stop and not gone for the second burger, not to mention the hot-fudge sundae (most of which Z and I wound up tussling over).

Betty makes the drive in three days when she brings Kat back home to the family farm for the annual summertime visit. Can we cover the full distance from Centropolis to J. City in the same period? Looks like we have a fighting chance. If we can average somewhere around eighty-five tomorrow we'll make it.

US of Amurka. We're seeing it. Lots of Old Glories flying and plastered onto cars and especially, to be sure, pickups. Occasional hostile glares as back in "Easy Rider" days. Meanwhile I notice Z's and my cohort have become the oldest generation out on the road -- not too many great-grandparent types go traveling around these days, it seems -- and the generation two behind ours appears to hold down most of the management positions in the so-called "hospitality industry" and the generation behind that, the pierced and tattooed ones who look as though they just hopped off a skateboard, are doing most of the actual manual labor. In other parts of the country the scorned "illegal

immigrants" are probably handling that work, but not in
the ferociously Cawk and conservative region we've been
passing through.

Pedophile priests.  They're dominating the national
news these days, to such an extent I almost expected the
streets to be filled with befrocked clerics copulating
with their tiny main squeezes when I landed in Catholic
epicenter Centropolis.  But I'm not really following the
story.  Such hysteria and self-righteousness on the
media and Protestant sides, such hypocrisy from the
Catholics and the family-values crowd.  I say let 'em
all stew in their own lusty juices for a while -- and
especially the racist parents who sent their kids off to
segregated Catholic "academies" rather than daring to
let them mix with the mongrel USAn public as opposed to
just the majority Cawk portion of it.

Other news I'm not able to follow.  It's a matter
of guessing what's going on from the headlines and
slanted right-wing summary stories in the abysmal
national daily paper that's been the only one available
at any of our stops thus far.  Apparently the status quo
is holding in the Mideast: Israeli attacks and sieges
continue in occupied Palestinian territory, U.S. pleas
get nowhere (because they're preposterously hypocritical
and really just designed to mislead domestic public
opinion).  Palestinians suffer, Arabs seethe.  A leak
from Washington says the State Department believes its
Mideast mission last week was intentionally sabotaged by
the Pentagon and its allies, which is to say the neocon
cabal in the White House.  And that's about all I know.

Z's already asleep on the sofa bed.  I'm looking
right at her.  She's stretched out on her stomach in a
yellow T-shirt under a golden blanket, shifting about
from time to time while seeking a position in which her
aching right hip will be comfortable.  Last night's shag
certainly didn't help that hip any.  But she's not
complaining, bless her.  "From now on until it heals,"
she said with a smile, "I'd better be on top."  And may
she be there often!  -- But she almost certainly won't
be tonight.  She's taken a sleeping pill and it's as if

[ Jyze of the Heavenly Year : Green Horse ]

I've taken two or three myself -- or rather I'm guessing
it is, because I've never taken a sleeping pill in my
life. (Could that be right?  As far as I can recall,
yes it is.)

    High-school kids carousing noisily out in the hall.
It appears to be some sort of prom-weekend mass soiree.
My first sight upon stepping into the hall with Mama E
when we arrived was of a covey of seemingly naked girls
rushing straight at us.  In teensy-weensy bikinis they
were, it turned out, bound for the indoor swimming pool.
What excitement!  From the continuing high decibel level
out there right now I have a hunch that scene might soon
be resurfacing in my nightmares.

    And an idyllic Heavenly Year moment a few dozen
miles back in the mountains: a sparsely wooded hillside,
steep, rocky, yet with lots of vivid green grass and a
herd of Black Horses, I'll call them, initial caps and
all, gracefully grazing in the mist, their bodies
arranged at odd angles because of the rocks and
steepness; and about ten minutes later it dawned on me
I'd been vouchsafed the archetypal vision of "Horses in
the Clouds" in the Year of the Black Horse.


                        [+1]


    When we awoke this morning at the mountain hotel it
was snowing.  Such nasty freeway conditions for the
following hour or two.  And yet -- we made it.  Mission
accomplished.  Eight hundred miles plus in a single day
-- through several mountain ranges, past numerous raging
rivers, past a continental divide, past deserts and
canyons and Native so-called reservations and even a few
small cities.  And now, four a.m., Mama E's asleep in
her new apartment and seems quite pleased with it, and
I'm just back from doing four hours of scoping work on
top of all that driving and I'm too wasted to jyze.  But
just in case I didn't already say it, though I'm pretty
sure I did, but I'm too far gone even to glance up a few
inches to check:  We made it!


                        131

------

14

------


Jyze playing catchup as it moves into the Blue
Sheep cluster.  That's why this entry is starting out in
the scope-office conference room with just thirty
minutes left until bus time.  And I'm worried about
cutting it close with the bus because earlier tonight
when I wanted to go out to deposit my check and score
some lunch from midtown chain burgers I found the main
elevators weren't working and I had to wait fifteen
minutes -- no lie! -- before the slowpoke freight
elevator finally showed up.  And last night I missed the
last bus for the first time in a year or more and had to
walk home.  And this happened, as is only fitting, in a
way at least, on the night when identities flip and
witches play tricks on you: Walpurgis.
    That makes today May 1st, Labor Day for all the
world other than Canada and the U.S. and maybe one or
two other benighted lands.  And because the commies made
such a big deal of May 1 -- workers, unite! -- the
cappies of the U.S. Senate at the height of the Cold War
had to make May 1 Patriot Day for us.  Rich old boys
will be rich old boys.  (In Hawaii, I remember, this is
also Lei Day, which seems to fit well with the maypole
theme.  -- And by the way, the leis I laid in to present
to Z and her mother at the airport have yet to emerge
from their protective bags in the Z-mobile's trunk.)
    I didn't make it up to the motel today, but
according to Z-spouse Mama E's feeling a bit perkier
now.  She's eating, she's unpacking, she's opening the
blinds to scope out the other residents as they pass by
in the courtyard (most of them, to Z's eyes anyway, look

132

"like active or retired bikers").  She's even talking,
Mama E is, about taking in some sun on one of the
benches out there -- though today the sun disappeared
after supplying two glorious blue-sky days for Mama E's
introduction to J-town -- which, however, except for
what little was visible through her windows, she never
saw.  Could be she's perking up because she's off the
antidepressants again -- they were making her dizzy --
but we're hoping she's passed a low point and she'll be
getting better by stages, at least up to a level which
will permit her to continue living independently, more
or less.  As she says herself: "A lot depends on if I
can walk or not."

   (In the midst of these jyze jottings no fewer than
three visitors have shown up here in the scope office:
Ross the night guard, Jasha the janitor foreperson, and
Chun the Chiusan janitor -- who presented me with a hunk
of sticky rice she made herself -- and now my time is
up, with scarcely any margin, because all three visitors
assured me the regular elevators are working again and
so I figured I could cut it close the usual way.)
              *              *
   Three hours later I'm back in the black armchair.
Black Horse wearing just his Heavenly Year birthday suit
and looking so pale and hairy.  And speaking of Horses,
I should note this before I forget: the Kentucky Derby's
coming up this weekend and Mama E's pumped for it.

   Z-spouse left me a brief note atop the Neapolitan
soy ice-cream carton in the freezer.  "I'm jess wild
about you!"  She's also said she'll be in my "thrall"
forever because of the "storybook rescue" that just went
down.  And so far she's being exceptionally sweet,
thoughtful, loving.  This past morning especially she
was loving, slipping naked between the sheets just as my
radio alarm began beeping.  And I, even though seriously
groggy, was up to the challenge.  And so was her bad
hip.  A "plan A" vagina dialogue followed -- logged in,
shot out, very comely for both parties.

   Today she returns to work.  The heap of e-mail
awaiting her will be formidable.  And an era of

frugality is about to set in.  She figures moving Mama E
out here and setting her up for her new life has cost
between five and six K so far, all coming out of her,
Z's, pocket, with lots of big expenses yet to present
themselves.  "This is entirely new to me," she marvels.
"I've never had a dependent before, much less my own
mother."  Except for me, that is, as an indie dependent
of sorts.  And I wouldn't want to be denying it either.
(Last week I broke a blood vessel in my ring finger
while assembling Mama E's dresser and since then I've
been forced to do without wearing my wedding ring -- and
to my surprise I feel oddly off-balance without it.)

While helping Mama E pack back in Centropolis, Z
came across an envelope containing some of her father's
personal belongings, including papers and ID cards.  She
left those out for me to peruse earlier today.  He was
born, I learned, in the year between the births of my
two grandmothers -- so in 1895, or three years earlier
than Z had thought -- and his birthday is just nine days
before mine.  1895: that's a Sheep Year too, and in fact
a Blue Sheep Year (one Heavenly Year of the long type
later Lady U was born under the same sign).  It was
especially touching to unfold a piece of crumbling
yellowed three-ring-binder paper and discover it to be a
handwritten will he'd carried around in his wallet for
years -- saying, among other things, he wanted to be
buried in a certain cemetery in Centropolis near the
gravestones of the family he'd worked for as a cook and
handyman in his thirties and early forties and remained
friendly with until the parents' deaths (and four years
ago Z and I, guided by Mama E, visited his grave there).

Also in going through various papers Z learned her
parents had married not just once but twice.  The second
one was in Centropolis in 1946, five years after she was
born; it took place because the clerk of the town in the
next state to the east couldn't locate the papers for
the first marriage, which took place there in 1940.  (Or
did it?  "Maybe it wasn't really all that official," as
Z herself says.  "Don't forget, LOML, official
interracial marriages weren't all that easy to come by

in those days in the buckle of the Bible Belt."
     And for news of the world in the Month of the
Dragon we've got this: our neocon regime cooks up a deal
with the Saudis (as nasty an autocracy as the world
knows and the country itself a seedbed of terrorists,
including fifteen of the nineteen members of the 9/11 Al
Qaeda hijacker gang along with the Al Qaeda leader, who,
incidentally, U.S. intelligence says has been spotted
twice this week alive and kicking in a certain obscure
Pakistani town).  And all this seems to have tamped down
the war tensions a bit, with an Israeli pullback
promised -- but nobody yet knows what either side wants
to happen next, meaning: what's the plan here?
     Meanwhile pundits are saying the U.S. invasion of
Iraq, previously believed to be set for this fall, has
been "postponed" until early next year owing to public
outrage at the U.S. in those Arab states which would be
needed as allies, or at least as silent tolerators, for
the invasion to proceed with minimal risk of U.S.
casualties.  Or so it's said.  But then some cabal
members have boasted that we can pull off this invasion
alone, meaning with no allies at all, and at any time we
choose.  "Regime change," that's what we're after.  We
rule.  It's so clean, so simple!  Just do it!
     A hundred years ago yesterday Congress voted that
the Chinese Exclusion Act, which they had passed twenty
years earlier and then extended for ten more years,
would remain in effect indefinitely -- that is,
permanently.  The shame!  I haven't seen a word about
this centennial anywhere in the mainstream media.
Luckily for me, however, that congressional act, though
it did apply to most other Asian nationalities, did not
apply to Filipinos, since the Philippines had recently
become a USAn colony ("possession" is the word I usually
heard in history courses) -- after the massacre of
roughly a third of a million resisters who sought
independence for their country -- and therefore Vincenzo
B., ironically enough, was able to make his way to the
U.S. some fourteen years later.
     One final note.  Last night, thanks to my

unexpected walk home, I was a witness as the witches of
Walpurgis made the moon travel backwards.  While angling
off the "high road" onto the steep downhill route into
the AQ I happened to glance up to see a sublime vision
of the gibbous lunar face hanging just above the
floodlit hilltop DC castle -- our own Harz mountains
stand-in, as it were, for the witchy gathering.  And
then by a parallax phenomenon taking place as I walked
eastward up the main AQ drag, the moon's position in the
sky also seemed to move eastward above the top of the
castle and then partway across the valley to the
southeast.  Odd how I couldn't stop marveling over this
as I ambled along -- but I couldn't.  (Though at the
same time I still kept a wary watch to my rear, to my
left, to my right, and ahead.  But no obvious dangers
materialized.)  (And best to JRX the name of that
mountain range.  And Hawaii too a few pages back.)


[+2]

Some days it's hard to hold to the plan.  This is
another of those.  Friday night, jazz turned up loud on
my hideaway radio (to override the stentorian and inept
and screechy quasi hip-hop playing down below), and ten
or twelve blocks straight up the hill Mama E is going
through what appears to be a rerun of the esophageal-
reflux crisis that set in motion the chain of events
which now has her living in J-town.  Or at least such
was the case a couple of hours ago.  My hope is that Z's
been able to calm her down and administer the meds which
the Centropolis doc prescribed for her.  But -- lots of
other things could be happening.
　　And: I'm just going to assume all's proceeding
passably well.  I must.  No other choice exists if I
hope to keep this Heavenly Year project on course and at
the same time continue churning out the work for Naomi
(hang on to my job, really).
　　And: I should mention this is what Z insists she
wants me to do.  In part she says so, I'm sure, because

she knows how much it means to me, but it's also because she's fiercely proud and wants to care for her mother as much as possible without disturbing anyone else's life. (Which isn't to say she's ready to give up her own life, and especially her work, for her mother's sake. If Mama E can't basically take care of herself -- with an hour or two of daily help from Z or me or both of us -- Z will be seeking an assisted-living situation for her. In the end it's Z's call, I figure, and this is what she says it depends on.)

Yes, it hurts not to be there right now. Z's going through hell, her mother's going through hell. -- Or no, I don't want to put things quite that extremely. It's difficult for both of them but before tonight things seemed to be on the upswing and certainly they were a lot better than I'd expected. Mama E seemed to be settling in and perking up, Z seemed to be getting back in the groove at work.

So there'll be ups and downs. Am I surprised or something? Let's hope this is just one of the downs and nothing more.

Earlier tonight we rode up to Karen K.'s place with June to pick up a fancy color TV for Mama E. It was when we delivered it to her that we discovered the crisis. She hadn't been able to keep anything down for more than an hour; the Mylantin did nothing; she'd just tried to call us. She sounded panicky, frightened; wanted to hit a hospital emergency room as she did in Centropolis the last time something like this happened. But the doctor back there told Z when she visited his office that the meds he was prescribing would suffice. He also said this kind of problem doesn't warrant emergency-room treatment and should be easy to deal with as long as Mama E recognizes what it is and doesn't panic.

That's where things stood when I left. Z was waiting for Betty to return her call. As a former geriatric nurse Betty's the one who usually has the best advice to offer about Mama E's medical care (and ours too for that matter).

[ Jyze of the Heavenly Year : Green Horse ]


     Tangles of guilt and morality, right and wrong.
The grim dance.  Primordial traumas bubbling back up,
for Z and for me too (my mother's final year, the run-
ins with Barb who in some ways was playing the same role
with our mother as Z is now playing with hers).  What's
best to do?  How much can anyone do?  Before this past
week, as noted earlier, I'd spent all of maybe five
hours in Mama E's presence and talked with her briefly a
few times on the phone.  When I met her she was already
past eighty.  Spouse of her daughter or no, in many ways
I'm just a peripheral figure here.  Thus I justify my
own periphery-hanging.  No moral certainties anywhere to
be found: I do and I don't want to move in closer.  When
I try to do exactly that I get burned and seemingly make
matters worse, at least at times, becoming a kind of
rusty and lopsided fifth wheel.  So I should do the
stiff-upper-lip bit and try to make myself available
only if needed and wanted.  What else can I do?



                          [+1]


     High wind-chill out there.  In here boxing's on the
tube and the jukebox is blasting something called "Can
You Feel The Rhythm" -- all the lyrics of which are
inside those quotes, unless I missed some different ones
at the start.
     And what about me?  Can I feel the rhythm today?  I
think I can do that, yes.  But -- it'll be a stretch.
     At one-thirty, just before the alarm went off, Z-
spouse crept in, slipped naked between the sheets,
pressed her frontside against my backside as we both lay
on our right sides and pressed her lips against my ear
in our still operative (more or less) "shag signal" and
then whispered, "You know what today is?"  "You mean...
Cinco?"  "Yes!  You remembered!"
     Could she really have thought I'd forget?
     Also known as our FF Day, First Fuck Day.  And as
protocol requires -- not that we need any protocol on
this -- we proceeded posthaste with the reenactment.

[ Jyze of the Heavenly Year : Green Horse ]

        And now here I am at the east-depot saloon, baddest
saloon in town, on my way in to work.  Five feet to my
right, half a dozen tough-looking guys are following the
boxing match as if they're part of it, fists lashing
out, feet dancing, beers spilling.  I'm back in my old
favorite side-entrance seat in the bizarre wooden niche
directly beneath the main TV screen, which is one of two
which serve the big open area between the bar and the
pool-table room.  It's the usual scene in here, folks of
all races, creeds, colors, and sexes, including a couple
of transgenders (which is not so usual here).  The
percentage of brutes and nasties is probably a bit
higher than usual.  The booth in the far corner is
packed with mean-looking Rususans who probably don't
care too much that today happens to be Orthodox Easter
back in the old country.  -- As over here I play the
scribbly Prince Myshkin role, as in "The Idiot."
"Smile, fool, you're on the air!  Feel the damn rhythm!"
        And yesterday was not only opening day of the
boating season -- a big event locally, and Z and I hit
the tail end of it when we stopped at our favorite
salmonburger joint overlooking the central urban lake,
which was still crammed shore to shore with vessels (and
so stressed out from the crowds were the kitchen staff
that they screwed up our orders in three different ways)
-- but it was also, I'll say again, Kentucky Derby day.
And Mama E, who now has a working big-screen color TV,
watched the derby and got all hopped up over it: she's
been playing the horses pretty much all her life.
        Friday night was, I'll say, a trial.  When I
arrived home at the usual time -- one-thirty a.m. -- Z
wasn't around and she obviously hadn't made it home
herself since dropping me off downtown.  Nor was there a
voicemail from her.  That was the night we'd arrived at
the motel to find Mama E in the midst of a reflux
crisis.  So what to do now, I asked myself, about Z's
absence?  I figured I was probably being punished for
something -- who knows what; the candidates were legion
-- and so I decided to wait it out, but with qualms.
What if I were wrong?  But the chances of that were

slim, I thought, and if something bad had happened I'd
be of little use anyway and wasn't wanted regardless, as
I saw it, or there'd've been a message.

I wasn't wrong.  Some forty-five minutes later Z
stumbled in gushing tears.  Her mother had begged her to
stay the night.  But the reflux symptoms immediately
vanished when Z agreed to hang on with her a while
longer, and Mama E was soon snoring up a storm.  "All my
life she's been trying to manipulate me by crying wolf.
She did it with my father too.  He reacted the same way
I do.  Eventually he would explode just like me.  The
only difference is I've learned it's better to explode
sooner rather than later, before it builds up into
something really bad."

Still in slack-cutting mode, I didn't explode
myself.  I tried gently to impress on her the importance
of not closing me out.  Communication and all that.
Maybe next time she could leave me a voicemail saying
what was going on?  She thinks I don't understand, can't
understand because I never went through with my own
family anything like what she's faced lifelong with
hers, but I say I went through enough; I know what she's
talking about.  Nana's Alzheimer's, Mother's nervous
breakdown, Barb's many freak-outs, not to mention the
strange and extreme behaviors of Ladies C and V and S,
among others (some of these behaviors induced by my own
bizarre behaviors to be sure, or so the ladies would
undoubtedly insist, and -- enough said).

I support my Z-spouse no matter how appalling her
treatment of her mother may seem at times.  It's
necessary for Z to be that way with Mama E and I know it
and respect the fact.  Still, it's impossible not to
feel sorry for Mama E, who after all is almost eighty-
seven years old, in poor health, uprooted from her
customary setting and ways, domiciled in a strange city,
immobile, scared half to death -- and still quite
capable of driving her daughter mad with a few perfectly
calculated gibes.  She doesn't even have to calculate
them; they've been a reflex of hers for decades.  That's
what Z says and I don't doubt it's true.

[ Jyze of the Heavenly Year : Green Horse ]

It's all one day at a time right now.  The first
doctor's appointment is still more than two weeks away
-- and that was the earliest one available.  Z,
meanwhile, faces the budget crunch at work; she's under
tons of pressure.  She's set "ground rules" for Mama E
regarding visits, calls, doing laundry and shopping and
so forth.  For the next couple of weeks I'll be
alternating with Z in making visits to the motel, one or
the other of us each day and sometimes both of us,
together or separately at different hours.  We'll see
what shakes out during and after this period.  (Some of
Z's friends are helping too.  Today Aida, who knows Mama
E from a Centropolis visit she made with Z a decade ago,
dropped by the motel for a chat and found Mama E quite
charming.  And Betty's providing frequent nursing tips.)
     And jyze?  Jyze will bend every effort to keep
itself going in the ways previously set up.  And if it
can't, it will try to find new ways, but in any case to
keep going.
     As for the world, more disgusting news.  Today's
banner headline has the U.S. withdrawing from the treaty
setting up the International Criminal Court.  The
neocons fear it would be used against the neocons
themselves, that is, the cabal.  I wouldn't be that
optimistic myself, but certainly it should be used
against them.  And then another story, clearly floated
by cabal insiders, lays out their plans to proceed just
as previously signaled with a unilateral attack on Iraq.
Total U.S. world domination, here we come.  Just a few
speed bumps to negotiate along the way.
     And a surprisingly pleasant letter arrived from
sister Barb.  She liked the new translation of "Zeno's
Conscience" which I recommended to her.  Z's reaction to
this letter: she now supports me "two thousand percent"
in my struggles with Barb.  But this isn't from
understanding our ongoing feud, which I don't really
expect her to do anyway; rather it's reciprocation for
my supporting her with her mother.  Which is fine.  Nor
do I expect any real improvement in my own relations
with Barb.  But at least she's trying to be civil and to

keep channels open.  And so I'll do likewise.
     -- All right, Blue Sheep days must come to a close.
It's the hour, it's the many things to be done, and it's
also the urgency to find a usable restroom because the
one here at the saloon has a long line and various
restrictions (you can't take your pack in with you, as
an example, for fear it's full of dope for dealing; and
there's no one here I'd trust enough to leave my own
pack with for even a moment, including the bartenders).


                        ------

                         15

                        ------


     Sitting on a rock in a little glade.  Nearby a
small stream gurgles and, a bit farther on, a small
waterfall splashes noisily -- or rather several small
waterfalls -- and a few birds are flitting about in the
trees.  But no monkeys are in sight, much less Fire
Monkeys, the tutelary spirits for this cluster.  The
glade, however, is located on a steep hillside and the
tutelary spirits would approve of that fact, since their
slogan is "Monkey Climbing the Mountain."  And this
sylvan scene really isn't so peaceful, and the
notoriously noisy Monkey spirits (sorry, Mom) would no
doubt approve of that fact as well.
     Also my favorite USAn poet of the prejyze era
would like this spot, I'm quite sure.  He's the one who
said he could never enjoy nature unless a subway
entrance was nearby.  As it happens, such an entrance
does stand not too far away, just beyond the last tree
in the glade and across the stream of the several
waterfalls.  "Metro Tunnel," the sign above it says.
This entrance isn't used much, but every now and then as
I jyze away someone emerges from it or enters it -- as

just now a fellow carrying what looks like a violin case
does -- emerges -- and he also wears a flaming-red
mohawk and black sag pants above combat boots and he
displays multiple facial piercings.  Could it be he's a
back-row violinist arriving for tonight's performance of
the Jyze City Symphony?  No, I don't think so, because
to my knowledge no performance is scheduled for tonight.

Just barely through the trees and shrubbery I can
make out various body parts of the Z-mobile in all their
mottled creaminess.  It was sheer luck I was able to
snag a parking spot so close by at the peak of the rush
hour in a setting such as this.  The wagon -- twenty
years old now -- is facing uphill at a sharp angle, its
front wheels admirably curbed.  A nearby sheer vertical
steel-and-glass urban cliff-face looms above it to a
height of maybe five hundred feet with no setbacks.
Buses grind noisily by between here and there.

Through another gap in the foliage I can see (as
now a chortling humanoid face briefly blocks my view) a
big black hammer slowly rising and falling and some
skateboarders striking sparks off concrete walls.  And
here, within easy reach, three different types of azalea
swaddle me in what might look to a passerby like
bouquets though probably not so to the flocks of pigeons
and gulls that turn this way until -- now!  When I blurt
"Over here, birds!"

The big black hammer rising, falling, is Hammering
Man, our sorry excuse for major public art that's
laboring away in front of the art museum, which stands
just across the one-way-southbound "middle road," with a
slice of the bay visible down the corridor behind it.
This where I sit is part of the garden of remembrance
outside the symphony hall, whose rounded glass lobby
windows hang overhead like another cliff face, a lot
smaller, starting some thirty feet up the hill.  Behind
me, across the two-way "high road," looms another very
tall building of much earlier vintage, 1930s classic art
deco, and it's known in Jyze as "scope south" because
for a period of six or seven years I worked there at
night on the eighteenth floor.  And a diagonal block

143

north and slightly east of that is the less picturesque
tower housing the current scope office where I've worked
nightly, more or less, and on the seventeenth floor,
ever since.  That one jyze dubs scope north.

We also have a poet's -- another poet's -- words
written in granite just up the hill, on the side of the
symphony hall, right next to the waterfall which feeds
the stream running by my feet.  (I should mention the
stream's only about a foot wide.  It reminds me of
ancient photos of the sluice system carrying water down
this same hill almost a century and a half ago, but some
eight or ten blocks south of here, to the sawmill and
other early structures of the original Cawk settlement).
This second poet is a man who happened to be a college
teacher of mine, which is the main reason I decided to
pop over here today rather than to some other Monkey-
spirited grove in the urban forest.  I never much liked
the man's poetry but he once wrote a recommendation for
me which probably changed my life or at the very least
made it much easier for me to become the jyze guy I am
today and also the Heavenly Year celebrant; and
therefore he certainly merits a mention in these pages.

A couple of years ago I jyzified a bit about this
poetry man too, and at this same spot except on a lower
level where there are tables, or I tried to do that but
probably didn't get very far because a guard ran me off.
Today they're letting me be, the guards, possibly
because it's still an hour or two before the crowd in
tuxes and fancy gowns (beneath anoraks in some cases)
starts arriving, if indeed they'll be arriving at all
today given that it's apparently the symphony's night
off.  But something else cultural might be going on.

My teacher's words inscribed in granite purport to
speak for the thousands of local warriors whose names
are also inscribed in granite in this garden and who
died in some of this country's more recent wars but
before we achieved such massive technological
superiority that we no longer needed to trade off lives
to achieve the aims of our leaders (for the Persian Gulf
War of a decade ago a single name is cited on the

memorial and for the "eternal" war on terror, who knows,
there might never be any, although I notice the savvy
designers of the garden here have provided several blank
granite blocks for future wars just in case.

My teacher's words, projected to come collectively
from the mouths of the fallen warriors:

> Whether our lives and our deaths were
> for peace and a new hope, or for nothing,
> we cannot say.  We leave you our deaths.
> Give them their meaning.  We were young.
> We have died.  Remember us.

When did he write those words?  I don't know, but it
couldn't've been recently since he himself died some
twenty years ago.  In those earlier days it wasn't
kosher, as it is now for many leading members of the
political party in power, to eulogize war casualties by
speaking of their sacrifice on behalf of the USAn
Empire.  Even a true-blue old-school USAn patriot like
my teacher might've found that a bit much.

But here I am paying my respects anyway.  Today's
his birthday.  He was born the same year as my mother's
father, exactly a century plus a decade ago, and often
reminded me of him during the period I studied with him
almost forty years ago.

-- And why is it I have the wagon today?  Because Z
was running late and at four I dropped her off at her
eye doctor's office a few blocks from here.  She was
sure her eyes would be too blurry from dilation drops to
drive home, and she wanted to do some shopping afterward
anyway -- blurry eyes or not -- so she decided to take a
bus home instead.  Then I stopped at a downtown chain
drugstore to buy a new foldable umbrella for my bag.  I
left my old one at the ORB the other night and someone
walked off with it.  It lasted for two or three years: a
pretty good run.  I'm proud.  But I couldn't take a
chance on going without an umbrella for even a single
day.  (And right now I'm feeling a few splintery little
drops -- gray clouds are rolling in from the southwest.
This may seem all too convenient but in truth it can't
even be called a coincidence; it's just another instance

of how it is around here.   -- And the invisible Fire
Monkeys chortle in the bushes.)
     Z's now talking about taking tranquilizers to keep
herself sane in her dealings with her impossible mother.
Her friend Irene suggested this.  She might not actually
do it -- she shuns most mainstream drugs -- but just the
thought that she could do it seems to have brought her
some relief, especially now with cava cava no longer an
option.
     I've given up on the notion that I can, much less
would want to, keep up in this jyze with the day-to-day
emergencies regarding Mama E.  The latest involves the
runs, diarrhea kind.  This week I was scheduled to make
four visits to her, but the first two have been canceled
because Z was called in earlier on the same day.  For Z,
lots of anxious adjustments.  The mygs are swarming!
-- For me some anxious adjustments too, yes, though
nowhere near as many or as anxious.  At least not yet.
     Other news, just today a scare with friend Olwen,
our marriage "officiant" (Sufi priestess and fine nature
poet).  She went in for a routine colon exam -- but not
so routine for someone who suffers, as she does, from
MCS, or multiple chemical sensitivity -- and the surgeon
managed to puncture her colon: the same kind of accident
that killed Z's and Olwen's friend Julie K.  But Olwen's
been patched up now and apparently is out of danger,
although she remains in the hospital.
     And I must go now.  Not because it's raining again
-- it isn't -- although I've brought forth my new
umbrella just in case.  Rather it's scope time.  As it
happens, the two J-days for this cluster fall on the
first and third of three grand-jury days.  It's rare for
grand jury to meet three days in the same week.  I've
got my work cut out for me.


                         (+3)


     -- Not a Dragon in sight.  But we do have a dolmen.
And some doves, mourning type, as is only appropriate,

but now no more than yesterday or tomorrow or any other
day in these turbulent times.  (But aren't all times
turbulent?  -- No, not to this extent, I'd say, not with
the lives of so many species including our own on the
line.)  And baseball fans are streaming by, on their way
to tonight's game against the Bluejays -- and on other
game nights I've been able to hear the roar of the crowd
from this very spot, but on those occasions the
fountains cascading from near the dolmen weren't yet up
and running, and now for the roar to be audible the wind
must be blowing from the ballpark's direction.  -- As
it's manifestly not doing now, as I was just shrouded in
a cloud of mist blown from the fountains to the north.
     -- So now I've moved to the opposite side.
"Cascadia," the fountains and dolmen are called as a
group -- another instance of public art -- and they're
made from basalt rocks representing our region's
turbulent volcanic past.  Some are laid flat at ground
level and they're polished up for easy sitting, with the
rocks arranged around the dolmen -- or stelae, maybe,
since the double uprights lack a cross-piece -- but
arranged in a vespers circle of sorts, as in camp days
of yore.  This is all part of plutocrat #2's holdings.
We're exactly one block north of the bank that was the
setting for Heavenly Year opening night.  ---
                         *
     (And right there the J-stick flew out of my hand.
While I was stretching.  It might've landed glancingly
on its nib as the flow now seems a little different, but
apparently no serious damage was done.  I have too many
layers of clothes on; I was stretching in an attempt to
smooth out some wrinkles pressing into flesh under my
belt.)
     Here too, on my new stone, I'm reminded of those
vespers sessions.  No matter where you sit, the smoke
from the campfire at the center follows you.  In this
case it's wind-borne spray.  -- I'll try the rocks to
the east this time.
                         *
     -- Here seems better.  But a scruffy vagabond in a

worn denim jacket with a tattered U.S. flag sewn on it
lurched toward me like a war casualty a few decades
after the fact and was clearly about to demand a handout
but I growled "Can't be talking right now" and he moved
along, dimly identifying me, I think, as a possible
tetchy fellow vintage battle casualty and in any case
one outweighing him by quite a bit.  But he's gone now
and I'm happy that he is, yes, I'll admit it.  In this
"Cascadia" area and in fact the whole plaza, which is
surrounded by fancy new buildings up to a dozen stories
tall (including the all-green-glass one built at a tilt
and shaped something like a diesel engine to fit in with
the nearby railroad stations), I'm at this moment the
only partaker of its extremely expensive serenity.

No Dragons present, no, for the last entry of
Dragon Month, and no Fire Monkeys either, but one of
those famously pterodactyl-like yellow construction
cranes is hovering a couple of hundred feet overhead,
and if it leaned its beaklike tip way down here it could
easily swallow me as a pre-dinner bonbon.  Or, reminding
me of a horrifying picture in today's paper showing a
wounded Palestinian clamped in place on a dirt road by
an Israeli robot, it could pin me on this rock until one
of plutocrat #2's functionaries arrived to check out my
bona-fides -- as indeed could happen at any moment
regardless, robot or pterodactyl or neither, and in fact
has happened to me once before with the human
functionaries patrolling this supposedly public spot.

No Fire Monkey present, as I say, but a whooping
siren has been blasting somewhere not too distant nearly
the whole time I've been here, and that reminds me of an
old nickname of mine, Howler, as in howler monkey -- but
self-bestowed, to show I was all too aware of my
relative lack of restraint as a haole (which is to say a
Cawk) while corraled up with my reticent zen in-laws of
that period: the Lady U era.

-- But turning elsewhere.  A swivel of the head, I
see the largest of the hilltop hospitals, almost as
castlelike atop its east-hill summit as the DC castle
(originally a hospital itself and built at about the

same time) is atop south hill.  And right behind the
east-hill hospital, not visible from here, is Mama E's
low-rise motel (three stories), where yesterday
afternoon I sat for several hours holding her fine
gnarled old hands until Z decided the time had come to
take her to the emergency room of another of the east-
hill hospitals.  That's a single block behind the motel,
from my perspective here, and its upper floors might be
among the highrise outcroppings visible as I look up
there now, and behind one of them Mama E might be lying
or sitting up at this moment, as her fifteenth-floor
windowside bed commands a glorious view of the downtown
and the harbor and possibly even this spot where I sit.

   And today, even though she's been newly diagnosed
as having a bleeding ulcer and a number of other serious
problems, and she faces more testing tomorrow (including
a colonoscopy just like the one Olwen went through last
week, and we can confirm now has apparently survived) --
today, I say, Mama E's in a marvelously cheerful mood.
Triumphant you might even call it.  This could be
because she's all drugged up but it's more likely
because she's been proven right in her belief that her
health is seriously deteriorating.  Or both.  Before I
left home we had a rollicking phone conversation.
Tomorrow I'll pay her a visit and we'll hold hands and
flirt some more.  "You'd better watch out," she warned
me today.  "You're getting a reputation as a good
husband!"  (She really did say that!)

   Ach, not to worry, because I know it can't last.
Not if I'm to have any hope of keeping this Heavenly
Year Heavenly for me in the way I desperately want it to
be.

   What else is new?  The most famous horse around
town and also the No. 1 stud kicked off the other day.
Died.  Went belly up.  Flew off to stud heaven.  I'm
talking about the horse named (by me) Jyze City Jake,
who managed to live a life spanning exactly one twenty-
eight-year Glennarian cycle.  He won the Triple Crown
and then, back around the time I entered into a state of
zen marriage with Lady U, devoted himself to a long

career of being literally at stud (carnally at stud too,
and worth more than half a million a pop at his peak).
     And this news.  The tragicomic standoff among
warring monotheistic legions continues at the Church of
the Nativity in Bethlehem, though a breakthrough is said
to be near and a conference will be held this summer and
all will be well and the obliteration of nations
harboring those who'd terrorize the Forces of Good if
only they could will continue on its merry way.
     (But here comes the same lurching drifter again and
he's looking even drunker and meaner.  Time for me to
hit the road.)




------


16


------



     Snake Month opens at the ORB cafe.  Also the first
entry of the Purple Rooster cluster, as I'm calling it,
in relation to deep-history year 4655, the slogan being
"Lonely Rooster."  And it's the day after USAn Mother's
Day.
     In the next room, applause for poetry.  I didn't
check whose poetry it is, but I'm glad places still
exist where one can hear applause for poetry.  -- And
half a mile to the north, a famous Chinese cellist and
his friends are sawing, plucking, blowing their way into
the second night's performance of something called the
"Silk Road Project."  A distant relative, I'd like to
think, of the "Heavenly Year Project."
     A splintery wind-driven drizzle is commanding local
air or otherwise this jyze would be going down outdoors
somewhere, although it's also chilly out there -- and
after an unseasonably warm and sunshiny three-day off-
jyze period.

150

[ Jyze of the Heavenly Year : Green Horse ]

One correction.  Mama E's room at the hospital was
on the fifth floor, not the fifteenth as I was thinking
at the time of the last entry.  The top floor there is
the twelfth.  Whether the fifth floor's visible from the
"Cascadia" fountain I'm still not certain.  Regardless,
owing to the hospital's hilltop location, her view to
the west was indeed terrific.  And she liked it even
more, she said, because it reminded her of the room back
in suburban Centropolis she's now left for good after
staring out its window for hours every day over a
twelve-year period.  That was a third-floor view, mainly
of rooftops and sky, maybe not much from a conventional
aesthetic standpoint, but still: one's own vista.
    So Mama E was a happy camper in the hospital room.
She enjoyed all the attention, we could see, and feeling
safe, and having a bevy of nurses who would come running
at the push of a button.  It didn't really matter that
she couldn't understand, especially after her hearing
aid went out, most of what they were saying.  And the
food was good, and she could eat again.  (Friday evening
she insisted I "help" her dispose of a big piece of her
grilled chicken and half her slice of chocolate cake --
she's not back to high-volume eating yet -- and I can
testify too: good stuff.  And at the price, which I
don't even know except those were probably the most
expensive hunks of grub I've ever bitten into -- at the
price, I say, it ought to have been even better.)
    The worst part of the hospital stay for her wasn't
the colonoscopy or any of the other testing, which she
passed with relatively flying colors (that is, the docs
could find nothing likely to be fatal in the near term
or unamenable to treatment at least of the pain-
deadening kind).  No, the worst part was that she was
facing a Saturday-morning discharge.  She couldn't hang
out there forever.
    So now she's back at the motel and she's nowhere
near as chipper as she was in the hospital.  (The
discharge was a nightmare for Z-wiff, dragging on for
six hours Saturday morning and early afternoon.)  Z's
decided it's best to find her a "group living"

situation, preferably in a private home -- literally a
household -- where she'd be one of four or five elders
residing in "semi-assisted" fashion.  The search for
such an arrangement will start this week.  Until we can
find it I'll be dropping by the motel on alternate days
as Z's relief person, or at least that's the plan as of
now.  In practice Z goes more often because some matters
only she can handle.

So far Z hasn't had to resort to her newly laid-in
stash of tranks.  She's definitely more "labile" than
usual -- apt to break into tears at the drop of a dish
of soy ice cream, for instance, or any word remotely
interpretable as critical from me or anyone -- but then
"lability" happens to be one of her most attractive
traits, at least at most times.  She seemed very
grateful when I reminded her that I'd grown up with a
similarly "labile" mother who'd likewise experienced
"nervous troubles" in her twenties and I'd probably be
a lot more worried if her, Z's, "lability" ever stopped.
I mean, I like live-wires!  I need live-wires!  I love
my Z-wiff live-wire!

And there's my Mother's Day tribute for Z, even
though she's never been a mother herself -- because she
says she feels like one now, mothering her own mother.
We had planned to do dinner with Kat and Betty at a
spaghetti joint on the waterfront, but Z was so worn out
from dealing with Mama E she decided to cancel it.
Betty and Kat did drop by briefly with flowers for Z and
a small stuffed Black Horse for me -- if you squeeze its
belly it makes a galloping-hooves sound and then
whinneys three times followed by a grand-finale nicker
sort of like the PHYZ-Z-Z-Z of a whoopee cushion.

-- And one reason I came here today, rather than
picking out some other warm room with a roof over it,
was that my mother visited this cafe with me a couple of
times (and maybe also once or twice with Rob).  Not too
many other places in this part of town can I say that
about.  In fact only one comes to mind: a restaurant at
the public market (both its second-floor bar -- the
booth where Jyze City's best-known artist of the

twentieth century used to hang out -- and its third-floor dining area with the marvelous bay/sound/mountains view, better by far than any hospital's).

Today, by the way, is also a crucially important anniversary for the USAn Empire that's finally daring to call itself by its proper name.  On this date our country launched one of the most successful wars of territorial aggression of all time.  At the cost of a mere eleven thousand U.S. soldiers' lives we acquired a territory larger than today's Western Europe -- making the Vikings of yesteryear look like the two-bit raiders they actually were.  This war wrapped just four years before the Cawk-invader village that would become Jyze City started going up at the very spot where I'm now writing -- its main blockhouse and its first building were just a stone's throw from here.  And if it hadn't been for that fabulously successful territorial grab (the so-called Mexican War) it's unlikely the state of the union I now live in ever would've existed.  Instead it probably would've become part of western Canada.

All that might seem like ancient history.  But it's not impossible that people alive today could've heard about it directly from people who were actually there. -- And just this week the cabal's underlings have ruled that certain people who actually were there, collectively speaking, no longer exist, even though they're right here in the flesh.  This is the Duwamish Tribe, whose chief allied with the Eurusan invaders because another local indigenous tribe was more powerful and also had its eye on this same piece of land since it offered some fairly good fishing spots, though it was too exposed to the elements for year-round living -- and for his agreeing to join this alliance the city later named itself after him.  And now our current cabal, as I say, has ruled the Duwamish no longer exist as a tribe, thereby overturning a ruling by the previous U.S. administration that they do so exist.

Not that there's a big uproar over this, except among the Duwamish and a few allies and sympathizers. The mixed European invader tribes who took over the land have more immediate wars and land grabs on their minds.

See, today's also the first day of Rab'i I, the Islamic calendar's third month.  1380 years ago the man who became the Prophet started his migration from Mecca to Medina on this date, and that's when the Islamic calendar began.  That tribe and others that later assimilated with it religiously -- often, I'll note, under extreme duress -- are the ones most on our USAn minds today.  Today's headline story says the Palestinian Tribe, which is one of those assimilators, will never, ever, ever be allowed to have any land of its own if the ruling right-wing Israeli party, firmly supported by the USAn cabal, has its way, and that ruling party intends to do whatever's necessary (recall it controls the tribal nukes) to make sure it does.

All of which is just a distraction, admittedly, from the crucially important issues of the time.  And this, of course, makes the distraction even more useful, simply as a distraction.

And so for me, to keep from going crazy, but also because I'm hooked and I can't stop and don't really see how matters would be or could be any different if I did -- for me, I say, this jyzey distraction.

And other distractions too.  Hunger, men's room, body maintenance, scoping work -- all calling me right now.  (As providentially the last applause for poetry sounds and people start filing out blinking into the real and definitely more prosaic world out here.)  (And I should mention I'd personally prefer to call this city by its Duwamish-derived name, but the jyze rules require me to call it Jyze City.)


[+4]


Had to let a couple of extra days go by.  Not to bemoan, though, because this right here and right now can hardly be beat.  Sun casting down beneficence and seals barking, mountains glittering, a twice-life-size statue of the famed Norski "explorer" of a millennium

ago steadfastly gazing westward over my shoulder --
though a mangy crow just landed atop his helmet.  And
this on his very own day, the "explorer"'s, or one of
them anyway: Norwegian Independence Day.

Not only that but it's also Meet Kat Day.  And the
first day of the Jewish Feast of Weeks, commemorating
Moses coming down from the mountain -- looking a whole
lot like the statue here, as I recall from the movie --
but bearing in his arms the world's first law book.  Or
so legend says.  And tomorrow at the new baseball
stadium (the team's on the road this week) we'll watch a
seventy-fifth-generation descendant of Confucius, June
Kung Q., receive her sheepskin certifying her as a Juris
Doctor, which is to say a master of the law books USAn
style, just like my very own father and his father
before him.  (And best to JRX Moses and Confucius, yes.)

All these sailboat masts, a "forest" of them, a few
swaying gently right now as a launch motors by: they
always bring Dad to mind.  Sailing did him in -- he went
out with a boom (that is, the one that bonked him on the
head as it suddenly swung while he tried to negotiate a
sharp turn in a race in which he was badly trailing; and
then he drowned, or at least that was the coroner's
verdict) -- but, as I strongly realize again every time
I come here, he'd love this scene.  Sailor's paradise.
His spirit just might be dwelling somewhere nearby.
Maybe he's one of these gulls or the figurehead crow
that briefly perched on the Norski hero's helmet.

In the central SQ plaza a mile or so east of here
the big parade is gearing up for a six p.m. launch.  I
stopped by that plaza just long enough to hear a group
of Norskis in traditional outfits belt out the Norski
national anthem for a crowd of mostly trad-clad Norskis
whose average vintage made me feel green in my skin --
as in the Green Horse.  At the Norski gift shop around
the corner I bought some Scandi horse cards even though
the horses depicted are all red and, even tougher to
take, of Swedish origin.  And I read in a guidebook that
roughly one fifth of Jyze City's current inhabitants can
trace at least some part of their ancestry to

Scandinavia (which I'd heard before but still find hard to believe).

On the far coast, meanwhile, "a furor erupts."  The government, it turns out, had advance knowledge about the terrorist airplane hijackings of 9/11 but did nothing to prevent them.  Well gosh, we're shocked.  My guess is it's about time for the cabal's deep thinkers to see to the staging or provoking of another attack to make all dissenters scram back into the caves from which they're finally daring to emerge, albeit in trickles.

Also, a treaty is signed, the U.S. and Russia. Stocks of nuclear weapons will be reduced by half or two thirds over ten years.  Or then again maybe they won't, since the treaty is nothing more than a collection of loopholes through which a thousand nukes could drop without anyone even noticing.  But for symbolism it does matter.  It would appear the Russkis, having abjured communism, are throwing their lot in with the cappies. It's now more or less official: North vs. South, Cawk cappies vs. everybody else.

And above those mountains out there a fleet of dirigibles will soon be hovering to guard the coastline. Today's OMP says so.  They'll be a lot more technologically advanced than the crude gas bags that watched in that same area for a Japanese invasion during World War II.  And a good thing too, because now their job will be much bigger and tougher: to keep out all drugs, terrorists, and -- no doubt most important in the long run -- "illegal immigrants."  Like, for instance, rusty freighters packed with people driven to desperation by global roasting along with our "rising tide sinks all continents except our own" globalization policy.

Here in J. City, speaking on the personal level, the Great Adventure continues.  At this very hour Z and her mother are meeting with a geriatric social worker at the motel, "exploring the options."  (And also Amanda the housecleaning specialist is making her quarterly appearance at our apartment, tidying up Z's portion and our common areas but leaving my portion as it is, as per my agreement with Z; and that's another reason I've come out here to the SQ today to do my celebrating, since I had to clear out of 203 at NUT dawn anyway.)

Earlier this week Mama E had a "break-in incident" which may or may not have been at least a little bit real.  Three times in one night she called 911 to report that bad guys were trying to break into her place.  Twice the police came out and the third time they were already there in the motel dealing with another matter.  They didn't see anything or find any evidence of trouble, although the next day Mama E insisted otherwise.  "I was right!" she cried even before saying hello when I arrived for my afternoon visit.  Z had dressed her down earlier for imagining things -- something like this had happened at least once before in Centropolis when Mama E was coming off antidepressants -- and now she, Mama E, was telling me the police had returned a fourth time at noon with a fingerprint team and found prints on the windows.

Mama E can be creative.  And this was the perkiest I've seen her yet.  Clearly she enjoyed all the attention, just as at the hospital.  Cliff, the motel manager, struck the proper tone of admiration for her valor as he installed a new chain lock on her door while I was there: I saw her eyes light up.  And who knows, the jerks in the next apartment -- they truly are nasty guys, fresh out of jail, newly lined up in evening restaurant jobs and this was their night off and they were partying, as Cliff told me, though somehow the cops missed this -- those bastards might've been terrorizing her a bit just for fun, pressing their faces against her window and making weird sounds.  Or maybe they were paying her back for turning the volume up too high on her TV or something similar.  Mama E herself told me they'd been tape-recording Z-wiff's outbursts and playing them back over and over, for hours.

So that was an exciting day.  And it was Wednesday, the scheduled day for this entry.  Thus the postponement.

Yesterday, Thursday, was quite different, yet the

effect was much the same.  This day it was depression.
The nasties next door hadn't acted up again but now Mama
E wasn't eating.  Full of apologies for all the trouble
she was causing me and Z-wiff.  Sad, imploring eyes.
Eventually it came out she was worrying about the
upcoming visit of the social worker -- did it mean they
were about to lock her away somewhere?  I did my best to
reassure her but saw no evidence of success.  (The day
before I'd done better.  I always know I'm getting
through to her when she starts telling me I'm the
spitting image of John Wayne.  "You look just like him.
You talk just like him!  You do!  You do!  Just like
John Wayne!")  (The same JRX for the notorious hard-
right icon as in previous jyze annals.)

At this point we're pinning most of our hopes, Z
and I, on Doc F, the visit with whom is now only four
days off.  It seems at least marginally possible some
deft adjustments in medication could start Mama E moving
in the right direction again, and then improvements in
diet, exercise, and social life could foster a positive
cascading effect.

Then again, the mother of one of Z's grad-school
friends died just last week, also at age eighty-seven,
and after making a visit to the emergency room for
exactly the same reasons as Mama E's last week.  Poor Z
attended her funeral on Wednesday during my sleep hours.
And the other prime nightmare these days regards Z's
friend Terri, who had to commit her mother to an asylum
when her roaring imagination -- at first much like Mama
E's of this week -- suddenly took her over completely.
Well, no, not "suddenly"; I shouldn't say that.  It was
a ten-year deterioration that involved all sorts of ups
and downs and more than one commitment to a dementia
ward.

So how about it, Norski hero?  You offering me some
firm spiritual guidance to carry me through this
adventure of mine?  Like, say, "Ever onward" or maybe
"Beyond the monster waves, more monster waves"?  This
hero first climbed up on his perch here, I can't stop
without mentioning yet again (as it seems I do every

time I go into jyze mode here), the very year and maybe
even the month I first arrived in J. City.  A sign, a
portent.  So hearken, J-man, to your guardian spirit!
Standing up there all alone.  Thousands of miles from
home, a thousand years from home, yet risen to the
heights -- a Lone Rooster if ever there was one.


------

17

------


    This spot ought to work all right, for a while
anyway, just so long as the rains hold off.  But they're
hinting they won't.  Splintery mist.  Yet the sun's
shining above the mountains far to the west, down the
street corridor and across the bay and the sound,
illuminating swatches of haze and mist over there --
like tomography views of thoughts the mountains are
having, I'll venture to say, with yellows and oranges
predominating -- so, colorful thoughts.
    A Chinese Buddhist storefront temple just down the
hill, a Japanese Buddhist "church" (according to the
sign) right across the street.  On the far side of a
warehouse rooftop -- one studded with amusingly
pagodalike chimney vents, reminding me of the view from
Mama E's window back in Centropolis -- stands the
steeple of a Chinese Baptist church.  And I perch on the
edge of a window well on the north side of the Natusan
center, propping myself in place with my foot against
the base of a small tree -- or call it a sapling.
    So this is a fine spot for infusion by the spirits.
And today, being Pentecostal Sunday, is an excellent day
for it, especially since it's also Buddha's birthday,
again, at least according to the Korean calendar.  And
those shafts of sunlight make for splendid spirit

chutes.  -- And also on the far side of the rooftop of
pagodas, the skyscraper procession poses on its hillside
ever frozen on the verge of marching down into the bay.
Horizontal bands of gray and silver, rollickingly lacy,
serve as celestial backdrop for spirit chutes and
skybuster procession alike.  And the rubbery squeaks of
basketball sneakers issuing from the open back door of
the AQ rec center, also across the street, are almost
indistinguishable from the gull cries which provide most
of the rest of the tweeter part of the soundtrack, with
roaring engines from the freeway a block down the hill
as the main woofers.

I'm on my way in to work after completing the
fortnightly provisioning run.  Spirits are excellent all
around.  The social worker has declared Mama E to be in
remarkably good shape for her age, nowhere near nursing-
home material.  And his advice is equally welcome: she
needs to be doing more things on her own, exercising,
using her mind.  So the bugle call's now going out for
what's known as "elderhelp."  A few tweaks of her meds,
we're told, and she'll be well on her way back from the
brink.

And June is now a Juris Doc.  We watched for almost
three hours at the baseball stadium as the movable roof
overhead rolled slowly in and out and in again on an
afternoon of highly fickle weather, much like today's.
The commencement speaker, sorry to say, was my ultimate
employer, in a sense, the U.S. Attorney for the western
half of the state, Grant M.  Not only is he a member of
the current in-party and a cabal appointee but he's a
rah-rah guy and a probable future political candidate
himself.  His first act at the microphone was to strip
off his academic cap and gown to reveal a baseball
uniform bearing his name where the player's name usually
appears (the uniform of course being that of our local
team in whose stadium he was speaking, and he donned a
team cap too); then he exhorted the graduates to go
forth and hunt down terrorists.  Seriously!  And he told
the story once more of the capture of the Millennium
Bomber from Algeria by way of Canada, making it sound as

if vast hordes of like-minded evildoers were trying to
sneak across the border even as he spoke.
    -- And by the way, right on schedule the cabal has
issued a new terrorist alert, predicting that a massive
"second wave" attack, following up on 9/11, could come
sometime in the next month.  It's doubtful, however,
this warning will be enough to undo the political damage
wrought by the recent revelations concerning the cabal's
preknowledge of the 9/11 hijackings and its do-nothing
response, so I think we can expect additional dramatic
developments.  Maybe Grant M.'s vigilante attorneys will
discover terrorist tunnels under the border with Canada?
    After the commencement Z and I snuck home for an
hour's nap -- I'd had to leap out of bed at eleven a.m.
-- and then hurried down to a fancy Chinese restaurant
in the AQ for June's graduation banquet.  The food was
sensational, dish after dish arriving via spins of four
very large lazy Susans on separate tables, with Peking
duck the piece de resistance on all four.  Relatives and
friends had flown in from as far away as Taiwan and the
U.S. far coast -- and many from the megastate to the
south, where June's two sons now live -- but
unfortunately I barely got to meet most of them.  Z and
I were quite properly assigned to the English-speaking
table, which was one step above the children's table but
well below the two Chinese-speaking tables, one for
friends and relatives and one for June's old college
classmates, with June herself perched on a chair between
those two tables and only occasionally popping over for
a word with us linguistically deficient locals.  But our
table was lively too, with several people I knew
present: Aida, Karen K. (who sold us the sofa-bed and TV
for Mama E), Z's coworker Neal S. (successor to Z as
editor of the utility's public newsletter), and June's
younger son Michael (now out of a job after being laid
off by the scandal-ridden Arthur Andersen accounting
firm -- pre-Enron, as if this made any real difference
-- and now thinking of going to law school himself --
"Look, Mom, if you can do it..." -- but also skinnier
and newly "angst-ridden," in Z's view; but to my eyes

he's just trying to rehumanize after his days on the college football team.  (Of course JRX the names of those unlucky corrupt corporations that got caught.)

When I met June's eldest brother and de facto family head as well as family superstar -- the one who's a highly regarded professor of high tech, about whom June's told me scores of stories -- I passed along the interesting historical fact that the indigenes of this area called the first white invaders "Bostons."  He seemed to get a large charge out of that -- he lives in the eponymous city himself -- but then he had to move on to the next outstretched hand.  Still, I found him surprisingly easygoing and personable.  And was also surprised by his mop-top of pure black hair, sort of like a modified version of the wig I gave Dad, oh, about thirty-seven years ago now at the time of the British rock invasion.  I'd been expecting this brother to be a lot more like Lady S's eldest brother, Hyu, but I guess June had just been sort of humoring me in portraying him as she did.  "Yes, yes, I understand, because my eldest brother is exactly like that!"  Of course it's also true I was meeting June's brother under considerably less stressful conditions than was the case for most of my dealings with Hyu.

-- Straight overhead a smooth bald spot has appeared, completely blue, in a sky whose gray has otherwise gone all roily.  The promise of a spectacular sunset will not be realized; the mountains have vanished.  As have the spirit chutes.

Pentecostals, it's said, are overwhelming the Catholics in Africa and South America and will soon be the strongest organized religious force on those two continents, which will also be two of the most desperate world regions as global roasting and the ecocrunch accelerate.  Will rusty shiploads of foreign Pentecostals flying crusader crosses be sunk by U.S. guided-missile drones launched from coastal-patrol blimps, say just on the other side of those same vanished mountains, as the assembled deities of our Judeo-Christian Greco-Roman heritage cavort high

overhead with their usual godly indifference?  I
wouldn't bet against it.

     Tomorrow, I should also note, is the anniversary
date for the convening of the Council of Nicea back in
325 C.E.  That was more or less the occasion when the
notion of Judeo-Christian-Greco/Romanism really got
going.  A Roman emperor was riding along and suddenly a
spirit chute angled down from the heavens and he was
infused with the idea that Christianity and empire just
might go well together, and shortly thereafter he called
in his council as a kind of rubber stamp and also a
calendar-making operation.  It came up with a lunar-
based formula for setting the date for Easter and
therefore, basically, all the rest of the days,
including today, Pentecost (or another name for it is
Whitsunday, based on the old practice of baptizing on
this occasion, everyone wearing white to signify
purity).  -- And in my Heavenly Year I see all these
pieces fitting ever so snugly into place.  Almost takes
my breath away.  -- As overhead, just like that, a roily
gray mop-top wig covers the blue bald spot along with
most of the rest of the sky and I concede I'd better not
be sitting outdoors like this for much longer.


[+3]


     On the hundredth day I'm back at Z-geist.  "The
first hundred days" -- traditional stocktaking time for
new government administrations and also for jyze
projects, among other complicated undertakings.  I even
skipped an extra day so jyze could set up here now.

     New twists and contortions of the zeitgeist.
Boggling, me cronies, I say boggling.  How remarkable to
be alive in these times -- and to be trying to give the
old 'geist a few kicks myself just for the heck of it.

     Skipped coffee at home so I could do it here.  But
it still took me a long time to reach this spot.  For
one thing, I couldn't put down the newspaper.  And Z
called with an update on the latest Mama E crisis.  And

I called brother Rob at work to catch him up on the past couple of months -- returning his call from yesterday just after I left the house -- and by the way, I don't believe I've mentioned yet that as of late January my little brother is a grandfather.  A strapping lad named Royce.  And down by the west terminal I watched a continental train pull out from the station thirty feet below street level (which is to say it pulled out from the original street level) and disappear into the downtown tunnel.  And then checked out the plaza at the new county building (I've never seen it open to the public before -- it offers a good close-up view of the new football stadium, which is officially opening next month) and another new Z-geist competitor, a sadly slick cafe.  And now here I am, as guitars strum and early gamegoers waving pennants parade by just outside the window, most of them having moments earlier passed obliviously with respect to jyze meanings under my lucky composite Brown Horse across the street to the north.

It's National Maritime Day.  Out in the bay fireboats are shooting off their nozzles and a trophy of the Cold War, a Russian submarine, is being triumphantly displayed (as in, say, those notorious instances of shot-down pilots of U.S. bombers being paraded through the streets of Baghdad or Hanoi).  -- And jyze is borrowing the celebratory atmosphere for the hundredth-day anniversary of its Heavenly Year fling.  Yayhoo!

Meanwhile the terrorist warnings are back and this time with a whole new set of enhanced bells and whistles.  Maybe I'm too skeptical here, but I see mainly cabalistic maneuvering in the wake of criticism over its recently exposed failure to heed warning reports last summer before 9/11 and to alert the public to the danger.  "You want warnings, we'll give you warnings."  So now they're saying a far-coast landmark -- maybe even the Statue of Liberty -- may be targeted for demolition in the next few days.  Apartment buildings or malls might be blown up.  Suicide bombings are "inevitable" (and really, who could doubt that; but "inevitable" without any qualifiers covers a very long

period).  And it's also "inevitable," the secretary of
defense tells us, that terrorists will acquire "weapons
of mass destruction" and try to use them against U.S.
"interests."  Because they hate us and our freedom,
see, and absolutely not because we ever did anything
nasty to them.  And also absolutely not because our
"interests" have expanded to include control of most
everything that exists on this planet, including, if you
let your skepticism run wild -- as you probably should
-- the terrorists themselves.

Our supreme USAn leader, meanwhile, is off to
Europe for the signing of the phony-baloney white
Patriarchy Club nuclear arms reduction treaty with
Russia.  Massive antiwar demonstrations are said to
await him at a stopover in Germany -- let's hope that's
true.

Oh fascinating world.  Wars threatening to break
out in Kashmir and Colombia.  Catholic Church reeling
over massive new pedophile-priest scandals and cover-
ups.  Iran has been declared -- by us -- the new top
terrorist threat, superseding Iraq (but is this just a
temporizing ploy?).  Astounding jade deposits are
discovered in the highlands of Guatemala, not far from
where Kat was born.  (Just think: if her parents had
kept her she might be on the brink of inheriting
fabulous wealth.  -- My eye she would.  It'll soon turn
out the highlands are owned by some big USAn mining
corporation under the terms of a secret treaty much like
the ones which in effect assign most of the rights to
minerals in Native lands in this country to pinkskin
resource corporations -- or for that matter like the one
which transferred to the U.S. the rights to the land on
which I sit at this moment: involved a few trinkets,
basically, and the presence of lots of highly persuasive
U.S. firepower, as in virtually all such treaty confabs
across the rest of the country; and what else is new?)

Is it any wonder why the Yellow Dog is heading for
the mountains?  (But look out, Dawg.  Remember what
happened to Al Qaeda in those mountain caves.  And don't
forget: your every paw twitch can be spotted by a

missile-armed USAn drone at thirty thousand feet.)
     Yesterday, I want to note, was our -- Z's and my --
lunar FF Day, making the bookend for the solar version
observed on Cinco de Mayo.  But this time we couldn't
celebrate properly.  We're both so damn worn out from
trying to keep up with Mama E.  -- And Z-wiff fears,
still, our relationship will be damaged by this dicey
situation and goes out of her way to show me she's
determined not to let that happen.  Cards, gifts, verbal
reassurances.  Not necessary, Z-babe!  But we're getting
off on it anyway.  And I try to reciprocate as much as
possible on the cards, gifts, reassurances.
     The long-awaited doctor appointment on Tuesday, Z
told me, went surprisingly well.  Doc F, or "Winnie" as
he's known to his former nurse Betty and so now to us
(though she's advised us not to call him that to his
face) -- Doc F, I say, is a Cawk originally from the far
coast, northern rural sector, and also, according to Z
(and Betty too), quite the charmer.  He declared Mama E
to be in pretty darn good shape, all things considered.
He's switching her over to Prozac (a side effect of
which during the adjustment period is nausea, cause of
today's crisis du jour) and trying to "bulk up her
stools" as part of a long-term remedy for incontinence.
     Tomorrow during my visit to the motel I'll be
attempting to prop up the head of her bed by fifteen
degrees to help counter reflux.  Z's legendary system-
working abilities are being tested to the limit and
she's seeking advice, counseling, help of any and all
kinds on various Mama E-related issues, including her
own -- that is, Z's -- ongoing mental health.  -- Oh,
and we've been getting rambling and obscene voicemail
messages from Mama E's longtime "boarder" Tito.
Presumably he's in need of bucks.  His free rent at Mama
E's old place in Centropolis will be running out at the
end of the month.  One frequent topic of conversation
between me and Mama E is the possibility that Tito will
show up in J. City at any moment.  Supposedly this would
be the last thing she'd want, but the sparkle in her eye
when she talks about the prospective horror suggests

otherwise.  I'll say this: he can swear impressively in
Greek.  Not that I can understand any of it.  Z had to
explain to me that "puta," which he calls her over and
over in the voicemail, means "whore."  But Z knows him
fairly well and isn't bothered; in fact she seems to get
a charge out of his tirades.  They probably remind her
of growing-up days in the old hood, which bordered an
area with many Greeks -- and that may be how Mama E came
to meet Tito in the first place (no one knows for sure,
and she's not talking).

My exciting news is that I've discovered a new art
gallery in the AQ.  It's a couple of doors east of the
restaurant where June threw her graduation party, and
that's when I first noticed it.  Since last year's
earthquake I've stopped walking on that side of the
street because big slabs of fallen bricks caused a
section of the sidewalk half a block farther east to be
fenced off.  Evidently the gallery opened during that
period.  It's run by a painter/calligrapher who
emigrated from mainland China a decade or so ago, Mr. X
(yes, his last name starts with an X), and he's good.
My eye was caught by some Chinese-astrology-based
inksticks displayed in the show window, and when I went
in to buy a few (for Horse, Snake, and Dragon years, at
four bucks a pop) Mr. X himself was the one who greeted
me.  For another ten bucks he threw in -- at half price!
-- one of his own eleven-by-fourteen inkbrush portrayals
of a Black Horse, and I've already hung this on one of
the bookcases at the hideaway.  Now I'm trying to
interest him in doing a somewhat larger version that
would include the ideogram for "Heavenly Year."

He seems fascinated with my jyze project, although
I'm not sure how well he understands exactly what I'm up
to: but then sometimes I wonder how I'm doing myself on
that score.  In any event explanations are difficult
because his English is very spotty and of course my
Chinese is nonexistent.  But I like the guy -- he's
forty, very friendly -- and I have hopes, though I
suppose they'll probably be dashed just because I look
like a typical AQ homeless Cawk vagabond and live in

ways Mr. X might find preposterous.  But he's an artist
and knows the "Tao Te Ching" almost by heart (he recited
a few lines, in Chinese of course) and so -- hopes!
     Several hours of phone talk with June this week.
The blow by blow and step by step of her big weekend.  I
probably should've cut her off at some point but I just
couldn't.  "Hello, buddy-buddy," that familiar voice
says, and I figure there goes a big chunk of the
afternoon.  I suspect I know more about her life and her
family than anyone else on earth who's not an immediate
family member -- and that probably remains true even
though I've already forgotten much of it.
     In other news, and so splendidly apt it is, I've
just received a mailing from the Social Security
Administration updating me on my account and explaining
my options for retirement.  It spells out my earnings
over the years all the way from 1960 when I put in a
summer assembling consoles on a Crest assembly line
while Dad was hobnobbing with the Crest execs one floor
up -- this within a mile or two of where the young Z
lived at the time, though of course I had no idea she
was there, except as a very general notion regarding
those sexy but hard-ass big-city girls -- and nearly
blinded myself in the process (but still learned a thing
or two about life in the big city, no question).  My
pathetic earnings record.  I don't know if the benefit
I'm entitled to is the rock-bottom minimum but I
wouldn't be surprised to learn that's the case.  My main
question right now is whether I want to go for
retirement at age sixty-two or sixty-five or seventy.  I
suspect in my tax circumstances sixty-two would be best
but at some point not too far off I'll have to do some
serious thinking about this.  And how apropos for a
Heavenly Year!
     Mr. X, I meant to mention, is a Metal Ox or "Ox on
the Way."  He was very surprised I could tell him this
just from glancing at the birth date in his brochure.  I
was surprised myself.  It's becoming part of my ingrown
symbology system.  My worldview!  Zeitgeist, take
notice!

[ Jyze of the Heavenly Year : Green Horse ]


------

18

------


     Well, it seemed like a good idea at the time.  And
yet also appropriately loony.  Start this one -- and
finish it too -- under the shadow of a lunar eclipse.
So I'm trying to do just that, at 3:13 a.m. on what by
Gregorian reckoning is Trinity Sunday: which means you
get not just the Holy Ghost this time but the Father and
the Son too, and all combined into a single troupe and
dancing, as nimbly as can be, on the nib of a J-stick.
     And still does seem like a good idea.  It can't be
kiboshed by the usual problem, overcast Jyze City sky.
The permacloud must be made part of the basic scene,
that's all, because the eclipse is visible from above
it.  Presumably.  There could be higher clouds too.  And
the almanacs I consulted could be wrong on timing (in
fact one insists on a 2:13 a.m. start).  Beyond that the
possible exceptions become philosophical in a way that
any self-respecting jyze neoprag is embarrassed to admit
he or she (or pick your pronoun) has thought about.
     A lone bird started sounding off moments ago --
before 3:30.  Dawn comes early in J. City these days but
not usually quite this early.  More likely for this
sensitive bird I'm the one who's brought on dawn -- by
turning on the light near the window with the bird-
bearing tree limbs hanging immediately outside.  Just
moments ago.  And now the cascade of birdsong.  The
whole neighborhood chorus is shrieking.  It's a highly
competitive business, bird-cries.
     And on the radio the jazz station is playing softly
and just a few hours ago a DJ informed us it's utterly
apropos to be listening to this station because it's

International Jazz Day (or it was until midnight by
Gregorian time, and so still is, as I figure, by NUT
time).  And it might as well be International Jyze Day
too.  Why?  Because we like it!  (So let's get down and
boogie!  Do the Fonky Honky!)
     When the USAn year turns a corner.  It's Memorial
Day weekend.  Three-day holiday.  At this moment two-
thirds of a continent distant the big engines are
revving for the 500, or about to.  Glass of wine here --
because I have no bourbon for special occasions and
couldn't afford it anyway.  And the Z-woman sleeps, but
not the sleep of the worry-free.
     Mama E again.  Another emergency-room visit, this
one running from six-thirty p.m. to one-thirty a.m. last
night by Gregorian count, and with the same results as
before: ain't nothin' wrong with this woman, the docs
declare, except maybe an overreaction to her meds
(Prozac the most likely culprit) and even in that case
by no means severe.  And on a full-moon Friday night the
emergency room was a battle zone.  I happened to arrive
home just as Z did -- such a fury she was in I thought
she was about to smash the car into all four garage
walls as she tried to back into our narrow parking slot.
     Now she's laying down the law with her mother.  I
mean, it's hardball time.  I'm backing her up a thousand
percent while also staying in red-alert damage-control
mode.  (Which reminds me: no new terrorist incidents
have taken place despite the cabal's warnings and the
advantage to them of staging such incidents.  Guess they
decided it was just too risky.  And our state's security
outfits apparently realized this too: none of them,
according to today's papers, even bothered to heighten
their readiness level or react in any other way --
except maybe with private hoots of derision.  It's the
old, old issue: how many times can the authorities cry
wolf?  And: just by the law of averages they're likely
to be correct on one eventually.)
     Enh, a little drama to keep the Heavenly Year
narrative zipping along.  I shouldn't be complaining.
     This entry, by the way, crazed to start with, also

[ Jyze of the Heavenly Year : Green Horse ]

falls under the aegis of one of my favorite Taoist
beasts, the Golden Pig.  Or Boar, which is almost as
good, and seems to be universally preferred by USAns
born during this one-twelfth slice of the cycle, for
example Jay the juggler and Olwen the poet, neither of
whom I've seen at all since this Great Adventure with
Mama E started up (or no, I briefly saw Jay as he
juggled in the upstairs hallway at the WOC -- juggled my
story as well as the six balls, a quick trip description
by me -- the only chance I've had to lay it on anyone).
     But it's turned out to be a kick-back kind of
night.  No calls, no messages (I just checked, having
spaced out the task earlier).  A slow-rolling eclipse
and it's due to peak about an hour from now, perhaps in
a clamor of birdsong even more riotous than what already
exists -- itself redoubled moments ago because I was
overheating and so opened the balcony door, at first
just a crack and then all the way.  The effect of the
wine, perhaps, on top of the sheer physical effort of
churning out the jyze.  Or letting it churn itself out,
I should say, or gallop itself out: a case of the Horse
of the Same Color (still Green) riding the jyze.  Or
rolling its chariot with the eclipse, could say.
     -- Oops, and I've neglected to mention it's also
the birthday of the great-great-grandfather of us all,
we USAn free thinkers, born 199 years ago, and wouldn't
he be amazed to see what his kind of thinking hath
wrought as we make the whole world knuckle under to our
notion of freedom (though as the coiner of the term
"hobgoblin of small minds" he might not have been too
troubled by the inconsistency, especially since we're
talking about mere political matters here -- and he
specifically cited politicians as bearers of the kind of
"small minds" he was thinking of).  (But here's Z.)  ---


                        [+2]


     Again I start out saying this probably can't go on
for very long.  It's the municipal plaza, just across

from city hall and down the hill from the county jail
(screams and cries issuing from which occasionally reach
me here).  And splinters of rain ride the air.  And at
the far end of the plaza a crowd of homeless men,
mostly, is gathering, though I don't think the free meal
is being served here tonight, or maybe it already has
been, though I see no sign of that (not much litter in
view and the trash bins are not overflowing).  But I
must be looking more prosperous than usual today because
several of these guys have already made their way fifty
feet or more down here to try to hit me up for coins or
smokes and two have clearly been of the nasty type.  If
the rain doesn't run me out -- and it appears to be
worsening -- they might.

Hunched over the J-book which is propped across my
thighs.  Hood up.  The food-service tent is also up now,
I see.  Old Glory stirring soggily in the drizzle.
Inscribed on the brown granite walls are mostly the same
veterans' names that appear on the lower but wider walls
at the symphony hall.  That's the new, this is the old.
The plaza here is looking tacky these days, its granite
walls streaked and pocked in places and the concrete
tiles underfoot bringing to mind a badly pot-holed city
side street.  And of course it's this memorial, not the
one at the symphony hall, that better represents the
true workings of cultural memory over the long term.

For what did these men (and surely a few women too,
though it's hard to find any evidence of this here) give
their lives?  Well, we know.  But then they thought they
knew too, or at least some did.  That the USA might grow
and prosper.  The system.  And now their memorial plaza
fills up with people for whom the system is not working.
Whether you say it's by choice or not, these people --
many of them military veterans themselves -- don't fit.
In their poverty and desperation they're equipped mainly
to serve as a reminder why others had better try harder
to fit, no matter how bad the fit.

A loudspeaker, omnipresent, female voice: "Will
those lying down in the plaza please sit up."  -- And
then from the same voice, a cheery "Thank you!"

[ Jyze of the Heavenly Year : Green Horse ]

        Memorial Day.  At three p.m. local time, in all the
nation's localities, one minute of silence was observed
for our country's fallen warriors.  This year in the
wake of 9/11 the business of memorial gratitude is
drawing a lot more cultural attention: it's up to a
whole minute!  And those European anti-U.S. war protests
I was hoping would occur, they haven't amounted to much.
The Stars-and-Stripes juggernaut keeps rolling.  ---
                            *
        Ever worsening drizzle drove me back to the Z-
mobile.  Now another front-seat entry, but also a
continuation.  The brown granite wall chiseled with the
names of Korean War vets blocks my view of goings-on up
in the plaza proper.  Eventually, though, it's all
coming down, this wall right here and everything else on
the grounds, to make way for, I think, part of the new
city-hall campus.
        Trees and skyscrapers.  This is a major downtown
street ("very high road") but not many cars are around
on a holiday.  Sparrows, pigeons, gulls, starlings.  Z-
mobile windshield stippled with rain beads but not yet
to the point where any are on the roll.  Some will be
soon, though, I'd wager, as the beads grow bigger and
bigger.  Rain sounding on the car's tin roof -- like the
feet of a flock of miniature dancing sparrows.
        I have the wheels because I just stopped by to see
Mama E.  My appointed mission: to break to her the
contents of the new law that Z's laying down.  New
protocol, new rules.  And I tried to do that.  But
probably mostly failed.  She was at her wit's end
because of the buzzing still being caused presumably by
a bad reaction to the Prozac.  Misery.  I did what I
could to buck her up and asked her to help me and
herself out by not pressuring Z too much.  Bromides and
hand-holdings and laying on of hands on her skull -- it
felt good, she said, but it did nothing to quiet the
buzz.  So now she's promised to do her best to hold on
until tomorrow evening's visit from Z, who hopefully
will arrive with some new ideas from Doc F, assuming Z
can get through to him (over the past four days no such

luck, but then, again, it's been a holiday weekend).
And I'm thinking I'd better show up tomorrow too to try
to buffer them, mother and daughter, from each other, if
I can.

One day at a time.

-- Still no windshield tears!  But the rain's let
up, that's why.  Suddenly not even a sprinkle.  This is
an utterly normal local rain pattern, something I'd take
little notice of if not for the demands of jyze, which
resemble those of TV networks these days: must have more
and more material!  No dead spots allowed!

But no.  Jyze allows dead spots.  It could stop
right now if it wanted to.  But it doesn't want to, not
quite yet.  Though before too much longer, yes.  And it
could start up again whenever it wanted to, and that's
another quality jyze doesn't share with network TV.

My original thought regarding today's entry was to
split it between the municipal plaza and the waterfront.
For the lunarly oriented -- and we're all just that, in
a sense, in our sublunary world -- this is a special
day, and that specialness could be best observed at the
waterfront.  I'm talking about gravitational pull.  All
things are interconnected, including the yin moon and
the yang sun and the yin/yang earth, not to mention us
much smaller heavenly bodies and even the seemingly not-
so-heavenly bodies, even the windshield beads waiting to
flow -- flow or go, evaporate, gather elsewhere for the
next big zigzagging opportunity.

Today, see, is a seasonal low-tide day.  Today the
ocean drains out of the bay and the sound in order that
it may swell with pride elsewhere, say in Korea where
many of the men whose names are etched in granite here
died.  And then roughly eight to twelve hours later, say
right about now, it may again swell with pride here.
But shortly after noon the second-lowest tide of the
year exposed lots of rarely seen bay/sound bottom and
the clammers and the barnaclers and many other kinds of
bottom explorers were no doubt out in force -- including
Wei and Alison, who called, Z told me, to ask if we
wanted to join them in their "mudlunking."  But she told

them we're already dealing with a different kind of low
tide these days, and they could easily understand
because in the past year both have gone through one or
more crises with an aging parent.
     -- Now resumed rain patter and the first tears.
But they don't roll steadily.  More like rabbits on a
hillside full of rabbits, first one creeps a couple of
crooked limping hops here, then another there -- and now
one does the full zigzag from near the top all the way
to the bottom, "in one fell hop-along."  And through
these tears I see the blurry living ghosts as they keep
arriving for their free dinner at the municipal plaza.
     I'm reminded of the fine movie Z and I saw last
night, Sherman A.'s "The Business of Fancy Dancing."
The pain -- all those spirits so far from the rez (the
real one).  The misery of the fancy-dancing windshield
raindrops.  The jail screams -- still audible because
the car window in the lee of the prevailing wind from
the southwest is cracked open.  Our very own south hill
appeared briefly in this movie, probably shot from
somewhere near the Natusan center where jyze was going
down last week.  But the shot wasn't focusing on the
hill; it was trained on the massive freeway
intersection, the picture of urban impersonality.  Other
shots showed woods near Jess's house where Z was staying
Thursday night, trying to melt away some of her tensions
in the hot tub.  And the golf-tee icon was in the movie
too, and several very familiar cafes and coffee shops.
For raw material we've only got so much to work with in
J-town, me or the talented Sherman A. or anyone else.
     The zigzag lines made by the windshield tears, they
quickly break up into a new series of beads
indistinguishable from the others.  Ashes to ashes,
beads to beads, tide to tide, tears to tears.  I'm
thinking the intensity of this beading activity owes a
lot to the wax job applied at the car wash the day
before Z was supposed -- this was back before the plans
abruptly changed -- to arrive at the airport here with
Mama E. in tow.  The wax, I could say, doesn't wane.
Not yet anyway.

But the light does.  Not until this moment, when the streetlights flicked on, did I notice.  Deepening grayness.  In Russia our supreme leader took a midnight walk on the Nevsky Prospect, where it's daylight all around the clock this time of year.  The press release made my eyes go wide: it said the prez had been preparing for his first Russian visit by reading "Crime and Punishment"!  I recalled Lady S telling me it was her reading of this same book at age thirteen that made her realize there were grays in the world, not just bright colors.  But I suppose the concoctors of the presidential image figured they could suggest their man was engaged in deep study of the battle between the forces of good and evil.  (And a JRX for the Russian street name, I guess it is -- or could it be a kind of extended lookout park?  Or both at once?)

And tomorrow we can celebrate the 1,141st anniversary of the Vikings' sacking of Paris.  To try to imagine my ancestors among them I picture my father in a horned helmet (historically inaccurate to be sure) and a furry tunic with leather calf thongs (like the actors in "The Vikings") and a big sword which goes wavy on me until it resembles the Filipino sword from World War II days which he proudly mounted on his study wall -- but whether he came by that sword in some sort of military operation on Luzon or perhaps bought it from a shop in Manila or even in Centropolis or somewhere else on the way back home, I don't know -- never thought to ask and he never volunteered -- and it's just very hard to keep everything in focus right now.  The sacking of Paris took place in year 3216 of the Celestial calendar, or close to it, so I suppose a few poets of the late Tang were still around brushstroking their miraculous "word temples" shortly before the dynasty collapsed.

-- A fight erupts on the sidewalk now, a few yards from the Z-mobile.  I mean this moment.  Heavily duct-taped backpacks (much like my own) thrown down in anger.  Lots of colorful language, highly repetitious.  And I discover that by twisting my head far to the left I can see part of the long line huddled in the rain up in the

plaza itself, only a couple of umbrellas in sight, gray
colors, vacant eyes, awaiting the arrival of the meal
truck.  Dinnertime tonight must be nine o'clock, because
as of yet no truck's in sight.  Dark clouds, and their
appearance on the scene must've caused the streetlights
to go on, photoelectrically.

The fight broke up fast.  But others look imminent
or at least seriously potential.

Two or three days a week I walk by this plaza.
Sometimes the meals are served here, sometimes they're
served at "Vino Meadows" by the courthouse or under the
nearby overpass.  With my worn backpack and jacket, many
if not most people must assume I'm headed for the end of
the line, and that's how I like it and want it.  But --
this scene, it's searingly sad and it's infuriating.
This doesn't have to be, here or anywhere.  Of course!
Let's look on the bright side, Mama E!

Okay, now jyze wants to stop.  The Golden Pig, also
dubbed the "Monastery Pig," jumps on the Black Horse and
together they head back to the monastery, which is to
say the hideaway.  Then, at least for the Black Horse,
onward to the scope office.  Then home, stage set south
hill, for a dawn "pillow-talk" liaison with Z in which
she'll certainly want the full scoop on how the big
scene went down with Mama E.


------


19


------


Nostalgia as it oughta be.  "Hey Jude," the
stretched ending, played live by a local cover band at
one of the taverns in the HQ triangle.  I'm sitting on a
bench just outside the entrance, my back to the show,
but I can hear it all just fine -- as a roar goes up and

break time's upon us.  And to fill the gap, reggae and
Latin and jazz flow in from other taverns to the left
and right and across the street straight ahead.

     Feet splayed oddly on uneven cobblestones.  I
hustled down here to pay my rent since tomorrow's the
1st.  Now fifty minutes or so for jyze before last-bus
time.  Which means it already is the 1st by Gregorian
reckoning.  Another great nineteenth-century USAn poet's
birthday has passed.  The World Cup is into its second
day in the joint venue of Japan and Korea -- the only
two countries I've ever visited, except for brief
passages through Canada and of course some very long
ones in the U.S., starting at birth (or some might say
nine months before birth).

     So this is just a start on the White Rat cluster.
But it's a good place for rats -- most of them, as it
happens, of the Norwegian variety.  As part of the
latest HQ cleanup campaign the metal dumpsters in the
alleys are being replaced with smaller lidded plastic
bins, and the abundant rats in the area, who love the
dumpsters, dislike the plastic bins and so are instead
invading the buildings in search of food and shelter.
I've seen several scampering around on the first floor
of the hideaway building in just the past week.

     Victorian five-ball lamps, also some three-ballers
-- the leafy trees down here look good in such
triangulating light.  Totem pole, the city's shame (one
of so many!), rising dignified regardless.  Chain-link
fence still surrounding the area where the restored
pergola will stand.  The eponymous chief, the bust,
eyeing it all blankly from the pedestal twenty feet to
my left, lights of the oldest cafe in town glowing
across the street as backdrop for the chief's famously
stoic gaze.  Long-suffering, yeah, could say that.

     I'm short on time tonight because I stayed too long
with Mama E and my scoping work took a bit longer than
expected.  It's been another busy week of Mama E crises,
with the latest involving severe leg and hip pain.  I've
had to bear the brunt of the caretaking because Z's
"been the boss" at work with Kent out sick.  Will Mama E

ever come out of her tailspin?  I still have hope.  I
finally met Doc F during an emergency visit to his
office on Tuesday and he seems both competent and caring
-- and maybe best of all, has a good sense of humor.

But still, the dreads.  When Mama E didn't answer
my call this afternoon to let her know I was on my way
over I feared the worst.  Every time our phone rings it
might be, again, the worst or anyway something very bad.
Every night when I come home, more dreads, especially if
the apartment lights are on (which I can usually tell
from a block away).  Z-wiff needs lots of calming and
consoling and encouraging these days.  Like last Sunday,
for instance, when I had to break off the eclipse entry.

But.  We're hanging on.  If anything we're tighter
than ever.

And this bit of good news: Mr. X at the AQ art
gallery is making me a special Heavenly Year calligraphy
work and he's promised it'll be ready Sunday.  -- And
that, by the way, happens to be Mama E's eighty-seventh
birthday, solar kind.

Friday nights in the HQ aren't what they used to
be.  Not here and not, from what I'm told, anywhere else
in the entertainment zone that makes up maybe half the
quarter.  Apparently Friday's continuing to slip as a
big steppin'-out night.  And the HQ's no longer the
hottest nightlife district in this town.  And the
baseball team's on the road, or otherwise a few groups
of postgame carousers wearing team gear and/or waving
team pennants would likely be roistering about.

Cover band back from break with another tune that
hails from my Mezzu days, "You Really Got Me."  Can't
help but smile at the deja vu, the ironies, the cycles,
the memories.  What the heck am I doing sitting here?
Fossil!  -- Imagine my father doing something like this
at such a vintage.  Parked on a bench outside a tavern.
And dressed like I am now, jeans and chucks and raggedy
henley and a couple days' beard.  Jyzing!

Warm night, lots of skin showing all around,
including up close.  Navels.  Short skirts.  Waistbands
of thong underwear riding above curvy bands of flesh and

then hiphuggers.  Cycles.  Sex.  It's forever hitting on
new ways to stay in fashion, sex is.

Haul out my trusty pocket watch and it says five
more minutes.  Now "Hang On, Sloopy."  Lord help us.
The preposterousness of whatever it is that decides
which pop music (or pop anything else) ends up
characterizing an era.

At this moment J-slinger G happens to be the
longest-haired longhair around.  In fact, other than the
cover band's drummer he's just about the only longhair
around.  Military types abound, though, so we know any
terrorists in the area will be lying low tonight.  Or
perhaps they'll be drawn here, who knows.  As if by
pondering this matter I'm not gladdening both sides.

-- Okay, hike on up the hill.  Maybe jyze will
return later for an encore -- if the home scene permits.

*          *

Yes.  A free forty minutes before bedtime.  Today
the birds didn't awaken until twenty to four and this
time it was the roar of a passing motorcycle that roused
them (the same big ol' hog, I'm pretty damn sure, that
frequently sets off car alarms at this hour).  Nor has
Z-wiff awakened at all, even though she left the bedroom
door wide open as per usual on Friday nights.  Tonight
was the office women's party for June at a restaurant
somewhere in the north end of town and Z wheedled a ride
home from Leola (deploying her fancy new wheels -- same
model as the old ones but now with an all-leather
interior, one of only twenty-five such dazzlers, she's
let everyone know, in the whole region) -- Z bummed this
ride, I say, so she could get herself well oiled on
tequilas.  Without doubt she was in need of a night off
and a five-star bender.

As am I.  But this jyze fling right here will have
to be it.

Oy, the news.  India and Pakistan edging ever
closer to war, deftly egged on by Al Qaeda, it seems
almost certain, as a kind of reprisal for the U.S.'s
Afghanistan invasion.  "You thought you could do all
this imperializing, Yanks, without consequences?"  Nukes

180

may well be used, the pundits say, of course with
horrific loss of life, and then -- will China come to
Pakistan's aid?  And then Russia to India's?

   Meanwhile Israel again smashes into Palestinian
towns, but this latest incursion doesn't even make the
front pages.  And the new U.N. report on the direness of
the global-roasting/ecological crisis -- "Earth on the
Precipice" -- scarcely draws any notice at all.

   The brouhaha over the FBI's bungling of pre-9/11
clues ends up just about the way everyone figured it
would.  The FBI takes the fall but says it couldn't help
itself given the supposedly tight constraints it was
operating under and its mission guidelines.  So now the
bureau's being reorg'd and beefed up to fight terrorism
as a first priority and the post-Watergate constraints
on domestic spying are being dropped.  Beautiful.
                         *
(The early dawn quiet was just ripped apart again,
this time by a big crash right outside.  Squealing
wheels, a horn refusing to shut off.  Someone's car
parked on the street is now a good deal less shapely
than it was five minutes ago.  And a guy on a bicycle
pedaled insouciantly by; I saw him when I stepped out on
the balcony to check out the scene.  -- And the noise
may've awakened Z, because I just heard the toilet flush
in our big bathroom.  -- But now she's gone back to bed,
probably with tequila-aching head aching a little more.)

   A note she left on the chair says she hasn't
forgotten it's still my Heavenly Year.  The note is
written inside a new pocket-size hardcover folder for
stickie notes.  I've been trying to find something like
this for years.  How does she do it?  So often she comes
up with terrific little surprise gifts for her G-man!

   Wednesday afternoon I dropped by Mr. X's gallery to
commission the Heavenly Year work.  It turns out he has
even less English than I thought.  Fortunately his wife
and two young daughters came in as I was trying to
explain what I had in mind for the painting, and the
older of the daughters -- a fourth-grader, I think she
said -- was able to serve as interpreter.  The results

were both encouraging and disappointing.  His literal
understanding of what I was after seemed good but now I
no longer felt we were clicking intuitively to the
extent we were the first time.  I hope I'm wrong.  And I
should be finding out Sunday.  (I'm paying him fifty
bucks, by the way.  That was my idea, not his.  He
probably would've done it for less -- maybe even for the
same half-price ten bucks I paid for the inkbrush Horse.
On the other hand some of his paintings hanging in the
gallery carry price tags well into the thousands of
dollars.  After I apologized for not being able to offer
more there was a moment of warmth; he put his hand on my
arm and assured me, "No, no, I will do" -- as if maybe
we were fellow artists understanding each other after
all.  That's why I still have hope.)
     Graying dawn, overcast, the streetlight still
glowing outside the window.  And the street's quiet now.
Did the owner of the mangled parked car ever come out?
Not that I know of.  A surprise awaits him or her in the
morning.  Before I even got out there, by the way, the
other car drove off with horn blaring nonstop.  Bound
for the police precinct to report the accident?  Somehow
I doubt it.


[+3]


     Sittin' on the old harbor steps.  -- Well, not so
old really, maybe eight or ten years tops.  They
materialized during my watch in this town.  For better
or worse, I therefore bear at least a sliver of
responsibility for their existence.
     But up near the top.  On a fine warm evening, just
past sunset, a bit of breeze off the bay reaching me
here.  I can see it down there, the bay, a couple of
truncated rectangular slices of it, framed by the two
decks of the viaduct with lights moving north on the
upper one, south on the lower, and in both directions in
the neon-lit rectangles below the lower -- that's the
"very low road" that runs along the waterfront.  (Maybe

I should be saying all this aloud just in case any of
the tourists are wondering about what they're seeing.
Half a dozen are scattered within hearing distance on
this level of the steps, though the faucetlike fountain
jets would probably wash out any words I spoke.  Several
folks are clicking away with cameras, with the clicks
entirely doused, for me, by the jets.  -- As a sliding
vertical ice tray of lights briefly fills one of those
truncated rectangles mentioned above -- a jumbo ferry.)

I'm half hidden in the greenery.  It's a canyon
here: big apartment buildings tower a few yards to my
left and right with very little in the way of setbacks.
Sitting behind windows at the staircase level, posh
diners, for a few of whom I may be a figure of local
color, albeit pink.  A hundred feet down the steps in
the plaza stands an empty outdoor cafe, chairs clustered
haphazardly around a dozen tables beneath half that many
tacky designer trees, with two clusters of globe lights
making for lots of intricate shadows faintly slipping
about on the stone tiles.  Sexy black lace, I'm
thinking.  And male wanderers with pocketed hands stroll
across it and dress themselves in it so to say.

I like the site.  The "venue."  But I didn't make
it down here as early as planned.  First a stop at Mama
E's delayed me long enough that I gave up on my
scheduled WOC workout (though I did stop by there anyway
to update Z and do a little friendship maintenance with
juggler Jay, who has two badly bruised wrists -- as he
showed me -- from botched handling of some rebar he was
working with at home this weekend; but nothing short of
amputation, he avowed, would stop him from engaging in
his regular WOC juggling session).  And then I got
caught up in browsing at the ORB, maybe because I needed
some time to recover from the downer of seeing Mama E.

She's suffering.  She doesn't know if she can hold
out until Thursday's doctor appointment.  Her repaired
hearing aid, which I picked up on the way over there,
didn't stop the buzzing in her head (tinnitus), as we'd
hoped it would.  Her right leg's still aching and she's
depressed.  She didn't want me to leave.  It was sad and

pathetic and we just have to bear up under it, tough it
out, keep on keeping on, hope for the best, prepare for
the worst -- "we" meaning all three of us.

And yesterday was her eighty-seventh birthday.  Z
and I took over a chocolate cake and bags of presents (I
worked on them most of Saturday night, as Z had earlier
on hers; mine included a brightly colored hanging salmon
cutout and a four-foot-tall loose-limbed jester, both
made of shiny cardboard, both with cartoon bubbles
appended containing humorous -- ha! -- uplifting
thoughts, and a "Life Gets Going Really Good at 87" bag
-- altered from "Life Begins at 50," which was the
closest to 87 we could find -- as if the closeness
mattered when the number had to be altered anyway -- but
I say this only to bring up the fact that there were no
"Life Begins at 60" bags -- and so this is it, right
here, this J-book: my surrogate "Life Begins at 60"
bag).

Camera flashes: these I can see.  Lots of photos
being taken here as is so often the case.  Half a block
at my back, above the top of the steps, Hammering Man
holds his hammer high and ready.  If I had a hammer, I'd
hammer in the evenings -- I mean, if I wanted the
tourists to go "Aw, look at that!" -- as one just did.

Mama E's birthday, I was starting to say, wasn't
much better than today.  The only point at which she
showed a few sparks of life was when she was scratching
maniacally at the Lotto tickets Z gave her.  And she had
a ten-buck winner!  (And Z's overall financial
indebtedness is increasing at the rate of about ten
bucks an hour, I'd estimate, if not more, and I mean
twenty-four hours a day, every day.  But this doesn't
seem to be bothering her and so it's not bothering me.
All in all she appears to be holding up pretty well.
Still hasn't used any of the tranks so far as I know.)

Why sit here on this day?  It has nothing to do
with Rats, or not intentionally anyway.  But it was 210
years ago today that a certain English sea captain,
after leading the first European "exploration" of this
area, almost entirely by frigate, and bestowing upon

many of the most prominent geographical features the names they're still officially known by today, came ashore and, pushing aside all the Natives who were already living here and had been for millennia, planted an English flag and claimed all this was now part of that distant country's turf.  I'm marking the occasion.  Certainly can't pretend it didn't happen, can we?

Also, today would be my parents' sixty-first wedding anniversary.  My age plus nine months of gestation plus another six months or so of post-wedding parental condom use makes sixty-one.  It's not even faintly a matter of coincidence that this arrival of the Heavenly Year will have, if all goes well, or anyway well enough, sixty-one clusters.

And then this: the new fiberglass dragons are mounting their light poles in the AQ.  By the time another Dragon cluster rolls around they should all be quivering in place and ready for prime jyze treatment.

Okay, I'm chilling out.  In a couple of senses.  The breeze off the bay, armed by these fountains here, pricks me with shivery water splinters, pretty much the same effect as standard J-town wind-driven drizzle.  And work awaits me at the scope office, three blocks straight up the hill from here, its wall of checkerboard lights already blazing away, I see, when I turn to check.

And finally, as a parting note, I have Mr. X's Water Horse Heavenly Year calligraphy painting.  And I love it!  And right below the Horse is, in Mr. X's own gorgeous calligraphy, the word "Jyze."  Written in this case with the first two letters atop the last two, going left to right Western style (except for the mid-word break).  And now I'm inspired to develop that logo into a signature-chop-like red ideogram myself and include it on the card I'm making for him as thanks.

------

20

------

Even the worst-laid plans may come to something.
And here I am right where I vaguely thought I might be
for the start of the Metal Ox cluster and so I guess I'm
all right.  But a rush job's arisen, possibly having to
do with the bush-league terrorist case I scoped for
grand jury yesterday (and which is already hitting the
news today).  So I can't stick around for long.
    And I couldn't drive up with Z, as also was
planned, to escort Mama E to her appointment with Doc F
-- after which, the plan was, I'd mosey down here to
the central plaza in the HQ, arriving just as the First
Thursday artwalk was getting underway.  But the
encouraging news is Mama E's had two quite good days in
a row and she's working on a third.  Cackling,
chortling, eyes sparkling!  And insisting lesbians were
making out in the trees outside her window yesterday
afternoon -- but maybe they really were, who knows.  Or
on the second-floor balcony passageway just behind the
trees.  Cliff the super confirmed some sort of party had
been going on up there.
    This excellent day.  This historic day.  Thirty-
five years ago the Six-Day War was chugging along (and
in a way it still is, with more Israeli incursions, more
Palestinian suicide bombings -- a dozen soldiers died in
one of those bombings yesterday).  Fifty-eight years ago
it was D-Day; the beaches of old Viking territory
Normandy were aswarm with Good Guys out to wrest the
homeland from Nazi Evil.  And 113 years ago -- what
brings me here today -- a big chunk of this city burned
to the ground.  The Great Fire.  Famously remarked the

author of "Kim" and "The Jungle Book" a short time
later, arriving for a visit midway on whatever imperial
errand he was running at the time: the entire city was
nothing but a "black smudge."

   -- Now a streetcar rolls by, cream and green, Stars
and Stripes snapping.  Clang clang.  Gulls plaintively
crying too.  All plaza benches are occupied by the
homeless and their belongings -- still hours to go until
the missions open for the night.  Dead ahead looms the
brick office of "America's bank," as one of the signs
says, on the very spot where the south blockhouse once
stood, city residents clustering inside during the one-
day Battle of J-town in 1856, the Good Guy homelanders
attempting futilely to wrest their territory back from
the forces of the Evil Invaders, our Cawk ancestors.

   And I sit right next to -- looking him straight in
the gas mask -- a kneeling figure wearing an ax in his
belt and carrying a nasty-looking forked tool.  Two
other similar figures stand on his far side pointing a
heavy hose toward the bank where the south blockhouse
stood and a fourth is crawling along behind the others,
and he too is gas-masked.  Or oxygen-masked, I guess I
should say.  All are life-size, or maybe slightly
larger, bronze statues, and I'm perched on one of the
cut-stone blocks explaining this is a monument to the
city's fallen firefighters.  Half a block to the north
stand the fire-department headquarters.  Tourists are
braving the swarms of homeless to snap photos of the
four bronze figures, the jyzer likely an unwanted and
certainly an unbronzed fifth figure in some of them.
Firefighters are hot right now, heroes of the hour, the
year, because so many died or suffered serious injuries
in the collapse of the twin towers.  Jyzers are not yet,
and are not ever likely to be, hot.  So we're pleased to
bask in a little inadvertent attention here, yes.

   ORB, only real bookstore, half a block to the west.
Folks milling around outdoor art displays to the south
in the next block of the plaza.  The gold-rush monument
across the street -- it's actually a tiny national park,
someone told me, though it looks like just another

storefront -- is closing for the day.  The Great Fire
made this city into a blank slate; the gold rush about
eight years later inscribed the modern city on that
slate, more or less, or so the historians inform us.

At the time of the anti-Chinese riots, just a few
years before the fire, this was Chinatown.  It too
burned to the ground.  The land to the east was tidal
mudflat up to that point, but it was soon filled in and
the remaining Chinese and various newcomers, including
many Filipinos who started arriving shortly after the
gold rush as a result of the conquest of their homeland
in the late 1890s by those same Bad Guys, which is to
say: we USAn Cawks.  And all this, from here roughly two
miles southeast up to the very street where Z and I live
on south hill, was part of the claim of one of those
early Cawk founders, often celebrated in local history
as a handsome and popular blond hellraiser pioneer dude.

Endlessly and renewably boggling it is, yes.
Outrage and atrocity are everywhere thickly layered,
like the pigeon droppings on yon glass pavilion roof.
(And the totem poles at my back, all three, seem to
offer nothing but eternal yawns -- although those might
better be seen as masks for totally justified fury.)

My Celestial calendar tells me we're at the start
of the "Grain Fills Out" fifteen-day period.  I'd say
this applies not just to grain but to flowers too, and
even trees.  Meanwhile India and Pakistan still quiver
on the brink of nuclear war, a million troops glaring at
each other across the Kashmir line -- and we of the
hyperpower can take a lot of credit for stirring up this
colorful drama, pundits say, with our destabilization of
the region via invasion last fall.  Our cabal does know
how to keep things hopping for just about everyone.

But for me the high moment of the week was the
release of a U.S. government report confirming global
roasting is for real and we advanced industrializers are
causing most of it -- and the report says what we should
do about this devastation of the natural world is "adapt
to it"!  Well, the very next day the cabal's ultra-right
brain trust made such a stink about the confirmation

that their appointed leader, our national president,
took it all back and said, in effect, global roasting
doesn't exist after all!  Meaning we don't have to adapt
to it!  And all's well again!
     Criminelly, can it get any loonier than this?
-- But of course it can, and it almost certainly will.
We're gonna have a whole century of this.  And if I can
hang on for the entire allotted maximum known human life
span I'll be able to witness about sixty percent of it.
     -- And just as the crowds here are turning frisky
-- acres of flesh on the strut, with postpunk tattoo
body-hype types pretty much making out in the trees --
I gotta pack it in and hoof it uptown and jump into the
gears of the machinery of justice to play my role as a
tiny and very far from indispensable cog.

                    *              *

     Back for an encore.  By Gregorian measure it's no
longer Great Fire Day, but I'm holed up in a federal
battlement across the street from the spot where the
fire started.  Nobody'd better try to attack me because
I'm under federal protection here and in this paranoid
era even a love tap would probably be prosecuted as a
capital offense.
     It wasn't a cow that caused it, as in Centropolis,
but it was something similarly trivial, seemingly, a
heated glue pot tipping over, and poof, city core gone.
Thirty square blocks.  I've read, though I still find it
hard to believe, that the column of smoke was visible as
far as ninety miles away in the state capital.
     The old ten-story -- or eleven? -- federal office
building stands over there now, something like a square
wedding cake in appearance, red brick with white icing
slathered on top and dripping down the sides.  It's of
roughly the same vintage as the DC castle on south hill
and looks equally castlelike.  Now, though, it's just an
historic also-ran, rendered as such by the big new
federal building -- forty stories or so -- at whose base
I sit, on a wooden bench, inside an octagonal open brick
watchtower of sorts, about eight feet high, right at the
intersection of the "edge road" and the steep uphill

east-west street to the north.  It's one of my favorite
places to pause for a rumination or two.

     A floodlit Old Glory ripples almost directly
overhead.  Foot traffic is light, and most of that is
bound for the pedestrian bridge a block to the south and
then for the ferry terminal.  Over a period of almost
seven years I trod that route myself five or six times a
week but usually much further along in the night, at the
tail end of the graveyard shift.  Two blocks farther to
the south is the HQ triangle and my hideaway office
which I'll be heading for in a bit to pick up a few
items before catching the usual last bus home.

     At the triangle I'll genuflect before the bust of
the eponymous chief.  As of midnight, maybe twenty
minutes ago, we're into his death day: June 7, 1866.
About two years before that my Norwegian great-
grandfather Bendyk was born, presumably in Sandefjords-
Stolen above Dale near the heart of the old Viking
stomping grounds.  When my father was two years old,
Bendyk typed out a letter welcoming him into the world.
-- It's a sign of advancing decrepitude, no doubt, but
I just can't stop being astounded by how recent all this
once seemingly ancient stuff is starting to look to me.

     -- Meanwhile no one's giving me any trouble here.
A roving panhandler tried to hit me up from a distance
but that's about it.  No federal guards have come after
me either and that's even more surprising.  Maybe
they've had to shrink their security perimeter.  After
the bombing seven years ago by homegrown Christian
Identity terrorists of another highrise federal building
some fifteen hundred miles to the southeast -- killing
167 occupants and bystanders -- this building here
became a fortress, and now since 9/11 it's even more of
one.  But -- this is how life is when you dominate the
world.  You've got to be ready to put up with a few
minor inconveniences.  Here and there the dominated and
the survivors of the massacres might even hold a severe
grudge against you and seek revenge.

     Another U.S. flag, I notice now, is planted atop
the wedding-cake building, but it's flapping pretty much

in the dark up there.  And gray clouds roll by, low,
like expanding puffs of cannon smoke.  And lights shine
here and there in various nearby buildings ten or twenty
or even forty or fifty stories up and the swing shift,
mostly of janitors and most of them immigrants, many
"undocumented," minimum wage, little English, and hard
workers too, is going at it.  They're my main
compatriots of the night.  And think of all the hundreds
of millions around the globe who'd love to have such
jobs -- who'd do just about anything to nab one.  And
soon may have to be doing just that -- anything -- as
part of their "adaptation" to the devastation caused by
global roasting under the guiding domination of this
very country.  Lordie it's gonna be a hoedown.

     The Great Fire was a kind of local early warning --
and early warming.  What kind of rebuilding will even be
possible after the Great Roasting?  And how long will it
take?  And who, other than mutant beetles maybe, will be
doing it?


[+4]


     Eclipse time again.  Yes, another eclipse, already,
and for this one the moon is interposing itself between
south hill and the sun.  An "annular" type: from the
perspective of certain points on earth it will appear to
make a "ring of fire."  Or maybe it won't, if the moon
isn't far enough out into its orbit.  Today's paper says
it's not, but at least one almanac says it is.
     Well, anyway, I've moseyed over to the park.
Hilltop park this time, two blocks due south of the
apartment.  I've brought my coffee.  Crown of the hill,
a fabulous view in all directions, though to take in any
of it you must peer between houses and also around or,
in a couple of cases, under trees.  It's three p.m. and
the "limits of umbra," according to that same maverick
almanac, should've been reached by now.  I'm not
planning to peer straight at the sun to see if that's
true, nor will I try the recommended protective method

of poking a hole in a card and looking at the shadow it
casts, but in theory the central eclipse here has begun.

     Going just by rule of thumb, eyeballing it, I'd say
it has so entered.  For a blue-sky day the sunlight's
weak, the shadows less contrasty.  But the difference
isn't all that great, and that's because (the same
almanac says) we're far enough off the central path of
the eclipse here that we're privy to only about forty
percent of the effect.  The birds, for example, are
still cheeping away at their normal clip, I'd say; few,
if any, are acting as if dusk has arrived early.

     But it is odd.  Something slightly ominous seems to
be lurking beneath the surface of the everyday.  As jyze
drama-meister I insist on this.  -- As a city bus
lumbers insouciantly by on the street to the east (our
street).  Kids play on the swings under the eyes of
watchful moms who are speaking a chirpy Cantonese, I
believe, amongst themselves, four of them.  Bypassers on
foot, hombres in supersag pants, float some spirited
Espanol this way.  At the moment I'm the park's only
easily identifiable Cawk.  And I'm smiling happily over
this: I always like being here.  And never more than
when I can grab my favorite seat on the wooden bench
under the long droopy limbs of the big oak, as now.
Gazing at the shallow kidney bean of the wading pool,
waterless at the moment (as for the entire time we've
lived up here) but not kidless or momless or birdless or
(for a minute there) squirrel-less.  Leaf shadows on the
bench and the cement path gently shifting about in
lovely interlaced kaleidoscopic fashion -- you think,
"Show me a law of complexity that can deal with this!"

     But I won't be here for much longer.  Today's one
of my days for checking in on Mama E, and I'll be
driving the Z-mobile so Z can pick it up to attend a
women's-group meeting tonight on the north end, and so I
must get it there by a time certain and therefore I have
my pocket watch laid out on the bench.  (Kids are
fascinated by this watch, moms are highly apologetic for
the disturbance they cause for the ill-dressed yet still
credibly elder jyzer and whisk them away.)

[ Jyze of the Heavenly Year : Green Horse ]

     This will be my first visit with Mama E since last
Thursday -- and that means the news must be good.  A mix
of "good" and "okay" days, actually; but no particularly
bad ones.  Z saw her Saturday and Z and I both felt we
could let her (and ourselves) have some peace Friday and
Sunday.  That peace for us felt odd, we agreed, and I'd
say now the oddness resembled that of this eclipse
(which is proceeding undisturbed and seemingly unnoticed
by anyone else here).  For the first time in a couple of
months worries about Mama E weren't blazing.  But it was
also as if we were playing hookey.  It was exceptionally
fine being off by ourselves but there was as well a
sense we were breaking some rule and a truant officer
might pound on the door at any moment.
     And it's a special day in a couple of other ways.
For one, the Month of the Snake is coming to an end --
just did this less than an hour ago, roughly in tandem
with the start of the eclipse -- and the new month,
following in the usual order, is the highly auspicious
and personally near-momentous Month of the Horse.
That's me!  -- Well, no, I'm Year of the Horse, not
Month.  My Month "pillar" is the Monkey.  But still, a
Horse person in a Horse Month lives well, so it's
decreed, and I'll do my utmost to convert this decree
into hard fact.  Or warm and cozy fact.  Or not fact of
any kind but being.  Suchness and thisness and newness
and deliciousness.  Thus the new zodiacal ontology.
     Also it's the last day of the first third of the
Heavenly Year.  The first panel of the triptych, a few
more strokes here and it's history.  With respect to
your lifetime you don't know when you hit the triptych
hinging points -- though up until recently I thought
they came at age twenty-eight and fifty-six; and now I'd
like to hope with the crazed intensity of a jyze fanatic
that the two "thirds" hinges hit instead at forty and
eighty, making your Heavenly Year even more Heavenly
because under this arrangement it becomes the midpoint
and thus in another sense the high point -- but when
you're engaged in yearlong jyze projects you don't just
hope, you know (underscore that!).  And so I know right

now this is almost it, the hinge.  Or it could be the
new zodiacal epistemology.  -- But no, not this next
double asterisk, I don't think, because I'm fixing on
popping up again in a couple of hours, after seeing Mama
E.  That's when the eclipse will be hitting its max and
if epochal events are to be sparked, they'll most likely
(following traditional eclipsian logic) occur then.
And besides, I have personal and world news to catch up
on, and that by itself (both types!) is epochal enough.

*       *

   Next hill to the north.  Me and a bunch of other
eclipse watchers are seated on the upper part of the
front staircase of the city's largest cathedral -- the
very one where Z and I attended the wedding of Ramona
and Pepe back in "Jyze Millennium" times -- as right now
the six o'clock bells chime -- and we're gazing out
above the downtown skyline at the slightly obfuscated
solar orb all mutedly a-dazzle in its diaphanous
swaddling of high white clouds.  Several observers even
have official eclipse-watching kits, perhaps clipped
from a newspaper (though if there was one in either of
today's local papers, I missed it).

   A massive bronzed double door rises behind me,
cluttered with human figures in bas relief, I guess is
how to say it.  Or maybe they're angels.  Possibly even
demons, posted there to remind all pagans they're
forbidden to enter.  Up above the doors, a stained-glass
Christ figure holds forth magisterially alongside a
legend almost like a cartoon bubble but giltier and
stretched out more.  The figure's asserting, "I am the
vine.  You are the branches."  That's what it says.  And
I say: oh yeah?  Who dis guy t'ink he is anyway to be
calling me a branch of him?  And if we're gonna be
cracking down on the basis of terrorist profiles, what
about him?  Look at that beard!  The robe!  The sandals!

   Eclipse just slightly past its peak right now, by
the paper's measure, or an hour and a quarter past it by
the almanac's.  Diluted light like a winter day yet it's
still warm.  And peace reigns up here, with birds, with
distant surflike freeway sounds, with kids cavorting and

194

off-duty priests wandering by, exiting, entering, like
the police HQ just down the hill at shift-change time,
only here the glances are at once more paternal (good
day, padrone!) and also more suspicious.  If I were by
myself I'd probably be shooed away.  But some of these
other step-sitters might be part of the flock, or I mean
true branches of the vine.  -- And what an odd metaphor!
You'd think in two thousand years they'd've come up with
something better.  Maybe tootsies of the multimillipede?
     Even though we're not far from the crown of east
hill, enormous 'scrapers rise dead ahead and their upper
stories glare down at us.  One of those 'scrapers is the
famously phallic tower which will someday house most
city government offices, Z's included, unless she
decides to retire first, which I'd say is extremely
unlikely given her, which is to say our, current
financial situation.  Beflagged hilltop hospital #1
stands a few blocks to my left.  For Mama E, who lives
just a block east of that, this is a low-okay day.
Left-leg pain is again worsening.  She'll be seeing the
doc for it tomorrow at noon, with Z as her escort.  The
magic birthday salmon is not doing its job.  I thought
maybe it had just unwound like a watch and so gave it a
few spins and thereafter it slowly revolved, regularly
reversing directions, in its corner above the sofa-bed
as we talked.  Anything to get Mama E smiling.
     She doesn't remember the full eclipse that darkened
Centropolis back in the early sixties, I think it was.
Only once every 350 years does any particular spot on
earth experience a full solar eclipse, so it follows
that the odds for any individual person to see one in
his or her lifetime -- without, of course, making a
special effort to do so -- are somewhere between one in
six and one in five, or if the 120-year maximum life
span is in play, one in three, or one panel of the max-
life triptych.  So we were lucky, we Centropolitans of
that era.  I still recall the darkness, the quietness,
the eerieness.  It was very easy to see how such an
event could be viewed by so-called primitive peoples as
being of profound significance, equivalent for today's

sophisticates to Friday the 13th to the hundredth power
or maybe a fifty percent drop in the stock market.

I promised news.  For the world we've got USAn
diplomacy hard at work to tamp down the crises in the
Mideast and Kashmir -- of which we've been, to be sure,
among the main fomenters.  We've got the cabal
announcing formation of a new Department of Homeland
Security ("biggest gubmint reorg since '47!") to try to
distract attention from new revelations of terrorist-
related malfeasance on the part of the FBI and CIA --
who, regardless, won't be affected.  And just today, the
"capture" is announced of an alleged Al Qaeda terrorist
from Centropolis, a U.S. citizen who supposedly was
trying to construct, all by himself, a nuclear bomb,
"dirty" type, with which to wipe a city from the map --
maybe Z's and my original home burg, C-town itself.  And
yet I thought I also heard the man had already been in
jail for a month.  So some clarifications are in order.

For personal news, I'll start with the hanging of
Mr. X's "Heavenly Year of the Water Horse" artwork,
newly framed by me, in my hideaway office.  All else
pales beside this.

Other than Z-wiff wishing our sex life would pick
up a bit -- she wrongly, I think, blames herself, but
it's clearly a matter of total emotional distraction for
both of us with Mama E.  I insist all's fine with us.
Friday night we attended a performance of "Migrations"
at an east-hill venue; Z's friend and mentee David M.
from the utility was a key performer on drums and did
beautifully (it's an Afrusan men's arts group: poets,
painters, musicians).  Saturday we mostly lazed around
except for a run to the arts store at the big south-end
mall where a sale was on (and I stocked up on gel pens
for use in making the remaining portion of the thousand-
card wedding gift when I can find enough time to do that
in an unrushed way, so probably not until next year).

One amusing story.  David M.'s son Omar is in Kat's
class at middle school.  Friday night was the end-of-
semester class dance, and when we saw David at
"Migrations" he reported hearing from Omar that Kat had

danced "all night" with a guy named Avery.  Next day Z
couldn't hold back; she had to pass the news on to
Betty, who not only hadn't heard about it but didn't
know who Avery was.  So maybe Z has unintentionally
brought some grief down upon Kat.  But probably not,
because Betty seems to hang pretty loose on such things.
According to her, Kat's still so innocent she thinks
oral sex is sex you just talk about.  Me, I think Kat's
not all that innocent, but still probably smart enough
and well-raised enough to stay out of trouble for a few
more years until it becomes irresistible.

But yes, Kat's drifting away from us, and the J-
town presence of Mama E with her many needs is only
accelerating the pace, and that's sad.  It's just very
hard now to find times when we can all get together.
Yesterday the four of us had plans to see a movie on the
downtown glitz strip but then Betty had to cancel them.
As a surrogate father figure for the kid I'm called on
to do less and less; I'm a fading shadow.  My current
sense is that I've fallen short in Kat's eyes in some
way -- maybe just because of age or glaring social
eccentricity -- or perhaps it's more a matter of my not
being there enough.  I regret this but I don't see any
way of changing things, at least not for a while.

As a pair of white-robed women -- vaguely angelic,
it can't be denied -- flutter out from behind one of the
big bronze doors and disappear around the corner.  And
yon fiery orb, though still partially eclipsed, is now
causing my racing J-stick to cast a noticeably more
distinct shadow on the page, meaning the end of the
phenomenon is near.  The other viewers, moreover, have
already wandered off and I'm all alone here, a tiny
jyzing figure perched on the stone steps at the foot of
the double-steepled front of the huge cathedral and
wondering what strange manner of creature the big bronze
doors might disgorge next.  Whatever it might be, I
don't doubt I could be woefully underpowered to deal
with it.  And so I'm thinking it's as good a time as any
to bid farewell to today's Heavenly spectacular and
wander on down the hill to work.

------

21

------


Starting this one in a state of flabbergastion --
and shock.  At midnight on an unseasonably warm night,
at least by the old standards.  Holding down a bench
outside one of the clubs in the HQ triangle.  Live
"classic rock" playing in there (maybe the club's
recent fling with Latin music is over, though I doubt
it: Latin is very popular right now).
    It's a Tiger cluster.  Black Tiger.  Black Horses
like Black Tigers, even if they're not supposed to.
"The Tiger Passing through the Forest."  No moon in
sight.  No non-zodiacal horses either -- the baseball
team is on the road again and no one's around to hire
carriages.  Graduation's Saturday at the U and so I
would've expected more carousing students.  Maybe the
legions of motorcyclists gathered at their usual club
cluster a block to the south have scared them away.  Is
the second Thursday of the month always big for bikers
or is it every Thursday?  I don't even know.  "Don't get
around much anymore" -- like hell!  But not around here
at party time, no.  Not if I can help it.
    It's also Dad's Gregorian death day.  It was a
quarter of a century ago last year and now, of course,
it's that plus one.  As a percentage the "plus one"
shrinks a little every year but the memories only seem
to grow more plentiful and stronger.  He was fifty-eight
and a half when he died, about fifteen months younger
than I am now.  I can't really take in this fact other
than as pure fact.  Whooom, a sailboat boom knocked him
senseless -- or was he already senseless before the boom
struck?  Was there a stroke, a heart attack?  We'll

198

never know.  As mentioned in previous annals, no autopsy
was performed.  (A coroner gave his verdict, yes, but
that's different: little more than an educated guess.)
     Dad, I miss you.  Funny thing is, this year I'm
coming to know you as never before.  Dad the human
being.  It's your death day but it's also, technically,
the first hour of Flag Day.  Apropos?  Would you think
so?  If you did, would you own up to it?
     -- But what's flabbergasting and shocking is
drawing me away from a mere -- even if it's my own
father's -- death anniversary.  And in this book
littered with anniversaries.  But -- speaking of
strokes.  A stroke hits someone near and dear.  Well,
no, not so near physically, or dear either except in an
elegaic sense, I guess I could say -- but it's real.  As
I discover.
     What happens is I find a phone message for me --
from someone named Glen Sandefjord.  And on the death
day of another Glen Sandefjord.  This message has good
news for me -- I'm a third Glen Sandefjord, not so
incidentally, and by birth order the one in the middle
of the other two -- and the message says he's now
planning to go to law school.  And he leaves me a number
which I then call at the first opportunity (after
discussing the matter with Z-wiff) and we talk for close
to an hour.  It could be a whole new era is getting
underway -- father-son era, I'm saying.
     And then I ask him how his mother's doing and he
tells me she's suffered a stroke.  It happened a month
ago.  She was paralyzed on the left side, arm and leg.
Most of the feeling is back in the leg but only a little
in the arm.  The prognosis is unclear.
     Lady S: the dancing Gray Rooster.  She who's a kind
of half-acknowledged guiding spirit of this Heavenly
Year celebration.  Mother of my only child (or the only
one known to have lived to walk the earth if you say
childhood begins at conception, as I do although in a
guarded and qualified way).  Great love back in the day
and so great love always, even though that love couldn't
live with itself and so, in my view now, couldn't have

been all that great, and even though I've used the term
"great love" about others and now do so more than ever
about the current love and mean it.  (Is it true that in
the present era you can't have a love if you don't think
of it as a great love?  Hollywood's to blame maybe?  I
suppose, but I still believe a great love is what I've
got here in J. City with the one and only Zoelie B.)
        What a day.  It could be I'm gaining a son here,
finally, after so many years of being closed out for
reasons I've more or less always accepted, even if
regretfully and painfully.  And at the same time losing
the sense of the wonderful and yet also hugely
perplexing person who is his mother being alive and well
in the world -- being who she is, relatively speaking.
        It's too much to take in.  I'm agog and aghast,
reeling.  I've already written to both of them: Elgie
and Lady S.  -- But last year they contacted me too and
it seemed relations were about to resume and then --
nothing.  And that contact came in this same month a
year ago, presumably triggered by the advent of Father's
Day, which falls again this Sunday.  Dad's death day and
Father's Day, with Flag Day in the middle -- I was
thinking I would concentrate my jyze efforts on those
conjunctions.  But Saturday is also the Dragon Boat
Festival, which in Korea is the Tano Festival in which
the girls get all dolled up and fly about on swings and
the spirits of the ancestors are propitiated -- and I'm
more or less a living ancestor for Elgie, and maybe for
Lady S too, in a sense.  (And now a raving drunk sits
next to me and emits a big noxious belch and I have no
choice but to quit my own raving.)
                    *           *
        -- And another slight miscalculation.  Two of them,
in fact, if not more.  First, this is the flag pavilion
at the J. City fairgrounds and we're still in the sunny
early evening of Flag Day but not a flag's in sight.
Where the pavilion itself used to be (where I sometimes
ate lunch during that World's Fair summer forty years
ago) is now a walled-in construction area.  What will
emerge from behind those walls, a poster tells us, will

be a different sort of pavilion, named for a local media
company that's putting up big bucks for naming rights.

And the second miscalculation, when I sat down on
this handsome magenta-colored bench on the western edge
of the lawn surrounding the international fountain
(which is spurting to the max at this very moment as
kids dash about so they'll wind up in the spray as it
shifts from zone to zone) I landed on something soft and
squishy: a big gob of pigeon shit. And then by reflex I
put my hand down to leverage a liftoff and my hand
landed on another gob of the same slimy stuff. Had to
wipe both deposits off on a nearby tree trunk, probably
looking something like a bear in heat.

But now I see I was wrong: not just one but two big
U.S. flags are in sight. One's atop the old armory
(visible above a line of leafy green trees if I sit up
straight) and the other, far bigger, also far higher, is
rippling as a flag oughta ripple but few ever do, on a
pole atop the giant golf-tee icon some six hundred feet
up. And a news helicopter is currently hovering near
it, presumably to shoot footage of impressive flag
action for Flag Day newscasts.

This year the flag, like firefighters, like Latin
music, is, yes, hot. You're a flag-waving patriot or
you're evil, one of the Bad Guys, anti-USAn: so the
cabal has proclaimed. At four p.m. "we all" voiced the
pledge simultaneously from sea to shining sea, or so I
heard someone say on the radio. Apparently I was the
only one who didn't -- but only because I hadn't heard I
was supposed to (I note this for the benefit of any law-
enforcement official checking out this jyze under
warrant of the U.S. Patriot Act -- I would've even said
the "under God" part, I swear, and "under the present
Emperor," as the Patriot Act requires in a little-known
codicil that applies mainly to aging sixties radicals).

And note this: the drunk who plunked himself down
on my bench last night was truly bad news. He showed
not one iota of respect for a working jyzer.

I came straight down here from Mama E's. Today was
a good day for both of us. She's on a painkiller now

for her leg and hip problems, which Doc F has come to
believe must be arthritic, since Tuesday's x-rays showed
nothing broken and no sign of a pinched nerve.  But the
doc fears the painkillers won't work for long and then
she'll need a hip replacement.  Oh no!  And in her
eighty-eighth year!  Today, though, I knew would be fine
because she called ahead of time and asked me to pick up
some "groceries" for her on the way over: milk, powdered
mini-donuts, and a slice of apple pie.  It turned out
Tito had called to ask her a favor, whose nature she
didn't specify to me but no doubt had to do with sending
money.  She told him no way, she was broke, he should
see her medical bills -- and she also said he shouldn't
be coming out here.  But the call lifted her spirits
regardless.  She showed me lots of old photos, including
a booklet about the Kedrowski family put together by her
brother Joseph, the one who recently died at age ninety.
Her father came from just about the same area in the
Austro-Hungarian empire as my Fritsch ancestors did, as
is reflected in my family's personal names, which
included a Vincent (my middle name for an hour at birth,
after Great-Grandfather Vincent Fritsch, before Dad
preempted it with his letter asking that the kid, if a
boy, be named for him -- one of my favorite stories) and
also reflected in the name Barbara, given to Vincent's
daughter -- Gram to me -- and to my own sister as well.
     We had a cackling good time, we did.  And I should
mention: when I arrived her room was full of smoke.
She'd burned her chicken nuggets to a crisp because she
still hasn't figured out how to work that durn
newfangled microwave.  To turn it off she yanks the plug
out of the wall.  I aired her room out with a fan and
one of her thuggish next-door neighbors leaned out of
his doorway with furious reddened eyes and accused us of
trying to burn the place down.
     -- And so, back to my own startling phone call.
This Glennar III, as noted before, is almost exactly the
age I was when he was conceived.  I was four months
short of my thirtieth birthday, he's about eight months
short of his.  And yet on the phone he sounds so young,

and not just in the timbre of his voice.  Was I like
this at his age?  Perhaps so -- still Mr. Earnest or Mr.
Innocent.  Or maybe it's just the way he talks with
elders, showing respect which seems exaggerated almost
to the point of parody (but then -- his mother is Asian
and in Asia it remains generally at least somewhat true
that elders oughta be venerated -- and especially in
their Heavenly Year).  He's sheltered in a way, no
doubt, still living with his mother, but this isn't so
unusual these days either.  Consider Olwen's son Trent,
currently living at home at forty plus.  Also, Elgie is
Eurasian or Eurasiusan in a country that doesn't exactly
encourage assimilation across racial lines -- in fact
neither of his countries of origin do.  As he told me on
the phone, all his best friends are Korusans, and this
would tend to limit his exposure to mainstream ways in
both of his cultures.  He even said one reason he wants
to go to law school is "so I'll have more diversity in
the people I know."  (He sounded embarrassed, I'm sorry
to say, to tell me all his friends are of Korean
ancestry, as if he thought I'd disapprove.)

Well, I hope he's growing up.  One good sign is
that in the past year he's taken a deep dive into
reading -- "at least a hundred books."  But like many
kids with backgrounds similar to his, his leanings are
toward math, science, and logic rather than disciplines
more heavily dependent on language.  It's the logic and
rationality of legal studies that attract him; he's not
as aware as he should be of the attorney's reliance on
language skills.  And I have to wonder how emotionally
mature he is.  One reason he wants to do law school is
so he'll be financially secure -- he won't even be
thinking about getting married until after he graduates
-- but then he also said he's looking for a woman who's
a basketball player so his kids will have "tallness
genes," and he seemed quite serious about this.  He even
thanked me for passing along my own "tallness genes" to
him (he says he's about my height, six-two or so).

But I shouldn't make too much of any of this.
We're very early in what's likely to be -- if it

continues at all -- a protracted shakedown period.  And
I shouldn't count on anything either -- as Z-wiff
reminded me when I told her about the call.  She's
worried "your heart will be broken again."  And so am I!
But then too I don't think I really have any right to
complain.  If Elgie and I can establish a relationship,
that's a bonus; it's something I've never expected.  And
I was pleased to confirm again that Z would welcome it
if it did happen.  She even offered her room for him to
stay in if we could talk him into coming up for a visit.

     She also views Lady S's stroke as a wake-up call
(another one) for both of us.  Eat well, exercise lots,
try to keep the mygs quietly roosting in place rather
than so frequently stirring them up.  She's right.

     I made a get-well card for Lady S.  Hope she
doesn't think it's too corny or sappy.  No question it's
pretty bad on both scores.  But I'm sending it anyway.

     -- As sundown nears and a chill hits.  The
fountain's now shut off.  The lower of the two visible
flags is in shadow but the one atop the grand icon is
catching the last rays way up there, almost in the jet
stream.  (Oddly, it reminds me suddenly of the flag
rippling atop the highest bluff in, or rather just
outside of, La Chavelle, Mentoka, back in "the Valley of
the Fathers" -- as it was first dubbed in "Jyzer.")

     O Dad.  It's because of you, I suppose -- at least
you far more than anyone else -- that I'm bothered now
to be worrying about what a patriot is and whether I am
one, and if so, in what sense, and what does that mean
in a world so threatened and most of all by the actions
of my very own country.  It's not satisfactory to say I
consider myself a citizen of the world first.  I equally
consider myself a USAn first -- "this land is my land"
-- and I know how I want this land to act in the world
-- meaning to protect the world's well-being, not
hyperaggressively aiming to control more and more of it
militarily/politically/economically.  -- And I believe
this wanting of mine is itself patriotic: the highest
and best kind of patriotism.  So sez I.  And so it goes!

[+1]

    -- And now it's Dragon Boat Day.  A fine blue-sky
afternoon and I've got a wooden bench to myself in the
pocket-size pavilion park at the heart of the AQ.  It's
back under the trees, this bench, and also under the
three-story-high mural of the Green Dragon -- roughly a
hundred feet long -- wrapping J-town in its coils of
good fortune.  Paint on brick, somewhat faded now, but
still a sight to behold.  (The wall constitutes the
south side of a low-income hotel bearing the family name
of our current supreme USAn leader and also the previous
one but one, his father.  But the matching names are
just a coincidence, for sure.)
    The Falun Gongers are meditating in front of the
red-columned pavilion.  A dozen of them seated cross-
legged on individual mats, motionless, as tinny music
plays and all around them life goes on as usual on a
Saturday afternoon in the AQ -- kids cavorting, old
folks sunning, low-incomers jawing, winos resorting to
swigs from bottles hidden in the traditional brown paper
bags -- and the great Tang Dynasty poets surely would've
said regarding all this, "Right on!"
    This is a holiday celebrating a poet from an even
earlier time.  He drowned himself as a protest against
injustice.  Hurrah for poets with a sense of justice!
It's also the fifth day of the fifth lunar month -- the
Five/Five Festival is another name for it, or just the
Summer Festival -- and its roots are the same as those
for the Tano Festival in Korea, so again we're back to
honoring ancestral spirits.  But in Korea, I suppose
because the population center is much farther north than
China's, it's also known as the Spring, not Summer,
Festival.  (Question: in some sense is Elgie regarding
me as a kind of living ancestral spirit who's
materializing back into his life?  Maybe so.)
    Just before I came over here to the park a Korusan
guy sold me a bottle of grape juice at one of the corner
markets.  He was watching a Korean-language TV show

making fun of the holiday, skimpily clad starlets riding
swings, flying off of them into the arms of skimpily
clad musclemen.  "Following the World Cup?" I asked.
"Oh, yeah, man -- go USA!"  "Not go Korea?"  "Go Korea
too!"  "But not go Japan, right?"  "Japan, boo, boo!"
Ah, with such multistranded intricacy the tapestry of
our time is woven.  -- And up the street I dropped in at
Mr. X's gallery thinking I would wish him a happy Dragon
Boat Day, but he was out.  The older man watching the
shop recognized me but didn't even try to communicate
via spoken language.  I held up both hands with thumbs
and fingers stretched out and said, "Five/Five Day,
China."  "Yes, Five/Five Day, yes!"  He lit up.  Said I:
"Say hello to Mr. X, happy Five/Five Day."  "Yes!"
     A huge flock of pigeons is surging about on the
bricks in front of the meditators, chasing tossed
crusts.  The meditators took a short break but now
they're back at it, hands in prayer position, posture
exemplary.  Falun Gong of course is the reactionary cult
making such hay in this country over its being banned in
China as a subversive organization.
     Speaking of crazy fundamentalists, one bashed in
the front passenger window of the Z-mobile last night.
Or at least that's my theory and the way I'll write it
up in the police report, which must be filed before
insurance can be collected.  It was down in the HQ and
the basher was a self-described "born-again Christian"
whose offensively aggressive offering of "the Good News"
I and several others had rejected -- but I'll have to
save the rest of the story for later.  In fifteen
minutes Z will be picking me up at the usual AQ Japanese
teahouse and we'll be attending a barbecue celebrating
the graduation of one of her mentees from the U this
afternoon (where a protest was set to face the main
speaker, a former U.S. secretary of state, regarding
her notorious remarks about the death of half a million
Iraqi children -- owing in large part to our imposing
draconian sanctions on that country, including on
medicines -- being a "justifiable outcome" of our
country's supposedly freedom-loving foreign policy).

[ Jyze of the Heavenly Year : Green Horse ]

    I'd like to be scribbling this within sight of one
of the newly mounted light-pole dragons.  They're a
sensation.  But I couldn't figure out on short notice a
good place to do that -- where, because of the minimal
time available, I could be sure of encountering no
hassles.  So another time for the new dragons.
    There's little sign of the Dragon Boat Festival
here in the AQ.  In effect it's been moved to later in
the summer during J. City's main festival period.  At
this early date chances are too high the weather will be
bad.  But what we're seeing today, as it happens, could
scarcely be better.
    -- As the Gongers start rolling up the meditation
mats.  I too, my figurative jyze mat.  The pigeons will
have more room to roam now as I see a pair of competing
crust-tossers at work -- no, three of 'em, an energetic
squadron of female Asiusan elders.  All, I'd say, are
close to halfway into their second Heavenly Year cycle.
And kids chasing the flocks, pigeons flapping wildly
about.  It's chaos out there!

                    *            *

    -- And so with the plants all watered J-time's
finally here again.  At half past four in the morning or
slightly later than that, dawn breaking with the usual
chirping prelude, the porch door open, cool air pouring
in -- and so it's not just Father's Day but the daytime
of Father's Day.  I'm chuckling over this.  In what odd
ways this has turned out to be a true cluster of the
fathers -- and with myself, such a poor specimen of a
father, unexpectedly thrust into the paternal spotlight.
    For the past several years I've been Kat's punching
bag for this holiday as her "sub" or "surrogate" or
"alternative" father or uncle.  Looks like that won't be
the case this year.  I'm sad about it too.  But on the
whole I've scored big this year.  What a hoot!
    Meanwhile it's still Dragon Boat Day by my own out-
of-phase NUT system.  I even considered opening our
bottle of rare Dragon wine to finish up the day with a
special flair.  But didn't.  It still stands in its
honorary spot atop the fridge.  And in the bedroom Z-

wiff at this moment reads the Sunday far-coast paper
which arrived with its usual loud thud half an hour ago.
She's giving me jyze space.  She's seriously afraid
she's alienating me by taking away from my jyze time
with all the Mama E duties and discussions -- bursts
into tears over this fear, even, as she's apt to do over
most anything, of course, especially in these super-
labile days -- but I assure her nope, it's just not so;
this kind of challenge is just what jyze likes and
needs.  -- And earlier tonight we got it on in a
relatively rare evening conjugation, so to speak, very
sweet, very strong for me: I've been highly pleased with
the way that particular part of my anatomy has been
functioning lately, in a kind of second adolescence
comparable in a way to the standard geezerly second
childhood (which may be coming next as regression works
its backward course).  So, I'm thinking, maybe the
expanded domestic and extended-family duties are
actually having an erotogenic effect on me.
     The luau, I want to report, went well.  The
backyard where it took place featured a fantastically
gnarled and thick-limbed plum tree.  Evander, the
honored graduate and the only male person of color
present (as opposed to various mestizas, to use Z's
preferred term), was magnificent in his lei and islander
grass skirt.  Kent and Dale, Z's current and former
immediate superiors at work, both attended.  I ate a lot
and talked little.  My favorite part of the evening was
a stop along the way at the magazine shop where Z and I
met.  Since that big day every single one of my returns
there has produced in me an almost seismic frisson.  I
can't stand inside the door without being rocked by her
presence outside just as I was on that day.  How corny
this is!  And yet how deep its meaning goes for me!
     The semiopaque plastic sheet taped over the empty
space where the car window used to be worked all right
but I had to open the driver's-side door every time we
made a left turn into traffic.
     How that window got stove in I'll never know for
sure, but my best guess is it was a case of collateral

damage from fundamentalist rage.  When the burly
proselytizer tried to give me his "Good News" leaflet I
merely said "Not interested, sorry," in my usual bland,
neutral way, and slipped past him -- I'd just exited
the car after parking it on the middle road, around the
corner from the hideaway building's side entrance -- and
the guy didn't seem at all upset.  But when I looked
back moments later as I was about to round the corner,
he was arguing with two young guys getting into a red
car parked right behind mine, and when they gunned off
one of them yelled, "Fuck you, asshole!"  As he'd done
with me, the proselytizer replied, "God bless you!", but
now much louder and more angrily.  I was worried he
might do something truly crazy -- violently crazy, like
attack someone -- but he wandered off heading away from
me and I thought that was the end of it.  But when I
came back to the Z-mobile maybe an hour later the window
was bashed in, with shattered glass all over the front
seat and floor and dash area, and the same was true of a
small yellow car parked behind mine where the red one
had been.  As far as I could tell, nothing was missing
from the Z-mobile.  By then no one else was around.
     The sword of the Lord.  A one-man crusade in a
crusading kind of time.  To this guy -- big and surly
but straight-looking, wearing a gold print short-sleeve
shirt and a crew cut -- I suppose I could've been evil
personified, a virtual fifth-column Al Qaedaist.
Goodness knows the FBI needs all the help it can get.
     Would this dastardly act also fit the definition of
religion-based domestic terrorism?  Well damn, it
should, shouldn't it?
     Around $500 it'll cost us, we figure, Z and I, with
insurance paying roughly two-thirds.
     -- Today's also Bloomsday, incidentally, and it's
feted big-time over on the other side of the state.  Why
there?  Who knows!  But I was reminded of something: I
neglected to celebrate Jyzeday.  I even forgot to put it
on my calendar.  Jyze began on the 3rd of April, 1994,
in a little-known literary mecca across the sound: the
basement "library" at U Acres.  Since another occasion

may never arise to memorialize the real Jyzeday in jyze
itself, I've decided to declare a substitute Jyzeday for
this year only.  Just what day it'll be I don't know
yet, but I'll be glad to have an excuse to liven up some
otherwise ordinary cluster -- to jazz up the quotidian.
Or -- maybe I'll just say that in this Heavenly Year
every day is Jyzeday.  Or better yet, say every sixth
day is Jyzeday, as is already standard -- but always cap
it like an official holiday.  Or maybe just imagine it's
capped.  Less to remember that way.

And finally, today's also the birthday of one of
the main inspirers of jyze.  The 239th birthday.  I've
referred to his influence many times before in these
annals but otherwise probably no one would ever guess
his identity.  It's the Japanese haiku master who wrote
"A Year in My Life."  What I can't figure out is this:
how was he able to stop after only one year?  And: why
would he want to do that after producing such a
masterpiece?  But then maybe he didn't want to; maybe
the times or his health or something else forced him to.
(Also this weekend the Juneteenth Festival was observed
in a park in the formerly redlined all-Afrusan district
between a few blocks north of here and the ritzy hood
well east of east hill.  -- And the protest against the
former secretary of state didn't amount to much.  -- And
tensions are supposedly easing in Kashmir.)

So to the fathers I say: many thanks!  My dad and
Zoelie's: I'd thought today's jyze would be focusing on
them.  Their different ways of fathering.  Those two men
came into the world twenty-two years and thousands of
miles apart but died within three years and ten miles of
each other.  Never met.  One a lawyer, one a lithograph
operator, but both very smart, handsome, charming men.
Both dedicated newspaper readers.  Both apt to disappear
from the house for a day or two during a battle with the
Mrs.  Both gaga over a difficult daughter.  They
might've had a lot to talk about if anyone could've
brought them together in the same room for a few hours.
Dad's wartime service in the Philippines, for instance.
Patriotism.  Their workplaces were within a mile or two

of each other -- they might even have seen eye to eye on
Centropolis politics.  Though I doubt it.  I like to
fantasize, idealize.  Tend to do it especially when I
get tired and drink wine.  -- So bottoms up and dive
deeply after the moon and take that, injustice!


------

22

------


     Half moon rising in blue sky just above the pigeon-
shit-bespattered noggin of the Filipino hero whose looks
remind Z-wiff more and more of her father.  White on
gray, almost a pretty sight, sauce drippings across the
cheekbones -- or it could be frothy champagne.  After
all, today's the man's birthday.  His forty-first, plus
a century.  At the moment no one else is here to observe
it, but back in the homeland -- of Vincenzo B. too
(middle name Regalado) -- it's a national holiday.
     Here it's official Juneteenth.  This is quite
something by itself, or at least it's gradually becoming
that, a little more each year.  And it's also the
twentieth anniversary of the tragic death in a midland
U.S. city of a young Chiusan man at the hands of racist
Cawks, and so tonight on the way in to work (and I'm
pausing along that route right now) I'll be checking out
the vigil against hate crimes to be held in his honor at
the pavilion park in the AQ.
     A busy day.  Second in a row I've had to be up at
noon, an hour and a half earlier than the current norm.
Yesterday I delivered the Z-mobile to the repair garage
out in the SQ for engine work; today I picked it up and
took it straight to a glass-work place a few miles even
farther north for the "Good News" window replacement and
some unrelated windshield-ding patching.  Total tab: a

little under a thousand bucks, of which insurance will
cover, it turns out, about four hundred.  And yesterday
the first of Mama E's emergency-room bills arrived,
eight hundred or so, the kick in the shin being that
Medicare will pay only about half.  Yipe!  The money
flying around!  All I can do is look on in awe.  -- As
the enstatued Filipino hero himself seems to be doing,
the object of his awe, however, appearing to be the DC
castle.  Or what is that expression?  Contemplative
dignity maybe.  When the statue went up a dozen years
ago the castle was still a hospital and the hero, of
course, in his lifetime was a doctor as well as a writer
and political leader in the fight for Philippine
independence (eventually crushed by USAn imperial
forces, but well after his martyr's death).

On the way out to the SQ today I was done in by
grogginess, inattention, and a confusing detour in lower
north hill.  I mistook one bridge for another and jumped
off the bus two miles too soon.  Had to walk those, and
they became closer to three because at the start I was
so disoriented I hoofed it several blocks in the wrong
direction before realizing my error.  But luckily I'd
given myself a big time cushion just in case and in the
end I was only ten minutes late for the window-repair
appointment.  And it was a splendid afternoon for a walk
in a part of town I'd never before checked out on foot.
Along the way I passed by the neighborhood P-patch where
Wei and Alison were married.  And it bothered me that I
couldn't figure out which house was theirs up on the
roof-jumbled and woodsy west slope of north hill, east
of the P-patch and maybe half a mile away.

Dogs on leashes here in the park, babies in
carriages (one so bulkily padded it appears it could
survive a collision with an SUV -- and pushed by a tiny
young woman speaking shaky Japanese with an older woman
who's presumably her mother visiting from the old
country).  Mixture of leafy and needly trees across the
street, all in gentle motion in the breeze, the shifting
textures a pleasure for the eye.  A couple of scruffy
Cawk homeless guys are holding down adjacent tables in

the shelter thirty or forty paces to the north, scaring
everyone else away.  I'm probably having some of that
kind of effect myself, though the fact that I'm pushing
a J-stick might make me look somewhat less fearsome.
    Z's in the first of three straight days of
performing the Mama E daily visit.  I did the previous
two.  The news there is not good: Mama E careens from
one ailment to the next, with little respite from the
menu of crises du jour.  Lately the severe leg pain has
yielded to nausea and that in turn to agitation/anxiety/
sleeplessness.  Z's back to looking into group homes.
Meanwhile she's dealing with new twists in the ongoing
budget crisis at work and also some continuing hip pain
of her own.  She's still doing well at maintaining her
spirits but I'm afraid she'll be facing more than she
can bear if Mama E's condition doesn't stabilize soon.
    So how am I faring amid all this?  Okay.  Luckily
I'm able to be a lot more flexible with my work schedule
than Z is with hers.  The hours I spend with Mama E can
be emotionally draining and so can the worries about
emergency calls coming in from her -- I'm the one she
tends to ring up now; Z's off-limits while at work or
asleep.  -- But I have time to myself when I can
recover.  And I like being able to help Z out in a time
of urgent need.  She and her mother are caught in a
tangle of love and pathology (as Z herself calls it)
going back sixty-two years as of this month -- including
Z's months in the womb -- and that of course makes the
pain of the current situation far greater for her than
anything it can possibly cause me.
    And there are good times in all this as well.
Touching moments.  Lots of humor.  Mama E's wrestlings
with the microwave all by themselves would make for a
couple of zippy sitcom episodes.  Her relations with
Terrible Tito.  Her weird subvocalizations and eyebrow
wagglings.  Her unending statements of thanks and
reassurance with complaints craftily interspersed.  The
hearing-aid squeaks and squawks.  The right-wing talk
shows and the tabloids read with a big Sherlock Holmes
magnifying glass, the many tabloid clippings she saves

for me and our loopy discussions about those.  Her
ceaseless movements.  Her nonstop puzzling about which
pill to take when and at what dosage, from which bottle,
with or without what kind of food or drink.  The scads
of pills dropped under the sofa-bed, accidentally or
otherwise, which make for, if you bend down and eye them
with a squint, a rock-littered moonscape.  -- But her
smile can light up even her gloomy room.  And when she's
having a good day (of which not a single one's cropped
up this week) she can be a barrel of laughs, at least
for an hour or so.  (Her repeated offers of this or that
for me to eat -- everything in the fridge and cabinets,
over and over again.  "You don't want a banana?  How
about a donut or apple pie, d'you like apple pie?  I've
got chicken in there, I don't want any more, have some
chicken, take it to work" -- on and on and on and on.
-- And at least once every visit she rediscovers I'm the
spitting image of that odious hard-right director and
star of "The Green Berets."

        But the world, what about the world?  Shouldn't it
be granted a few sentences in here?  This being a Gray
Rabbit cluster in which the Rabbit is "Running through
the Forest"?  So here's my own news sprint.  Another
Israeli outrage, taking over a big swatch of Palestinian
land for good as retaliation for a suicide bombing, and
the U.S. just twiddles its thumbs, except for announcing
that something called "preemptive response" will become
our formal foreign policy, basically, and forget all the
treaties we're signatories to.  We're boss of the world
and that's it.  If we feel like attacking, we'll attack.
If we want to go with a nuke, we'll go with a nuke.
Anyone got any problems with any of that?  If so,
prepare to be obliterated.

        -- Meanwhile the Filipino hero is playing the wise
bartender up there on his perch, saying nothing, saving
his best bits for moments when the patrons tire of each
other.  -- And I'm almost ashamed to say I just turned
down a chance to take a picture of a family in front of
the hero's bust.  "Can't, I'm right in the middle of
this."  No problem, though, because a woman in polka-dot

shorts with a babe swaddled in aluminum tubes and red
canvas on her back happened by at the perfect moment and
she did it.  Filusan J-towners, I'd say.  Handsome
family too.  The hero plays his appointed statuesque
role and as a writer himself must be pleased to see I'm
hanging in here with the J-stick with which I'm also
making sure he, the "doctor/statesman/martyr/genius" (as
the dedication says), gets his props from me on his day.

And this propsing having been accomplished --
however minimally -- I can leave now and by doing so
encourage (as no one else is present at the moment) the
birds to return to their statue-top perch.  No
disrespect intended, Mr. DSMG!


[+1]


A few minutes before the big moment.  Or an hour
and twenty minutes if you look at it another way.  But
I've set up out on the 203 balcony to do my jyze thing,
wearing sweatpants (maroon) and a hooded sweatshirt
(black), both of which I'd hoped I wouldn't be needing
to use again until sometime in September or October.

It's five a.m. or maybe a minute or two before and
it's plenty bright enough to go at it without turning
the outdoor light on.  The hazy rosy band above the
mountains on the far horizon -- above the in-city hills
as well, and above the white mist rising just high
enough off the lake to make its surface shape visible in
some places where the lake itself ordinarily isn't, sort
of like a cake risen above its pan; and from here only a
few narrow unrisen blue slices are ever visible
otherwise) -- that band is rosiest, I say, with some
gold mixed in, at the spot where the sun will be edging
above the peaks at five-eleven, according to the papers.
It'll be at its farthest-north point of rising for the
entire year.  Because today is, jyze fans, what?

The summer solstice!  That's right!  And around
here the solstice is a very big deal.

An occasional car barrels by down below, each one

headed south so far.  That's counterintuitive since
downtown is north and many more people work there than
anywhere to the south, or rather anywhere to the south
within commuting reach.  There might be an explanation
for this -- there must be! -- but never mind.

Birds getting into it something fierce, I'd say
about a dozen of them, maybe more.  Quite a racket.
Nowhere do I see a light on and hundreds of windows are
in view from here, possibly even thousands -- and
certainly thousands if I were to bring out my trusty
monocular and train it on the facing hill to the east.
Yet it's still quiet enough up here, even with the birds
squawking away, that the rumble/roar of the freeway
down in the valley makes for a consistent bass line,
though it's neither percussive nor rhythmic.

Brightening, brightening.  The sun's target spot is
bright orange now and the aura is much larger.  I have
to stand up to look, however, because it seems I didn't
pinpoint the spot so well earlier after all.  My view of
the real rising spot is almost perfectly blocked by the
semicircular crown of a heavily leafed tree which itself
rises well above the roofline.  Here and there shreds of
orange shine through the upper part of the tree -- I
notice now -- looking sort of like the last embers in a
vertical bed of coals -- and...any second now.

Hey -- there goes the first northbound car!  And
now a northbound garbage truck and right behind it
another car!  The law of averages at work.  Z-wiff
meanwhile sleeps.  Usually I'd be going in there right
now ---

(But here she is!  "Where are you?" she mumbles
groggily from inside the door and around the corner.
The surprise voice from the balcony, as with Romeo but
even better it's her G-hub: "Ya wanna watch the solstice
sunrise?"  And Juliet enters in her sexy short red robe
and rubbing her eyes.  "Sit on lap okay, just a minute?
Ooh, you're so cold!"  "And you're so -- hey!")  ---

*          *

Now I'm stoop-sitting in the HQ triangle.  Still
about two and a half hours left of solstitial daylight.

[ Jyze of the Heavenly Year : Green Horse ]

Is this the day that's longer than any other?  You'd
think so, but I have a hunch, based on a tickle of
memory, it's not.  Today, again according to the papers,
offers exactly sixteen hours of sun-up time, from five-
eleven a.m. to nine-eleven p.m.  Tack on an hour or so
of non-full nighttime at both ends, dusk and dawn, and
you've got around eighteen hours of daylight.  In other
words, today is about as nontypical a day as can be for
a night worker in this city -- or for that matter
anywhere else in the northern hemisphere.

And what a day this maximally atypical day has
been.  Gorgeous.  It still is now: looking across the
tree-crowded triangle at the sun-washed brick and stone
of the hideaway building.  The eponymous chief, the
totem pole, the crowded benches.  At the sidewalk cafes
scattered here and there every table is occupied.  A few
minutes ago three separate groups of forty or so taking
the underground tour were simultaneously visible as they
tramped from site to site, like separate herds on the
move in a single corral.  And here's a red double-decker
tour bus, open-topped, I haven't seen before, pausing as
its PA spiels the tale of the fallen pergola that's now
being remounted -- the first section just went up this
week.  As two horse-drawn carriages pass each other
going in opposite directions across the main
intersection, both horses black -- Black Horses, yes --
and both Horses (now again capped) seeming to wink at me
even with their blinders on because -- it's our year!

Summer begins today.  Summer is the official
zodiacal season of the Horse.

Am I wrong or are things starting to break my way
right now?  All the pain and suffering to one side it
still seems like it.  If Elgie really is about to become
a functioning, interacting part of my life then it must
be so.  In that case a lot will change, not necessarily
in any material sense but in the way I look at things,
and here I'm referring to some of the major decisions
from earlier in my life.  What once seemed questionable
might now start to look more justified or at least
acceptable -- and therefore I might be better able to

admit to myself it was questionable in the first place.

(Despite the large crowds down here this evening the feel of the place is laid-back and easygoing. Mellow, yup, I'd say so. Most likely that's because the baseball club is on the road. Nobody's rushing to get to a game or to make a quick buck off folks rushing to a game. Even the attempted scams are slower-paced and the panhandlers almost gracious.)

-- So yesterday the book arrived, the one Elgie promised to send. It's called "Positive Quotations" and it's a collection of exactly what the title says, thick and heavy like a reference book but with all negativity and criticality (not to mention hypercriticality) banished, except for a number of barbs directed at those who think critically and have some negative thoughts about, say, current U.S. foreign policy or political power structure or, you know, racism, sexism, imperialism and global roasting and like that. It seems to be a product of the phony-baloney "Morning in America" moment of roughly two decades back and a kind of companion volume for certain far-right tomes extolling so-called family values. But it's not too flagrant about any of this, and a glance through the index turns up numerous respectable literary figures, so it can't be all bad (but some true troglodytes of the antediluvian right also get a bunch of play, so neither is it all that far from all bad or say essentially bad).

Not that any of this matters a whole lot. Not yet. I'm giving the kid the benefit of every conceivable doubt. Period. Nor will I yield to the natural didactic urges stemming from my fathering instinct, such as it is -- or at least not yet, and not in any way that might be construed as a critique of him or the way he's been raised. His mother and I see the world much differently -- in fact, it might even be said that's why he exists -- and first and above all else I want to respect his attachment to her. -- And obviously I'm reminding myself of this because I suspect at times I'll be urgently needing the advice. The battle between Lady S and me over many of the values I expect to find

Elgie's adopted as his own is also, of course, at least
in a sense, the reason she and I were never able to live
together for long or in the end stay together.  I can
already see that this battle is reflected in who he is,
and I don't doubt I'll be coming across many more ways
in which it's the case, nor that there must be still
more -- probably a great many more -- I'll never
recognize or understand.
    Not that it matters!  Or so I hope.  And being
myself a person riddled with hard-to-expel deposits of
"positive quotations," I'd be betraying my own nature
not to show some optimism or at least possible-ism here.
And do feel both!  -- I'm even thinking this
rapprochement with Elgie, if such it really proves to be
(see, I'm also riddled with deposits of doubt and
negativity), could open the way to an attempt at one
with sister Barb as well.  And to say this shows just
how strongly I feel (as of right now) things might be
breaking my way.  Without question the estrangement from
Barb goes the deepest of all.  Can it be resolved or
dissolved or buried in a fashion that makes a
significant brother-sister relationship possible again?
As opposed, that is, to the almost totally perfunctory
and trivial one we have now?  Probably not.  But maybe.
A very weak but still nontrivial maybe.
    -- And here's a tourist duck, of the motorized
kind, like the ones I first saw in Mentoka Dells half a
century ago.  I hear "original sawmill" and I hear
"owner's cookhouse."  Both of those used to stand here
in the early days after the Eurusan takeover of this
turf.  It was a gathering place too, for community
meetings as well as entertainers and politicos.  Had any
J-slingers been around at the time, this likely would've
been a prime spot for jyzing, just as it is now.  And to
say this -- to be sitting here jyzing as the spiels for
tourists ring out -- makes me feel sort of historical
myself, as in a lifelike statue of Man Scribbling While
Sprawled on Stoop.  As in "The Anti-Thinker."
-- Delusions of squalor!  Or just ordinary fantasies
really, the sort of thing many fictions are made of.  No

fiction, no Hollywood; no Hollywood, no making over this historic triangle into a vaudeville stage.

For future set designers, it's the granite staircase in front, flight of six stairs, with a rounded stone arch about, oh, fifteen feet high at the apex, painted a subdued off-red, and I'm stretched out on the upper three steps on the right side as you look eastward from the cobblestones, propped against the side of the arch and the bottom of the black iron gate which extends across when the building's closed -- it's open now, though no one's come in or out while I've been here -- and at the elbow of the same arm I'm J-sticking with is the J-book spread flat on the landing.  In my work jeans and gray henley and four-days-unshaven state I'm looking, as Z observed earlier when I met her at Mama E's place to drop off the car, "even more rough-trade than you did yesterday."  (She'd been with the amusingly kitschy and campy gay social worker Marshall -- who was "assessing" Mama E -- when I first came in and this was actually how she'd warned him I'd look.  Later she said she thought he was coming on to me.  Ha!  But then the thought became arousing to her, she insisted, as well as disturbing, and she wrote a long note laying it all out. Ten pages!  And day before yesterday she wrote me a four-pager!  Wotta hunka burnin' wife!)

-- And tomorrow, by the way, is her conception day. We figured it out several years ago.  It had to be a certain steamy Saturday night in 1940 on Centropolis's north side -- same flat she grew up in -- because Saturday, and no other time, was when "ootchimagootchi" (couplings) happened with her parents and also because her mother's pregnancy went to full term.  Of course you can't know for sure under normal circumstances (as my mother could, for example, and did regarding my own infamous December 7th conception day) but we've declared tomorrow to be the one.  And this year it happens to fall on a Saturday.  Even though we're planning to see a movie with Betty and Kat tomorrow afternoon we're still hoping to work in a timely reenactment of the conception act itself.  Having another person living nearby who was

also present for that glorious occasion sixty-two years
ago -- was the other star of the show along with Papa V
-- should make things even kinkier than usual.

So: is this the moment when the Gray Rabbit stops
running?  The sun line on the hideaway building is up to
the top floor now.  In a short time the only Heavenly
Year summer-solstice day there'll ever be for me will be
as gone and done for as is the only summer-solstice day
of Jyze City's originary year.  So be it, of course, and
for all days, amen, and may tomorrow be another day
every bit as marvelously unique (that's not even a
positive thought -- it's just a run-of-the-jyze hope and
wish with the usual acknowledgment of a whole spectrum
of possibilities, pro and con, built right in).


------


23


------


Feels like a midsummer day.  And it is -- and for a
lot of folks back in the lands of the former Viking
empire, the, underlined, Midsummer Day.  Last night was
the merrymaking eve of same, with bonfires roaring and
beer kegs flowing.  St. Hans Day it's also called, in
honor of the priest known in the English-speaking world
as John the Baptist, but I don't see any need to make a
lot of that, or him.  The Baptists are not covering
themselves with glory these days as they, in alliance
with various other sects, go about forming their own
Christian empire that will make all the others look
minor and merciful.  (And JRX that priest's name.)

Instead it's a fine time to focus on the Green
Dragon.  Matter of fact, one of those is curled around
the telephone pole on the far side of the street in
front of the Chinese market up here in the southeast

corner of the lower AQ.  It's one of the dozen or so
dragons newly patrolling the AQ boundaries -- and
sensationally so, as just about everyone seems to agree
-- but it's the only green one I could find.  And green
matters.  Green is Wood.  Green is green.  Green is "the
Cheerful Dragon" -- sort of as in the Jolly Green Giant
(JRX).  And this is the cluster of the Green Dragon.  In
the era of the Green Horse.  A woodsy, yangsy, frolicky,
prosperous time for all.

     As here I sit on a low concrete fence -- and it's
all greenly vine-colored, as is the high wall behind it
-- just two feet from the edge of the busy six-lane
street that runs directly beneath the great arch of the
south-hill high bridge.  Or it's seven lanes if you
count the one that's closest to me, which is maybe four
feet wide and is intended for bicycles, with a stylized
international symbol of a bike-with-rider laid out flat
on the pavement right in front of me.  Squashed flat is
just what you risk being, too, as an urban bike rider,
with traffic as it is these days.  But a good number of
bikes zip by anyway at this hour, maybe two or three a
minute on average, appearing suddenly from behind an
outcropping of shrubbery to my left, pedaling hard on
the long uphill pull toward the freeway underpass a
block to the east.  An on-ramp and an off-ramp up there,
lots of traffic on both, and two panhandlers with
cardboard signs working one, three more posted at the
other -- it's unusual to see that many at once so close
together -- and all but one are familiar figures to me
(one was up on the high bridge yesterday with his dog --
he's been hanging out in this hood ever since Z and I
moved into it; at the moment he's living out of a
shopping cart he parks in the recessed, little-used
doorway of a warehouse across from the Natusan center).

     And the "boys of summer," meaning the baseballers,
are back home.  That's the reason for the constant
stream of foot traffic beneath the Green Dragon.  Game
time's about forty minutes from now.  If I were sitting
on the other side of the street I could see both
stadiums and also the DC castle lording it over the

whole scene from about five hundred feet up, building
height included.  But there's no place to sit down over
there.  And over here there's no sidewalk, so I'm spared
any close scrutiny from the walkers -- but I do get
glances from startled bicyclists.  "Hi there!" I said to
one who happened to come along as I was looking up and
our eyes met -- friendly and cheerful I was -- but no
response.  I'm too unexpected here and too close --
probably scary to some.  A swift kick to the bike frame
could topple the rider into traffic.  I imagine some of
them will be calling the city tomorrow demanding an
immediate cutback on this shrubbery.

So what's new on this grand day?  (Blue skies, T-
shirt warm -- and the downtown skyline looking on too, I
neglected to mention earlier.)  Well, lots.  Best of
all, Z and I just happened to have Kat staying with us
overnight on the weekend of her first date ever.  The
date went down at a midtown movie theater yesterday
afternoon and both parental units agreed it should be a
group outing with parents serving as chaperons (and Z-
wiff tagging along as Betty's auxiliary to keep the
numbers equal on both sides) (it was way too early in
the day for me to play that role).  The movie was
"Undercover Brother," a spoof of seventies black
exploitation films.  The guy was Avery, the same one Kat
danced with "all night" a couple of weeks ago -- "sort
of your typical white guy except cuter in a boyish way,"
Z reported to me later.  Now we're waiting to hear the
early reviews from the principals themselves.  But Kat,
she was cool beforehand, seemingly not nervous at all.

At the start Kat and Betty had brought me a belated
Father's Day present, a big tray of strawberries picked
from their backyard garden by the first-dater herself.
Delicious too -- but either these or some leftovers from
Aida's graduation party for Charles (high school coming
up for him) flipped my stomach to fritz state for the
rest of the weekend.  -- And speaking of hot stuff,
today has first-ever vibes of a related kind for me --
and I wasn't a tenth as cool about the initiation as Kat
was about hers -- but I'll save all that for later.

[ Jyze of the Heavenly Year : Green Horse ]

     Z, meanwhile, has had another "tough love" talk
with Mama E.  This weekend brought two new crises; the
talk was Z's response to one of those, and the other one
(a repeat of Mama E's break-in paranoia) seemed to be
retaliation for the talk itself.  Part of the tough
love, insisted on by Z, is a reduction in our visits
from daily to four days a week.  Wednesday and Friday
will be (tentatively) my days.  I'm backing Z all the
way, unconditionally, mindlessly if necessary.  Our
newest worry is that Mama E's now for the first time
talking about staying over at our place on nights when
"they" try to break in.  We're figuring the latest
medication change -- she's off the antianxiety Zyprexa
-- is the cause of these delusions and so we're calling
for a resumption of Zyprexa, even though it probably
brought on last week's two days of "zombiehood" (which I
don't think I've mentioned before now).  It's beginning
to look as though anything we try will induce a serious
downside.  Minimizing those downsides, maybe alternating
them, that's our more realistic goal now.  Eliminating
them -- not too likely.
     Other news, local kind?  A cop gets killed in Leola
and Gerry's burban hood, he's pink, the shooter is brown
(and a recent releasee from prison, and naked when it
happens, dashing around in the streets, and overcoming
pepper spray to grab the cop's own gun to off him with).
This incident will be used to block any serious attempts
to reform the racist police practices endemic to this
region and so many others.  Depressing.  And on south
hill a Cawk bus rider assaults a driver, causing the bus
to lurch out of control and plow into a pickup driven by
-- Matt B., "retired landlord," as the newspaper story
describes him.  We haven't seen Matt (a/k/a "Zonker" for
his deep suntan and long golden locks) -- haven't seen
him yet, I say, to ask about it.  But the bus route
involved is the one both Z and I use between the hill
and downtown when we don't walk or drive.  The last
statistics I saw said it was one of the three most
dangerous routes in the city for on-bus crime and police
dispatches.  I witness minor incidents as often as

several times a night on the 1:15 bus home but the
overall atmosphere has seemed less tense for the past
year or so.  The growing number of Hispanic riders
(mostly non-English-speaking) may account for much of
this, because they tend to try to stay out of trouble,
many or perhaps most of them being in the country
"undocumented."

     -- Keep on smilin', Green Dragon!  But just know
this: massive fires are burning across the USAn west, a
new famine is threatening millions in Africa, Israel is
invading Palestine yet again -- and none of this, bad as
it all is, is the truly bad news, except for one sorry
fact: the really bad news still isn't recognized as
being bad.  Or, worse yet, many people -- and what
really matters, the ones with power -- consider it good
news.  Material "progress."  Wealth.  Mansions.  Budgets
up.  Greenhouse gases up.  Glaciers melting.  Oceans
acidifying.  Animal species vanishing.

     Oh the complexities.  Can this drive to "progress"
ourselves to extinction be reversed?  It's not
impossible.  But how?  First things first, how to awaken
people to the urgency?  Or rather, since USAn polls say
people are aware of the urgency all right and yet by and
large still want to do little or nothing about it, how
to awaken them to the severity of the urgency?  How to
jujitsu the focus on terrorism to a focus on ecological
apocalypse?  How to get from modernism and postmodernism
to a new ecopragmatism?  -- Or a new metaphysics based
on global stewardship.  Makes me shudder, that term
metaphysics.  Just call it a new set of operating
principles under which life on earth would become
sustainable.  For right now it emphatically isn't, and
it's becoming less so every day and the pace of this
lessening is itself accelerating.

     (Yike, here comes a woman climbing over the fence.
What's back there I don't know -- homeless encampment
probably.  Part of "the jungle."  And since I've ranted
myself into the usual corner I might as well be moving
along anyway.  -- Carry on, ye Cheerful Green Dragon!)
                    *         *

-- A mere hour later and here's the spot.  "Where
the kid became a man."  Well, no, not quite.  Where the
kid with a cherry became a kid without a cherry.
     It's FFE Day.  That's First Fuck Ever, and I'm
talking about for me.  It's the fortieth anniversary.
Before last month I'd long since forgotten the exact
date -- if I'd ever taken note of it at all -- but I was
able to figure it out from the letters I sent home from
the J. City World's Fair.  Yesterday, the 23rd, was my
first "date" with Kristi K., whom I'd met a few days
earlier in the armory food arcade, where she was an
employee at, of all places, a candy booth.  Tomorrow,
the 25th, was the day of our trip up into the mountains
(the story of which I've been telling for years --
staying on too long at the mountaintop, then at deep
dusk inching back down literally on the seats of our
pants and nearly slipping into free slide several times,
then finding the car's battery dead and hitching back on
the freeway).  (But those mountaintop hours made it all
glorious.  Cozied up naked in a little makeshift tent,
because a light drizzle began when we got up there and
never did stop until we arrived back in the city.)
     The cherry-losing night was not so glorious.  It
was a backseater and the car -- Warren T.'s fin-bearing
sedan in which he and I had driven out all the way from
the far coast -- was parked at the curb across the
sidewalk and grass strip from where I sit now.  On this
side of the sidewalk is a double wall of riprap with a
curving stone staircase rising gradually between the
walls.  The address number is 910 -- the sign is new,
and so is the wooden deck up above, I think, but
otherwise it seems to be pretty much as it was back
then.  We usually parked on this street because spaces
were hard to come by down on the main drag two blocks to
the west and were almost always available up here, maybe
because the homes are big and have garages (although
several three-story brick apartment houses are within
view and were also present, I'm pretty sure, back then).
     I don't remember exactly the hour but it was very
late by my standards at that time.  Maybe one a.m. or

even later.  There were no disturbances that I recall,
no interruptions or distractions.  We had a blanket
pulled over us.  Other than that, funny thing, the
details are mostly gone.

So why am I here now?  Because of that old saw
about your life having three crucial moments: birth,
marriage, death.  But death I'm splitting into two for
this annal, with the sixty-year moment as part of it (so
that it can be properly celebrated), and the same goes
for marriage, except I'd have to split marriage into
more than two since I've been married three times (or
four if the faux "zen" one that lasted eighteen years
were included).  So instead I'm designating FFE to stand
in for all three or four hitch-ups and thereby
sidestepping any show of bias regarding them.

"From kid to man."  Not really, no -- to repeat.
But a transition for sure.  And at an age just two
months short of my twentieth birthday I was certainly
old enough for a kind of initiatory crossing of the bar.
And Kristi was a good one to help me with it: far more
experienced than I was (though I'm sure I tried hard not
to let on this was the case), very sexual, a good sense
of humor -- and she liked me a lot, but not so much that
an emotional disaster would've resulted if things hadn't
worked out for us.  And as I've implied already, they
didn't.  We stayed in contact and had several continent-
crossing liaisons over the next two years and then three
more years later met again in the megastate to the south
for a brief encore -- but our entire cumulative time
spent together in the flesh (whether clothed or not) was
maybe ten weeks tops.

Eeeesh, what terrible scribbling.  At sunset.  I
sit on the third stair on the curved staircase at 910,
now just two months short of age sixty (solar)(me).  And
a couple of joggers go by, and so does a hand-holding
gay pair (probably wouldn't've seen that around here
then), and so does a wary woman with a big dog.  Across
the street an even warier old man -- I'd say at least
two decades my senior -- rolls out his recycling bins.
"who are ye and what's your mission?"  Ha -- I'm putting

these words in his mouth but only because he's putting
them in his eyes and glaring them at me.

    Who am I?  Artsy-looking grungy old longhair codger
with backup-J-stick-bearing shirt pocket and an odd
pendant hung around my neck.  Sez "Jyze" on it.  Lord
help us!  (Why "Lord"?  Sheer Christian-empire instinct,
that's all.  Or call it mindless reflex.)

    Could blather a bit about sex, I suppose.  For me
it was always, no question, one of the main electrical
sources, so to speak, making my world go around, and
still is.  It did so even this very morning, I'm pleased
to report, with an FFE Day quick "ootchi" pop with the
Z-wiff -- though I didn't announce it under that rubric
or disclose anything before or after about its
historical significance to me.  (Why not?  Because in
recent years I've sagely declined to speak with her
about past sexual involvements in anything but the
blandest generalities.  I can only wish I'd been wise
enough to decline similarly with others across my whole
sexually active span of forty years.  But in that case
those years probably would've been much different, so
no, I take it back.  I did what I did and it was usually
good or better than good, at least for me (but I think
for the woman too), and it was occasionally not so good
and in any case it was what it was and what I've got now
is the result (in part) of all that and I like what I've
got now a bunch and I also love it and I know the Z-wiff
does too.  And now I sigh and say these words might not
come anywhere near to nailing the matter with precision,
but they'll just have to do.)

    Dusk.  Quiet evening, a Monday evening just as it
was back then.  A few bugs flitting about.  The globe,
after all, is heating up.  -- But no, I'm not going
there.  Not again!  Not so soon after the last time!
-- And on an evening of Heavenly and lustily married
lustalgia.  Sigh again.  Trees and flowers, lots and
lots of maple leaves intricately interlaced and for the
moment holding stock still as a few bedding-down birds
twitter and flutter.  A dog barks.  Night's coming on.
And I'm scrambling for the exit.

[ Jyze of the Heavenly Year : Green Horse ]


[+1]


        Little bit of paradise here.  Terrace gardens in
climax state -- the flowers, that is -- on a sunny warm
blue-sky early evening.  Steep hillside and I'm up near
the top, hunkered down on a wooden bench.  Among all the
laughing daisies and geraniums and fuchsia floats a
grizzled J-slinger face with awe etched on it -- gasp!
-- and in that cross-sound view of partially mist-
obscured mountains resides such aching wistful beauty,
enough to make the sublimest existing postcard picture
of the scene crumple itself up in raw envy.  Aw, and now
a tiny ferry comes chugging into view to provide that
necessary point of merely human perspective -- just in
case the grizzled jyzeface falls short.
        A wooden bench built into a wooden platform or
deck, I guess, fenced, all the wood wabi-sabily
weathered, projecting out over the hillside with its
rows of small terraced garden plots and its intricate
pathways fringed with debarked timber and scattered live
fruit trees, and here and there a human figure laboring
away in nonlaborlike slow motion and one leaning against
a tree trunk admiring his own handiwork (and every last
one of these human figures -- I count seven -- Asiusan
or at least Asian-looking and all wearing floppy wide-
brimmed straw hats, four conical and three not).
        And the vast industrial panorama to the southeast
as well, the harbor with its clusters of orange cranes
(all seemingly asleep right now), the stadiums (game
three of the current series getting underway before
fifty K or so folks who've forked over a lot of dough to
gain the live perspective) (it's on TV too), the orange-
brick DC castle of south hill with, beneath it, tiny
vehicles crossing the deep waterless moat on the
sweepingly curved high bridge, which is painted green.
        Yes, it's only today that I'm finally getting to
the officially decreed Cheerful Green Dragon Day.
Monday was supposed to be the warmup.  Today -- the wild
climax.

[ Jyze of the Heavenly Year : Green Horse ]

     By sheer coincidence Z-wiff bought a Green Dragon
necklace at the solstice fair on Sunday (she took Kat to
see it in the morning while I was asleep).  The necklace
part is made up of shiny green fins like those rising
above the Dragon's spine; the pendant is a ball around
which a Dragon is chasing its own tail, and maybe tale
too, and the ball also looks like the earth with the
Dragon being the continents -- which is the feature she
especially liked.  I meant to ask her to let me wear it
one of these three days but I didn't get around to doing
that until too late -- in bed this morning -- at which
point she said her heart was set on showing it off at
her downtown leadership group's banquet tonight (that's
where she is right now).  She felt bad about declining
my request, though, and so left me a substitute, a
copper funnyface, as in a comedy drama mask, which I'm
to imagine vertigrising into a Green Dragon.  I've got
that funnyface right here, pinned on my shirt, as one
more bit of necessary human perspective.
     I've just come from a sad two-hour visit with Mama
E.  Earlier today the crisis du jour, prompting four
phone calls from her, was extreme dizziness -- she made
it sound desperately bad -- but by the time I arrived a
difficulty with swallowing had arisen and she'd entirely
forgotten the dizziness.  She begged me to stay on past
my announced limit of six-thirty, and I did, until
seven.  It made no difference.  Will she survive through
the night without me?  Most likely.  But also maybe not.
This is just how it is now, and it's like this virtually
every day.  About all I can do is give Z some respite
from dealing directly with it.  The sad truth is our
being with Mama E seems to bring her, Mama E, little, if
any, comfort, and that's doubly true with me -- the son-
in-law, the near stranger.  Equally sad, I can only take
so much of being with her myself.  When you come up
against the grim facts of death and dying you get some
hard lessons in the necessary limitations of, yes,
again, the human perspective.  -- Or hard review
lessons, I'll call them.  Nothing really new here
except, again, the particular human details of it.

So...onward.  What else is Heavenly Year jyzifying
about if not moving on while you still can?  -- And by
the way, if any of this sounds a bit overly weighed down
with hokey wisdom excretions, I say blame the moon in
all its fullness infusing the nights with delusion after
delusion of Heavenly enlightenment.

Out in the world of politics it's ugly again.  The
cabal announces a new plan for the Mideast in which the
Palestinians will by and by be granted nationhood if
they meet various conditions the severity of which ought
to make even the most righteous right-winger blush with
shame.  And never mind any more on that for now.  Today,
meanwhile, the leaders of the so-called G-8 nations --
the eight being ours and our major cappie hench nations
-- are meeting to decide what crumbs to throw to Africa.
They're convening in a remote Canadian village so that a
protest like the one against the WTO here in J. City
three years ago can be avoided, with air patrols filling
the sky and a large contingent of troops guarding the
single road leading in and out of the village.

And so back to matters of merely personal
significance.  Today, as it happens, features two
anniversaries of note, and both are lunar.  For one,
it's Z's conception day again.  -- And to think the
woman in and through whose body she was conceived was an
hour ago hanging onto my thigh for dear life!  (And she
still wields a grip that a professional wrestler might
envy, except it's bonier -- and come to think of it the
wrestler might envy the boniness too, because it can get
your attention fast.)

And then the other lunar anniversary brings zen-
wife Lady U into these pages for the first time in
calendrical fashion.  It's her lunar birthday.  Today
she hits -- hard to believe -- the beginning of her
fifth Great Year (a Great Year in Chinese zodiacal terms
being, in case I haven't noted this before, a complete
cycle of the twelve totem animals and thus a span of
twelve ordinary years).  Just where she is while hitting
it I don't know and don't want to know.  Well, no, I
wouldn't mind knowing but I think it's not wise to

pursue the matter.  That zen hitch-up's still close
enough in time that any prolonged direct exposure to it
might be potentially painful, and not just for the Z-
wiff.  Later on, though, I expect I'll be delving more
deeply into it or trying to -- wisely or not -- as I can
hardly do otherwise since it occupies such a large chunk
of my personal history in the later years and most of it
happened right here in J-town or not far from it.

    In honor of these two anniversaries I stand up and
spin around twice, J-stick in hand, and the flowers nod
respectfully as my body parts brush by.  In the distance
a pair of gigantic orange dock cranes stand touchingly
close to each other and seem to symbolize something
really big, like, say, the immortality of loving
pterodactyl mates.  Hawks swoop and soar.  Mountains
fade into a mist tinting toward golden.

    -- But wait, there's still yesterday to mention.
Yesterday it was fifty-two years ago -- and I still
remember the occasion with surprising clarity -- that I
learned at the back driver's-side window of a long black
car freshly parked in Uncle Hank's driveway in the
Centropolis burbs that the Korean War had started.  And
my father, who was in the army reserves, and my mother
blanched.  And thereby my life over the decades to come
and right up to the present was majorly changed.

    And now push on.




------


24


------




    If I sit here observing long enough -- the leafy
trees, the statue of the eponymous chief (a different
statue of him), the monorail pylon, the rooftop radars,
the frisbee-like great saucer floating high above --

[ Jyze of the Heavenly Year : Green Horse ]

I'll be able to become them and witness the world
through their essences and eventually I'll be able to
write about them in a fresh and original way.
     It's worth a try.
     Ventured here from a wooden bench in that other
cobblestone triangle at the other end of downtown.  It's
late enough that most cafes are closed but bars aren't
and neither are most bar/cafes such as the one a couple
of doors down to my left, or southwest.  I'd be
launching this session in there except it's much too
crowded and crazed.  No surprise really -- I gave it a
look-see only because the new edgeville espresso joint,
a few blocks south of here, was closed, and that was a
surprise.  Maybe it shouldn't've been -- I've never
visited the place before -- just driven by -- but it has
the look of an artsy late-closer like the primo javahaus
and several others I like.
     When I left the apartment at eight I promised the
Z-woman that tonight for a change I'd try to bring the
wagon home in one piece.
     All week terrorist warnings have been sounding.
It's said they've got their eyes on our town again.
It's said a major operation will shatter the Fourth,
coming up this Thursday.  What a couple of crocks!
-- Or most likely they are.  The odds would be just as
infinitesimal even if the cabal were dealing out truth,
which of course it isn't.  But still, this terrorist-
alert stuff gets to you.  So when, as Z and I drove home
at the end of our provisioning run earlier tonight, we
saw a massive black cloud billowing up from the vicinity
of the fairgrounds -- just about the spot where the
arena would be, it seemed -- we both had the same
thought (though actually we'd assumed at first that the
cloud was just an unusually dramatic raincloud, because
other such clouds only slightly less impressive were
visible elsewhere).  The thought: dirty bomb!
     Okay, so if I'm down here now it must not've been a
dirty bomb.  The bar/cafe would probably be closed, yes
(though to my knowledge it's never been closed for any
reason at all).  The fleet of insta-cam trucks belonging

to the TV station headquartered across the street
wouldn't be snoozing in their parking lot -- but they
are.  (And again it's probably not a good idea to be
jyzing in a drizzle, hoping the thickly leafed maple
hanging overhead will offer enough shelter.  Already
I'm hovering over the J-book to see if my head will do
the job since the leaves are partially failing at it.)
    Drunks staggering by.  A punk couple getting
surprisingly affectionate.  A panhandler or two working
hard at coin extractions.  But all this is as nothing
compared with the normal street bedlam in my home
triangle.
    What did cause the exceptional cloud I don't know.
News radio told us nothing.  Four times in the space of
three blocks we had to pull over to make way for a
blaring fire engine.  But the real origin will likely
remain a mystery as far as these pages are concerned.
Which is all right: it fits right in with the times.
(And Z loves a good mystery, and she'll be the first
reader of these pages, so as the popular injunction
goes: bring it on!)
    -- It's a different geared saucer up there now, I
see, no longer aglow.  The aliens must not work a night
shift.  The red light at the top seems to be flashing
but it's really not; the illusion of that stems from the
leaf action of the maple right here.  -- And the chief,
holding forth in his robe atop the pedestal at the
center of the pond, he's mostly hidden in the leaves
too, but his legs show the reflected yellow neon from a
Thai restaurant at my back: my main source of light too.
    Big new business scandals busting out all over.
The week-in-review section of the far-coast paper,
Sunday edition, asks if capitalism itself will do in
capitalism.  Wall Street is on edge.  What if the market
were to crash?  What if irrational exuberance suddenly
gave way to highly rational extreme caution?  Yet on the
other hand it's just business as usual, nothing to get
excited about -- not when dirty bombs might be going off
in your very own former hood at any moment.  And truth
to tell even this scary stuff is pretty much the usual.

Also interesting, our notoriously left-leaning regional circuit of the U.S. District Court has ruled that the Pledge of Allegiance should be banned from schools because the phrase "under God" violates the doctrine of church-state separation.  Hilarious!  The right wing's trying to stir up a patriotic furor over this and they're having no trouble at all in doing so.  Imagine, to ban "under God" at the very moment of the first Christian crusade of the new apocalyptic era!

And much is happening on the personal front as well.  Mama E, for instance, again called 911; this was later that same night I last wrote about her.  Five aid personnel and three cops showed up.  Z and I didn't hear about it until the next morning and could scarcely contain our relief once we knew she was all right: because Mama E had been able to get to the hospital without calling on us for assistance.  Later I talked with her and I've never heard her in a better mood.  It was a triumph to her too, and doubly so, because she'd also proven to us again that something really was wrong with her.  What was it this time?  An entirely new malady: a bladder infection!  -- But the cops complimented, she kindly let me know, both the flying salmon and the dangling jester I'd given her for her birthday.  I wonder if she also told the cops they were gifts from her son-in-law, John Wayne (standing JRX).

The hospital released her Saturday, and since then she's been on a new kick.  When we call she doesn't answer the first couple of times, and then she picks up only to croak "I'm okay" and then immediately hangs up.  She's done this with me, with Z, with nephew Jacob calling from Centropolis.  What's going on?  Who knows!  Presumably she's miffed that Z didn't stay on with her longer after her release on Saturday -- but the doctor said there was absolutely no reason to keep her at the hospital and Mama E couldn't stay awake anyway.  The next visit was set for Monday -- tomorrow -- and we decided to stick with that unless she called asking for assistance.  She didn't.

Fun and games.  It's crazy.  It's also more or less

typical for this kind of situation, or anyway not too far out of the ordinary.  That's what they all say: docs, nurses, eldercare workers, other kinds of social workers, and other daughters -- friends of Z's -- who've tried to deal with elderly mothers in failing health. Not that any of this makes us feel a whole lot better.

Loud music coming out of the cafe/bar whenever the door opens; the draft it creates is pushing a black plastic bag across the cement bricks in distinct little lunges, although the music appears to be doing this all by itself.  No one else is daffy enough to be sitting out here at this hour in the drizzle, which is now mixed with sprinkles.  Several human-male-piss-like arcs of water shoot out at the chief from the edges of the pond showing no respect at all for his considerable dignity, and they also create a sound more like real rain (and there's an occasional mysterious sploosh as if a line of mutinous frogs were being forced to walk the plank).

A matched pair of chrome-domed, earringed, tattooed, clodhoppered, sag-shorted gay dudes clomped by holding hands a moment ago and I was surprised to see them enter the bar/cafe, which is a raucously straight kind of joint -- or so it's always appeared to me -- and sure enough, after taking one glance inside, the pair popped right back out and resumed trudging up the street.  And this reminded me: the whole town is gay tonight.  Z and I didn't make it to the big pride parade on east hill and then were doubly embarrassed to learn that Z's nephew Jacob joined the one in Centropolis -- embarrassed and astounded.  Jacob?  Somehow his daughter must've shamed him into going: that was Z's theory.

-- Just sneezed twice, and hard enough each time to blow another bag or two across the square.  Extreme weather shifts will do this to me.  Before the arctic front blew in we had a marvelous skein of near-tropical days.

By now, I should mention, we're about an hour into Half Year Day.  That's what I'm told they call it in China, though they must be thinking Gregorianly when they do so.  (It's also the Chi-comms' birthday party.)

The first six solar months are over, the second six are coming in.  For some corporate bookkeepers it's the end of the fiscal year and therefore they can launch into a new volume of elaborate distortions and obfuscations.

More leaping imaginary frogs but no monorail trains.  One hundred and eighty degrees to the rear, craning my neck, I see neon signs at street level.  Low-rise buildings, they're part of the charm of this area, though in many places you have to squint pretty hard to call it charm.  But I've always liked it around here, maybe for that very reason.  The pizza joint across the lane to the northwest is new to me but not much else is. The poor chief, 24/7 he has to watch that red neon pizza sign revolve -- he appears to be gazing straight at it -- and it tints his face red too.  As if in embarrassment for us at the seeming confirmation of our Cawkian racial stereotyping (we pinkskins).


[+1]


I'd been hoping to end this cycle with a profusion of green.  Set up in the climax rain forest over on the peninsula, something like that.  Or the arboretum here in the city.  Or the greenbelt on south hill.

What jyze must settle for in real life is the green corner of the living room at home.  Or greenest, I should say, because here no corner's without its motley collection of potted plants, freshening the air but also, as per the warnings on some of them, possibly causing mold.  But I don't worry about that too much; it's the look and the feel I go for.  This living room lives.  It grows.  It rocks.  (And soils.  And pots. And sheds.  And thirsts.  And thrusts.)

Main thing is, I'm worn out.  It's been another tough couple of days with Mama E.  But now comes a kind of break: she's been admitted to the hospital for a "psych eval."  In fact she's already there.  "It's a murracle!" cries Z-wiff's note, and she has every right to feel that way.  The pressure on her from Mama E's

demented behavior -- quite possibly it really is some
form of "senile dementia" -- has been terrifying.

Yesterday when Z went over to the motel she found
Mama E curled up in shit- and piss-fouled sheets.  Not
quite in a feral state, but almost.  She hadn't been
taking her meds.  -- And I won't go on from there.  But
today when I took her in for her previously scheduled
appointment -- handing her off to Z when she arrived
after work -- Doc F was able to see what he wasn't
prepared to see before -- in part because Mama E is
usually able to act fairly normal if she wants to.  The
question now is whether she retains any control at all
over the spasms of not wanting to.

At one point I asked her why she'd done what she
did this weekend.  She just gave me a mysterious smile
-- almost a complicitous one, as if to say, "You know
why and I know you know why and you know I'm not going
to acknowledge why and you know why I'm not going to
acknowledge why" -- and then changed the subject.

Do I know why?  It appears to be a matter of
willful resistance -- punishing Z-wiff for not treating
her mother as her mother wants to be treated and feels
she deserves to be treated by her daughter.  But how can
it be called willful if she's lost control of her
actions to the point where they're obviously working
against her own best interests?

Earlier today Z petitioned the state to start the
process of qualifying Mama E for acceptance in what's
called an adult family home.  If Mama E will accept it
herself, that's likely to be the next step, though it
could take months to accomplish and then more months to
see if it will hold.  If it doesn't hold, a harsher kind
of institutionalization would likely follow.

It's sad, it's awful, but right now the relief at
knowing there will be at least some relief for us that
may also be relieving for Mama E is so great it's
elating.

-- Aiieee!  The denial of death (as in the riveting
Ernest B. book of a quarter century ago -- and yes, I
met him once as part of my editorial duties in MSM #2 --

and the man himself has been dead for almost that long):
just a brief exposure to an experience like this is all
it takes to make you understand why that particular form
of denial is sometimes so necessary.

Today, by the way, I'd hoped to be jyzing out in
the middle of the rain forest at noon, since that was
the exact midpoint of the solar year (only in leap years
does it fall on the 1st of July, and even then it still
occurs at noon because the last six months cumulatively
remain slightly longer than the first six). But of
course that was a pipe dream so far out it was more like
a two- or three-pipe dream -- of "B.C. bud," say, which
for the past two decades has reigned as No. 1 on our
local weed potency chart, as I know from being a close
reader of grand-jury transcripts for all that time.

Am I ever able to rouse myself early enough to be
jyzing at noon? Only as a by-product of emergencies
rumbling in from the outside world.

-- That note a few paragraphs back about potted
plants causing mold, it also comes courtesy of Z's old
college friend (roommate for a while) Fritzi, who last
week rang Z up while in town for a convention. They
hadn't seen each other in ten years. Fritzi teaches air
quality in the MSM #2 schools. She also has a lot of
funny college stories about Z to spill. We met her for
drinks in the lobby of her downtown hotel Saturday night
after she and a rowdy gang of fellow, but all female,
conventioneers got back from a baseball game -- and so
the hilarity couldn't go on for long with both Z and
Fritzi being confirmed lifetime larks, meaning early
risers and early to-bedders -- while I'm just about the
ultimate owl.

The best story: Z intentionally shocking a roomful
of very proper U of Mentoka sorority girls during a
double date with Fritzi in Lahontan -- one asking Z
about the pin she was wearing and Z saying "It's two
flies fucking." In those days Z was the "siren," Fritzi
was the "siren-enabler," dolling her up and sending her
out into the night. Then in '67 Fritzi moved to MSM #2
-- barely a month or two before I did -- and met her

husband there just as the Summer of Love was gearing up,
and they're still together and still living in the same
house they bought back then for forty K, and this house,
now worth close to a million, is located less than half
a mile to the north of my own main turf in that town
back in the day.  She even recognized my name, she said
-- swore this "on the Torah" -- from old newspaper
bylines.  And her husband, Alex, has taught writing and
USAn lit for years at the same high school Elgie
attended.  I liked this Fritzi -- very warm, witty,
open; puts her hand on your arm when she's talking to
you just the way I sometimes do -- and infamously did
with Z on our first date and therefore it almost became
our last date -- and I'm hoping we can get together with
Fritzi again, and meet her husband, before too long.
     Which means: the chances of our traveling down to
the megastate this year have now gone up again.  But
only slightly.  Must keep in mind Mama E's condition.
     -- It's dawn.  Dappled inky clouds, looking to my
eye like dark blots on a gray-blue blotter: right out
the window.  Birdsong here and there but only in the
warmup stages, like singers in widely separate rooms in
a music rehearsal building.  No call-and-response, I'm
saying.  Or is there ever?
     And I'm wondering whether Sirius is visible.  The
Dog Star.  I'm thinking maybe it's absconded from this
quarter of the sky at this season, leaving behind just
its reputation: when Sirius shows up the Dog Days are
beginning.
     And on this day by NUT time exactly 149 years ago
-- July 2, 1853, and so the same year as the Cawk
invaders' initial conquest of J-town -- the infamous
USAn Black Ships sailed into Tokyo Bay.  And if they
hadn't done that, I wouldn't be here, or anywhere, to
note this fact.  I wouldn't exist.  And much, much else
in the world would also be different, yes.
     Enough? Enough.  And so how did it go, this second
Great Year?  A cloud of dust, galloping hooves, the
hearty cry of "Hiyo, Green Horse, away!"  -- Making room
for the fiery, the magnificent, the impassioned ---

BOOK C

[ Jyze of the Red Horse ]

------

25

------


    A slice of moon pushes up from the smoking shards
of the fireworks.  A few hours ago we watched from the
balcony as the stormy sky above the lake lit up in
pulsing flashes, from as far north to as far south as we
could see.  After about five minutes, though, it got
old.  And the wind turned chilly.  The bedroom beckoned
(and not just to Z-wiff) -- for sleep.  Now the last
cars have had plenty of time to careen home from the
bars at closing hour and it's unusually quiet out there.
Or it seems that way, maybe just by contrast with the
earlier incessant boomings.
    But it's still the night of the Fourth.  And it's
also the inauguration of the Red Horse era.  A new jyze
volume!  The volume of the authentic prime Heavenly Year
Festival itself.  The volume, what's more, of the middle
quintile, the Monkey Month, the visitation of the
ghosts, and the Golden Mean.
    For us, the wiff and me, it was a fine day.  For
Mama E it may have been fine also, let's hope, because
she's been admitted to the hospital again and that's
where she seems to like best to be.  Or did I mention
this in the last entry?  Suddenly I'm thinking I did.
But since it's the overriding concern of our life right
now -- Mama E's health status, that is -- it bears
repeating.  And the latest word is she's been resisting
the nurses' instructions, perhaps in part because all
three, Z tells me, are East African, and two are males.
Nor is she taking well to the proposition that she's in
need of a "psych eval," although in truth that's the
main reason she's been hospitalized.

[ Jyze of the Heavenly Year : Red Horse ]

    How much longer she'll be in we don't know -- two
or three days maybe.  We're trying to make the most of
the respite.
    All week the media have been full of warnings about
terrorist attacks aimed at disrupting Independence Day.
Patriotism is popular again, at least for some.  Flags
are flying and I don't mean radic-lib flags.  Doubters
and dissenters like me and Z and most of our friends and
for that matter a large majority of the population of
Jyze City are necessarily keeping a low profile (as of
course I for one would be doing anyway).
    My bus book for this week has been a contemporary
philosopher's collection of replies to her recent essay
on patriotism and cosmopolitanism.  In championing
cosmopolitanism she makes it sound so dry and abstract I
actually experienced a resurgence of the kind of
patriotism I felt as a kid, before starting to learn
what the USA is really up to in the world.  For a short
time I even thought I might be able to hang on to some
part of that resurgence.  I even came up with a modest
proposal for patriotic reform that would again make the
U.S. a country I could feel proud of.  But my enthusiasm
for it has already evaporated.
    It would be simple, though.  What really counts for
most USAns is the idea that we're a free people -- the
idea of freedom.  So I say let's just adjust a bit what
we mean by freedom.  Even the looniest right-wing gun
nuts don't say every USAn should be free to own a
personal H-bomb.  They accept that freedom must be
restricted in some respects.  So let's restrict it for
corporations and plutocrats in whatever fashion might be
necessary to prevent them from shaping government policy
in ways that cause this country to (A) dominate other
countries, and (B) push the world toward eco/climate
catastrophe.  And that's pretty much it.  I mean, sure,
capitalism has been immensely successful in terms of
creating economic and military power.  These two big
problems (A and B) are a result of its success and they
will eventually -- soon -- cause its own destruction and
quite possibly that of civilization itself, so let's

make some adjustments, okay?  The other problems
regarding racism, sexism, militarism, nuclear armaments,
wealth distribution, out-of-control consumerism, one of
the worst pandemics in world history (AIDS), and so many
other matters, those we could get a handle on under
present arrangements if we'd just make these two crucial
adjustments regarding freedom.

Maybe tomorrow I'll start feeling better again
about this reform proposal.  Today, though, the specter
of our rampaging neocon-inspired war fever has got me
feeling way way way down about the proposal's chances.

But then here's my king-size box of cornflakes with
the U.S. flag vigorously a-ripple on the front and the
Declaration of Independence displayed in several
different flagborne fashions on the back, none of them
really readable.  -- Well, no, the Declaration's just
there once; the other flags are saying other things --
"Remember Pearl Harbor" (certainly the jyzeman can't be
opposed to cultural remembrance of his conception day)
and other rousing slogans in the spirit of "Don't Tread
on Me."  The part about overthrowing our government if
it's become tyrannous, that's not decipherable on the
flag with the Declaration or any of the others.

*          *

It's still the same day, Gregorianly, although
sixteen hours deeper into it, and we're just reaching
not the farthest-in but the farthest-out moment of the
entire year.  It's the orbit I'm talking about --
Earth's.  The planet's.  Its orbit around that which
right now seems to be balancing atop the farthest-north
peak of the mountains to the west and casting rays of
gold across the sound and the bay.  Old Sol I'm talking
about, by cracky.  It's also -- that dazzling orb now
seeming to consume itself -- hanging directly above the
far reaches of north hill.

Oh what a day it is: Aphelion Day!  With ridged
bands of clouds at the horizon making for spectacular
ever-changing rosy-orange celestial settings.  Fabulous
rippling waters.  A ferry glides out, no lights on yet
though it's dark enough for them in that southwesterly

direction.  All this as seen from a waterfront park, out
at the end of a wooden pier, me and roughly a dozen
other observers, while behind us a group of paramedics
and cops ready a scraggly-bearded street dude about my
age, I'd guess, or maybe a bit younger but more worn
down by the street life, for lifting onto a stretcher.
     "Wotta view!  Looks almost like the sky's on fire!"
     "You're so lucky to be living where you can see
something like this any time you want!"
     I don't think any of these celebrants are enlisted
in a tradition which makes a lot, or anything at all, of
Aphelion Day.  If only they knew!  We're three million
miles farther out than we were back in January.  The
planet's going around a bend -- hang on or you might fly
off -- might keep sailing out tangentially into a wholly
unexpected celestial neighborhood.
     Now in the narrow mouth-shaped gap between clouds
and mountains the final burst of color -- a sexy rose.
     Last night the big fireworks display was blasting
away right here.  Today the far-coast paper reveals the
Pentagon's plans for attacking Iraq from three
directions early next year.  A quarter-million troops, a
massive bombing campaign against "thousands" of targets.
Why?  Because Iraq might have -- the evidence is murky
at best -- a few of the "weapons of mass destruction" of
which we possess tens of thousands.  And we don't like
Iraq anymore, although we sure did when we allied with
them against Iran in the eighties and encouraged their
use of just such weapons (call them WMDs) and even
provided some to them in the form of poison gas.  And
Iraq has all that easily accessible oil.  And most of
its people practice the same religion as those who
launched the 9/11 attack last fall.  And that's about it
really: our casus belli.  So wave those flags!  Fire off
those Roman candles!  We've got another war to fight!
     Today is also, I absolutely must mention, the solar
birthday of the woman with whom I lived for far longer
than any other: Lady U.  She's now twelve years older
than I -- "the old man" -- was the year we met.  The
gull perched at this moment on the fence post a dozen

feet in front of me is eyeing me curiously -- might be her spy, I feel, or even her reincarnation, in a sense, if I wanted to pursue the thought.  But I don't.

Here's a four-deck jumbo ferry coming in, with lights shining but without sound.  The Lady U gull flies away.  All the other celebrants are gone too, although here come a couple of new ones.  The guy on the stretcher's also outta here.  To the south I see the lights of both stadiums -- games taking place, or at least one game.  Why the new football stadium's lit up I don't know for sure -- maybe it's just a rehearsal for the workers -- but I'm impressed.  Huge twin white arches.  And then the bright harbor lights to the south, gigantic cranes standing guard.  Mountains silhouetted against blue sky to the, yep, west.

Yesterday we attended a Fourth of July barbecue thrown by a friend of Z's from her J-town leadership group.  He's a shop owner in the HQ and so introduced us to a number of local people he'd invited, including the co-owner of the firehouse tavern (the high-spirited, husky-voiced Chelsea M.).  We missed a cameo put in earlier by ex-mayor Jon R.  I ate about two pounds of salmon.  And I met Z's "flower lady" friend from the A-mart, Jean H., whose husband, also present -- they're both Chiusans and natives of MSM #2 although they lived in Italy for many years -- turns out to be the painter Victor H., who also contributes reviews to the same AQ weekly Z writes for.  We wound up driving them back into town and joined them in a gallery "trot" on the other side of the HQ triangle and then visited their splendid fourth-floor walk-up studio/loft.  Vic and I seemed to hit it off pretty good; we exchanged phone numbers. He's very self-effacing; I was raving about Mr. X's work -- he who painted up my jyze Black Horse -- and at that point I didn't know Vic was a painter himself; he'd said nothing about it.

-- This past paragraph has gone down under a bit of duress.  Two homeless guys came up and are now sitting just a few feet away and I sense potential trouble.  So it's time to split.

[+2]

     -- On Tanabata evening I asked myself if there was
anyplace downtown where I could feel excited about
cranking out some jyze.  Any "venue."  And here's the
spot I came up with.  Same as the one I tried to come
up with a week ago, to wit: edgeville espresso, the new
one.  But this time it's open.  Two hours until closing.
Plenty of free tables.
     But no stars are visible out there.  Umbrellas on
the move, yes.  So with wet feet I recall (by way of
nostalgia-riddled mind) the kimonoed children of
Inagoyama (JRX) bearing poems and notes on bamboo
sticks.  "Make a wish upon a star."  Or two stars in
this case, the forlorn lovers of the Silver River (a/k/a
the Milky Way) -- but ecstatic on this night, the
occasion of their one yearly meeting.
     An old Chinese legend which was often brought to
bear on the love life of my Red Horse era, sometimes
even by me, but especially by Lady S.
     It's a little warm in here, I notice.  Just as it
was back at the scope office.  And this is how it oughta
be according to the Chinese farmers' calendar, which
declares today to be the first day of the "Slight Heat"
fifteener.  As the long Independence Day weekend
sputters to a close with absolutely no evidence of the
raucous new patriotism -- or any kind at all -- visible
from where I sit.  And I can see scores of apartment
decks.  Not a single flag on view, I'll testify, to give
proof of its continuing existence through the night.
     Old oak table here, it reminds me of the one I
lugged from apartment to apartment in MSM #2, except
this one's nicely refinished (just the way Mom used to
do it in the early Gatewood years -- including the
birthday cart which I don't doubt would be deployed to
great effect in this Heavenly Year if she were still
around -- and in theory could be so deployed regardless,
since I think Barb has hung onto it in Mother's old
apartment -- but almost certainly won't be, or at least

not that I'm likely to witness, and so it goes).

But Elgie did send an e-mail.  It's dated a week
ago this past Friday, although I didn't see it until
yesterday.  (Z's been having trouble with her internet
hookup.)  This, in fact, is my first e-mail ever.  The
jyzemaster, it seems, is a little behind the digital
curve.  And what's more wants to stay right where he is.
Will respond with pen and ink only.

As expected, Elgie's seeking help in applying for
law school.  Not the monetary kind -- not yet -- but
advice and possibly some sort of "strong
recommendation."  Advice, anyway, I can do, and maybe
some vetting of applications.  But since he makes no
bones about what he's trying to accomplish -- gain
admission to a high-ranking school so he can join a
high-ranking firm and make lots of money -- I guess I
should be equally candid about being less than wildly
enthusiastic about such a set of goals.  So here I am
about to be my father all over again, but in reverse.
Too bad the attorney vocation coming down from Gramps
skipped a generation -- from Elgie's perspective it's
too bad, that is.  Or at least he might think so.  But
if it hadn't skipped that generation, his mother and I
never would've met.  Of that I have no doubt at all.

His message is disappointingly formal and
businesslike -- except for the salutation, "Hi, Pops!"
The tone is deferential in what I recognize to be a
filial Korean way.  He's ordered the books I
recommended, so what should he do next?  I'm hoping to
loosen him up.  But I understand he's in a dicey bind,
living with his mother, asking for help from his father
from whom he's been estranged almost all his life and
considering going away to school (a majority of the
dozen schools on his list are in the eastern half of the
country).  Would his mother accompany him or is he about
to leave her behind just after she's suffered a stroke?
I expect it'll be a long time, at best, before he'll
open up enough to me to be ready to discuss such thorny
questions.  (Lady S, incidentally, hasn't replied to my
note as yet, nor does Elgie's e-mail refer to what her

reaction was to it or, for that matter, to her at all.)
   -- An hour until closing.  Customers are down to
two on this side of the room.  The armchairs at the
other end are still groaning with some sort of group
meeting.  I'll bet at least half of those bedecked
apartments up there across the street are empty.  The
dot-com crash has left my former hood here grossly
overbuilt.  The old has mostly been chased out but the
new is a long way from being born, except materially.
   Folksy music here.  Thick green rug.  It's all
right, not too blatantly techie even though you're
clearly an outlier if you're doing your jyze or anything
else by hand instead of by keyboard.
   Medically, Mama E's still being evaluated.  Z's
been on the verge -- a number of verges -- of freaking
over the nonstop maternal display of resistance.  I'm
still trying to be a calming influence.  A tough week
ahead once Mama E gets out again.  It'll be my job,
we've agreed, to talk turkey with her.  She may push
intransigence to new extremes even as her health
deteriorates.  I'd say she's well past the stage where
the traditional villagers would've carried her up to the
top of the mountain and left her alone to meet the gods.
Sounds cruel, is cruel, but it might be even more
merciful than cruel.  However: we're not giving up.
Will keep trying to help her get over the hump and
moving back toward independent living with frequent but
reasonable assistance from us.  She won't be eligible
for Medicaid for at least two months because of the
existence of a six-K insurance policy in her name which
must first be cashed in and "spent down" to below two K.
The "spending down" could be done immediately on
existing bills, but she still won't regain eligibility
until September.  So it's pretty much official now: a
strong Mama E subtheme will continue all the way to the
end of the Red Horse period and perhaps well beyond.
Contrapuntal, this subtheme, most likely.  But I'm ready
to be surprised.  And of course hoping to be.
   Yesterday after visiting Mama E at the hospital we
headed up to the Yuke (university quarter) where we did

the full circuit: bookstore browsing, both dinner and a
movie at the cine cafe, then vite/supp and grocery
shopping on nearby streets.  The big hulking co-protag
of the Norwegian film "Elling" reminded Z of me and also
reminded me of me -- yeek.  Norski halfwit who likes to
bang his head against walls, literally, in moments of
frustration.  Whenever I hear Norwegian spoken I'm
instantly transported back to Turtle Rapids.  Just
think: it's likely I'm related to just about everyone in
Norway.  (In truth this actor in the movie looks even
more like our recently unearthed "lost branch" cousin
Ron H.).  And good news: the cafe portion of the movie
theater has reopened, and it's now operated by the same
folks who run the cafe in Z's old hood where we tete-a-
teted (ha!) on our Meet Day, and the new operation looks
good and feels good and the food's good and it even
appears the place will still be good for jyzing.  I'm
planning to give it a shot there one of these days.
     And more news.  Larry B., Naomi's husband, will be
receiving a national award as the leader of the team
that prosecuted the Al Qaeda-linked "Millennium Bomber."
Naomi will be accompanying him back to Justice
Department headquarters in D.C. for the ceremony, and
this means I'll probably have no work the week after
next.  For me this'll be crunch time for sure.  The
question is: do I borrow the rent money from Z or do I
cash in the deep-reserves account?  That account's
perilously close to the cutoff point which I promised
myself I'd never let it dwindle to.
     So I'm mulling.  As the Horse Month -- but not the
Red Horse twelve-animal Great Year -- comes to an end.
And I want to mention this: I listened to a tape of a
radio program about neopragmatism -- Z ordered it as a
surprise for me -- and for the first time I heard the
voice of another longtime hero of mine, and one still
standing: Neoprag Brother No. 1.  He didn't sound as
lugubrious as I'd come to expect from various written
descriptions.  Nor did he sound as patriotic as I
feared.  Some of his most recent philosophical/political
moves have made me very uneasy -- I don't believe you

should or even can be loyal, as he argues, only to your
own language community, nor do I think breathable air
and potable water, among a number of other necessities
for most forms of life, can constitute anything less
than a "philosophical" absolute  -- but the man's still
up at the top of my list of great thinkers of my
Heavenly era, which is to say: the past sixty years.

All mulling aside, however, this joint will soon be
closing.  Time for me to hie on up the street for a
teriyaki special.  And after that, hole up at the
hideaway for an hour or two and scratch out a letter to
Elgie.  "Son, as you head off to law school you should
be aware...."

Strike that.  Mull some more while on the hoof.


------


26


------


Well, it's another spectacular summer day in J-
town.  -- But not only that, no.  It's pavilion park in
the AQ on the day before the opening of the AQ street
fair (which is really, to my mind anyway, the delayed
celebration of the Dragon Boat summer festival).  And
it's also the opening paragraph of the long-awaited
cluster of the Purple Sheep, a/k/a the Fire Sheep or
"Lonely Sheep," which refers to the Chinese year 4665,
in the Great Year of the Red Horse and the Heavenly Year
of the Black Horse.  -- But "long-awaited" -- couldn't
that be said of all sixty-one Heavenly Year clusters?
It could!  And I'm saying it, one cluster at a time!

On the way in but it's still early.  Skipped most
of the home breakfast ritual -- everything except the
three pieces of honey-slathered orange-bread toast (with
the third piece tossed in to make up for missing my

cornflakes).  A bottle of iced coffee rests on the bench
here.  And in front of me an unusual scene: the roofs
for all the street-fair booths are laid out in stacks of
three or four, filling up the entire park except for the
funky little red-columned flying-eaves pavilion at the
center.  The roofing material for the booths is a shiny
white vinyl (recalling old-time majorette boots),
dazzling in the sun, and the peaked frames make the park
appear to be buried in huge snowdrifts -- but abstract
or geometrical ones, maybe as an early modernist would
paint an Arctic scene.  And yet it's framed by the usual
AQ setting, with redbrick buildings mostly three or four
stories tall predominating, a dozen nearby trees gently
shaking, cars rolling, people strolling, birds swooping.
-- As I peer at it all while tucked deep beneath shady
limbs in the isolated northwest corner of the park.  (I
can see only the heads and sometimes the shoulders of
passersby moving along above the drifts.  It's like the
outdoor winter scenes in the Japanese film version of
"The Idiot" set in snow country: people walking from
building to building in a labyrinth of narrow outdoor
snow hallways dug head-high or even higher.)
     -- And with much to mention.  A definitive change
in Mama E's status.  A growing political brouhaha over
corporate accounting scandals, with the cabal on the
defensive (partly because the big kahuna himself is
directly implicated) and the stock market sinking
rapidly.  A week of chance meetings and bump-intos for
both the Z-spouse and me -- and an interesting long
three-scotch rap session with my new friend Vic H.
     So Mama E first.  The news is that Doc F is now
saying she's gone around the bend.  She's "in and out of
dementia," unable to care for herself, needs twenty-
four-hour attention.  A nursing home is most likely the
next stop, but an adult group home is a possibility if
she can regain some mobility.  That's all being
evaluated now.  She's been transferred over to a
"nursing facility," as they call it, just half a block
from June's dorm on the Jyze City U campus and still
within easy walking distance of south hill.  It's

actually more like a halfway house for convicts, as I
see it, but here the crime is sickness and old age and
you're being prepared for either a return to society or
a journey to the Big House in the Sky.  During my first
and only visit there so far it reminded me of an elders'
version of "Fellini's Satyricon."  Limbo I guess is what
it really is.

But it could be a lot worse.  Four patients to a
room, curtain partitions, a potty for each bed, lots of
aides to change diapers and tend to other problems.
Halls teeming with folks in wheelchairs or using
walkers, a few laid out on gurneys, many asleep or
nodding out, some groaning, some showing stunning
corpselike visages -- but lots of quirky life there too.
"Oh my, how tall are you, young man?" -- a tiny elder
Cawk woman in a very large wheelchair, inquiring of me.

Mama E is still in an early adjustment stage.
She's refusing to eat in the cafeteria or to allow the
male aides of recent East African heritage (I'm
guessing) to assist her in diaper changes.  She's hiding
food she dislikes (which is most of it) in the
wastebasket -- just as I used to do with asparagus and
liver in boyhood days.  But she can still scratch away
at a lottery card with the best of them.

For Z this is also a juncture time.  Her mother is
"officially" declared to be demented and so Z can no
longer hold her responsible for the many bad things she
does.  The long hard fight is over -- or anyway this is
how it feels to her much of the time.  What we're facing
now is new and disorienting.  It's exhilarating in one
sense -- free at last! -- but also terribly sad.  She's
writing poems about the mystery of her mother's dreams.
And she talks with me a lot about all this, on the phone
during the day and then for up to an hour (or roughly
twice as long as usual) when I go to bed before she gets
up.  She continues to go out of her way to bring me
little gifts because she feels she's "forcing" me to
endure all this turmoil with her mother.  Apologizes
over and over.  And I tell her over and over it's not
like that, and it's not.  Sounds like soppy nonsense, I

suppose, but it's at times like this that love goes deepest and means most -- and is the best.

-- Oh Lord, Lord, here he goes again. Will someone please hose this man down with ice water.

(Where have all the pigeons gone? The Falun Gongers and tai chi-ers? The pensioner bench-hangers? Long time passing! Everyone but me seems to think the park's closed -- me and a couple of squirrels chasing each other around in the densely branched squirrel paradise overhead. Maybe some "Park Closed" signs are posted but if so they're in Chinese. I do see several possible candidates.)

Chance encounters I mentioned. Z ran into Vic H. at a bus stop in the HQ (turned out later he was on his way to be sigmoidoscoped -- that is, to get a lightstick shoved up his ass in pursuit of "presidential polyps" -- so-called because the cabal chieftain himself suffered the same indignity just last week) and moments later along came my cousin Kar, recently arrived in town for the summer. He's now director of a foundation about which I know little -- but it champions biodiversity and sure does sound important -- and to Z he looks much older and more harassed and even emaciated. "Glen always was huskier" was his reply to her observation that he seemed thinner. "We've got to get together" was also said and I'm expecting and hoping we will.

For my own random encounters I have Howie P. and jugglin' Jay. Howie's a coworker of Z's and I bumped into him on the street outside the city offices and he was eager to tell me about the seminar he attended recently at a prestigious far-coast university, one week long, British satire the topic, a famed USAn literary critic in charge. Jugglin' Jay happened upon me at my favorite back-corner table at the ORB cafe. Two weeks ago a big photo of him performing at the national jugglers convention at the J. City fairgrounds made the front page of the B section of the FAP. This summer he's working on seven-ball juggling and building a porch on his and Melanie's house. I tried to wangle an invite for dinner -- Z and I have never seen their house, just as they've never seen our apartment, and we've been friends for almost five years now.  A slow unfolder of a friendship.  Don't know yet whether the attempted wangle worked, and that probably means it didn't.

And then tying one on with Vic.  I tried to drop off a book he'd expressed interest in with Jean, his wife, at A-mart but she'd already left, so I headed for their loft.  He was home, not in much of a working mood after his sigmoidoscopy, so invited me up.  It seems he likes to have an excuse to knock back a drink or two. (Jean explained to me later about medical restraints stemming from his quintuple bypass, the ghastly scars from which were on display on his legs that evening -- from artery transplants, I'm assuming.)

And it was good.  And just as we got to politics roughly three hours later -- and I'm afraid politics would not have been so good -- Jean arrived home and it was time for me to be moving on.  Mostly Vic and I exchanged life stories, with the emphasis on his, and rightly so.  He's seventy-three (a Snake person like the Z-woman, but he's Earth and she's Metal), he grew up mostly in MSM #2's Chinatown, went to art school down there, painted some locally famous murals, moved on to Norway on a Fulbright -- he speaks Norwegian! -- and then hobnobbed with the Abstract Expressionist crowd in FCM #1 before winning a Guggenheim which took him to Rome, where he wound up staying for thirty years.  Jean, daughter of a family friend from a town near MSM #2 and twenty years his junior, paid him a courtesy visit in Rome during a European tour and, in essence, never left (became his second wife, I believe -- many of these details are obscured in a scotch mist).  -- And a fine sunny evening it was too, the interior of their fourth-floor loft in a century-old building a visually rich sight if ever there was one -- in fact close to my ideal for urban living, thus meaning for any kind of living.

Vic's had exhibitions all over the country but apparently not too many recently.  "I just can't get a show in this town!" he grumped.  I went audacious -- presumptuous -- and quipped about "who needs shows anyway." This seemed to stun him. And he seemed to be worrying a little bit that I was out to exploit him somehow (like what -- make him into a Heavenly Year jyze character? -- well, if he'd like me to sit for a portrait I'd gladly do it). One thing he is doing these days is writing a lot of book reviews for the AQ weekly mentioned before. It turns out I've been admiring his reviews -- very gracefully written, especially on arts-related topics -- for years and never knew he was living within a few hundred feet of my hideaway office.

We've got a lot to talk about. But his kind of culturedness may be too Old World for me -- or mine too callow for him, put it that way. Opera, classical music, classical painters -- that's not my world. Jean is a live-wire, though, vivacious, easy on the eyes, fun to be around. She's very protective of him and at the same time all wrapped up in their son Ro -- who's twenty-one and a student in Romance languages at the U and still lives with them up in a small loft within their large loft -- but I sense she too for some reason is wary of me. Maybe it's because I haven't made much of a mark -- okay, basically no mark at all -- in the arts world. It would figure they'd go for accomplished types. Adele U., who's been seeing Vic and Jean at community events for years, says she doesn't think they're too conservative, which is my fear owing to a few throwaway remarks of Vic's -- about the need for more respect for authority and so on. Jean worked as a researcher ("leg woman") for the Jyze City three-dot columnist Colman R. for years and he certainly wasn't conservative. Then again V&J are apparently close with Bruce O., the Japusan HQ bookseller and gadabout, and I've never been able to warm up to him (and just yesterday I learned from Jean, as I was dropping off some clips for Vic at her flower stand, that Bruce had suffered a stroke only hours earlier).

But I'm making an effort here. Reaching out. Chances for real friendship are rare and they become even rarer, it seems to me, as you move into or near your vintage years. Vic said much the same himself.

But he also said he worries about "the cost of the
emotional investment" -- I guess because he's lost a
number of good friends to death in recent years.
     Speaking of which -- reaching out, that is -- I
sent off another long letter and assortment of clips to
Elgie.  So far from him there's been just the book and
the one e-mail -- nothing I consider to be a serious
effort at personal communication.  But again I'm still
hoping.  From his mother, meanwhile, nothing, period.  I
suppose my card must've offended her somehow.  For sure
it's something that's happened before.
     -- Late afternoon now but otherwise little's
changed.  A flock of pigeons did arrive but seemed
puzzled by the dazzling vinyl snowdrifts messing up
their playground -- and keeping away their pigeon-feed
tossers -- and soon took off.  The sun is sneaking in
beneath the trees behind me -- over the roof of the post
office -- and causing my head to cast a strange befurred
shadow that jerks lumpily across this J-book page.
     I got work to do.  It's climax week for the big
grand-jury case that's been breaking my brain and
toasting my eyeballs for months -- and recently it's
been grabbing lots of headlines too.  A world-renowned
surgeon falsifying records, intimidating witnesses, the
university's illegally begotten profits running into
tens or hundreds of millions -- the main scene of all
this nefariousness one of the hospitals just a couple of
blocks from Mama E's room at the motel -- which room
now, incidentally, she'll likely never be seeing the
inside of again -- and the person who's deciding whether
there will or will not be a plea bargain in the GJ case
and, if the latter, what the terms of it will be is none
other than the same war-drum-beating cabal appointee
Grant M. who spoke at June's graduation last month.


                    [+3]


     -- Had to skip an extra day.  Lots of work to push
out before Naomi's departure for Washington with Larry

to receive the terrorist-prosecuting award.  Not enough
work, though, to make up for the lost week.  I've
developed a case of the financial jitters.  And in this
I'm joining most of the rest of the country.

    "Panicky markets."  Cabal supreme leader under
fire.  So of course we of the dissenting type are
issuing warnings.  Expect (A) a new series of terrorist
alerts, (B) an actual terrorist incident (either staged,
provoked, or simply allowed to happen), or (C) an
expedited timetable for the upcoming invasion of Iraq,
previously "scheduled" for early next year.  Or all
three.  Or maybe an expanded war somewhere else.
Colombia maybe?  Venezuela?  Philippines?  North Korea?
Iran?  All of the above?  Axis of Evil only?

    Meanwhile I'm starting into a week's unexpected
vacation from scoping.  I'm planning to devote a big
chunk of it to catching up on periodical reading.  And
tonight I'm right back downtown on my usual turf,
picking up a paycheck.  Earlier, a workout at the WOC
with the Z-woman -- our first together in several weeks.
Then some cleanup on my own at the hideaway.  Now, after
depositing the check, I've drifted two blocks downhill
to the outdoor cafe at the art museum.  At this hour --
a little after midnight -- it's closed, of course, but
no matter.  Stacked black metal chairs chained to heavy
round black tables.  Stacks six or eight feet high --
you can't sit on them, obviously; it would be like
climbing up to a highly unstable lifeguard's chair.  I'm
perched on the stone base of the fence separating the
blocklong stairway from the sidewalk and street.  Two
blocks up the hill I can see portions of both of the two
highrises which are the only places where I've worked
("day job" type, that is) for the past twenty years.  On
the hillside below them, the symphony hall and another
truly huge 'scraper.  Then here, then the harbor steps,
then the waterfront, then the water.

    No moon.  But a warm night.  A crimelight,
tastefully disguised, shines directly overhead, causing
the leafy branches to cast quivery shadows.  Before I
could even sit down a cop car flashed its spotlight at

me.   "Radio cabal headquarters we've got a possible
terrorist incident unfolding at the art museum in J-
town, might be just what they're looking for to justify
their Iraq invasion."  But since sitting down here I've
been given a pass by two watchperson teams.  They might
think I'm one of this year's rare foreign tourists and
I'm sketching the ancient stone camel and the ghostly
Chinese scholar stationed in the semi-dark on the grand
staircase inside, just the other side of the glass.
     The extra day I had to skip was Bastille Day.
Guess that's only as it should be in this year when
securite' trumps liberte', egalite', fraternite' (but
come on now, is there any year around here when that's
not the case?).  Yet still, "like all days" (and I ain't
kiddin' either), it's a special day.  First, it's the
climax of Bon Odori; the lanterns are being lit to help
guide the spirits of the dead back to the other world,
candles floating down the river, bonfires blazing in the
hills above town -- but not here.  That's the original
Bon Odori back in Japan I'm referring to.  Ours here
takes place next weekend, presumably to avoid a conflict
with this week's AQ street fair.  And the original for
Bon Odori itself, the Chinese "Month of the Dead,"
doesn't begin until about three weeks later -- which
also happens to be the start of my Heavenly Month.  So
good times lie just ahead.
     (Now the lights flash on above the grand staircase
inside.  It's janitor time.  The camel and the scholar
-- both suddenly looking much stonier -- will soon be
feather-dusted.  Latino-looking guy in a red henley just
like the one I'm wearing except not quite as faded is
pushing a mop around at the moment, sort of helter-
skelter, not following a rigid pattern.  If he had paint
on that mop he might be creating a work that would merit
hanging on the walls in there.)  (Bad joke.  Catcalls!)
     The other way today's special: it's one of my
wedding anniversaries.  Three of them fall in July --
speaking of the solar calendar and solar anniversaries
now.  As of today it's been twenty-eight years since the
hitch-up with Lady S, the mother of the son, who'd

already been born and in fact had been walking for five
or six months at the time.  As it happens, it's my only
unconsummated marriage.  Well, in a sense.  It was
consummated before, of course -- preconsummated, I guess
one could say -- and then postconsummated after we'd
agreed to separate again.  By traditional standards it
was even less of a marriage than my first one (with Lady
C, the drama student).  And the third one, with Lady U,
was less still by those same standards: it was never
official at all.  The fourth, of course, is the one I'm
in right now.  Going great guns, it is, by any standards
I know of.  For me the fourth time's the boggling charm.

(Now the grand staircase lights go out.  Just like
the lesser artworks up in our apartment, the ones here
apparently don't require a nightly feather-dusting.
-- And time to break out my pocket watch.  Last-bus
anxiety starts up.  -- Yipe, it's later than I realized.
Must split in about twenty minutes.)

So it's actually the 16th by Gregorian count.  At
the time of the first atomic explosion, fifty-seven
years ago today, I was two.  The British prime minister
back then, told of the bomb, famously said, "It's the
Second Coming in wrath!"  I just learned that today.

The AQ street fair was a gas.  Wei was spiffy in
yellow bermudas (the shame!).  The Z-woman grumped that
I wasn't holding her hand enough -- but this was because
she kept running off to greet friends or to check out
things for sale beneath those snazzy white vinyl roofs.
Dinner at the fine old Japanese restaurant around the
corner from the teahouse, an intriguing tour of the
teahouse hotel (it's the Hotel La Chevalle all over
again up there), Chinese ice-cream cones at A-mart and
Z's cone broke off and her arm looked like it did when
it was set in plaster for her fractured wrist two years
ago (this as we sat at J-town plutocrat #2's dolmen
fountain).  And I introduced everyone to Mr. X and his
family at the gallery, but very briefly because he had
several customers waiting.

Today Z learned her mother will probably be rated a
"level 2," meaning she can go to what's called an adult

family home.  We'll soon begin the search for a good
one.  But Z's very unhappy with Aida, who's been making
frequent moralistic comments -- all to the effect that
truly good daughters don't warehouse their elderly
mothers -- and of course this is the last kind of thing
Z needs to be hearing right now.  So she's planning to
have a "tough talk" with her, Aida, tomorrow.
     -- Last few lines here.  Of all the things
screaming to be said, pick a couple.  I'm disappointed
it's not looking as good as I was thinking with Vic and
Jean on the friendship front.  Did I maybe say something
offensive during our scotchfest the other night?  Yeah,
probably.  (As part of my Heavenly Year no-holds-barred
celebrating I'm getting into the habit of doing things
like that, it would seem.)


------

27

------


     Starting out in the dark again -- but with good
enough light.  Perched on the edge of the raised
platform of the streetcar stop at the HQ central plaza.
Around the corner from the major cluster of nightlife
action sites, but on a Wednesday night the scene there
is, not unexpectedly, subdued.  More's going on under
the trees right here in the plaza.  And through the
crowns of those trees, the floodlit pyramid atop the
great white tower, forty-two stories up at the blue-
lighted tip, rendered impressionistically alive by
intervening shifting layers of leafy branches.
     Perched here, the Yellow Monkey.  And why?
Because behind me lies -- or stands actually -- that
same smallest national park of them all (most likely).
It's what's called an "historic park," meaning it's an

262

ordinary storefront containing lots of small artifacts
and moderately enlarged photos celebrating an event that
happened a thousand miles north of here.  And today's
the 105th anniversary of the arrival in town of the ship
bearing news of the gold strike up there.

Yesterday the chairman of the Federal Reserve Bank
(an acolyte of the execrable "Atlas Shrugged" author)
chewed out the corporados for what he called "infectious
greed."  Of course that's exactly the quality that built
this country.  Certainly it built Jyze City -- gold
rushes, land rushes, military-industrial rushes, dot-com
rushes, among many others.  And wasn't it our USAn
supreme leader #40 just a couple of decades back who was
lauding greed for the large role it played in bringing
on "morning in America"?  Isn't greed more or less the
national watchword?  "In greed we trust."  How it is!

No streetcars at this hour.  Laughter and yakkety-
yak under the trees, a couple of boom boxes dueling,
lots of homeless folks curled up on the benches or on
flattened cardboard boxes or newspapers spread on the
bricks and cement.  On a night this warm who wants to
risk sleeping in a shelter?  It's safer out in the wild.

My vacation week.  So far so good.  Except this: we
learned Mama E will be allowed to stay at the nursing
facility for just one more week.  Z's had to launch an
urgent search for an adult family home.  She's working
from an inch-thick list, moving outward from south hill
by zip codes, calling first to ask about vacancies, then
driving around checking them out.  Today's the first day
for implementing this plan so I don't know how it's
going yet.  She's having to take tomorrow off and borrow
more money.  The mygs are flying for sure.  I imagine
she'll be hitting the Wellbutrin tonight.

I'll be inspecting the semifinalists with her this
weekend.  Until then I'm charged with being the one who
visits Mama E at the nursing facility.  At this point
she's more in dementia than out, riddled with paranoid
fears about her roommates and the nurse's aides.  But
she's eating better and seems to be suffering less pain.
As always she apologizes frequently for being "such bad

company."  Her main message for me today, repeated ad
nauseam, was to tell Z to tell Aida not to bring along
any friends if she comes by tomorrow, as at one point
was the plan.  But with the new housing emergency it's
not likely Aida will be showing up.  She'd go only if Z
went also.  And as mentioned before, Z and Aida are not
on the best of terms right now.  But I can't explain all
this to Mama E.  No point in even trying.

A long socializing stretch lies ahead for me.  Kar
tomorrow, Vic Friday (I'm pleased to say he called
finally), and brother Rob Saturday.  Lots for a Yellow
Monkey clinging to the mane of a galloping Red or Black
Horse to jyze about -- or at least I hope so.

The government let the nefarious neurosurgeon at
the U cop a plea.  Front-page headline news.

-- And it's best to be moving on.  The jyze rush is
over for tonight.  But it'll pick up again later in this
Gregorian day (it's past midnight and has been since the
start of this entry).  And I've been panhandled only
twice so far.  Street lamps visible under the trees, in
the trees -- it's a gorgeous sight.  Bricks, monuments,
totem poles, cobblestones, sprawled sleeping figures,
neon of beer signs glowing in bright colors along the
peripheries -- it's almost, except for the neon and the
totem poles, a nineteenth-century Parisian park scene as
painted by, say, Mr. X up in the AQ.  (I'd say Vic H. in
the HQ but as far as I know he doesn't do the kind of
quasi-Impressionism this scene all but begs for.)

                   *           *

-- Some sixteen hours later.  Here's the cine cafe
in the Yuke, an outdoor seat by the fence overlooking
the steep cross-street hillside and its sidewalk
striders -- gliding down pretty much, or laboring up
(you could learn a lot about crowns here -- of heads,
I'm saying, the hairy kind, some more than others ---


                   [+1]


-- At that point cousin Kar came up, arriving quite

early, just as I had done myself about five minutes
ahead of him.  Several hours of talk followed, over
dinner and numerous glasses of wine.  The wine did me in
(and the roast lamb at the Greek place didn't agree all
that much with him).  Now, some thirty hours on, I'm
giving it another shot but at a different venue.

Northern tip of the HQ triangle.  To the south the
entertainment strip throbs along the edge road.  I'm
sitting on the table-less outdoor platform at a small
Italian restaurant which has long since closed for the
night.  Aural cacophony surges over this spot, mostly
from the triangle itself -- conversational, vehicular,
musical (several live bands and all drawing swarms of
dancers).  I'm a happy guy.  Where's the moon?

Tonight it's house bourbon that's doing me in.
What an exceptional week this is turning out to be!
When did I last socialize like this?  If ever!

This Vic H., I love the man.  And what a phenom he
is!  My fears that I'd offended him last week were
baseless and foolish.  Tonight he brought along a draft
volume of his autobiographical reminiscences for me to
have at in editor mode.  I showed him the hideaway, my
inner sanctum very few others have visited.  I learned
he studied for a doctorate in philosophy at the U of
Oslo under the master of Deep Ecology himself -- just
needs to write the thesis and he'll be ready to go (not
that he intends to do that after a gap of forty-five
years).  We sat outside at the firehouse tavern on this
splendid summer evening and gabbed for hours as the
goths in black with brightly colored mohawks and a dozen
slave vessels' worth of chains lined up for the S&M-
based show at the club across the street.

Such a fine coincidence that we met, Vic and I.
Our stories are reverse images in a pair of facing
mirrors full of intriguing flaws (although in terms of
recognized accomplishments his trajectory undeniably
rises a magnitude or three above mine).  He hitched up
with a Norusan woman in the U.S. and Europeward they
sped, to the mountainous Nordic peninsula of her
ancestors, and though they stayed there for only a year

or so, his life especially was reshaped thereby.  I
hooked up with a Korean woman visiting the U.S. and was
drawn to her mountainous Northeast Asian peninsula on
the other side of the world and stayed there for only a
year or so and yet my life was likewise reshaped.  I'm
still marveling over all this -- and much more -- and so
is Vic.  Nor does either of us hesitate to do it openly.

     But I shouldn't assume too much.  Nothing's certain
and everything's fragile.  (As a guy in a black-and-
white jester outfit bounds by just to prove the point.
Howls and whoops go up too, but not for any reason
related to the jester as far as I can see.  And here are
three young hook-nosed Latino-looking gents in white
sailor suits with strange hats -- on shore leave from,
I'd guess, the Ecuadorean "tall ship" sailing vessel
that came in yesterday.  These summery days in the HQ
it's unusual to see a female whose midriff isn't bare --
but here's one right now in a classic little black
cocktail dress and nasty spike heels she can barely
navigate on as she teeters across the cobblestones.)

     And then there's Kar.  He's not happy, I learned,
with the biodiversity foundation.  He's at odds with the
board.  He's again got applications out.  His hair's
thinning and Z's right, he does look more than a bit
gaunt and haggard.  But I'm feeling more comfortable
with him now.  We go back together about half a century.
We talk politics and the conversation quickly grinds to
a halt because we think so much alike in this realm and
it's all so depressing/infuriating right now.  (Today
the stock market fell another four hundred points or
about five percent in a single day.  If such losses
continue, the moneyed classes will turn against the
cabal and lots of nonmoneyed folks will suffer too --
but if the upshot is that this country might conceivably
hang a political U-ie in the near future, of course I'll
be pleased and so will Kar.  There's also a possibility,
we agreed, some form of martial law will be imposed.)

     Today Z and I looked at the first of the two "adult
family homes" on the semifinal list.  (Adult family
homes -- hey, is that sort of like an adult theater or

an adult bookstore, a lewd and licentious site for
performing polymorphous perversities with full-grown
family members?)  Actually it's terrific -- a large
burban-style dwelling on the west side of the city
(conveniently situated roughly halfway between Rob and
Gail's place and Betty and Kat's), in a woodsy setting
with an impressive view of the downtown skyline to the
northeast across the bay, fifteen or twenty minutes from
south hill by car, and the woman who basically runs it
is Filusan (her husband is ex-military Eurusan but he
has an outside job with our local aerospace/"defense"
leviathan).  Mama E seemed happy when we told her about
the place -- to my surprise and Z's too.  Yesterday Mama
E took a fall at the nursing facility while trying to
navigate on her own the two steps to her commode.  It
jostled her brain: today she was the liveliest I've seen
her in weeks.  But still -- deterioration continues and
is obvious.  Will she be able to hack it at an "adult
family home"?  Next Tuesday we'll be taking her either
to the one I've just mentioned or to a very similar one
in the north end of town -- harder to get to for us but
possessing the advantage of being run by a trained nurse
and her husband (and in this case they're both Filusans,
though he too has some sort of full-time outside job).

I brought my watch down from the hideaway without
the backpack it usually rides in.  A first, in fact.  It
says eleven minutes to one.  Soon back up to the
hideaway, then homeward by bus.  -- Hello, three sexy
women, all in tight jeans, high heels, and black bare-
midriff tops.  Hello also man in red bermudas carrying a
suit on a hanger over his shoulder.  Hello black-leather
motorcycle couple revving at the light, her hands
squeezing his bared pecs from behind.  Many cabs in
sight.  Horse-drawn carriage too.  Pedicab.  Naval
captain in dress whites.  -- Do like to scope out the
cavalcade.  I'm glad, though, I no longer have to be out
there hustling for sex and love and adventure, or
fighting off the urge to be.  Can sit here enjoying the
spectacle and thinking heavy thoughts, light thoughts,
nonthoughts.  Peak summer weeks coming up.  Heavenly

[ Jyze of the Heavenly Year : Red Horse ]


Monkey Month just about to swing in.  Somehow it's all
hanging together, this Heavenly Year experiment.  Got
some excitement stirred up here in the jaded heart of
the old General Jeep!  And plenty more to come!


[+2]


     Now doing my jyze thing on the steps leading up to
the Buddhist bell.  Visible through the shrubbery on the
other side of the bell is the circling mass of Bon Odori
dancers waving their foldout fans in time with the
throbbing bass drum and the shrill recorded female
singer voices.  That's a temporarily closed main street
they're doing the ritual dance in, honoring those who
have passed before.  All types too: young and old, all
races, all kinds of garb -- even some summerfest
pirates.  I've recognized a dozen or so faces, including
Z's friend Aida, her brother Ray and his wife Vivienne
and their two kids, and Amalie M. -- but none from my
own pre-Z J-town life when I almost always attended this
festival (with the Japusan Lady U).  Big crowd on a
glorious summer evening.  Teriyaki smells wafting by,
mmm, I could go for some of that.
     Z-spouse and I were here together earlier for a
while.  I took her home so she could start preparing for
the upcoming workweek as she likes to do on Sunday
evenings.  I walked back down the hill (nabbing my first
ripe blackberries of the season from the huge patch at
the northwest end of the high bridge, a favorite of the
folks who emerge hungry from the greenery underneath)
(but getting at the best berries reminded me, shame to
say, of tarbaby and the briar patch) and passed the
staging area for the AQ parade -- aswarm with majorettes
and Chinese drill teams, high-school band uniforms,
tubas antically ambling about on human legs -- and then
turned east instead of west at the main drag, which I
rarely do, and walked up a few blocks to the main J-town
Japanese Buddhist temple.  Festivity regained but this
time in jyze mode.  (As now the sound track switches to

live taiko drumming.)  Down in the central AQ the parade
will be starting soon and I hope to catch the tail end
of that a little later.  (Why?  Because it's a parade!)

At the moment I'm sitting under the edge of the
bell-pavilion roof.  The wooden columns and beams are
reassuringly thick and indeed must be to hold up all
that heavy metal.  Earlier we watched the bellringer at
work as he pulled back, using a rope, the log hanging
horizontally about six feet up, then released it to
strike the bell.  Deep resonant boom.  "The temple bell
falls silent but the flowers keep ringing."  I didn't
realize it until today: the temple across the street is
celebrating its centennial this year.

A flute now -- shakuhachi type, I think.  It brings
back Japan days for me, the small-town bathhouse where
the owner's daughter practiced her shakuhachi as the
foreigner soaked naked within her sight.  Bon Odori
always does well at evoking nostalgia.  Plangent
moments, bell-like, sweet fading after-thrums.  I sit
here alone -- "the Lonesome Howler" -- sheltered from
the crowds except for a few folks crunching by on the
gravel paths.  Some impossibly cute kids in kimono are
dancing around in circles on the round stone by the pond
and some impressive goldfish are lurking below, cruising
slowly this way and that.  Red and white Japanese
lanterns bob like very large fizz bubbles above the
booths and the heads of the crowd across the street.
Shafts of sun find their way through trimmed bonsai
branches -- seem to lay across the branches almost
horizontally at this late hour as if mimicking the bell-
stroking log.  So these must be the flower-striking
logs.  Memory flowers, briefly abloom, I've got whole
cherry orchards full of them for the years with Lady U
and Lady S and my extended stays in Japan and Korea.

Up early today for inspection of the other finalist
adult family home in the far north end -- quite near, in
fact, a rental house I once shared with Lady U.  I
agreed with Z-wiff: this one's even better.  Benita, the
thirty-something Filusan nurse who runs the place, seems
kind and firm and capable and also has a good sense of

humor.  It's worth driving the extra miles.  I expect
we'll be seeing a lot of movies at the nearby bargain
theater.  Not with Mama E, though, unfortunately, unless
she makes some miraculous progress first.

On the way back we stopped at the nursing facility
to tell Mama E about the results of the search.  She was
suffering too badly from an upset stomach to show much
reaction -- until, ironically, we mentioned that
Filipino food would be served for some meals.  Then she
brightened.  Her husband Vincenzo used to cook for her
and he was, from everything I've heard, very good at it.
Anything I rustle up for Z, as she doesn't hesitate to
let me know, falls far short in comparison.

-- We're back to the circle dance now.  What a
sight!  It's hard to tear my eyes away.  Always has
been.  It's about the only chance most of the folks out
there ever get to be a terpsichore before a seated
audience (and some standing) of hundreds or maybe
thousands.  Ooh the varieties of self-consciousness, the
permutes and combos -- and all mixed with pleasure and
excitement.  Such a happy scene it is!


------

28

------


Clear the two potted hardy fuchsia off the old
redwood chair and plop myself down.  Jyze time!  And it
could scarcely come at a finer moment.  About a quarter
through the fifth watch by the Taoist way of reckoning,
which is to say about half past three a.m. by local
Daylight Saving Gregorian, and the night's so mild I'm
wearing just shorts and a sleeves-chopped-off henley and
I'm feeling no pain at all.  Not even any slight
discomfort.  For J-town a night this mild is a rarity

even at the height of summer -- though not for much
longer, almost certainly, with global broiling moving in
so fast all the glaciers around here are melting like
ice cubes in a cool drink left out in the sun.
      Peaceful night too.  The moon, nearly full, has
long since passed out of sight, but swarms of stars are
atwinkle even though the air's plenty murky.  It's so
quiet the buzzing from the transformers mounted on the
telephone poles across the street sounds abnormally loud
-- almost as loud as the crickets on a hot Mentoka
night (and brother Rob says he's hearing crickets during
his late-evening strolls for the first time ever in J-
town).  Few cars go by -- and when they do, tonight I'm
promising myself I won't record the fact -- unlike that
previous balcony entry which turned out to be little
more than a traffic log.
      Earlier today Leo the Lion came roaring in with hot
breath.  And with this cluster the Golden Earth Rooster
is flapping in too -- "Rooster Announcing the Dawn."
Most likely it won't be doing that in this part of town
-- just the usual feathered suspects here -- but out on
the west side Rob, again, hears an authentic rooster
crow almost every morning.  And well he should, since
it's coming from the backyard of the house next door.
      Technically this cluster is starting out on time,
but for me we're still in the day previous.  By NUT time
it's midevening of Monday the 22nd.  But this is also
the last official day of my vacation and tomorrow,
meaning Gregorian Tuesday, might turn out to be an
unusually busy day if I also have to go back to work (I
won't know about that until I hear the message Naomi
will be leaving at noon).  The day's already certain to
be busy enough -- and wrenching, and probably comical
too -- because in the afternoon we'll be moving Mama E
to her new home.  Well, no, as I realized the instant I
wrote the word "certain," it's far from certain.  This
is how everything is with Mama E.  But her release from
the nursing facility is scheduled for "early afternoon,"
and her new home -- the one in the north end, farther
away from us here but more homelike and also more

medically competent, we're pretty sure -- is expecting
our arrival sometime between two and eight.

(No bugs out here either, by the way.  Not yet.
But this will likely be changing too.  When I arrived
home tonight several mosquitoes were hurling themselves
against the glass lobby door with the bright light
behind it.  I don't think these skeeters have perfected
high-altitude flying yet.  It's hard enough for them
that they're at the summit of one of the city's higher
hills; fifteen more feet up to this balcony is more than
they can handle on their first night out on their own.
First night I know of, anyway.  Before now it's probably
been too chilly.  -- And our usual local feathery
heralds of dawn are now hard at it.)

What a fine vacation it's been.  So relaxing!  This
past evening it capped itself with a bit of serendipity:
I bumped into the Z-woman near the far end of the high
bridge as she walked home from the nursing facility.
I've also greatly enjoyed the three convivial evenings
in a row with first Kar, then Vic, then Rob.  Each
afternoon or evening I've worked out in relatively
leisurely fashion, I've soaked in the whirlpool, I've
caught up on periodical reading and I've copy-edited the
first half of Vic's eighty-page "Cicatrix" manuscript
(and I'm pleased to say it's fascinating and well-
written for the most part and yet also -- this pleases
me too -- I think maybe I'll be able to help him jack it
up to a publishable level).  -- Oh, and not least, for a
change I've been getting more than enough sleep.  And
that ought to prove useful in the hectic days ahead
before Mama E settles in, if she ever does.

Meanwhile: the stock market keeps tumbling and lots
of people are very worried.  On top of everything else
could it be we have a worldwide depression starting up?
Sunday a mammoth corporation filed for the largest
bankruptcy in U.S. history, almost doubling the previous
record set just a couple of months earlier.  The
government's doing nothing: it's too compromised by its
deep ties to the failing companies and their fraudulent
business practices.  In effect those companies are the

government, or a large part of it.
    Fabulously interesting times.  And they're likely
to become even more so.  "The wonder and the terror
beyond."  (Eyes of fire burn through the ordinary!
-- But no one needs eyes of fire to burn through our
current ordinary.)
    And I wanted to launch this 28th jyze cluster
tonight because July the 22nd, as I've mentioned, is a
special day for me.  How run-of-the-mill can it be when
it's an anniversary of one's own wedding?  So then how
extraordinary does it become when it's the anniversary
of two of one's own weddings?  The drama student and the
diver/dancer: Ladies C and U.  Yup, rock-solid facts.
    The Year of the Purple Sheep was the year of the
first wedding -- in an upper-midwestern cornfield -- and
the Year of the Yellow Horse, eleven years later, was
the year of the zen wedding outside a central-mountain-
state phone booth.  Of these two marriages, it was the
latter, the self-proclaimed zen one, utterly unofficial,
that lasted.  Its staying power exceeded that of the
cornfield wedding by over seventeen hundred percent.
    (Oh the sky is lovely as the black slowly
transmutes to indigo and navy blue, revealing three
squiggly dark clouds brushstroked halfway across the
eastern horizon even as a few stars directly overhead
continue twinkling -- and the classic evergreen behind
the house across the street gradually materializes too.
And the clamor of the stand-ins for the Golden Rooster
continues.  And this isn't a traffic report but a cop
car just floored it down below and zoomed off as distant
sirens sounded -- the very first local crisis du jour to
come to light -- at least as these jyzer eyes register
it -- at the dawn of the new day.)
    Marriages.  To think I've had four, and three
official, and one currently active, and the total will
never again increase (knock on chair-arm redwood, which
I notice has become respectably weathered, just like, I
hope, me: being a truly married man now, indubitably in
it for the long haul -- or for the haul anyway, whether
long or short or something in between -- and it'll only

273

[ Jyze of the Heavenly Year : Red Horse ]

be the reaper that ends it -- I'd bet a bunch on it).
     Fifth watch must be about to blink out.  -- But
first I wanted to mention that both of those July 22nd
marriages served to increase the numbers of the human
race, as marriages are traditionally intended by society
to do.  But in each case the increase was very brief and
unremarked by the census bureau, although the so-called
pro-life forces would've counted them if they'd known.
Therefore I suppose I could say I've more than done my
duty both for society and the human race and also for
the genes whose existence and replication we're all
hormonally driven to promote.  Yet in the end I turned
against those genes, or was complicit in the turnings
against them -- they were only copies, after all, the
genes, and not even the cloned kind, which at least are
one hundred percent copies -- and thus I both remained
true to my genes as they are, the originals, the museum
version, and also spared a vastly overpopulated world.
     So that's it for now.  Vacation just about at an
end except for the last sleep.  If possible this jyze
will resume later in the Gregorian day, but I'd say the
odds of that happening are slim (knowing that just by
writing this, my contrarian nature will be provoked to
improve the odds -- unless including this parenthetical
note decreases them again -- decreases -- increases --
gotta stop on one or the other, she loves me or she
loves me not -- she loves me!)
                    *              *
     -- And she does.  Or something does.  Because now
it's roughly twelve hours later and an opportunity has
arisen for me to tack on a few lines.
     Most likely this will be the last jyze session ever
hosted by Mama E's motel.  I'm sitting at her card table
a step or so from the little kitchen, with the four-
foot-tall loose-limbed jester cutout hovering over my
left shoulder: "Jes lemme know when ya wanna hear
anudder bad joke!"  (That's what's written -- by me --
on the cartoon bubble emerging from the jester's mouth.)
     Door to the courtyard's open a crack, fan's on.
The preview-of-the-future heat wave continues.

[ Jyze of the Heavenly Year : Red Horse ]

    Up at one.  A labile Z-wiff under extreme stress.
Mygs, yes, again doing their myggy thing.  She even
objected to my wanting to listen to the top-of-the-hour
two-minute news capsule (to see if the world's fallen
apart on this day when some pundits predicted it would).
She said I've never put news over her needs before; I
said she's never objected to my listening to two minutes
of news headlines before.  Besides, it's a J-day -- news
is a must!  (The market's down another percentage point
but the center seems to be holding so far.)
    So off we rode to the nursing facility.  And to our
amazement we found Mama E in the best spirits we've seen
from her in weeks.  A priest had been in to bless her.
And ever since she fell on her head, she cackled to us,
everyone had been extra-nice to her.  We wheeled her out
(the facility had kindly presented her gratis with a
surplus wheelchair) and loaded her into the Z-mobile and
rolled northward.  In under thirty minutes, because
traffic was light, she was in her new room.  -- And all
along the way she was so talkative not even the roar
from the open windows on the freeway could stop her.
    It's a large ranch house, all one level, in a
residential neighborhood with a church on the corner
across the street and two lots to the east.  Tony's the
resident caregiver, as they say; he's there most of the
time, a Filipino man in his mid-thirties, I'd guess, and
friendly with the five resident elders (or at least he
puts on a good show when visitors are around -- but I
think he really is gentle and friendly).  Two of the
residents are developmentally disabled -- I don't know
in what way technically, but symptoms of spasmicity and
lolling heads, gaping jaws, rolling eyes were hard to
miss -- and these two may fall a little short of being
elders.  The other two are older women probably in their
seventies, one Afrusan and one Eurusan.  The Afrusan,
Pauline, doesn't talk much and goes off to a day center
for several hours five times a week.  The Eurusan,
Muriel, does talk and seems the liveliest of the bunch;
she's probably the best hope for a friend for Mama E.
    Soon Benita, the Filusan nurse, arrived and guided

us through an informal admissions procedure in Mama E's
new bedroom.  Benita's thirty-eight, Z says, and has
four kids of her own but she clearly knows what she's
doing with fading elders.  She and Mama E hit it off
right away -- Mama E told us afterwards she was reminded
of Z's Filusan friend Aida.  And as noted before, the
food served is Filipino -- not always but often.  At
Benita's request Mama E rattled off her food likes and
dislikes at great length, boggling Z and me.  Benita
even wondered aloud to Z and me whether we'd been
exaggerating Mama E's poor health status.

So hopes are high on all sides.  And I think I'll
leave it at that for now.  It's good to feel hopeful
while you can.  Tomorrow, who knows.

Outside, the little courtyard fountain splashes
audibly here at the motel where Mama E no longer
resides.  A songbird belts one.  Tenants laze on benches
and dangle their feet from the second- and third-floor
balconies as music plays softly.  Old Cliff the manager
came by a few moments ago, sweeping the sidewalk with
the steady rhythms of a true Zen (capped kind) devotee.

And now it's all for naught from our perspective.
Two months remain on the lease and with vacancies high
these days we'll probably have to pay for both months.
Karen K. has said she'll buy back the sofa-bed -- for a
third of what Z paid her for it!  But Z's not squawking.
The new dresser I assembled and this card table with the
two folding chairs will go up to Benita's place, as
we're calling it.  Other items Z paid a bundle for are
probably bound for storage: microwave, color TV, fan,
round table, tub chair, etc.  We'll see.  We'll see!
This weekend will be the time for hands-on dealing with
all this.

What I'm wondering is if Mama E will want the
jester and the big "health salmon" with the shiny purple
and red body and green fins that's swimming overhead in
the corner.  It's blowing a big cartoon bubble that has
written on it, "Stand under me for 'Magic Fin' J-town
Salmon good-health vibes."  If Mama E doesn't want it, I
do; I figure we'll be needing it ourselves all too soon,

Z and I.  In fact we already need it.  Everybody needs
something like this!  Always!  And there's only one!
   And it's time to march on down the hill.


[+2]

   -- Got java, will jyze.  And free java too.  Z gave
me a debit card presented by our local coffee colossus
to attendees at a J-town leadership-group function.
Seeing me place that card on the counter, the barista at
the AQ east-station franchise, realizing she had no drip
coffee ready, must've assumed I'm a regular -- even
though I look more like the homeless men passing by
outside in droves today (and I look thus every day, if I
can manage it) -- and she kindly said she'd "buy" me the
coffee since she was making me wait so long.
   One more proof of the old adage: got plastic, will
prosper -- until, that is, the world chokes on it.
   So now I too am sitting outside.  Like numerous
others of my scruffy ilk I've laid claim to one of the
wooden benches on the surface level of the station
complex.  Each bench is partitioned across the middle to
prevent sprawling or sleeping, and that's all right by
me: I'm not tired right now.  And I don't like seeing
areas like this turned into homeless encampments --
though I like even less the shortage of beds for the
homeless in more-appropriate locations, and still less
yet our society's determination to create ever greater
numbers of the homeless.  It's the system, folks!  It's
just one of a number of evil Faustian trade-offs we've
made in the decency-for-power arena.  Rogue nation!
   Getting-off-work time.  Going-to-the-old-ball-game
time.  Skateboard time.  Cooling-off time -- it's been
overcast light-jacket weather all afternoon after a long
spell of glorious days with a few scorchers mixed in.
-- And here in the ongoing personal jamboree of Jyzer G
most of the arrows still seem to be pointing up.  -- Or
is that really true?  No, I guess it's not.  But the
fact that Mama E appears to be settling in all right at

Benita's place makes it seem so.  Even the darkest news
looks brighter.

What does it mean that Z's recent exam revealed new
vaginal growths?  Hopefully not too much.  The last time
this happened, several years ago, she had to undergo a
D&C procedure, a "scrape-out," and she might soon be
facing another one.  The earlier growths proved to be
benign.  Her mainstream doctor (who's also my mainstream
doctor, and my only doctor, though I haven't seen her
since the day we met a little over five years ago and
remain in fierce denial, like most of your standard U.S.
male persons, as Z likes to point out, vis-a-vis any and
all medical needs I may have) -- our mainstream doctor,
Karen, I say, thinks Z might just have naturally thicker
vaginal walls.  But for years Z's been taking hormones
in herbal form and the latest medical reversal on the
effects of those hormones on postmenopausal women is
worrisome.  And the last thing she needs right now is
more stress.  But now she's got it.

For me there's also some deepening money stress.
It's not life-threatening or anything like that but it's
nagging away regardless.  Will I have enough to pay my
rent next week?  It's gonna be close.  If the amount of
work I'm getting doesn't pick up, every month will be
close.  Some months I'll probably fall short.  Then
what?  The deep reserves are shrinking alarmingly, even
faster than our region's glaciers -- though not faster
than the stock market itself in which roughly two thirds
of the deep reserves are invested.  I'm just going with
the meltwater flow and keeping my fingers crossed (which
isn't easy when you're jyzing away with a J-stick, not
to mention when scoping at the keyboard).  After all,
this is my lucky Heavenly Year.  The way I see it, it
oughta be less likely now than at any other time in my
life that something should go seriously wrong.

Baseball fans hurry by, some bearing cushions.  I'm
happy to say my natural posterior cushion hasn't
withered away just yet.  If it had, my list of potential
jyze venues would need major revision.  But excitement
and anxiety are in the air; our J. City baseball team's

lead is down to one game and tonight's the opener of a three-game series with the team that's closing in on us. Monday night brother Rob and I will be seeing a game on reduced-price tickets he obtained through his employer, but that game will be against the cellar-dwellers. "Every game counts now," Rob reminds me. True, but games against the onrushing second-place outfit count twice as much. Of course he knows this perfectly well.

Wednesday night was the full moon -- last one before my very own of the Heavenly Month. It's looking good, the moon is -- no matter how strong the peer pressure, it should never go in for a facelift. When you think of it, is there anything that's changed less over the years? I like pondering the proposition that not only everyone in the world but also everyone who's ever been in the world is or has been looking up, or out, at pretty much the same beautifully weathered and pockmarked face gliding by on a regular basis. The Tang poets, for instance, or the Persian ones, or the ur-person way, way, way posthumously dubbed Lucy we all descend from. Having an area of stability in your life -- even a few of them -- never hurts. -- Well, never? No, not never! But on the whole it's a good thing.

Last night at 8:50 p.m. I observed a moment of silence (while at the keyboard, as it happened, at the scope office, working on the dep of a Romanian-born sculptor who now can barely lift a chisel after an auto accident on the freeway bridge visible from our balcony at home: the rear tire of a truck exploded without warning right in front of him) -- observed a moment of silence, I say, in honor of the great urban poet of our modern USAn era, alluded to in these pages several times already, who died at that moment on July 24th in the Year of the Red Horse, thirty-six years ago, when he was run over by a kind of dune buggy.

You roll your dice, you take your chances. -- But these pigeons here, they've got it good. An elderly Asian woman, presumably of Chinese descent, with a cane and an expansive purple quilted jacket, keeps tossing out handfuls of grain for them, like a pioneer woman

seeding a field.  She must have a big pouch under that
jacket.  And she probably uses the cane to fend off
anyone who'd bother her; her footwork is quite agile.
Soon every pigeon in J-town will be here and I'll have
to pull my feet up off the ground or maybe just scram --
as the great flock parts before me.  The Conference of
the Mourning Doves!  (A few are brown and white like old
Kook and Little Kook, former mother-and-child residents
of our 203 balcony.  We haven't seen them in recent
months since Z had to give up their care and feeding.
It's good to think other folks may have adopted them.)
     And one of the new fiberglass dragons has taken up
residence on the pole across the street outside the
east-depot saloon.  Happily enough it's a red one, with
yellow markings.  But it does look a bit skinny.  Ever
since Jean told me that many in the Chinese community
find the whole set of dragons -- fashioned by a Eurusan
outfit -- too skinny, they've seemed to be emaciating
before my eyes (and some of their spatial alignments,
Jean said, are seen as being Feng Shui-ishly incorrect).
     I stopped by to visit with Jean in her flower stall
one day and she told me Vic had "greatly enjoyed" our
evening out together -- but she thought she might've
enjoyed it herself even more.  "I got to light some
candles and put on my music and just kick back all on my
own -- it was like paradise!  This almost never
happens!"  Now she tells everyone Vic's in a happy state
these days -- "He's found a new playmate!"  This is the
week their friend Bill W.'s in town (he's a very good
Chiusan journalist I met thirty years ago in MSM #2; and
the timing will be tight but we might have a chance to
do several decades' worth of catching up).
     Hope Vic's ready to roll up his sleeves and get to
work with me on his stories next week.  -- Hope he
doesn't mind all the blue marks I've made on them.  Hope
he can compartmentalize the editor a good safe distance
from the friend.  (As a boy Vic too had a fox terrorist
-- I mean, terrier! -- that was truly an unintentional
error! -- had a fox terrier, I say, as a pet, and he
lost it in a similar fashion.  His was Spot, mine Pogo.

[ Jyze of the Heavenly Year : Red Horse ]

He also had a pet chicken named Henry and one night
after dinner he discovered Spot had just eaten Henry.
Only a few bloody feathers remained.)



------

29

------


     Is this cement animal at whose side I'm sitting a
dog?  I'm assuming it is.  A guard dog.  Two of them, in
fact, one stationed on each side of the steps here at
the front entrance of the big new building -- commercial
on the first two floors and residential on the upper
five -- on the main east-west drag in the AQ.  On the
other hand they could be lions.  But they're definitely
white, reflecting that this is a Metal Year, and they're
fierce, with teeth bared, and to me they look like --
Dogs, yes, capped.  "Temple Dogs" even, maybe -- which
would be apropos because that's the type of Dog
associated with the year 1970, which is year 29 of this
extended (sixty-year) Heavenly Year.  And it's also just
right for guarding the entrance to this jyze cluster.
     The temple here is devoted to commerce.  Fittingly
enough!  Four lanes of traffic meanwhile course by, much
of it consisting of departing baseball fans.  Half a
block west stands the freeway atop its familiar
colonnaded overpass, with ceremonial carp swimming and
dragonflies zipping round and round the supporting
columns of bright yellow and orange.  Directly across
the street here, shoppers rummage in the large sidewalk
bins of one of the many warehouse produce marts in this
part of the upper AQ -- colorful mounds of melons and
apples, peaches and grapefruits, along with many other
fruits and vegetables with only Asian names that I'd
have to see the labels in English on the bins to

remember.  And all that produce is protected from the elements by blue tarps and flowery beach umbrellas.

And it's raining out there.  More like misting actually, but produce still needs protection and so do walkers and so do jyzers.  And this jyzer right here has not only the snarling Temple Dogs -- that's the moniker I've settled on -- for protection but also a high arched plaster overhang.  Also helpful is the fact it's Sunday and most of the businesses in the new building seem to be closed for the day -- or otherwise I'd probably have been chased away long before now.

Mostly gray overcast.  The orange-brick dot-com castle atop south hill, prominently visible above the roof of the small set-back Vietnamese cafe (formerly a service station) to the left of the produce mart, is aswirl in the gray like a massive Tibetan mountaintop monastery.  A typical J-town day in the season when overall typicality is least likely to show itself.

A metal expansion joint on the freeway is beating out arrhythmic percussive accompaniment for these words, like, say, a broken background tape for a do-it-yourself hip-hopper.  If a trailer truck goes by, that joint gets three, four, even five stupendous whacks.

Earlier today Z-wiff and I visited Pista, the big Filipino summer festival, in its usual site at a lakeside park on the south end.  An hour of wandering there left us thoroughly soaked: mist and condensation droplets from the tall trees (which were gorgeous today, almost like a scene from "Snow Falling on Cedars") -- those droplets working inward on our clothes, sweat working outward.  Yet the crowd was larger than ever, numbering in the thousands.  Filipinos, after all, comprise the state's largest non-European ethnic, as opposed to racial, minority.  And can any other state say that?  Not that we know of.

I love wandering around at Filipino events.  For one thing, do the women of any other USAn ethnic group dress even half as sexy?  (That's the Spanish part of the heritage at work, Z says, and she's definitely one who knows about dressing sexy.)  For another, nowhere

will you find more mixed couples to study for clues to
the impression you might be making yourself as part of
such a couple or how you might make a better one.  For a
third, you've got all those tightly knit family groups,
often with an elder or two in tow.  Today we saw several
in which the elders were probably no older than
ourselves and yet they were all tending to what appeared
to be great-grandchildren.  And then there are the
glitzy show-biz spectacles on the main stage: only
Filipinos can compete with gays for camping it up
Hollywood style (especially those Filipinos who are gay
themselves, although maybe they shouldn't count because
the combo is just too unfair).  And finally there's the
fact that Z seems to know approximately every third
person and it's always great fun to see how they react
to me -- today one woman said, "Oh, how could I forget
you -- I've seen you at these things for the past twenty
years!" (in fact I attended my first Pista five years
ago, and I've missed at least one since then).  -- And
also Z feels compelled to buy something at every booth
that's occupied or sponsored by someone she knows.  This
is one reason she may be J. City's champion hoarder of
unwearable T-shirts and unlistenable CDs.

Last night was the big downtown torchlight parade,
the start of the main week of the summer festival.  Up
to half a million attendees were expected.  We thought
we'd be among them, but the closest we came was watching
about three minutes' worth on the tube -- and that was
plenty.  Not just for me, but also for Z.  She hates the
crowds, even on the tube.  I hate the tube but I don't
mind the crowds themselves when seen in person, or at
least not for the torchlight parade.  I like to watch
the parade turning the last corners down in the HQ and
then breaking up outside the stadiums.  Parking's not a
problem for me because I can just walk down, and of
course she could too.  But the hours don't fit with her
schedule -- the parade doesn't even start until her
usual bedtime, which at this time of year is right
around dusk -- and since the parade's shift a couple of
years ago from Friday to Saturday night I no longer have

a chance to watch it on my way in to, or while taking a
break from, work, or not as a rule anyway.

I'll leave my annual rant about the summer festival
itself until later.  Suffice it to say the part I go for
is already over.  Now starts the militaristic part,
which this year will no doubt be worse than ever, a kind
of enactment in spectacle mode of the post-9/11 Patriot
Act.  (Rumor has it the grand jury will be tackling a
couple of new terrorist cases this week.  Scoping those
into good clean USAnese, what could be more patriotic
than that?)

Today, by the way, is also Parents Day.  "In what
country?" Z-wiff asked when I told her.  "Ours!" I
declared; "It just hasn't caught on yet."  And then she
scored big with me by wondering aloud if Congress should
declare an official Heavenly Year holiday for all those
turning sixty.

-- So yesterday we initiated what will likely
become our new Saturday routine.  After I was good and
awake, well coffee'd up though not yet as thoroughly
newspapered up as I'd've preferred, we motored about
fifteen miles northward to Benita's place to see Mama E.
Our visit didn't go very well -- she was back to a
semidepressed state, showing little interest in us or
her new surroundings -- but then we weren't expecting
miracles.  (Even so, Z-wiff said I looked "stricken" the
whole time.  If true, though, it was because I was
trying to get across to Mama E how disappointed I'd be
if she didn't at least make an effort to adjust to her
new life.)

Then, after saying our farewells until my next
planned visit on Tuesday -- when I'll be on my own -- Z
and I did a drive-in fast-food dinner, a stop at two
shoestores in search of slippers that'll fit Z's
nonstandardly shaped feet, and a grocery run on north
hill before finally heading home, skirting downtown
because the crowd was already massing for the parade.  Z
said she'll no longer be scheduling social events for us
on Saturdays.  And since it's tough for us to socialize
together on any other day owing to our conflicting work

regimes, we'll obviously be cutting back on our mutual
social life, at least for a while.

Is this a bad thing?  Not necessarily!  But for
Heavenly Year jyze it might be.  Jyze without a social
dimension is jyze diminished.  But -- perhaps other
dimensions can be discovered, explored, enhanced.

And so -- Temple Dogs, you did well.  Many people
have come by, some of them distinctly odd characters.  A
few fairly radiated hostility.  Yet none succeeded in
distracting me more than momentarily.  And the produce
mart successfully closed for the day -- with all the
bins rolled inside it's now just a nondescript warehouse
over there fronting on an ordinary sidewalk.  Thunkety-
thunk, traffic continues to sail by on the freeway and
also on the main drag down below, and in both cases it's
still mostly outbound.  A few weeks back a Chiusan woman
was run over at the crosswalk half a block to the east;
this stirred up a community storm and now the city has
vowed something will be done because the AQ does too
matter and this street is not just a getaway ramp for
burban-bound commuter traffic.  But it'll take time
because complex interests are at play, to be sure, with
numerous powerful oxen to avoid goring.

So Temple Dogs of the AQ, I'm leaving but you've
still got your work cut out for you.  Just as always.


[+3]


-- Word's out: fleet's in.  So I've sought the
protection of another pair of Temple Dogs.  They're
the only accessible ones I know about in the immediate
area.  They guard the front-stairs entrance to a small
Chinese office complex in the southernmost part of the
AQ.  Plainly what they're meant to do is protect this
establishment from people like me, especially at times
like now -- midafternoon, Hour of the Monkey (four
p.m.).  But I'm enlisting them for another purpose.

Festival promoters say we're lucky to have a fleet
visit this year.  According to them, the half-dozen big

gray warships (with the biggest, an aircraft carrier,
due in tomorrow) are needed on the front lines to do
battle with the far-flung terrorists.  Those evildoers,
of course, have no ships at all, except maybe a few
small motorboats they can plow into our warships when
they're moored in foreign ports -- those of our
neocolonies, for instance, and tributary states.  But
the truth is the ships are needed more here to serve as
jingo drums.  Otherwise they wouldn't be here.

A fine blue summer day so never mind.  The last day
of the solar month named after the supreme leader of
another big empire, albeit in an antique era, a certain
Julius.  That means it's also the last day I'll be
living in a solar month in which I won't be either a
sexagenarian or a post-sexagenarian.  I'm enjoying this
fact conceptually.  Tomorrow the burden of venerability
increases -- though so too do all the attendant honors
and rewards.  I wish!  -- And I'm vowing right now to go
proactive in trying to goad some into being.  Just as a
pastime, I'm saying.

Meanwhile markets are yo-yoing.  Down ten percent
one week, up ten percent the next.  Nothing like this
has been seen, we're told, since 1933.  Congress churns
out laws to crack down on rogue CEOs -- ha!  Meanwhile,
as predicted earlier in these pages, various high-
ranking cabalists -- meaning in this case the
president's cabinet -- step up the war talk.  Yup, they
say, maybe we'd better move the launch a little earlier,
to this autumn, perhaps right around election time.  So
now such a prospect is being truculently bruited about.
Is it really possible a more bellicose bunch ever held
the reins in this deeply militaristic country of ours?
(which laughably likes to think it's irenic to the
extreme except when its hand is forced.)

Tomorrow the Blue Angels -- a name highly apt for
this era of resumed Christian crusades -- start their
practice flights, roaring by at about five hundred feet
above a good number of J. City hoods, including the one
next to ours.  Every year they're my wake-up nightmare
for three or four days, usually about ninety minutes

before my alarm goes off.  White-noise machines and
earplugs are useless before the onslaught.  Looking
straight east from our balcony we can see the jets
flying at its level or slightly above, the wings
seemingly within easy slingshot range.

I'm a day late with this entry because I took
Monday night off to see the ball game with brother Rob.
Sunday night I wound up at Vic's loft for several hours.
Yesterday I went out to see Mama E -- with whom there's
a new crisis du jour today.  And tonight I'll have to be
down at the scope office to start work on two full days
of grand jury.

On all of which more later, except maybe the grand
jury.  Yesterday I learned the terrorist cases have been
transferred to a jury on the far coast, southern sector.
In that particular district they're known for patriotic
pliancy to the max -- or to be plain about it, for
hangin' juries, including the grand kind.  What will
replace those cases here I don't know, but apparently
there is something.  (And here I sit being gaped at by
passing workers and clients.  Have the Temple Dogs never
before today allowed anyone of Cawkish stripe to sit on
these stairs?  This is the impression I'm getting.)

-- Fifty yards to the right and up the equivalent
of a couple of stories, the freeway and a row of
sentinel evergreens.  Fifty yards to the left and down a
couple of stories, a school playground featuring
splendid Chinese murals which Vic H. cautiously told me
he much admires and then walked this back with "well, up
to a point, let's say."  A noodle-making company stands
across the street; it boasts big tiles on the facade
with roses apparently hand-painted on them.  Of the
downtown skyline only the upper third of the tallest of
Jyze City's numerous terrorist-attractor structures,
"America's bank," is visible from here.

But these chucks are made for walkin'.  Two miles
to go before I can scope.  And on the way in I'll pump
some iron to build Temple Dog strength.  And shower and
shave so as to be able to pass the scope-office scruff
test (though actually it's only in my mind -- unlike all

         [ Jyze of the Heavenly Year : Red Horse ]

these other outrages, I tell ya).
                         *         *
     -- Z-wiff astonishes again.  Arriving home at the
usual time I find a gift from her on my chair.  Not just
any old gift.  It's something I eyed longingly for weeks
in the show window at the wooden-toy shop -- and never
mentioned to her.  Thirty bucks, too much for me,
especially this month (though now I'm in the clear on my
bills, if only just barely -- and of course meanwhile
the cycle starts all over again).
     A window full of foot-high cast-iron (not wood)
replicas of the ancient Chinese terra-cotta grave-
tending soldiers.  And their horses!  The horses a dark
gray verging on black.  And tonight I find one of them
standing proud on the coffee table in front of my chair.
Better by far than any White Temple Dog.  -- And a
loving note from Z.
     Somehow she knew I would covet such a Black Horse
and cherish it forever -- even in the grave or from my
scattered ashen state.  This Horse will be appointed to
look after my remains.  (It's dusty or looks dusty -- in
fact looks ancient, as if it really was dug up from a
two-millennia-old grave.)
     Oy.  And such timing!  Just as we cross into the
solar version of the Heavenly Month!
     This halfway through the fifth watch.  A cooler
night than most of late.  I'm holding down the corner of
the couch by the greenery and the puffing locomotive of
the Fookin' Fogies Lub Klock (also purchased at the
wooden-toy shop and made entirely of brightly colored
plastic).  Cup'a health wine.  The far-coast paper says
we all need more vitamin D than we're getting.  I'm warm
enough in just a sleeveless henley.  This year I'm
seeing a bit more sun than usual -- just because more's
been in view -- but as a nightscoper and daytime sleeper
I still need much more D than the average pink person.
     As predicted, at grand jury they're turning the
heat up on a couple of CEOs.  We've got our own local
version of a massive accounting scandal.  A tough job,
rapid-fire quoting from documents without saying exactly

where the quotes are coming from in the documents and
intermixing ad-lib paraphrases with true quotes -- a
nightmare to scope -- but at 250-plus pages it's saving
my ass on this month's rent.

And the baseball game.  It was on Olsok's Eve two
nights ago that Rob and I saw it.  He'd never heard of
the holiday but he knew about the king it's named after
back in the old country -- a local guy who lived just
across the inlet from Sandefjords-Stolen a thousand
years ago.  Was he the one who welcomed in the
Christians or the last one to try to fight them off?
Damned if I remember and I neglected to ask Rob.
"Viking King."  It's quite possible some loyal
Sandefjord-family minions went down with him in the
great battle.

A perfect evening for baseball.  We sat high in the
upper deck of the right-field bleachers where the view
of the bay and the sound and the mountains beyond was
superlative at sunset.  Rob's much more into our J. City
team than I had previously realized and has been, he
tells me, since about seven years ago.  It took him a
full decade after his arrival here in '85 to mourn the
loss of his Centropolis favorites sufficiently and then
transfer his allegiance.  He also now knows much more
than I do about what's going on in the baseball world.
I found it odd suddenly being the rube after growing up
as the one in the know on just about everything in his
eyes because I was ten years older.  He brought along a
paper bag full of snacks -- grapes, chips, sandwiches --
and we nibbled from that bag all the way to the end.  I
confess I enjoyed observing the antics of a nearby group
of baseball fanatics from Japan at least as much as I
did the game itself.  The loud train whistles sounding
during the national anthem were also a kick.  No Olsok's
Eve bonfires, however, were visible in the nearby hills.
-- And of course the nearest of those hills, looming
before us about a mile away as we climbed the staircase
to the upper deck, was our very own, Z's and mine, south
hill.

It was on Olsok's Day, if there really be such a

day, that I drove up to Mama E's new place on my own for
the first time.  The best moment occurred when I asked
what she'd like to do during future visits.  She gave me
a hand signal that said bye-bye to the adult family
home.  Ouddaheah!  Funny eyebrow waggles.  Cracked me
up.  But then she allowed as how escaping Benita's place
wouldn't be possible for her: she can't get around much
anymore, often needs help even to make it to the toilet
(and sometimes doesn't get all the way there regardless).
Admittedly I was relieved when Tony arrived to help usher
her to the dinner table using her walker -- it meant I
could leave.  It's not clear she's lost the will to live,
it's not certain she's continuing to deteriorate as
rapidly as before, but I fear this is how it is in both
cases.  Our hopes of at least stabilizing her situation
for a while may not bear out.

And then back two days to that terrific Sunday
evening at Vic's.  We always sit in a cluster of small
chairs in the center of the loft living area, drink
scotch, talk on and on about so many things.  On this
night it was mostly his stories and the potential for a
terrific autobiographical book that shines in them.  I
think I helped him see some of that potential which up
until then he hadn't quite grokked.  I told him I'd help
him out with editing and constructive criticism -- all
the way to the end.  And Jean seemed warmer to me -- she
even got some lipstick on my shirt while giving me a big
tight long-laster of a hug.  Then she was off to deal
with some unexplained emergency -- but was the book I
saw in her hand a bible?  That would explain a few
things -- but also make me wonder about some others.

Vic's a few months shy of seventy-three, as much
older than me as I'm older than Lady U.  He's had
several tough health setbacks in recent years but seems
okay now and is still very sharp mentally.  I just hope
he can stay that way for a good long time -- and for at
least that long I don't start losing it myself.  I see a
rare kind of friendship developing here.  You're lucky
if it happens to you two or three times in your life.

-- And that's going to have to do it for the Temple

Dog.  One last howl and on we move.  To bed!  (But look
at that marvelous Black Horse, will ya?  Jes look!)
    Arrrooooo....




------

30

------


    Here's something new yet not so different.  And in
any event: short.  Because work awaits.  Heaps of it.
But enough time to stop here at the tiny four-columns
park for a kwikjyze -- to kick off in just the right way
the Silver Pig entry and summer anti-festival weekend,
I'll call it.  Because, yes, we're at the solar entrance
to the Heavenly Month.
    I trekked around the back side of east hill, that's
what.  Instead of turning west after crossing the high
bridge and hiking down through the AQ as I usually do, I
kept on going straight north, up past the Jyze City U.
campus, about fourteen blocks in all, then turned west
down the commercial corridor with its many hip cafes and
taverns and boutiques to -- here.
    In four and a half years of walking in to work from
south hill I've never done this before.  Why not?  Beats
me.  It's a block or two longer, I suppose, because the
other way involves two long diagonals, but it's also
somewhat more level.  -- Well no, I always like going
through the heart of the AQ, that's the main reason why.
But this route also has its points of interest.  (Of
course if I want to stop at the hideaway the AQ route is
much shorter.  But I don't always want to do that.)
    All we have left here are the columns, the four
just mentioned, with a dozen good-size leafy trees
grown up around them.  Four benches.  Greek-like ruins.
Excellent close-up hillside view of the north end of

downtown, with the greenly overgrown convention center
and freeway park to the left, the frisbee-twirling-atop-
golf-tee icon to the right, the freeway itself running
in its deep cement ravine just beyond the columns, out
of sight from here but emphatically not out of sound.
     Setting clear enough?  Ha -- as now another gaggle
of picture-takers arrives.  Convivial I'm not today.
Grouchy's the word.  But forgivably so, I insist, given
the Blue Angels' sleep-destructive fly-bys of the past
two days -- with two more still to go.  And the grand-
jury scoping this week is again at maximum degree of
difficulty.  Half is a health-club-equipment scandal,
the other half still more alleged Islamic terrorism.
Aptly enough today's OMP went with the first story for
its front-page headline, the FAP with the second for
its.  When this sort of thing happens I'm always swept
by the delusion that I'm Mr. Insider, but it never lasts
for more than about three seconds.
     Leaving home this afternoon I at first walked west
across the hilltop itself in hopes of catching a glimpse
of the fleet docked along the river and the southern
reaches of the bay.  And was surprisingly in luck.  Awed
by the hugeness and the ominousness of all that floating
gray steel with the big gun barrels pointing every which
way, including at south hill.  Straight ahead far below,
longer than the combined width of the two stadiums just
to its north, the black silhouette of the aircraft
carrier.  It forcefully reminded me of the carriers in
my model fleet of half a century ago, when I was gazing
down from my bed as they cruised the rug on the floor.
(Not that I haven't seen these silhouettes before in J-
town, especially during my ferry days.  But because of
the angle, this one appeared to have dropped down in the
middle of the south end like a huge new building.  The
river's fairly narrow at that point -- the water not
visible at all from my hilltop vantage.  For that reason
the scene down there also recalled photos of ships that
appear to be stranded in the middle of the desert as
they pass through a completely obscured canal.)
     What's it cost to maintain all this armed might?

[ Jyze of the Heavenly Year : Red Horse ]

Well, as we already knew, more than what the next
sixteen biggest national spenders pay for theirs --
combined!  Of course without this might we'd lose much
of our world dominance and our economy would go kerplunk
and the billionaires wouldn't be as rich and lots of
folks couldn't afford home swimming pools or SUVs.  And
yet maybe then life on earth wouldn't be doomed?  The
odds of human survival would go up significantly?
     -- I'll probably have to be scoping every night
this weekend, through Monday.  Yet tonight I'll be
seeing June at two a.m. for a bar-exam rundown; Saturday
Z and I will be visiting Mama E and then meeting Jay and
Melanie to see "Sunshine State" (a rare late-show
outing); Sunday evening Kar might be dropping by the
hideaway to read Sandefjord family letters from the
thirties and forties; and Monday evening I'll be meeting
up with Vic.  Busy, busy.  Hey, what's this, all of a
sudden I've got a second life!  (But do I have a second
wind for it?  Well, yeah, I think so.  Surely I can huff
one up.  Huff and puff while you still can, sez I.)
     Sun angling in.  At first I was sitting in the
shadow cast by a column but the shadow's gradually
shifted to my left.  My presence here is now fully
revealed -- I'm all lit up.  Parades of hill-dwellers
trudge by on two sides, heading home from work, mostly
the young and tattooed.
     -- And before I go I must pass along this sad news:
Mama E's dementia is progressing.  In Doc F's view it's
irreversible.  She "fell off a cliff," as he put it,
when her brother and her step-daughter Camilla died last
spring and winter.  Z-wiff says she, Z, is now able to
let herself feel the sadness more.  She'd hoped to be
able to have some good times with Mama E and fate hasn't
allowed for much of that, so she's thinking she'll start
doing things with her anyway -- taking her for rides and
whatnot -- even if most of the pleasure of it (maybe
all) will be lost on Mama E.  Last night on the way home
they stopped for burgers at one of our favorite spots
and that seemed to work out well.  Tomorrow we're
planning to hit Mama E's longtime favorite, a certain

franchise burger joint (in fact the same chain whose
ferry-dock franchise provides most of my softie cones
and whose Centropolis franchises used to provide several
of Mama E's chief hangouts of the past twenty years).
    And that's gotta be it, kwikjyze kaput.


[+2]


    Midsummer's night -- if I'm figuring right.  Nobody
bothers to keep us posted on these things.  And it's the
middle of that night.  Bottom and the gang are cavorting
out in the shrubbery -- or is it just a couple of lusty
cats?  A cheese-slicer-thin arc of moon is rising
(though doing so semi-stealthily behind roiling mist of
varying thickness) -- meaning the Sheep Month is just
about done.  A night or two of dramatic darkness will
follow and then -- BLOOEY!  Lunar Heavenly Month!
    I've kept quiet up to now about this being the "Pig
in the Garden" cluster.  But I just made the rounds of
our indoor potted garden, touching each of these leafy
beauties with the long wandlike spout of Z's ancient
brown watering pitcher.  I'm root, root, rooting around
for the home team.  Strange how I enjoy so much this
watering and plant tending.  My boyhood years offered no
hint of such a predilection.  A diviner back then
might've predicted I'd go for penny poker and board
games in my fogey phase.
    This from the black armchair, J-book spread across
the usual hairy bare pale pink Cawk thighs.  Here's a
small blue mug of cheap cabernet I've already been
nursing for almost two hours.  For a change the radio's
off even before the morning news comes on.  Balcony
door's open just a crack.  Streetlight's glowing at the
center of our biggest window, above the couch, but
otherwise all's black out there except for a few
scattered hillside sparkles in the distance.
    This chair's a wreck but no way can I give it up.
When the springs failed I stuffed the base with
newspapers.  When the seatcover wasted away I replaced

it with a triple layer of towels topped by a mint-
condition forest-green one.  Over time the contours have
adapted themselves to my three or four favorite sitting
positions, including the one where I rest my right leg
on the right chair arm.  A reading lamp with a three-way
bulb hangs inches above my head (Z's afraid my pineal
gland will be overstimulated as a result but concedes no
major symptoms of this have appeared so far).  Tables on
both sides bear magazines, books, pens, clips, post-its,
stapler, notebooks, a cat-face-shaped cupholder made by
Kat and Z working together and presented to me on my
birthday last year.  The usual low rough-hewn coffee
table standing at the center of our cluster of couch and
two armchairs serves also at one end as a hassock for
me, though at most times it's so piled with items I have
to settle for the extreme corners.  At the center of
that coffee table stands the splendid new Black Horse.

    Ah, such a night!  Midsummer and I'm midway through
the cycle of sixty.  With the "wrapping" of this entry
it'll be thirty animals down, thirty to go.  But because
the final cluster will be a repeat of the Black Horse --
that's what the Heavenly Year's all about, the cycle
beginning to repeat itself -- because of that, I say,
the actual midpoint of the book will appear halfway
through the next cluster, with thirty animals out of the
way before that cluster and thirty to go after it.  At
that point my life will already be half done, bookwise.

    To transfer this "half done" concept to real life,
I'd have to hang on until I reach what's said to be the
current maximum age for humans -- meaning in order for
the years I've already lived to constitute half my life.
So there it is again, the fabled 120.  Does even one
person in a billion make it to a second Heavenly Year?
Well, but then maybe before long science will have some
of us (the ones with big, big bucks) making it to third
and fourth Heavenly Years.  Maybe most of us, who knows.
My generation may be one of the last for whom the notion
that living to age sixty makes any kind of celebratory
sense at all.  -- But then again, as noted, the odds
that the human race will soon self-destruct are high and

daily increasing.  So all this is just the sheerest
Heavenly Year fantasy.  And why not?  The transience of
it all!  The effrontery!  Have at it, human mayflies!

   So it's August.  Congress shuts down, the cabal
chieftain goes off to his ranch -- in both cases for the
whole month this year.  So can we maybe ease off on
expanding the empire for a while?  -- Unlikely, correct.

   For a late snack I indulged in a huge bowl of fresh
blueberries with vanilla ice cream mixed in -- and a
couple of cookies June laid on me Friday during what
will probably be the last of her post-midnight drop-ins.
This time it was just for bar-exam postmortems.  If it
turns out she failed this one, she'll just keep trying
-- she doesn't give up.  As she said herself, it doesn't
matter when she passes it because whenever it is, now or
ten years from now, she'll still probably be "the
world's oldest beginning lawyer."  Today she's moving
out of her student dorm room and returning to her
house in the burbs.  Last year's dot-com stock-market
crash pretty much decimated her fortune, she says --
only she knows how big it really was, or is now -- and
so she'll be hanging on to her city job until she passes
the bar and can find attorney work that pays roughly the
same or better.  Then, I'm sure, we'll be seeing even
less of her.  In the past four years June and I have
spent hundreds of hours together, most of them right
here between the hours of two and four or five in the
morning.  It's been one of the odder relationships of my
life and of hers as well -- maybe it would make the
upper tier of all-time odd relationships, period, here
or anywhere.  No matter: we've both relished it.

   In other social news of the personal type, Jay and
Melanie canceled out on the movie last night and Kar on
the office visit tonight, and a good thing too, in both
cases: I needed all that time for scoping and could've
used even more.  Mama E wasn't too demented or too
depressed, and an intriguing flare-up occurred when she
insisted on our taking back Z's framed high-school
flamingo painting for fear someone would steal it off
the wall at Benita's place.  Z broke into tears and

said, "I'll cry all night if you don't keep it here."
Mama E's reply: "I'll cry even more than that if you
leave it here."  For a few moments they were locked into
what was clearly a replay of a lifelong dynamic.  But
then Z, recalling her recent realization that her
mother's behavior should no longer be treated as
intentional or manipulative but simply as symptomatic of
her dementia (even when it may involve an element of
intention or manipulation as well), gave in.  -- And
after we left Mama E we stopped at the far-north book
arcade for dinner and an extended browse.  And both
mornings, for the second weekend in a row, some real
good loving, complete with "invag money shots."  Papa
got his pop back!  And mama got her squeezebox
squeezin'!

     And tonight a note.  For the first time in two
weeks Z checked her e-mail and found a ten-day-old
message from Elgie saying he'd like me to edit his law-
school application essay and to give him a call any
night after nine.  Z's just too distracted these days
for this e-mail system we set up with Elgie to work as
planned.  Snail mail would be a lot faster -- and
preferable too, at least for me.  But I don't think the
kid would go for it.  Handwriting skills are
disappearing, or so we hear.  My J-stick makes me a
dinosaur twice over.  This is almost as odd as the
plant-watering -- and to think that as a kid I was out
there practically on the scientific cutting edge (among
my peer group, I'm saying).

     From Elgie's mother, still no word.  I'll have to
ask him what's going on with her.  (I make note of this
just so I'll feel the surge of deja vu that comes with
doing so.  And sure enough, I'm aswim in it.)

     Speaking of things at least primitively scientific,
today is day number 2,452,800 by Julian count, and it's
also the anniversary of the Julian count itself, its
inception, or anyway the birthday of its founder.  The
count runs in cycles of just under eight millennia
before it starts over, and that'll be happening, in
theory, in another dozen or so centuries.  The Julian

period began in 4713 B.C.E., which is to say it's
roughly the age of the Chinese calendar plus the
Christian calendar plus a lucky 13.
     -- And just to show I'm not neglecting all
financial details in this cluster, my rent at the
hideaway received its annual COLA bump this month.  It
rose all of two bucks, from $181 to $183.  So once again
the bursting of the dot-com/tech bubble shows a good
side for me.


                       ------

                        31

                       ------


     At the center.  Center of the annal, center of the
year, center of the city too.  In theory, anyway, as far
as the city part of that goes.  Downtown plaza, the
triangular public square, sitting on the stone stage at
its center, near the fountain, just as -- right this
moment -- the water shuts off and the cascade curtain
disappears except for a few odd trickles and sneeze-like
afterbursts.
     Am I centered?  Am I centered?
     All around on all three sides, big buildings.  Poor
light here, from the globe lamps shining along the
street behind me; that's why I'm sitting on the stage
itself rather than on one of the steps leading up to it.
Those steps offer more shelter from the bay breeze,
which is chilly tonight, but up here the light's better
and I'm safer, I think, since I'm out in the open -- "on
stage."  Down in the grove toward the south end of the
plaza, the acute angle of the triangle, dark shapes are
moving about, not identifiable from here.  But
regardless I'm always on the alert outdoors at night on
the city streets -- I'd be a true urban crazy not to be.

[ Jyze of the Heavenly Year : Red Horse ]

     Those first words "at the center" hit the page at
exactly 11:53 by the jeweler's clock that's clearly
visible a block down the avenue.  That's when the lunar
year crossed the midpoint.  The calculation's mine,
though, and could be wrong, just as I now think my
midsummer night's calculation was wrong.  Probably last
night was true midsummer's night.  But no matter, I'm
going with my original calculation in both cases.  It's
another of those Heavenly Year prerogatives.
     Strictly speaking the new lunar month -- Heavenly
Monkey Month for the J-slinger -- doesn't start until
shortly past noon, meaning later today by Gregorian
count since we're now eight minutes past midnight.  So
I'm figuring I'll make this a two-part entry.  I'm even
planning to get up early so I can be there for the
rollover J-person-on-the-spot.
     Meanwhile it's apropos to be writing in such poor
light.  The new month begins with the dark moon, which
is to say no moon at all.  Out in all that darkness --
and in this J-book too, and here in the triangle, and
maybe over in the grove with the shadowy movements --
the hungry ghosts are gathering, as they should be for
the start of hungry-ghost time.  -- And the chill wind
is apropos as well, along with a few tumbling fallen
leaves I can see here and there, because, even though by
the pope's measure we're still three and a half days
short of mid August -- we've just now crossed from the
Gregorian 12th to the 13th -- the calendar from the
Celestial Kingdom says today is "Beginning of Autumn."
     Between eight p.m. and half past eleven I was up in
the scope office rushing out a job.  Just as I was
leaving, Chun appeared with her hoover.  From here I can
see the lights are still blazing on the seventeenth
floor of our building -- a block and a half south --
which means she's still working up there.  My pal.
Speaks maybe a few dozen words of English.  From time to
time she brings me Chinese goodies to eat -- she seems
to think she's training me to appreciate a superior
cuisine.  It's a kick and so's she.  In her mid forties,
with two daughters in their twenties, an accountant

husband -- they live on south hill a couple miles south
of us (learning even these minimal facts took months).
Warm and friendly yet also very proper.  Sexy too -- but
I'm a true-blue married guy and scarcely even notice,
except for the record and purposes of eroto-aesthetic
appreciation.  Same for her in the way she sees me, or
at least so I'd like to think (because so she's
indicated, seemingly, mostly by gesture).

Three days, three noteworthy events.  (As a medicaid van shrieks by, lights flashing, slows briefly and
whoops goonishly at the intersection.)  Long talk with
Vic Monday night, long visit with Mama E Tuesday
afternoon, long phone talk -- two and a half hours! --
with Elgie Tuesday night.  More later on those, or I
sure do hope so.

Meanwhile what news from the big stage?  Iraq
"debate" intensifies.  What kind of attack?  How big?
When?  -- But not whether.  It's a done deal, senators
say.  Outrageous!  Any voices opposing an attack are
excluded from the "debate."  For the current era this is
a typical outrage, of course, but that fact serves only
to make the outrage even greater.

And the economic crisis appears to be deepening.
Now South America looks ready to go blooey.  Will our
own recession here, thought to be over as of a few
months ago, turn into a "double dip"?  Suddenly "double
dip" is on every lip.  And I say: read those lips!

Oh, and that other Mideast crisis has been
continuing all along.  A wave of suicide bombings in
Israel as desperate outgunned Palestinians try to fight
back from the occupied lands.  Israel grinds down with
weapons we USAns are paying for.  Now our own secretary
of defense -- the man from Gatewood!  my homey! -- tells
the world those occupied lands long ago became part of
Israel; it won them fair and square in the '67 war.
Does this mean might makes right?  Does it mean, for
example, Japan and the Philippines belong to the USA
now?  Eastern Europe to Russia?  Stay tuned for details.

This entry, I should note, comes under the aegis of
the Black Rat.  Another cycle of twelve is launching.

[ Jyze of the Heavenly Year : Red Horse ]

On Hiroshima Day, which was yesterday, I could find
not a single pundit or feature writer linking the
200,000-plus civilian deaths intentionally caused by our
nuking of that city with the issue of civilian
casualties caused by terrorists -- the three thousand at
the twin towers, for instance.
-- And already it's one a.m.  I've paused too often
as people wandered by.  Groups of three or four, lone
individuals, some less then friendly but none so far
making any serious trouble.  Two pushing big grocery
carts heavily laden with personal belongings, one with a
black spaniel leashed to it.  A guy sucking at a
milkshake through a straw walked around the borders of
the stage here as if on a tightrope -- did it twice --
both times veering off at the last second to miss me by
a couple of feet.
Public square.  City center.  Hot vortex -- though
mostly empty at the moment.  A guy cleaning with a hose
now.  No cars in view, no other movement.  Still, quiet
center.
Yeeha, for this far!  -- And now the bus.

*              *

So I made it out of the sack by Monkey time with a
quarter hour to spare.  The jyzer's doin' the Monkey,
yes he is!  -- But for how long, I'm wondering.  A whiff
of mortality here.  I wake up with a pain in my gut and
it's not like any I've ever had before.  Upper stomach.
It's not bend-over bad but it's worrisome anyway.
Where'd this come from, I wanna know.  What's going on?
The hope is it's gas gathering at an unusual spot.
Antacid pills provoke a few belches -- maybe that's a
good sign.  Sitting on the throne does nothing.  So you
wonder: an ulcer?  Stomach cancer?  Heart attack cue?
Up until now the gut has been low on my list of
likely mortality gotcha zones.
-- A few more small belches.  This, all will agree,
is an inelegant way of kicking off the true Heavenly
Month.  But that word "apropos" pops up again.  "Puts
the fear of the reaper in ya."  Yeah, well, but I
thought it was already there.

[ Jyze of the Heavenly Year : Red Horse ]

So then I ask:  Is this how the hungry ghosts make
their presence known?  Again, "apropos."  They're
hitting the hunger center.  "Hitting" almost literally:
like the reverbs from a punch in the solar plexus.

But easing, I think maybe.  As I sit here hunched
over at the dining table in unit 203.  Sunny day and it
seems strange in this room, I suppose in part because I
so rarely see it at this hour.  Angles of light are
odd.  Sounds coming in from outside also.

-- Now the biggest belch so far.  This is hopeful.
I can start to see the comical side.

Lying to my left atop the table is the new issue of
one of the weekly newsmagazines which I couldn't resist
picking up at the ORB last night.  Its cover story is
"Visions of Heaven," with details from a centuries-old
oil painting featuring angels and cherubim and whatnot.
The subtitle: "How Views of Paradise Inspire -- and
Influence -- Christians, Muslims and Jews."  The chief
influence we're seeing these days, it's obvious, is far
from Heavenly.  But then what else is new?

To leap from the horrifically sublime to the merely
pathetic, last night was our yearly SHAN (South Hill
Alliance of Neighbors) block party.  As in previous
years, the east-west cross street to our north was
closed for a block, hotdogs and burgers were grilled, a
Girl Scout troupe did fancy drill-team exercises.  Fifty
or sixty folks showed up, mostly drawn by the free grub
provided by the SHAN hardcore, of whom Z-wiff is one.
Unfortunately I couldn't make it this year.  Sorry as
they are, I still enjoy these little get-togethers.  And
Z put in just a thirty-minute "cameo plus."  I forgot to
ask her if terrorism was the theme this year, like
neighborhood crime watch was the past couple of years.

Matt B., owner of the two-story motel-like
apartment house a block north of us, was there.  I saw
him earlier in the day as he sprayed water on a new
concrete sidewalk he's putting in.  "I keep trying," he
joked, "but I just can't get this stuff to grow."  My
reply: "Have you tried nightsoil?"  (Matt's bald spot is
growing, though, I noticed, and maybe as compensation

his remaining hair is longer -- almost as long as mine.)
And the large peace sign gracing the side of his shed
sort of like a big bull's eye is freshly repainted,
truly an act of courage in these belligerent times.  The
door of the shed was open and I could see his monster
motorcycle in there looking all dusty.  Matt's just back
from a series of major out-of-state biker gatherings.
He said he tries to hit two or three every year.  And
from a letter of his published in one of the local
dailies last year I know the man can turn a mean phrase.
His values are an odd mix of hippie, biker, and
landlord.  One of his favorite pastimes is to wander
around the hood looking for opportunities to gossip or
kibitz -- if you want to know something about what's
going on around here, he's the one to ask.  And he's
probably put in more work than anyone else on our new
hood P-patch, which remains, however, a work very much
in progress.  It's across from our homewardbound bus
stop, laid out on a hillside too steep for a street.
     -- Had no idea jyze would be taking me there.
Meantime my gut's feeling much better.  Can afford to be
flippant about it now.  However, time's running short
and I haven't even begun to do justice to all the hungry
ghosts.  I figure I probably have more than most people
-- these ghosts being acquaintances who have died while
bearing some grudge against you.  Or at least I have my
share.  And I'll try to let them have their say in these
pages in hopes they won't give me another big gut scare.
Nothing like it ever before, really!  -- But they'll be
around for fifteen days, the traditional period,
rampaging away and at the same time clearing the ground,
psychically speaking, for the core Heavenly Year
celebration which will start up a couple of days after
they depart.  (It's just coincidence, to be sure, that
my birthday falls in the same month as the hungry-ghost
period, which has been observed in the first half of the
seventh lunar month for millennia.  A happy coincidence,
I'd even say.  Gives me a metaphor on which to structure
the kind of yearly accounting I've always liked to
engage in -- felt compelled to engage in, really -- at

birthday time.)
     And now I turn to the question of breakfast.  Will
I be able to eat?  More urgent still, will I be able to
drink coffee?  And then, less than an hour from now, I'm
pledged to deliver the car to Z downtown so she can make
her Thursday visit to Mama E.

                    *              *

     -- Here's a kwikjyze postscript from the black
armchair midway through the fifth watch.
     First, I felt normal all day after leaving the
house, the stomach pain was gone, but now it's back
although nowhere near as bad.  My current best guess is
it's caused by a rotten vite or supp.
     Second, maybe I should say something about the
unreliable narrator.  Of course there's no such thing as
a perfectly reliable narrator.  But I do the best I can
to be accurate and get things right and also be frank
about any failures I'm aware of in those respects.  My
intentions are good and I ask for conditional trust --
also known as suspension of disbelief -- except at times
when it's clearly unwarranted.
     I bring this up because it turns out I was
apparently wrong again on time.  First midsummer's
night, now the start of Heavenly Monkey Month.  Worse
yet, I pried myself out of bed ninety minutes early this
morning for nothing.  The Heavenly Monkey didn't become
official until 4:17 this afternoon, or maybe 3:17.  At
this point I'm throwing up my hands and saying either
time will serve well enough.  Best to focus my efforts
on getting the next one right, whatever it may be.
     And finally, I realized I haven't mentioned
anything about the essay Elgie sent up via e-mail.  I
didn't see it until Monday night when Z-wiff brought me
a copy she'd printed out at work.  I'd made a special
trip home to call Elgie about it at nine p.m. -- the
hour when he becomes "reachable live," according to his
e-mail -- but the essay stunned me so much I felt I
needed a day to digest it before calling.
     In Z's words, he comes off in this essay as
"extremely naive for a twenty-nine-year-old young man."

And I'd say: that's exactly right.  He reminds me of my
college-freshman students in Korea: he's determined to
go right out and solve humanity's biggest problems by
this weekend at the latest.  Has he been living in his
own fantasy world?  Sheltered and protected, yes.
Spoiled, no doubt.  More shocking yet, at least to me,
he sounds like a serious Christian.  He announces
proudly that the Bible is his favorite book -- just as
our current supreme leader did -- and "Positive
Quotations" is his second favorite.

I learned a few other things about him.  For
several years he ran his own internet music business
which "made" (his word; he doesn't say whether the
revenue was gross or net) up to $140,000 a year.  Before
that he was employed by a Hollywood studio in a music-
related job; then after the internet business folded he
worked in sales and marketing for a "large company"
which he doesn't identify.

His ambition now, as he states in this essay, is to
go into patent law.  Prospects in the wellness industry,
he says, look good.  And I'm wondering: did he just make
all this up for the essay?  Maybe so.  He never
mentioned any of it on the phone.  -- And he also talks
about "solving the problem of aging" and mentions that
he believes computers will soon be able to "answer every
question."  (Like, for example, why we exist?  Which
religious version of heaven is the correct one?)

And yet: the writing isn't too bad -- though it is
sloppy -- and I can see he's tried to follow a few of my
suggestions.  He's even included some information about
my side of the family, although every single fact is
garbled.

Later that night, and again the following
afternoon, I put in a couple of hours drawing up a list
of suggestions for the next rewrite of the essay.  Then
Tuesday night I again came home early so I could call
him (and drove back down to work late, staying there
until past four a.m., as I'd also done the night
before).  But I'll wait until the follow-up portion of
the Black Rat cluster to delve into that call.

[ Jyze of the Heavenly Year : Red Horse ]


[+2]

     Doing what I can to center myself.  Recalibrate.
Work up a sense of where I really am.  Which is here:
right arm leaning up against the "City Datum," as it's
called.  In fact those two words are inscribed in stone.
Cornerstone, it is, of my very own hideaway building.
As my peripheral vision reports feet and lower legs
parading by within inches on both sides.
     Just an extremely narrow ledge, also of stone, to
sit on.  The rest of the step is made inaccessible by a
closed wrought-iron gate painted glossy black.  The
elevation here is "18.79."  That's feet, I'd say, above
sea level.  And these inscriptions were carved well
before the big global-melting rise in sea levels began.
     This being nine o'clock of a hopping Saturday
night.  Three or four blocks to the south the first
football game to be played in the new stadium is
probably reaching the fourth quarter along about now.
When it's over, a big fireworks display will erupt.
     Sitting here much longer could cause a severed
tailbone -- mine.
     I like it that this "datum" is located on my
building.  This is the ultimate reference point for all
surveying done in J. City and probably the whole county.
It's all laid out from here.
     Surely this is as solid as reference gets.  It's
foundational!  As much as it can be, it's all nailed
down -- or could say set in stone.  Or stoned.
     But you can't sit too close to the hot center for
more than a few minutes or you'll broil.  Or, the cold
and stony center and you'll freeze and turn to stone
yourself.  Not only that but the nightlife crowd is
literally stumbling over my feet at times.  This seat
warn't made for sittin'.  As the music throbs and
dissonates, half a dozen different bands.  All live.
And I've hung on here way past my shatter point.
                    *              *
     -- Now a concrete block just outside the stadium

parking lot.  Wow, spectacular scene!  As I hear a
broadcaster say they'll just let the clock run out.

Two huge white arcs across the southern sky (and
unless I'm wrong a slice of Heavenly moon is hiding
somewhere behind them), banks of bright lights, upper
decks packed beneath the overhang, roar upon roar,
raucously stomping feet.  Loudspeaker vibrations so loud
the words are hard to decipher -- powerful echoes
bouncing about and canceling parts of each other out.

I was heading for one of the old wooden baggage
carts parked behind the west train terminal but then saw
they were all occupied by other football freeloaders.
As are scores of cars parked outside the fence, radios
blaring the game broadcast.  From much of the lot the
huge video replay screen inside the stadium is fully
visible.  I imagine when the regular season starts we'll
see massive crowds out here.  -- As a freight train
rumbles by some thirty or forty yards to my rear, three
engines, two sporting orange livery and one green, the
elephantine trumpeting sounding triumphant -- and now
comes the thundering herd.  Of humans, I'm saying, from
the stands, even before the finish.

Quite a scene.  The playing field of adolescent
dreams.  It twangs deep resonances in me too.  Also some
negative tuning forks, so say dissonance forks.  The
site of powerful cultural conditioning, and nothing's
subtle about it.  Rah rah, hit 'em hard, the good guys,
our guys, the home team, dominate!  Destroy!  Kill kill
kill!  We rule!

-- As everyone waits for the clock to run out so
the pyrotechnics can begin.  Here's the Fourth of July
personal and up close -- where you can be burned by
falling embers.  (As into the station rolls a regional
passenger train originating from the second major city
to the south, I hear the station PA announcing now --
silver cars snaking through the petrified forest of
columns to my left -- or rather the cars are going by
the station and into the tunnel, then via a newly opened
switch re-entering the station rolling backwards.

The Z-woman dropped me off at the hideaway on her

way home.  (Have to tilt the J-book down a bit to gain
enough light to jyze by, but once I do there's plenty:
most of it coming from the stadium game lights.)  An
afternoon with Kat and Betty, first all four of us
visiting Mama E, then all four (but not Mama E) hitting
the far-north book arcade for burgers and browsing.  Kat
was cranky and limping from cuts on her feet suffered at
a beach party Betty threw for her as a delayed birthday
celebration, since her real birthday party back in
February had to be canceled on account of illness.

"First game in this place ever!" a shirtless young
dude in amusingly super-saggy pants and backwards
baseball cap just cried out with delirious glee.  And to
think that over the next half century or so (global
roast and other factors permitting) a large proportion
of what most USAns know about our fair city will come
from cameras trained on this stadium and the one for
baseball standing directly behind it just a block away.
So here's a very early sample of that knowledge.

I can smell the fireworks even though they haven't
gone off yet.  Are the fuses already lit and burning
down?  Someone points out that a man's perched atop the
clock tower of the terminal about 250 feet up, above the
clock itself, silhouetted, sort of like the tramp
clinging to the clock hands in "Modern Times."

Big roars of the crowd.  Why?  This ball game's all
over but the roaring!  And the refs' whistles -- those
are clearly audible.  Seven minutes left, someone says.
Can't be, sez I.  Way too much.

Screech of rail brakes.  Shirt-sleeve night.  The
size of the investment -- much of it public money, of
course, and it's benefiting the world's third-richest
man, our local plutocrat #2, who owns the team as one of
his many lucrative hobbies and sidelines.

Bus engines are turning over in the parking lot.
Choppers materializing visually like mutant fireflies.
Train bells clanging.  Massive disembarking crowd
cheering, pennants waving.  Rumbles the PA: "Breaking
away for a twenty-yard gain, the Black Horse busts some
Heavenly moves!"  (I mean, it could be saying anything.

It's impossible to decipher what it's saying.)

Z-wiff, I'll declare again, she sump'n else.  Now she's feting me righteously for my Heavenly celebration. Each night she leaves a new message on a foldout card strung on a Heavenly Month necklace, each one numbered as part of a count-up to thirty, representing my solar birthday on August 30th.  And almost every night a new gift.  Last night it was a copy of a Life Magazine (JRX) photo book celebrating the magazine's first sixty years, published in 1996, with mushy X-rated comments written by Z on many of the pages in sparkly purple gel ink.

-- And here we go.  Stadium lights dim, fireworks ignite.  Red white and blue, this book page glows all three colors by turns, smoke roils and boils, someone nearby cries "Amurka, you crazy!", loud booms and crowd roars, "Best show in town."  Between every word in this paragraph a hyper-loud burst as a kind of ultimate punctuation.  Still sounding!  -- Surprise, at the front entrance too.  -- It's shrouded in white smoke just like the day the predecessor dome blew up on this very spot. WHOOOOSH, WOW!!  Red white and blue's phantasmagoric glare!  (And still more!  -- But that's enough for jyze. Try to beat the briefly stalled stampede to the exits.)

*       *

-- From where I sit about four hours later.  Black armchair, three a.m.  Tick of a couple of clocks, sniff of stadium fireworks (yes, still lingering even way up here on the hilltop).

The smoke cloud drifted both south and north.  The southern part ran into the prevailing breeze from the southwest and therefore floated up south hill to wreathe the top -- made a pretty sight with the floodlit DC castle glowing orange inside it as I walked up through the AQ and crossed the high bridge.  At the same time from that bridge I could see the HQ and environs obscured in the other main body of the cloud, only the tops of most of the buildings clearly visible, with the spire of the great white tower rising out of it like a huge blue-tipped traffic cone.

And then I opened the door and there was the Z-

babe spread naked across the bed devouring one of her
whodunits. "Hey you, home already?  -- Wait, you can't
read your new card until midnight!"  She had the lamp
turned on by the bedroom armchair, ready for me.  And
only just now, several hours later, have I re-emerged
from the bedroom.  As almost always the stack of
periodicals waiting to be read is nowhere near as much
diminished as I'd been hoping it would be by this time.

Walking in the dark along the west sidewalk a block
north of here I banged smack into a low-hanging
blackberry spear protruding from the steep embankment.
Only an instinctive blink spared me from a sharp poke in
the eyeball.  The eyelid and skin around the eye are
still stinging a bit, especially when I forget myself
and rub them.

Also the ceiling in our large bathroom sprang a
leak this afternoon.  The new tenants upstairs are
sloppy when taking showers and Raphael's handyman Wayne
hasn't gotten around to patching the grouting at the
base of their tub.  This leak was our biggest domestic
excitement since the garbage disposal went on the fritz
a couple of months ago.  And the fritz is what it's
still on now, by the way; we've decided to just live
with it like that.  We rarely use it anyway.

As for the other updates, best to limit myself to a
few comments about the call to Elgie.  I'll tackle Vic
another time since I'm quite confident now there will be
many more times with Vic.  With Elgie there may be too,
but I'm not really all that sure about anything with him
just yet.

So Tuesday night, after going over his essay for a
full day while letting the new information about him
sink in, I called and we talked for the previously noted
two and a half hours, and that doesn't include a half-
hour gap while I waited for him to call me back because
he has free post-nine-p.m. phone service.  It turned out
he'd lost my number and in the end had to wake up his
mother -- yes, Lady S herself -- so she could give it to
him.  (Evidently it took her a long time to find it.
And that may be because it's been a couple of years

since she last called.   -- And she still hasn't replied
to my get-well card or had him say anything to me about
it.  So I gather it must've upset her in some way.  I
won't even try to guess what that might be.)

     And now I must anticlimactically admit not a whole
lot of substance came to light during this call.  I
asked many questions but for the most part he answered
minimally and didn't really pick up on any of the cues I
tried to give him.  I did learn he's still unemployed
and he was out riding his bicycle at the beach earlier
in the evening for an hour and a half.  The one new
development since we last talked, he said, is that he's
now thinking of joining Americorps for a year while he
waits to start law school.  The main attraction of this
is that, though the pay is low, it does offer a five-
grand scholarship which he could use for law school.
And this in turn suggests my hunch may've been right:
his main reason for contacting me this summer was the
hope of soliciting financial help.  But I'm happy to say
he's been proud enough not to ask directly.  And I'm
also proud enough myself to say I'm not intending to
offer any.  But then again: I might.  If things went
exceedingly well between us for an extended period -- if
he showed me he intended this resumption of relations to
be permanent and to take on some real substance -- then
I might decide to give him part of what remains in the
deep-reserves account Mother left me.  (As of today that
amount stands at just slightly over forty K -- it lost
$2500 in the last month alone -- and I still owe Z eight
K of it.)

     No decision about that for a while.  Maybe I'll
wait a couple of years to see if he's really serious
about law school.  I have my doubts he'll want to stick
with it.  To me his talents would appear to lie
elsewhere -- maybe something more directly related to
math, at which he did so well in school.  In our dawning
digital age those skills would likely be much more
valuable than any verbal ones he may have (but I, sorry
to say, see little evidence of, and Z says the same).

     At one point I asked him how his mother's

recovering from the stroke.  "Pretty good," he said; she
doesn't have much grip with her left hand and she walks
more slowly than before, but otherwise she seems about
back to normal.  Well, I joked, did that mean her sense
of humor was back to normal too?  When he seemed puzzled
by this, I reminded him he'd earlier told me the one
good thing about the stroke was it had seemed to improve
her sense of humor.  He chuckled but that was it: didn't
answer.  (Is this the usual fear of a child of divorce:
being caught in the middle between the alienated
parents, being pressured to take sides?  -- But to put
him in such a bind is the very last thing I'd want to
do.  As always, it's my intention to support to the full
his mother's choices regarding him.  But sometimes it's
not so easy to avoid reminding him I see many things
differently than she does and would've made many
different choices regarding his upbringing.  So far,
though, I think I've done all right.  It's my hope
we'll be able to talk openly about all this someday --
utopian hope probably.  Fantastical.)
     And I learned this: she, Jang, Lady S -- his mother
-- won a silver medal for her age group in an important
marathon in Seoul which she entered at age sixty -- in
her Heavenly Year!
     And the rest of the call dealt with editing.  He
sat at his computer and typed in changes and took notes
on my suggestions.  He usually caught my drift quickly
enough and wasn't inordinately defensive.  He showed
flashes of a self-deprecating sense of humor which I
hope will manifest more often as he loosens up with me.
But then what else can you do but laugh at yourself when
you spell "niche" "nitch"?  And lots more like that.
It's clear enough writing has never been an area of
strong interest for him, just as, until recently,
reading hasn't.  But he's thinking he can teach himself
how to write adequately in the next year, and I think he
probably can -- at least up to the standards of most
lawyers.  But will he enjoy the life that comes with
lawyering?  Hard to believe.  But then it's difficult
for me to see how anyone could enjoy such a life, and

yet at least a few naturally litigious/contentious souls must do just that.  And maybe some other kinds of souls also do, scattered sparsely across the land.

He's hoping Americorps will be able to offer him some sort of forest-ranger job where he'd have nothing to do most of the time but study legal books to gain a head start on everyone else in his class.  He also likes the idea of breathing fresh air (the apartment where he and his mother live -- I'm almost sure it's just one apartment -- is in downtown MSM #1).  Sounds to me like he's also looking forward to getting away from home.  But Lady S may have different ideas for him, and now with her being in a stroke-recovery phase he may have an even harder time resisting her.  Just as, say, I often had a hard time resisting her myself.  And maybe he doesn't want to resist her at all -- what do I know?  He's an only child and by her own choice she's devoted a big chunk of the past thirty years to raising him by herself, often under considerable constraints and hardships (as he says himself in his essay).

But how deeply does he see?  Maybe he can't afford to explore his own emotional depths -- maybe that's the cost of having such a woman as his mother around all the time -- and of not having his father around.  He seems to admire way too much a male boss at his most recent sales-job workplace, a gung-ho type who generated millions in sales for the company.  -- But I don't want to be forming any judgments here just yet, not even of the provisional kind.  Instead I'll try to summon a few positive quotations of my own and keep my fingers crossed until the bones ache.  (Which for a longtime pen-squeezer and keyboard-basher such as myself might start happening much sooner than I'd like.)

-- "Hi!" says the Z-wiff, wandering in.  Four-twenty a.m.  As good a time as any to bring this session to a close.  The Red Horse rises.  (But first this last note: we left it that Elgie will send up his rewritten essay by e-mail and then leave us a telephone voicemail saying he's done so.  And he's agreed not to try to have the application ready by the first day it can be

submitted -- the time when the gung-ho boss mentioned
earlier insisted he should fire it in.  So progress
seems to be occurring already, at least a wee bit.)


------

32

------


   No moon in sight.  No hungry ghosts either, but I'm
sure they're around.  The moon, I've just learned, is
gone; the newspaper on the bench here tells me it set an
hour ago.  Half past eleven now.  I came over to the
ferry terminal because I knew the fountain here would
offer a wide view of the sky.
   The hungry-ghost period doesn't start, the way I
figure it, until I see the moon.  But the later in this
fifteen-day period I see it, the more intense the
visitation will be during its remaining days.  And if I
don't see it at all, Katie bar the door -- except doors
don't work against ghosts.  (But ghostbusters do.  Maybe
I can learn a few of their tricks.)
   How do I know they're around, the ghosts?  Well,
for starters, and to repeat, what else is the pain in my
gut all about?  Hungry ghosts, again, strike the hunger
center.  (And it is still paining me, though not as
badly.  This might be because I'm showing those ghosts
some respect.)  -- And then the other reason I know
they're around is I'm thinking about them so much.  Who
exactly are they?  What exactly is needed to propitiate
them?  Beyond the ghost goodies I set out for them, that
is.  On the desk in my office I've laid out seven
chocolate power bars I think they might go for.  This is
following my hunch they number seven.  And another hunch
is they haven't been eating nutritiously.
   -- As one pathetic drifter after another tries to

hit me up for a smoke or change.  More ghosts right here
quite possibly.  Every single one of my millions of
ancestors has good reason to be angry at me.  Am I not
complicit in letting the only home they've ever known --
the planet Earth -- be destroyed?  Of course everyone
else alive today is likewise being besieged, or should
be, by millions of ghosts for that same reason.  But not
too many people seem to be noticing this just yet.
Maybe they haven't realized the panhandlers aren't the
usual ones; they're just wearing panhandler disguises.

     Ferries glide in and out.  Nothing ominous about
this unless you think about it.  Nowadays all the
ferries are accompanied by little Coast Guard
antiterrorist gunboats.  Ghostbuster boats, you could
call them.  So far as anyone knows they haven't sighted
a single terrorist and yet we know from the highest
authorities that they, the evildoers, are all around us
and among us.  The panhandler ruse is one of their
favorites.  Some dress up as Natives like the ghost
spirits which J. City's eponymous chief warned us about.
Others are known to be the cause of our gridlock traffic
jams, which they succeed in engineering through car-by-
car takeovers of driver spirits, converting good
burbanites into road-rage maniacs.  And look what
they're doing to the economy!

     Water splashes in the fountain.  No water shortage
there.  (Not yet.)  Cars whiz by thirty to forty feet up
on the viaduct.  Oil we've still got.  Don't forget
who's running the world!  The night sky's so clear the
stars are twinkling in double time (and did I just see
one of the forty Perseid meteorites predicted to be
making Brownian flashes up there tonight?) -- no sign at
all, in any case, of the "brown cloud" hovering over
East and South Asia, as described in today's OMP, and
estimated to be causing half a million deaths annually
in India alone.  We can even justifiably claim this
particular outrage is not all our fault, we USAns.  As
rulers of the empire maybe it's our responsibility,
true, here where the buck stops (and starts -- and to
repeat again, that's one of the slogans for the Heavenly

Year of the Water Horse: "The buck starts here" -- as in
bucking bronco, as in "Don't try to ride me, frickin'
empire") -- but the ultraconservatives so renowned for
demanding personal accountability from their cultural
opponents don't bother to ask the same of their empire.
Maybe later for that, after all the terrorists are
cleaned out and order is fully restored and enforced.
(It'll take fifty years, they say.  Until then, tough
luck for those who find themselves under a brown cloud.)
    Dock lights.  Huge floodlit orange cranes.  A late
horse-drawn tourist carriage, the horse (a white one)
wearing a straw hat with its ears poking through and the
driver a matching hat but without visible ears.  Under
the viaduct's lower level, through the empty gap, a view
of neon-lit night spots of the HQ entertainment zone --
a few still open at this hour, including the one across
the street from the hideaway building's side entrance.
(Speaking of panhandlers, the powers-that-be want $11
billion to replace this viaduct.  It's all but certain
to collapse in the next big earthquake.)
    So it's purge time.  That's what this ghostly
period is for.  Get it all off your chest so we can move
on to -- move back to -- business as usual.
    At home tonight version two of Elgie's "personal
statement" awaits me, downloaded and printed by Z at
work.  Oddly, though, Elgie didn't leave the promised
voicemail alerting me he'd e-mailed up the new draft.
Three times we went over this.  Again, not an auspicious
sign.  It was sheer luck Z noticed the file while
searching for something else.  I glanced at the new
version: it looks better but at the same time almost
entirely unrelated to the first one.  He also sent up a
copy of a personal statement written by a friend of his
who's already in law school -- where, I don't know --
and Z says Elgie's seems to be modeled closely on that
other one.  (I did notice a paragraph dealing with his
mother's stroke.  It said something along the lines of
"How were we to know she'd been living on nothing but
cheese, yogurt, and ice cream?"  That doesn't sound like
Lady S to me.  Owing to her long career in dance she

always watched her calories carefully and was also
extremely nutrition-conscious.  I was the one whom she
accused, and rightfully so, of neglecting nutrition
principles because I ate too much in the way of meat and
potatoes, sugar and dairy, and especially too many
"empty calories."  So: another little clue she's gone
through some big changes.  -- But a marathon runner who
eats like that?)
     -- From time to time pulses of ferry riders
thunder by.  Light planes buzz overhead patrolling the
harbor.  Ferry terminal guards with big dogs sniff
around.
     Still no moon -- this fact tending to confirm the
OMP's prediction regarding time of moonset.  From our
perspective here skyscrapers seem to peek over the top
of the viaduct if I tilt my head up a bit.  No fish
stink in the air -- but lots of auto exhaust from the
ferry waiting lines.  Tomorrow's my day to see Mama E.
Z tells me Margo, her eldercare counselor, says it's
okay to be thinking about cutting back on the number of
our visits per week.  The lights were already off in Vic
and Jean's loft up on the fourth floor when I walked by
their building at eleven-thirty.  Ominous black boats
glide by in the night like Commodore Perry's infamous
Black Ships (Perry, that's my middle name -- for real;
and thus, I suddenly realize, no JRX is needed for it --
and I was called General Jeep by Gramps Perry, who was
possibly named after the commodore -- though I'm just
speculating) and here's an aid car too, flashing lights,
red white and blue, and a big whooping siren, but now
gone already like a bad-trip apparition.  (And just for
form I'll mention it's the cluster of the Gray Ox, "Ox
Outside the Gate," that hard-working beast, and this
terminal is known as "the gateway to downtown Jyze City"
and was exactly that for me for almost seven years.)


[+2]


To ward off the ghosts I sought out one of my lucky

spots.  Also I paid my respects, as I always try to do
when I'm in the HQ, to the lucky composite Brown Horse
across from Z-geist.  And I'm carrying my lucky wooden
Jeep pen with me ("There's Only One" is the advertising
slogan inscribed on it) as a supplement to the lucky
jyze pendant and I'm wearing the lucky "Word Temple"
button (an orange one today).  I ain't superstitious --
but a procession of seven ghosts just crossed my trail.

It was two nights ago I spotted the ghost moon for
the first time.  I'd just emerged from midtown chain
burgers carrying my double-stack in a white paper bag,
on my way up to the scope office, and there as I waited
for the light it took me by surprise, materializing out
over the bay, low in the sky, straight down the street
corridor -- due west.  Moons don't often come at you
from the west in this city and new ones even less so.

Later that night the bus I was riding had to make a
detour around a crime scene in the AQ -- about three
hours earlier, the driver told me, a man had been
murdered there.  Turned out this happened shortly after
I'd walked by that very spot.  (As I often do on the way
in.  It's near the yellow and orange colonnade beneath
the freeway overpass, a few feet from where I scribbled
out the frozen-fingered snowfall entry last spring --
and maybe sixty feet from the light-pole-mounted dragon
which was the first of the new bunch that Z and I
spotted, then jumped out of the car to take photos of --
in fact the murder happened right beneath that dragon.)

Six blocks due west of said homicide scene I've
found a new lucky spot.  A century and a half ago when
J-town was in its very first year of Eurusan control
this area was underwater out in the tideflats.  Now
vehicular traffic is flowing by, eight lanes of it, and
lots of foot traffic too (early arrivals for tonight's
baseball game), and down below, causing the granite
block on which I sit to tremble at times, heavily laden
railroad traffic (and checking overhead, I see a
terrorist-size plane too, and gulls circling the west-
depot campanile -- whose clock is hard to read but I
think it says 5:25, and everyone in sight, except maybe

the people behind glass in cars with closed windows
indicating the presence of air conditioning, is sweating
-- as a cab pulls up and four grown Cawk men of roughly
male-menopause vintage tumble out, all wearing Jyze City
baseball caps and jerseys -- practically roll across my
feet like clowns at the circus -- "Well, hello there,
Pierro Cawks!")

Also as a reminder of the perils of the times, Z-
wiff went in yesterday for her endometrial biopsy.
Hopped in the saddle so the doc could insert her
apparatus -- a female doc, yes, but the penetration
still felt "clunky" to Z.  Now we wait a few days to
hear if she'll be needing a full D&C, as she did the
last time.  Or the news could be even worse than that,
though the doc says the chances of this are very low.

So we propitiate our ghosts.  Not that we're
superstitious.  Well, maybe she is, though I've seen no
strong evidence of it.  Me, I'll say it again: I ain't.
The language of superstition is often more effective
than the language of emotional abstraction for
expressing fears and hopes, guilts and shames -- that's
why I go for it.  And the fondness of certain artsy
types for this more colorful language is no doubt the
source of many superstitions which eventually establish
themselves in popular culture and thus become authentic
(as in "believed to be a description of reality," as
per the spiritual wing of philosophical pragmatism: "if
you believe it, in an important sense it's true").

So I sit on this brown polished-granite cube
inscribed with a yin/yang symbol -- just like the South
Korean flag -- and I feel lucky.  A couple dozen of
these cubes are strewn, evenly spaced, across the
triangular area of this tiny park just east of the east
depot and behind a bus stop: I'm reminded of cubes of
baled hay in the Mentoka farmland I passed through
several times a year in my youth, well before farmers
switched over to baling in giant round cylinders --
except this field here in J. City has half a dozen trees
growing in it and no tractor could possibly make it
through.

This late in the rush hour only about a third
of the cubes bear perchers awaiting buses.  But all of
the cubes are engraved with railroad memorabilia of one
sort or another, including one with the logo of the line
whose tracks passed within a few blocks of the hospital
where I was born in Lahontan and, 125 miles southeast of
that, both of the Gatewood houses I grew up in, and
going in the opposite direction from Lahontan passed
through Mentoka Falls of my grad-school years and within
a few miles of Turtle Rapids of Sandefjord ancestral
lore and eventually ended up two thousand miles farther
west at this station right across the street here.  End
of the line, correct.  (But I still say I ain't
superstitious.)

     -- How is it the yin/yang symbol can be considered
a bit of railroad memorabilia meriting engravement on
this cube?  Well, here's how: because a certain railroad
(not the one referred to above) back some 130 years ago
when it was going transcontinental made it part of its
logo.  That's all there is to it as far as I know.

     Fifty feet to my left a primeval grove once stood
and that's where the longtime indigenous locals of this
area launched their attempt to expel the Eurusan
invaders holed up in the blockhouse across a small tidal
inlet.  Shells rained down from the black USAn ship --
much like Perry's -- anchored just offshore and routed
the locals.  That early version of the Battle of J-town
was fought right here.  And we Eurusans don't even have
a monument in the area commemmorating our great victory
over the savages.  What, are we ashamed or something?

     -- Meanwhile most of the clouds have dispersed and
while looking up at the indecipherable clockface I see,
a few degrees off to the right and at the same height as
the face, a ghostly daytime sickle of moon.  Dinner
hour -- it's gotta be hungry.  And busy, as control
center for who knows how many billions of ghosts.

     My ancestors, I think, are probably resting more
easily than most.  At least they've got one descendant
who's thinking about them.  And not just now!  More than
anything else ancestors want to be remembered.  They'd

like mausoleums and regular ritual observances, no
doubt, but being sensible and intelligent they'd surely
prefer deeply felt remembrance to merely material
monuments and empty ritual services.  They'd rather be
engaged in matters of moral dispute -- regarding their
support of slavery, say, or indigene-cleansing -- than
be mindlessly approved of.  They certainly do have a
bone to pick with me (and all their other descendants)
with regard to preserving the only home they've ever
known or can hope to know, which is this earthly abode.
True, they'll go on existing here even if we blow the
place to smithereens, but the trouble then will be the
lack of propitiators for them.  And when you're a
ghost, there's not a whole lot else to look forward to.
     But it's not the ancestor ghosts I'm really
worrying about.  They know I care about them and they
know I'm doing the best I can to see that their home
planet remains favorable to the propagation of further
generations of propitiators.  Rather the ones I'm
concerned about are the ghosts of Elgie's half brothers
and half sisters.  Seven of them, I figure.  They're
following me around right now.  They'll be following me
up to the scope office -- I have to show up there in
just twenty minutes.  They'll let me do that, too,
because I've bargained with them: I'll engage them
directly later tonight at home.
                    *              *
     -- Again it's a night so fine I can crank out some
balcony jyze -- barefoot, in shorts and sleeveless
henley only.  As with all basically terrible things,
even global roasting has its good side.  You're a lot
more likely to experience it, though, if you're well
situated to start out with.  Nothing unusual there.
Which doesn't mean it couldn't be at least partially
compensated for.
     The dreams of Heavenly dementia.  (On this balcony
I might query, "Wherefore art thou, Elza?"  But we know:
she's those same fifteen miles due north at Benita's
place, where the latest word is that she asks for help
from Tony, the caregiver for all five house residents,

every ten to fifteen minutes all day long.)
     A few stars visible up there but only dimly.
Monday's murder under the dragon did merit a squib in
today's "Briefs" in the OMP.  Today's fifty-seventh
anniversary of V-J Day merited no mention at all in OMP
or FAP, and same's true for the fifty-fifth of India's
Independence Day: the bloody yet inspirational birth
moment of the excellent novel "Midnight's Children."
Those big, big tribes that fought back against Western
colonialism, of course including our USAn colonialism,
and are continuing to do so half a century later, we
just don't like to think about them any more than's
necessary -- which is to say, precious little.  So far.
     And then the seven ghosts.  I welcome you, ghosts!
I offer you more than just power bars.  How about
eternal tribute?  If you would so have it, may it be
jyzified right here and now.  Without me, I want you to
remember, you'd've had no life at all.  Nor was I the
one in any of your cases to decide you must become
ghostly -- I merely concurred in each of the decisions.
(Well, only in five of them.  The sixth I didn't know
about until it was a done deed.  And the seventh is a
special case I'll get to in a moment.)  But I'll also
confess I'd've been mighty unhappy -- or so I believed
back then, and still believe today -- if any of those
decisions had gone the other way.
     In Japan, I've read, whole cemeteries are devoted
to ghosts of this special kind, and that may be true of
Korea and China too.  (Today is also Korea's Liberation
Day, I neglected to mention earlier, also first
celebrated fifty-seven years ago, marking the end of
thirty-six years of harshly oppressive Japanese colonial
occupation.  We USAns had a hand in Japan's colonialism
too, though you rarely hear about it: we agreed not to
object to their colonization of Korea in exchange for
Japan's agreeing not to object to our parallel -- almost
simultaneous -- colonization of the Philippines.)
     One of Elgie's half-sibling ghosts partakes of
Lady K essence; one of Lady C essence; one of Millie W.
essence (she a generous comforter of the jyzer during

the chaotic era of Lady S versus Lady V showdown); and
three of Lady U essence. But those last-named three,
for them there was no real choice, or so the doctors
declared. A creaturely creation taken to term would've
meant the end of both Lady U and the creation; and so
the two creations that followed, also partaking of Lady
U essence -- DNA essence is of course what I'm talking
about here -- never would've happened. Therefore,
ghosts No. 5 and No. 6, you should be especially kindly
toward ghost No. 4; without No. 4, no you. And the same
goes for No. 5 as well as No. 4 with respect to No. 6:
so be especially kindly twice over, No. 6.

Finally, here's the story on No. 7. This is a
collective ghost. It may have no existence at all or it
may be multi-essenced. It's the Ghost of the Unknown
Abortion. (There's that stark word at last.) In that
impassioned era there may've been other co-creations
partaking of other essences as well as mine. It was a
joyous and libidinous and tumultuous time. But if there
were others, I never learned of them.

Am I sorry for the pain and suffering I helped
cause others? Yes. Am I sorry I followed my heart?
No. Am I sorry others followed theirs? No. Do I wish
I'd been a true Boy Scout (or unhypocritical family-
values reactionary, of which few if any have ever been
known to exist) and insisted more fiercely on marrying
Lady K, say, and she'd eventually yielded to that
insistence and we'd stuck together forever with no
straying and so none of the other six ghosts would've
been created and the first creation could've put off
becoming a ghost for a Heavenly cycle or two? Well, it
might've been nice, I suppose. But much more likely it
wouldn't've been. So no, I don't wish that. And I'm
sure the creaturely creations of Lady K's later
relationships -- two such creations that I know of --
wouldn't either.

Do I think my views spread across a whole
generation have weakened the nation's moral fiber? Not
hardly! Those views, what's left of them after the
ceaseless poundings they've taken from the legions of

the corporados and the family-values types, are just
about the last hope this nation's got as it hurls along
its collision course with itself.  Or are there maybe
other hopes springing up I don't know about?  I hope so!
(Hope springs eternal, you betcha.  But hope will also
soon be complicit in ushering me and everyone else off
to ghost city.)
     So there, you spectral seven.  Before much longer
I'll be joining you and we'll be eight.  And then later
Elgie -- unless he realizes his cockamamie dream of
inventing immortality -- will be joining us.  The
numinous nine who partake of Jyzer G essence.  And wotta
motley crew we'll be!  Might as well lighten up and
enjoy ourselves!  And later on we could well be joined
by others -- maybe millions of others, though clearly
that depends mostly, and in fact entirely for the first
crucial step -- as far as I know -- on Elgie.
     So no, I ain't superstitious.  I welcome you,
ghosts.  Are you really out there?  Hiding behind the
telephone poles or lampposts or trees in the primordial
grove, making sure no Black Ships are lurking?  None are
anchored here across the street.  Come on over and let's
party!  -- But we'll have to make it quick, because it's
my bedtime.  Gotta save our serious partying for another
occasion.  Just let me know when you think's good.


------


33


------


     Ten straight up on the big public-market clock.
I'm straight up myself as well, standing, using the top
of a newspaper vending box as tonight's jyze platform.
This at the busy corner across from the market on a
Saturday night.  And directly above the newsstand

diagonally across the intersection hangs the one, the
only -- the Monkey Heavenly moon.

     Granted I can just barely push this J-stick along
tonight.  To be able to make it to Vaughn and Renee's
wedding on the shore of the utility's reservoir up in
the mountains to the southeast I had to rise at ten
o'clock this morning -- equivalent of two or three a.m.
for the sunny-side-up world.  We got home from that
journey early enough that I could squeeze in an hour's
nap before we met Jay and Melanie to finally catch
"Sunshine State."  But now I'm draggin' again.

     But.  But.  Today's my first birthday of the
Heavenly month!  Not a terribly noteworthy one, it's
true, but yet one that must not go unmentioned.  The
Julian-shadow birthday, as I call it.  Which is to say:
if the Gregorian calendar reforms hadn't been
implemented in this country exactly a quarter of a
millennium ago (that is, well before it became an actual
country), but otherwise all else had been the same ever
since (admittedly quite a hypothetical), my birthday --
and everyone else's -- would've fallen thirteen days
earlier.  That's twelve days for the adjustment in 1752
and one more day to account for the slippage that's
occurred in the two and a half centuries since then.

     And why celebrate at this particular junction?  As
traffic rolls noisily by on the bricky street, revelers
whoop, streetpeople panhandle, horny males slip into the
porn arcade (whose brilliantly bright marquee lights
cause the market building across the street to flash
spasmodically as if it's a nightlight on a timer gone
wacko) -- and the pulchritudinous nightlifers of August
strut their stripped-down and gussied-up stuff (many
headed for the big rock venue half a block to the south)
-- it's because today is the market's ninety-fifth
anniversary and I was hoping to get in on the tail end
of the festivities.  Which I've done, but it's the very
tail end: the cleanup already underway behind lowered
wire gates.  And yet it's still lit up like party time
over there.  And of course it's during cleanup hours
that we of the nightscoper world are used to partying.

[ Jyze of the Heavenly Year : Red Horse ]

O ye seven specters: are we not having fun?
So much going on these days.  Ten or twelve blocks
to the south down the old edge road, in the HQ triangle,
the newly reconstructed pergola was officially unveiled
today.  The tall ships sailed into the harbor with
anachronistic brio (two days ago actually) and are now
tied up nostalgically over on what I think of as Lake J-
town.  It's the twenty-fifth anniversary of the death of
the first great Cawk rocker -- "the King" -- and the
media aren't letting anyone forget about it for a
second.  And that's just the really big stuff.  Then
there's this: both OMP and FAP have my birth date, solar
kind, emblazoned in their front-page headlines today, as
if it must represent something truly important.  This is
because the union for major-league baseball players has
announced they've called a strike for that day, August
30th -- unless, that is, certain conditions are met.
Most likely a strike won't actually occur, but right up
until the deadline I'm expecting maximum drama to build,
focused on that date.  And what more could a celebrating
Heavenly Year J-slinger born on that date ask for?
-- As hoped, the specters and other ghosts have
been wielding their clout with the deities on my behalf.
Already the results of Z-wiff's biopsy are in and she's
fine.  A minor polyp was causing all the bleeding.
Stretch limos nose by.  Boom boxes with wheels and
engines roll by, pulsating and vibrating with the beat
like sets of monster drum traps.  An Old Glory ripples
inconspicuously and yet, to be sure, somehow ominously.
The moon dips perilously, seemingly.  Sizzling beef is
in the air, also a whiff of potent weed.  At this hour
no one wants to buy a day-old OMP (like the ones in this
box), so I'm not being asked to step aside or move on.
I've done my best to cheer up June, who's still
suffering post-bar-exam depression.  Her younger son,
Michael, is about to take off for a one-year teaching
gig in China before starting law school.  My own son has
just begun what's intended to be a one-year stint as a
paralegal at a Korusan law firm in his current home city
(he swerved away from Americorps for unexplained

reasons).  New good friend Vic I'll be seeing again on
Tuesday.  Mama E's former longtime boarder (and likely
lover) Tito has moved to a mountain city north of the
border and wants us all, Mama E included, to motor up
for a visit -- "It's only a seven-hour drive!"

Three years ago at our wedding Vaughn L. caught the
bouquet.  Today he married Renee, the woman he's been
living with for seven years.  The ceremony, both
newlyweds told us (separately!), was inspired by ours.
"We tried to get the same warm feeling."  The setting
was superb: abundant wildflower meadows, the city's
reservoir, wooded hillsides, craggy gray mountain
outcroppings looming across the reservoir.  Waterdrops
falling on kettledrums of various sizes and pitches
standing in the garden made for a marvelous random
tympanic effect (a first for me).  Z and I vicariously
relived our wedding day through Vaughn and Renee.  On
the way home we figured it out: this was the eighth
wedding we've attended together, not including our own.
That's 1.6 weddings per year.  Before marrying Z I
averaged maybe 0.2 weddings per year, and that includes
those for all three of my own pre-Z marriages (even the
zen one).  For this occasion today Z pleaded with me to
wear my hemp wedding outfit and for that reason I did.

-- I've just made myself useful.  A young woman
with a fancy silver glitter spot painted on her
prominent right cheekbone needed to borrow a pen in
order to endorse a check to deposit at the ATM so
conveniently located right outside the entrance to the
porn arcade.  I obliged -- but not with my J-stick, god
forbid!  Nor with my lucky wooden Jeep pen.  But I felt
I could safely risk losing a ballpoint editing pen since
I have a near-full twelve-count box of such pens at
home.  -- Said the young woman as she handed the pen
back and very briefly glanced at this page: "Oh, you're
sketching!"  (Well okay!)

Pink neon of the big public-market sign, red
clockhands.  And I'll acknowledge it's hard to get used
to the sight of all these scantily dressed youngsters.
Pulchritude on parade, it's the marching order this

year.  Gasp and then gasp again.  Saudi Arabia this is
not.  I mean, are we a Great Satan of a country or what?
All hail the restorative powers of decadence!  -- And
the area just south of here, by the way, a year ago
constituted itself as a marketing zone and christened
itself the west-edge neighborhood.  That name has taken
on new meaning since the attacks of 9/11.  The official
slogan for this hood: "Never a dull moment!"  But so far
I've not once heard the term "west edge" in use.

     -- So last night a second long editing phone talk
with Elgie, this one lasting from two a.m. until almost
five.  His excuse for not leaving the promised voicemail
alert for me was that he was "shy" about possibly waking
us up.  I suspect this really had more to do with fear
of Z-wiff answering the phone.  Understandable enough.
After all, she's his mother too, albeit of the step
variety, and they've never even met.

     This call left my earlier impressions of his
general goals and state of knowledge unchanged.  But
there was less awkwardness, I felt.  I find him
generally likable but scarcely know what to make of him.
He again told me of his hope of meeting (during his law-
school years) a woman "as tall as or taller than me."
That's the only qualifying characteristic he mentioned
for a potential mate.  He confirmed, quite without
embarrassment, that he's looking forward to getting away
from his current living quarters for a few years.  His
mother's doing much better; he's confident she'll be
able to take care of herself.  "She even has a maid
service coming in to help her."  (Is that a feature of
Medicare, I wonder?  If so, it could be said I'm her
enabler in this.  Since we were officially married for
well over the requisite ten years I believe she's
eligible for Social Security coverage and she's
definitely old enough to qualify for it.  But I don't
really know how it works or what's going on.  It's also
possible she's come into a considerable inheritance --
but if that were the case I doubt Elgie would be taking
a job as a paralegal.)

     Next step in the evolving relationship with Elgie

will come in a few days when he e-mails up the next
draft of his essay.  My big curiosity at this point:
will he want to keep channels open with us after he's
sent off the applications with the essay included?
(He's planning to apply to between ten and fifteen law
schools.  At the moment he's most interested in two
elite northeastern far-coast schools because he thinks
they'd offer him the best chance to land a high-paying
job with a top firm, and he seems to like the idea that
this job would probably be in that same part of the
country.  He's straightforward about wanting to broaden
himself and finding Koreatown in MSM #1 "too
confining.")
     -- Moon's been sliding sideways and down but is
still smiling on this odd scene.  Ninety minutes of
standing in one spot, though, and I feel I've had just
about enough.  The crowds are thinning out a bit but
also becoming more boisterous and literally bumptious:
from time to time a passersby crashes into me.  "Oops --
'scuse me while I kiss this guy!"  -- Or the sky.
     And this is the Green Tiger cluster!  How could I
neglect to mention it?  "Tiger Standing Still."  But no
more on that for now because I'm outta here.  Will walk
the west edge to my office and do what I gotta do --
check out the new pergola as well -- and then bus home.


                         [+2]


     Nearly a virgin bench -- one of two (where there
used to be four) -- beneath the newly reopened pergola.
In its emptiness it beckoned to me as I came around the
corner into the triangle.  But I had to grab some
coffee first -- I'd skipped the ritual at home so as to
gain a little jyzing time down here.  Tonight I must
head up to the scope office a bit early (Naomi has an
all-day job, unusual for a Monday, and she's also left
me four hundred pages of grand jury to final).
     I stood in line at the triangle chain coffee shop
across the street keeping an anxious eye on this bench

through the window.  At one point it appeared a homeless
woman would claim it and my heart sank -- looked like
I'd have to settle for one of the aluminum sidewalk
tables outside the coffee shop.  But as it turned out
the woman was just setting down her backpack and
sleeping roll for adjustments; she soon moved on.  So I
rushed over and grabbed the bench.

One side of it actually.  A white-bearded guy with
lots of shopping bundles just plopped down on the other
side, to my right.   -- And a motley array of maybe
thirty visitors trundles by: the underground tour.  As
they head down the stairs by the datum cornerstone of
the hideaway building, a similar procession emerges from
the alley across the street by the old merchants' cafe
(which is back to offering live rock music on weekend
nights, featuring again this week the same excellent
funk-rock band: they're usually blasting away over there
when I come out the door on weekend nights and I like to
go over and listen for a while if time permits).

Pedestrian prose!  Well, I'm sorry, Adam Z.  But
then it's your fault I'm particularly aware of this
shortcoming after reading some of your "Mysticism for
Beginners" earlier today while gobbling down my peach-
topped cornflakes (and banana-, strawberry-, and
blueberry-bottomed: that is, massively fruited, to use a
word Elgie deployed in his essay, as in "fruited plains"
-- and he also described himself as having become a
"fruitarian" as a result of his mother's stroke, and I
had to ask Z exactly what that term meant so I wouldn't
be taken as an ignorant old fossil by my newly
rematerialized son, and then on the phone he wondered
aloud if use of those terms made him sound like "some
kind of nut."  I said no, to get that kind of reaction
he'd have to use the term "nutarian" -- lame, yeah, but
he did chuckle a bit).

White-bearded Cawk guy takes off, tall pigtailed
Native man descends.  At first he wants to talk but I
tell him I've gotta do this now and happily he's letting
me be.  I did learn he was under the impression the
earthquake of 2001 (Mom's Birthday Quake) knocked down

the old pergola.  I quickly filled him in on the
eighteen-wheeler truck that turned the corner too
sharply a month before that quake; and just then another
tour group arrived and the guide started telling the
same pergola story while practically standing on my toes
and I asided to the Native guy, "There you go, see?" and
he listened until the guide finished up (as the first
row of tourists gaped at us two weirdos holding down our
bench and one twisted his head all but upside down
trying to scope out the content of this J-sticking).

They're like crowds of ancestor ghosts, I'm
thinking.  My ancestors, the Native's ancestors,
everyone's ancestors.  They're checking out the scene
before delivering final judgment.  But we all know what
the final judgment will be.  -- Certainly the black-
marbled head and torso of the eponymous chief, resting
atop its pedestal a few yards to my left, knows.  (The
Native guy left, though, and was briefly replaced by a
small nervous Cawk guy with curiously fluffy blond hair
who was casting paranoid glances in all directions -- on
a bad drug trip, most likely -- and then flitted off
like a frightened bird and I was alone again on the
bench, and I still am.)

Arriving home last night I found a line of five
horse statuettes parading across the living-room couch.
A note said: "Can you guess who brought these over?"  I
checked them out and saw all five were made in China.  I
figured it had to be June.  And I was right.  Today I
called to thank her and she said she'd come across them
while "dismantling" her home of twenty-five years up in
the northern burbs and thought of me.  "It's better you
have them for your Heavenly Horse Year and then you can
decide if you want to throw them out.  Don't feel any
obligation to keep them."

But I will keep them.  They'll be my lucky Heavenly
Year June's Horse Herd.  Evidently she first bought them
for her ex-husband but I didn't press too hard on that.
And she said something that touched me.  I'm not to tell
Z about this, but when June's lonely in these law-school
postpartum days she imagines her mother is in the room

with her and now also her good friend from Taiwan who
died two years ago and sometimes even -- me!  It's the
first time she's ever said anything quite so intimate to
me.  -- If we'd met back before I knew Z we might've
become lovers, I daresay, but it never would've lasted.
Instead we can be friends and, because she's also Z's
friend, the relationship can last.  There's full three-
way trust and also, I believe, full three-way awareness
of the benefits and how unusual it is that something
like this can work out.  Certainly it's a first in my
life.  (Or the trust is close to full, I should say.
Z's a bit cautious, so make it ninety percent full for
her, and surely that's good enough.)

    August dog days.  They're continuing, mostly fine
and warm, although some ominous clouds are moving in
from the southwest right now and a chill wind is rising.
The war drums on Iraq are pounding ever louder; a story
in today's far-coast paper describes the massive arms
buildup at U.S. bases in our Mideastern tributary states
such as Kuwait and Oman.  My reading of the letters
pages makes me think a fairly strong antiwar movement
could soon emerge.  Under the circumstances of the
ongoing War on Terrorism (sic sic sic), however, it's
likely the government will crack down openly on dissent
in the same way that, roughly three decades back,
another bellicose U.S. regime tried to do.  Unless the
out-party gets its act together for the elections this
fall -- and maybe even if it does -- the chances look
better than ever that by early next year this country
will be under a kind of de facto martial law.

    But right now we're in the countdown to Heavenly
Fest Days -- ten, nine, today is eight.  Just a couple
more celestial touchstones to pass and we'll be there.
-- And the pigeons coo their amazement!  And the
century-old bricks weep with joy!  And even the steel-
hard new pergola (its black iron columns so shiny, its
overhead copper framing for the glass panels so
pristinely ungreened) -- it trembles with giddy
anticipation!

[ Jyze of the Heavenly Year : Red Horse ]


------

34

------


     Bad timing.  Too much work and the work too time-
consuming.  But I'm here anyway to get in a few jyze
licks.  And a few's all it'll be -- about forty minutes'
worth.
     I stopped at the first place where I could see the
moon.  Today's the day it goes full.  It's up there now,
like a beat-up Japanese lantern hanging by an invisible
black string between the upper floors of highrise X and
highrise Y a couple of blocks down the old middle road.
Illumination round!  -- Don't I wish.  But it's round
all right, and glowing a slightly silvery white, and
very bright.  Yayhoo, Monkey moon!  Last lunar fullness
of my pre-recycled life!
     As it happens, I'm perched on a stone ledge in the
garden of remembrance.  Water trickles down by my left
hip -- water dimly lit up from below, as in underworlds.
This is good, this is right -- in mondo ways -- because
tonight's also the night we festively send all the
restless ghostly spirits back to the underworld.  If I
had candles with me and a means of floating them I'd
launch them down the stream right here.  It would be a
lovely scene.  "We leave you our deaths.  Give them
their meaning."  (But this otherworld isn't really
"under"; it's here, there, everywhere.  And so it's not
really "other" either.  It's just that a special time is
passing, temporarily, which is to say it'll be back next
year, and every year, forever -- barring human
extinction and a few other types of catastrophe -- and
each year with a bigger crowd of ghostly visitors than
ever before.)

[ Jyze of the Heavenly Year : Red Horse ]

     And then finally, among auspicious events, just
moments ago the sun passed into Virgo, according to the
charts.  (And now the moon, as if it were a big round
white throw rug being very, very slowly pulled in on a
laundry line, seems to be passing into a quite large
skyscraper window -- or you could say it's moving into
highrise eclipse.  Just a slice of it remains visible.)
     Thus the stage is almost fully set.  Heavenly!
-- As a Blue Rabbit of the mind scampers by.  Red Horse
nostrils flare.  And for the third time in a page and a
half of jyzing I reply to a mixed query/plea: no, sorry,
I don't have a smoke, I don't have a light, I don't have
spare change (in that order, by three different men).
     The ghosts and I now at least seem to be on good
terms.  For one thing, they've noticed that we of the
surface world are considerably more restless and
agitated than they are.  It appears the universe may be
going through one of those flip-flops, similar to when
the main Atlantic Ocean current reverses its clockwise
direction (as it could be doing again any decade now).
It'll soon be a mad scramble -- though not necessarily
voluntary -- to get from surface to under.  And then
what will the meaning of Heavenly be?
     "Give us our meaning!"  -- And today a new way of
doing this hit the media.  Carbon from a loved one's
cremated body will be hardened into a diamond (using a
patented and highly expensive process, to be sure, so
maybe not all possessors of bodies will want to or be
able to partake -- probably only a very few will -- and
so other ways of giving meaning haven't yet become
obsolete) and the diamond will be set in a ring or
brooch or maybe even a tooth, it's suggested, and the
loved one's spirit will gleam forever, restless or not,
and that will be the loved one's meaning.
     -- Well, it's a start.  Next we'll be patenting
ways to inscribe stories on the surface of those
immortal diamond souls -- jyze stories even -- and the
stories will grow longer and longer, like holy books
inscribed on the head of a pin.  And with this extreme
miniaturization and the simultaneous ongoing expansion

of the universe it's possible sufficient space will
always exist for recording all the stories that ever
could be told.  And I'm talking about the material world
now, not any mere virtual one.

     (It's been a fine couple of days.  Busy.  Yet a
relaxed evening with Vic on Tuesday and a good visit
with Mama E yesterday afternoon.  Scoping's been heavy
and so my money worries are over for at least another
six weeks, even though for the long term they've
increased.  Peaches are in season.  The kitchen sink's
acting up again -- what a drain!  And I'm thinking I
must be at the peak of my game for this cluster and the
next one.  -- Well, it's a thought anyway.)

                    *         *

     -- So here's what's happening at mid fifth watch.
This time of year it's still pitch dark and birdless at
this hour, yet warm enough I can be naked, even with the
balcony door open.  And am right now.  When a car passes
by below it hits the iron plates currently covering
holes in the street dug yesterday for purposes of laying
cable: WHAP-WHAP!  If they're going very fast -- and
many are, as always at this hour -- there's a third WHAP
(more like a utensil-drawer drop in some instances) when
the car hits the ground again.

     In the bedroom Z-wiff's coughing a bit.  On the
phone today she said she had the sniffles and might use
them as an excuse not to visit Mama E tomorrow.  Most of
the weekend, after all, will have to go to cleaning up
her old east-hill apartment, which has now been rented
to someone else for next month, thus saving Z a bundle
since the lease doesn't expire until the end of October
-- or is it the beginning of October?  No, I think the
end.  That the turmoil over Mama E has been going on for
almost four months now is already hard enough to fathom.

     Horses everywhere I look in this room.  June sent
over two more today, both painted on a small bamboo tray
in a piece called "Horse Tending," attributed to a Tang
Dynasty artist whose name I'm actually familiar with.
Very fine tray!  I'm intending to come up with a way to
make good use of it.  For now it's going atop the small

row of books to my left, with the Jeep cap on top of it.
(I'm still supposed to be donning this cap as a signal
to Z when I'm jyzing and want to concentrate -- a signal
not to talk -- but haven't done that yet this year and
very rarely did it back in "Jyze Millennium" days.)

What else is happening on the birthday front?  Not
much.  I've agreed to set aside most of three days, from
Friday evening through Sunday of this coming week, but
for what I don't know yet.  Maybe, as on other
birthdays, Z's planning a retreat somewhere.  Not a big
bash, I hope.  The more private and intimate the better.
The "real" birthday, the traditional Western solar one,
is a week from today, but the lunar one is just four
days off, and I'm thinking of that four-day period
between them, and including them, as one big lunisolar
birthday extravaganza.  I'm even considering laying out
forty or fifty bucks for a large bottle of my favorite
bourbon, which I pretty much gave up entirely earlier
this year owing to the cost of drinking a glass of
cabernet each night for health reasons (though I do like
the wine -- just not as much).  So obviously all the
stops are coming out that can come out.  Wild doings
ahead.

On the reacquaintance-with-the-kid front, no real
news.  He started his new paralegal job this week and
presumably that's why draft three of the personal
statement hasn't arrived yet, although he promised it
for last Sunday night.  (I guess he's again "shy" about
leaving a voicemail, this time to warn me about the
delay.  But what the heck, I'm easy.  And perhaps he
already senses this, or down deep always knew it.)  At
one of the glitz-strip chain bookstores yesterday I
happened across -- by sheer luck -- the section for
college guides and it contained no fewer than four books
devoted solely or in major part to preparing personal
statements for law-school applications, so today I left
him a voicemail listing those books.  One of them
included a suggested timetable for various steps in the
application process, and according to that he still has
seven or eight weeks before the optimal filing time.

[ Jyze of the Heavenly Year : Red Horse ]

And I should say: I've been grateful myself to have a
few extra days' respite on editing his statement.

     With Vic it was just a good evening, four or five
hours of leisurely talk as we strolled around from venue
to venue in the HQ -- first a stop under the lucky
composite Brown Horse, then one at Bruce O.'s bookshop,
then one at the waterfall garden park, then one at the
new municipal gallery opening up in the civic center,
and finally one at the sidewalk cafe of the bookstore
bar on the edge road.

     For more than twenty years I've been walking by
Bruce O.'s shop and wanting to meet him, but the few
times I've tried to chat him up he's been all but
totally unresponsive, so I long ago stopped making the
effort.  But because he and Vic are good buddies, this
time was different.  The quadruple-bypass twins, the two
of them -- but Bruce is only six weeks into recovery
from his stroke.  And yet -- so animated!  A lucky
survival -- had he not been in a room with three doctors
present when the stroke hit (while he was hooked up to a
oscilloscope, or whatever they're called, while walking
a treadmill) he'd've been a goner for sure.  Even
indoors today he was wearing his trademark yellow snap-
brim rain hat.  I wonder, did they manage to get him to
doff it before he was anesthetized?  Or did they wait
until lights out for him and remove it themselves?

     By happenstance Evan W.'s wife, Moeko, was present
in the shop when we arrived.  Though she and I have met
several times, she didn't recognize me or recall who I
was when Vic introduced me -- not until I added that I
was the one who'd sent her and Evan the perpetual wooden
Christmas card last year, you know, Zoelie B.'s husband.
Then she remembered -- said she'd loved that card.

     It was Moeko who reminded Vic about the municipal-
gallery opening, so after chatting for an hour or so in
front of the waterfall (where on some occasions in the
past Vic and I must've both been present at the same
time, since he's visited the site quite often for years
and usually, like me, in the late afternoon) -- after
that, I say, we went on up to check out the gallery

opening.  The one big disappointment there was that not
a single Vic H. canvas was on offer.  Why? I asked.
"That's a good question," he said grimly.  There was an
Evan W. canvas, however, and also the man himself was on
hand -- for his day job he works a few feet away from
Jean, Vic's wife, in the A-mart produce department --
and we gabbed a bit with him and, again, Moeko before we
had to stop because the mayor was about to deliver a
speech.  A crowd of forty or so, including many of the
artists who'd done the paintings on display -- all from
the city's art collection -- applauded politely as the
TV lights flashed on.  Who knows, maybe on that day this
jyzer right here made his first J-town TV appearance
ever -- possibly even on four different channels!
(Though I can think of a few other possible times,
especially during politcal demos.)
     Vic's been working fiendishly on his stories.  He
says my suggestion that he tell the tale of his rejected
Chinatown mural (this happened half a century ago down
in MSM #2) as a concluding chapter has enabled him to
see the stories as a single whole for the first time, or
at least in a much more unified way than before.  And he
had a present for me: an envelope containing the revised
versions of the stories I read before and also several
new ones.  Going over those will be my free-time task
for the next couple of weeks -- if I have any free time.
But sooner or later I will, and I'm looking forward to
reading those reworked stories.
     Ulp, ulp, the fifth watch ended almost twenty
minutes ago.  And it's still dark out there.  I was
fooled!  So now I gotta run.  Run for bed!  And tend
real quick to several neglected chores along the way.


[+2]


     Sittin' on a bench in the park.  Hilltop park this
is, or officially south-hill playground, a two-block
stroll due south of 1511.  Lazy Saturday afternoon.  My
favorite bench over by the waterless wading pool is

occupied, drat it anyway, so I've hunted down the only other shady bench in the park. This one faces south toward the baseball/soccer field, the elementary school, and the big southern volcano (which can't be seen today owing to haze and clouds claiming that quadrant -- and claiming all other quadrants too, except for a raggedy-edged round patch directly overhead looking, once again, like a bald spot and revealing a blue celestial scalp).

A fine site for the very last entry of my official solar pre-elderhood. -- But wait a minute, I'm making it sound as if I think I'm about to become a fossil merely because, by the way of counting one's years taught by the culture I've grown up in, I'll be clicking over into sexagenarian territory. But not to worry: I know living beings no matter how old are unlikely to fossilize overnight. It's probable I'll still be good to go for at least a while.

For Z-wiff the afternoon is not a lazy one; she's over cleaning Mama E's former apartment, and I'll be joining her there later. We'd been hoping to catch a touring lefty carnival of sorts with Wei and Alison this evening -- one of the few sparks of dissent in view on the national scene this summer -- but we couldn't work out the timing. (As a big jet passes overhead just above the clouds and right through the bald spot. The flight path from the main J. City airport still runs directly along our street here, but usually the jets are up quite a bit higher. -- Any long-term significance to this altitude change? Can't say I know of any just yet. But also can't say I'm not suspicious.)

So where have all the neighbors gone? Only two other park visitors are present, and they're both sitting on my favorite bench. I suppose lots of folks are off on vacation (which has always been one of the banes of my birthday week: fewer people around to attend the party). Others are probably working in their gardens or watching a ball game on TV or -- who knows what. What do people do at this time of the afternoon these days? Mainly stare at pixels?

Coming here always brings Kat to mind. We had lots

of fun in this park back before she started morphing
into an adolescent with a whole new set of hormones in
play.  Snowball fights, swinging, frisbeeing, nerfing,
merry-go-rounding until we were both too dizzy to stand
up.  (A lone pigeon just crept up on me from behind.
It's pecking at the ground within leg's reach to my
right and looking up at me between pecks with a
dissolute but pleading eye.  Pigeons must get fed a lot
from these benches.  This one's grossly overweight --
clearly a contemporary USAn pigeon.)  -- And here comes
the ice-cream truck with its familiar loop of insipid
jingles: all being snatches of standard tunes, many
wholly inappropriate for one reason or another: "Jingle
Bells," the Marine fight song, etc.  Maybe that's why
the truck doesn't draw out any kids?  It doesn't even
bother to slow down as it rolls by the park.

     From this spot a long-distance view opens in all
directions.  But none of the views are much good.
Truncated corridors appear here and there between houses
and under the crowns of trees.  In effect you're sitting
in the shallow caldera of a small volcano with a few
jagged gaps in its walls, which are the houses and
apartment buildings, and only two of those structures
more than three stories tall.  -- Or it's even more like
an old USAn hilltop fort, quite sizable, with a few
gates open in the walls in the belief the enemy whose
land we're in the process of stealing won't be attacking
us for at least another hour or two.

     I came here today because my Celestial calendar
says we're at "Limit of Heat."  Does that mean the
upcoming fifteen-day period's as hot as it gets or that
today marks the end of the hottest period or even that
today's the last day when it's possible to have heat?  I
don't know.  But whatever it might mean, I wanted to
experience it myself firsthand.  This is the outdoor
place I could do it with the least possible effort.

     And today my very first "outside" birthday message
came in -- "outside" here meaning other than from June
or Z-wiff.  It might be my last too, so I should savor
it.  It's a voicemail from Wei and Alison, presumably

thinking they might not see us again this week after we canceled the carnival.  They do a spirited version of the traditional happy-birthday song.  Wei's harmonizing sounds a little off-pitch at times but still impressive.  Alison calls me "Glenneee-eee" at the end -- her singing voice is unexpectedly sweet.  I'm bemused by this serenade but also of course delighted and touched.  Now I'm trying to think of something I can sing back to them as a thank-you.  Maybe "Too Much Horsey Business."

During my most recent visit to Mama E, as I sat next to her on the deeply upholstered loveseat where she spends almost all her waking hours, she clamped an iron grip on my left forearm and looked me hard in the eye and said, breaking into a wide grin, "Next week is your big week!"  (But yesterday she was in "high dementia," Z said, leaving her, Z, weeping for hours after her visit and then for another hour when I arrived home at the usual 1:30 a.m. last night.  Mama E was demanding to go to the emergency room but didn't want Z to tell Tony or Benita, her caregivers, about it.  It's been more than six weeks since her last such visit.  We figure she'd probably been making them quite regularly for years back in Centropolis without ever letting Z know and now in J. City she's had to go cold turkey and she's jonesing for the drama and attention.  The trouble is, as always, maybe some new development really does merit emergency treatment.  How can we ever be sure? -- Well, I can think of a few ways, yes.  But none of those are detectable right now, thank goddess.  -- Such as finding her lying on the floor out cold or worse, what I mean.)

-- A Latino man in a baseball cap (Astros) with the brim pulled low over his eyes and a big black dog lunging at the end of its leash: their sudden appearance galvanizes the pigeons and also me.  At first I didn't see the leash -- just the big black dog crashing into my right peripheral vision.  Shades of old Mikey leaping out from the bushes as I headed up the side walkway at 1511 back in TJM days.

Life's aburst with adventures.  For pigeons and

nonpigeons and quasipigeons alike.  (Foghorn sounding
from the bay, train whistle accompanying it, another jet
flying low, a trolley bus rolling by -- maybe this is
the site I should've chosen for that center-of-the-
world feeling -- and it offers a top-of-the-mountain
bonus -- cherry on top.)

    This year my extended birthday celebration
coincides, I'll note here, with the convening in South
Africa of the third Earth Summit.  Hopefully it will put
into a bit higher dramatic relief our country's shameful
act of opting out of the Kyoto Accord and going its own
reckless way on global roasting and the ecocrisis as on
everything else.  The rest of the world must figure out
how to tie down this 8,000-pound gorilla that is us or
we'll make the sky fall for sure.  Already it -- the sky
-- seems to many to be doing just that owing to massive
floods in Europe and Asia, massive droughts elsewhere,
massive glacier melts, massive extinctions, massive
acidification of the oceans, massive soil depletions,
massive disease and pestilence (West Nile disease
reaches our state!) -- but of course all this is only
the beginning.  Or rather not the beginning -- not even
the prelude -- it's just a few of the lesser instruments
of horror tuning up in the end-times orchestra pit.

    As for our country's avowed fifty-year war to wipe
out evil, the supreme leader has now let it be known
he's a "patient man" and he really hasn't decided yet
whether he'll order an attack on Iraq or, if so, when
it'll be.  Meanwhile preparations continue apace.  But
the chieftain is feeling a little heat because of new
financial scandals and the outbreak of what some are
calling "a real debate" on Iraq.  But as far as I can
see the only "real" debate is still between right-wing
factions as to the best tactics for producing "regime
change" in Iraq -- that is, for turning it into another
USAn tributary state under firm multinational-corporate
control, with the profits from all that Iraqi oil (used
mainly to fuel USAn SUVs and give an in-your-face boost
to global roasting) -- with all those profits, I say,
lining the usual power-elite pockets, perhaps along with

those of a few key Iraqi quislings.  Until this "regime
change" is accomplished all true-blue USAn patriots will
rest uneasy.
     -- Another goldang gloom-and-doom rant.  This is no
way to end the last of the pre-recycle entries.  I'm
supposed to be celebrating!  So maybe I'll come back
tonight and go for something calmer and more
traditionally philosophical.  Or better, maybe something
bluesy and melancholy, nostalgic, allowing for a little
haunting of my reveries....
                    *              *

     So after doing the moving -- the first load of Mama
E's stuff, now stored mostly in various niches (or
"nitches") and crannies here at 1511 -- it's been a
night of relaxed reading.  I did call Elgie but a party
was in progress -- or sounded more like howling regress
-- at his friend's place at one a.m. and he agreed to
call me back tomorrow afternoon.  Z hit the sack early,
plumb tuckered out from the cleaning labors.
     Jyze or no jyze tonight I asked myself.  If jyze,
what's the peg?  Maybe better no jyze so as to let the
reservoir refill for the big birthday-week jyzathon.
     Then at the last moment a peg appeared.  Or rather
it was there all along but I didn't notice it.  It's
already Sunday morning, almost five a.m., and at
midnight Monday night the big bash will begin.
Therefore today is my last full normal from-rising-to-
retiring Gregorian day of being a non-elder.  That's the
peg.  Solarly speaking it's my last day to whippersnap.
     And about what?  That, of course, is the rub
concerning this peg.
     Lots of sky in view from the black armchair but no
moon.  Quiet sifting of the fan, balcony door open,
jazz playing softly on the radio -- probably the last
tune of the night.  The stack of discarded newspapers
has mounted to an all-time high or close to it, right
here next to the chair.  I can put my hand on it -- and
do.  It sways but stays upright.  But the addition to it
of the upcoming Sunday papers could easily topple it.
-- And here comes the public-radio news again but the

extended kind, not just headlines.  Best to flick it
off.
     No point in launching into another rant either.
It's just a fine gentle night.  I'm grateful to be able
to experience such nights.  Grateful to have made it
this far in a life that by and large -- and despite the
many sorrows I've brought down on myself and others --
has been a run of pretty damn good nights and days as
well.  With the world I have some quarrels -- well, just
one big, complex one really; the others I can let slide
more or less permanently -- but with myself I'm at
peace.  These are the really, really good years.  I
don't expect them to end tomorrow just because I'll be
crossing this arbitrarily drawn line into elderhood.
Knock on newspaper stack!  (In my biased view this right
here -- bringers of news (and lit) -- is the highest and
best use for trees.  Otherwise, and for the most part,
far better to leave them in the ground.  -- But of
course both of these statements are much too simplistic.
And yet still welcome under the jyze rules.)
     So -- keep slinging it, Jyzer G.  But on the other
hand right now go grab yourself some sleep.  Gird up for
the dag-nabbest celebration of a lifetime -- coming
right after this short break.


------


35


------


     It's happening at midnight, here on the same
outdoor steps at the east-depot complex where I began
this exercise in shameless autofestschriftian self-
indulgence (not to say solipsistic decadence) exactly
seven lunar months and nineteen lunar/solar days ago.
Only major difference is this time the moon's up there,

perfectly positioned at thirty degrees above the horizon
and the A-mart parking lot and maybe twenty degrees
above the glowing orange-brick DC castle.  A gibbous
moon, a Monkey moon, a moon howling like a gibbon.

        You made it!  You're ancient!  You're ancient and
yet you're still not completely history!  You're still
on the go!  Even while seated!  You deserve
congratulations of the highest order!

        -- I'm expecting the security guard to come along
any minute now just as before and try to kick my ass off
this concrete step.  A short while ago I got the boot
from another spot where I was thinking about setting up
for this grand moment -- three blocks to the north at
the western entrance to the AQ where the two Red Dragons
stand watch, or hang watch would be more accurate, on
their lampposts.  It was my intention to sit on the
steps of the waterfront-streetcar terminus across the
very high road from the Dragons; the moon looked like a
great glowing truncated pearl or perhaps a beach ball
suspended on their extruded tongues where they almost
met above the middle of the street.  But that terminus
is shut down now because of construction and the instant
I stepped inside the yellow warning ribbon a loud
tapping sounded from a second-floor window of the ten-
story building that's going up next to the station.  A
guard glaring and wagging his finger hung over me like a
childhood vision of the discipline monster.  Apparently
he'd been keeping an eye on me as a suspicious character
as I scouted out the site.  I lingered a moment or two
to show I'm not easily intimidated and then skedaddled.

        It's very important to have a Red Dragon in sight.
Two are not necessary -- just one will do.  And luckily
I've got one here, sort of.  It's the big metal Dragon
coiled around the cylindrical pole outside A-mart's main
entrance, just to the rear of the large stone lantern.
Ordinarily this Dragon isn't Red -- it's an ironish
brown, maybe slightly rusty -- but I chose my spot
carefully so the Dragon would pick up reflections of the
red safety lights of the baseball stadium, hidden behind
the edge of the bank building to my right.  So it's Red.

[ Jyze of the Heavenly Year : Red Horse ]

It's a Red Dragon and this is a Red Dragon cluster.  In
the Great Year of the Red Horse.  A fiery time.  All
these Reds represent the element Fire.  Passion reigns
supreme.  But it's a lucky time also.  Regarded by many
as the most auspicious of all times of year.

        As days go, however, it's been a screwy one.  I'm
more than slightly discombobulated by all the
excitement.  Haven't made it in to work yet -- had to
return to 1511 early to pick up the Z-mobile so I'd be
able to drive myself home later when I've finished my
scoping work long after the buses have stopped running.
Then at our door I stuck my key in the wrong lock -- the
one that's been broken for years -- and was surprised
when the door wouldn't open.  I thought Z-wiff must've
left it locked on the inside, as she's done on several
other occasions, so I rapped on the door a few times and
when no response came I was making ready for a mighty
macho moment: breaking down the door (it's actually
quite easy to do).  -- But then she appeared, baffled,
asking me through the closed door who I was; and when I
confirmed it was just the old G-hub she swung the door
open on her naked self (except for the waist-encircling
"blue inner tube" she still wears at times on weeknights
to protect against back problems).  "What are you doing
here?  Why didn't you just use your key?  Is something
weird going on?"  -- And she told me the living room was
out of bounds until midnight.  I apologized and
explained and tucked her back in and rushed off so I'd
be down here by the appointed time -- saving the big
surprise in the living room for later.

        Earlier, leaving the house in midafternoon, I took
the winding western road off the hill so I could load up
on special libations for the Heavenly double birthday
party.  -- Found the state liquor store with no trouble.
Like our house and like lots of other houses and like
many warehouses and even a stadium or two down in the
reclaimed tidelands area it rests almost directly atop
our recently discovered branch of the J-town Fault.

        Glancing up now.  Sail along, silvery half moon!
-- Looking as though you've been shot straight up out

of the central tower of the DC castle -- like a half-
disintegrated white-hot cannon ball.  Which if it goes
straight up must eventually come straight down.  And if
it did, it would wipe out one of the last and largest of
the dot-com wonderbizzes.

   -- So I say this is an auspicious time.  And I've
got a reason and I mean an unexpected one.  It still
seems way too good to be true, and it also seems I
must've planned it somehow to happen just when it did,
but the timing obviously is just sheer dumb good luck.
And things could still go wrong; to name a couple, an
earthquake could swallow the whole hill or the silvery
half-cannonball could fall on our apartment since it's
only a few hundred yards south of the DC castle.  And
regardless, let me record the good news in this J-book
right now while I can.

   My son says he wants to meet his father!  Glen III
wants to meet Glen II (actually Jr.)!  It wouldn't truly
be our first meeting -- I lived with him for about
fifteen months when he was an infant and was in his
company for a total of maybe a dozen hours during his
early teen years -- but it would be our first meeting as
adults.  If it really does happen.  But here's the
stunner to me: he proposed it!

   I'll have to save the specifics on this until
later.  I haven't even made it in to work yet -- as I've
already said -- and soon the bars will be closing.  But
I do want to note the third Earth Summit is getting
underway in South Africa and also all day it's been
Women's Equality Day in the U.S. and for both of those
reasons we cheer this day.  And Mama E is showing quirky
new signs of life and I'm wearing a six-day beard (just
to give myself and any passersby an intimation of how
I'll look as a confirmed graybeard) and the White House
is now suddenly claiming that the congressional
authorization of the 1991 use of our armed forces to
"roll back" the Iraqi invasion of Kuwait also authorizes
an attack on Iraq itself now, eleven years later.

   Back on day one of the Heavenly Year I saw a number
of Old Glories when I sat on this same spot.  Tonight

not a single one's in view.  Does this mean anything?  I
hope so.  But does it mean the superhawkish cabal in
Washington will pull back on its war plans?  Dubious.

But now I'm an elder by lunar count.  Maybe that
durn cabal will finally start listening to me.

The Z-mobile's parked a block up the street.  Even
in the midst of high festivities there's still scope
business to be taken care of before I head home tonight.

*          *

Sixteen hours later and by NUT time and also by the
jyze rules it's a new day but I'm suspending both of
those heuristics for this special occasion and sticking
with Gregorian time.

Meanwhile I've worked at the scope office,
celebrated at home, slept, caught up on newspapers, and
now I'm on my way back in for more scoping.  Drat the
luck!  Another heavy workweek!  But it's driving the
wolf from the door and so I welcome it.

Oh such a fine day it is.  I've come in this far
via the east-hill back path and all along the way tables
and chairs have been set out on sidewalks but with few
available seats, including here at the primo J. City
javahaus; I had to wait several minutes before I could
grab the one I'm holding down now.  On my left a row of
smokers is emitting enormous I'm-da-coolest plumes which
slowly drift this way but on my right a small evergreen
is working hard to filter the air and on the sidewalk
below stands a cold bottle of root beer, so what's to
complain about?  (As for latching onto a table inside,
perish the thought until maybe ten p.m.)  (As now a
couple of colorfully spandexed men dismount and chain
their fancy mountain bikes to the hitching post and
sashay inside hand-in-hand.  More power to you, dudes!)

Me the shaggy hippie type, ponytailed and now a
full week gray-grizzled.  Some might say I'm way out of
my element here.  I say not so.

In shades.  Bright late sun blasting straight up
the street corridor all the way from the waterfront.
Abundant traffic fumes adding to the smoky mix.  Jagged
mountains out there farther to the west, almost hazed

out.  But the skyscraper shadows here just east of J-
town's big downtown cluster are sharp and lengthy.

So it's still the same day, and therefore still the
day of days.  Front-loaded, this double-double, but also
back-loaded, because another day of days will be coming
up in just fifty-six hours or so.  "What a scam he's got
goin'!" Wei reportedly proclaimed to Z at lunch today,
referring to me and my four-day lunisolar birthday (not
to mention the fifth birthday earlier this month
("Gregorian shadow") and the sixth back in February
("Birthday of Humanity")).  The card companies and the
gift industry ought to glom onto the idea, Wei went on;
thar's gold in thet thar moon.  -- And it's still not
out, by the way.  Not until quarter past ten tonight.
And I'm wondering: should that one be considered my
lunar-birthday moon or was last night's the one?  Only
tonight's moon rises during the Gregorian twenty-four-
hour period of my lunar birthday, but last night's was
visible for a longer time (by a factor of three) during
that same period.  And to this I say: why should I have
to choose?  I'll take 'em both!

Last night I didn't arrive home until 5:05 a.m.
Right away I poured myself a celebratory drink from the
big new bottle of primo bourbon and then used it to wash
down some leftover chicken -- hadn't had a thing to eat
for fifteen hours, since breakfast -- and then opened
the two wrapped presents (each with a funny card) the Z-
woman had left on my chair.  Wotta wiff!  Wotta scam
I've got going, you betcha!  A book of 1940s songs, a
video of newsreels from 1942 -- and a promise to
serenade me with my pick of the songs.  So I made my way
straight to the bedroom -- right at the usual time, as
it happened -- but with drink in hand and moving already
a little unsteadily.  And in very high spirits.

Just the husband she always dreamt of: staying out
on the town all night, coming to bed at dawn stinking
drunk.  As she'd observed a few times before, when under
the influence I often become "highly attentive sexually"
though not necessarily in ithyphallic fashion.  And that
was so on this occasion.  But we had a rollicking good

time regardless.  Lotsa smacks and licks and lotsa yuks
too.  Elderman!  -- And after half an hour she had to
get up and go off to work just as if it were a normal
kind of day.  (Her best line of the night: "Oooh, I
think I'm slickin' fer a lickin'!")

     And going off to work is what I must be doing
myself before much longer here.  But I'll be back later,
jyzing away some more, because during these four days of
high holiday I'm allowed to do that.  For this special
period even jyze's most hallowed axioms get relaxed.

     In the mail today, a magazine-size package from
sister Barb.  I haven't opened it yet.  It might be
wiser not to open it at all and just write her with
profuse thanks but without mentioning whatever's in the
package, just in case it's something to make my heart
sink (as has been true several times in the past).
-- But no, the elder brother -- now doubly elder -- must
not prejudge and will try hard not to judge at all.

     -- As the sun sinks behind a mountain.  Half's
still showing, like the throw-rug moon in skyscraper-
window eclipse the other night.  But down here on the
street all's no longer a dazzling golden haze.

     Before moving along I must mention today's news.
The snarly-mouthed neocon veep gives a predictably
hyper-hawkish speech on Iraq -- and his key rationale is
that we must attack them before they attack us!  That
nasty Iraq is going to attack the poor defenseless
hyperpower!  And with what?  Sandbags maybe?  The veep
can provide no evidence whatsoever that Iraq possesses
even a single "weapon of mass destruction" (while we of
course, as noted before, have tens of thousands) or any
connection at all with those evil-to-the-marrow Al Qaeda
terrorists.  And yet the cabal's plans for a "regime
change" attack lurch ahead unimpeded.  The world thinks
we're mad -- because we are.  Power mad.  Guilt-driven
what's more.  And in numerous ways in absolute denial.

     -- Sun's completely gone now.  Just a band of
golden glow hanging on above the sharply cut mountain
silhouettes.  Root beer's gone too except for this one
last swig -- skoal, you golden geezer!

[ Jyze of the Heavenly Year : Red Horse ]

(I'm just a bit hung over, I must admit, from last night's overindulgence.  Knowing what this slight headache comes from, it almost feels good.  It feels even better when I remind myself that further overindulgences lie ahead during this high-scam bash.)

*          *

-- Back again for a lunar encore.  Lunar, loony, selenocentric, moonstruck, I don't know.  Another double-stiff one here.  The corner of our unit 203 "great room" with all the greenery and the puffing "Fookin' Fogies" klock.  Way across the room the magic-fin salmon swims -- slowly rotating -- just below ceiling level.  And outside the window here stands the hilarious new "It's a Boy!" Heavenly Year stork.
As I walked toward the house from the bus stop I could see something unusual: our balcony light was shining.  It's a big white globe the size of a soccer ball -- the moon effect, I was thinking (as the ever more gibbous real moon kept an eye on all this from its perch above the mountains to the east).  Then I saw more strangeness up on the balcony -- an extremely large bird, it appeared.  Not until I was standing on the side walkway a story below the balcony could I see it was indeed a large bird: a stork, in fact, about five feet tall, wearing a top hat with "It's a Boy!" written across the crown, and a bundle suspended in a sling from its beak.  And not until I got up here and examined the bundle closely (cackling sporadically) did I realize it's shaped like male genitals and has goofy words about the J-slinger written in the spaces for the baby's description: name, weight, length, etc.  And not until I was back inside moments later, ensconced in the black armchair and gazing out at this bizarre bird, did another dimension of its aptness occur to me: what the Heavenly birthday stork is bringing me this year is indeed a boy.  My own boy, Elgie.  A bit delayed but -- for real!  (If it works out.)
This Z-wiff, over and over again I'm astounded by how she can outdo me at my own game.  ("It's a Girl!" "It's My Girl!"  "It's the Girl of a Lifetime!")  -- And

now I'm oiling myself up for another bedtime "midnight
creep," so to speak, though at five-thirty a.m., and
this one will make last night's look like a bumbly early
rehearsal.  And what will I be wearing?  Why of course:
my birthday suit!  (Groan groan groan and so be it.)

   -- But I do want to say a few words about this
"new" son too.  His proposal that we meet came at the
very end of our forty-five-minute talk Sunday.  It
stunned me with its sheer unexpectedness.  What he
suggested was this: that I join him on his tour of law-
school campuses when he learns which ones have accepted
him (he's quite confident a number of them will) and
must choose among them.  Yikes -- that would cost lotsa
bucks!  "Well, maybe I could do one or two," I
stammered.  "I mean, it would be a trip to do them all,
but...."  He also said: "It would be a good way for us
to get to know each other."  Was this a dream or what?

   And earlier he'd sounded genuinely excited when I'd
said I could send him, if he'd like, a lot of material
about his ancestors on his father's side.  "I'm older
now," he assured me.  "Maybe I wasn't ready before but I
am now."  He even asked me to include a list of the
vites & supps I take.  And was startled to hear I weigh
somewhere between 215 and 220 now.  "I'll just be a
stick next to you!" he cried (he weighs 170).

   All this knocking me for a loony loop.  As did the
news that the car he drives is a black Mercedes
convertible, a '99 model, bought new when his dot-com
business was flying high.  "I told you he was a fox!"
was Z's comment upon hearing this.  A mover, she meant.
Swift with the distaffs.  "It's a boy toy!"  Well,
maybe, but that's not the way he comes across to me on
the phone.  He sounds both too dreamy and too practical
for that.  (JRX on the brand name up there: shame on me.
And on him too, in my view, for rolling on such wheels.)

   And then this: he seemed startled to hear he's the
age right now, almost to the month, that I was when he
was conceived.  "I was born in '42, you know," I said.
"Conceived on Pearl Harbor Day.  Did you know that?
Your mother must've told you.  That's one of my favorite

growing-up stories."  But he hadn't heard it.  A pause,
and then: "So Dad, does that mean -- you mean you're ten
years younger than her?"  Now he sounded shocked.  And a
moment later: "I'm embarrassed to mention this, Dad, but
I don't even know when your birthday is -- what date, I
mean.  Let's see, if I'm the same age you were...."
"Well, Son, I'm a little embarrassed to tell you too,
but as a matter of fact it's this week.  It's my
Heavenly Year, you know, Year of the Horse and all that,
the Water Horse, Black Horse, same as the year I was
born, the cycle of sixty starting all over again."
"That sounds sort of like what they have in Korea."
"Exactly right -- and not by coincidence!"
     But enough of that.  More to the point, he's
working on his applications and he likes his new job as
a paralegal.  He's planning to sell the fancy wheels to
help pay for his first year of law school -- meaning
he's broke, or near broke, just as I figured.  As he
ages a bit some of the baby fat is melting away and he's
revealing himself to be a chip off the old block.  And
now he appreciates the old block itself a lot more too:
his boss, an Ivy League law-school grad, is very bright,
he told me, and has two daughters who are attending the
"best college in the country -- Adams!"  (Meaning I'll
soon have to perform a bit of jujitsu on the facts for
him and explain why I ended up my career there in such
ignominy -- and proud of it!)
     The next installment on this miraculous tale will
be next week, I hope.  He's vowed -- "really, really" --
he'll focus his full attention on the personal
statement, version three.  (Z-wiff said she'd never
heard me talking on the phone in a tone quite like what
she was hearing as she slipped in and out of the room
during this call.  Not exactly avuncular, according to
her, but very close to downright patriarchal.  And here
I thought I was warm and encouraging!  -- But yeah, I
can see why she'd hear it that way and maybe he would
too.  I'm still more on guard than I want to be.
Progress, though, is surely occurring.)
     Huh?  Am I losing it here at six after five in the

a.m.?  The glass of lunar-birthday libation is empty
-- that's a tip-off right there.  Almost time for the
bedward creep.  But I do want to say things have reached
a high point.  I've been hoping for years that something
like this Elgie resurfacing would occur.  Now the
Heavenly lunar birthday has a meaning bigger to me than
that of just about any other day in my life.  And: it
fits the occasion.  It expresses who I am, how I've
lived, who I want to be.  A big crescendo moment here.
"Peak experience" -- this is it!  Can't be topped!

But I can close the book on it too.  Move on.  For
after all, this is just one day of four.  (As the steps
of the paper-delivery guy sound -- a bad toss, I can
tell, because instead of returning to the car after
tossing it he keeps going toward the lobby patio and I
hear him toss it again over by the door -- and now as he
leaves he clears his throat right beneath my open window
here -- a surprisingly intimate little moment.)


[+2]


An outdoor bench at the downtown plaza.  The
fountain roars and a nodder nods (a vigorous one too,
taking up a whole bench a few paces to my left).  But
I've finally found me a space-time cranny for jyzing.
Just a tiny one, though, big enough to let the jyzer
make his mark with minimal details and that's it.

Already it's close to dusk on the second inner day
of the Heavenly double-double.  Surprises and glitches
galore forced me to cancel the entry planned for the
first inner day.  Another full night of grand jury still
lies ahead.  Traffic was terrible coming back in from
Benita's place tonight -- a trip that usually takes
twenty or thirty minutes took almost two hours.

Most of yesterday afternoon's potential jyze cranny
went to phone talks with June and Vic as well as the
usual one with Z, and all of them quite long.  Vic
hadn't realized it was my birthday; he was calling
because he needed directions to my hideaway office.

He'd gotten lost inside the building, he said, while
trying to deliver his latest batch of "Cicatrix"
stories.  June was sad again -- still the bar-exam
postpartum and uncertainty, the big changes in her life.
She was in FCM #1 last week, leaves for the megastate
tomorrow.  She's not pleased with son Michael's new plan
to teach in China for the next year.  I said I thought
it would be a great broadener and eye-opener for him.
He's about a year younger than I was when I left for
Korea -- which is to say he's Elgie's age.
        And then a tough night of grand jury with a ninety-
page expedite order to top it off.  I had to drive back
down at 1:30 a.m. and didn't get home again until twenty
to five and I was totally wasted.  Jyze was impossible.
        And then this afternoon at Mama E's, just me and
her.  I furnished the cake and candles.  She could eat
only a few crumbs.  My birthday present from her is
"John Wayne's America," a book on the workings of
celebrity by a writer I admire.  I showed her the front-
cover photo of the conservative icon himself playing the
role of Rooster Cogburn -- complete with eyepatch -- in
"True Grit."  "Yep, it's you," she cackled.  "But you
look better on the other side."  (That one shows the
icon in his sleek younger days as "the Kid," I believe,
in "Stagecoach.")  -- But those were pretty much the
only good moments.  She told me she's developing the
shakes -- wanted to go to the doctor tomorrow or maybe
call 911 immediately.  I'm handing off to Z-wiff on this
one.  She's skipping work tomorrow, Friday, by the way
-- my big day -- and after I get up at my usual early-
afternoon hour we'll be heading off somewhere private
for most of the Labor Day weekend.  It'll probably be
her view that this "shakes" business has more to do with
Mama E's feeling abandoned -- meaning it's payback.
Probably at least partially true too.  (It was Z, of
course, who picked out the John Wayne book and painted
the Red Horses Black -- with some Red still showing
through, just right -- on the nifty Chinese bag she
found to wrap the book in.  And last night, staying
firmly on message, the gift on the chair was a splendid

Chinese pen box with a mash love note from her inked in
among the ancient ideograms adorning the outside.)
      Flags rippling.  Music of street musicians
clashing.  A slight autumnal chill in the breeze.
      Any last thoughts as a pre-elder of the solar type?
Tonight's the last time I can make a claim to that
appellation, at least by the sixty-year standard --
which after all is the one I've adopted as my own.
Starting about three hours from now I can maybe still
qualify for pre-ancient but no longer pre-elder.


                         [+1]


      -- After all this buildup the day itself ought to
be a big echoing silence.  And it might be yet, or close
to it.  But not here as it's starting out at a very late
hour.  Not if the birthday kid can help it.  Almost half
past five in the a.m. -- I'm again suspending NUT time,
as is only appropriate for a solar birthday -- and
admittedly I can barely keep my eyes open.  Didn't get
home until an hour ago and as I came in the door Z-wiff
serenaded me with "Happy Birthday Again" from our bed.
I lay down next to her and we nuzzled and updated each
other in the dark for a while and then she donned her
robe and accompanied me into the living room.  Several
handmade banners were stretched across the room at odd
angles ("because my M'bao loves banners so much") and
the neon glowboxes were all aglow and a wrapped present
and two cards were awaiting me on the black armchair
(where I'm sitting now, and libating too, for an almost
unheard-of fourth straight night).  I said I wanted to
wait until this coming afternoon to open the cards and
gift.  She was disappointed but still okay with it.  She
said I'm to pack an overnight bag and around five p.m.
we'll be hiking down to the waterfront -- that's all
she'd tell me.  But she was sorry to hear I hadn't had
time to stop by the hideaway earlier after seeing Mama E
-- something birthday-related awaits me there too.
      "You're spoiled," she pointed out.  And ain't it

the truth!  (But in my defense I'll note I've done a
good deal of spoiling of her too, especially during her
own Heavenly Year last year.  And will soon be doing
even more to try to get back ahead of the game.)

A hard-rock-loving longhair crew was laying new
carpet in the hall outside the scope office tonight.  My
eyes are still stinging from their glue fumes.  For a
late snack I had two scoops of someone else's salted-
caramel ice cream from the office fridge (it's been in
there for weeks).  Tonight's scoping was the high-speed
pinball-tournament type -- my senses are still racing.

Baseball strike on or off?  Nobody knows.  The
deadline's here -- the 30th.  Yes it is!  And everyone
cares!  Or so's you'd think from the media uproar.

Ten to six in the morning on the bewitching day.
Obviously I'm incapable of coherent thought.  Words are
going down, I can see that, but what are they saying?

They're saying: having writ, this J-stick hereby
retracts so as not to impede the race to the sack.  But
will step back in later and race again itself, maybe
against itself, but try for true lofty official-biggest-
day-of-a-lifetime focus.

*      *

-- And here I am in Heaven.  Or as close as I'll
ever get to it, and it's pretty damn close.  It's a room
at the teahouse hotel in the AQ -- the hotel that
occupies the four floors above the teahouse itself.  And
not just any room -- it's a corner room.  Not a bridal
suite or a honeymoon suite or a presidential suite but
all those and more rolled into one: the Heavenly Year
Suite!  It sez so right on the door!  In handwriting (on
cardstock showing lotsa hearts and flowers around the
borders) that closely resembles the Z-woman's.

It's somewhere around three a.m., so technically by
Gregorian count the Heavenly birthday is over -- but not
so by the way I'm back to counting now.  By NUT time
it's still Friday the 30th.  "It's your day!"  And
asleep in the white-bedding-swaddled iron-framed bed at
whose foot I hunch over in a plush white circular
armchair of uncertain vintage jyzing merrily away in a

circle of light shed by a hilariously rickety spare lamp
provided by Don, the caretaker: asleep in that bed, I
say, is the wiff of the millennium. Who's pulled out
all the birthday stops -- in fact the celebration still
has two days to run by her reckoning. This is just the
first stage of a three-day wild weekend overlapping with
the four-day lunisolar bash. She insists and I happily
acquiesce. As she says: "We need this! We deserve it!"
     Windows open for a refreshing cross breeze,
authentically antique white lace curtains stirring
gently inside the pulled shades as gulls cry in the
distance. (As with humans, some gulls work -- maybe
even prefer -- the night shift.) A train whistle cries
too and not very far away: I can hear the rumble and
think maybe I can feel it faintly (it's entering the
downtown tunnel two blocks to the west). Reminds me of
the passing freights at the Hotel La Chevalle, as does
this hotel itself: very similar turn-of-the-century
vintage -- turn of nineteenth century into twentieth,
I'm saying. And just about everything in this room
looks to have survived most of the past century if not
all or maybe a little more than all: dresser, bed, a
primitive wooden armoire (if that's the word for a
closet on wheels), even the sink in the corner -- which
in turn reminds me of the two SRO hotels I lived in
about a quarter century back.
     Lots of history here. Up until World War II this
area was the heart of Japantown. Here and at the very
similar hotel next door, and at a number of others
nearby, hundreds or maybe even thousands of Asian men,
including many Filipinos, lived alone in single rooms.
The historic Japanese theater is just a block up the
hill, the terrace gardens where jyze likes to hold forth
almost across the street.
     It's the perfect place to be on this occasion.
That immediately became clear when we arrived. And
before then I didn't know we were coming here. Z's
canny misdirections -- "At about five o'clock we should
walk down to the waterfront" -- had me utterly fooled: I
visualized a ferry trip, an inn somewhere on the far

side.

     She hit on this idea almost two months ago --
shortly after we toured the place in early July.  She
knows my mind and heart.

     Further proof of that: her main gift, opened after
my breakfast this afternoon (and a slight meltdown over
a neglected piece of birthday ritual -- "The missed
stitch that allows the tapestry to be beautiful").  It's
a mola!  And not just any mola, but one of a Black
Horse!  Framed beautifully, in warm brown rounded wood,
by our WOC friend Melanie, Jay's wife.  And picked up,
the mola itself, by a work friend of Z's who visited
Panama this spring.  Z's comment: "It's the only way I
could hope even to approach the portrait you did for my
Heavenly Year birthday."  (So I must say that portrait
turned out to be far more of a success than I thought
and in ways totally unexpected.)

     First the hand-in-hand stroll down from south hill
at five p.m., Z's backpack-on-wheels in tow.  Then,
after stashing our packs here, we continued on to the
hideaway, encountering unexpected crowds en route.  We
hadn't realized it, but the baseball team's back in town
-- and the strike that provided the week's chief
headline drama (which for one day it had to share with a
wild bus takeover that ended up in a crash that left
dozens injured just ten blocks south of our apartment)
-- the baseball strike, I say, was averted at the last
moment.  And on the other side of downtown the big end-
of-summer festival was starting up at the fairgrounds
(but we've both avoided this festival for years because
of the extremely large crowds it draws).  Families and
other small groups in from the burbs for one or the
other attraction were nearly mowing each other down on
the sidewalks in their eagerness to get to the venues.

     -- And we slipped through to the hideaway where
she'd planted a marvelous bouquet of -- "bawoons."  Big
ones!  With a patchwork circus-horse beauty as the
centerpiece!  (She'd thought I would encounter this
bouquet Thursday night before going to work but I'd
returned from Mama E's too late to stop by the office.)

And onward.  Pick any restaurant -- it was my
choice.  I froze.  Coming up with something she'd go for
too was no easy task.  We reviewed the options together
and finally settled on a popular fish house on the
waterfront.  Basic J-town with a touristy tinge, but as
she said, "It's a lot better than -- " and then she
mentioned several other places we've visited in the
past, usually at my suggestion.  Personally, though, I
thought it even better than that, with our booth located
far enough out on the pier to offer an excellent view of
the ferries gliding in with such stately grace less than
a hundred yards away.  One plate of salmon, one of
halibut, and we switched plates halfway through.  Hand-
holding across the table, sappily reminiscing, toasting,
addressing expressions of gratitude to any deities who
might be listening in for permitting such a miraculous
"last-chance romance" to blossom for us, knock on wood.
    And a stroll back to the hotel, with a stop at A-
mart to load up on snacks.  Mine, grape juice and
kettlecorn, I've been working on for the past hour.  And
because it was already well past her normal bedtime when
we arrived and I was still way behind on sleep and
knocked groggy by drinks at the fish house, we quickly
hit the sack.  Cool breeze tickles and we're dozing off
in each other's arms and also, literally, faces, almost
lip to lip: very lovely!  Yet at the same time listening
in on the many unfamiliar street noises -- half a dozen
different languages, boom boxes, gunning hillside
engines, lovers arguing -- in English (about which club
to hit next) -- on the sidewalk maybe twenty feet below
our third-story windows.  (Likable urban views from
these windows too -- landmarks of the area, great white
tower and west-depot campanile, ballparks, bay and
mountains -- with larger buildings looming up the hill
to the north, including the newly acquired municipal
tower, some sixty stories tall, where Z's future office
will be located, probably starting early next year.)
    Going back, I was pleased too by a voicemail in
which June sang "Happy Birthday" and then by a brief
visit she paid us on her way to the airport to attend

her Taiwan college's class reunion in the megastate --
June all dolled up in a flowery black dress and bearing
a dinner-for-two gift certificate for me and Z
redeemable at a fancy new Lake J-town restaurant and a
card with the handwritten note "To be happy at 60 is a
great accomplishment" (the unwritten subtext being that
she's not so happy herself right now but hopes to be by
the time her own sixtieth rolls around next year).

And pleased by another gift certificate, this one
for our local art-house theater chain and ordered for us
from afar by sister Barb, and also by the card Keith
made and the long, serious letter Barb wrote -- a letter
that avoids the major issues between us, as always in
recent years, but also avoids offending and is otherwise
quite thoughtful -- enough so that I'm ready now, I
think, to make a further conciliatory move and proclaim
forgiveness. As a wise elder I'm hoping to be able to
deal much better with her moral exasperations and harsh
criticisms (neither of which categories I expect to
cease). If I can't do it, so what, we're just back to
where we were. If I can, I think the gain (net over
increased exasperation, say) could be considerable.

And pleased by a matted' "LX" (Roman numeral 60)
Vic made for me as a birthday gift, including it in the
envelope also containing another story of his that he
shoved under the door at the hideaway. A note explains
the "LX" is cut from Buddhist lucky paper money and the
background paper is an Italian declaration form for
customs. That he would do this for me (and on such
short notice -- not until Wednesday afternoon did he
know this was my big day) means a whole lot: like maybe
I really do suddenly have the kind of friend I've been
wishing all my life I could find. -- Not the least of
the many wonderful surprises this Heavenly Year has
brought. (Sentimental sap I am and proud of it.)

Then again I haven't heard a word from either of my
brothers. With Rob it's understandable and even
traditional; at some point roughly halfway between our
two birthdays we'll get together to celebrate both of
them at the same time (but even so I was hoping to hear

from him today).  With Jeff it's painful.  I know, I
know, this is how Jeff is, how he's always been, but
it's not how I want him to be with me -- never has been
and less than ever is now.  Over the long haul none of
the attempts I've made to encourage him to keep in touch
have succeeded.

    -- Deepening night and quieting too, except for a
flurry of nearby sirens about twenty minutes back.  So,
yeah, some painful twinges.  Some around aging too.  Of
course!  I don't want to be decaying, breaking down,
withering, shriveling, doddering, losing it, suffering,
dying -- any of that.  But...it's such a conversation
stopper.  Jyze-stopper too.  Life-ender.  Who wants to
be fighting it -- there's that as well.  Not a dilemma,
just a lemma, as it were, and as elementary as they get
and with no way out (unless you count cryogenics or
other kinds of high-tech medical miracles, and I don't).

    Also this note.  It's something I've been saving
ever since I read the excellent "Marking Time" for TJM.
With all due modesty I'll mention now that those of us
born on August 30th can claim a special relationship
with the beginning of time as just about everyone knows
it.  We 8/30s are people of the origins.  We descend
from the calendrical Garden of Eden.  Genesis R us.

    How so?  Because on this date in 30 B.C.E. the
Emperor Augustus marched back into Rome after
dispatching Mark Antony and the armies of Cleopatra
(leading to her self-dispatching with the asp) -- and
with Augustus's arrival began the procession of seven-
day weeks as we now know them in the Western world and
most other places as well: Sunday followed by Monday,
Monday by Tuesday, etc., which has continued unbroken
right up to the present.  And in everyday life this is
the calendar that matters most.  Over the course of the
centuries months have been dropped, years, dates (such
as those of the Gregorian twelve-day leap) but the
succession of days has always remained the same.  ("Day
by Day."  Everydayness.  The quotidian.  One day follows
another.  Diary.  Daybook.  Chronbook.  Jyzebook.)

    Does this matter?  Only symbolically.  But then one

could say that symbolically is the only way anything can
matter.  How bestow meaning otherwise?  Not even a knock
on the head or a kick of a stone ("I refute you thus!")
or a confirmed scientific hypothesis can do it.

It's a stretch, sure.  A very long stretch!
Stretching and bending, they matter too.  Especially as
you get along in years.  As the J-slinger is now doing
as he moves into senior J-master mode.  You can be quiet
too, and that's all right.  Or you can stretch and bend
and pass things along symbolically (or semiotically), in
ways themselves more or less obtrusive.  Luckily you
don't have to be making sense when you're doing this.
You can try, though, as a way of adding something extra
that some might appreciate to the long, long list of our
ways to celebrate life on earth.

Bird cries in the night.  Choruses of them, cry
answering cry.  Outside this fine old AQ hotel on the
southern slope of Jyze City's central hill in the year
of the Chinese lunar sexagesimal cycle (which also
matters a lot!) 4700.  As at this instant the Z-wiff
flings herself from left-side sleeping to right-side
sleeping with a surflike splash of white comforter.  And
I, though the J-stick will surely cry out in protest,
must, with the next in the endless chain of days, and
almost endless chain of birthday days, just about to
dawn -- must call it, I say, a night.  Heavenliest of
Heavenly nights!

------

36

------


Here it is right on time, the turn into autumn.
And what could be more apt as I creak off into my
autumnal years?  It's not drizzling at the moment,

though, and my heavy shirt makes the chilly breeze
bearable, and therefore I'm risking an outdoor jyze
session at Z-geist.  Aluminum chair, aluminum table,
hard by a street corner with a view, a good specimen of
a Year of the Water Horse flowerbox hanging nearby, its
miraculous six-foot-long bushy braid of trailing
nasturtium vines seeming to sit tall -- very, very tall
-- in the chair opposite, today's jyzetime companion.

For me Labor Day always arrives like a kind of
epilogue the weekend after, or roughly every seven years
two days after, my birthday.  Then a new volume in the
life starts up.  First day of school in these parts is
tomorrow.  In ancient Egypt the new year started right
about now -- which is how it happened, in brief, that
the aforementioned Emperor Augustus, freshly returned
from Egypt, made his proclamation about the endless
cycle of weekdays to start on what would much later
become the birthday of the future Jyzer G.

And happily it was a quarter millennium ago
yesterday that the Gregorian twelve-day correction came
into effect in the far-eastern part of what is now the
USA, with the calendar jumping ahead so that Thursday,
September 14, followed the next day after Wednesday,
September 2.  The procession of weekdays was maintained
even if that of the dates wasn't.  Also as part of the
same correction the year was redefined, with its
starting date moved from March 25th to January 1st.  So
today in a sense is the anniversary of time as we know
it in a different way, in addition to the weekday cycle
-- we USAns and everyone else who's forced to pay
attention because, as it's at last been openly and
officially declared, World Empire R Us.

That very first year of modified time as we now
know it, 1752, was however reduced to 354 days because
of the calendar jump, so at least from the standpoint of
day counts it was more like time as those who follow the
lunar calendar, with its ordinary years of 354 or 355
days, have always known it.  So actually it was the next
year, 1753, that, since it contained the full number of
solar-orbit days beginning on January 1st, was the first

full year of time as we now know it.  That means we have
another big anniversary to look forward to, with
concomitant major celebration, on this coming January
1st: a quarter millennium of time Gregorian.  (But as
far as I'm aware, no one's making any preparations yet,
mainly because no one seems to know about it.  Word just
isn't getting around.  Only jyze is on the ball here, as
far as I can tell.  It's got the scoop.)

     As I say, that first year in 1752 was shorted
eleven days.  That's why I've come to think of this
period starting today and lasting through the 13th as
the Shorted Days.  In the history of Western time going
back at least fifteen centuries these eleven days have
appeared once less than all the others (except February
29, which of course is a special case).  Each year we
should be feeling a psychic duty (as certainly I am
right now) to live each of these eleven days with
doubled intensity as if to make them two days in one and
thus do our best to restore balance on the grand scale
of Western history.  And this effort in turn should make
us more aware of ways to restore balance to world
history as it's been affected by the heavy imbalance
(not to mention devastation) caused by Western history
itself, not just Western time, especially during, say,
the past five centuries, or in other words the quarter
millennium of today's anniversary doubled -- restore
that balance with the appropriate intensity, yes.

     So these are once again special days, although of a
different kind.  (As the sidewalk foot traffic brushing
by picks up at rush hour, exposing my protruding left
knee to peril.  And what you think of this, nasty green
giant tablemate?  -- who seems to be wearing the Z-
geist sign suspended above the flowerbox as a kind of
crown.  Its lightbulb logo is ferociously crackling out
ideas and decrees.)

     -- And there's yet another way these days are
special.  To some this too might seem a bit hokey.  Viz:
today I'm starting into the nonwombal months.  The
approximately nine months between conception and birth
we first experience through a wombal filter, as it might

be called, while riding in a cushioned and fully
curtained sedan chair of sorts; but the roughly ninety
days between birth date and conception date we first
experience unfiltered, uncushioned, and -- raw.  That
may have something to do with why the three months of
fall to me seem not only autumnal -- especially this
year -- but also somewhat brutal.  And yet also --
fresh.  It's not to be denied, for me they're almost
springlike.  Like the crocus and daffodil, like just
about everything green except the evergreen and various
other winter greens I'm out in the world for the first
time, glistening and hungry as a newborn babe.  It's all
new to me.  And this counteracts nicely the autumnal
effect.  It's like the Heavenly cycle is starting over
right here.  Or like -- I'm reborn!

     Or at least that's another take on things besides
the drab old quotidian one.  (But the quotidian is not
drab and old!  It's got, for instance, screeching gulls
and, right across the street, the quake-damaged redbrick
hotel -- which, according to the papers, is now about to
go the way of all aging structures and be replaced by a
slick office building, and that's a shame -- and right
beyond that, the lucky composite Brown Horse (which I've
not as yet today genuflected to) -- and diagonally
across the parking lot to the Horse's right the basement
comedy club where jyze once sat in the window seat at
the "Sleeping Dog" bar upstairs gazing out on all this,
including the very spot where I'm sitting now, until a
bus pulled up for its break and blocked the view.

     -- And I'm about to move on: head for the Brown
Horse to pay my respects and then to the WOC to meet Z-
wiff for an elder bone-building session.  I'll come back
later with the news of the day and the story of the last
third of the glorious Heavenly triple-double birthday --
which includes one startling new development.

                    *         *

     A quarter of a day later, under the maples in the
HQ triangle.  Or under one big maple, to be precise,
though plenty of other maples stand nearby.  I'd hoped
to be sitting on my favorite triangle bench at the foot

of the totem pole, with Victorian five-ball cluster
lights shining on each side, a fenced-off area
protecting my back, and a clear view of anyone
approaching across the cobblestones. For a year and a
half that bench was out of reach inside the pergola
reconstruction zone, but now it's accessible again.
Tonight, alas, someone's already claimed it. A reader,
apparently homeless, with lots of gear staking out the
rest of the bench to keep disturbances to a minimum.

Other than mine, that's the only bench in the whole
triangle that's occupied. But at least no rain is
falling. Desultory snatches of live music bounce around
among the buildings -- stray guitar plucks and riffs --
triangulating, could say. At my back the tattoo place
is open but empty. The only action I've seen was at the
bail-bond office run by my former second-floor neighbor
who's now relocated next to our building's side entrance
just around the corner. Three neofolkies, I'll call
'em, Cawk and female and extremely innocent-looking,
were in there negotiating with big bald Afrusan Sherman,
who's seen it all and in triplicate. My guess is the
neofolkies' consorts got busted, perhaps while trying to
score some bud in the alley behind our building. (Does
Sherman perhaps control the action in that alley? It's
not unthinkable. But it might be actionable to suggest
it, so I'd better dare to say no: of course he doesn't.)

An unexpectedly light scoping night. I was able to
spend a little time with the Heavenly balloons up in my
office: the big "Happy Birthday" on a field of daisies,
the even bigger flying circus horse (a white one, but
outfitted in colorful circus tack and bearing on its
belly on both sides a big black number written with a
wide marker in Z's hand -- "60" -- which is not
referring to a speed limit, no, but still a limit, yes,
and an elastic one, true, but again only within limits).

Earlier in observing this is the time of year for
fresh starts I neglected to mention one example of such
a start that seems particularly apropos now. It was
exactly twenty-three years ago today that Lady U and I
rolled into J-town to start our new life here, pulling

a big U-haul trailer behind Dad's old Hornet (whose
brakes never did recover from the trip of close to a
thousand mostly mountainous miles) (and JRX that car-
model name).  That was the last, so far anyway, of my
many fresh starts in a new city.  And because Lady U was
with me, it was less completely fresh than some.  But
the timing's good for this cluster of the Purple Snake,
because it was during the Purple Snake year -- 4675 on
the celestial calendar, 1977 in the time of our time
(and in our culture) -- that Lady U and I first met in
my former lifetime city No. 11, two years before taking
off for J-town.  The eighteen-year period with her is
what I think of as the second act in my adult life.

And now a quick recounting of the events of the
third double day of the Heavenly triple-double.

Saturday, curiously enough, began the last of the
major events of J-town's sesquicentennial.  This was a
reenactment of the Duwamish Tribe's canoe journey into
the heart of what's now called, in jyze, Jyze City.  Z-
wiff was out of the room late Saturday morning when I
was awakened, probably by street noise coming through
our open window at the teahouse hotel, but then I heard
the surprisingly loud roaring of a very large crowd.
"That can't be for the arrival of the canoes," I sagely
thought.  And no, it wasn't; it was the multitude
warming up at the nearby football stadium -- the brand-
new one.  And the roars weren't even spontaneous, it
turned out; they were practice roars for TV.  A moment
later I heard the stadium PA announcing they would now
do a practice run on the national anthem.  And they did.
It reminded me of boyhood times when I was lying on the
grass in our front yard back in Gatewood and a hymn sung
by the congregation at the community church half a block
away would come floating in on the breeze.  (It was hard
to get back to sleep at the teahouse hotel, but only
because I was so excited by the new setting.)

Next, breakfast at the teahouse itself.  A walk
home.  A fossils' nap.  Then a splendid picnic with
Betty and Kat -- surprise! -- at the south-end Japanese
garden.  Kat was adorable and maddening by turns, and

sometimes simultaneously, as usual.  Mostly she read a book while the elders gabbed.  Betty hauled out a set of bona-fide Jyze City World's Fair glasses she'd come across this summer at her uncle's farm some fourteen hundred miles to the east.  We doused ourselves with mosquito spray.  Took lots of pictures.  Ate roast chicken and potato salad and a birthday chocolate pie with fruit topping and candles that couldn't be blown out because no one had thought to bring matches to light them with, and no one nearby had any either.

Sunday's surprise was another birthday dinner, this time with Gail and Rob at our favorite retro fifties diner over on their side of town.  We'd hoped to find a free table in the outdoor section but arrived a few minutes too late; it was closed.  Between dinner and dessert Rob, as is customary, stepped outside for his pipe-tobacco hit.  It was a relaxed and happy repast. The meatloaf was everything meatloaf can be and the mashed potatos lumpy in a way that seemed to enhance the flavor.  Hit tunes from my adolescence, even though somewhat scratchy, in most cases sounded far, far better to me than they did back then.  The whole evening was sort of Golden Pondish, I suppose, but also much livelier than that.  A fine and fitting close for Heavenly Cycle No. 1 for Jyzer G.

Next day, Labor Day, I did what I usually do on Labor Day: labored.  Went off to work at five p.m. facing a massive night's task because I'd taken Friday off and the Justice Department was waiting on me.  The right-wing born-again attorney general's hot breath, I swear I felt it, and it was corrosively foul.  It was brown-level alert and then some.  But I did my duty.

Z-wiff, meanwhile, could finally take a deep breath or two of her own.  Her astounding birthday labors were finally over.  She had done herself -- and me -- proud for sure.  -- Yet she wasn't quite done.  When I arrived home that night I found a handmade card of the folding pop-out type on my chair, with the cover saying "Thass not all, folks..." and then on the inside: "Z&G continue to live happily ever after!"  And this note on the back:

[ Jyze of the Heavenly Year : Red Horse ]

"Dere's always more Heavenly Hoopla for M'bao" -- and
that written inside a heart.  Ain't she fantastic?  Gush
gush gush, mush mush mush.  (If I haven't mentioned it
before in this annal: "M'bao" is her acronym for "My
beloved and adored one," as "LOML" is "Love of My Life."
I'd say they're both at once serious and tongue-in-
cheek, tilting situationally this way or that.)
     -- And then finally the surprising new development.
This I can cover in a couple of sentences (and I have no
choice anyway as bus time approaches) and then expand on
later.  That's the point of it: it will be expandable.
In a nutshell: I wrote sister Barb a long letter, a
couple of hours' worth of high-speed scribbling, and
toward the end I slipped in a paragraph saying I think
maybe we ought to get together one of these days.  So I
guess all this Heavenly marinating is mellowing me and
I'm ready to stop being such a grump with her.


[+2]


     Artwalk night in the HQ.  Most of the action's in
the central plaza nowadays, the leafy expanse laid out
northeast-southwest and extending across the middle of
two full blocks.  Artists spread their wares on the
bricks and cobblestones and the crowd mills and grazes.
On each side stands a row of century-old brick buildings
three or four stories tall in most cases, many with
galleries or shops open on the ground-floor level.  At
the moment I'm sitting in the sidewalk-cafe section of
an Italian coffee shop in the southeast corner of the
plaza, facing out toward the action.
     On the other side of the column to my left a torch
singer performs.  "Give it up for Julia!" the emcee's
urging now.  I'm mostly hidden back here.  Perfect spot
for jyzing, well lit by overhead lights shining inside
the shop where a long line waits patiently.  I did some
waiting there myself to score an orange drink in the
kind of cup that entitles me to sit here -- the shop's
name printed on it -- and I lift it conspicuously

whenever Mr. Tough Guy Security Dude clanks by.

Considering we're in the Shorted Days -- and it's also the first day of school citywide -- the turnout for Artwalk is surprisingly good. What's more, it seemed rain was imminent, but the mass of dark clouds angled northward and my opening appeared.

I'm midway between visiting Mama E and putting in a few hours' scoping. If the job's light, I'll use the extra time to work on Vic's stories. We're meeting tomorrow and I've done less than half what I'd hoped to.

Today and tomorrow: an interesting couple of days moonwise, with sister Barb's and brother Jeff's lunar birthdays occurring back-to-back this year. Solarly they're ten days apart; Barb's was yesterday. Rob and I are both grappling with what to do about Jeff's on the 14th -- he who never contacts us. Or so rarely anyway. But we do know we'll be regathering, Gail and Z included, with Kar and Kerani next Tuesday evening at Rob's place -- we worked that out on the phone yesterday and today. This Month of the Rooster, starting tomorrow, is looking to be another busy one socially.

So where was I? (Concentration is a little difficult here. Amped-up echolalia rules.) Was about to say autumn political season is cranking up fast, that's what. Off-year elections still two months away, but long before·then -- in fact soon, before the end of Shorted Days -- the one-year anniversary of "the events of 9/11," which everyone is predicting will break all records for USA-style self-congratulatory sanctimony. "Patriot Day," it's been decreed to be. The media are already awash in it as cabal members chortle behind the sleeves of their villainous black trench coats. And the day after that, 9/12, the supreme leader himself will be addressing the United Nations and it's expected he'll be talking war on Iraq. USA the indignant wronged party, don't you know, as if we haven't terrorized the Mideast for decades and killed hundreds of thousands there, and most of them civilians. But never mind, we're doing what we must do to thwart evil and keep the oil flowing and remind everyone who's boss while also expanding the empire as the Lord has declared we must.

Meanwhile here at artwalk business appears to be good.  As the sky darkens, the trees are lighting up from underneath, making for a beautifully textured natural arcade roof.  The stock market is plunging again, by the way, a hopeful sign for those who'd like to see regime change take place in the U.S. as soon as possible.  If I put out a cup it might fill up rapidly with coins and bills -- apparent artist person hard at work, sketching perhaps, obviously in need of alms.  I'm glad I brought along my heavy sweatshirt.  And I wanted to mention that "The Sources of Anti-Americanism" is the topic for a conference of twenty so-called scholars of far-right stripe convened by the cabal's PR honchos in the nation's capital.  It's meeting behind closed doors, with no members of the press allowed -- wouldn't want the secret findings to leak out so that the evildoers could use them to stir up even more anti-empire trouble.

At midtown chain burgers last night -- I'm still more or less a regular there -- I witnessed an unusual occurrence.  When I first came in, a well-weathered homeless man was stretched out motionless on the floor in the dining section with several aid-car personnel frantically tending to him as people at nearby tables calmly chewed away at their double-stacks.  This in itself wasn't anything unusual; as the guy standing next to me in line observed, "Happens all the time -- whenever they're running low on raw meat to feed into the grinders."  What was unusual was that when I left just moments later, a second person was stretched out motionless on the floor right next to the first -- it was his female companion.  As I overheard a medic explaining to a cop who'd just arrived, "We've got us a double whammy -- two heart attacks!"

-- While I've been jyzing, a young tattooed fellow in an apron has been stacking outdoor tables and chairs. Only three chairs are still in use, along with one table: mine.  No pressure, though -- and that's nice. But things could change at any moment.

While on my way down to work last night before the

"double whammy" incident I had to detour up a block to the very high road to skirt a crime scene.  A six-block area, centered on the high road and a block and a half straight up the hill from the hideaway, was cordoned off because a sniper was holed up in the low-income hotel right above one of my usual bus stops.  I've had garbage tossed at me a few times from the upper floors of that hotel -- probably most everyone who uses the bus stop has -- but I've never been shot at.  It can be a scary stop at times, yes, but the alternative, two blocks north on the high road in front of the building where Z-wiff works, is sometimes worse because the lighting's not as good there and usually fewer people are around at one in the morning (protection being in numbers).

And now I'm an old guy too.  But what can I do?  I just try to stay alert and keep out of harm's way.  It's a shame this country doesn't care enough to make its cities reasonably livable.  Nothing new though.  Priorities.  Trade-offs.  Livable cities just don't fit with cut-throat capitalism and world domination.  The urban rez.  Be grateful you've got it, peons!

-- Time's up.

*       *

A black-armchair kwikjyze.  We're already four hours into the anniversary of the day more than five millennia ago when the Mayans believed the universe began.  Or at least so it's reported, and so I passed it along in a voicemail to our favorite person of Mayan descent, El Kato, requesting that she confirm or deny after consulting her deep soul.  So far no word back from her one way or the other.  But I'll note that for the Mayans the universe began about four hundred years before it did for the ancient Chinese, but about thirteen hundred years after it did for the Christians of a few centuries ago and roughly the same time as it did for the Jews.  This adds up to a kind of cosmic consensus, it would seem, except -- well, obviously it leaves out a lot of other views.  Yet isn't this how it's always been in cosmology: agreement can be reached only if a lot of views are left out?  And so it seems to

373

continue today.

     All this as a preface just so I can mention one peculiar fact.  If I'd been born seriously Jewish, today would be the anniversary of my circumcision.  And maybe it is anyway.  Who knows?  -- Although this is something I could possibly research.  At one point I even intended to do so but I lost my focus.  I can say this, however: right now I'm feeling a kind of phantom glow where the old foreskin used to reside.  Isn't that a possible sign?  Or maybe it's just the warmth of the spotlight of jyze attention shining on the site.  In any event, if I'd been circumcised on this date, and if I took with appropriate solemnity the orthodox Jewish notion that life does not properly begin until a child is named and, in the case of a male child, circumcised, then there would be a sense in which today is -- once again, and may the procession go on forever! -- my birthday.

     It's another stretch, though.  And so: best to snip off the flimsy notion from the staff of jyzerly fact.

     Lunar zodiac's hard enough to absorb all by itself. Jeff's lunar birthday, Barb's.  Cluster of the Purple Snake ending, Month of the Monkey ending, Great Year of the Fire Horse ending.  "This is your life.  Give it its meaning."  "Morph the old symbol system into something more apt for the times without violating it."  "Make voyages.  Attempt them.  That's all there is."  (That last quote is a voice from almost forty years ago suddenly piping up all on its own -- the author of "Cat on a Hot Tin Roof," no less, as cited by someone else in a fine goofy novel called "The Dud Avocado," if I'm remembering right.)

     -- Nonsensical though these kwikjyze words are, it seems they don't want to stop.  It's as if the birthday week was the peak extended moment of all time and anything that follows must truly be a kind of postscript.  And that's true -- in a sense!  But I'm also recycling myself and heading into a new Act II -- in a couple of other completely legitimate senses.

     And enough of that.  Step back and make way for the Great Year of the Yellow Horse!

BOOK D

# [ Jyze of the Yellow Horse ]

## 37

Waterfall gardens park.  A gorgeous afternoon.
Dapple reigns -- and some of the leaves causing it (in
tandem with the golden orb) are turning brown, as is
only seasonally correct.  Silvery blue cascading over
glistening dark brown, the whole northwest corner, up to
just below the third-story windows (several of which
boast white curtains gently swelling out), and the gulls
are ecstatic.

So here's where the Yellow Horse starts its run.
It's a jyze express, twelve stations, each and every
delivery guaranteed.  (This park is dedicated to a large
national parcel-delivery service which began on this
site.  The park is payback for business incubation.)

Every time I come here I wonder why I don't do so
more often.  The air's good, the setting's gentle on the
eyes, the contrast with the surrounding urban scene is
invigorating (a wall maybe twenty feet high stands on
three sides -- an old brick building occupies the fourth
-- and the roar of the waterfall drowns out most city
sounds).  There's even a guard to fend off the more
obviously obnoxious interlopers.  It's just a few steps
off my usual beaten path from south hill to the
hideaway, which is two blocks north of here, just as Z-
geist is two blocks south and the ORB two blocks west.

But -- it closes at quarter to six.  That means to
enjoy a free ninety minutes here I must leave the house
by half past three.  If I get up somewhere between one-
thirty and two and make breakfast at home, coffee
included, a departure that early is difficult to pull
off unless I skip most of the chores and give up on

reading the papers, and even then I'd have to rush more than I'd like.  And these days I can't afford to fall behind on reading the papers.  It's a jyze necessity.

So that's why.  Today's an exception, however, because, though I did do the chores, I didn't make coffee at home and I read most of today's far-coast paper last night after arriving home (it's still being delivered between one and two a.m. most nights).

And what's going on?  A big fizzled adventure over the weekend.  And just today the third version of Elgie's personal statement finally came in, two weeks later than he "really, really" promised, and in Z-wiff's view the task of editing it will be, as she put it, "daunting."  And the media (mainstream type anyway) are full of war talk and the expected vast upwelling of national sorrow and angst and righteousness along with acres of hokey pop analysis -- all generated by the one-year anniversary of "the events of 9/11."

Today's also Chrysanthemum Fest in Japan as well as in the AQ here, or rather the northern and central sectors of the AQ.  Mums are yellow -- we need some for the Horse of this Great Year.  In fact we had some early mums that sat in a pot for a month on our living-room window ledge, but by last week they were done and just yesterday they hit the compost bin.

And the high holy days of Judaism are continuing, as are the short profane days of jyzism, not to mention the Shorted Days of the Gregorian leap.  Stroboscopic phase-shifted transition is still in process.  (I see the guard's now making what will likely be his last round.  The head count in here's already dropped from some two dozen when I arrived to exactly three, and none of us looks to be the kind of well-heeled world traveler who might give the guard pause about closing up a little early.)

The big fizzled adventure?  It started with a voice message around noon Saturday (while the Z-woman was out and I was asleep).  It was Tito the Greek, Mama E's former roomer and presumed lover for a decade or more off and on, onetime pro wrestler, habitual gambler, three hundred pounds plus -- in Z's estimation probably closer to four hundred by now -- he who's saved Mama E's life at least twice and perhaps more.  The message was hard to decipher because of his thick accent but it was clear he was in J-town and wanted to see Mama E "today" and he was all but pleading when he wasn't demanding. But -- he left no way for us to reach him.

As it happened, Saturday afternoon we'd planned to visit Mama E together, Z and I, and we went ahead with that, checking our home phone from time to time for voicemail from Tito.  Mama E was adamant: she didn't want to see him and she didn't want us to see him either.  Z pressed her to say why.  She wouldn't, other than to admit -- something she'd never told us before -- he'd "taken advantage" of her in the past.  And she mentioned the gambling, the creditors chasing him, the possibility that an ominous-sounding "they" might even have followed him out here.  She also insisted Z and I are "above" him, which Z found fascinating for what it implied concerning her mother's notions about class. When I asked, "He doesn't carry a gun, does he?", Mama E gave me a significant look and said, "He has, yes."  (Z thought this was just a scare tactic.)

We'd already agreed between ourselves, Z and I, that we'd see him but wouldn't give him Mama E's address or phone number.  Probably he was hoping to borrow some money from her -- or maybe more than just "some" and probably more like confiscate.  But as it happened, he never called again, or at least he hasn't up to now. Too bad!  We figure he probably caught a ride down with a Canadian friend (as noted before, Tito's now living some seven hours' drive northeast of here) and they slept in the car -- maybe played the horses or hit the casinos first -- and left for home the next day.  -- And if it happened once, it could easily happen again.

(The guard's retreated to his office and the count of park occupants has risen to eight, including a conspicuously well-off touristic couple taking photos and speaking with what sounds like an Australian accent. Therefore my chances of being able to hang on here until the official closing hour are looking much better.)

And two meetings with friends made this weekend one of the best of the year for me.  Sunday afternoon Z and I visited Olwen at her home near what we all call Manny Lake.  Her son Trent was "felled," she said, an hour beforehand by a migraine but we had a wide-ranging dining-room talk with Olwen on her own, including much reminiscence about our wedding over which she and Trent presided quasi-Sufi-style three years ago this month.  Originally the plan had been to attend a Sufi picnic on this afternoon, but Olwen had vetoed that idea not long after proposing it: she decided she didn't want to "shock" anyone with how much she'd aged since last attending one of these picnics six or seven years ago.  Z thought she did look older -- her face more lined -- but I found her full of life and delightful (she's relieved because her brother Carey's cancer appears to be in remission).  Then again when I hugged her before leaving she seemed even frailer than Mama E.

On Friday an excellent evening with Vic.  Jean was down in the megastate -- tending to her own aged mother, exactly Mama E's age (or no, I think that's the father; the mother is maybe three years younger) -- and so Vic brought out the scotch and we talked writing and art for a couple of hours up in the loft.  Best of all, he showed me an album of family photos going back to the nineteenth century in China and we went through it slowly, photo by photo, and many of the characters in his stories that I'm editing took on faces and bodies (and clothing) -- it was fascinating.  (Also to see Vic himself going through life phases and exploits of many kinds.)  "At this point," he observed, "you probably know me better than anyone else on earth -- better than my own mother and father ever did."  (Someday I hope to balance this out -- after all, I've got some photo albums and writings too.)  Then we ambled over to the AQ and he showed me a number of his favorite restaurants before we settled on one for a late dinner.  After that we stopped by the nearby AQ pavilion park, where a kung-fu movie was showing outdoors and Vic's longhaired

[ Jyze of the Heavenly Year : Yellow Horse ]

twenty-one-year-old son Ro was among the audience seated
on folding chairs in front of the screen, which was
mounted on the side of the pavilion itself (all of which
reminded me of watching movies projected onto a side
wall of the Jondahl store in Turtle Rapids during
summertime visits when I was a kid).

Vic says he feels beholden to me for all the help
I'm giving him with the stories.  "I was getting bogged
down -- you've gotten me going again."  But I feel I'm
gaining just as much if not more from him.  If we have
some political differences, they no longer seem
insurmountable -- they might even be quite minor.  I'm
learning much about China and Chiusans, about the USAn
coastal art worlds and lots else besides, but that's not
the main part of it either.  Mostly it's that over the
course of his life as a whole he's gone through much of
what I have but from a perspective which in many ways is
the reverse (obverse?) of mine.  We can bounce things
off each other endlessly, knowing the other will
understand and yet also be intrigued by the differences,
with lots of new insights generated on both sides.

-- More on all that later.  Or sometime.  Right now
it's the guard's last round for sure.


[+2]


This whole Heavenly Year project is predicated on
the notion that anniversaries matter.  History matters.
Calendars matter.  Memories matter.  All of which is so
not just at a personal level but socially and
culturally, locally and nationally and internationally,
familywise and friendswise -- and for that matter (for
all matters that matter) wisdomwise.

A sentencious start, that.  But if ever there was a
day for it, this is it.  Today sententiousness has a
license to go wild.  But I'll try not to let that happen
in this jyze any more often than it has all along.

Where's this coming from?  A semisecluded nook in
the outdoor ground-level plaza of the AQ bus station.

[ Jyze of the Heavenly Year : Yellow Horse ]

Hanging vines tickle the back of my neck and shoulders
and the slatted bench imprints itself in inch-wide bars
across my posterior (as Mother would call it, if she
wasn't feeling French enough for "derriere") -- imprints
itself in a hidden jail-suit pattern, I'll say.  A block
to the west the knockoff of the Venetian campanile
stands tall, visible down a surface corridor running
between the bricky old east depot and one of the taller
new plutocrat #2 buildings behind it to the south.  A
brilliant powdery blue sky serves as a fine backdrop for
all this.  A frisky bay breeze is trying to flip the J-
book pages and strip me of my coffee napkins and is also
putting a little extra sizzle in the vines' tickle.
     So on this date in U.S. history our government,
working with the usual mercenaries and rightist
quislings, effected "regime change" in Chile.
Underwrote the murder of many thousands, including the
democratically elected leader of that country.  Stabbed
democracy in the back.  The same thing we've done in
numerous other countries (in some cases to be sure
democracy wasn't yet in place -- just more or less
peacefully threatening to be).  It was all part of our
hegemony project; it just wasn't openly called that yet.
Now it's all hanging out.  Empire-building, that's what
we've been doing all along and are doing now.  Only at
this late date do we come out and openly admit it and
even boast about it at the highest levels of government.
     To those who've been aware of this all along --
which means a majority in the world but probably only a
small and near-powerless minority here -- it would not
have come as a surprise that people wanted to attack the
United States as a matter of retribution for our attacks
upon them over a period of many decades, or in fact for
the entire 226-year course of the country's existence.
The only surprise would be that an attack -- executed by
a "special forces team," as we call our own men we send
on such missions, of fewer than twenty -- could succeed
as well as the one that occurred on the far coast a year
ago today, September 11th.  In terms of loss of life it
was not so notable: more people die of malaria every

single day.  In material costs it was bigger but still
negligible if viewed as a portion of, say, this
country's gross domestic product.  On that scale the
USA's bombing of Yugoslavia a few years earlier probably
did more damage, as did a number of the many other USAn
bombing campaigns of the past half century.  But in
symbolic terms it was major.

To the world it becomes clear the hegemon has some
vulnerabilities.  To the USAn mainstream it becomes at
least thinkable that our highly aggressive and often
violent way of interacting with the world in pursuit of
our hegemony project can lead to some nasty
consequences.  A consciousness may be dawning -- though
it's not much in evidence yet, as the warmongers
inevitably dominate the early reactions to the 9/11
attack -- that some major changes need to be made in
those ways of interacting, or else the world will turn
ever more angrily against the United States and we'll
become an ever more militarized state in response.

Does this mean I'm what the right wing in this
country calls a BAFer -- a Blame America Firster?  Well
of course it does!  Anyone who pays any attention at all
to world history -- just the past couple of decades'
worth is enough, but best to go back the full two
centuries for the definitive case -- must be a BAFer.
Blame others too, to be sure -- does anyone anywhere
lead a truly one hundred percent pure and blameless
life? -- but let's get the blame hierarchy straight.
And let's focus on the world as it is right now.

The human race itself is at risk as never before.
The crunch century is just beginning.  The first few
shots have been fired in the war to force the West, with
the U.S. at the helm, to change its resource-gobbling,
ecosystem-shattering, nuclear-weapons-brandishing, non-
Western-peoples-oppressing habits.  If the West can't
come up with a way in which the rest of the world can
prosper on a more or less equal and Earth-sustainable
basis, the rest of the world in its desperation will
bring the West down, one way or another, if the West's
own egregious practices don't accomplish this first all

[ Jyze of the Heavenly Year : Yellow Horse ]

by themselves.
     A national dedication to achieve this worldwide
goal is the only fitting tribute to the thousands of
USAns (and a few from other countries) who died in the
attacks on FCM #1 and Washington, D.C., on this day a
year ago, as well as the thousands of non-USAns who've
died overseas as a result of our knee-jerk military
reaction to 9/11, in Afghanistan and elsewhere.  These
people died (as have tens of millions before them) in
large part because of our brutal imperial and
neoimperial policies.  Yes, it's that simple.  And we
could give all their deaths at least a partially
positive meaning by reversing those policies.
     Today is also, by the way, Enkukatesh, the
Ethiopian New Year.  Most people of Ethiopian descent in
this country (Jyze City boasts up to twenty thousand all
by itself) are lying low for the holiday this year,
celebrating quietly at home.  They're too easily made
into Muslim scapegoats by the large faction of USAns who
want to Blame Islam First (but wait -- aren't many of
these Ethiopians Coptic Christians? -- but no matter,
they look like those other Mideastern villains who are
daring to fight back).  But the point is: this day or
any day can be the day of a new beginning.  We're still
in the high holy days of Judaism: the random call is
sounding for redemption, forgiveness, renewal, new
beginnings.  We're still in the profane Shorted Days:
how better to restore them to fullness?
     But none of this will be happening.  After a day of
"rolling requiem" -- worldwide, we're supposed to
believe -- our colossally unwise supreme leader is
probably at this very moment delivering a war-prep
speech as his 9/11 condolence display and tomorrow will
certainly be doing more of the same in a much-hyped
address to the UN.  The big question now, as before, is
whether the invasion of Iraq will be happening soon and
unilaterally or later with our tributary states and some
European allies (hench-countries) bribed and/or strong-
armed into being on board.  Some pundits are predicting
the invasion will be delayed for as long as two years,

384

until election season in 2004.  I think it's much more
likely we'll launch it soon, probably late this fall,
possibly even in time for our off-term elections in
November, and then set up another war for 2004, probably
with North Korea or Iran (the other members of the "Axis
of Evil" triumvirate proclaimed by our USAn neocon
cabal) or maybe Syria or Colombia or Venezuela.
     Oh, the shame and ugliness of these days.  This is
not how a Heavenly Year is supposed to be!
     -- But I'm still going for the Heavenly regardless.
To live our lives continuously in thrall to war and
politics is itself to become the enemy.  A truism, yeah,
but no less true for that (as with so many truisms!).
     And then there's our own finitude.  Jean H., Vic's
wife, reminded me of this maybe ninety minutes ago when
I dropped off some edited pages for him at her flower
stall.  Jean waving happily in her bright green apron as
I walked up through the produce section -- I liked that.
I felt welcome.  But she has it tough these days -- the
docs have given her mother a year to live, her father
only three months.  Part of the reason Vic is working so
hard on these stories -- doing little painting, she says
-- is that he too "feels the finitude."
     As does the J-slinger.  As he certainly should in
his Heavenly Year.  Right now, for instance, wearing
shades with a certain kind of lens (I forget the name --
these are the ancient ones, very expensive, that Lady U
gave me back in the days when she was part-timing at the
optician chain store and essentially could get them for
free if they had a slight flaw, as these supposedly did,
though I don't know what it was and have never noticed
anything remotely flawed about them) -- with these
shades on, I say, I can see my age quite clearly.  That
may even be their flaw!  But I look down at my thickly
haired bare right forearm and for some reason these
lenses make the white hairs stand out.  In normal light
or with normal lenses they're pretty much invisible --
look brown like all the rest, or at most sort of golden.
With these lenses I see their truer color.  Or just: the
truth their color represents.

[ Jyze of the Heavenly Year : Yellow Horse ]


------

38

------


     The Heavenly Birthday Horse is literally hoofin' it
on my shoulder.  That's why it behooves me -- right
there a Z-wiff-type pun if ever there was one -- to be
sitting here at my hideaway desk, so I can feel the
weight of the lucky Horseshoes.  In brief, the Horse is
climbing down from its commanding position.  It's
literally true that my shoulder is what's holding it up.
It's a partial truth, though, nonetheless, because even
if my shoulder weren't present, the Horse would still be
suspended in the air above my desk; it would just be at
a somewhat lower level.  About seven inches lower, I'd
estimate, or roughly the width dimension of this J-book.
     All three balloons are shriveled, but the Horse is
most shriveled.  It's leading the downward charge.  Much
of the inner thigh of its left rear leg (the one my
shoulder is holding up) is pressed flat against the
outer thigh, the work of some sort of suction effect
resulting from the likely fact, as I see it anyway, that
the empowering substance of the balloon's rise (helium)
is itself rising to the highest point within the Horse's
body, to wit, its head and shoulders and withers.  For
that reason they're "head and shoulders and withers"
above the rest, and then some -- although not much.
     In the next day or two, maybe three or four, the
balloons must come down.  So I'm seizing the moment to
get jiggy with them.
     Sunday night about eleven-forty, a third, meaning
forty minutes, into the third watch.  Blues play down
low on the radio.  Atonement should be everywhere
because this is Yom Kippur.  Instead revenge and fury

are everywhere, or so you'd think from the way the media
are depicting the world these days.  But I haven't seen
the slightest evidence of those primary emotions
anywhere else but in the media.  Of course I make it a
major point of my life to avoid, if I can, the places
where those emotions would likely be found, and the
media places most of all -- except the newspapers.  For
me they still serve as the main enablers for the reality
principle.  (It's a principle not to be ignored but
neither to be embraced without caveat.)

I'm late getting to tonight's jyze session --
opener for the cluster of the Golden Sheep, and in the
Sheep Month as well -- because I was putting together
materials on family history for Elgie and began noticing
how much of its content I've already forgotten.  Is X
related to Y?  How?  A familiar urge arose to restore
old connections in my mind and maybe come up with some
new ones.  Blink, ninety minutes passed.

Last Tuesday at brother Rob's, by the way, we
brought forth the photo of Grenjad S. and his wife,
Vaehild R., our double-great grandparents who lived in
Sandefjords-Stolen, Norway.  It's the only known photo
of them and Kar had never seen it, since it cropped up
only recently through the efforts of Ron and Karl of the
"lost" Karl S. branch and Kar hasn't met them yet.  A
fine moment -- out on Rob's deck, late sun shining
through the fabulously twisty branches of the corkscrew
willow as strains of classical music washed over us from
Rob's jerry-rigged speaker system, attached by looping
wires to the garret window of his study one story above
the deck.  Unlikely family resemblances were noted.

(News at midnight interrupts.  What fresh
abominations?  On Tuesday our supreme leader warned the
UN it had better authorize a U.S. invasion of Iraq or
we'd go ahead and launch it on our own.  Some in the
peace party even viewed this as a small triumph since
only worldwide protest has brought the UN into the
picture at all.  Meanwhile advance military headquarters
are being set up in the Mideast for U.S. commanders --
"war games," they say, will now be played.  The latest

informed-outsider predictions focus on January or
February as the time for the tanks to roll for real.
Winter months, they say, are better for wearing gas
masks in the desert.  -- And what about corporate crime,
sputtering economy, shattered liberties and ever-
widening inequality here at home?  War trumps of course.
It's hard to see how this won't be the story over and
over in the years and decades ahead.  -- But we must
have hope.  At least there's some talk of resuscitating
the old peace movement.  Well and good!  And yet it's
all just a distraction from the truly profound issues --
the ecocalamities ahead.  Those, after all, if you dig
into underlying causes, are a large part of the real
reason many of these wars are being waged.)
     But regardless it's been a fine week here on the
surface at the compensatory local level.  You can't
battle all this craziness if you don't have a life.
     On lucky Friday the 13th, dinner at Holly R.'s new
apartment, just her and Z and me.  It's a run-down
three-story building in the central area, with long
straight halls "like bowling alleys," as she said, but
the eastward view from her back corner apartment is
stunning -- put me so much in mind of 1616 in MSM #2 I
could've wept: steep house-crowded hills, lake,
mountains.  The splendidly warm and good Holly -- works
nights at a hospice and tries to stay one jump ahead of
the IRS because she's withholding war taxes and has been
doing so for twenty years.
     Yesterday, Saturday, we hit a new street fair on
east hill with Wei and Alison.  Many of the usual
street-fair suspects and attractions were present, with
an unusually large number of beady-eyed cops glaring
from side streets, and we four were just about the most
elderly attendees.  It seems the youth of today, even
the rebels among them, don't take much to street fairs.
Tattoos and piercings, in your face rather than laid-
back -- but then this has been the case for two decades
or so, ever since the punks started to seriously grow
their numbers.  A new peace movement might remedy this.
-- Dinner at a repurposed former counterculture

restaurant, now a cabaret which however still serves mostly organic food. "Lounge culture." Not really Z's or my kind of thing. But enjoyable anyway.

Today's visit to Mama E again brought Z to tears. But she recovered quickly. We tried setting up a card table and playing gin rummy but Mama E wasn't interested. Nothing interests her right now. Something -- maybe a new medicine, maybe just a worsening of her dementia -- has her feeling bad. This isn't really new, and neither is her unwillingness to try to distract herself from her own suffering. She just can't do it -- apparently. We're back to hoping for the occasional good day. (A stop for salmonburgers at our favorite Lake J-town drive-in on the way back boosted Z's spirits somewhat. But she still warned me again she might start mainlining Wellbutrin, the strongest of the tranks.)

Earlier Z had pointed out to me some crossed-out entries on our calendar. This is the week we had originally planned to pick up Mama E in Centropolis. That was just seven months ago! -- This is also -- I let Z know, not to be outdone by her on calendar awareness -- Respect for Elders Day in Japan, a national holiday. It's also the solar birthday of my mother's mother -- my beloved Nana, almost as much a mother to me during my first three years on the planet as my real mother was. From my packed storehouse of memories of her the one that pops up most often these days is her saying at the age I've just become or possibly the age I'll be next year, "I'm just an old Methuselah now" -- quite amusingly too. Good old Nana picking the last minuscule shreds of meat off those Thanksgiving turkey bones. Ending with an Alzheimer's dementia of her own that started with confused street wanderings but didn't take her all the way down for more than a decade.

And yesterday was brother Jeff's solar birthday. He hits the old speed limit, the gas-saver one: fifty-five. I'd like to know what he's up to but I'm almost afraid to find out. This economy must be hurting him and also Angie with her interior-decorating business. He wouldn't want to let any of us know. He might give

up -- do who knows what.  If he felt cornered, that is.
-- Binge on alcohol at this point, I'd guess.

Cousin Kar, I should mention, has taken a job with
yet another conservation outfit and is thinking of
making himself into a "grizzly specialist."  Z, who sees
scores of application essays at work every year, helped
me out immensely with a rewrite of Elgie's "personal
statement"; then I added my two cents' worth (literally
about two percent of the changes were mine) and I'll
mail it off tomorrow or Tuesday.  I haven't had a chance
to get as much done on Vic's stories as I'd hoped and so
I hesitate to call him.  (And the cuts on Elgie's essay
are extensive; I don't know how he'll take them.  It's
my impression, and Z's as well, that he's been rather
thoroughly sheltered from criticism so far in his life.)

-- And this cluster is "Sheep Running in the
Mountains."  No moon's in view yet -- tonight is
overcast -- but at the end of the week comes the long-
awaited Moon Festival and with it our lunar wedding
anniversary, Z's and mine.  We're going out dancing --
yes we are!

(This Horse balloon has been kicking me all the way
through this entry.  Now I'm taking it seriously:
letting myself be kicked out, busward.)


[+2]


We've got drizzle and we've got blustery wind.
Plans go awry again.  I'd like to be sitting at the
picnic table in the little corner park.  Instead I'm
crammed behind the steering wheel of the Z-mobile.  But
the location here is ideal.  A search up and down nearby
streets found only one open parking space, and that
happens to be right in front of the spot where I used to
live.  Me and Lady U, our first J-town apartment.  The
door was on ground level, up about three feet from the
sidewalk.  Hedges.  What the lady loved to call a
"purple penis tree" (lilac).  A high wooden fence to
the right concealing our tiny patio, with the garage on

the other side serving as its side wall.

Oh, nostalgia, indulge indulge -- but of course not too much.

I'm on my way back from Mama E's.  I usually roll right through the old hood here as I head downtown on the main surface street (meaning non-freeway) one block to the east.  Today I'm stopping for a few moments.  But just a few.  It's a ritual thing.  Jyze has reached cluster No. 38, and in my thirty-eighth year this became my home turf.

All the buildings in view are the same as back then with one crucial exception: the one on our old lot.  The sprawling nineteenth-century farmhouse with all its add-ons is gone, replaced by a nondescript -- except it's gray and blockish and three-story -- apartment building.  Its imminent construction was what forced us out seventeen years ago, though by then we'd been living for three years in the small "carriage house" in the back corner of the same lot.  That too was demolished.

The university's not in session yet but enough students are around already that the feel of the area is much the same.  Back then we blended in easily -- especially Lady U, who at twenty-four when we first arrived in town was near the average age for a university student, and she looked even younger.  I could still fake it myself as if I were a slightly older grad student.  I was comfortable here then, period.  I might even feel that way today.  -- But I doubt it.  Better to be away from the student world now.

When I arrived to see Mama E, she told me to close the door, she's got bad news.  Big drama.  But all it is, it turns out, is the buzzing in her head.  It's back.  She doesn't want anyone in the house to know; she's afraid they'll make her leave.  I promise her I'll tell only daughter Z about it.  I also agree to smuggle out a piece of salmon from her dinner plate.  It's too tough; she can't chew it.  But Tony will be pleased if he thinks she's eaten it.  I protest but eventually agree to do it if she'll give me a big kiss on the cheek.  She immediately obliges.  The salmon, I should

note, is so soft it crumbles in my fingers.  Wrapped in
a couple of napkins, it rests on the car seat next to me
right now, awaiting my next move.  I promised her I'd
feed it to the birds in the alley.

-- But why am I so busy I'm two days behind on the
jyze master plan?  Simple -- it's all Elgie's fault.
He's deluging me with rewrites on his various customized
personal statements for particular law schools.  Also
I'm ghosting recommendation letters which he'll then
give to the recommenders to sign.  That's how it's done
these days, he assures me, except for a few sorry old-
fashioned types.  Z's helping me out with all this or
I'd be a well-roasted goose.  We're both dismayed by a
lot of the stuff Elgie writes, but -- well, play the
hand you're dealt.  Even if it contains jokers spouting
appalling reborn-Christian cliches.  Whatever else might
be said, the lad certainly can sound earnest.

I wrote him a long letter about the effects that
taking religion public could have on the kind of career
in law he's said he wants (big firm, big prestige, big
bucks).  I've also sent off lightly annotated -- with
stickies -- versions of the Chandler-Hutcheson genealogy
and the book about the old Sandefjord stomping grounds
in Mentoka, meaning Turtle Rapids and environs, and
included photos of all his paternal ancestors going back
to his great-great-grandparents.  Tears welled as I
wrote the farewell message from his grandmother -- my
ole maw! -- dictated from her deathbed, now emerging
from her mouth in a cartoon bubble from a copy of the
college-years photo of her in the genealogy.

I talk with him almost daily.  Yesterday he was
stuck answering the phones for the law firm where he's
just started working as an untrained paralegal -- he
sounded embarrassed to be revealed to his father as the
lowest flunky around.  But that's absurd.  Doesn't he
realize his father's a flunky too, and at a point much
further along in his career?  -- But probably at some
level he does realize this and it bothers him.  Thus he
insists on seeing me as an important writer.  But he
doesn't push it too much.  I might stop enjoying the

flattery and puncture some useful illusions.

In Z's view it's a kind of cosmic joke.  Payback.
Revenge of the deities!  But I have more hope for Elgie
than that, and of course also more attachment.  (Nor do
I want to sound like she's disparaging him.  She's been
great.  But as she said herself: "I just have to get
over my silly notion that he's going to be a younger
version of you.  It's a different world out there now.")

-- One other startling bit of news.  Vic's son Ro
got assaulted at the symphony-hall bus stop last
Saturday night.  A cross-racial incident: he was in a
hurry and a little cocky with three Afrusan dudes and,
as Vic said, made just one mistake: he ignored a warning
to get out of their space and tried to push through them
to reach a bus that was about to leave.  One of them
blindsided him with a blow to the face, opening a gash
and pushing his teeth in.  The cops would do nothing.
Vic and Jean escorted him to the emergency room at the
public hospital, which was hopelessly overcrowded, and
then to the nearby private one (Mama E's favorite) and
they didn't get out of there until almost four a.m.

I didn't hear about this until yesterday.  With the
focus on Elgie's needs I haven't been able to do much
editing for Vic and so have put off calling him.
Yesterday I stopped by Jean's flower stall with an
envelope of edits for her to pass along to Vic and she
told me the story about Ro -- and she was frantic enough
even before this incident owing to the deteriorating
situation with her own elderly parents.  Today I called
Vic and we had a good talk.  Ro, it must be said, is a
little too macho in his street ways; he's endangering
himself.  He attended a tough J-town high school; he
should know better.  He's developed some of that Bruce
Lee don't-take-no-shit attitude with an odd Italian
street-kid twist to it.  (JRX on the actor's name.)

Symphony hall, that's one of my two main bus stops.
I know just how nasty things can get down there.  You
don't challenge guys on the street.  You steer away from
all situations where a confrontation looks even remotely
possible.  That's my lesson learned from more than

twenty years as a nightscoper dealing with those same
streets and bus stops.
     -- Out in the bigger world, new fascinations.
First worldwide protest forces our cabal to go through
the UN with its war threat on Iraq; then Iraq surprises
everyone by saying it will comply with UN demands by
letting arms inspectors back in.  They call the cabal's
bluff!  So now our supreme leader is seeking
congressional approval to attack anyway.  If he doesn't
get it, he'll still attack.  He'll probably get it, but
he's made no compelling case (because none exists).
Most in the opposition party are caving to war fever
stoked by cabal lies and gross exaggerations transparent
to anyone who pays the slightest attention to the news
(much as in Vietnam days).  Will the UN also cave and
provide cover for this unilateral U.S. power (and oil)
grab?  That's not yet a certainty.  Nonetheless, the
odds favor war before the end of the year -- meaning the
lunar year.  The cruise missiles could be winging off
just as this Heavenly Year jyzefest shuts itself down.
     And here I sit in the car nostalgivating.  That
fall twenty-three years ago when Lady U and I first hit
town had a similar feeling.  The Iran hostage crisis
broke out, the war drums were pounding.  Mideast-looking
students in this area and throughout the city were lying
low and watching their backs at all times.  But now's
significantly worse.  Eco/climate crisis is much further
along and there's no countervailing power in the world
to keep USAn rapacity in check.  We're in the early
years of endgame and most of the world sees us as the
main bad guys, and they're right.  It's not necessary,
in my view, but it's true: the corporate interests, the
military-industrial complex, the plutocrats have a death
grip on the USAn wheel of state and no one knows how to
wrench it away from them before it's too late.
     That's my squeak for today.  The J-slinger that
squeaked.  Sittin' on the dock of a lost past, knowing
a ton of work awaits me tonight even before I get home
and start in on Elgie's stuff, and tomorrow Amanda's
bringing her one-woman-dervish housecleaning service to

unit 203 and I must prepare for this cyclone in numerous
ways -- most important, by taping off and putting up
signs to indicate "no clean" areas.  (This morning at
Z's request I snipped some hair from the middle of her
crown, clearing a circular area around a mole she's
having removed.  It brought back the early days when she
gave me a haircut so I'd look more "nineties."  In
exchange back then I was allowed to visit her apartment
for the first time and I discovered she was a clutter
person just like me, and the way for romance -- and
future employment of cleaning services and the like --
was cleared.  Of course that story's told at some length
in "Jyze in Love" so -- enough said.)


------

39

------


     -- And then some plans go right, as in well.  At
least I think this one is doing so.  Moon Festival!  At
a few minutes past midnight it's just starting up.  But
there it is, the selenotic object itself, glowing big
and fat and juicy, high in the southern sky -- the mouth
of the vatic salmon of family lore.  Floating huge above
the bay -- as I hold down a table in the park next to
the public market, the scenic overlook that rides the
upper edge of the bluff running along the waterfront.
     Just as I did three years ago plus a couple of
days.  And then as now the mythical creature surfaced in
the middle of the bay shedding silvery cascades and rose
slowly like a marvelously shapely dirigible and then,
after a suitably dignified pause, opened its great round
mouth to pronounce its blessings on the marriage of G&Z.
(Just as in the altered fabulist painting of the scene,
done with spectacular prescience a century ago, more or

less, and now hanging in altered-art form in our unit
203 hallway, the centerpiece of the thousand-card
wedding offering from G to Z, still not quite complete
but closing in on that goal with a mere hundred and
forty cards, give or take, to go.)

This notoriously nasty spot.  I'm the only one here
right now -- it must've been swept clean not too long
ago -- but a rowdy bunch is hanging out across the old
"very low road" under the glass shelter.  I'm keeping
an eye out over my right shoulder.  Seems I'm pretty
well concealed from them.  But things could change at
any moment.  If I stop abruptly, that's probably why.

Roar of traffic on the viaduct maybe thirty-five or
forty feet below the lookout railing.  A tour boat
gliding picturesquely by for some strange reason at this
late hour about a hundred yards offshore, cabins fully
lit and hauntingly empty.  A small paper bag tumbling
and scraping by on the cement deck here (scrappily too)
-- I'm hyperalert.

Somebody left a cheap jacket on a seat at the table
behind me.  White simulated-leather arms, badly cracked,
like an ancient high-school team jacket.  An old urine
trail leads from beneath it past my feet.  By "old," I
mean no longer frothing but still wet.  It's blocked at
its head: unable to cut a path any farther through the
dust and debris.

Oh but I'm happy here.  Don't have long to say
anything, though, which is sad.  The presence in unit
203 of cleaning dervish Amanda turned my workday upside-
down.  Coffee at the hideaway, finals at the scope
office, then a workout at the WOC, then dinner at the
hideaway (the three Heavenly balloons sagging badly
now), then a quick walk straight north up the edge road
so I could be here at midnight.  Boisterous edge road.
Baseball crowd just out (much later than usual),
sidewalks packed on both sides of the street with fans
all headed north, revelers cavorting and styling in
warm-weather finery, street musicians and panhandlers
and roving flower peddlers -- a light-wand peddler too
-- working extra hard, doing what they gotta do because

[ Jyze of the Heavenly Year : Yellow Horse ]

this is their main chance for the evening for sure.
     Aha, forgot to mention what's hanging over my left
shoulder -- the whole up-close romantically lit downtown
skyline.  Just scoped it out in spite of myself.  But
moon still magisterially aglow out over the bay.  This
night the first I've seen any part of it this month.  A
dramatic entrance it made: I'm leaving the WOC, going
south, thinking it should be up there somewhere -- it's
not -- I cross the street and it slides out from behind
the slender upper stories of the great white tower --
who'd ever have thought it might be hiding there!
     Tonight Z's off with her main grrrl gang -- a
"pajama party" at Aida's.  Tonight also Sukkoth,
another Jewish holiday, is launching -- to celebrate and
give thanks after forty years of wandering in the desert
(and for what Israel's doing to the Palestinians now it
ought to go wander forty more years in the desert out of
sheer shame) -- it began at sunset.  And for much of
Asia, including the Celestial Kingdom, this is fall-
festival weekend.  Mooncakes and grave-tendings,
primping for the ancestors, thanking the appropriate
divinities for all that's gone well in the previous year
and brought forth such abundance.  Big fat bright
harvest moon!
     Later today (by Gregorian measure) Z and I go
dancing.  Steppin' out on our anniversary.  To both of
us the lunar observance seems more apt than the solar,
which doesn't come until Wednesday.  We picked the
wedding date for its being the famously fullest of full-
moon days (or I did, but with Z-deep's -- at that point
she was not yet a wiff -- with her enthusiastic
agreement).  And tonight, though it's still Friday
night, and though Saturday is the Moon Festival here and
everywhere -- tonight is the night it actually becomes
full, at one minute before seven a.m. our (NUT) time.
     Oh I don't want to go.  But...carry on for me,
oracular mouth of vatic salmon.  The one-fifteen last
bus waits for no one, however exhilarated.  -- And it
would seem I've made it through this bay-watch
extravaganza safely (despite creeping/scraping bags,

more of 'em, seeming like small animals sneaking up on me) and so I'm even more reluctant to split.

*        *

Now three hours later at home and things are not as expected.  The apartment's cleaner, yes -- and Amanda respected all my "no-clean zone" signs this time -- but the Z-woman's not off pajama-partying.  A note on the hall floor explains: "Sorry -- my back went out so I came home."  (Wish she hadn't included that first word -- and I wonder why she did.  She couldn't possibly think I wouldn't want her here.  I guess it's a joking reference to some repartee from last night.  She asked then what I'd do tonight when I came to bed and she wasn't in it.  "Guess I'll go right to sleep," I said, "just to see what it's like."  Ha ha -- just kiddin'! But lately our "pillow talk" sessions have been lasting longer and longer and I've been more and more fatigued during the workday as a result, because I basically have no choice but to keep prying myself out of bed at the same time in the afternoon.  A couple of nights ago we set an "ironclad" new outer boundary of 5:38 a.m. for the start of my sleep time (I won't even try to explain why it had to be that number rather than, say, a nice round 5:40).  Last night we overshot it by twenty minutes.  -- But don't get me wrong, jyze fans.  This is not a truly serious problem.)

Z's injured back, however, might be.  Once or twice a year it goes out and recovery time seems to vary from a few days to several weeks.  I worry this might be worsening with age or just from happening so many times.

The Moon Festival anniversary dance party will probably be a scratch.  And I was planning to wear my old all-hemp wedding outfit again, along with the even more venerable "original courtin' shoes."

A quiet evening at home likely lies ahead.  Not my first choice, but still: fine with me.

Meanwhile I've put my foot down with Elgie.  I left a voicemail for him at the law firm where he's working; it said I wouldn't be writing the two recommendation letters on behalf of the state senator and the Korean professor.  Both were just too far out of my comfort zone, I said, and let it go at that.  I also said I'd be willing to edit the completed drafts if he wants to send them up.  I may regret that too if they turn out to be anything like earlier ones.

Why the reversal?  The "context" info he provided at my request was grossly inadequate.  About the senator he could say only that he, Elgie, will be meeting with him next week.  Beyond this, talking with Z about it I began to think I'm being too pliable with the lad.  As she rightly pointed out, I have a long history of being subjected to his mother's attempted manipulations -- or maneuverings as I usually try to call them -- and it wouldn't be too surprising if he were carrying on the tradition.  To Z he's sounding more and more like an extremely sheltered kid to whom no one's ever said "no." (That was indeed an issue between me and Lady S during his infant years -- and fairly typical, I've since learned, for Korean/USAn mixed child-raising.)  Z also expanded her "cosmic joke" reference a little further, saying it's almost as if he's been intentionally designed to possess a whole series of qualities which are highly irritating to me, starting with the TV-evangelist God business and working on down through so-called positive thinking, yearning to make the big bucks, apolitical rightwardness, etc. etc. (and that second "etc." there is fully justified, I insist -- but to heck with citing more specifics for the indictment).

It's not that I haven't been thinking these things myself.  But it's good to have her come up with them on her own.  She speaks her mind and I'm glad of it.  (It bothers her that Elgie's been sending all his e-mail to me via her e-mail account and yet he's never addressed a word of thanks or any other kind of word to her.)

Well, so he's still a kid at twenty-nine and seeing himself as the center of the universe -- could it be it runs in the family?  The paternal line as well as the maternal?  It just skipped a generation with me?  Ha! -- No, I'm not giving up on him.  I hope he won't be giving up on me.  But I must draw the line somewhere.

[ Jyze of the Heavenly Year : Yellow Horse ]

I'm glad I've now done that.  My guess is it won't be
the last time I'll need to do something like this.
    What else is there to say?  Well, the cabal makes
it doubly official: we're out to dominate the world
militarily and in any other way that matters to people
who love money and power more than anything else.  The
administration sent its "National Security Strategy"
document to Congress today.  It's a lightly disguised
version of the right-wing plan that shocked the world
when it was first leaked at the end of this supreme
leader's father's term in the same office in '92.  No
other country will be "allowed" to challenge our
military supremacy.  You hear that, China?  You're in
the crosshairs, just as you feared.
    Meanwhile Congress is being whipsawed to sign a
blank check for the cabal on dealing with Iraq.
Detailed war plans are ready.  If the UN doesn't do as
we demand and fails to authorize an invasion, then we'll
invade on our own say-so -- it's an open threat.  The
justice minister of Germany calls our supreme leader a
Nazi -- says he's acting like Hitler -- and Washington's
furious.  Apologies fly.  But the truth is that in
certain ways the Hitlerian gleam is unmistakable.
Demands and threats, saber-rattling, plans for a
thousand-year USAn reich.  "Master race" talk isn't out
in the open but no one could possibly believe it's not
there behind closed doors.  (JRX the Hitlers.)
    -- Will I let these horrific developments mar the
one and only Heavenly Year Moon Festival of my entire
life?  No way!  I sit in the black armchair, softly lit
living room, radio playing low, tail end of the fifth
watch -- no one else is up in the house or for blocks
around, probably, the street outside is quiet -- what
better time for it?  Plants galore, horses galore.  Not
a single newspaper-clipping scrap anywhere to be seen.
This "great room" here is freshly cleaned and thus ready
for some serious entertaining.  We've booked dinner
guests for the next three weekends, including some
who've never been here before.  Will Gerry and Leola be
rattled?  How about Vic and Jean?

[ Jyze of the Heavenly Year : Yellow Horse ]

     Tick tick, the hand moves past straight up.  If
we're gonna make the new pillow-talk deadline work I
must do my bit and slide in there early.  The magic
fingers had best limit themselves to a back massage
tonight.  She'll have tales of the new casino which the
grrrl gang hit before the pajama party (for a tribal
benefit -- gamble in good conscience!).  Probably a
bawdy dream or two to report as well.  She's been on a
roll with those lately -- last night her big flame of
almost a quarter century ago, Brian S., popped up in one
for the first time in months.  She'll also want to fill
me in on the utility's reaction to a muckraking critique
that ran in the FAP, the more conservative of the two
local dailies, yesterday, written by one of their scab
columnists.  It focuses on the annual employee picnic at
the same retreat where Vaughn L. and Renee got married a
month ago.  As it happens, I wrote one much like it
myself roughly thirty years ago about the utility in MSM
#2, but I'm playing that down with Z so far.
     And there's the badly depressed June.  The grrrl
gang is circling protectively around her.  My own
efforts to rally her have failed completely.  Z's theory
is that of the four known factors involved -- law-school
postpartum, selling the longtime family home, fear of
the awaited results on the bar exam, and son Michael's
decision to teach in China for a year before starting
law school -- it's the last-named of those that's
bothering her most.  This is the first time Michael's
gone against her wishes in a serious way.
     Okay, enough speculation, let's go talk that pillow
talk.

                    *            *

     -- Jyze will now try for a Moon Festival nightcap.
Same setting as a few lines up -- black armchair, fifth
watch, a grand Glennarian NUT-time extension on the
Gregorian Saturday that started at midnight twenty-eight
hours ago.  On the couch a big stack of Sunday papers
awaits culling (all those ad inserts) and reading
(tomorrow, NUT-wise).  The ice cubes crackle in another
kind of nightcap, half a glass cup with a Christmasy

outdoor scene painted on it, salvaged from the grab bag
of ol' Maw's lesser kitchen contents after her death.

How often will it happen that the full moon of the
eighth lunar month -- Moon Festival moon -- will fall on
a Saturday in September, as it has this year and also
did in the year of our wedding?  You'd think one year
out of seven, but surely not, because some will be in
October.  It's safe to say we won't see too many more in
our lifetimes -- speaking of Z-wiff and me, the
whooping-it-up married duo.  It would take a lot of luck
for the number to be bigger than two or three -- and a
fair amount for it to be even that big.

So, seize the night!  -- And we did, to the extent
reasonable caution in view of physical limitations would
permit.  We did after all do the dinner and dance, but
we made it out to the dancefloor only once -- for a tune
my college-era band used to play at functions not all
that much unlike this one: "Johnny B. Goode."  Tonight
it rocked the Visayan Circle.  Some things never change.

I couldn't wear my full wedding outfit -- it turned
out it was stuffed into a bag waiting to be cleaned.  I
donned the pants anyway, and substituted my new hemp
"shirt-jac," which is at least a little bit like a
Filipino barong.  Z called it a Norwegian barong.  The
main difference is it's not transparent and so you can't
see the henley underneath -- a distinct improvement, if
you ask me, for these more northern climes ("more"
relative to the Philippines, not Norway).

First stop was the south-hill garden club.  This is
part of the ritual now -- we peek in the windows and
recall the glories of our wedding reception there -- the
wedding-cake cutting, the money-stuffing, the Li'l
Filipinas' serenade, the toasts and speeches, the line
dances.  Then we walk the grounds -- with their orchard
and gardens befitting the ownership -- and sit in the
old wooden gazebo as squirrels scrabble and scuffle in
the roses nearby (only at that spot have I seen more
than one squirrel at a time on the hilltop).  We renew
our vows and I get all sappy.  I'm admittedly the
connubial leader in that regard, the chief sap.  How

absurdly well this hitch-up's worked out for us!
-- Then, on the way back to the car, we both stepped in
a well-concealed patch of manure fertilizer and had to
frantically scrape off our shoes in a kind of
anticipatory dance step -- doing the Manure-Off! --
before driving over to the Scandi quarter.

Turned out our friend Willis E. was the keynote
speaker for the Visayans.  The former Black Panther can
do whatever's called for when it comes to politics.  The
setting was a grade-school gymnasium with one of the
basketball hoops hanging directly above our table.
Roast beef, salmon -- not so tasty.  Z-wiff sort of
vaguely knew many of the attendees but no real friends
were present to make for lively interactions.  Only in
J-town and one or two other U.S. cities, we learned, is
there a Visayan Circle; usually all the Filipinos from
the various regions meet as one.  The Visayas are a
group of islands, including the one Z's father emigrated
from in 1916 and very close to the one where a certain
celebrated Western so-called explorer "discovered" the
Philippines and claimed them for Spain; and then the
island next to that is where the Visayans claimed the
explorer, as it were, for themselves, doing him in for
his sheer hubris.  And rightfully so!  Foreign invader!
Sneak attack, just like Pearl Harbor or 9/11!  -- All
this info, except for the last part, was right there in
the program.  I happened to be glancing through it as
the crowd belted out the Star-Spangled Banner.

And during the drive back through downtown, and
especially as we crossed the high bridge, the festival
moon, about a third of the way through its circuit of
the night sky (no cloud anywhere), was at its grandest.
You could see so clearly the frog and the lizard and the
rabbit of ancient Celestial Kingdom lore.  Of course
it's hard to think of anything to compare with the moon
in boringness, so when it takes on meaning and
transcends itself, that's truly something.  For sure
nothing could be more Heavenly.  (And it staged an
encore a few hours later when I went out to pick up the
papers -- old luna so splendidly fractured and laced by

403

the leafy trees of our stone garden path.  -- Or more accurately, the concrete walkway outside the side entrance of our building.)

     -- One other news tidbit, and it's a disturbing one.  In talking with Betty tonight Z learned Kat's school counselor called Betty at work with the warning that several of Kat's classmates had reported Kat had talked about killing herself.  Kat herself says she didn't mean it seriously, and it's hard to conceive of her being suicidal -- she's so animated, takes such strong interest in so many things, from reading Harry Potter tales to playing sports -- but it's still a shocker.  We've scarcely begun to absorb it.  -- And would like to dismiss it as preposterous.  But -- Kat's hormones are kicking in.  There could be something to it.

     -- And it's an early blue dawn out there.  It snuck up birdlessly!  Means I'm an hour late for bed -- which is okay because it's Sunday morning and Z will sleep in.  But evergreen silhouettes standing against a band of orange above the mountain cutouts.  Apparently the "It's a Boy!" stork -- now perched indoors, in the large corner planter -- is the only bird around at the moment.

     And I'd say it's been a great day.  It's something you always like to do -- live a day as the high point of the year -- and this year, as an unexpected benefit of going Heavenly, it's coming closer to happening for me on a regular basis than I ever would've dreamed possible.


                         [+2]


     A brief stop at the HQ plaza on the way in -- the last lap, the home stretch.  A seat on the steps of the central pavilion, across a cobblestone stretch from the double totem poles whose top figures are hidden up in the trees.  And peeking above the crowns of those trees to the right of the poles, the pyramidal spire atop the great white tower.

     Why stop here?  Autumn leaves are scuttling around

the square, chasing each other in tight circles as
pigeons and gulls and clusters of human vagabonds look
on in amusement and celebration, for today is the autumn
equinox.

Or officially it is.  It seems the equinoctial day
for the whole nation is decreed by media consensus back
on the far coast, where the equinoctial moment came at
12:56 a.m.  That means it took place here three hours
earlier, halfway through last night's second watch, and
so here the equinox arrived yesterday.  But this wasn't
generally recognized and so it might as well not have
happened.  No matter: jyze is saying it did even while
still accepting, grumpily, the mainstream verdict.

Nor is it any longer the Virgo month or the summer
season -- two more Heavenly birthday circles we've now
passed through and all the way out of.  Instead fall and
Libra.  No longer "I analyze"; now "I balance."  Libra
also came in last night in these parts, exactly at the
moment of the equinox.  But today's the first day of the
Libra sun.  And all around the plaza here this new sun's
lighting up the old redbrick storefronts as seen beneath
tree branches.  It's a pretty sight, calming and hope-
inducing.  The totem figures, behind their impressive
show of timeless fierceness, are surely smiling.

On the way down I made a drop-off at our usual dry
cleaner in the southern AQ.  My wedding outfit and my
dress pants (such as they are) must be ready for an
upcoming cascade of major events.  Saturday is Paz and
Tobey's commitment ceremony.  Wednesday is Z-wiff's and
my solar wedding anniversary.  And several other
engagements will be coming up in following weeks.  Unit
203 is as clean and orderly as we can ever hope for it
to be, meaning, as noted before, the window of
opportunity for dinner guests is wide open and a number
of same will soon be clambering in.

Vines and bricks.  Squabbling crows.  A wino
dispute which meshes nicely with that of the crows.  On
this date Augustus Caesar was born, or otherwise, again,
August 30th almost certainly would not have been the
first day of consecutive Monday-through-Sunday Western

history.  On the phone Z tells me more files from Elgie
have arrived on her e-mail site.  I'm impressed by a
"Novelist Speaks" piece in today's far-coast paper --
the author's got it right about the telling detail and
the reportorial high.  What I'm wondering is why she let
herself get hooked on newspapering for so long.

Bells chiming -- it must be quarter of.  I'm due to
meet Z at the WOC in fifteen minutes.  If I'm lucky I'll
be able to come back to these pages for a second round
-- maybe even beneath the triangle totem pole -- between
the WOC session and the scope-office session, the latter
of which shouldn't be too demanding tonight: maybe
thirty minutes at most.

(Just now the first panhandler hit of the
afternoon.  "How you doin', bro?")

*          *

-- Lucky me, I've got the best bench in town.
Unlucky me, I can't stay here long.  Thirty minutes
maybe, forty tops.

A little after eleven p.m.  A Monday night and the
HQ triangle's quiet, relatively, though I can hear
snatches of live music coming from three or four clubs.
As I exited the hideaway building's side door, a tall,
extremely long-legged woman in some sort of Tahiti
outfit was uncoiling from a car parked right in front of
me.  Strangely, our eyes locked -- maybe she was afraid
I was a crazy about to attack her.  I smiled.  She
smiled back, though warily.  We went our separate ways.
I looked back to see how she was doing.  She didn't look
back, or at least not while I was looking back.

Eight or ten sets of large curious eyes -- hostile
eyes, maybe, and especially if they're paying any
attention to deep history -- are looking over my
shoulder from the totem pole standing about eight feet
behind me.

Tomorrow will be tricky.  Before delivering the car
to Z-spouse at her office at five I'm planning to pick
up flowers from the public market and some anniversary
balloons at the party store over by the fairgrounds --
maybe a gag gift or two as well.  At five I'm also

supposed to be dropping by Vic and Jean's loft to
discuss some edits and do some socializing.  To be able
to pull all this off I'll have to put in a full night's
work at the scope office tonight.  It'll be tight.

At the WOC Z reported Elgie had sent her a "cute"
e-mail note introducing himself (as I'd suggested he
do).  She also said his latest draft of the personal
statement looks "about as good as I think it's going to
get and still be him."  She thinks it'll be acceptable
with a few mainly grammatical changes.  Those are what
I'll be tending to after work tonight.

Yesterday's visit with Mama E didn't go well.  Z
got into it with her for being so unremittingly
negative, then broke down and wept.  I couldn't do much
but twiddle my thumbs and stare out the window at the
birdfeeder action in the front yard.  Today Z had six or
seven different matters she had to take care of for Mama
E from work, including filling out for Medicaid what's
called (with extreme lack of euphemism) an "irrevocable
funeral agreement."  She also saw Margo, her eldercare
counselor, and with her permission did more weeping
there.  She worries that I don't want her to weep in
front of me; she thinks I might want her to keep a
"stiff upper lip," just as her mother wanted her to do
as a grade-schooler in the face of discrimination for
being Asian (being called "Jap," "Chink," and also
"crip"; being chased through the streets by nasty white
boys).  I told her she's only half right; I try to help
her keep a stiff upper lip when it's necessary -- how
else can she do her job? -- but I'm open to all kinds of
expression from her and have been all along and during
this time she's expressed all kinds of things to me in
just about every way possible.  Have I objected to any
of this?  Have I been anything but receptive?

She eased off -- said I was right.  Apologized.
And everything was okay again, or at least it seemed so.
To me it's remarkable we haven't faced far worse
tensions over this horrifically difficult and painful
situation with Mama E.

-- Can't say much more.  Wish I could take a few

moments to really feel the location.  Street lamps,
flowerboxes with magnificent dangling nasturtiums still
profusely abloom (the trailers are seven or eight feet
long in some places), accents, echoes, a whole row of
bench sleepers wrapped in blankets.  Neon colors and
steady, quiet, fully-leafed trees.  Bracingly fresh air
-- not too fishy -- off the bay.  Cars, cabs,
bicyclists, drunks, panhandlers, cops on horseback, cops
on bicycles, cops on foot.  And I'm this sixty-year-old
man and now it's not a new fact to me anymore, it seems
almost ordinary -- except the year's still Heavenly and
will remain so for all twenty-two jyze clusters still to
come and I'm promising they'll be as lively as I can
make them (with lots of help expected from our bimbonic
supreme leader and his vicious crusader cabal).


------


40


------


    The idea tonight was to slip far away from the
madding throng.  Instead I find myself back at the
foaming center of it.  "Under the pergola, down by the
ba-ay."  On all sides the normal commendable Friday-
night froth and frenzy.  The Water Horse in his Earth
Horse incarnation at the outset of a Silver Rooster
cluster in his Heavenly Year wouldn't dream of putting
down the animal spirits of others.  And they're bursting
out all over on a warm night like this.  Here's a
snorting equine right now!  And look at all the
microminis and bare midriffs in those parallel lines
outside club X and club Y across the street.  VRROOOM,
VRROOOM, big wrist-twisting, testosterone-spewing action
as a pair of black-leather-clad and majorly zippered
harleyquins wait for the light to turn green.

[ Jyze of the Heavenly Year : Yellow Horse ]

    "Whatcha got goin' there, player?  Writin' it all
down, eh?"
    Next bench to my right, a couple of lazy
panhandlers sporting a makeshift fishing pole are
dangling a sign out into the passing stream of partiers
-- sez "Fishing for beer!"  Getting lots of laffs but
maybe not so much cash.  -- And now a guy's taking a
picture of them (and also, inadvertently, of me jyzing
about him photographing them and me).
    -- As we all await the Iraq decision.  Is the U.S.
about to seal its doom, as Emil A., savvy editor of the
alt-weekly, thinks?  Stay tuned.
    Wednesday was the anniversary of another
"explorer's" sighting of the Pacific 489 years ago and
claiming it all, every last drop, for the King of Spain.
It was also the anniversary of the inauguration of
Greenwich Mean Time 326 years ago.  Therefore it must as
well have been the anniversary of the wedding of ZAG and
GAZ -- three whole years ago.  And so it was!  (We're
speaking solar anniversaries here, and the Gregorian
version of same.)
    She, the bride, wore her J-book earrings, I wore my
"Krazy bout Z" dogtags.  I even hauled out my true
wedding ring for the occasion, the first time it's
adorned my hand since last spring when its bulk caused a
messy break in a blood vessel in my pinkie.  (And the
inscription on the ring's inner liner still seems to
read "ZAG," as the one in hers looks like "GAZ" -- but
in both cases the seeming "A" is actually an ampersand.)
    We met outside her office and off we went to the
preselected Lake J-town restaurant.  A fine use for the
gift certificate the descendant of Confucius had passed
along to us, after herself receiving it as a law-school
graduation gift from a friend (she's started taking an
antidepressant now, June has, sad to say, as her
postgraduation blues deepen -- and Z-wiff and Aida are
worried enough they're thinking of calling in her older
son, Adam, from down in the megastate).  A window seat
at the restaurant, bourbon and margaritas as float
planes took off on the lake just outside.  Salmon on a

cedar plank with a berry glaze.  A good relaxed time --
we're relationship vets now.  It's our leather
anniversary!  And to celebrate appropriately she wore my
old handmade fringed brown leather shirt from the early
'70s -- the hands that made it being Lady V's.  And the
leather, actually, is horsehide.  (Even way back then I
knew I was a Horse.  But I don't think that was why the
Silver Cat picked out that hide.  She thought it was
supersexy, that's why.  And on Z it still is just that.
I wonder: would Lady V appreciate the irony?  By now
just maybe she would.  Back then I suspect the sight of
the Z-woman so attired would've inspired another attack
of the Valkyrie -- Valerie being her name and Kyrie a
nickname, as jyze may never have mentioned before.)

At nine o'clock, after dropping Z off at home --
she worked up a triple-margarita buzz -- I went to work.
Scoping kind.  For the first couple of hours I was
hitting keys more or less at random -- had to go back
and redo the first fifty pages after I sobered up.)

(Big Afrusan guy just blew in -- startled me as he
yanked out a large "donation" sign he'd stashed behind
the bench I'm sitting on.  For an instant I thought he
was going for my neck.  Nor was he a real friendly dude.
Now he's setting up over by the oldest of the local
saloons (in fact the oldest in town).  And I say: can't
we all just get along here, party hearties?)

The next morning Z apologized for being less than
her usual raw and raunchy edgy-vivacious self, not just
at the restaurant but for the past nine months or so.
"Nonstop packed-in-cotton-batting feeling" is how she
described this period.  Said she's felt battened-in ever
since her half-sister Camilla died.  Is that how I've
been seeing her? she asked.  Well, yeah, now and then, I
said, but nothing like nonstop, and it's not as if it's
unexpected or something I think she should be able to
easily shake off.  What with Mama E's condition it's
been a time for double mourning and seriousness.  Truth
is, she, Z, has handled it all impressively, and also
juggled the Heavenly Year expectations of her crazed Z-
hub equally well while doing it.

            [ Jyze of the Heavenly Year : Yellow Horse ]


     Another aspect of this, both the postpartum June
and the currently partum Betty (who's feeling rejected
by Kat as "the child" wants to spend more and more time
with her friends and less and less with her mother) --
both June and Betty, I say, and Z says too, are
emotionally needy right now during a period when, again,
Z's empathy reservoir is running low.  As a consequence
she doesn't want to be expanding her social circle at
this point (as she told me at the WOC today, explaining
why she'd rather take a pass on inviting Vic and Jean to
see a movie with us on Sunday).  Makes sense to me.  No
doubt it's also not a great time for the G-hub to be
engaged in an elaborate yearlong jyze project.  But
she's voiced no objections to that -- in fact she's bent
over backward to encourage it and to indulge its
gargantuan obsessiveness -- and so I certainly don't
want to be making waves about any of this other stuff.
     Tuesday I dropped by V&J's loft for a fine few
hours.  Jean arrived home after I'd been there a while
and this time she stuck around -- put on "her" music
(which is mine too, or at least was this time: some very
fine late-forties bebop) and broke out the candles and
rustled up dinner for the three of us.  Very sweet of
her.  Lively talk for a couple of hours.  How she misses
the old "carefree" bohemian life (only recently did she
take the flower-lady job: to help pay Ro's college
expenses).  Rattled on amusingly about racial
stereotypes and the graying of pubic hair.  Ro seems to
be psychologically recovering from the bus-stop assault
but the dentist has warned that one of his teeth might
eventually turn black.  Vic and I, by mutual unspoken
agreement, let the spotlight shine on Jean all evening.
She's almost twenty years Vic's junior, an independent
spirit ("just like your wife," she likes to say to me)
but also devoted to him.  Animated and emotionally very
warm.  Always now a big hug for the J-slinger.  (And Ro
stopped me on the stairway: "Hey, I just wanted to thank
you for the way you're inspiring my dad!")
     Every few days I find an envelope from Vic under my
hideaway door -- more rewritten pages.  The man's a

scribbling fiend!  I'm more determined then ever to keep
up with him on the editing even as I fall further and
further behind.
       (As three skateboarders thunder by on the street at
about fifty miles an hour after zooming down the hill.
-- And here's street-cartoonist Darren, who often sets
up in front of one of these pergola benches: he's
picking up the old bedsheets he uses for displaying his
cartoons -- or no, he's laying them down, and now it
appears a couple of cops are giving him a hard time --
or maybe they're just going after the blustering wino.
-- So it seems, as the wino moves along and the cops do
too.  On this occasion anyway street art gets a pass.)
       -- Today's high point was another phone talk with
"Pups."  (I'm jokingly calling Elgie that when he dubs
me "Pops.")  He was worried because the revised personal
statement hadn't arrived yet.  I assured him it was in
the mail -- snail mail -- and it ought to be there any
day now.  Sigh.  Pops, he be such a din-o-saur.  Pups's
phone message was so soft-spoken and stumbly it took me
three replays to decipher it.  To what extent this is
persona and to what extent the deep Elgie soul my sense
is still less than sure.  In the live call I learned
he's currently unattached romantically but he had a
seven-year relationship with a "girl from down here,"
meaning MSM #1.  But extracting info from him is tough,
no matter what the subject; he volunteers little and
answers questions with extreme reticence when he answers
them at all, unless they happen to push just the right
button.  He likes to talk about law school, health, his
reading.  He'd received the two family-related books I
sent down but had almost nothing to say about them.  He
did volunteer that in old pictures from Mentoka days
"you look like Josh Hartnett -- you know who that is?"
I said I'd heard the name but that was about it,
revealing my obliviousness to pop culture hot with
twenty-somethings.  "Dad!  He's a big heartthrob in the
movies!"  I couldn't hear him that well.  "He's in
'Heartthrob'?  I don't think I've seen that."  Yes,
those were my exact words.  What a ditherer!  "Jes call

me Metheuselah."  (And of course JRX the actor's name.)
     He did manage to talk -- or charm -- a female aide
to a certain megastate legislator into writing the
recommendation letters for him, so that's one issue
we've been able to sidestep.  (Elgie had lunch with the
aide and the legislator himself on Wednesday.)  He's
still planning to apply to fifteen law schools; he's
been told getting in is often just a roll of the dice
depending on unpredictable diversity needs and whatnot,
and I suppose that's true at least to a degree and
especially for the "second-tier" schools.  He's no
longer talking about retaking the LSAT if he doesn't
score a "first-tier" admittance.  And yes, it's a little
disconcerting the way he speaks with such gung-ho
resolve about this or that plan and then a week later
it's completely off the docket and seemingly forgotten.
     Lights!  Sirens!  Action!  -- It's somewhere in the
next block down, out of sight, but several squad cars
zoomed by, one lunging up over the curb right in front
of me to get around a row of cars stopped for the light;
and now I can see the flashing blues and reds reflected
off the upper stories of the building where Evelyn H.,
my divorce lawyer from three years ago, has her office.
Could it be another dastardly topless scene is unfolding
down there?  Scores of partiers are rushing over that
way from outside the clubs here in the triangle.  I,
however, must pack it in and trudge off in the opposite
direction, scope office bound.


[+2]


     Colossal Heads on display up above.  Also lots of
normal-size heads floating by down here, many wearing
team hats and some with mouths chomping on hotdogs.  But
directly over my own head a truly colossal Colossal Head
hovers, a "Roman Spectator," as it's officially labeled.
Farther up the concourse beneath the stadium overhang
hover five or six others.  An Elvis.  A Lauren Bacall.
An Ivory Coast mask.  It's art.  Eternal observers of

the thronging sports-mad down below.  (And JRX the
celebrity names.)

I couldn't stay away.  Today our guys are taking on
the Vikings.  The game's starting late because it's on
national TV -- forty minutes from now, at half past
five.  Thirty minutes after that I'll be meeting Z at A-
mart, which is a few blocks east of here.  "Here" being
the entrance steps of the city's and the region's
largest and newest public venue.  The cine-cafe theater,
where we'll be seeing a movie at seven, is surely one of
the smallest and among the oldest film venues in the
city or region -- maybe even the smallest.  (What does
all this size stuff mean?  I ain't speculatin'!)

Here and there a Viking hat and every single one
inauthentically horned.  A big crowd over to my left
queued up for terrorism inspection before entering the
stadium.  Security is omnipresent and some might call
that an understatement.  The air's fragrantly smoky from
a long double row of concession tents lined up along the
walkway (which is technically the same one that runs
through the HQ plaza, I believe, but closed off now,
maybe permanently, here as well as there).  From the
braid of wafts my nose can disentangle burger, hotdog,
bratwurst, pizza, popcorn as my gut rumbles nonstop.

Moments before I sat down here a demo passed by,
entirely encircled by cops in black on bicycles with a
large group of police reserves trailing on foot and
helicopter gunships hovering overhead, although no guns
were visible from where I stood -- a demo, I say,
protesting a long string of police killings of black
men.  And rightfully so!  Make your voices heard!  (Just
this afternoon Z suggested we display antiwar signs on
our windows, both apartment and car.  Of course I
immediately agreed.)

"National TV, national TV" -- the words most often
heard from the babble of the throng.

The Roman Spectator stares straight ahead
unblinkingly, as if drugged, but probably just bored.
He's seen all this before in numerous other settings.
Bread and circuses, the inevitability of imperial

collapse, shrug and yawn.

But it's a fine day for a spectacle.  Shafts of sun illumine the billowing clouds of cooking smoke.  Meanwhile a few thousand more people have disappeared into the entrance maws (surely many of those folks are now among the ones I can hear roaring and stomping up there) and the lines are shortening quickly.  And the entrance steps sport far fewer last-minute gnawers.

And so I say:  Go, Vikings!  Maraud!  Give J. City what for!  Fire up war-weary mythical imaginations!

-- A block to the south stands the baseball stadium, black-roofed, useless, dead now.  It's the last day of baseball season but the team's on the road and they're last year's heroes anyway -- dead, dead, dead -- didn't even make the playoffs this year.  (Cheers!  Wild hope stomps the stadium steps over here!  Toss them some raw meat!)  True, the J. City gridders themselves are off to a zip-and-three start, but eventual playoff triumph remains at least theoretically possible.

-- And now with surprising suddenness I'm being exposed.  A few stragglers are still arriving but most of the crowd's made it safely inside, leaving just me and a scattering of other questionable types out here, along with the same very large mass of security folks with nothing better to do than focus on non-revenue-producing misfits such as myself and my motley compatriots.  And I get the strong impression it would be best for me to move along right now.

*      *

Seven hours later I'm jyze-ready at the scope office.  First time in months I've set up for it here.  But speaking of time -- don't have a whole lot of that.  Thirty minutes.  Just barely enough to limber up the J-stick.

Little change in this room, I'll note, since my last visit (nonjyzing).  The video camera aims straight at me, but no red light's in sight and the big monitor screen's blank -- no national TV for this jyze hoedown.  At the other end of the glass-topped table the memorial photo of the late twin towers hangs serenely.  My

computer squats on its cart in the far corner, behind
the coatrack.  The office security system is still on
the blink, as it has been for most of the past year.
The firm's too cheap to spring for repairs.  We could
lose our grand-jury contract because of this.  But the
chances the feds would get wind of it are low.

Naomi's been so burned out on grand jury she gave
it up for the month of September -- handed it off to one
of her backups.  At the same time she's making a bigger
effort to find work on Mondays and Fridays -- days she
normally takes off quite often, especially during heavy
grand-jury weeks -- and so for the month we're actually
coming out a little ahead.  We'd be doing even better if
the local courts hadn't called for a crackdown on what
they call "format shrinkage," in which the number of
characters in a line of transcript gradually dwindles,
in this case from the high fifties to the high forties.
Now they're enforcing the rules strictly, or are saying
they will, and we're back up to sixty.  That means our
income from transcript production on any particular job
is reduced by about a fifth.  It's a heavy hit!  Yet so
far we're getting by all right.

I'm also being hammered by the stock market's
ongoing decline.  In the eyes of investors, the
widespread financial scandals are merging with the fear
of a wartime oil shock and a general loss of confidence
(well merited!) in the economic system itself to cause
the biggest losses seen in decades.  Yet I'm doing
nothing about it -- not even thinking of closing my
deep-reserves account.  If I lose it, I lose it.  I
can't shake the feeling it's not really mine to do
anything with.

*

Time's up.  Chun the Chiusan janitor just came in
and we jabbered a bit in our usual near-nonsensical way.
She asked me to read a note written in English and taped
to an odd-looking red plastic box.  "Anyone want this?"
is what it said, I told Chun.  "I want!" said Chun.

*         *

-- A few last words with my Jeep cap on (and the

416

blue quilt pulled over my naked legs because nights are
suddenly much chillier).  And why was this quilt from
Z's room set out in folded form on the couch when I
arrived home?  Presumably so June could sleep on it if
she happened by tonight.  It would've been too big a job
for Z to rearrange everything in her room so June could
sleep there.  We're all trying to do what we can to help
June survive her crisis.

But why the Jeep cap?  Because today's the birthday
of the man who gave me the nickname Jeep -- and also
gave me his first name as my middle name and gave me my
own first name as well by giving both of those names to
my father first (and my family name too, of course, by
direct patrilineal descent).  It could even be said he
gave me my other last name, the real last name strictly
in terms of word order, because if he hadn't bestowed my
first three names on Dad first, I wouldn't've needed a
Junior at the end of them.

Had he not died (forty-four years ago) he'd be 113
today.  It's quite a stretch but it's not impossible to
imagine him at 113.  For one thing, he'd probably still
be a member of the Sons of Norway.  He might even still
be playing tennis.  And he'd almost certainly still be
playing the stock market.  But I don't think he'd be
drinking the way he did after the scandal years, or
there's no possible way he'd've reached such a venerable
age.  The general feeling in the family has always been
it's a miracle he reached seventy.

Shortly after he died Aunt Greta wrote in a letter
to my father (I still have it) that he, Perry, was the
finest, most upstanding man she'd ever known.  But I
wonder: did she feel that way because she was, and still
is, a rock-ribbed right-winger just as he was?  Or was
it the chicken and not the egg: she became a right-
winger because she admired him so much?  I think it was
the chicken, because my own father became a right-winger
and yet he didn't get along well with his father after
1945 and thought him "weak" in later years.  But then
again: shattered idealization of Gramps on the part of
several of his kids had a lot to do with this turn.

[ Jyze of the Heavenly Year : Yellow Horse ]

     Well anyway, Gramps, I always thought you were
terrific.  Thanks for all the names, for the many gifts
(that big yellow toy excavator especially), for the
warmth and affection -- and for all the many genes you
channeled my way via Gram and Dad.  I'd like to try to
identify them one by one but that would get just a bit
complicated.

     In place of gene analysis, a few words about Paz
and Tobey's commitment ceremony.  Poor Paz, she wept all
the way through while struggling to read her lengthy
handwritten pledge.  After the second or third sentence
not an eye remained dry in the audience, including mine.
Paz was tuxedoed, Tobey gowned; flowers were strewn; two
classical guitarists played (and for a brief but painful
minute a boom box blasted some nasty funk from the yard
next door).  Gwen took an awkward yet somehow still
graceful and definitely sexy spill on the hillside (she
was wearing a very short dress) as she approached the
seated audience; Jess got caught up in a bocchi ball
tournament and arrived late.  It was the first time I'd
seen Gwen and Jess together since before our wedding.

     I did my best to rouse June from the zombie state
produced by the antidepressant.  At the reception
afterwards -- at the same site, but indoors, a hall
reminiscent of the garden club where Z and I held our
reception -- spirits were high and mildly subversive, as
befits a group of lesbians cruelly denied the official
benefits of the married state despite the many benefits
they provide society (Paz and Tobey have been together
ten years and own a house and two cars, consume heavily,
pay lots of taxes, and both are valuable city
employees).  Everybody danced with everybody.  I knew
maybe two dozen people there.  Z and I have both been
declared honorary lesbians.  When the mic went around
the room for toasts she delivered a punchy one that
brought the house down.  We had a fine time together: it
was almost as if we were reliving our own wedding
reception.  And could anything be more appropriate for
our anniversary week?

------

41

------


Back room, a familiar Yuke coffee shop.  Revives a few memories, yes it does.  Who's denying?

Up at the U bookstore a new novel-writing phenom is reading, he of self-proclaimedly heartbreaking effect and staggering genius.  A big crowd.  I'll admit I took some subversive pleasure in being only slightly interested.  I did think I heard Mentoka State University and even the term "Mezzu" mentioned as he read from his new book -- that is, it must be in the book -- and my ears perked up.  I listened for a few sentences.  That perked them down again.

Java in the alley, half a block from where Lady U rehearsed in Leslie M.'s studio.  Here's where we met afterwards -- scores of times.  In those days high partitions stood between the booths back here.  No more. And now I'm alone in the room.

It's a Dog cluster.  Black Dog.  "Family Dog."  And so much is happening!  -- This as once again a new year gets underway.  This time it's a new fiscal year, our very own.  Fiscal things are not looking good in the USA right now; that's no doubt another major reason the cabal has the war drums pounding away.  Rightists deny this, of course, but some of them can't help winking when they do.

About four centuries after the Celestial Kingdom gathered itself into being, a bear (beating out a tiger) mated with a god and Korea came onto the scene -- today's the anniversary of that divine/bestial copulation and therefore I have a son who's now applied to eighteen USAn law schools (not a mere fifteen), as

attested in yesterday's e-mail.  But he's decided not to
go for early admission, and that means I probably won't
be meeting him in person before the Heavenly Year ends.
It'll be next spring before he learns where he's been
admitted, if anywhere, and so whatever campus tour we
might make would be delayed until then.  (Why not go for
early admission?  Because not all schools offer it,
that's why, and therefore he might be required to decide
on whether to accept a second-tier school before knowing
whether he'd been accepted at a better one.)

What else is happening?  The deadly poker game over
Iraq continues.  The new angle here is we now have our
own local player in it -- the older brother of Z's (and
Aida's) former lover Kirk.  He's had the gall to
challenge the rush to war, and he's doing it while
visiting Iraq with two other congresspersons.  Therefore
the cabalian superhawks are calling him "Baghdad Ed" and
they're furious.  We in his district -- all of J. City
and a swath of the burbs -- are proud of our Ed,
supporting him by three or four to one.  Out here in the
urban portion of the far, far upper corner we have
something the east-coast medialand seems sadly short on:
perspective.  Not to mention strong progressive values.

Sunday we're marching against the war.  Even though
the march starts in the early afternoon, I'm planning to
join it, with Z.  This is one of those rare occasions
when it actually might matter how many people show up.
One trouble, though: the alt-weekly says the March is
Saturday.  The website confirms Sunday, but still --
that there could be such a major glitch this late in the
game is not a good sign.

As I drove northward to see Mama E this afternoon I
snuck in a few glances at the freighters moored out in
the bay.  They're backing up because of a lockout of
longshoremen whose contract has expired.  The shipping
companies, emboldened by the cabal's antilabor stance,
are trying to break the union.  The result could be a
damaging hit on the economy at a time when it's
vulnerable.

October surprises.  Any others the month has in

store?  Today an Iraqi vice-president proposed that the
best way to ease tensions between his country and the
U.S. would be an old-fashioned duel between the supreme
leaders, theirs and ours.  A combat I could go for.  The
final third of my Heavenly Year -- also launching with
this cluster -- could use some high international drama
like that.

I spent the ninety minutes with Mama E trying out
various offbeat ways to make the buzz in her head go
away -- acupressure on her palms, shoulder raises, neck
compresses, anything I could think of.  Nothing worked,
sorry to say, but she seemed to be having a good time
with it, all things considered.  I know I was.

The good news is that she had laser surgery on both
eyes Monday and she's seeing better now -- can read her
tabloids just using glasses, dispensing with the huge
Sherlock Holmes magnifying glass.  But as long as the
buzz continues she doesn't feel like reading, watching
TV, doing anything at all but listening to that buzz.
And of course she doesn't want to be doing that either,
but she has no choice.  It varies in pitch, she says,
from low to high, which is the worst: "Means it's
getting angry."

Z's been having a very tough time with Mama E
lately.  She did heroic work to shepherd her through the
laser surgery.  She's now awaiting word on the state's
decision regarding Medicaid.  The paperwork has been
horrendous.  Also new problems have been cropping up
with prescriptions.  Dispiriting stuff, and massively
time-consuming.  Over the course of a week she must make
dozens of phone calls, wait forever to get through to
doctors and social workers and counselors and
caregivers, take time off from work to pick up
prescriptions -- and of course things often go wrong.
The details on all this -- forget about those.  I'm
ready to schiz out myself just thinking about them.
She gulps down her herbal "Exhilarin" capsules by the
handful but has managed to stay off the hard stuff so
far (the Wellbutrin).  I try to be there for her as the
comforter/distracter.  Her tears cascade onto my chest

in the pillow-talk hour and at other times as well.

But onward!  For good stuff, a couple of hours with Vic and Jean and Ro yesterday at the loft on the first day of Ro's new semester and then a stop with Vic alone at a spiffy downtown gallery for the opening of Catherine S.'s new show, very chichi.  For bad stuff, a bicyclist ran a red light and smashed into the driver's-side door of Betty's car, seriously injuring himself and shaking her up pretty badly (his face pancaked against the top of the door window just as she glanced up from inches away -- she said it was like a bank robber in a nylon-stocking mask).  Fortunately Kat was off at a school retreat at the time (one of the parent chaperons for this event being Z's coworker and friend David M., the one whose son Omar is in Kat's class).

For more good stuff, landlord Raphael and his chief handyman Chad came by this afternoon and the bathroom ceiling's now patched up (last month's bathtub overflow in 303 directly above us eventually caused a cone of paint to hang down from our bathroom ceiling, looking like a huge cream-colored wasps' nest).  And the kitchen sink is draining properly again.

For more bad stuff, it's rainy and cold -- looks like the jet stream's already executing its annual spoilsport southward course change, meaning more Arctic weather is blown down our way -- and I'm carrying my hooded jacket with me again for the first time since late spring.  The sky was a battlefield this afternoon: squadrons of low gray clouds charging in all directions, hovering angrily, hissing.  Quite a spectacle, actually, and probably for that very reason a major cause of the massive freeway traffic jam that forced me to shift to my alternate backroads northward route to Benita's place (and the fifteen-mile trip still took an hour and twenty minutes -- almost as long as the projected time for the visit itself).

So why am I hanging out in the Yuke at this late hour?  Well, Naomi left a message saying today's scope job canceled, so I have only an hour's worth of finals to do at the office.  And I wanted to use a bookstore

coupon I've been hoarding ever since my birthday to pick
up a copy of a very good contemporary Chinese novelist's
new nonfiction "Return to Painting" (because he's also
an excellent painter).  It includes a long essay on
aesthetics and politics.  It seems he takes the detached
art-for-art's-sake view -- politics has no place in art
-- but with a few twists that are intriguing.  All my
life I've been wrestling with this question.  Lately an
article by my neoprag fave-rave (whose seventy-first
birthday is tomorrow) has been forcing me to revisit the
question in search of new arguments to support my strong
belief that staying engaged matters as much for the
caring artist as for the caring citizen.  "Caring"?  Am
I presupposing what I want to argue for?  Well, no.  If
you don't care, fine, make art about what you do care
about.  Maybe others will care about it too.  If you do
care about political matters, then to deaden that caring
is also to take some or all of the life out of your art.
I believe this -- fiercely -- and especially for myself.
    Will I have more to say on such a contentious
topic?  Maybe not.  Not unless some revelation comes
along.  Meanwhile better to try to walk the talk and of
course then jyze the walk.
    -- By now Lady U would've tossed her dance bag on
the booth seat opposite.  "Oh man, wotta night!"  I can
still hear it.  Can still smell the liniment.  This
would've been toward the end of our really good days --
and then came the Year of the Black Dog and those days
were gone for, yes, good, and in both senses, forever
and a bettering, considering that the change eventually
allowed me, much later, to meet and hitch up with a
certain Zoelie B.


[+3]


    A few hours ago ten thousand people clamored around
this spot where I'm sitting now, all demanding "Not in
our name" and "No Iraq War."  A fine afternoon, a
bracing experience, but will it be enough to make a

difference?  Not likely.  Maybe in the longer run and as
a small part of something much larger, after the
movement has some time to build.  There's a slim chance
it could turn things around at that point.  Slim, but
better than none.  It's even better than fat, as in "fat
chance."

Not "a few" hours ago.  Eight.  But here I sit on
the stone steps in the downtown plaza, beneath the giant
staple, right where the rally speakers stood.  Now as
far as I can see not a single soul's lurking about
anywhere in the plaza -- a nonjyzing soul, that is, or a
nonjyzing nonsoul for that matter.  Tomorrow's a
workday.  For me tonight's been a worknight.  Ordinarily
I'd be catching the last bus home right about now, but
on this occasion I've got wheels.  The Z-mobile's parked
two blocks due south in front of the scope building.

And I'm in a bad way for time.  Tomorrow evening
brother Rob and I will be celebrating his half-century
birthday (in our ritual birthday way, meeting at our
favorite railcar diner), and I've yet to come up with a
gift for him.  Nor have I had a chance to so much as
glance at the Sunday papers.  And after rising two hours
early, before noon, so Z and I could arrive at the rally
on time, I'm dead tired now.  A one-hour nap earlier
this evening fell far short as a recharger.

So these few pages and the Black Dog's done.

At one point my plan was different.  I'd scribble
first outside the fairgrounds playhouse where
"Indigenes" was performed (with Lady U in a key role),
then here.  A bigger workload than expected scotched the
"Indigenes" part of that.  A choice had to be made.
Today's doings beat out those of twenty years ago.

A coppery glint -- I'm reminded I'm wearing a new
wedding ring, bought for five bucks at yesterday's Tree
of Africa festival.  It fits better than the original
one, which endangers the blood vessels in all my fingers
except the index and gets in the way when I'm typing or
pumping iron or loving, among other crucial pursuits.
I'm retiring that old ring to an honorary spot in the
living room near where Z's white platform wedding shoes

hold forth on their plinth.  She's approved the shift.

Tree of Africa with Gerry and Leola was fun.  A big cathedral which I used to hoof it past forty years ago on my way to see Kristi K. out in the Yuke.  The acoustics in the main sanctuary were not good for the all-star African band with its wildly pounding bongos and congas -- the echoes were so bad they gave Gerry a headache and he had to take shelter in Leola's fancy car until it eased off.  (He's another Water Horse, by the way, born three months after me on what twenty-one years later would become JFK (JRX!) assassination day, and he pleaded with me to read him a passage from this Heavenly Year jyzebook, and I did, the one about the vatic salmon, and he commented on it thus: "I'm not sure I understood it.  But don't get me wrong, I like it.  It sounds just like you."  This was almost a rave, right?)

Shops and office buildings surround me, department stores, all silent, only a few lit up.  Puffy fog clouds roll by like tumbleweeds just slightly above the tallest buildings.  It would be a good time for the city to do some soul-searching if it were of a mind to do any.

We arrived at the east-hill park for the rally at one -- turned out the march wasn't scheduled to pull out until three.  All that rushing for naught!  So then we retraced some of our steps to partake of brunch at a certain popular eatery on the main east-hill drag, and we waited there for the march to catch up with us.  Oddly, although we'd both chowed down there dozens of times over the years, we'd never done so together before the previous night, when we stopped in with Leola and Gerry after Tree of Africa (Leola's sister Renny is convalescing from chemotherapy, tended to by Leola on a hospital bed set up in G&L's living room -- so Leola may need R&R these days even more than Z does).  Today Tad, a member of Z's book group, showed up at the same eatery by chance and joined us at our table and wound up marching most of the way in with us -- not happily at first, because he'd been fighting with his gay lover Cesar, but then happily, yes, after he received a makeup call from Cesar on his cellphone.  So in that sense it truly was a doubly successful peace march for Tad and Cesar. -- And at least singly successful for lots of others too, myself and Z by all means included.

The marchers stretched curb to curb for a dozen blocks or more, heading south at first, then straight west while descending the hill to the plaza where I sit now. Sun beating down the whole way -- I got sunburned. Huge papier-mache puppets, seas of signs, Uncle Sam on stilts, a large cloth peace eagle, a seventy-five-foot-long cloth missile, and drums drums drums (most of the way we strode along right next to a raucous drum corps). It was the mid or late sixties all over again. Someone handed me a U.S. flag converted into a hand-shaped peace sign identical to one pasted on my motor scooter back then; I waved it like an elder possessed.

For lots of folks the march with its rallies at both ends was a spirit booster. Dissent against the cabal's outrageous policies is still in an early enough stage that you can feel lonely and isolated -- until something like this happens. We saw dozens of people we knew and were heartened by the diversity of the crowd, racial and otherwise, e.g., gender and age.

Another march is scheduled for the 26th of this month. Given today's success, it's likely this next one will be much larger. Similar rallies and marches were held in cities across the country today. What were the numbers? (The perennial question.) If as big as here, hope still springs even though it's, as it seems I can't stop saying, way slim.

-- Oops, just now I almost got whacked by a flying peace sign. A swarm of skateboarders showed up and they're tossing around leftover signs like frisbees. No lie -- this one whizzed in like a missile and lodged in a crack between stones not six inches from my left hip -- quivered there like an arrow. Laughter from the skateboarders. A few choice words from me -- I coulda been neutered here! -- but then I calmed down -- noticing I'm vastly outnumbered.

Yeah, and I'd say if I want the peace -- such as it is -- to hold I'd better head myself on out right now.

------

42

------

A shrill gray day at the north-end marina.  Shrill
because wheeling flocks of gulls and crows are
skirmishing out over the forest of sailboat masts.  As
the verdigrised Viking of a thousand years ago looks out
from his pedestal some twenty feet behind me and maybe
fifteen feet up with typical Norski impassivity -- and
it's his official day in the USA!  That's why I'm here,
to commune with the spirit of a man who knew something
about imperial reach.

What they're calling a great debate is going on in
Congress this week.  The issue's great, yes, but there's
no real debate -- the system's too deeply corrupt now
for real debate to take place on any important issue.
Congress will support the cabal's agenda.  With
"preemptive" war against Iraq the U.S. will start down
a path it won't be able to exit.  Or I should say it
will continue past the point of no return on the path
it's already on.  Collapse will be inevitable a few
decades down that same path, if not sooner.

So whatcha say, Viking man?  At least you had the
sense to turn back.  You saw how badly you were
outnumbered by those no-good Skraellings, as you called
them.  The cabalist neocon crusaders running our country
today see the rest of the world in just about the way
you saw the Skraellings -- and the numerical odds aren't
much different either -- but the crusaders think they
can prevail by sheer firepower and the supposedly self-
evident superiority of the USAn way as defined by them.

It won't happen.  I'm apologizing right now on
behalf of my generation who failed to stop these

lunatics, though many of us did try and some are still trying. (I realize the "Stop War" button I'm wearing these days ain't gonna do much.) Because of the decision being rubber-stamped in Congress this week tens or hundreds of thousands will die soon, tens or hundreds of millions within a decade or two or three as the wars multiply and the ecological consequences of capitalism-gone-wild kick in. Not that it hasn't been evident for a long time that this would probably happen. But still, you can't help but cry out when passing a major milepost on the road to apocalypse. This is one of those.

European observers detected some slight reason for hope in the speech our supreme leader gave Monday night. They think he hinted a USAn invasion of Iraq could be averted. I don't think so; I think he was just playing the game. But I hope I'm wrong.

Mr. Viking, you with me on this? You and the other ancestral spirits?

-- And it's an unusually good day to visit a nautical setting. That's because just yesterday the cabal chieftain invoked the Taft-Hartley Act, forcing the longshoremen back to work without a new contract. The economy's too fragile, he said -- not in those exact words -- and war materiel needs to be moving. He didn't mention the other major reason, although it's scarcely a secret: right-wingers are out to break the unions. (Well of course they are! That's not news! Didn't jyze refer to this just last week? They're cappies! They've been trying to do it for more than a century! -- And the horrible thing is they may finally be succeeding.)

During a lull in the gull-vs.-crow wars I hear the distant barking of sea lions. Or are those the screams of outraged dock workers?

(By the way, a take on the world political crisis very similar to mine showed up in an analysis called "The Threat from America" in the current issue of a fortnightly book review out of London. It's only the second such article I've come across this year in which the effects of long-term social and economic changes caused by eco/climate crisis are seen as the big picture

against which all else must be measured and judged.)
     And here I sit.  It's also just another day.  Nor
did I travel all the way out to the SQ simply for the
purpose of communing with the Viking ancient (though
maybe I would've anyway; I've done it before, and some
of those visits have even been written up in other J-
books).  The more practical purpose was to pick up the
Z-mobile, which underwent a tune-up and also had some
rattles quieted at our usual auto shop.  Three hundred
bucks.  Z-wiff pays.  And as it happens, the other major
way in which she's a sugar mama for me popped into view
today.  The city distributed a notice about the cost of
her health-care plan for next year, and to keep me on
the coverage will set her back an extra fifty bucks a
month.  She didn't hesitate a moment, though.  And joked
later: "I wouldn't sleep at night if I didn't do it."
     It's true I don't use the car much and I've never
availed myself of the health care.  If I were on my own
I can say flatly I'd have neither a car nor health care.
But I'm grateful to have access to both now, especially
as age threatens to reduce my mobility and make me
increasingly vulnerable to health problems (such as body
breakdowns, rattles and the like).
     -- And here comes some light drizzle.  Surprise!
Or call it heavy dank.  Or -- more like showers all of a
sudden.  Best to hightail it outta here.  Gimme shelter!
                         *
     Maybe twenty minutes later.  I lucked out -- first
with a parking space, now with my favorite window table
at an SQ chain coffee shop (the one with the big comfy
armchairs which are almost always already in use).
Across the street the six-flag cluster above the
triangle is seriously aflutter (it's Old Glory -- or Old
Shame to me these days -- and the five Scandis).
Umbrellas don't know which way to aim.  Building-huggers
sidle along, silhouetted by lit-up shop windows.
     On the far side of the room a fire roars in a
fireplace.  Gas and fake logs and actually it's more a
faint hiss but still I'll fall for the Z-worthy pun and
say at least it's hearth-warming.  Flickery flames, old

folks seated nearby, heads nodding, eyelids lowering
nonstop by degrees.  Reminds me: this week Z and I
became card-carrying members of a funeral home located
about three miles east of here.  If my corpse is found
lying in a gutter somewhere, the finders will know what
number to call -- unless they'd rather just make off
with my wallet.  I was disappointed the card says
nothing about my funeral plan being "irrevocable."

On Monday night, Rob at the railcar diner.  Last
night, Vic at a little-known but very fine Chinese joint
in the AQ.  Happy nights!  Rob didn't know quite what to
make of the new Black Dragon paraphernalia I wound up
laying on him for his fiftieth birthday -- so he'll have
a full decade to work up to his Black Dragon Heavenly
Year.  And Z and I went in together to buy him a hemp
shirt marked down by half.  "I can't believe we're all
fifty or older now," he said several times, referring to
himself and his siblings, of course including me.  It's
good to be reminded once in a while of his perspective.
The rest of us have all been fifty or more for eons!

"Over 50 Crisis Center.  It takes a geezer to help
a geezer."  -- So said the hand-lettered sign which I
came upon posted in our interior hallway at home last
night.  I wondered if something had happened to Rob, but
it turned out the sign was referring to June.  This week
she finally learns whether she passed her bar exam.  Z
and Aida have already decided to do an "intervention."
Saturday we'll drive up to June's place out in the burbs
and help her pack for a stay at Aida's.  Her zombie-like
state is worsening, Z says, and may be turning suicidal.
Is it just a loss-of-face thing?  Just a matter of
coming from a long line of champion exam-takers going
all the way back to Master Kung himself?  Well, no.
It's isolation, loneliness, aging, lost friends, lost
investments, all kinds of things.  It's June -- an
unusually high-strung woman, like Z, like my mother,
like Ladies S and V.  And no doubt quite a few others.

Meanwhile the kid keeps madly applying to law
schools.  Twenty-two is the latest count, and he says
this is it, no more.  Another top-ten northeastern urban

far-coaster is the final one.  He sent me a shoddy
pastiche of statements written for other schools and
requested that I redesign it for this new one.  What
troubled me most, he again failed to leave a voicemail
saying he'd sent it via Z's work computer -- despite our
earlier talks about this and his "really, really"
assurances.  But I did the revision anyway.  And now
with my immediate usefulness to him seemingly coming to
an end it'll be interesting to see whether he wants to
keep up the relationship, and if so, how and to what
extent.  So far he's failed to respond in any way to the
books, photos, long letters I've sent him.
     And what else?  It's pumpkin time.  Z, always
seasonally aware, always a live-wire (except for her
"down time" and "introspective periods"), left a
colorful little pumpkin-like squash on my chair several
nights ago, a lonely face drawn on it, and each night
she adds a new cartoon bubble of commentary to it.
Wotta wiff!  -- And a new "planet" half the size of
Pluto has been spotted and named, and it's the name I
like: Quaoar.  Its diameter is about the same as the
distance between here and MSM #2.  The mention of which
triggers this: sister Barb still hasn't replied to my
birthday letter.  The chances of a grand Heavenly Year
reconciliation with her are starting to look less good.
     I'm pleased to say a new book is out about the last
day on which I didn't exist on this earth, either as a
living physical presence or -- after my coming demise --
a fading ghostly body of words.  "December 6," it's
called, and it's about life in Japan the day before the
attack on Pearl Harbor.  In an interview the author
foolishly brags about having spent only a grand total of
four weeks in Japan before writing it.  Wotta jerk!
     Last weekend a big gun battle, gang-related,
erupted outside a nightclub on the "very high road" near
the northern edge of downtown J. City -- fifty shots
fired, two dead.  Rob often walks by that spot on his
way to catch a bus home.  The cops say the violence
level downtown is nowhere near what it was ten years ago
and my own observations would confirm that.  But it's

getting scarier again, no question about it.
     I gotta go.  And in more ways than one (drinking
too much coffee causing one of them -- and now a root
beer).  But first I'll mention this: it's a Gray Pig
cluster and the slogan is "Pig in the Forest."  The Pig
is the last in order of the twelve animals and the Gray
Pig (Water Pig) is the last of the sixty-animal cycle,
equivalent to the final year of a century in Gregorian
terms.  The next year -- which is No. 43 or, in my own
Heavenly cycle, 1984 -- it all starts over again.  And
speaking of starting over, another reason I've got to
get going here is that it's a grand-jury day.  Naomi's
back in GJ harness and therefore so am I.  The docket's
said to be full: sex-slavery, terrorism, drugs,
corporate scandals.  I'm salivating.


                         [+2]


     It's not a lickin' stick, it's a bumpin' post.
Sign says so.  Brand-new, never been used, just
installed here at the AQ streetcar's southern terminus.
It's a sled on the tracks with a pneumatic bumper
mechanism at one end, designed to halt a runaway
streetcar.  If a runaway hits the bumper, the bumper
compresses and then the sled itself slides a few feet to
hit another bumper, this a rubber one anchored in a big
concrete block.
     About a year and a half ago a runaway smashed into
a concrete block here -- a different one -- causing a
number of injuries.  Since then this terminal stop's
been closed; it's been moved "temporarily" around the
corner to the northwest.  And a new building's been
going up right next to the shelter at my back -- which
is why I couldn't sit in this spot on my lunar birthday
(the guard appearing in a window above to shoo me away).
But the area's open now, although the streetcar's not
yet running to this final corner, the original terminus.
Soon, though, maybe, it looks like.
     And we've got a runaway in the nation's capital.

Even the appearance of a real debate got canceled.
Congress has voted the cabal can do as it likes in the
Mideast -- a three-to-two margin in the House, three-to-
one in the Senate.  Crows the supreme caballero: "Now
the world knows that the United States speaks with one
voice."  The headline in our little local lefty rag gets
it right: "U.S. Declares War on World."  Even if an
invasion of Iraq is somehow averted, this remains the
case.  It says so right there in the cabal's strategic
document.  It's official policy now.

As the cars roll through the intersection here.
The sweetest rush hour of the week: Friday afternoon.  A
glorious sunny day, but with a "bone-chiller" cold snap
due to arrive tonight (which is to say, we'll be going
subfreezing).  That's why I decided to grab this chance
for an outdoor jyze session here at one of my favorite
spots.  It's unlikely, but if gloom season starts up a
little early -- and if the occasional drizzle breaks
aren't serendipitously timed -- I might be shut out on
outdoor venues for the duration of the Heavenly Year.

Gates of the AQ.  Twin dragons chinning atop light
poles.  A diagonal block up the slope of east hill the
top-floor windows of the teahouse hotel of Black Horse
birthday renown are still catching some late rays, as I
can see from here.  Beyond that, way up, past a canyon
maze of structures, "Old Shame" flutters atop the
hospital (the war against death rages on but we won't go
there anymore).  The east-depot market has moved a few
doors south to a corner location diagonally across the
intersection from me.  It's spiffed up a bit, the better
to serve the classy clientele of plutocrat #2's cluster
of new buildings, including this one going up at my
back.  Not a cloud in sight.  Many pedestrians, mostly
Asian and young, the females almost all dressed pretty
much alike in tight hip-hugger jeans and midriff-baring
tops, we males enjoying the spectacle.  And the females
themselves seem to be enjoying it too -- hair tossing
smartly about, some snazzy runway struts.

Me, I'm no longer a player in those games, not even
a gaper or ogler, or at least not openly so.  Just

another old fogey dispassionate observer, detached and
disinterested behind my shades, yok yok.
     Big deep rumble of a freight train passing by below
street level, heading into the tunnel.  Engines.  So
many engines around here!  Every time the light turns
red, jyze is presented with a new audience as cars back
up on the very, very high road right in front of me, the
nearest vehicle usually within arm's reach.  They're
seeing a weird jyzer-person at work up close.  "Hey
dude, scribble sump'n for me!"  (Nobody's said that yet.
Or anything at all.  Everyone's cocooned behind glass.
Wary too.  They probably think I'm a street-corner
panhandler working on a new sign.  -- And I'm grizzled
today, a full five days' worth, and this black-and-white
chuck currently propped on the shiny pneumatic tube, I
know there's a hole in the sole and it's showing -- it's
in-yer-facing all these gussied-up solo drivers.  Some
may be mentioning this as they converse on their
cellphones.  -- I say that because, here as elsewhere,
it seems at least half of the cellphone talk I overhear
is devoted to nailing down the speaker's location at
that very moment.  Or maybe half's a little high.  Say a
third.  -- But then who am I to object when a similar
portion of jyze is devoted to much the same thing?
Location, location, location: here it surely is!)
     Next I work out.  The Z-woman won't be there; she's
seeing Mama E this evening.  Keep them muscles movin'.
A feature in today's OMP describes the oldest tree in
the world so far as anyone knows, dubbed "Methuselah,"
of course, a bristlecone pine perched on a megastate
mountainside about ten thousand feet up.  It's believed
to be five thousand years old, which makes it roughly
three hundred years older than the Celestial Kingdom and
only thirteen years younger than the world itself as a
famous Christian bishop opined a few centuries ago.
When I turned the page and saw the picture of this tree
I identified with it immediately -- it reminded me of a
certain photo of myself taken at the south-end Japanese
garden a month ago -- gritty, scrubby, bristleconey.
(What this paragraph is, it's part of my ongoing project

of talking myself into getting used to being old.  It's
not a conscious project but I just can't seem to help
myself.  It's like customizing -- or age accustomizing,
call it.  Adapt and adjust or you die, and then you die
anyway.  Rage or be graceful, go with or against the
flow, you still gotta go.  Deal with it.  Or don't.
Doesn't matter!  -- Except maybe to certain projected
future observers, one can hope, just as I'm turning out
to be a (presumed) projected future observer for a
ragtag group of my urjyze and protojyze predecessors.)

*          *

Little bit of a nightcap.  Did some strawberry
shortcake for supper -- a celebration, with Z providing
the makings.  A DSHS worker passed the word to Benita
that Mama E's been approved for a full Medicaid ride.
That translates to three grand a month plus the cost of
medicines and miscellaneous services.  A whole lotta
bucks!  Mama E was shocked to hear how much her new
state of residence thinks she's worth.  Consider all
those people (half the world population or so)
struggling to get by on a buck or two a day!  What we're
talking about here is the fruits of hegemony.  Most USAn
economists, of course, are in the pay of the hegemonic
system and prefer, at least for public consumption, to
see things otherwise on the "fruits of" question.

But jyze has returned for an encore tonight for a
different reason.  It's now five a.m. of a new day by
local Gregorian Daylight Time and that new day is --
Columbus Day.  He who sailed the ocean blue in the year
that for me is an internal dyslexic-like inversion of my
year of birth, 1942, going by Christ-based time since as
he approached death Columbus famously came to believe he
himself was the resurrected Christ.  But as indigenes on
this continent have been pointing out for close to five
centuries, he was one very nasty man -- a genocidal
maniac, among many other notable negative qualities.  A
review in this week's glossy far-coast lit weekly lays
out the basics of that story.  Even sketches his visit
to Iceland in 1477 -- but unaccountably fails to mention
the strong possibility that while there he got wind of a

435

certain heroic Norski's Vinland voyage almost five
centuries earlier and decided to replicate it along a
more southerly course.  But apparently Columbus died
still believing the lands he had run into were part of
China, not a whole "new" continent or two.

Since then, half a millennium of genocide and
rapacity.  In this country the plunder paid for a lot of
scientific progress and also a lot of slaves, and those
two categories taken together translated into immense
industrial and military power, thus compounding manyfold
the original real-estate swag.  So great was the amassed
wealth that the ruling class could afford to buy off the
discontent of their subalterns by sharing a bit of it
and guaranteeing certain freedoms.  Eventually things
got to the point where a Mama E could go on Medicaid at
36K-plus a year and the cabal in D.C. could announce
it's taking over the world.

What a fascinating cluster you've been, Gray Pig.
The end of the animal line and you did yourself proud!

-- One last bit of news.  Recall the winding
western path that the first Eurusan settler relied on in
mounting and dismounting the ridge that Jyze knows as
south hill, which ridge he claimed as his own property a
hundred and fifty years ago when the two-pronged
European invasion launched by Columbus -- following the
heroic Viking's lead -- reached this region and snatched
it away from the local Skraellings.  That path later
became the paved road which in the current era some
seven thousand drivers, mostly hilltop residents, use
daily to get on and off the hill.  And yesterday,
because a construction worker noticed some shifting of a
column supporting the bridge that carries that road over
the main north-south freeway, the bridge was closed for
an indefinite period.  Likely cause of the shifting?
Damage resulting from the Georgianna Chandler Hutcheson
Sandefjord Birthday Earthquake of 2001.

-- "There you go again, blaming it all on your poor
mother."

Certainly not.  But neither am I denying her
influence on my life was considerable.  And remains so.

------

43

------

First, because it's a gorgeous day (another one!).
Second, because it's lunar Double Nine day and the
Celestial advice for this day is to get yourself and
your family up high, out of harm's way.  And third,
because I've been wanting to return here and, again, as
the weather changes I might not have another chance to
do so.  -- Which is a mandatory geezer tack-on clause, I
suppose, for the justification of most anything.
    It's the AQ terrace gardens.  A little before four
in the afternoon.  Earlier I drove the Z-mobile down to
hand it off to the Z-woman and she in turn drove me up
to the Japanese theater, visible from here, just past
the top of the gardens.  So for once the walk to reach
this deck was downhill all the way (though no more than
eight or ten steps).
    Everything basks in golden light.  Not a cloud to
be -- what?  Seen, yes!  The sun's hot on my right
shoulder; it's time right now to take off my long-sleeve
black outer shirt.
    Done.
The bay's a dazzly silver -- and all but
motionless, with several large container-laden ships
moored out there.  Flashes from cars on the freeway a
couple of blocks to the east thread their way through
narrow needly gaps in the evergreens.  On the far side
of the AQ valley the orange-brick DC castle, looking on
this day to be made of sunbaked adobe, presides
impassively atop the northern prow of south hill.  A
dozen blocks to its right the new football stadium winks
-- it's like the top half of a giant steel eye seen

obliquely from above, with X-braces for eyelashes.  Last
night the 49ers were in town and wrestled our boys down.
I hiked through the roaring canyon during the opening
moments and was allowed to pat the muzzle of one of the
beer-company Clydesdales.  Big horse.  Good horse.  Good
Horse Year Horse, little streaks of black in its muddy-
brown composite all-Horses type of hide.

*

    -- I've just shifted seats as my neck was starting
to simmer.  Now I'm looking straight at a group of
Korusans working in a garden on this same terrace but
three or four plots to the west.  I can translate a
simple word here and there.  "Yes!"  "Ouch!"  "Look at
this!"  One woman's wearing a green accountant's
eyeshade that puts me in mind of the one Popeye used to
wear half a century ago.  Several people are out on the
decks of the big low-income apartment building rising
above the gardens at their northwest end.  By my count
fourteen balconies are visible and two are showing "Old
Shame," two are displaying "No Iraq War" signs (just
like ours in the window at home and on the Z-mobile's
rear bumper), and three are given over entirely to
satellite dishes -- it's a kind of instant poll on the
war, I guess, and probably as accurate as any.
    Big sunflowers here.  Apples red on the trees
(heavily laden, just like the low-riding container
ships).  Best of all, a big hardy fuchsia bush dangles
red blossoms with purple bells within arm's reach.
-- So deliciously you can almost hear them tinkle.
(Without doubt you can hear some merrily cheeping birds
flitting about in the tree behind them.)  Except for a
few reddish-brown leaves on the arbor vine to my left,
autumn's not yet putting on much of a show here --
unless you give it credit for the overall appearance of
greenery in ripe harvest-like profusion.  And you
should!  (Here's a pair of dancing butterflies --
swallowtails.  And I love the weathered gray wood --
especially of the staves, each a different length and
cut -- of the fence separating the area up here from the
row of plots being worked by the Korusans.)

[ Jyze of the Heavenly Year : Yellow Horse ]

     My own half-Korean offspring, I'll mention right
now, has left two messages in the past twenty-four hours
saying he'd like me to call, he wants to "chat."  Hmm.
Hope there's no ulterior motive here.  But then -- so
what if there is?  In reply I left him a message at work
(he was out) suggesting it might be a good idea to set
up a regular weekly "chat" time.  After all, we've got a
heckuva lot of catching up to do.  And I've got a ton of
fatherly wisdom to impart, built up over the years, if
he wants to hear it, or even just a small portion of it.
My latest thought is I ought to be very direct with him
about my opinions, even if many of them -- as surely is
the case -- clash with his.  I'll see if I can persuade
him to lower his guard a bit so we can both talk more
frankly.  Not that I haven't been trying to do this
before now.  But a renewed effort.
     In a little more than an hour I'll be meeting Vic
at his loft.  Looks like this too is about to become a
regular thing.  He proposed it in a note I found under
my door yesterday (along with the usual stack of
corrected manuscript pages) -- a "boys' night out" every
Tuesday.  For me Tuesday night's a scope night but it's
usually relatively light so I'll give it a try.  One way
or another I'm sure we'll be able to work something out.
(This Saturday Vic and Jean will be coming over to 1511
for dinner.  It might be a little awkward.  You never
know with couple dynamics.  The closeness developing
between Vic and me might unbalance things between Jean
and Zoelie.  It'll be interesting to see.)
     Saturday Z and I helped June move down from her
ritzy burban digs for the therapeutic stay at Aida's.
It was sad to see June's near-zombie state as she moved
through the dusty rooms of her very large home.  She was
helpless even to choose a week's worth of clothes; Z had
to do it for her.  Then an even sadder moment followed
at Aida's as the three of us sat on the couch in her
small den while Aida checked the website for the bar-
exam scores.  This time the list of names of those who
passed was finally posted, and June's name wasn't on it.
She didn't react much that I saw, but then that's just

it: she's not reacting to anything.  Earlier she'd said
she was more worried about overcoming her depression
than passing the exam.  Now we're all worried about what
might happen next.  She assured Z and Aida she's not
suicidal and asked them not to contact Adam, her oldest
son.  "What could he do anyway?"  But Sunday Aida called
Z and said she was already climbing the walls because
June was following her around "like a sick puppy."
    Can I do anything to help?  Not much, I'm afraid.
When we're together June gives me long sad significant
looks and of course I try to smile encouragingly back.
If I had scads of time to devote to her, maybe I could
get somewhere -- but then Z, I'm sure, would be uneasy.
So I'm stymied.  The best thing I can do seems to be to
play a backup role, much as I do with Mama E.  June
herself says Z would object if June and I were to meet
alone too much and she evidently prefers not to risk
that.  So I just hang about on the fringes.
    Mama E?  Nothing much different.  I'll be seeing
her Thursday.
    Yesterday I called Rob on his actual birthday.
More and more as the years go by I realize how fortunate
we are to be living near each other.  So many similar
interests!  One prime topic this time was the most
recent report on world temperatures.  Once again this
year is shaping up to be the second hottest on record,
and it has an outside shot at being the first.
    And this week's world events?  A big terror bombing
in a Bali nightclub packed with Westerners, a sniper
picking off everyday folks in the USAn D.C. area.  It
appears the gap between France and the U.S. on the Iraq
issue is widening, meaning the UN Security Council might
not kowtow to U.S. demands and therefore the cabal might
choose to go it alone on Iraq, just as it's been
threatening to do for months.  At least then our nasty
unilateral ways would stand fully exposed and
indisputably confirmed.  U.S. public-opinion polls
continue to show increasing doubts about the wisdom of
such a blatantly aggressive move, but few analysts think
this will have more than a slight delaying effect, if

even that, on the war plans.

   Meanwhile the Scandis give a former U.S. president
the Nobel Peace Prize -- like all the other Nobels it's
paid for largely by interest on sales of dynamite during
the high colonial era -- and along with it they deliver
a richly deserved lecture to our current supreme leader
on his evil ways.  But of course he's not listening, nor
are the rest of the caballeros.

   -- So on Double Nine Day you read poetry and play
games and drink wine in a high place.  That's what
tradition decrees.  (Wei's spending the day making an
Alaska-Native-style kayak.)  Meanwhile this is the kind
of day, tradition also notes, on which disaster might
strike down in the lowlands.

   But I don't think so.  Not today.  And why?
Because with this cluster of the Green Rat, as mentioned
earlier, Heavenly Year jyze starts into a whole new
sixty-animal cycle.  It just has to be a lucky day -- a
day to celebrate.  And so I'm going to go do that,
beginning right now.  -- But first vamp just a tiny bit
more right here.  Take a last sip from the coffee mug I
brought from home as a wine surrogate.  Note the
lengthening shadows which have swallowed all the apple
trees to my left but not the ones higher up the hillside
to my right, beyond the nicely aging cedar garden shed.

   -- And now the sunflowers are cackling.  Time to
make myself scarce.


[+2]


   Here's a familiar spot.  I interlock with it as the
old Lincoln logs used to do with one another and
probably still do in the millions of nostalgia sets of
same reportedly being sold these days.  It's the
substation minipark in my former hood up in the Yuke.
It was built in the early years when Lady U and I were
living across the street, and so long has it been around
now that all the lettering's worn off the park sign
except for the park name itself, and that's quite faint.

[ Jyze of the Heavenly Year : Yellow Horse ]


     Basketballs thudding on the small court a few yards
behind me down on the lower level.  Years ago it
might've been me tossing up all those clangers.  The
small picnic table down there is piled high with coats
and backpacks, so I've come up to one of the benches
facing the figure-eight stone table on the upper level.
I'm ringed by familiar trees and looking out from under
them at several familiar buildings.  Recalling how the
sidewalk flower strip at the base of the big apartment
house across the street to the east used to yield a
bumper crop of velvety-red snapdragons every year.
     The picnic table down by the hoopsters, that's
where I scribbled out the last pages of the "Howler"
screed back in '82.  I was waiting for Lady U but she
didn't show up and that meant it was over with her --
the screed had found its ending.  Drama.  With that
catharsis complete, I then went straight up to the house
and started the long process of getting real again.
I'll grant I must've loved that woman one heckuva lot to
have willingly gone through so much over her.  Maybe in
its own way it really was just as much as I've loved any
of the others -- as if you could ever measure! -- but
for sure it put me in a world of hurt for a long time.
So I remember it now with a peculiar fondness, as I do
the several other major worlds of hurt over the years,
interlocking with them in that same Lincoln-log fashion,
might as well say (it's so USAn!).
     Feet crossed at the ankles out on the infinity
stones, left arm propped on bench and cradling J-book.
It's like easing back into a favorite armchair.  Many,
many hours I put in here writing or reading or just
pondering in this same slouchy posture.
     -- As darkness creeps in and the streetlight pops
into view in the branches of one of the low trees,
seeming to hang there like a miraculous glowing oversize
peach.  Behind it somewhere the recently risen gibbous
moon, probably blocked by the big apartment house.
Thunk, thunk.  An all-hours court.  More than a few
times I'd be lying in bed at four a.m. and they'd be
going at it over here.  When the court light was turned

off, the nearby streetlight did the job well enough.
For serious hoops it could be augmented, and often was,
with car headlights, like beach volleyball.

Marvelous weather continues. Me, I'm heading back
down to work after another goofy and sad visit with Mama
E. Z's on the outs with her right now, fed up with her
nonstop complaints and crafty maneuverings during
Monday's twin doctor visits. Mama E begs me to tell her
daughter to call. "I can't sleep, I'm hurting in the
heart so much." I promise to do my best.

What for news? A new international crisis, that's
all. North Korea, a charter member of our crusader
cabal's "Axis of Evil," for some odd reason decides this
is the moment to let the world know it has a secret
nuclear-weapons program. Does this mean we'll have to
be attacking them at the same time as we attack Iraq?
Of course we just might've been planning to do that
anyway. But will they retaliate by obliterating Seoul,
as they could easily do, and/or other parts of Korea or
Japan? Will Lady S's family be victims of a Seoul
bombardment for the second time in half a century?

Our cabal chieftain has put out the word he'll
grant the UN a couple more weeks of dithering and if
they haven't decided by the end of that time to yield to
his Iraq ultimatum he'll just order up an invasion on,
yes, his own. Most likely he'll consign this new crisis
with North Korea to the back burner until after Iraq's
cried uncle and a few hundred thousand Iraqis are dead
meat. Then, POW, North Korea's kaput. No compromises
with evil. The more it pops up, the more we'll stomp it
down, and the more God will love us. And of course the
rest of the world will be endlessly grateful.

-- The light here's becoming quite bad. The
streetlight by the basketball court is out, I see, and
the court light itself is completely gone, pole and all.
Some of the neighbors in the big successor apartment
building standing across the street on our old lot must
be better complainers than we were. And so right now no
more thunks. I should go too and return to the jyze
later -- because there's still more news to spill.

[+1]

Improvising here.  It's good for you!  A day later
and a jyzetime short.  I just scrubbed the toilets --
and don't worry, Z-goose, I washed my hands afterwards.

Trouble is, Vic's line's been busy for the past
hour and a half.  That likely would be Ro talking with
an inamorata.  I need to be getting a message to Vic
about a slight modification of our plans for tomorrow --
no movie's appealing to Z and me, so unless he wants to
hit the opening at the art museum, I'll just drop by and
pick up him and Jean and we'll come straight here.
(Which is why I'm scrubbing toilets -- I drew the joker
in our usual last-minute division of labor.)

Again I'm missing out on the HQ-triangle totem
pole.  One hundred and three years ago today a
contingent of city fathers stole it from a Tlingit
village in Alaska -- in much the same way the U.S.
plutocrats are about to go in and steal Iraq's oil.
Preach, preach!  I thought I'd be down there right now
consulting the totem oracles for advice.  But the
weather did, as promised, turn cold and cloudy
overnight, so maybe it's best I sit here in the black
armchair and consult long-distance, as it were.  (How
long?  Roughly 1.8 miles, same as the distance to V&J's
loft, which is a few doors to the west on the far side
of the triangle.  In the end I might go down there
anyway to deliver a note.  But I worry Vic wouldn't get
it.  Or I could buzz, but if someone answered I'd have
to go up and they -- he and/or she -- might feel imposed
upon.  Better just to wait and keep trying to call.)

It's six on the nose.  Z-wiff won't be home until
later; she's doing dinner downtown with Leola tonight.
June left a message; she'll be able to get back to her
burban home by herself on Sunday.  Just going by the
degree of animation in her tone, she's feeling better
but still not all that good.

Today's news: I don't want to let my hopes rise too

high, but it appears the U.S. is blinking at the UN in
the face of worldwide uproar.  We'll agree, in effect,
not to attack until after inspectors go back into Iraq
in search of "weapons of mass destruction" (the kind
we've decreed they can't have but we of course can and
do, by the tens of thousands).  After the Iraqis have
jerked those inspectors around for a while, we'll return
to the Security Council and ask if it's okay yet for us
to obliterate Iraq, and they'll say sure it's okay --
that's their part of the compromise.  Or so it appears.

Why's this good?  At least the principle of seeking
approval from the UN for your unprovoked attacks is
preserved.  "Go right ahead and sic 'em, Big Dawg!"
We're more than ten times Iraq's size in population,
incomparably more powerful economically and militarily,
so I'm wondering: will the UN insist on our granting the
Iraqis a handicap?  Will we be asked to give them a few
hundred strokes?  Will the UN make the U.S. play the
course blindfolded using only a putter?

No one's saying this yet, but I'm thinking it's the
North Korean mea culpa nukem that's caused this U.S.
blink.  Suddenly potential world "trouble spots" are
proliferating like mad.  Maybe the cabal is rethinking
the advisability of fighting as many wars at once as the
"Axis of Evil" and its outrigger nations and sympathizer
terrorist bands (or call 'em freedom fighters 1980s
style) want to give us.  Bring 'em on -- not!

Yayhoo!  Now another try at putting in a call.

*

Success!  We're all set for tomorrow.  And no
museum opening; Vic already saw the show up in Canada.
And it wasn't Ro doing all that talking on the phone.
Rather it was Vic's first son, Mark, who's a small-town
cop in the northern part of the megastate and close to
three decades older than Ro.  He popped into J. City
unannounced while racking up miles for his motorcycle
club.  To stay in the club you must log so many miles
per month, hit so many states.  He crashed in the loft,
called home, took off again, headed for the next two
states to the east to add them to his list real quick,

sort of like a fast-food stop -- before returning home.

So at half past five tomorrow afternoon we'll pick up where we left off on Monday.  That was a beautiful friendship-affirming talk up in the darkening loft as the sun, visible through the three large western windows, set behind the mountains across the water.  Vic flatters me a bit by talking about me as an artist like himself -- saying things like "we're not as well known as we should be" -- and of course I lap it up.  As he also said, we both recognized immediately that we had a great deal in common and saw the world in similar offbeat fashion.  (Am I taking note of this in jyze every time I see him?  Probably.  It seems so miraculous I can't stop raving about it.)

-- Speaking of No. 1 sons, I did talk with my own for more than an hour the other night.  It went well -- the best call so far.  And better yet, he agreed we should do it regularly -- once a week, Tuesday nights, one-thirty a.m.  He insisted it's a good time for him even though he gets up at eight to go to work.  About six hours' sleep is just right for him, he thinks.  (And he's expecting to be a centenarian someday -- starting say in about seventy years and four months.  But it's true, as I told him, that a recent "scientific experiment" -- ha! -- determined that people who sleep less tend to live longer.  I won't believe it, though, until a whole lot more confirming evidence is in.)
-- He even said he'd like to talk more often than once a week.  I'm the one who's putting a limit on it.

Most interesting, I learned his seven-year love relationship was with a Chiusan daughter of a pastor and mortuary owner living in a small midland U.S. city.  Lan-Lan T. -- what a lovely name!  A college romance -- he realizes now he'll probably never have another like it and "she was really a good one" (just the phrase his mother often used in this kind of situation).  Why'd it end?  "I messed up.  I really messed up bad."  The split came two and a half years ago when he was at the peak of his DJ-star popularity and yielded to a groupie-like hit on him.  He says now not a day goes by that he doesn't

regret losing Lan-Lan.  Ironically, they both studied
for the LSATs together back in '95 and then she went on
to law school ("not a top-tier one") more or less in his
stead while he set off on his internet/DJ trip.
Afterwards she failed the bar exam -- shades of June --
and she hasn't taken it again and now she's running her
own fashion-design company and has a new boyfriend.
(She's five-six, by the way.  That's far short of his
current ideal, which he still insists is serious.  "It's
not shallow like it sounds," he avers.  Oh, but it is,
it is.  But at least height is easily quantifiable, he
said, unlike, for instance, beauty.  But if hard data is
what he's seeking, he could get it on reflexes too, I
pointed out, not to mention vertical leap or I.Q. or
bank accounts, and he said he would chew on that.)
     And I brought up the shelteredness I sense in him
vis-a-vis political matters.  He acknowledges he's
pretty much ignorant in that realm.  He doesn't even
read a newspaper.  After I'd delivered a long (but
gentle) harangue on the need to be conversant on the
great issues of the day he lamely asked if I thought he
should renew his expired subscription to the further-
right of the two major U.S. newsweeklies.  Yikes!
     But it's a start, this talk.  We're on our way.
(And I should note this: he still hasn't volunteered a
single comment about the letters I've written him or the
books and articles and photos I've sent down.  I have to
squeeze things out of him and I haven't even begun
trying on those.)
     Almost seven now.  Tonight I'll have to be a
scoping maniac.
     -- But last night's shocker, I almost forgot.  At
nine-thirty or so -- the usual time -- I hit midtown
chain burgers to pick up the usual twice-a-week bag of
two double-stacks with lettuce and tomato only, hold the
cheese.  I found a notice on the door saying the place
was closed down permanently.  All of a sudden!  Out of
the blue!  I'd been there two nights earlier and saw not
a single sign such a calamity was in store.
     I've been doing the double-stack thing there for a

decade or more.  Occasionally I would hit the only other
fast-food franchise open late evenings in the area,
three blocks north near the plaza, but that closed last
year, and probably for the same reason: it was becoming
a magnet for "urban riffraff."  People on the streets
had nowhere else to go.  And now there's nothing.  The
scores of swing-shift janitors who bought dinner there
will be out of luck for hot meals.  I'll have to start
making sandwiches again, or subsist on power bars and
veggie juice and bananas or apples or whatever I can
find at the grossly inadequate and expensive mom-and-pop
stores down on the middle and low roads.
    -- And the Green Rat grins Greenly and says,
"You're outta here and it's about time!"


------

44

------


    Blue Ox.  Hunter's Moon.  Good coffee.  Good jazz.
So jyze oughta be raring to go.  But the J-slinger's out
of sorts today.
    And thirty-seven minutes just won't do.  But that's
all I've left myself.  Then onward to the WOC.  I've got
an appointment with the Z-spouse.
    ORB cafe here.  In a couple of hours the "December
6" author will be arriving to read from his spyboiler.
All ears will be focused on it -- what should be
subtitled "The Last Day Before the Coming of Jyzeslinger
G."  Or wait, I think I've used that line before.
    It's cool and gray outside, incipiently drizzly --
if you clap your hands you can squeeze a drop or two
from the air, it's so humidly thick -- but nonetheless
the jyze could've gone down out there.  Should've.  But
I vacillated.  I considered half a dozen potential

venues -- no, more -- in the AQ and elsewhere along my usual inbound path. None felt right. I wound up here, upstairs. A "quick check" of the magazine stands for new arrivals led to extensive browsing. I couldn't resist.

Why so? Prosaic reason: because the address for Z's office has been summarily changed to a building where she won't be working until next year (the infamous Towering Penis building, the city's second-tallest, just four blocks straight up the hill from the HQ triangle). And for some unknown reason the magazines we subscribe to at her office address are not being delivered at either building. We didn't learn about this until last Friday but apparently it's been going on for some time now -- it's hard to say just how long. Maybe a month.

The ORB has some of the back issues. I can't afford to buy them. Next time I come they might be gone. So -- urgent extensive browsing.

Meanwhile it's become a certainty: the U.S. has blinked. Blinked and backed off. Suddenly cabal spokespeople are allowing as how it might not even be necessary to achieve "regime change" in Iraq so long as the alleged weaponsofmassdestruction (it's become one word, as a pundit on the left points out in one of those urgently browsed back issues) -- as long as the alleged WMDs, as I'll call them, sticking with my more concise previous practice, are eliminated. In other words: war's no longer a certainty. The cabal may be seeing it can't get away with naked aggression without putting itself in a world of angry backlash.

Of course the same loonies are still in charge in Washington. Their policy of world domination, officially announced in the outrageous NSS document released last month, is still in place as far as I know. But -- a ray of hope in the gloom.

To write about later there's Vic-and-Jean night, and also the new Horse necklace I'm wearing (a froufrou cube strung on it saying "We are the hero of our own story," which to me seems a plausible and even admirable but yet grammatically troubled statement).

And the full moon arrived on time.  Hunter's Moon is what it generally goes by in this solar land.  It's bright in the early evening and extends the hunter's hunting time, except when all the animals have already been hunted and/or climate-roasted to extinction.

Blue Ox, that's the cluster.  It's a Babe to be sure, as in Paul Bunyan's bulky ungulate helpmate.  Of all the sixty horoscopic animals this one might be the likeliest to have a bar named after it.  Or is that true only in Mentoka and parts nearby?  (City Park in Mentoka Falls boasts a huge statue of Bunyan with Babe.)  -- And the White Horse and the Black Horse would be close runner-ups in bar-name likelihood.  White Horse Inn, that's where Mom and Dad did the first night of their honeymoon, I do believe, and also maybe their first overnight together in the year between meeting and marriage.  Their FF spot!  (But I have to check on that. It's noted in Mom's diary -- discreetly, but she told me what the entry really means.)

And onward to the WOC.

*          *

Some eleven hours later.  No longer out of sorts -- just tired.  But mellow!  With one eye I'm keeping watch for Orionids, but it's strictly for show.  Halley's Comet could roar by two blocks away and no one would be able to see it under these heavily overcast and misty conditions.

Middle of the last watch.  And here's something a bit interesting.  For seventeen years October 22 was a special day for me, the anniversary of Lady U's and my meet day, and we always celebrated it as our prime anniversary.  Now she's gone from my life but the special day still packs a slight frisson, as does her birthday ("Born on the 5th of July!").

So three and a half hours into October 22 -- half an hour ago -- I came across a newspaper article saying Lane A. is returning to town as the artistic director for the town's number-two theater company.  It's the same Lane A. who directed "Indigenes" and was the first in the company to try to hit on Lady U.  She sought

450

advice from the jyzer on how to handle the tricky
situation.  The advice worked too, but perhaps only
because it was Marco R. she'd had her eye on from the
start.  Just could be she used Lane A. as a kind of red
herring with me.  Or Marco R. used Lane A. as a kind of
stalking horse, right.  Or maybe Lane A. gallantly stood
aside for Marco R., who was after all an old college
buddy he'd persuaded to come out from FCM #1 to play the
lead in the show.  Later that year Lane A. married the
well-known actress Mika P., whom Lady U and I met in the
same "Indigenes" period, but Lady U decided against
attending the wedding, in part because Marco R. would be
there.  It was a defining moment in the resuscitation,
such as it was, of our own (zen) marriage.

I do have a past.  It's popping up like crazy these
days.  Or so it seems to me.  This might be because
overall I've cut more ties to my past than most people
have.  I've never gone to high-school or college
reunions or any other kind of reunion, I've rarely kept
in touch with old friends and lovers and workmates.  For
years I wasn't even in the phone book.  I'm still not on
the internet and never will be as long as it's legal not
to be.  So when I get two out-of-the-blue hits from the
past in a mere six weeks it seems big.  Of course one of
these, true, is just a passive media hit.

-- Better to drop all that now and say a little
about the dinner with Vic and Jean.

Have the Z-wiff and I ever been more nervous about
hosting dinner guests?  Not that I can recall.  But we
did it our usual way, with me tending to the cleanup and
Z arranging the dinner, most of which came from a deli.
Free-range rotisserie chicken, our favorite, from the
north-hill market.  Roasted veggies, Italian bread,
tossed salad, blackberry pie with vanilla ice cream.  We
even had some candles going.  Drank three bottles of
wine.  V&J provided a bouquet of pink sweetheart roses
and a sackful of mixed fruit from A-mart where Jean
works (but neither of those gifts came from an A-mart
used bin, she assured us even before we could ask).

Next to their magnificent loft our place is

strictly run-of-the-hill.  Jean kindly proclaimed it
"charming."  After dinner we sat in the cluster here
(I'm back riding the black armchair right now) and
chatted until past ten-thirty -- quite late for Z, but
refreshingly early for V&J.  "Now I can go home and read
in bed!" marveled Jean, who quickly moved down from the
high futon couch to the floor during the talk session,
while Vic stayed up there on the couch with his feet
amusingly dangling.  Jean's a yakker for sure: I'd never
realized before how much so.  "Oh gee, do I have to tell
the story of how we met -- again?"  But tell it she
vivaciously did, for about half an hour virtually
uninterrupted, with masterly pauses at all the laugh and
gasp lines -- the works.

Do we get along as couples?  Maybe not as well as
I'd like.  Z seems to find Jean a little too culture-
vulturey and a lot too talky and says straight out that
Vic isn't her kind of guy -- too reserved, stodgy-
seeming, I guess.  She thinks he ought to do something
about his hair, which I happen to know is his pride.
She thinks it's too straight-looking, too passe', "too
'Kookie, Kookie, lend me your comb.'"  I enjoy them both
-- V&J -- and like Vic a great deal and think his hair's
fine, especially in terms of quantity; I wish I had half
as much.  Z's maybe not patient enough to appreciate
some of Vic's finer qualities.

How do they see us?  A strange couple, no question,
but artsy, maybe too overtly political, certainly not
widely recognized or celebrated as many of their friends
are and Vic himself is.  I've made myself useful to him
and therefore I get to have a chunk of him.  He's
mentorly for me and yet we also hit it off and enjoy
each other's stories -- not least because they're often
revealing in an inspiring way (even mine!), providing a
new angle on similar events in one's own life.  But for
us to keep clicking over the long haul I'll probably
need to show him some work that's as good in my field as
his is in his, meaning his painting.  And I don't know
if I'll ever be able to do that.  (It's not that I don't
think my work's good enough.  It's just I don't know

when it'll be ready for showing, to him or anyone.  And
he's almost seventy-three.  He's thirteen years ahead of
me just as I'm thirteen years ahead of Lady U.)  (And
that also puts me seven years ahead of Jean.)
     -- Okay, I've pushed this all the way to the limit.
If I don't get ready for bed quick, the Z-wiff will be
rising on her own and she won't be pleased and I'll have
to stop anyway.


                          [+2]


     It's another anniversary of the beginning of the
world.  Happily, it's also an anniversary of the end of
the world, so we can push ahead here under a kind of
balance.  -- But for how long?  (Which is a rub with a
whole lot of friction in it, no question.)
     And the blue skies are back.  But an autumnal
chill's persuaded me to take the jyze indoors again.
I'm even willing to settle for a chain coffee shop.
I've wound up at a round wooden table the size of a
manhole cover and not a single sign of wear is anywhere
in sight -- on the manhole cover, on the barista, in the
shop, out the window.  Wabi-sabi this site is not.
     But have I got news!  Not to reveal just yet,
though.  Some stage-setting and throat-clearing first,
just so I don't have to feel too much like the earnest
cub reporter leading with the hot stuff.
     The unworn view out beyond the glass is the AQ
depot complex -- trees, stones, dolmen, lots of brick
and glass.  Plutocrat #2 toys.  (Just be happy he's our
plutocrat, punk.  -- Screw you, reactionary voice
bubbling up from my swampy brain backwater.)  Far left,
A-mart; far right, stadia and port cranes.
     The fall colors during my walk down were looking as
good as they get around here.  Over the past six weeks
the greenbelt below the high bridge has slowly modulated
to something closer to an orange-and-rust belt.  With
perfect timing as I came adjacent to the bright yellow
bigleaf maple near the north end of the bridge a very

large leaf fluttered down in front of me like a starfish
settling slowly to the bottom of an unusually limpid
lagoon.  Could I avoid stepping on it at the last
moment?  It wasn't easy.  "Dance, mere human," barked
the starfish as if waving a six-gun, and I did.

Last night staggering out of Vic and Jean's place I
ran into such a splendid Hunter's Moon, hanging like a
blank white eyeball next to the midsection of the great
white tower.  Halloween's coming!  I rarely see the moon
from that angle in that part of town.  -- And upstairs
Ro and Jean banged on bongos in a demo for the J-slinger
as the World Series played silently on the tube -- from
MSM #2!  Recalling for me (and no doubt for millions of
others) the nationally televised World Series earthquake
of thirteen years ago when ol' Mom was living down there
-- the urgent phone calls.  Jean presented me with a
pair of cords Ro no longer likes, just my waist size but
(as I learned today when I tried them on at home)
baggier in style and quite a bit shorter in the legs
than I can comfortably let myself be seen in.  Vic had
just come in from his new door-watch job at the
convention center.  Their rent went up, Jean told me
(just like Z, she's refreshingly forthright about such
things), and she said to Vic, "You'd better get a job,
buster."  If he feels it's a comedown, he doesn't show
it.  I'll say this: knowing about it makes me feel I'm
one of the family.  Hey, I do that too -- you gotta love
a jyzer with a day job.  Sling paint, sling jyze, same
diff (pretty much).

On my Celestial calendar the fifteen-day period
starting today is marked as "Frost Descends" and the
lunar animal is dubbed "Ox in the Sea."  Today's also
the little-noted day the swallows traditionally depart
from Capistrano (JRX) -- an occasion much less
celebrated than their springtime arrival there and for
that matter probably soon to go extinct, if it hasn't
already, owing to climatageddon.  And it's even the day
on which the sun sign of Libra gives way to my father's
sign, Scorpio (and the autumn chill is forcing the
spiders to move indoors in lemminglike waves all over

town).  And as of today exactly 101 days remain in the
lunar year and thus also in Jyzer G's Heavenly Year.
Spotty days most may well be if the standard odds hold.
     For "lesser" news, France and Russia continue to
throw dirt in the cabal's eyes at the UN.  Accordingly
the media note discreetly that our "war exercises"
scheduled for Oman in November will be delayed until
December.  (Again I say we have North Korea's nuke fess-
up to thank for the cabal's blinking.  Suddenly at least
some of the neocon fanatics seem to be noticing that
their idiot foreign policy is already blowing up in
their faces.  -- But that doesn't mean they'll scrap it.
Most likely they just want a little time to rejigger the
marketing effort.)  -- And the far USAn coast remains
under siege by a sniper who's so far offed a dozen
people in the D.C. area.  In the halls of power at least
a few cabal supporters must be taking notice of this too
-- what a single determined person can do with an
ordinary rifle in the nation's capital and nearby.  WMDs
are not necessary.  Are we really sure, the caballeros
might be asking each other, we want to be making even
more enemies all around the world?  How about making all
the world an enemy?  Might this not cut into the
monetary tribute we're due as the mightiest of them all?
     -- All right, enough tantalizing on the big news.
Here it is:
     Elgie's coming up for Christmas!
     It was an extraordinary ninety-minute phone call
between 1:30 and 3:00 a.m.  He had a bad case of the
hiccups through much of it.  I learned all sorts of
intriguing details about his life, including the fact
that his money problems are just as bad as I sensed from
the beginning a couple of years ago -- no, worse.  Much
worse.  It was a confessional moment -- "I've really
messed up, Dad.  I'm really sorry."  -- As if he'd let
me down!  But his mother he truly did let down.  As he
said, he had just two things "on my desk" still to take
care of: his offical bankruptcy and -- his mother's!
Caused by him!
     Christmas isn't solid yet.  He's the one who

proposed our getting together.  He was ready to head
this way sooner -- ready to drop everything and hop on
the next plane, or so it seemed.  I said it would have
to be December or January, contingent on Z-wiff's
approval, and we agreed it would be good to aim for the
holidays (since work will likely be slow for all three
of us then).  In bed this morning I dropped the bomb on
Z.  "Oh my god -- he'll be staying in my room?"  But she
reacted well -- and should've, because she's been urging
me to invite him up here ever since our first contact
with him, to repeat, two years ago.  "I can't wait to
tell Aida at lunch today!"

Then I passed along the news about his financial
situation.  Warning bells started clanging.  -- But
she's a born worrier.  "Tsuri."  I've told him I can't
help him financially -- and he's not asking me to.  His
mother can survive on Social Security (thanks to me!)
and sporadic help from her family in Korea.  He'll be
applying for loans for law school and selling his fancy
wheels and working hard to earn a second-year
fellowship.  He's sobered up after a wild '90s ride.

Today Z's thinking about dates to propose for his
visit.  In a few days I'll be calling him back.

Another reason not to feel too sorry for him: in
order to pursue the law-school idea he quit a job in
sales for a Korean conglomerate -- still unnamed -- in
which he was making ten K a month.  He decided
bankruptcy was preferable, not just for himself but for
his mother as well.

He was riding high into early 2000.  His internet
company was netting $14,000 a month and he was investing
much of that in dot-com stock.  Then the company reached
a size that would no longer allow it to fly under the
radar of the large national corporations -- "the big
boys."  They pulled the rug out from under him by
"bribing the music industry," as he put it, to change
the rules regarding CD usage.  (His biggest competitor
was the same outfit that provides closed-circuit TV and
music to the health-club chain that runs the WOC and
many other such chains nationwide, including the one in

MSM #1 where he works out.)  Suddenly his income dropped to a thousand a month, and that happened just as the bottom fell out of the stock market.  To cover margin calls he maxed out his credit cards, whose limits had recently been increased to an incredible $180,000 on the basis of his business success.  When this failed to cover his losses, his mother used up her savings and maxed out her own cards.  It wasn't enough and they both went bankrupt.  Then she had her stroke.

Not long after the bankruptcies hit the poor kid took up Christianity.  What attracted him about it?  "It just seemed so logical," he said with supreme innocence.  The Ten Commandments appeared to fit right in with his existing values.  And some flashy right-wing TV preacher won him over.  Yeek!  -- But at least it all sounds as superficial as a lot of other things about his '90s life.  It can't be too deeply rooted yet.  Can it?

Another reason he needed an anchor during this time was the romantic crisis he went through.  That also fell into the category of "I really messed up."  It turns out he went back and forth between Lan-Lan (she of the seven years) and Faith (the unsubtly named pastor's daughter -- I had this confused before) -- flip-flopped between them a total of eight times!  His mother must've thought the genes responsible for this shameful behavior came straight from me.  Over our dozen years did she and I attempt seven reconciliations?  Not quite.  Four or five maybe.  And the same with me and Lady V.  And several of those were bouncing between Ladies S and V.  But not eight!  -- Still, I can relate.

(Holy moly, time's zipped by.  Sun's angling in at the far end of the shop and illuminating my toes.  Gotta race for the WOC.  -- But I'll be back later with another tranche of startling news.)

*          *

Capping it at 3:20 a.m.  True enough, there is more startling news, even beyond what I was referring to at the coffee shop.  The latest is that two arrests have been made in the D.C.-area sniper case and they're a father-and-son team from -- two satellite towns of Jyze

City!  Those two towns -- small cities themselves,
really -- are about a hundred miles apart and I sit
right on the line between them, a little closer to the
one to the south, home of the father.  Afrusans both,
and the father uses an adopted Islamic name.  Look out!
     No wonder grand jury was cut short today.  All the
agents who were supposed to testify were probably
ordered to drop everything and pursue this case.
     Will links show up to earlier alleged J-town terror
incidents?  To anger over local police shootings of
Afrusans?  As yet few facts are being released.  Public-
radio news speculates the two snipers might be part of a
larger operation.  (Z's reading the far-coast paper's
story on the case in the bedroom right now.  I figure
it's at least six hours behind the radio news.)
     Meanwhile Chechnyan Islamic militants are holding
six hundred Russians hostage in a Moscow theater -- also
right now.  This moment!  As I jyze!
     Earlier, though, as seen through streaming hilltop
fog, the big bloated Hunter's Moon was pulsating
gorgeously -- all glowingly ablink.  The note Z left on
my chair before going to bed says so too.
     Oh the crises.  And what was exactly forty years
ago today?  A presidential speech to the nation
announcing the blockade of Cuba because Russian missiles
had been spotted there.  -- Or no, we're already into
the 24th.  That's Black Thursday on the FCM #1 stock
exchange, seventy-three years ago today (Vic's birth
year).  If it ain't one damn crisis it's another!  And
right now what we're going through are just minor
episodes compared with what's ahead as eco/climate
disruption proliferates and becomes the ultimate
multiplier/intensifier for all other conflicts.
     So by those yardsticks I suppose the news about
Elgie's bankruptcy isn't such a big deal.  So then how
about this: he says he not only wants to marry a woman
who's six-three or more so his kids will have a shot at
the NBA or WNBA, but he wants to have ten kids!  This
guy's living in cloud-cuckoo land, no question about it.
Even his own friends have pointed out he'll have to

marry an Hispanic woman if he wants that many kids
(since Hispanics, at least in stereotype, are
religiously opposed to birth control; and not even in
heavily Hispanic MSM #1 is there an abundance of such
women who also happen to be six-three or taller).  Elgie
himself acknowledges (when pressed) that these notions
of his are "just dreams" -- but what curious and
revealing dreams they are!

I learned this too: Lady S's elder brother, Hyu, is
still around and still heading up the family and living
in a highrise condo now in the very "Mud Village" where
his sister and I set up housekeeping when Elgie was just
about to turn one year old.  It's become a forest of
highrises out there, the kid tells me.  I guess Hyu has
dropped the feng-shui objections he raised to the site
back then.  He retired a few years ago from his longtime
job as dean and professor of English lit, but he still
accepts missions on behalf of the government.  The
latest was to travel around the U.S. presenting
auxiliary South Korean medals to USAn Purple Heart
winners from the Korean War.  I saw an article about
this in the OMP (or FAP?) a few weeks ago -- a local guy
who received one of the medals was featured.  Hyu might
even have been in the picture.  He might have been
staying at a downtown J. City hotel as I labored away
within shouting distance at the scope office.

Their mother is still alive too -- Halmoni, as I
knew her, Grandmother -- but she's in a nursing home
now.  Elgie wasn't sure of her age but I'm figuring she
must be ninety-three or so.

I also asked Elgie a number of questions in both
blockbuster areas: politics and religion.  About
politics he said, "I don't really know anything about
it.  I don't have any politics.  What you said is true,
Pops, I need to start learning about the world."  About
religion he seemed so nonplussed I quickly dropped it.

Still and all, it wasn't just a flabbergastion,
this talk, it was also deeply moving.  I felt for the
poor guy as he bumbled out his bankruptcy explanations
between hiccups.  I thought maybe I really could help

him out -- be an anchor for him.  A father figure who
just happens to be his probable (highly) blood father!
He sounds lost and desperate behind his easygoing and
imperturbable and willfully positive veneer.  I nearly
wanted to weep when he told me in such earnest Pops's-
approval-pleading tones that he's ordered a copy of the
dictionary on USAnese usage I recommended to him -- told
me this for the fourth or fifth time!

He did say his mother isn't really a Christian --
"She's more into nature and things like that."  Which is
a relief to know -- sounds like she's the same old
quasi-Taoist.  On the other hand he said she "hasn't
been very sociable lately."  Apparently she's not too
happy about his driving her into bankruptcy and whatever
role that may've played in causing her stroke.

Despite all the nonsense he spouts he's got a lot
of charm.  He says nonchalantly that he's "always been
pretty popular" and makes sure I realize the problem for
him isn't finding a woman, it's finding "the" woman.  It
seems a couple of female employees at the law firm are
already fighting over him.  No big deal, though; he
assured me he can handle it.  Same as the bankruptcies,
law school, whatever.

This evening at the WOC Z and I settled on some
dates for his visit.  New Year's week is our first
choice, Christmas week second, M.L. King week in mid-
January third.  Visit length of ten days is the absolute
max given our limited space in unit 203 and our out-of-
sync schedules and various other commitments -- not
least to (A) Mama E and (B) jyze.  I'll be presenting
these options to him on the phone as soon as I can.  And
I'm imagining things we might be doing together, the kid
and I.  What I'd like to show him of the city and my own
past as currently archived in the hideaway -- the whole
dang six-decade Heavenly Year of it.

Turned out to be quite an Ox cluster, yes it did.
Have I mentioned lately that the kid's an Ox himself?
And a Water Ox, what's more, just as I'm a Water Horse.
It's elementary!  -- But owing to our different yin/yang
influences my animal is Black and his is Gray.

------

45

------


Something like eighty-two is the age the actuaries
predict for my death.  Of course they're not talking
about me personally, or at least not necessarily; rather
it's the average age of death for my age-sixty USAn
cohort forecast on the basis of mortality tables.  And
cluster No. 45 in the Heavenly Year annal -- this
cluster right here -- is roughly the equivalent,
relative to the sixty-one clusters of the full annal, of
age sixty in my predicted life of eighty-two years.  In
other words, as of now I've progressed as far in the
jyzing of this annal as I have in the living of my
entire predicted life span.  In both cases I'm a little
short of three quarters done.
     -- But never mind.  The new point of interest is
that, as of this very minute, jyze is going down in an
hour which doesn't exist.  That's one way to put it.  Or
it's the twenty-fifth hour of the Gregorian day.  Or
it's the only hour in Earth's full orbit around the sun
that repeats itself under USAn calendrical rules; and
therefore, following the maxim that history repeats
itself as farce, farce is what this entry's sure to be.
     In yet more other words, at two a.m., three minutes
ago now, time "fell back."  Daylight is no longer to be
saved; we're on standard time again, which is, for me,
at this hour of the night, Nightscoper Upside-down Time,
also known as NUT time.  What a moment ago was three
minutes in the past is now fifty-six minutes in the
future, and as the first number increases the second
will count down to zero, which will then become two
o'clock again.

[ Jyze of the Heavenly Year : Yellow Horse ]


    Z-wiff sleeps, meanwhile, wasted from today's peace
march.  I'm ensconced beneath the unzipped blue sleeping
bag in -- the black armchair!  A couple of hours ago I
spoke briefly with first-and-only-known-surviving-
offspring (or highly probable offspring) Elgie and told
him I'll be paying for his flight up here (and then the
one back to MSM #1 -- the whole bloomin' round trip).
And when will this visit take place?  "The sooner the
better," was his expressed view last week.  But as of
tonight he'd neglected to check with his employer about
when he'll become eligible for vacation days.  Being a
new employee he'll almost certainly, I'd say, fare more
poorly on being granted time off than he's currently
thinking he will.  I said, "I have to warn you, Zoelie
and I don't live exactly a mainstream life."  "All the
better!" he cried, sounding quite sincere.  He was at a
friend's birthday party, calling on his cell, voices
murmuring and glasses clinking in the background -- thus
the call's brevity.
    Here's the point (as the clock ticks off its
nontime -- so uselessly, so wastefully!): this Heavenly
Year project now has what looks to me like, barring some
dreadful unexpected turn, the ideal shapeliness for its
concluding quarter.  The long-lost father meets up with
the long-lost son.  The torch gets passed after all.
Nature cycles on.  The arc of one life rainbows down
toward its pot of golden ashes as the other arcs up
toward a glory yet unknown.  The hoary themes of East
goes West and West goes East achieve what could be
called an ultimate expression -- of sorts.
    And so on.  And: ya gotta love it!  Especially as
it takes on real life and flesh and no doubt all kinds
of exasperating true-to-life detail.  Or on the other
hand I could quit right now -- keel over, victim of
maybe a heart attack or, like Lady S or Vic's friend
Bruce O., a stroke -- yet still knowing the shape is
there for the uncompleted saga.  I can step off the
stage happy!  -- Kerplunk, vanishing forever into the
brassy deep of a new metaphor: the orchestra pit.
    That's why I'm glad this is the cluster of the

White Tiger.  That powerful beast.  And what month is
it?  Month of the Dog!  For that matter, today's the
three-hundredth day of the Gregorian solar year.  All of
this makes cluster No. 45 -- keyed to Gregorian solar
year 1986 and Chinese lunar year 4684 and zodiacally
dubbed "Tiger in the Forest" -- makes it, I say, a very
good turning point as the annal heads into (in lunar
terms) its final quarter.  Last 440-yard lap of the
outdoor mile!  Not to mention that in crusader churches
everywhere today is Reformation Sunday, marking the
schism that proved that, for those who still doubted
even after orthodoxy once again split into two vastly
different new orthodoxies, the Pure Path at least up to
that point hadn't been so pure after all, since all
those worshippers who turned out to be unorthodox from
its perspective had previously been on it.

   -- Did the roughly ten thousand marching against
the war today in Jyze City make a difference?  In morale
for folks like me, again, yes.  But the corporate media
don't bother to tell us the number of marchers in other
U.S. cities, just as they didn't for London a month ago
when, as it turns out, up to 400,000 hit the pavement.
"No Blood for Oil" and "Regime Change Begins at Home"
-- the two most common signs of the day here along with
"Not in Our Name" and "No Iraq War."  If only all four
could score!  (Awful thought: if our crusader cabal did
call off the attack, the chieftain would be declared a
hero of peace!  Yet the plan for world domination would
remain in place -- might even be realized more quickly
and smoothly.  -- But I'd still go for calling off the
war.  Fight your battles one at a time.)

   Here's the question.  A think-piece in a glossy
far-coast monthly magazine (it's edited by an execrable
neocon fellow traveler who calls himself a liberal, so
-- beware!) predicts a U.S./Europe schism not unlike
that of Christianity itself half a millennium back, with
today's newly united Europe emerging as the stronger
state -- the true dominator.  Is this likely?  I think
not.  I think it's neocon rabble-rousing.  I see the
Cawks eventually uniting against the world.  Ugly

racialism.  It'll be the ultimate us-versus-them,
because otherwise "them" will be too dangerous from
sheer power of numbers (not to mention depth of utterly
justified outrage).  It's the logic of capitalism as
well: big money unites for self-protection when the
chips are down.  The result, catastrophic beyond
imagination, with not much, if any, habitable planet
left. Who to read this jyze then?  Ha!

  That's my rational fear.  But it's hope, however
foolish, that keeps me marching.  (And it's obsession --
and love too, of course -- that keep me jyzing.)

  -- On the coffee table here, two photos of Elgie he
sent up to us, along with one tossed in "for fun" of a
blond TV star upon whom he declares he has a "big
crush."  "You know any like her up there you can fix me
up with?"  In both photos he appears with some Korusan
buddies and among them he's the long-faced, big-nosed
one, literally, as opposed to round- or pentagonal-
faced, small-nosed or bridgeless-nosed.  Good-looking
guy I'd naturally say as another long-faced big-nose.
His only discernible flaw is a slightly protruding
canine tooth (and without being asked he's let me know
he's wearing braces right now to bring that arrant tooth
into line).  His hairline's fairly high but not
noticeably receding.  Z says he has a "tender-around-
the-eyes, deer-caught-in-the-headlights look" which can
also sometimes be seen, she asserts, on me, "though not
quite as extreme."  In my view she pushes this one too
far in both of our cases, his and mine.  And I'm pleased
to see he looks none the worse for wear after his
struggles of the past few years and appears quite
comfortable and happy with his friends.  And yet -- he's
told me he wants to move beyond them.  And in one of the
photos he's wearing a sheer black see-through net T-
shirt -- and the urge to wear a shirt like that, Z
jokes, he must've inherited from her (she was an early
adopter on see-through dresses back in the sixties).

  The stepmom.  She says some of her old friends will
howl when they hear.  She "designed" her life, she likes
to say, so as to avoid the snares of motherhood and

heavy family responsibilities.  Of course I tried to do
much the same from the paternal angle.  I might've gone
for raising a family if I'd been an early financial
success as a writer, but the writing always came first
and I always knew the odds of success in that realm were
stacked against me, early or late or any time between.
Z and I have lived similarly in this respect and our
willingness to accept as much on both sides is, I
believe, a big part of our compatibility as a couple.
     -- So I've decided I'll be cashing in the deep-
reserves account.  I'll use part of it to pay for
Elgie's visit from start to finish.  Mother would be
very pleased to know the money she left me, or at least
part of it, was serving such a purpose.  -- But it'll
only be a small part.  The balance I'll put into
certificates of deposit timed to mature yearly, to help
me keep the wolf from the door over the next decade or
so.  And soon I'll have to decide if that yearly income
on top of Social Security (elected early) would be
enough for me to survive on.  That is: should I retire
from nightscoping year after next?
     Retire!  Gadzooks!  And so much still to do!
     -- As the twenty-fifth hour comes to an end.  It's
now two o'clock again.  In fact 2:07.  Almost got
trapped in the hole in time -- lucky to be able to climb
back out while still clutching this J-book.
                    *           *
     -- More than twenty-four hours later, but it's
still the same day for jyze purposes.  The standard
jyzeday can be up to twenty-nine hours long, as I
calculate it, from mid third lunar watch or 12:01 a.m.
of the Gregorian day to end of the fifth watch or five
a.m. of the following Gregorian day.  Under special
circumstances a jyzeday might go even longer, from start
of the first watch of the lunar day until end of the
fifth watch of the following lunar day, or exactly
thirty-four hours.
     Well yippee!  And I note in any case we're out at
the nonspecial extreme for today.
     And what kind of jyzeday has it been?  One that

keeps me asking, and also keeps the Z-woman asking, am I
losing it in the same way Mama E is?  We hurried out to
make it to Tala's birthday party on time and I left the
stove turned on, my second cup of coffee still warming.
Worse yet, I absentmindedly tossed a cardboard cup in
the regular trash instead of the recycle bin.

Reminding me: Z has gallantly passed the recycling
baton to her protege David M. as of this week.  She
wanted to attend a big recycling conference in D.C. but
invited him to go in her stead.  This doesn't mean she's
about to fade graciously into the sunset, though, she
assured one and all, perhaps herself included in some
sense.  She's weighing which of several ripening issues
she wants to take up as her next pet cause at the
utility, with environmental justice still in the lead.

(And she's on the H-rag again.  In case I haven't
explained that term lately, it means she's suffering a
herpes outbreak.  Worse, almost, her herbalist has given
her something called "Black Salve" to apply to her
vagina every day for two weeks in the hope it'll prevent
further polyp growths.  If it works, great -- but is
there any reason to think it will?  None that I know of.
But I still support the idea of consulting an herbalist
if you happen to be a person who believes in the healing
power of herbs.  I believe in it in some cases, but not
enough to accord an herbalist my blind faith.  Which
isn't to say I have any greater faith in mainstream
medicine, except as a treater of last resort.)

What kind of day has it been?  (I got sidetracked
there.)  A ship nearly keeled over down at the docks.
The World Series ended, and MSM #2 wasn't the winner.
USAn mainstream media (but not media elsewhere) gave
short shrift to the worldwide mass protests against the
cabal's war plans.  Russia ended the theater siege in
Moscow by piping poison gas into the theater, killing
more than a hundred hostages -- many of them members of
Russia's own ruling class.  Our U.S. chieftain leveled
another threat, and certainly not for the first time: if
the UN doesn't decide this week as he demands, the Truly
Evil Empire (that's us, folks) will attack Iraq on its

own.  Even the conservative FAP sees this for what it is.  Its front-page headline echoes a famous one from a quarter century ago: "CABAL TO WORLD: U.S. WON'T WAIT IF U.N. DOESN'T TAKE LEAD."  (Actually this headline uses the cabal chieftain's name instead of "CABAL," but I refuse to accord him the honor of a JRX mention.)

For Tala's birthday we just put in a cameo.  I was happy because I got to eat bulgogi beef and because Serafina, the bantam fighter -- still without a job -- gave me a big hug and a slightly lingering kiss on the neck, adding to my growing suspicion that she might like me all right after all.  Z-wiff showed around Elgie's photos and everyone oohed and ahed.  Sera's mother (and of course Aida's as well), Mrs. D, said it best: "You have a very handsome son -- he doesn't look anything like you!"  Even Mr. D, skinnier from his cancer treatments but still quite animated, got a big hoot out of that one.  The only disappointment of the visit was that we never even glimpsed the birthday girl (she's ten now) or her sister or her cousins, except for my favorite of the flock, Maricel.  The others were all playing hide-and-seek upstairs and couldn't be bothered with adult flapdoodle.

Perhaps I should also mention that today, the 28th of the Gregorian month, is the birthday of the cofounder of our local software behemoth.  This is J-town plutocrat #1, the world's richest person in the latest rankings.  (Local plutocrat #2, the world's third-

richest, is the other cofounder.)  It's quite possible
#1's house is visible from our balcony.  If our unit 203
were up a story higher, it almost certainly would be.  I
hadn't realized it before today, but this man was born
the same year as Lady U.  And then they were
kindergartners together, first graders together, second
graders together and right on up the golden ladder.
Peers.  For some reason I find this hard to fathom.
     But I can't pursue it any further.  Time's up.
-- Don't want to pursue it either.  Money equals power:
it's not news.  The news itself is not news.  And what
also isn't news but is what we should be paying
attention to is -- the same old boring yet horrifically
deepening planetary eco/climate crisis.  That's it.  The
Heavenly word -- over and out.


[+1]


     Slip about five pages of the alt-weekly, folded
once, under the table leg to steady the jyzing surface.
Pour the spillover coffee pooled in the saucer back into
the cup.  Crack open the J-book to affix the new sixty-
cent stamp next to the two thirty-four-centers showing
the "Happy New Year" Water Horse and the rainbow-bright
"Happy Birthday."  The sixty-center has a prominent
white "60" up in the corner above an image of the Grand
Canyon -- abyss for the Heavenly Year geezer to gaze at.
     And let fly!  It's open-mike night at the ORB cafe.
Looks like a rapper who goes by P-Dawg is doing the
emceeing.  But that's in the other basement room, closed
off from the cafe proper by shuttered internal windows.
I'm sitting at my usual table in the partially hidden
back corner.
     And it's Devil's Night.  Not too many people seem
to be aware of this.  It's the night of mischief-making
that precedes trick-and-treat night, which itself is the
first day of Hallowtide, which then continues for the
next two days -- the Days of Death.  These also are no
longer a big deal if you're USAn -- probably they never

were -- which only makes sense since we're so
notoriously death-denying and death-defying.
    Applause!  Laughter!  Reader number one is a hit!
-- But now the bus person tells me the cafe's closing
early tonight, at eight o'clock, and that's just fifteen
minutes from now.
    This afternoon an exhausting three hours with Mama
E.  The cabulance rolled up to the east-hill clinic
entrance at the very instant I did.  As we waited she
scratched at a lotto card with a quarter just to have
something to do -- but she was lively and looked good
with her new short haircut.  As our seventy-minute, it
turned out, delay in the outer waiting room wore on
she had two bathroom emergencies, and on both occasions
we made it to the head in time, old Mama E hobble-
whizzing along behind her walker as I ran interference.
We also studied together the collection of tropical fish
in the huge waiting-room tank -- especially a big
spotted yellow one shaped like a railroad gondola car --
and such quizzical eyes it had!  Then another long wait
in a patient room before Doc B, the ENT specialist,
finally appeared.  He spent all of two minutes with her,
pronounced her ear infection "improved," said to come
back again in a week.  It's either a benign tumor or a
form of skin cancer; excision under local sedation will
be necessary when the inflammation "minimizes."  By a
miracle the new prescription was ready within thirty-
five minutes, just as the cabulance pulled up again.
    Open eyes.  Death coming.  (Mama E's biggest
problem these days is with her eyes: "They just want to
keep closing all the time."  Second is the interminable
buzzing of tinnitus, but yesterday she was able to read
an article about it and was comforted to know millions
of others suffer from it.  After learning this, the
buzzing sounded less loud and more musical -- she told
me so herself.  On the phone she asked Z for Tito's
number.  Thus it was a very good day.  Or as Z explained
it: "We B. women, having our hair cut starts those
hormones perkin'.")
    And then I rambled straight west down east hill

just as in the old days after visiting Mama E at her
motel.
     -- Looks like I won't be getting the boot from back
here after all.  They've probably forgotten about me.
As long as the reading goes on they have to keep the
area open even if the cafe's closed; there's no other
way out for the attendees.  Go P-Dawg!
     -- But no.  I can't stick around.  Things to do,
places to go, Devil's Night mischief to wreak.  Later,
though, if at all possible, I'll slip back into the jyze
seat.  I don't want to be done yet!
                    *            *
     But I am done -- all done in.  Not a thing I can do
about it.  So just a facesaving squib and I'll crash.
It's 5:27 a.m. and Devil's Night has worked its mischief
on me.  Tomorrow, though, I'll be starting right back in
with the next cluster and what I hoped to fit in here
tonight ought to fit in a whole lot more easily there.
     And the White Tiger fades into the foresty fog.
First just stripes remain and then those too fade to a
Cheshire gray.




                    ------


                      46


                    ------



     So my biggest year of them all enters its fourth
quarter as I loll in the same old black armchair.  Any
problem with this lolling? None.  It's allowed!  As a
Heavenly way of being it's even encouraged!
     As of four hours and eight minutes ago we're into,
by Gregorian count, the middle day of Hallowtide.  It's
a Day of the Dead, first of the matched set, and also
the first day of the old Celtic year.  So this right now
is yet another New Year's Eve -- in both senses.  How


                      470

long's it been since the last one?  And this one won't
be over until dawn -- by my lights anyway, not to
mention its own.  And in the meantime yet another new
beginning.

I did no begging at all on Beggars' Night and
didn't witness any either.  But lots of folks were
stylin' and costumin'.  They were out there on the
streets, on the buses, in the shops -- ghouls and
zombies in the lead and Frankenstein monsters not far
behind.  Z called at two to report that her "Persona
Challenged" outfit -- a mix of different costumes from
past years, as in multiple personalities -- had failed
to win anything at the office party except an "everyone
gets one" prize.  Over at Vic's place Jean modeled the
Madame Butterfly outfit she'd fluttered around in all
day at work, assuring me that the huge pair of blue
butterfly wings sprouting from her back were well worth
the thirteen bucks she'd paid for them.  Vic showed off
an electrified pumpkin a friend had sent over.  I wore
the same lame button as last year over my usual jeans
and khaki workshirt.  It says: "This IS my costume."

No candy, no cookies, no goodies at all.  Other
than the fructose kind, no sugar on Halloween.  Z and I
both figure we ought to be shaping ourselves up to meet
the kid.  He's her son too, and she's quite adamant
about this contractual and official fact.  (I do marvel
occasionally that her stance on the Elgie matter puts a
night-and-day spin on the one Lady U used to take.  Then
I remind myself the circumstances are night-and-day
different too.)

Meanwhile: North Korea is playing tough.  And I say
good for them.  They're obviously correct that the U.S.
is threatening them and they have a right to protect
themselves.  Presumably the rest of the world -- and
especially the countries we've said we have in our
military sights -- is catching their drift as well.  But
if so, no one's letting it be widely known.  The latest
word is France and Russia will fall into line next week
on our Iraq attack -- after the off-year U.S. elections.
The chances of having a hot war to liven up the last

month or two of the Heavenly Year still look excellent.

Again no response from sister Barb to my birthday letter sent almost exactly two months ago.  The hope of reconciliation's fading fast now.  I did what I could -- tried -- went as far as I could go.

Nor is it a sure thing Elgie's coming.  He still hasn't called back with the dates.  I interpret this to mean he's facing resistance on taking vacation days so early into his stint at the law firm.

Which means hot war is looking better and better as the way to go.  Live fireworks, roasting human flesh. Sweet.  A fine time for the J-slinger to bow out.

Once this Heavenly Year is history will I ever jyze again?  Can't rule it out entirely.  But before starting up an encore volume I want to be sure all my other stuff's in shape.  Or at least figure out what this other stuff is.  By "stuff" I mean writings -- the oeuvre.  What to keep for, or as, and what to cull from, the oeuvre.

Z's little hand-painted pumpkin-like squash grins up at me.  So does the recent photo of Elgie she artfully cropped and framed and stationed on the coffee table right next to the cast-iron Black Horse statue.

Nine or ten days still to go on her black-salve yoni treatments.  She left the insertion device on the ledge by the bathroom sink to gross me out -- it's a big fat hypodermic-like injector and it's usually soaking in a two-quart pitcher of water with greasy black remnants floating on the surface.  Yipe!  -- But funny too.  It inspires cackle duels.

I read the first chapter of "The Modern Mind," the prodigious tome I sent Elgie (a new copy) to help him beef up his worldview.  By my lights it's way too gaga over science.  But for that very reason he might go for it.  If it would start him thinking about the larger issues, then maybe later on I could come up with something better to nudge him toward a more informed view on some of those same issues.  It's worth a try. Isn't this a major part of what fathers are for?  And then I suppose I'll have to engage in the more or less

obligatory overcompensation in areas where my own father
fell short.  Open expression of emotions, for instance.
Does Elgie need this?  Maybe not.  But then why does he
seem to be making such a fetish of logic?  Could he be
rebelling against his highly emotional mother -- as I
did against mine?  (But probably I rebelled even more
against my highly rational father.)

I'm wearing my slippers again -- first time since
midspring.  Moccasins actually, moosehide with a half-
dollar-size hole worn in the middle of both soles.  If
the bare floor in the kitchen is too cold I stand
bowlegged on the outer edges of my feet -- the outsteps,
as they might be called, and maybe even officially are
called.  Also I'm wearing heavy long-sleeve henleys
again.  Vic had a glowing radiant heater going in the
loft (which with its high ceilings is far too large for
space heating).  Mid twenties tonight.  But no snow's in
sight.  No moisture of any kind -- the serious rains are
coming late this year or perhaps won't show up at all.
The three dry months of August through October have been
the driest ever in the era of local European/Eurusan
occupation and annexation.  Z's unit at the utility is
again gearing up for public drought education.

What kind of cluster is it?  It's the Purple Rabbit
type, also known (especially in Vietnam) as the Fire
Cat.  The Chinese slogan is "Rabbit Looking at the
Moon."  But the moon's slimmed down to a nice neat
fingernail trimming or maybe by now it's vanished
entirely, until, I'd guess, shortly after election day.
Then it will rise on a landscape which I don't think
will be utterly transfigured in political terms, no.
But then again an outside chance remains that the more
right-wing of our country's two major right-wing parties
(and there are no other major parties) will gain control
of both houses of Congress, in which case the U.S. death
spiral will tighten and quicken.

The "antiwar impulse" is said to be gaining
strength -- even the far-coast-megalopolis paper
acknowledges this.  But that impulse will be flattened
once the cabal issues the official "Let's roll" on Iraq.

[ Jyze of the Heavenly Year : Yellow Horse ]


Yet since it's the only hope in sight -- in-country, I
mean -- I might as well keep pulling for the impulse.
So that's it -- that's the plan for now.  Go impulse!


                        [+1]


     -- And happy Celtic New Year, you old jyze
reprobate.  -- Muttering to myself again.  Down at the
hideaway, sunk deep into my other main armchair.
Blatantly ignoring my own jyze rules.  But what the
heck, I ain't no saint.  So today wants nothing to do
with me, because it's All Saints' Day.  Or All Hallows.
Referring to "Saints" as "Hallows" reminds me for some
reason of referring to the judges of the highest court
in the land (those pompous frauds) as "Supremes."
     Mr. X's Black Horse is snorting at that one.
     Live jazz blares down below -- bad jazz, I gotta
say -- and clashes with the rockstalgia of the joint one
door to the north.  It's Friday night.  I've blown most
of the early evening grazing in the meadows of my own
retro-prose, a/k/a protojyze and urjyze.  It feels good.
I'm like a second-childhood fossil poring over an
ancient scrapbook.  Once in a while I can even remember
something about the events described in these pages that
isn't there already in the written words.
     Just for kicks I'll be stretching out this cluster
to the limit.  The Hallowtide stretch -- a fun time for
self-subversion.
     Last night when I hopped out of the black armchair
after finishing up with the jyze I was startled to see
the last skinny-nail-clip moon of the Dog Month hanging
right there outside the window above the couch.  It had
snuck into view while I had my head buried in a book --
this very book it's buried in again now -- not at all a
first for me.  I almost yelped with pleasure.  Oooeee, I
do love those lunar surprises!
     Tonight the Russian janitor, Ivanka, and her
daughter Svetla are painting the restrooms on our floor.
For bladder relief I have to hike three stories up.

[ Jyze of the Heavenly Year : Yellow Horse ]

    With midtown chain burgers closed forever I have a
new dinner routine.  At the start of the week on the way
in I buy a bunch of bananas and a bag of tomatoes at one
of the produce warehouses in the AQ and a loaf of whole-
wheat bread at one of the HQ mom-and-pop markets and
stash the stuff here in the hideaway.  For dinner three
slices of bread, a banana, a tomato, and thou, choco
power bar, lying beside me in the Jyzer Ink wilderness.
Tonight, though, I'll be hauling the whole feast up to
the scope office since I'm running so late.
    Standing in the corner behind my left shoulder is a
new poster.  It's a clever ad for the annual jazz
festival which is currently tuning up around town.  It's
in the form of a political yard sign, and it reads:
"Vote Yes for Jazz" and in smaller print gives details
on the festival.  Yard signs are everywhere these days
with the election just four days away.  This one I found
poking out of a planter containing a big potted tree in
the upper AQ.  My way of voting yes for jazz was to
pluck the sign out of the planter, wooden stake and all,
and march all the way down here holding it aloft,
drawing lots of stares and even a few honks and raised
fists.  My plan is to convert the word "Jazz" to "Jyze"
and mount the whole sign, stake included, on the large
bookcase across from where I sit.  But not anytime soon.
Most likely it'll become a post-Heavenly Year project.
    And that had better be it.  Time to don once again
the scruffy outer garments of my nightscoper costume.


                        [+1]


    The expanded J-week staggers on.  It's not as hoped
for or as planned.  A bug is trying to take me down --
first one in a couple of years.  I'm battling it with
vitamin C and bourbon.  Can just barely swallow.  The
next twelve hours will tell the tale.
    No doubt about it: this entry will be utterly
incoherent but also mercifully brief.
    The plan for tonight was to take this show on the

road to David and Stacy's Day of the Dead party.  I even
brought home a stack of photos of all the important dead
people in my life, meaning the ones whose deaths came
during my lifetime.  Mom and Dad, all four grandparents,
all uncles and aunts, Peter M., Karen A. -- the only
exception being my childhood friend Kevin, cut down at
age ten by leukemia.  The photos were to go on David and
Stacy's mantel or one of several nearby tables with all
the other attendees' Day of the Dead photos.  Then I was
planning to hunker down in an armchair for a bout with
the J-book as the others partied around me.  I'd even
consented to dousing my bad hair with glitter in
deference to the spirit of masquerade.

Yesterday belonged to the saints, the pure, the
immaculate, the sanctified.  Today's for all the souls.
No, not all the other souls.  I'm sorry, but if you're a
saint you can't possibly have a soul, at least as I
understand the word.

-- And it's last-legs time.  J-stick-getting-stuck
time.  Coughing, throat-clearing time (but the throat
doesn't clear).


[+2]


On a beach chair beneath a palm tree -- a phony
palm tree as it happens.  I'm trying to steam away the
last vestiges of the malady.  I'm still not convinced it
wants to leave me.  But the tale the next twelve hours
told was a good one.  Yesterday almost all symptoms were
gone.  Today, better yet.

It's early Election Day eve.  This is the WOC, the
jacuzzi in the converted vault in the basement of the
former bank.  It's also the first day of the new lunar
Month of the Pig.  And it's Diwali light-festival time
in India -- somewhere in this town lots of people are
celebrating that (as the Polish Film Festival also
proceeds -- but this year Z and I are skipping it
because her struggle with her mother over the past many
months has provided her, Z, as she told me, with just

about all the Polishness she can bear.  When she arrived
home tonight she snuck up on me as I bent over our
mailbox in the garage and gave me a big hug from behind
and then informed me she'd just broken into tears while
telling her counselor Margo how "wonderfully supportive"
her husband has been during the Mama E ordeal.  Then she
broke into tears again right there in the garage and I
just about did the same.  Squeeze squeeze squeeze!).

(A guy just plunged feet first into the whirlpool
and sent a flight of water drops winging this way.  Some
hit my legs but it seems they missed the J-book.  Waves
bounced around in the pool, though, reminding me of Lake
J-town after yesterday's big Alaska earthquake: huge
waves sloshing around in the basin, tales of thousands
of dollars of damage done to many of the houseboats
moored there, including the one belonging to our friend
Madge I., whose insurance is already maxed out, she's
told us, owing to the extensive smoke damage sustained
by her east-hill condo in a fire last spring.  The
quake's epicenter was more than 850 miles to the
north (and fortunately in a largely uninhabited region).
For me, hearing about all this sparked one of those
knee-jerk all-things-are-connected moments -- which is
far from physics-type quantum entanglement, or so I'm
informed, except sort of metaphorically.)

-- Also of interest: the magazine in J-town's
combined Sunday paper (OMP/FAP) ran a big spread on the
AQ teahouse hotel, and the third-floor corner bedroom
where Z and I partied on my Heavenly Year solar-birthday
night was pictured, along with some other hotel and
teahouse features, right there on the magazine cover.
And Z-wiff learned from a utility maintenance guy that
the orange hammer made of hard rubberized plastic I
found on a table at the sidewalk cafe across from her
building last spring -- and it's been christened "Thor's
Hammer" by Z and displayed on our coffee table ever
since, right next to the cast-iron Black Horse (which is
still wearing a double set of leis from Paz and Tobey's
commitment ceremony along with a necklace of the
miniature birthday cards Z left on my chair, one for

each night during the month of August) -- that strange
tool, she told me, is officially known as a "dead-bolt
hammer."  She asked the guy because he was carrying one.
They're used to minimize damage to the surrounding
surface when you whack a "dead" bolt to loosen it.
     And this: the court's finally issued its decision
on the antitrust case against our local software
behemoth.  Lots of folks around here are doing a jig
because the biggest tech company in the world escaped
with a slap on its carpal-tunneled wrist.  For big biz
these are happy times even as the country's being
corrupted to the core.
     So that's the wet part of today's entry.  Now I
take the plunge again myself and try to drown the bug
for good.


                         [+2]


     -- And the doo-doo just keeps deepening.  In an
appalling upset right-wingers now control both houses of
Congress as well as the White House.  The gloom-and-
storm season is here.  My sore throat and cough that I
thought I might've vanquished have relapsed.  The UN
Security Council appears ready to cave to U.S. demands
regarding Iraq.  Our country is now assassinating
alleged terrorist leaders in foreign countries using
missiles fired by drone airplanes.
     But then on the other hand this is the first day of
Ramadan, a time to celebrate especially this year (by
this time next year, who knows, maybe our missile-firing
drones will have "taken out" all of Islam and started
going after non-church-attending Christians).  And I'm
not really feeling so bad physically.  And this is one
of my favorite nights of the year: Midautumn Night.  And
it's also my father's lunar birthday -- he would've been
eighty-five.  As it happens, the Russian revolution
began eighty-five years ago on the same night, the
upheaval known as the "October Revolution" (but that was
before the Soviet Union converted to Gregorian time,

meaning the anniversary now falls in November) -- so my father was born on the very first day of a new historical era in much the same way I was conceived on a similar kind of day.

I'm black-chair-sprawled. A few scattered storm-blown raindrops are pelting our south "great room" windows. As so often for these topping-off entries this one is starting out halfway through the fifth watch. Z-wiff is still asleep on the futon in her bedroom (to avoid my germs), "naked-hubby-body-deprived," as her note laments. I too lament! We need to get back to geezer horseplay (or Horse-and-Snake play). And soon will if positive thinking has anything to do with it, as Elgie of course would insist it must and so I will too.

My dream about Elgie last night must've been a Midautumn Night's dream arriving a few hours early. He did some bad things -- including "playfully" twirling an infant over his head, unaware he was endangering its life -- and I royally chewed him out for that. I suppose symbolically it was my own foolish guilty conscience lambasting my other and better self for having "endangered" Elgie's own life by not being there to raise him in my own image.

According to my Celestial calendar, tomorrow "Winter Begins." The timing couldn't be better. We're heading into a kind of reverse nuclear winter that may well wind up devastating the planet, including its vastly overlarge, and yet still wildly proliferating, human population. After last night's elections the Eco/ Climate Catastrophe Clock should be advanced another couple of minutes toward midnight. It was fifteen minutes before the hour; now we'll make it thirteen. But is there still hope we (or those who follow us) can turn the clock back? Of course there is! And if I start losing that last bit of hope, "Positive Quotations" is ready at hand for quick reference.

Earlier tonight on the way in I stopped off briefly to see Vic. Jean happened to be there and was in rare form, spinning out tales of her teen-years "Splendor in the Grass"-like romance with the son of the president of

a big MSM-#2-based national bank -- getting laid on the
floor of his family's mansion (and nearly laying me flat
with the casual way she used that "getting laid" term)
-- and her dread that she's going to run into the guy
again every time she returns home to tend to her aged
parents (who have just celebrated, or are about to,
their seventieth wedding anniversary).  She also
presented me with a paper sack filled with an extremely
fragrant type of lime leaf -- called caffir, I think she
said -- and commanded me to "bruise the leaves lightly"
and then sprinkle them into a hot bath "before you and
your wonderful bride jump in for what I guarantee will
be a very sexy soak."  Vic just sits back and smiles
fondly as Jean performs her lively and charming act.
Much like me, I suppose, when Z gets rolling on hers,
which is often in a bawdy spirit much like Jean's.
    Most of today's grand jury went to testimony by
east-hill druggies against a bad cop who specialized in
shaking them down for hard drugs which he then sold to
support his daily weed habit.  It was some of the most
addled and tangled Q and A -- but hilarious as well as
pathetic -- I've scoped in twenty years of grappling
with this stuff, a spectator twice removed (sitting late
at night in an empty office where I can laugh out loud
and talk back to the screen as if I were right there in
the fully occupied grand-jury room, and often do).
    Time's just about up.  Doggone!  -- By which I also
mean the Dog Month's just about gone, except for this
last little bit of overlap as the Pig grunts in and
forces the Purple Cat/Rabbit to slink/hobble off the
stage.  Still no word from Elgie, by the way -- whassup
with that young man?  Maybe I should just sit back and
wait -- see how long he can string this out.  Meanwhile
the prime rate took another half-point hit today,
meaning if I do withdraw my money from the deep
reserves, it'll earn that much less interest in CDs.
It's really just to squeeze out a few bucks to pay for
Elgie's visit that I'm thinking of doing this.
    Ha -- there goes Z-wiff's alarm.  Dee-deep, dee-
deep.  I gotta split.  Head on in.  Perfect timing.

------

47

------


    The Yellow Dragon curls around the upper third of
the light pole across the street from A-mart.  It's
either chasing something that got away or it's twirling
just for fun or maybe it's impaled on the pole and ready
for roasting.  I could be sitting in the lower section
of the A-mart food court right now taking in its antic
act.
    But if I were doing that I wouldn't be doing what I
really, really need to be doing.  Which is this: soaking
up steam in the whirlpool room at the WOC.  Again.  All
alone in the basement inner sanctum on a Friday evening.
And stretched out on the tiles beneath the potted palm
over by the big round vault door, as if the windstorms
of the past few days had reached down here, several
detached five-foot-long palm leaves.  A deciduous palm
tree!  Made of plastic!
    I'm not well.  I'm not terribly sick either, except
for the coughing in bed at night -- or strictly
speaking, during my usual daytime sleep hours.  Not even
widely advertised over-the-counter cold remedies can
stop it.  And during waking/working hours I sort of drag
through my appointed rounds.  Only when I'm sitting here
in the steam heat do I feel at least a little bit good.
    But I did stop by at A-mart on the way down and
paid my obeisances to the Earth Dragon mentioned above.
I was too late to say hello to Jean or Evan W., who has
several fine poem-paintings appearing in the new number
of a Japanese journal I've been a fan of since shortly
after my stay over there (it's in English).  That was my
other purpose in visiting A-mart: to pick up a couple of

extra copies of the journal for Olwen and Vic.

Earlier during my inbound trek down I had to plow through sidewalks clogged with tree limbs and many, many leaves blown down by the wind.  The gusts hit at just the right time to strip the golden bigleaf maples bare. (Reminding me, a few days ago massive flocks of starlings descended on the phone and electrical wires strung above the high bridge roadway.  It was an amazing sight, with thousands of birds perched on the wires -- there are eight or nine of them, in an upper and lower stave -- looking like the score for a fantastically complex symphony.  And the way the birds were constantly flitting about, seemingly never satisfied with their own pecking or perching order, brought the score to life: it became, in an unusual sense of the term, live music. When the spacing between birds shrank to about two inches, the whole line started scooting down one by one like dominoes falling.  Several times I saw a crow come lumbering up, big as a helicopter, it seemed, and the dominoes started tumbling in both directions as the starlings gave the crow plenty of landing space -- about eighteen inches on both sides, it looked like.  Bumped birds flew off in a squawking snit and squeezed into a space on another line, causing new flurries of shifting. Classic musical chairs but for the birds.  -- And then that same night I came across a marvelous description of the "murmurations" of huge airborne flocks of starlings written by a nineteenth-century English poet -- this in a collection of short diary entries, arranged by the month and day when they were written, which I've been reading more or less daily for the Heavenly Year, doing my best to stay in sync (that is, reading on November 8, for example, all the entries collected for various years under November 8 -- today).)

News?  As widely predicted, the UN Security Council has buckled to U.S. demands: it's unanimously passed a resolution calling for Iraq inspections to resume and warning that if Iraq refuses, "serious consequences" will follow.  Russia and France did manage to persuade the U.S. to withdraw an automatic war-triggering clause

and to stretch out the process a bit.  If Iraq balks,
the council will take up the issue again -- but any
aggrieved nation can attack them, Iraq, another clause
says, if it doesn't want to wait, and this clause was
not removed.  And we all know well our cabal guys are
aggrieved and won't want to wait.  But they might wait
anyway if the council looks easily bribable.  (And a lot
of oil will soon be available for doling out to willing
coconspirators at fire-sale prices.)

What does this mean -- will there or won't there be
a Heavenly Year war?  If all the various timing matters
are stretched out to the max, the first USAn attacks
might not occur until early February -- right after the
Water Horse gallops off the stage, chased away by the
rampant Water Ram.  But if Iraq balks early, either by
refusing to let the UN inspectors in or by denying them
access to certain allegedly suspicious sites, we could
still see some major fireworks in time for Christmas.
For a Holy War such as this one the timing would be
entirely appropriate.  If we're really quick about it we
could start bombing mosques before the end of Ramadan
holy month (that would be early December) and then
launch a massive invasion as our Christmas present for
Muslims everywhere.

The cabal, of course, is saying it doesn't really
want a war, all it asks is that the Iraqis roll over and
let themselves be stripped of their ability to defend
themselves and control their natural resources and then
everything will be fine.

-- So that's today's U.S. Empire Progress Report.
Meanwhile, twisting the dial back to local news of the
personal kind, I can pass along the word that Betty's
concerned Kat is becoming too sexual.  At a recent party
Kat went off to a bedroom with two boys and had to be
hauled back outta there by Faye, Celine's mom.  Also,
Z's worrying about Betty's views on abortion, which
suddenly appear to be surprisingly negative (we'll try
to feel her out some more on this).  Z told me her own
story about almost going in for an abortion -- the
closest she ever came, back in college; and she was

ready to do it -- but the alarm turned out to be false.
    -- Time's running out.  I do want to mention this
will be the last cluster to go down in J-town's official
Sesquicentennial Year, which comes to an end next
Tuesday with the 151st anniversary of the arrival
of the main body of the Cawk invasion party in what's
now the western part of the city.  But my own version
continues, because I say J-town didn't really begin
until the pioneers moved across the bay to what's now
the HQ.  Not until much later did the city grow to
include the original landing area on the west side.  If
the arrival of the invasion party there counts as
official J-town pioneering, so too should the even
earlier arrival of the first Cawk south-hill settler,
along with several others in areas which would later
fall within city boundaries.  (And by the way, it just
happens that today is also the 197th anniversary of the
arrival in 1805 of the first Eurusan land party to cross
the western half of the continent to our region.  So
it took only 46 years from the first land exploration
until total takeover and town-building time.  -- Call
that the prime genocide period, with a secondary mop-up
period following, between 1851 and 1889, the year of our
statehood here -- and the anniversary for that is
Monday.  Clearly our imperial forces of that era saw
the stormy month of November as an excellent time of
year to make things official.)


[+1]


    -- Here's one from the love nest.  A nightcap --
and it's nightcap number two.  Two highball glasses'
worth.  Good whiskey's supposed to drive away bad bugs.
Or is that an old alkie's tale?
    Hearts dangling on strings, some two dozen of them
of varying sizes and at varying heights, red ones and
blue ones and fuchsia ones, all gently astir from the
draft caused by my breathing.  Purple sheets on the bed,
books and towels stacked to the ceiling, the Jyze Gang

celluloid cowboy on guard in life-size cardboard-cutout
form -- mementos and knickknacks galore.

On Saturday nights I usually sit here while Z-wiff
sleeps, the radio tuned down low to, depending on the
hour, blues or jazz -- sit here in my old green
armchair, bought used during my first week in town back
in '79.  You been a good old armchair, you hear,
armchair?  And what's more you're no more broke down
than you ever were.

Z turned the phone off when we arrived home at nine
and I've left it off.  I'd feel like a fool sitting
around all night waiting for it to ring for a second
Saturday in a row.  If the lad's going to blow off our
carefully laid-out and agreed-upon plan, I'll let him
compose me a voicemail about his preferred next step.

We went out and saw a movie tonight but took it
very easy.  Wandered around for a while afterwards on
the east-hill main drag, hitting several bookstores and
card shops, then doing a late burger dinner at the usual
drive-in up there -- happened to grab a premier parking
place good for observing up-close the long quadruple
lines in all their boggling and comical and inspiring
and heartbreaking and never-ending typical east-hill
nightlife melangerie -- then found it hard to leave even
though many cars were waiting for parking spaces.

The movie was "Bowling for Columbine," a partisan,
manipulative, and basically accurate evisceration of the
USAn culture of violence.  It's sad to see productions
like this work so hard to demonstrate what the
government now blatantly declares: we're out to dominate
the world.  Yesterday it was radical heresy, today it's
a yawner -- and in both cases it's the flat-out truth.

Of course matters are more complex than the movie
makes them out to be.  Idealism of the USAn "freedom and
democracy" type will serve as a better cover for our
hegemonic designs -- cabalian cynicism will eventually
be overturned when the current out-party gets its act
together, say maybe about 2006 or 2008.  But the
corporate-powered expansionist thrust will still be the
same and thus so will its military push and the eco/

climate calamity that will all but inevitably follow.

What can be done?  Not much.  But regardless, just for starters: expose, expose, expose.

Short-term, here's the latest word on the Iraq crisis.  The Iraqis have seven days to accept or reject the UN resolution calling for renewed inspections.  If they accept, inspections will begin no later than December 23rd.  They must be completed within sixty days, and the inspectors will report any violations or discrepancies to the Security Council.  If the council doesn't consequently call for immediate armed enforcement of the resolution, the U.S., according to our supreme leader, will act on its own.  "Zero tolerance" is the watchterm.

Funny thing -- none of the media analyses I've seen even suggests the U.S. might plant evidence -- say a vial or two of anthrax in the basement of an Iraqi aspirin factory.  Yet story after story lays out possible ways the Iraqis could "cheat."  And it's widely known -- though little remarked -- that the U.S. planted CIA operatives on the earlier inspection teams.

Accch, but so what.  Isn't the outcome preordained and doesn't everyone know it?  Has the U.S. already spent billions readying its invasion force just for the fun of it?

Okay.  So enough on that for now.  Next step in the unfolding major public drama of the Heavenly Year is Iraq's response to the Security Council's resolution.  They have one J-week plus a day and not one minute more to come up with it.

Meanwhile today offers a couple of interesting anniversaries.  First, Krystallnacht in Germany -- another explosion of racism and violence.  And fifty-one years after that -- to the day! -- the Berlin Wall came down and the Cold War reached its symbolic end, opening the way for the U.S.-fashioned "New World Order" and the final stage of our self-immolating (though obviously as a society we're far from realizing this) hegemonic push.

-- In another era the reigning regime might've sent someone like me off into exile.  While awaiting regime

change back home I'd be doing literati scribblings --
about ephemerality and nature's cycles and whatnot.  And
I wonder: in some peculiar way is that happening to me
now as well?  Is that what jyze is really all about?


[+2]


     So now, delayed one sixer plus two days owing to
jyzer illness, it's obeisance to the Yellow Dragon.  Got
me a window seat, lower level of the A-mart food court,
hard by the bubbly fountain with its fortune in good-
luck coins sparkling in distorted underwater ovals like
a thousand laughing eyes.  Ya-ha!  And out there the
Dragon itself curls fiercely around its pole against a
backdrop of the central portion of the downtown skyline,
with the east-depot complex standing to one side and the
former blue-tile-roofed home of A-mart to the other.
And the skyline is impressively vertical, up to seventy-
five or eighty floors atop various levels of a steep
hillside, with everything still all lit up because it's
only six p.m. and the air's post-rain sparkly clear --
as now a big green truck arrives and parks just outside,
pulling a commercial curtain on the whole scene.
     I know it's six because a woman at the next table
asked me the time.  No question about it, she was
flirting with grimy ol' me.  I dug deep into my bag and
came up with three minutes to six.  "Ohmigod, my bus is
at six!  I thought it was so much earlier!"  Zip, gone,
end of rare but spirit-boosting flirtation.  (Before
that she asked about this jyzebook and mentioned she was
planning to buy a copy of the recently released journal
of the currently most famous of Jyze City's dead white
males, the grunge-era rock icon of "Smells Like Teen
Spirit" renown.  Oddly enough, Z-wiff brought home her
shopping items from the south-end discount mart today in
a cardboard box stamped "Journal of [icon name] -- Do
Not Release Until [such and such a date, which I've
forgotten].")
     When I left the house the Z-woman was still there

because it's a holiday and she devoted most of the day
to preparing her room for Elgie's visit.  But will this
visit really happen?  I promised her I'd dispatch a note
by snail mail asking what the heck's going on.  "Tell
him we gotta know the dates," she urged me, "so I can
space the cleanup stages as far apart as possible."

Today's not your usual monolithic holiday.  It's a
multipurpose one -- and yet I still must drag myself
down to the scope office to churn out some lightly
corrected finals that will take me all of forty minutes
tops.  On the other hand I'll have plenty of time to
indulge in another thorough steaming at the WOC.

First and least important, today is a holiday I
never even knew existed.  Yet to the colonial rulers of
certain of my foreparents it was certainly notable.
It's Martinmas!  To those unruly Swedes (yet not so
unruly during the several centuries they ruled Norway)
this was the day when autumn's work ended and winter's
work began.  It was also, symbolically, the hinge
between late middle age and early old age.  It all goes
back to St. Martin of Tours who lived about the time of
the Five Dynasty period in the Celestial Kingdom.  If
the weather turned unusually warm during late autumn for
another set of colonial rulers of my foreparents but in
this case the ones on my mother's side, the English, it
was called a St. Martin's summer -- that was before they
honored the victims of their North American invasion by
calling such a warm spell here an Indian summer.  (And
JRX the saint's name.)

It's also Armistice Day.  "At the 11th hour on the
11th day of the 11th month the War to End All Wars
itself came to an end."  True enough, for USAns anyway.
With the one exception of World War II -- which was
really just Act II of World War I, so shouldn't count
separately -- we've never again officially declared war
since then.  All our dozens of extensive acts of war in
this period (Korea, Vietnam, Cambodia, Laos, Grenada,
etc.) were mere police actions, so-called, slapping down
restive parts of the empire.  In no case did the number
of "enemy" casualties exceed the five million required,

apparently, for a real war to be declared.  Our current
police action in Afghanistan, labeled part of the War on
Terror, is, after its first full year, nowhere close to
the five-million minimum.  Since, however, it might
reach that level well before its predicted end in fifty
years -- speaking now of the overall War on Terror --
nomenclature change may become necessary.

Armistice Day in this country long ago morphed into
Veterans Day.  This is the day we honor the million-plus
USAn warriors who've given their lives so that we might
survive and what's more in surviving accord the
warriors' lives their meaning ex post facto.  And how
many of those warriors, I wonder, understood that they
were making the ultimate sacrifice so that the United
States might one day rule the world?

And today is Admission Day for our state.  Just
forty-three days after my Gramps was born, this far
corner of the homeland moved up from provisional
territorial applicant to a full-fledged member of the
empire's core group of states.  What had been a mono-
coastal nation a century earlier at the time of the
revolution now spanned -- a continent!

But far more important locally, today is a holiday
because it's the birthday of another local rock icon
who's a male and dead but not white (that is, not
completely white, which in legal and racist terms in our
empire is of course, as everyone groks, the only kind of
white there is) and not mainstream USAn at all except in
retrospect, although he performed the most famous
version of all of the national anthem: and jyze figures
it doesn't even need to state his name via JRX since
everyone already knows it.  Born not 43 days after
Gramps but 73 days after -- me!  The J-slinger!  It's
the rock icon's Heavenly Year too!

-- This window picture with the Yellow Dragon at
its center, I've neglected to mention it has a
reflected overlay.  It's a life-size white origami
crane, handsomely underlit, that flies directly above
the lucky-coin fountain.  White crane -- longevity
symbol, Celestial symbol.  That's the whole Celestial

cycle hanging up there, and now that I look again I see
this is what the Yellow Dragon's trying to get at from
its perch at the top of the pole.  The succulent white
crane hovers tantalizingly just beyond the Dragon's
reach.  And the green truck, I should note, has left.
     Symbolism run amok.  Meanings all too stark.


------

48

------


     "WORLD WAITS ON IRAQ REPLY."
     Headlines screaming!  No one breathing!
     -- But that was yesterday.  Early.  Very early.  By
morning the reply arrived.  Iraq says, "Come on in and
take a look.  We're clean."  U.S. scoffs.  Media scoff.
But now the drama point shifts to December 8.  By then
Iraq must produce a list of all their bad stuff.  One
misstep and kerblooey, they're chopped terrorists.
     Meanwhile much hotter news.  Appears we didn't
succeed in offing the other world-class arch-villain
after all.  The Al Qaeda leader, he's baaaack.  A taped
message warning the Empire we're in deep shit, his boys
gonna take us out.  Ninety-five percent likelihood it's
really him, say the experts, and climbing.  (To me the
voice sounds too young.  I wonder if it might be one of
his many sons.)
     Electrifying news, this, in the Muslim world as
well as here.
     So now we see how the twenty-first century plays
out.  Soap-opera showdown, us versus them, cowboys and
Indians, and meanwhile the planet goes to hell.  And
everyone with it, eventually, cowboys and Indians alike,
bystanders too (except there aren't any -- "If you're
not with us, you're agin' us" -- this is what our leader

keeps on saying -- except it's not true for most of us and most of them).

But let's be clear about fault. It's ours. Far, far, far beyond anyone else's. "Blame USA First." Let's do it! Because we deserve it!

-- This from the Z-geist cafe. The right spot for such big thoughts. And the local news is good. Very local, I mean, like the old three-story redbrick hotel still being propped up across the street. World events permitting, it'll be saved. Historic J-town to the rescue. The tiny museum celebrating gold-rush days will be taking up residence there.

Personal news good too. Two hours ago I talked with Elgie. "Oh, was I supposed to be thinking of a date?" -- No, he was just kidding. He hadn't forgotten but his boss had been involved in a big trial. "I guess I should've called to tell you that." "What, and not keep us guessing? Where's the suspense in that?" We settled tentatively on the MLK week in mid-January. If necessary he'll take the week off without pay.

I also called Lynn at the investment firm. Got Robbie instead; she said some nice things about missing Mom (mine, that is; her southern soulmate). Time to close down the account. "Not much in there anyway," I said. "Too true, too true." She murmured something appropriately sad and almost apologetic (but not quite) about the state of the market and the economy and I concurred and murmured something so she'd know I didn't blame her, which I certainly don't. At one point she misheard a remark of mine and wondered aloud if I'd moved rightward politically "like everyone else." She must've been talking about her big-bucks investors. But Lynn, her assistant, will be calling tomorrow and we'll work out the details on the transfer. End of an era. (And end of my memory. It's clearly coming. I couldn't even recall my own zip code -- or rather area code. But then it's one of those numbers I take pride in not being able to recall, so why worry? Just learn to take pride in forgetting more and more. Or call it maintaining the near-pristine blank slate.)

[ Jyze of the Heavenly Year : Yellow Horse ]


     Back to Elgie.  At one point he asked, "Do you
think I'm pathologically shy?"  It seems a law-school
forum is coming up and the schools he's applied to, all
twenty-two of which will be represented there, have
advised him to show up "unless you're pathologically
shy."  It's like a traveling sales show, I guess, along
the lines of the harvest festival that hits J-town every
year in late autumn.  I dispensed fatherly advice.  But
he does seem sort of shy, yeah.  No matter!  He also
seemed a little more relaxed during this call.  "We have
a lot of catching up to do" -- he said that with a
laugh.  (Joked about jumping out the window too -- and
the firm he works for is on the twenty-ninth floor.)
     I called Z-wiff right away.  The pressure's off a
little bit, she agreed.  Holiday focus can go elsewhere
and then afterwards it'll be Elgie's turn.  Just so long
as he arrives before the Heavenly Year ends, I'm okay
with it.
     So then: jyze gets egg on its face again.  When I
saw Vic Tuesday he said he'd been under the impression
that J-town's great Afrusan rock guitarist's birthday
was "right around" his.  Turns out he's right -- it's
the same day!  And that's not November 11th, as I'd been
thinking -- why I don't know -- for the guitarist; it's
November 27th!  But I had such fun with it on the 11th,
I'm not changing a word in this J-book.  And maybe now I
can have even more fun with it on the 27th.
     I'm still hacking away at night.  Can't shake this
damn bug.  Z's determined, though: she's moving back to
our bed tomorrow night "even if the germs eat me alive."
     It's Z's kind of cluster.  Snake time!  And Vic's
too, and my father's.  The Golden Snake this is.  Vic's
Heavenly Year (1989).  And for me the last cluster of
the Yellow Horse era.  Next J-week I move into the
Heavenly endgame, last of the Horses, the magnificent
White.  A bad year for a woman to be born under the old
dispensation -- no man wanted to marry a White Horse
woman.  -- Or wait, was that the Fire Horse?  I think it
was.  Red Horse.  Anyway, it's Kat's year.  Stomp all
over those old sexist superstitions.

[ Jyze of the Heavenly Year : Yellow Horse ]


     Updates?  Mama E's going into the hospital for a
day next week -- cyst removal.  Or maybe it's a minor
skin cancer (this is the same growth on her right ear).
Last week a first: she called to thank Z after a visit.
Next day, though, she had the shakes and desperately
wanted to hit the emergency room.  Day after that she
was scheming with Tony, her caregiver, to keep us from
hearing about the shakes incident.
     June's spirits seem to be improving, though very
slowly.
     Our calendar's already groaning with holiday plans.
     Jess returns from MSM #2 today.  Her brother's
trial is in the decision phase, jury out.  What a tale
it is: former city prosecutor, now on trial himself for
stabbing a homeless man who accosted him.  His life's
disintegrated since I ambled alongside him up at the zoo
four or five years ago, small-talking, as his wife
(they're divorced now) and kids gamboled up ahead with Z
and Jess and Gwen.
     Poetry reading about to start in here.  As long as
there's still a zeit with at least a dollop of geist to
it there'll be poetry.  Read away!  I'll be pushing on
to the ORB (a book I ordered has arrived) and then the
scope office -- work to do ("Don't wanna rush you," says
the guy, and I truly believe him).


                        [+1]


     -- And where do I celebrate the birthday of the
Golden Snake?  The baths, of course.  The WOC.  Where it
seems the winds are blowing again -- I have to cover the
spread-open J-book with a white towel and a plastic wet-
clothes sack, except for a narrow rectangular space left
open for jyzing.  (Reminds me of the old TV news-show
technique of highlighting a document sentence by
sentence on screen as the newscaster reads it, with the
rest of the document darkened.  "The moving news bite,
having bit, moves on.")
     -- And jyze has moved on to the next day too.  I

thought I'd be here last night, but a miscue with Naomi
cost me a couple of hours (she forgot to leave a tape of
deposition steno at the office).  So it's Friday.  The
Ides of November, except November has only thirty days,
so the Ides falls on -- how does that go again?  The
14th?  Is there an Ides at all?  J-slinger needs
reference help.

I'm a Water Horse, I'm in my element here.  Dad was
a Fire Snake, so he wouldn't be.  Earth absorbs Water
which douses Fire.  His death certificate says he died
by drowning.  But he liked palm trees and tropical
temperatures and beaches.  And vaults too.  Baseball as
well, but tennis more.  Ballroom dancing, suavity, big
words, pretty women.  Cigarettes.  Martinis.  Artichoke
hearts.  He could hover over columns of figures with the
best of them.  Also played a mean, and sometimes mean-
spirited, devil's advocate for dinner-table arguments.

Today I talked with Lynn and closed down the deep-
reserves account.  In ten days or so she'll be sending
me a check for about forty grand.  Eight of that I owe
to the Z-spouse, so thirty-two is the remainder of my
heritage from Mother (and from Dad via the payoff to her
of his life insurance some twenty years earlier).  The
account is worth roughly three-fifths of what it was
when I received it after Mother's death (one quarter of
her estate minus expenses).

Where'd it come from?  Luck, privilege, hard work.
Both Mother and Dad were born Cawk in a majority Cawk
country which discriminated ferociously against anyone
not Cawk.  Both had fathers with advanced degrees.  Both
were college grads themselves and Dad had two advanced
degrees (law and business).  Both devoted themselves to
work and raising their kids.  When Dad died at the early
age of fifty-eight, he had good insurance coverage and
good elite connections -- he and Mother were personal
friends of the president of the insurance company which
issued the policy.  That man, who conveniently lived
just a few blocks from our house in Gatewood, decided
double-indemnity benefits would be paid for an
accidental death in Dad's case, with no investigation of

the coroner's ruling that drowning was the cause of
death.  Years later, when Mother's investment of those
benefits went sour, she successfully sued her investment
counselor for the amount lost plus a large penalty.
This is why she still had an estate to divvy up for her
children.  (That and the general upward course of the
stock market in the post World War II "USAn Century.")
     Dad would not be pleased with the kind of life I've
led since his death, just as he wasn't pleased with my
adult life before his death.  He applauded
"independence" in a son or daughter but he wasn't one
for risk-taking involving the arts and he certainly
wasn't one for radical or subversive politics.  Yet I
like to believe he also would've envied my life.  He saw
it as his mission to live uprightly and in some sense to
vindicate his father's mistakes (especially the ones
regarding the financial scandal, supposedly caused, at
least to Gramps's way of thinking, by depredations of
liberal politicians and laws back in Great Depression
times).  But underneath he, Dad, wanted to live a wild
life himself, at least to an extent (as he had done in
college), and take lots of risks.  Had it not been for
the outbreak of World War II he'd've gone off to the Far
East to seek his fortune -- the "slow boat to China" of
a thousand dinner-table conversations.  Instead he went
off to the Far East with the U.S. Army to protect other
people's fortunes and also the opportunity to make one
himself someday.  By the time the war was over he had a
wife and two kids and no vocation -- he was twenty-eight
years old, almost Elgie's age now.  The rest is law
school, suburbs, working hard, business school, gaining
promotions and being careful not to endanger stock
options.  (And, on the side, not even known of to the
rest of us, including Mother until after his death, lots
of romantic and/or sexual affairs.  In his mind that
may've been -- probably was -- what remained of his
projected wild life.)
     O Dad, I do you little justice with a nutshell
account like this.  You live on for me, though, in many
ways unrelated to any of it -- your "bio."  We had our

battles but hostility is not what I feel now, and except
for isolated furious moments it never was.  Not only did
I love both of my parents but I also liked them!  Of
Oedipal strains and fractures there were -- I thought --
very few.  I liked the man's humor!  I even liked his
warmth!  (Others thought he was too sarcastic and too
emotionally cool or apt to hide behind interior walls.)
Dad, you were even open to negotiation.  You said you
were sorry.  You had a good curveball.  In politics you
were not what I thought you should be, true, but it
wasn't hard to see why you thought what you did.  We
shook our heads over each other's "follies" (as viewed
by the other) but we forgave each other.  That's how
I've come to see it.  I hereby confirm it again.

     He's been gone for more than a quarter century.
I've had a lot of time to think about all this and I've
actually done quite a bit of that kind of thinking.
Would he be bothered by my digging around in family
history?  I believe not -- he was starting to do the
same thing himself shortly before he died.

     -- It comes down to this.  Sustained attention is
difficult.  You dig, you keep in touch, you appreciate
the flashes of reconnection, both voluntary (stimulated
by revisiting papers and photos) and involuntary (all
others).  More may not be possible.  For me anyway.


                        [+2]


     -- Can't break out of this Z-geist habit.  Can't
whip the bug either.  Today it's a disheartening
weakness that makes even J-stick-pushing seem like hard
work.  Why? I ask.  Why me?  It's the lament of our
times.  And saying this is itself a second lament of our
times.  Or go ahead and leap: of all times.

     Whine.  Whimper.  I'm outta whack and outta pop.
Immediate cause is a night of little sleep.  Hack hack,
whoop whoop.  Limp limp, lame lame.

     In the bathroom at the scope office last night I
ran into one of the lawyers from the firm down the hall.

[ Jyze of the Heavenly Year : Yellow Horse ]

He'd been cooped up in his office all weekend working on
a case which goes to trial Wednesday.  He looked even
worse than I felt.  I thought: there but for the love of
jyze go I.  I also thought: Dad, I never really knew ye.
Never really understood how you must've suffered.  At
the sight of me this other lawyer probably felt -- and
maybe Dad did too in some hidden way -- there but for
the love of the law go I.

    As the fourth of the five "Great Years" grumps to a
halt.  Hiss ye Golden Snake!  Rainy, gloomy, blustery
day.  Just in time the Christmas decorations start
popping up.  Giant silvery evergreen trees hidden deep
in sumptuous lobbies.  At the moment this whole corner
of the HQ is fenced in by street construction projects
-- makes it feel as if we indie-coffee-shop types are
under quarantine.  Half the fences are for creation of
the fancy new esplanade leading to the football stadium,
the other half for repair of lingering earthquake
damage.  The lights on the street corner just outside
are blinking red, all four, all the time, as they have
been ever since shortly after the quake.  A streetcar
rolls by a block north of here, visible up the street
corridor, flags aflutter but soggily so.  I can see the
old iron fire tower atop the six-story building to the
north -- it hasn't been used in, oh, a century or so.

    Already anticipatory regrets are beginning to stir
for all the fabulous jyze venues the Heavenly Year will
inevitably be missing out on.  Cold and/or rain or snow
will be scuttling, most likely, all but one or two (at
best!) of the potential outdoor sites.  The intriguing
freeway Park, jyze'll never make it there.  A certain
hidden highrise plaza.  A dozen different sidewalk
cafes.  Other parks.  Hilltops.  Cemeteries.

    I should've been more diligent.  Shoulda pushed
myself harder!  -- But it's my Heavenly Year.  Too much
such pushing wouldn't've befitted my newly bestowed
elder's dignity and pace.

    I've even failed to convene a jyze session of any
kind, indoor or out, in the old far-north-end hood.
Could still stop in at the bus-stop saloon out there --

it remains up and running, probably still draws in some
of the same old gang of tipplers and codgers -- but it's
too late now to do this during the appropriate era, '86
to '89, Heavenly Year clusters 44 through 48 standing
for my age when I lived out there from late '85 through
mid '89.  That's dead as of last night.  But I suppose I
could still make a postmortem visit.  (It was the cough
that did me in.  It kept me from calling on Mama E
during the appropriate era.  I figured I would drop in
at that saloon on the way back home since I usually pass
right by it.)
     So now the question arises: will I make it out to U
Acres in the province across the waters to pay my jyze
respects?  During the appropriate era?  At all?  The
holiday crunch is looming.
     Glistening streets, streaking auto lights.
Umbrellas, fedoras, slickers over hooded sweatshirts.
An antifashion show to gladden the heart of such a one
as I (who in recent times can't seem to fight off the
deluge of "such a one" and "ye" clause constructions).
     Inspectors arrive in Iraq.  U.S. war-prepping dials
up another full twist.  How many billions are we blowing
just on these "readiness measures"?  Obviously it's a
poor investment unless we can take over Iraq's oilfields
as our just reward, and even then all the profits will
go to the oil companies (who of course are big fans of
the cabal, several of whose members, including el
supremo himself, are ex-execs of oil companies).
Thousands of Iraqi children die every month because of
"sanctions" we've been unilaterally imposing on the
country for a decade (after bombing its infrastructure
to smithereens) but you rarely see a word about this in
the mainstream media.  It's all the diabolical Iraqi
leader's fault, see.  We threaten to kill thousands of
children a month if he doesn't follow our bidding, he
resists (not surprisingly, knowing we mean to off him),
the children die, and it's his fault.  And what does
this say about us?  (Nothing new, that's for sure.
We've been using these same tactics ever since the early
days of ethnic-cleansing of Amerinds, and of course that

went on for centuries and still does go on.)
     Lecturing again.  "Preaching."  Who wants to hear
it?  Not me!  I'm the choir!
     It's confirmed, by the way.  "Scientifically."
"Near certainty."  The voice is the Anti-Christ himself.
The Al Qaeda leader, yes.  (At least a dozen times in
disparate sources I've encountered what I'd bet a bunch
is an apocryphal story about a kid seeing video of this
man on TV and asking his father, "Daddy, who is that man
who looks just like Jesus?"  -- The tip-off is that in
some of the stories the boy and the father are German,
in others English, in others USAn.  "Urban legends."
Nonetheless it's true, the man himself does look like
certain famous Western artists' conceptions of what
Christ looked like.  One therefore imagines Christ will
start looking significantly different in future Western
artists' conceptions.
     Meanwhile a new alert's hanging over us.  Homeland
Security honchos are warning that Al Qaeda is planning
"spectacular" new attacks which will take place in the
U.S. sometime in the next two months -- which is to say,
during the last and final and climactic part of my
Heavenly Year -- or in other words the White Horse
"Great Year," which launches with the next cluster.  I
forget what official alert level we're supposed to be on
now, but it's up there, although of course it mustn't
inhibit any of our holiday spending -- the cabal leaders
themselves have been explicit about this.  But I find it
deliciously apt that they're using the term
"spectacular."  Society of the Spectacle.  The prime
governing principle.  Spectacular fear!  (All this also
reminds me of westerns, good Cawk folks hunkering down
inside the stockade, evil indigenes "on the warpath"
around it, high alert: soldiers up in the corner
guardhouses peering nervously out.  And why USAns are so
frightened: now it's Jesus Christ himself out there on
the circling horses, leading the war chants, shooting
the flaming arrows.  -- And in a sense, of course,
that's exactly right.  It is Christianity gone wild
that's about to do us in, and in more ways than one.)

Also big news today: it's Mickey Mouse's birthday.
He's about halfway between my age and Vic's.  -- And I
should note I made a special card for Vic.  It shows J-
town's great Afrusan rock guitarist striking a monster
dissonant chord and in a cartoon bubble he's saying,
"Even for a crazed Water Horse it's a no-no to declare I
was born on any day other than Vic H. Day!!"  Something
like that.  And now I'm starting to see all sorts of
material timed for the guitarist's birthday.  J-town
plutocrat #2 is throwing a big sixtieth bash featuring a
live performance by another great Afrusan guitarist,
this one from Centropolis and still going strong in his
mid sixties: the "Damn Right, I've Got the Blues" man.
        One last note and I'm done.  In today's paper an
Israeli "settler" in Palestine is quoted as he occupies
a new piece of territory under the eyes of Palestinians
cowed by Israeli armed force (much of it paid for by
USAn taxes, of course, including mine and Z's).  He says
of the Palestinians, "They can stay if they're good and
they accept that God has given this land to us.
Otherwise they must go."  By "us" he means the Israelis,
naturally.  And this says it in a nutshell for USAns too
as we move to perfect our domination of everyone else.
God has given "us" the world.  If other people do what
we think is good, they can stay in the world, although
only where we tell them they can stay and under such
conditions as we specify.  They can be "free" as long as
they follow our rules.  They can be "democratic" and
elect their own rulers as long as their rulers follow
our rules -- which after all are God's rules.  They can
join in the "free market" as long as they follow the
rules of the "free market" and accept its results, and
if those who set the rules of the "free market" also
have much more money and can outbid them for anything
and everything, including all the resources of their own
country, so be it.  Oh, and they must disarm.  And then,
finally, peace will reign in all of God's kingdom.
        Z-geist, you must now carry on without me.  I'm
headin' on down the road to the jac at the WOC.

# BOOK E

# [ Jyze of the White Horse ]

------

49

------


White Horse.  Right here, representing both the
cluster and the "Great Year," peering down its furry
muzzle at this page from its perch on a columnar
pedestal at the entrance of the hideaway building.  On
the front steps of which I sit.  Taking in the late-
afternoon, late-autumn scene.  But on a weather-break
day.  Blue skies.  Happy totem pole.  Gleeful naked
trees, every last leaf stripped away.

And so begins the white album.  (Just spilled my
coffee on the step beneath my thighs.  Some of it got on
my jacket.  Oh well.  It's an awkward reach down there
and I wasn't paying enough attention.  It's an
occupational hazard for J-slingers because focus must go
elsewhere, i.e., to the J.)

And it's the last of the "Great Years."  Last,
except for a single separate cluster at the very end of
the exalted Heavenly Year.  Last, maybe, of the whole
jyze series (because I'll probably need the rest of my
years -- such as they may be! -- to type it all up and
wring out the repetitious and truly stupid stuff and
otherwise try to make sure the words are saying what I
want them to say and the punctuation's where it oughta
be -- period.  Comma.  Exclamation point!).

The White Horse looking over my jyzin' arm is one
of the red-carpet-riding miniatures I bought at A-mart
at the start of the year.  No other White Horses around
right now -- though you do see them from time to time in
this town, hauling cops or pulling tourist carriages --
so I brought this one down for luck.  It's about two and
a half inches long and two inches high.  No doubt this

scene here in the doorway seems bizarre to anyone who's
looking closely, but then if ever there were a spot
where bizarreness is the norm, this is it.

As of last night (when the Leonids were streaking
across the sky) just forty-two days remained in the
solar year.  More good luck.  Any forty-two I come
across, I try to show proper respect.

Visible straight ahead, which is to say west, half
a block away, fourth and top floor of a century-old
brick-and-stone building, are V&J's triple arched north
windows.  Last night Vic and I hiked up the edge road to
a local franchise restaurant for its cut-rate happy-hour
burgers, then stopped by at the hideaway and I showed
him some of my photo albums.  Keeping things balanced,
since he's showed me some of his.  Next to his mine look
skimpy and callow.  The crew-cut burban pink guy in his
suit and tie or sports uniforms.  Vic doesn't show his
reactions much -- probably I'm fortunate.  In any event:
another fine evening.  Talk of age, people dying off,
the fear of declining creativity -- but he's charging
ahead anyway and I'm trying to keep up with him.

Eschatological talk, that's what much of it was.  A
longhaired guy passing out leaflets room to room
upstairs right before I came down here used the term.
It occurred to me I should seize on it for this project.
Radiant eschatology homespun, right here, five cents.

WOC next.  Time for my comeback on the exercise
floor.  Tonight Z-wiff, sorely aggrieved by our long
doctor-ordered abstinence and avowedly super-hot to
trot, returns to our marriage bed.

A dozen yellowish-tan fallen bigleaf maple leaves
litter the concrete around me.  I give a huff, the
nearest one rises slightly and sidles away a few inches
like a lazy starfish.  If I were coughing now the way I
was last week the sidewalk and maybe half the triangle
would be swept clean.  But at this late stage I settle
for the occasional rear-guard hack.

-- When did the lights go on?  They're on now, all
around the square, five-ball Victorian clusters (and one
broken three-baller).  The buildings light up from

inside -- and with no signs of movement in there they
seem like life-size blowups of the old-timey miniatures
in fancy model-train layouts.

November 20th, sitting outside, not even wearing a
jacket -- not bad.  Dis da life!  (Not saying diss da
life.)  When I picked up this coffee across the street
at the chain joint the "Hallelujah Chorus" was playing
inside.  They're starting the season before
Thanksgiving, the barista told me (and could be speaking
for lots of businesses), because Thanksgiving falls so
late this year.  In all these office windows (many
belonging to barristers and barristas, that is, lawyers
as homophoned in latteland) I see only one Christmas
tree -- and that's not in an office, it's at the chain
coffee joint itself.  (Reminding me: it's a good thing
my jacket is not too far from coffee-colored.)

Night janitor Ivanka arrives for work and says to
me, "My my, you're here early."  She didn't notice the
coffee spill staining the steps.  Not yet.

In Germany it's Buss und Bettag, or Repentance Day.
I have plenty to repent, no question, but I'm putting
all that on hold for now.  It's also Revolution Day in
Mexico -- and I'll pass on that too, though Lord we
could sure use another one of those up here in El Norte
(but nonviolent please) and for the sake of the whole
damn world, yeah.  And then it's UN Children's Day
everywhere, and so I'll mention Kat, born in the Year of
the White Horse.  I gave her a horse exactly like this
one on the ledge here to my right -- two of them, in
fact.  But Saturday night she didn't show up to see
"Real Women Have Curves" with Betty and Z and me and it
seems she's just about faded from our life, Z's and
mine, or rather she's banished us from hers.  And that's
life!  But it's also sad.  We're still hoping to be able
to do something about it.  But as yet we know not what.

On the front page of the far-coast paper, a U.S.
senator, just about the only one in that august chamber
to stand up against the post-9/11 deluge of hard-right
reaction and bellicosity, is celebrated for turning
eighty-five.  Turns out he was born five days after Dad.

   And it's noted in that same paper that the Cold War
"officially" ended on this date a dozen years ago -- in
the Year of the White Horse.
   The tiny steed on the ledge is nonchalant about all
this.  I, though, am pleased to have such a finely
echoic day for starters.  Starters of what?  Yes, I said
it already: the last full Great Year.  Or maybe: the
last J-book ever.  Boo-hoo, yup.  Right on!
                    *          *
   Eleven hours later.  Marvelous night of soupy fog
-- after arriving home I watched out the window as the
full moon sank out of sight in it (reminding me of my
long-ago caddying days: a golf ball fading into the
depths of a water hazard, blue-greening out).
   Z-wiff awaits me in bed -- oh, about forty minutes
from now.  An excited note about our "reunion" greeted
me on the chair.  This morning she noticed I hadn't
placed my usual cup of frozen fruit in the nonfreezer
part of the fridge for thawing and she prepared one for
me.  It was very touching to discover this (even though
I'd intentionally skipped the thawing -- I knew I'd be
leaving soon after rising, with no time to slice the
fruit).  Earlier in the evening yesterday she'd seen me
walking across the high bridge toward downtown as she
drove home.  Blaring horn, I gave a two-armed wave, and
she then (as she wrote in a note later) burst into tears
thinking how we've had to give up so much of our prior
way of life since Mama E appeared on the scene to
reorder our priorities.  Later she cried herself to
sleep over this.  She's in a labile state for sure.  She
often is!  But she's resilient too -- bounces right back
with new insights, new determination, new plans.
   Wotta wife.  I can't say enough about this.  And
yet I can scarcely say anything, it's so overwhelmingly
true.  But this time around I ought to be focusing on
other matters anyway.  That was the decision going into
the Heavenly Year (after obsessively jyzing up the Z-
woman in the previous three annals) and I haven't done
too badly at sticking to it.  But she's always a big
part of everything and the number-one focus of my life

whether I spell it out in these pages or not.  Just how
it is and has been from day one, meaning ours together.

Mama E's ear operation has been proclaimed a
success.  She's already back at Benita's place and also
back to her old tricks.

Our young protofascist caballero -- crusader cabal
dude No. 1 -- he's off in Europe right now beating the
war drums, again threatening anyone who dares to go any
way but ours.  The madness of this course becomes ever
more stunningly evident -- except to the jingoistic USAn
public and its fanatical neocon leadership cadre.  Not
all the public but enough.  War fever!  Let's take over
the globe!  Yay!  Rah!  Kill!  USA!  USA!  USA!

Payback time has scarcely even begun.  The current
crop of infuriated terrorists is nothing compared to the
nasties ahead.  But of course this is fine with our own
fanatics.  All the more reason to keep us toeing the
line at home.  (It's basically martial law we're in now
even if it hasn't been officially declared.  And that's
where we'll be for fifty more years as the high chief
has already stated.)

Local news?  The sound's in even worse shape than
anyone thought.  The OMP -- i.e., the slightly less
right-wing of our local dailies -- is running a top-
quality investigative series about it.  But at the state
level the yahoos are still in control, with popular
initiatives cutting tax revenues to the point where
nothing much can be done about anything.  Jyze City's
the exception: funds for the extension of the monorail
just eked out an electoral victory (it wasn't confirmed
until yesterday when the last of the write-ins were
counted, two weeks after the election; going into the
final day the monorail trailed by exactly three votes --
but in the end it won by over eight hundred).

Upon arrival at the scope office tonight I again
found the room where I do most of my work completely
rearranged and almost impassable.  A table had collapsed
during the day shift.  I lost more than an hour clearing
paths and making necessary adjustments -- time I could
ill afford to give up because this was the first night

of a heavy three-day grand-jury period.

     -- I haven't mentioned a new work habit.  I've
compromised a bit with the computer age.  I now punch
the "News" button on the big screen in the ground-floor
lobby as I'm coming in to work and/or leaving -- get the
"top five" stories as the worst of our local TV stations
rates them on its website, with about a dozen words
allotted to each.  Usually it's "if it bleeds it leads"
local stuff, but once in a while a big breaking national
or even international story appears and I'm glad I've
checked.

     -- I'd like to keep going but nope, can't
disappoint the Z-wiff.  Or myself, true.  First things
first.  Whoopee, honey, hyar I come!


                         [+2]


     Straddling the days.  In the night.  It's the 22nd,
it's the 23rd.  It's Friday, it's Saturday.  It's a
famous day, it's a not-so-famous day.

     Later during this less famous day, in a last-minute
shift of plans, I'll be driving over to port jingo.  Z-
wiff insists I take the Z-mobile and she'll catch a bus
to her hair appointment.  She's long had plans to spend
the evening with Aida.  Until I clear some space in our
basement storage closet here -- by shifting most of its
contents to my old storage unit across the water -- we
can't begin clearing space in our bedroom so we can move
things there from Z's room, making that room habitable
for Elgie, assuming he really does come (and I've still
heard nothing more from him after extracting his promise
to "soon" let us know his plans).

     The point is, it's better to make this first move
in the game of musical storage as soon as possible.  And
who knows when another possible time for the trip will
open up.  Looks to me like our calendar's pretty much
full from now all the way to the week after New Year's.

     This coming week, by the way, after doing
Thanksgiving dinner at Wei and Alison's, as has become

de rigueur, Z and I will be shifting operations over to
southwest island for a few days of house-sitting for
Gwen and Jess (whose brother, to chase after another by-
the-way, has just been acquitted on the charge of
assault on the homeless man who in fact, as the jury was
persuaded, had first assaulted him).  I'll probably
stretch out the jyze schedule again so I'll have a
chance to do an entry or two over there.

Why's today, the 22nd, famous?  For one thing, it's
JFK (JRX!) assassination day.  And isn't that enough?
For my generation it surely is.  It's what Pearl Harbor
Day was for my parents' generation and 9/11 is for
the current one (when you're at the point of celebrating
a Heavenly Year you definitely have to count yourself
out as a member of the current generation for epoch-
dating purposes).

Life changed then.  And it also changed on the
less-famous today, the 23rd, at least for me, if the
date is looked at in lunar or NUT terms.  Before today I
had no life, after it I had one.  That is, it's the
lunar anniversary of my conception day, which also was
(say it again, Jeep!) Pearl Harbor Day.  And a fine
night it is for a lunar anniversary, the selenotic orb
just past full and winking like the incandescent golf
ball I mentioned earlier but retrieved now from the
glowy chemicalized water-hazard depths -- winking
through shifty layers of fast-moving clouds going every
which way but down (or so it seemed from my hilltop
perch after bouncing off the super-lively and crowded
Friday-night last bus).

And today Vic left me a note I'll treasure.  He
says, "Thank you for sharing the pieces of your past,
the photographic tesserae in the Glen Sandefjord mosaic.
I think we share a friendship and commonality that goes
beyond the verbal, visual or obvious.  It's almost a
Nordic thing" -- and then goes on to tell the story
about two Norwegian guys who meet, pour drinks, one says
"Skoal," the other says "Shut up.  Did you come here to
drink or talk?"  And he informs me of a bargain
photocopy rate at one of the nearby chain copy shops.

Gotta love the guy.  And I do.

    Today's boggling FAP front-page headline: "IS IT OPEN SEASON ON USANS?"  Just because three get shot overseas in one day!  -- And on the very same day more than a hundred Nigerians die protesting the upcoming Miss World Pageant in Lagos -- which pageant has now decamped for London.  A more fitting place to be sure. But yes, it is open season on USAns, and it's surprising it hasn't been widely noticed before now.  Our present policies are as good as painting bull's-eyes on the backs of all USAns traveling out of country.  If we're lucky the blowback will succeed in scaring us into changing those policies.  But I doubt we'll be lucky in that way anytime soon.  The policies are exactly what keep the power-mad in power and the money-mad in moolah. (And...let's not forget: the policies also keep many of the rest of us in power and moolah.  Giving up the policies will mean giving up a big chunk of the current "USAn way of life.")

    The Celestial calendar marks today the 22nd as the start of the "Slight Snow" fifteen-day period.  Winter's here for real.  Forget that sentimental falling-leaves nonsense; we're talking serious freeze-ups.  And today the 23rd our two major in-state university football teams clash up in the Yuke, big blowout, rowdiness to beat the band, a very good day to be heading out of town.  I played football myself as a youth and so I feel I can get away with saying it: real human beings don't play football.  Repent, USA.  Hut one, hut two -- make us relinquish the football!


                          [+1]


    -- Fourteen hours on.  Where am I?  Blink-blink. It's the usual root-beer stand at the mall in the old home port, just across the street from the storage unit. I'm still thawing out from a three-hour stint over there, unpacking, shifting stuff around to make room for the new arrivals, searching for various items, going


                          510

through another file drawer of Mother's papers and photos.  And with only a bare lightbulb for heat.

At no time do I feel the sadness of ephemerality as strongly as I do when immersing myself in Mother's file drawers.  She labored so hard to leave behind a well-ordered record of her life and the lives of her parents and the rest of her family.  Thousands of letters, photos, mementos, all labeled, chronologically arranged, often bearing short notes explaining the item's meaning to her and/or to others.  And now they all sit in locked filing cabinets inside a locked storage unit in a town she visited exactly once in her life.  Nobody ever sees the contents of those cabinets except me, and I look at them briefly maybe once or twice a year for an hour or two.  And I show brother Rob a few things I think he might be interested in.

The hope that someone will still care about us when we're gone.  How forlorn it is, how sad, how pathetic.  Of course it's the same hope that's the driving force, or one of them anyway, behind all this jyzing.  "That we may not have lived in vain."  But we do live in vain!  These jyze scratchings, even if they did come to mean something to a few readers in the future, does that make the living any less in vain?  It's small consolation -- tiny -- minuscule -- and I jyze on regardless.  Just for the love of doing it, really.  Why else did Cold Mountain keep doing his thing, Sei Shonagon hers, Pepys and Issa and Pessoa and Tsvetaeva theirs?  The love of doing it and the faint hope someone will care someday.  That's all it comes down to.  (And those writers' names of course can appear here only via JRX.)

Each time I go through these file drawers I find priceless new items I've overlooked before.  This time it's a packet of photos showing Dad evolving over a period of half a century, from early grade-school days to the death photo which ran in the local Gatewood weekly.  Middle school, high school, college, military, workplace I.D. cards with photos.  "The Snake" of his college fraternity with a couple of his girlfriends of that era (Mother writes "the Snake" comment on the back

of one of the photos) (and of course neither he nor she,
as far as I know, was aware the Chinese zodiac likewise
casts him as a Snake).  Also I came across a letter Dad
wrote to Popeye from Manila in the spring of '45
explaining exactly what his duties were -- or rather he
wrote it from "what's left of Manila."  Water shortages
will continue, he notes, until "we root out the Japs"
who at that time were still holding the reservoirs up in
the mountains.

The drawers also contain copies of hundreds of
Hutcheson and Chandler family letters (and a good many
others as well) going back to the early 1800s.  Will I
ever have a chance to read them before I'm gone too?  If
not, one reason will be that I must organize the papers
and letters of my own life to add to the heap.  Another
couple of file drawers for someone to try to figure out
what the hell to do with two or three decades down the
road -- and that's if I'm lucky.

This on my conception day, lunar version.  One of
the newly discovered photos shows Mother five or six
months pregnant with me -- and in the note appended she
says she's pregnant with Barb!  It's the only obvious
error I've ever spotted in any of her memorabilia.  (How
do I know it's an error?  The photo's commercially date-
stamped "May 1942" in tiny print on the back, lower
right-hand corner.)

These photos and letters are so precious.  Nothing
else remains of these two most important people in my
life!  O mortality, thy sting, how painful it can be!

Earlier, on the way here, I took a gander at the
old U Acres abode.  The house itself looks about the
same.  Someone seems to be living up in the barn now --
the scaffolding is gone and the structure looks sturdier
somehow -- and the uphill part of the two-acre vacant
lot, which had been partially cleared last time I drove
by for a look, has now been fenced in for horses.  I saw
four of them, all black.  Right outside the windows of
my old writing shed, a field of black horses -- which is
to say, Black Horses, capped, yes, and almost uncannily
like that scene we happened upon in the mountains during

the trip back from Centropolis with Mama E last spring.
    Each time I come over here, the house and the town
seem to regain a little bit more of the rustic charm
which drew us to them in the first place but soon began
to dissipate under the strains of daily living and a new
kind of extended intimate exposure to each other, Lady U
and I, in rural isolation.
    -- A man with a mop and a bucket says this section
will be closing now.  The other section has just one
empty booth, and a dozen folks are waiting in line for
it.  The walls here are plastered with snapshots and
those folks in line all look like they might be pictured
in them.  They deserve that booth and I don't.
                    *              *
    Ooh yeah, fine thick fog.  The streetlight across
our street is just a diffuse glow.  Z-wiff sleeps.
Plants are watered (potted-earth sniff lingering in the
air), periodicals read, a few sections of tomorrow's
bulky far-coast paper glanced through.  It came out too
early to include the result of our big intrastate-
rivalry football game.  But we now know China's economy
is still growing rapidly and that's good for those of us
who want to see the current Cawk-controlled unipolar
world relegated to history.  And I've got my Saturday
night glass of the good good bourbon.
    An uneventful journey back.  I stopped at the
drive-in by the bridge over the lagoon, indulged in a
large softie vanilla cone.  The bridge market where Lady
U almost took a job -- and who knows, if she had we
might've stayed together to this day (though I doubt it)
-- that market, I say, has changed ownership and is
converting to something more like a convenience store
with a deli.  The drive-in features a new three-panel
mural of the bridge next to which it sits -- but there
is no drive-in depicted in the mural itself, and so no
mural within the mural.  Reflexivity and infinite
regress are out of fashion in my old stomping grounds
over there, or more likely they just never were in.
    Lynn did leave a message the other day saying the
check from the deep reserves is in the mail.  It still

hasn't arrived.  Presumably Monday will be the big day.
She asked me to call if I wanted to know the amount,
since she wasn't sure it would be kosher to leave it on
the voicemail.  I didn't bother calling -- I didn't want
to have to say goodbye to her again.  In her voicemail
she sounded faintly resentful, I thought, almost like a
spurned lover, and I doubt this would be because of the
lost management fee, which was tiny by her standards (my
account was by far the smallest on their books, with
Rob's the second smallest and Barb's the third -- and
Jeff long ago cashed in his).  I think she, Lynn,
enjoyed all four of us as offbeat types -- not your
usual high-pressure investors.

I've already come up with a list of purchases to be
made with the two thousand bucks I'm intending to hold
back from reinvestment in certificates of deposit at Z's
credit union.  The bulk of the two K will go for Elgie's
visit -- if it really does happen -- but I'm also aiming
to buy a new backpack, a pair of jeans, a winter jacket,
two shirts, a dozen pairs of socks, two more pairs of
chucks (both black-and-white), and a couple of bottles
of bourbon.  And a hundred bucks' worth of books.  And a
couple of subscription renewals.  And maybe a laminator
so I can mount some of my wedding-gift cards for Z on
the cabinet doors in the kitchen without fear they'll be
ruined by grease spatters.

-- WHAP-sliiiiiide.  That would be the Jyze City
combined Sunday paper, the OMP/FAP.  It's an hour late,
probably because of the fog but maybe because of late
coverage for the big game.  No time, I guess, for the
delivery person to run it back to the end of the side
walkway for the WHAP without the sliiiiiide.

And I'm all done in.  Time to bid the White Horse
adieu in its cluster form.  The next clusterly Horse
that comes along will be Black and that'll mean we've
reached the end of the annal.  No epilogue this time
around, just as there is no prologue.  Heavenly entries
only!

[ Jyze of the Heavenly Year : White Horse ]


------

50

------


        A miscue and so I'm not holding down the bar at the
HQ-triangle tavern.  I thought it would be open until
two a.m. but it was already closed at half past eleven.
So here I am right back up in the hideaway.  The corner
armchair.  It's way too cold for outdoor jyzing.
Triangle tavern, jyze will stop by another time.
        It's Silver Sheep cluster.  Loud rock music's
playing as is often the case up here, but this time it's
coming from the office above mine rather than the saloon
below.  And the last of my "Happy Birthday" balloons has
fallen.  I'm wondering: should I pump them up again for
Elgie's visit and the annal-ending celebration, right
before all that's Heavenly reverts to pumpkin?
        Cluttered room too.  A bit of mold in the air from
the books and letters I retrieved from port jingo.
Seven years of unheated storage and untreated dampness
will do that.  Big stacks of reference books.  Ahead lie
years and maybe even decades, should I be so lucky, of
trying to make sure the words in all these jyzical pages
-- as I was saying last week -- are the right ones,
starting 'long about the first of the Gray Sheep Year.
        I pray I should be exactly that: so lucky.  And
tonight's a good night for praying.  It's the first of
the five Ramadan Nights of Power.  Tonight and every
second night for the nine nights following, as I
understand the setup, are jackpot semifinalists for
praying.  One of those five will be declared the
equivalent of a thousand months of praying and only the
Supreme Spirit knows which it is, so you're best off
going down on your knees and elbows and forehead all
five nights.  That way you're sure to hit the jackpot.

And that in turn means a whole lot of Muslims will be hitting it big prayerwise on or before December 4th. Consequently, on or before that date, if Allah is listening, the U.S. should go up in a big puff of smoke.

Inspections are starting tomorrow in Iraq.  That country's leaders have studied the small print in UN Resolution 1441 (authorizing the inspections) and say the game is rigged; the pretexts for starting the war are already there.  A former UN inspector in Iraq, a USAn, predicts the softening-up bombing campaign will start before Christmas, with the invasion itself coming the last week in January -- just in time to end the Heavenly Year of Jyzer G with a big bang.

Yesterday was St. Catherine's Day.  She's the "patron saint" for philosophers, so as a college philosophy major and a lay philosophy student ever since, I figured I might have a special "in" with her, and therefore I did some praying for luck yesterday too. The flocks for whom she's the guide are a varied lot, including not only philosophers but "maidens and mechanics."  With such a wide scope she may lack the focus necessary to break through to the Supreme Spirit (or the Supreme Spirit Council, if, as one might guess, that's a more apt description of heaven at the top). Chances for a breakthrough might be better on Thursday, which will both present a twenty percent likelihood for a thirty-thousand-fold increase in praying power and also be USAn Thanksgiving.

And tomorrow's Vic H. Day.  I met with him tonight and he assured me he too will be doing what he can to get the message through to the appropriate deities.  In addition we went over a list of questions I'd written out concerning the stories in the middle chapters of his book.  After a couple of hours up in the loft we turned the place over to Jean (it's her day off and she wanted to amp the music up high and kick back with a glass of wine) and adjourned to the ORB cafe and then, when that closed, a nearby Vietnamese restaurant, just around the corner from Z-geist, which of course shuts down early or otherwise we'd've gone there.

516

[ Jyze of the Heavenly Year : White Horse ]

Vic works with a couple of re-covered reference books (dictionary, thesaurus) hailing from the sixties, well-thumbed, pages yellowed and even browned around the edges -- keeps them atop the computer base right beneath his monitor screen.  Jean put me in mind of a celebrity chef as she juggled stir-fry dishes on the raised kitchen platform.  "You're like two students in there," she said, as we labored at the computer, "working on a project that's due in the morning."  She and Vic are both fuming over a very loud New Age musical group that's moved into the loft directly behind theirs.

Me, yesterday I covered Mama E's follow-up visit to the east-hill clinic and all went smoothly, with a cabulance again hauling her back and forth.  The growth on her ear turned out to be benign.  The only problem on this day was that the appointment went off on time and quickly and so we had to wait ninety minutes for her return cabulance, which must be scheduled days in advance.  For many of those ninety minutes leg pain had her up and chugging around the lobby with her walker.

Z-wiff's calling me "Mr. Sendfore" these days.  She bought us a "family membership" at the AQ museum and the card came back with that last name for her husband.

And it's now official: we're all being protected by something newly called the Department of Homeland Security.  Heil!  But it'll probably be a few years before they're out nabbing subversives like me and Z and the majority of J-town's residents.  News analysts say it'll take that long for all the conglomerated departments to learn how to communicate with each other.  Their employees will number a mere 170,000.  Slimmed-down conservative government, don'tcha know.

How many cylinders am I hitting on right now?  Not too many.  Time to give it a rest, while still holding forth the possibility of a revival later tonight if the spirit's upon me, Supreme or otherwise.  Because just about any old spirit will do.

*       *

Back three hours later for the encore.  Transported from one form-fitting armchair to the other.  Along the

way I saw half a grapefruit, with the rounded part
facing down and the straight edge tilted slightly off
the horizontal, hanging above the silhouetted evergreens
of the in-city ridgeline to the east.  I also watered
the plants, slapped together a peanut-butter sandwich
for supper (with baked potato chips and cranberry sauce
for "accompaniments," as they say), and read two
newspapers and one lit mag.  Not a bad night at all.
   The moon wasn't yellow or pink.  It was a white
half grapefruit.  Breath vapor was pluming impressively
from the contingent of swing-shifters, myself included,
as we filed off the bus at our hilltop stop.  A merry
bunch -- in fact the current mix on the last coach of
the night is my favorite for the whole time I've been
riding it.  The stars were unusually clear -- meaning
you could actually see a few.  One of the women from the
halfway-house group, Inez, a Latina with marvelous thick
hip-length black hair, even called out to me, "See ya
next time!"  The bus driver for Monday through Wednesday
nights has been hitting on her for weeks and she just
laughs it off.  She has twenty-six days to go and she's
free -- her sentence served, including time off for good
behavior.  What she's being held for I don't know.  Most
likely, though, as is almost always the case in my
experience with this particular halfway house (we have
five or six up here on the hilltop), it's dope-related.
   I count three buddies on this bus and a racially
diverse lot they are: an Afrusan guy, an Asiusan guy, a
Latusan guy.  I'm the only Eurusan regular at this
point.  Dennis, the Afrusan, is a foreman on the swing
shift of janitors at the public market; he's from the
far southeast coast, divorced, has a girlfriend in FCM
#1 whom he met in MSM #1 on his way back from the
Philippines; he's a sweet guy, laid back, but also a
spinner of far-fetched yarns and you never know what's
true and what's not; your best bet is to go with the
flow and express good-natured incredulity every now and
then to show you're not a total gull.
   Chan, the Asiusan guy, is of Chinese heritage, thus
Chiusan, works in the kitchen at downtown's hottest

[ Jyze of the Heavenly Year : White Horse ]


Asian-fusion restaurant, age maybe fifty, very slender,
speaks scarcely a word of English but loves to goof and
be playful; we communicate through improvised language
and he always pulls the stop cord for me before I can
get to it and then flashes a mysterious eyebrows-raised
smile and waves out the window as the bus pulls out.
    Hector, the Mexusan, is about five feet tall,
round-faced and ponytailed, reads lots of history in
both Spanish and English. He's always telling me about
his favorite stories in the news -- the walking Chinese
fish showing up on the USAn far coast was last night's
-- and asking questions about strange gringo customs.
Tomorrow he's taking the train down to MSM #2 to spend a
day and a half with a friend and then returning on the
same train in time to get to work Monday evening.
    I almost always sit with one of these guys. No
more reading on the bus. But most likely it won't be
long before all three change shifts or jobs and I'll be
reading again. It's unusual to run into friendly people
you want to be talking with on this route. And it's
risky to start up anything because once you start it's
hard to put it to a stop if that should seem advisable.
This time, though, I seem to have lucked out: a trifecta
no less.
    -- Someone's stirring in the other room. I think I
know who. So now'd be a good time to sign off.


[+2]


    Thanksgiving Day -- but late at night. Otherwise
it's not the usual place either. A green armchair in a
corner of Jess and Gwen's "great room" (which is
admittedly a whole lot greater than our own "great room"
at 1511) off in a woodsy stretch of southwest island out
in the middle of the sound. Z-wiff sleeps upstairs --
steep stairs, lipped, and she wasn't used to that and
nearly took a spill as a result -- and so do old Cy-dog
and Erfa, the new near-clone of Kiba -- and down here so
do a couple of black cats -- they're sleeping at

519

opposite ends of the couch -- and one of the cats is
neurologically damaged from mistreatment as a kitten and
walks with a comical stagger: a very touching and
lovable creature, though also clawsome.

     This island's only a twenty-minute ferry ride from
the west side of the city, maybe not even that.  Owing
to a "police incident" it appeared for a while our boat
was bound for a secondary far-side port where I
occasionally caught a ferry to the city back in my
commuting days.  A kindly deckhand set us straight on
the ferry's sequence of stops and also explained his
theory on why old Chinese coins have holes cut in their
centers: something about Dragon power and anchoring in
the earth.  Sounded reasonable to me, I said, but there
was probably a practical reason as well, and I repeated
what Vic had told me: that in ancient days traders were
the main users of coins and they wore them in strings
around their neck to make travel and counting easier.
But in general I thought the deckhand had it right: a
good myth that partakes of the reigning cosmology will
trump mere pragmatic explanations every time.

     Jess built this house mostly by herself.  An
impressive job.  High open-beam ceiling, lots of windows
-- two sides of the "great room" are about two-thirds
glass.  A gray stone fireplace stands just to my right
but it's probably not usable at the moment owing to a
burn ban the island's been under for several days.
Tomorrow Betty and Kat arrive.  Tomorrow night after
everyone goes to bed, and Saturday night too, I'll work
on Vic's stories at the big round wooden dining table.

     Earlier we did the annual Wei and Alison
Thanksgiving feast.  Two of Wei's cousins whom he only
recently met attended along with two other regulars,
Mari and Kirby, mother and son, combined ages a nifty
double-Heavenly 120.  Only in the past couple of years
has Wei started taking a strong interest in the Japanese
side of his heritage; the family held a reunion at the
USAn World War II "internment camp" where Wei's mother
and her four siblings and their parents were locked up
for the war years.  Unfortunately the Cawk ex-banker

husband of one of the cousins rattled on interminably about his travels and complaints about various airlines. That was Lowell. And his wife, Dora, wasn't much better. The Mentoka cousin, Sabina, is an artist and seemed to have interesting things to say, but she was constantly overridden. Z was surprised Wei and I didn't challenge Lowell on political matters. But I think it was clear to all but her it would've been pointless.

So -- Thanksgiving. A key foundational myth. Pilgrims, not pogroms. Our very first USAn supreme leader -- also a slaveholder and indigene fighter and exploiter -- himself commanded us to give thanks to God for our blessings. In other words, let God shoulder the guilt. It was all His doing, see, His plan, that we should dispossess these other folks of their lands, their livelihoods, their lives. When academics talk about the psychological "necessity" of religion they usually don't mention this part of it. Instead we give thanks that we are the stompers rather than the stompees. Thank you, God, for making us Cawks stompers.

But the small-group togetherness is nice. Recognition of the need for kindness and generosity is good. Acceptance that life itself is a blessing (irrespective of religion!) is also good.

As for our upcoming stomping of Iraq, we're presently once again in waiting mode. Inspectors are inspecting, Iraqis are letting them inspect, but the next major trip wire's not until December 8th. At that point Iraq is supposed to present a list of all its WMDs. If that list doesn't match the one we've compiled for them on our own, that'll be it: "material breach of 1441." Iraq, you're USAn lunch.

How'd we come up with this list of ours? Nobody knows. Informants, I suppose. How do we know we can believe the informants? We don't. Does it matter? (We ourselves, to repeat yet again, have tens of thousands of WMDs. Anybody want to try to do anything about it? Our allies Israel and Turkey are in violation of more UN resolutions than Iraq is, and Israel has nukes, although they refuse to acknowledge this. Will we stomp all over

these malefactors?  Are we in favor of the evenhanded
administration of justice?  Are you kiddin' me?)
     Don't mind all this, it's just rantin'.  A few
short paragraphs, no big deal.
     -- The day after I wrote that the old gang of mine
on the bus couldn't last for long, Dennis, the janitor
foreman at the public market, told me he's moving to FCM
#1 next week.  Gonna get hitched to that woman he met in
MSM #1.  (Why the rush?  He showed me her photo.  Wow!)
     Can't help but notice I'm coughing again.  Nothing
too serious yet but I sense the possibility of another
relapse.  This bug is sweeping the city right now.  My
case is minor compared to some I've come across.  Z's
friend Madge I. at work (she of the houseboat and the
funky dance steps) has it so bad her coworkers evacuate
their group office when she comes in and do their work
out in the hall.  Or so I'm told.
     Or it might be that what I've got is something
else.  An allergy maybe.  Country living.  The quiet
here reminds me of my earlier life in the backwoods with
Lady U.  A deeply pot-holed gravel road.  Jess put up a
curtain in the upstairs bathroom with the tub because Z
felt too exposed there.  The property is isolated and
the woods surrounding it are supposedly full of wackos.


                        [+1]


     And now for a nightcap at the house in the woods on
the island.  For this one I've switched over to the
round teak table.  A fancy black faux-industrial light
fixture hangs down low, just above my head.  The night's
every bit as black and quiet as last night was, except
for an occasional stirring from the bedroom down the
hall where Kat and Betty are sleeping, or trying to.
     Earlier we had some Hanukkah candles going.  A
boxful of them -- forty-five in all, roughly half blue
and half silver -- stands so close to the front of this
J-book it casts a shadow over the upper right-hand
corner where I've writtem in the page numbers (one for

this volume, one for the annal as a whole).  But I couldn't find the matches to fire up one of those candles for jyze ceremonial purposes.

At the same time it's still Ramadan, though not a Night of Power.  It's also Buy Nothing Day, but no one's paying any attention to that except for a few un-USAn true believers.  And since by solar measure we're well into Saturday, it's the third anniversary of the protests against the WTO -- now known by millions simply as "the Showdown in J-town," the start of the popular phase of the movement against corporate globalization -- and it's also Bonifacio Day in the Philippines, commemorating the revolt against the Spanish which in short order led to colonization by the U.S. under the command of the father of my own father's World War II boss -- and this latter man, the son, in turn was one of only two men in history who've been de facto emperor of both the Philippines and Japan.  The other being, of course, the authentic wartime emperor of Japan.

Then it's also -- today is, Friday -- the seventh anniversary of my mother's death.  From a Buddhist point of view, I'm told, this is an especially important mourning day.  At dinner tonight and then again later with Betty (as she did some sewing) I spun out "Mom stories."  Some people call this Black Friday because it kicks off the Christmas shopping madness.  I suppose I could call it that because it's Mother's death day, and in past jyze annals I'm pretty sure I've done just that. But it no longer seems so dark.  On the contrary, it's a good day for remembering her -- she seems to come more vividly alive -- and so it's a bright day.

Then a surprise tonight: Kat stayed up late after Betty and Z had gone to bed and she and I talked heart-to-heart for more than two hours.  Maybe Betty and Z put her up to it -- "Give the old subunk a break; he feels you're drifting away from him" -- but I don't think so. She asked lots of questions, some of a very intimate nature.  At one point she hauled out a condom from her jeans pocket -- said her friend Celine had given it to her this morning.  But she, Kat, has a boyfriend (Avery) and she wants guidance.  Not about condom use per se, at least not yet, but about kissing, about what boys like, about what might be a good Christmas present for Avery.  And about career and life things.  "Glen, what did you want to be when you were twelve?"  (Answer: more than anything else a great baseball player, but I also liked science and science fiction and still read lotsa comix.)

All this went down on the other side of the table right here.  Kat morphs into a young woman before my wondering eyes.  She'd love to be a Blue Angel -- meaning one of those daredevil crusading pilots.  She doesn't want to bring kids into a world so ecologically endangered.  Her math, she's very upfront in admitting, needs a lot of work.  She wants to learn Asian calligraphy (and as we talked she did a decent sketch of an egg laid out on my palm -- for an art-class assignment).  She wants a tattoo on her right shoulder blade -- either a rose or her signature image of a cat face, designed by herself.  She wears glitter in the corner of her eyes and she's strikingly beautiful, more so than ever, with sensational full lips and a very wide and dazzling and deeply dimpled white-flashing smile.

Can I help her grow up in a way that will enable her to realize a good portion of her potential?  I think so, if she'll let me.  And now I have some renewed hope she will.

-- So it's been quite a day, yes it has.  It also included a good quickie boink in the upstairs bed as Betty and Kat were supposedly about to roll up in their car (but then they called -- they hadn't even left the house yet).  Then a trip into the island's tiny central town for grub and newspapers -- I wasn't about to do without printed news for four days straight.  Then a roast-chicken feast at this table right here as J&G's grrrl-music CDs played loud in the high-ceilinged room.

And "Mr. Sendfore" is already forgotten, I'm pleased to say -- the name itself, that is.  It was my moniker for much of the Silver Sheep entry but that's where it's ending, I hope.  (As in Z crying out from the bedroom up there, "I'm sending for Mr. Sendfore!")

------

51

------


    HQ triangle tavern.  I finally make it.  And the
one and only window seat.  Looking out on the Christmasy
cobblestone scene.  Twinkly stars hanging in the trees.
    At midnight.  Live music, soulful kind, very loud,
and the blue neon of a "Cocktails" sign to jyze by --
glowing at eye level on the window a foot to my right.
    As December rolls in.  And Hanukkah rolls on and so
does Ramadan.  And Advent pops up and so does friend
June's august ancestor's lunar birthday.  In this
cluster of simultaneities involving four great lineages
of the more or less spiritual type we have something to
cheer about for roughly three out of every four earthly
souls.  And then on the dark side, it's World AIDS Day.
Just in the past year more people have died of AIDS than
live in the entire Jyze City metro area.  Maybe a
billion will perish from it in this century -- an
article in today's paper predicts this -- but I'd guess
eco/climate catastrophe will cut down many of those
predicted victims before AIDS can do it.
    But of course we USAns must focus all our energies
on vanquishing the evil Iraqis.  And after that, or
rather while we're at it but the process may take a bit
longer, on eradicating the evil religion of Islam.
Another think piece in today's paper informs us of this
latter necessity.  Supposedly it's the view winning out
at the "highest levels of the Administration."
Civilizational clash -- in the long run, see, we'll all
be better off for it.  And when we're done with the
ragheads, China should prepare for the bull's-eye to
shift to them.

[ Jyze of the Heavenly Year : White Horse ]


    These are exciting times to be approaching the end
of one's allotted span on the planet.
    -- Meanwhile a new tree grows in the triangle.  A
Christmas tree, this is, with white lights and
trimmings, rising from a plastic-lined plywood cube
packed full of earth.  First time I recall seeing a live
Christmas tree here.  It shimmers directly in front of
the main entrance to the hideaway building, visible from
inside through four porthole-like wreaths, one in each
door window.  And to get in the side door -- the front
entrance is grill-gated over at six every weeknight --
you now need a swipe card, as of today, although the old
combination lock will remain operational for another
week.  Transition time.  One more small instantiation of
the spirit of the age: electrodigitation.
    The band here's funky but too loud.  I usually like
loud, but not this loud and especially not this harsh
kind of loud.  The lead singer goes by the name of Spicy
and is exactly that; she's belting out a paean to "cunt
juice" at this very moment.  A first for me, I'm pretty
sure, hearing this term in song lyrics with live musical
accompaniment.  In truth the tune's not all that
lyrical, but that's the fault of the other words too.
    Today Jess and Gwen got "fogged out."  Jess called
in a semi-panic to tell us this, their flight having
just been canceled because it lacked "fog equipment" and
our whole region was fogged in (and still is).  Z-wiff
calmed her by saying she'd stay on at the house (J&G's)
another day, since she was planning to take tomorrow off
anyway.  I couldn't linger with her, though, having a
big batch of finals to get out, so she drove me down to
the ferry dock and I sailed across to the west-side
terminal and then bused in.
    For an hour or so it was the old life -- the one I
was living a decade ago, plus and minus three years, so
seven years in total.  A car ride down to the dock (only
an occasional treat back then; usually I arrived by bus
or bicycle), a twenty-minute wait in the terminal with
other night workers, then lining up outdoors in the mist
as the ferry glided in and offloaded, the walk up the

ramp ahead of the cars, the rush for booths on the main passenger deck, the rumbling engine, the wisecracking deckhands, the faint shoreside lights slowly sliding by outside the windows.  The main difference is that the ride from the island is too short to get much of anything done, including even a brief nap.  The guy in the booth behind me played a hand or two of solitaire and talked to himself.  I felt akin to him.  I still fit in just fine with the always-oddball night-worker crowd.

Band stops.  I might as well too.  Other than band members and bartenders, I'm now the crowd here.  I'm the one, the troglodyte.  But I've got my December storage payment to mail -- forgot all about it when I passed by the post office and now I'll have to hike back up there.

*         *

-- Later.  Too much later.  It's already past six in the morning and I should be in bed.  And the bed's right here, stretched out invitingly (though unmade) in front of me.  But first I need to add a few paragraphs to the short evening entry above.  Jyze can't stand pat on just that triangle-tavern blurt.

So here's the bad news.  The check still hasn't arrived.  It's been eleven days now.  This is not a minor matter -- we're talking almost forty K.  Lost in the mail?  Or did Lynn maybe fail to mail it?  Set it aside while waiting for me to call to find out what the various holdings added up to and then forgot about it when I didn't call?  Seems to me the chances of its being ripped off from the mails are slight and of hanky-panky at her investment outfit even slighter.

But still -- forty K!  This is way bigger than any other sum I've held or almost held in my hot little (actually not so little) keyboarding/jyzing hands, whether it was my own money or someone else's.  It's about three and a half times what I make in an entire year, or about two thirds of what the average J-town household does, or somewhere between a hundred and four hundred times what the average Chinese factory worker does (while working fifty-five or more hours a week).

Other news?  A brief Thanksgiving greeting from

Elgie was among the voicemails: he wants me to call.
Because it was a holiday I suppose I should've rung him
up anyway -- meaning on the day itself, and whether or
not he called first -- but I've been peeved enough by
his failure to follow up on his assurances to me about
"soon" that I just blew it off.  Note to self: try to
remember this is a kid (though he'll turn Gregorian
thirty next year, so that word also should be in quotes)
-- a "kid" who's facing bankruptcy proceedings right now
-- and not only his own but his mother's as well.
     Meaning I've got another call to make tomorrow.
     Otherwise all's as it was when we left for the
island.  Ciro gathered up our newspapers as they came in
and deposited them in a bag outside the 203 door.  Z
snuck a card into my pack before taking me to the dock
and then left me a voicemail here saying where to find
it.  Funny card too -- built around the thrill that's
professedly hers when she gets a glimpse of bare jyzer
tush and flopping loosey-goosey jyzer genitals while the
dude himself thrashes around naked in bed in the bright
daylight of J&G's uncurtained upstairs bedroom.  (Not
that he does all that much thrashing.  Maybe she's just
making all this up.  But he doubts it.  Still, he rarely
thrashes.  She's the champion thrasher of all the ones
he's encountered over the years and she also knows how
to flash flesh with the best of 'em when thrashing,
bright daylight or no -- and if he hasn't noted this
before in these pages he should go right out and enroll
in an "Essentials for Jyzers" webinar.)


                        [+2]


     Took a day off in search of answers to some key
questions.  Found some too, and got some news, and now
I'm back on the last of the five Nights of Power (and
the sixth of Hanukkah) -- stopping off at the west train
station on the way in to work.  For a leisurely jyze.
     "Anyone else going south?"  A doorman calls this
out just after the PA announcement of the departure,


                        528

last call.  "The whole damn country's going south!" I
want to yell back -- the obvious thing -- but I choke it
down.  Meanwhile a big rumble out there and off they go.

A million people pass through this station annually
now, most of them riding the new commuter trains.  At
the moment only one other person's sitting in here (the
cathedral ceiling was truncated years ago, by the way,
to save heating costs) and he's ensconced about five
feet from me and he's stinking up the joint.  A street
guy who came in to use the microwave which I happen to
be sitting next to.  Terry, from Centropolis.  I
overheard him talking with another drifter a few minutes
ago, but he left.  And I'm not moving.  I like this seat
because it's right under the "No Loitering" sign.

Another big rumble, only bigger.  This time it's a
northbound freight, then eastbound, eventual destination
probably Centropolis.  Whole lotta shipping containers
rolling by, bright colors flashing through door glass.

So all right then, the setting's set.  Now, first
up: the answer to the $40,000 question.  I called Lynn
Monday afternoon.  Her first words: "Uh-oh, does this
mean you didn't get the check?"  I explained the
situation and she signed off to do some "checking
around."  When she called back twenty minutes later the
culprit had been identified: it was the big corporate
broker they work with, a "bit of a glitch" there.  The
broker would mail out the check immediately, she said,
or they could deposit it into my account electronically
if I preferred.  Given my recent bad experience with
receiving it through the mails (even though it wasn't
the post office's fault) I did what I rarely do (when I
have a choice) and opted for electronics.  And last
night when I checked at the bank machine near work, the
money was there.  By a full order of magnitude it was
the largest number I'd ever seen in my bank account.

The final accounting on the deep reserves was
40,420 dollars and some odd cents.  I'd been thinking it
might be as low as 38K, so I was pleased.  I'm working
up a special list for Santa this year.  Ever since the
last time I took an extra chunk out of the deep reserves

-- was it two years ago? -- the long-term upkeep needs
have been accumulating, like maintenance on a building
that's going to seed.  Now I'll do what it takes to keep
this dilapidating pile of bones functional.

Next up, Elgie.  (Terry the noisome has departed, I
should note, and a station janitor in an orange vest has
come by, shining a flashlight under the chairs and back
behind the vending machines.  "Looking for money," he
admits with a grin.  This fortune-hunting is his own
private thing, I'm pretty sure.)  -- With Elgie there's
no news but there's also good news.  The no news regards
his visit to J-town: he still hasn't asked his boss for
time off.  It's just very hard to do, he says.  And now
he's learned one of his coworkers, while he was
dawdling, has requested a two-week vacation in January.
(So I miswrote; some news was also concealed within the
no news.)  And in a small firm they can't both be taking
off at once.  I asked him to put in for one of the weeks
in January when the coworker will be there, no matter
when it falls, though midmonth would be preferable.
He's promised to talk with the boss tomorrow.  He and
the coworker should go in together, I advised; that
would make it easier for both of them and the boss as
well.  He seemed to like that idea.  He's -- again! --
promised to call me as soon as he has a date certain.

The real news -- and this he broke to us in a
voicemail yesterday, his second in a week (the other was
the Thanksgiving greetings) -- is that his first
response to a law-school application has come in, and
it's an acceptance!  The school ranks seventeenth on his
list of twenty-two, but it's a triumph anyway.  The hope
is they'll keep the spot open long enough for him to use
it as a fallback in case no one higher on the list
admits him.  He's not expecting to hear from most of the
other schools until January or February.

A boost for his self-esteem.  And after all the
humiliation he's gone through with the bankruptcies over
the past couple of years he definitely can use it.

He's also started a night-school course in biology.
By next fall he hopes to have completed five more premed

courses, and he believes this will qualify him at most of the schools for a special cross-disciplinary program in biomedical patent law. I assume this means the notion of taking a preparatory legal-writing course (my suggestion to him) has gone by the wayside. I expect he'll regret this later, but maybe not.

And I learned his mother's made more progress in recovering from the stroke. Her left arm was useless at first, but now she can lift a cup and swing the arm when she walks. And the left side of her face was frozen in a slight frown, but now it's animated again and in sync with the right side. This too is very good news. Lady S, after all, is a presiding spirit in these pages, even though she doesn't know it and probably would be displeased if she did know it. Or, again, maybe not. She's a private person but also a performer -- just like the other female Heavenly Year presiding spirits, all four: Ladies U and V, the Z-wiff, and good old Mom -- but she, Mom, not to the stage born as the others were.

He who jyzes can loiter here. She who jyzes too, presumably. I know I've never had any trouble with it. One other loiterer is on the premises at the moment, a snoozer in a muddied pea jacket and navy blue knit cap, presumed Afrusan, with black plastic trash bags containing his presumed worldly goods. No one else. He seems to have some clout with the uniformed woman sweeping the floors, also presumed Afrusan.

In other news, but still big -- just not personal in the same way -- the war drums pound ever more feverishly as the cabal issues new jingoistic warnings: if the evil Iraqi chieftain doesn't fess up by the deadline on Sunday, we're going in. But the Iraqi chieftain seems to be complying with the inspection regime, so the U.S. might find itself in a bind. In effect our cabal's saying the Iraqi chieftain must prove a negative: that he has no WMDs. But unless the inspectors find some or the cabal has evidence not yet revealed, he can say he's complied with the UN demands, and it's at least possible the Security Council (specifically, permanent members Russia and France,

maybe China) will refuse to sanction an attack.  If this
happens and the U.S. attacks anyway, it's likely to
trigger massive protests and backlash worldwide, and of
course especially in the Mideast.

We may know the outcome as soon as Sunday.  Or the
cabal may take a few days to make it appear we're paying
attention to the list of weapons the Iraqi chieftain
will be submitting on Saturday.  Flashpoint could be
approaching.  Or maybe the cabal will wise up.  A slim,
slim, oh so very slim chance.

(Now I discover I was wrong.  Me and the knit-cap
snoozer are getting the boot.  No train's due in for
three hours.  "Fifteen, twenty minutes," says the
uniformed and armed security guy, "then I'm closing up."
I wonder about that -- they're required to keep the
place open -- but I'll play the obliging vagrant and
move on right now, well ahead of the deadline.)

*          *

-- A few blocks away, half an hour later.  A table
boasting an antique gooseneck lamp in the ORB basement
café (which is book-lined floor to ceiling most of the
way around).  In the other room a Sandinista is about to
start reading from her memoir -- although maybe it's a
novel, I'm not sure, or perhaps a memoir in the form of
a novel, just as this paragraph here is part of a memoir
in the form of a novel contained in a jyzebook -- but a
fictional jyze memoir, to be sure, a kind of running
autojyzographical roman a clef focused mostly on the
present.

This cluster began on the first day of a new month
and so do today's entries.  Just before midnight last
night -- but in the first double-hour of the new day,
a/k/a the third watch of the night -- lunar month number
eleven rolled in.  Or it can be considered lunar month
number one, since with this month the cycle starts over.
It's once again the Rat Month, for those who flout
tradition and apply the Celestial animal names to the
months.  And I'm one who does that.  It's the Rat Month!

I'm skipping my usual Wednesday-night WOC visit
tonight.  Too much to do, including over a hundred pages

532

of scoping, a stop at the triangle copy shop, and some
setup work for the next Heavenly Year cluster, because
tomorrow I won't have time to do it (suddenly I'm one
heckuva busy guy again -- and still catching up on daily
reading I didn't, because couldn't, get done at Jess's
place: the far-coast paper and various periodicals that
arrived at 203 while we were away).  And in a sense I
can't go to the WOC anyway, because technically it no
longer exists.  As of yesterday it's been sold to
another chain of gyms.  But night boss T.J. tells me the
changes will be few, and those few, he says, will be for
the better -- maybe even including lower membership
dues.  (Lots of talk these days about the coming
deflation, the odds for which are said by supposedly
expert economists to be about one in five, and of course
by paying less for the same product we at the WOC would
be doing our tiny bit to bring it on.)

Burst of applause for the glamorous ex-Sandinista.
Too glamorous, I'd say.  High-fashionably dressed.  Chic
and sleek and of money she reek!  To my mind not at all
your typical or preferred Sandinista.

Each day I peel back another window on my Advent
calendar.  This one says "4" on the outside and "21" on
the inside and shows a Black Monkey hanging from an
evergreen branch, banana-munching (I'm imagining all
this because I don't have an Advent calendar yet; but
last night Jean said A-mart carries a good selection of
them and she'd score one for me using her employee
discount).  -- Again it was a fine couple of hours with
those wacky Chiusan surfers Vic and Jean.  Again I
staggered off half-snockered, as Jean always notices --
even offering to help me make it down the stairs.  This
round it was bourbon for the first time (Vic noticed
scotch wasn't my drink of choice at the restaurant last
week).  Jean told lots of stories, including one about
her woman friend who likes to say "suck my dick" (it's a
hot phrase among the liberated-women crowd these days,
Z-wiff included) and another about a student working the
Swedish balls in her morning exercise class whom she had
to tell to tuck his testicles back inside his shorts.

Jean likes to talk about sexy stuff.  Vic tends to fall
silent once she gets going -- often he'll pick up a
stack of edited pages I've brought back to him and start
flipping through them, puzzling over margin comments
while she yammers entertainingly on.  And last night she
told me -- as Vic sat nodding in agreement -- that he
regards my editing talents very highly.  "Surely not as
highly as I regard his writing talents," quoth the
quick-thinking, tongue-loosened-by-liquor J-master.
     Tomorrow is June's solar birthday.  I'll be taking
her to a free showing of the new Korean movie "The Way
Home," meeting Vic and maybe Jean at the theater.
They're the ones who came up with the tickets.  Z won't
be joining us; she's got a can't-miss meeting.  She
suggested I invite June in her place as part of the
general continuing campaign to pick up June's spirits.
(And here I'll mention that Z tells me Mick U., head of
another branch at the utility, has the hots for her,
meaning Z.  He's begging her to transfer over and go to
work as his assistant.  "My branch needs you."  His
branch, right.  -- But all part of the daily palaver.)
     Jess and Gwen finally found a plane with working
fog gear and made it back home Monday.  For Z the night
she was alone in that isolated island house was "very,
very scary" -- although she'd stayed there alone before
and thought nothing of it.  What's new now?  "I hadn't
really stopped to consider what the situation is out
there."  (I think a whodunit she was reading may've
contributed as well.)  And Betty, in talking with Z on
the phone, mentioned she was very touched to hear about
the talk Kat and I had on Friday night.  "It's by far
the longest conversation she's ever engaged in with an
adult."  I mulled the matter and decided not to say
anything to Betty about the condom Kat produced during
that conversation.  Flashing on a view of it in the palm
of her hand like a diamond.  The cackle of the Black
Monkey.  "Elegant Monkey," the zodiac says.
     The gorgeous Sandinista drones on.  The cafe
empties out.  The crowd for the reading is good.
Upstairs the early Christmas shoppers are clomping

mightily on the wooden floors.  Creaks galore!  Books
selling like mooncakes!  -- And now big applause sounds,
a long breaking wave, by happy coincidence also nicely
timed to apply to the last jyze sentence of the evening.


------

52

------


   Time for another celebration!  And so I'm stopping
by at the AQ teahouse.  What's more: I've managed to
grab a good table.  It's the middle one alongside the
wall opposite the counter, the "Wall of AQ History."
Shakuhachi music playing.  Varnished wood, bared brick,
ancient tea-making implements and crockery on display --
everything about the place is tasteful.  Including the
coffee!  -- And upstairs, the hotel of my Heavenly Year
solar-birthday celebration.  Our now coincidentally
famous room on the third floor northwest corner, as
depicted in the local Sunday OMP/FAP's magazine spread
(a laminated copy of which is displayed on the counter
to my right -- and with the invisible ghosts of ZAG &
GAZ engaged in frenzied eroto-action on the bed).
   On the way here I stopped by A-mart to drop off a
present for Jean: a single sprig of pink gladiolus tied
with a red ribbon to a can of chicken soup with egg
noodles.  Last night at the movie it was obvious she was
coming down with a bad cold, and I knew from phoning Vic
earlier this afternoon that she'd soldiered in to work
today because they can't do without her at this busy
holiday time.  The florist at the nearby AQ shop
confided she had never before tied a flower to a soup
can for a customer or anyone else.  Jean said it was
also a first for her: no one's ever brought her a flower
meant for her and her alone at her own flower stall.

And I presented her with a card from Z thanking her for
the lotion and bathtub herbs she'd sent over via
"Glenmail."  And then I beat it out of there before
things could get awkward, as they usually soon do owing
to the press of her work.  (She said I'd just missed
seeing Vic.  And then Evan W. shambled by, his bald head
and schlumpy posture and green produce apron all taken
together making him look like he'd stepped right out of
a ukiyo-e sketchbook.  Funny thing: the two best
painters in the entire region -- or at least I know of
no one else as good -- cross paths up to several times a
day in the corner of the A-mart produce section.)

So what's the celebration about this time?  Well,
first it's another of those multifaith festivals.  For
Muslims it's the joyous Eid feast, for Jews it's the
last day of Hanukkah, and for Christians (orthodox and
not) it's St. Nick's Day -- this particular St. Nick
being an important bishop back in the fourth century
C.E.  From him derives, supposedly, the whole Santa
Claus and Christmas gift-giving tradition.

A second reason: I'm now debt-free.  This as of
five a.m. today.  I wrote Z a check to cover the eight K
she loaned me which allowed us to get married, and I
stuck it in one of her white wedding shoes along with a
little note and the usual stone-heart love token and set
them all atop the day's newspapers in the message spot
in my black armchair.  (How's it feel to be debt-free?
Feels like I oughta be celebrating!)

Third reason: this is the start of a big
anniversary cluster.  Gray Rooster.  There were big, big
doings sixty-one years ago.  But I'll get to those
tomorrow in a special jyzeday entry.

Meanwhile the war drums pound, the networks shriek,
the army reserves double down on their calisthenics.
One headline screams that our supreme leader says their
supreme leader "IS LYING."  Another wails "USAN
POPULARITY PLUNGES WORLDWIDE."  The cabal asserts --
offering no evidence -- it has solid evidence the Iraqis
possess proscribed WMDs.  Insiders speculate a massive
bombing campaign -- "softening 'em up" for our invasion

-- could start any day now, though certain
sentimentalists want to hold off until after Christmas
Day for symbolic reasons (they don't openly say this,
but it's not hard to guess what they're thinking; and of
course they don't want to be seeing headlines like
"SANTA FIRES MISSILES DOWN IRAQI CHIMNEYS").

Here in J-town an upsetting Heavenly Year death.
Rich D., a very fine local Cawk guitarist, creator of
the world-famous "Louie Louie" guitar lick, role model
for the two local guitar superstars mentioned earlier --
and a fine jazz and blues musician as well; I've heard
him live numerous times over the past two decades and
even spoken with him a couple of times for a few minutes
while he and his band were on break -- went down Monday,
the day after his sixtieth birthday (in honor of which a
big party was thrown at which he was the featured
performer).  Heart trouble.  Heavenly today, in heaven
tomorrow.  Needless to stress too much, that could be me
too, just slightly delayed.  Or anyone.  And will be one
day for sure, me and everyone, though the degree of
delayedness and suddenness will likely vary widely.

So bye-bye, Rich.  You were a good old picker.
(And forty years ago this fall the fabulous Nomads with
the 'slinger on bass guitar -- thump-thump-thumping in
the most elementary way -- were pounding out, though we
didn't know it, the Rich D. arrangement of "Louie,
Louie" at house parties in various college towns roughly
three thousand miles east of here.  My unbrilliant and
very short career in rock -- how the images do linger.)

-- And for hilarity, this.  Suddenly it's admitted
Bigfoot is a hoax.  The perpetrator died recently (at
Heavenly Year plus twenty) and his brother has now
fessed up, with a photo of the departed holding the
phony Bigfoot feet gracing yesterday's OMP right beneath
the war-drums headline.  Two carved wooden feet worn
sort of like a diver's finned flippers.  In such ways do
fabulous beasts enter the cultural imagination and gods
be born and cults and religions take root.

Other news?  The evening with June was -- how shall
I say? -- okay.  Considering.  It was her Heavenly solar

birthday minus one, it turned out.  She wasn't quite as vacant and moony as she has been, but her depression continues.  She apologized for being "poorly groomed." We wound up hitting a French restaurant near the theater for an early birthday dinner.  I did my best to engage her.  I subtly tried to stir up her hormones (on the theory they might command her mind to reconnect with reality).  Like Mama E, she at times seemed normal.

As with many free movie showings, this one was oversubscribed and big crowds had to be turned away. Vic and Jean were late; we weren't able to hold seats for them (they were lucky to find widely separated single seats).  "The Way Home" was touching -- the Korean granny with her marvelous lined face and carved hands reminding me strongly of Elgie's Korean grandmother ("halmoni"); and the traditional ways of the isolated mountain villagers, meant to contrast with the modern ways of the kid raised in Seoul, to me themselves looked somewhat modern and prettified compared with what I saw in the Korean countryside and even the Seoul burbs just a quarter century ago.  But regardless I was deeply moved -- tears welled up several times -- and not only because the personal resonance was so great (kid being raised by a single mom, clash in the kid between tradition and modernity, absence of father, suffering of grandparents, disapproval of clan -- not to mention familiarity of gestures, language, social setting) or because I so rarely get to see a Korean movie.  And this one was very well done.

But it started late and ran a bit longer than expected.  Afterwards June became more than a little panicky because she'd promised to pick up Adam at the airport at 9:20.  We had to duck out on the quick round of drinks we'd planned with Vic and Jean, and then when June seemed to become disoriented while crossing the street in front of the theater -- nearly walked into the path of a bus as she studied Adam's e-mail -- I decided I'd better drive her to the airport, and did, arriving just as Adam emerged from the baggage-claims area.  It wasn't quite the equal of the rescue of Z-wiff and Mama

[ Jyze of the Heavenly Year : White Horse ]

E in Centropolis last spring -- on the scale of pink-
knight heroism, I'm saying -- but June seemed very
grateful -- afterwards gave me the biggest smile I've
seen from her in many months.  (Earlier she had raved
nostalgically about how happy she was during those late-
night 203 visits of the law-school period -- "I was
too busy to notice then but now I really feel it.")
        -- Oh how fine it is scribbling in the teahouse.
It's indoors, it's well-lit, it has windows only to the
north (or no, also one facing downward into the storage
room with its poignant array of belongings left behind
by building residents during the Japusan "internment" of
World War II and never reclaimed), and it's too early in
the month anyway, but these hours have had a kind of
moon-viewing feel to them.  Quiet celebration!  Good to
be alive amid all the impermanence!  -- Good even to be
impermanent since it's a prerequisite for aliveness!
Alive and, yes, J-sticking.  On a pentimento table,
layers of newspapers from the '40s, sepia toned, merging
into the brown of the wood underneath -- and I'm adding
my own layer in a way and then I'll be making room for
those to follow (as a journal-bearing patron awaits a
table and so I'll yield this one to her).


                        [+1]


        Strange how hard it is to look at this night
straight on.  Is there maybe something to the primal-
scene business?  -- Well sure, think of the taboos.
(Think of them if you can, that is, maybe by declaring
you can't.)
        Sixty-one years ago today.  More specifically
tonight, but first today.  In their tiny garage
apartment in a small southern town near an army base.
The newlyweds -- it's been a few days over six months
since the ceremony -- are sprawled out on the bed and
one of them flicks on the radio and a moment later they
hear the news.  Shocker!  It means their imminent
separation, who knows for how long.  Maybe forever.

Maybe his death or severe injury.
     What they'd been doing that left them sprawled out
on the bed that Sunday afternoon, I don't know.
Evidently it wasn't what you might think newlyweds would
be doing -- at least not in a way that could've led to
the creation of the world's first full-fledged jyzer.
That came later the same night.  How do I know this?
It's written right here in the journal that belonged to
my mother.  Or no, not quite.  What's written is this:
               It was on Dec. 8 that Glennar was
          conceived -- quite elegant, n'est ce pas?
     Is "elegant" exactly the word she wanted?  Maybe
not.  But then, for whatever light it may shed, December
8 is the Feast of the Immaculate Conception.  But Mom
wasn't Catholic, nor was Dad.  Earlier in her college
years she'd broken an engagement in part owing to the
sacrifices asked of her by her then-fiance, who indeed
was Catholic and yet not ready to make similar
sacrifices himself.  So the light shed is scanty indeed.
But the choice of that word "elegant" (the one adjective
she left behind describing the event, even if on the
surface it seems to apply only to the timing of the act,
not its execution) was itself a kind of Elegant
Conception -- maybe just short of Immaculate.
     But December 8th, a Monday that year, would last
until midnight, so how do I know the night of the
Elegant Conception was the night which started on the
7th and ended on the 8th?  (Talking solar time here, of
course, and Gregorian "new style.")
     I know because my mama told me so.  It was
"sometime very late that night."
     After they heard the shocking news about Pearl
Harbor, Dad donned his "civvies" -- "said it would
probably be the last time," she wrote, "and it was" --
and they went out to get something to eat and then drove
to the base where he was stationed, outside of town, "to
see what was up.  Much excitement & tension in the air."
     And then drove back to their apartment, arriving
very late.  Imagine the thoughts, fears, confusions,
needs, excitements.  Adrenaline and many other kinds of

hormones pumping, no doubt.  The intense talk.  I know
for sure one thing they talked about: he might die, and
this might be their only chance to conceive a child.
The timing in terms of her menstrual cycle seemed about
right.  Before this they were using "protection,"
meaning condoms, but now they wouldn't.  And as
serendipity would have it....
     The early morning hours of the 8th of December, but
still the night of "the day that shall live in infamy."
Later on the morning of the 8th the U.S. president went
before Congress and uttered that famous phrase about
infamy, and just hours after that the senators voted and
the U.S. was officially at war.  So on the Gregorian day
I was conceived the U.S. went to war.  "Army Horse."  Of
course it's too much to say it's been at war ever since.
But if on the one hand that was the last time the U.S.
officially declared war, on the other hand it's hard to
think of a time since then when it hasn't been
unofficially at war.  The waging of war without the act
creating war -- sort of the reverse of Immaculate
Conception?  Well, no.  But the official Christian
designation for the day somehow seems appropriate.
     Dad returned to the apartment to sleep later in the
week, but by then it was too late in Mother's cycle for
conception to occur.  (She told me this herself more
than half a century later.)  Each morning he left for
camp when it was still dark.  She wrote:
          I never knew whether it would be the
          last time we'd see each other, or not.
          At night I used to lie in bed & listen to
          the troop trains pulling out.  They
          rattled the entire apartment -- the bed
          even shook from the vibrations.
     So they must've shaken up the future jyzer as well.
The mini, submerged, soon-to-be homuncular -- but as of
yet scarcely even cellular -- 'slinger.
     As it turned out, Dad's orders didn't come down for
another ten weeks or so -- and then he went for further
training in a far-coast state, upper sector, and Mother
was able to accompany him.  Not until mid April did he

ship out for the South Pacific, and Mother was there in
MSM #2 to see him off (and thus I was too,
embryonically).  But they stayed only until the end of
the month in the tiny garage apartment where I was
conceived.  It was a "hectic" time but they tried to do
Christmas the right way, even though "with the heaviest
of hearts."  Then on Christmas Day Dad was, she wrote,
"just a kid."

>        ...[Early Christmas morning] he yanked
>        me out of bed, & midst much gayety we
>        opened our stockings and gifts.  Glen blew
>        on a crazy whistle from Mother S's box, &
>        paraded around the house in bathrobe &
>        slippers tooting & grinning.

-- And I, from my secret observation post, cheered
the Old Bull on.  As I guess I must've also done during
some even more intimate moments during those four-plus
months before he sailed from MSM #2.  Let's give it up
for Mom and the Old Bull!

Sixty-one years ago tonight.  Did he maybe "parade
around tooting & grinning" that night too?  Maybe right
about this time?  Should've!  And even if he didn't, I
can picture it.  (Thanks for the image, Ma!)

Night of infamy.  Terrible, tragic times.  Yet I
can't look upon them in a completely solemn and sober
way.  Even on the darkest of nights, new life, new hope!
And now in our own terrible and tragic times -- with the
outlook quite likely even bleaker than it was then, with
human existence itself clearly hanging in the balance --
I can't help myself, I'm seeing them in the same way.  A
miracle can happen here!  Make love not war!  And make
haste about it!  (But not too many babies, no.  Make
love to the world.  Care.  Act.  Spread the wealth
around.  Redeem.  Resist the haters.  Sequester carbon.
Dismantle the nukes.  Imagine peace.  Make peace.)


[+2]

The mayor declares a drought advisory -- better

start shutting the water off when I'm brushing my teeth
-- but the winter rains are already back.  Flurries of
tippy-taps from the windows and an occasional swoosh of
wind.  A poinsettia, dark waxy green and bright velvety
red, preens on the coffee table -- blocks my view of all
but the muzzle of the Heavenly Year Horse, and a sprig
of Z-bought mistletoe dangles from that muzzle.
     Deep, deep, deep in the night.
     "Frida" at the Metro was better than I expected.
The title character herself was not much like Lady V
after all.  Afterwards a spectacular moon-viewing scene
from the side deck at the Lake J-town fish house: a
lunar crescent dangling just above a thick ground-
hugging fogbank from which the saucer atop the giant
golf tee emerged on one side and the triple radio towers
of north hill on the other, with the lake down below
entirely fog-free and aglitter with confusing
reflections of all the above and the brightly lit-up
Christmas boat plowing through the reflections, its wake
fracturing them even more.  And then the crescent slowly
sank into the fogbank, or seemed to, with its bottom
point faded to vanishing while the top point still stuck
out above like a nose snatching one last breath (a
synchronized swimmer vertically descending feet-first
comes to mind).  All this added an unusual savor to the
fish house's signature salmonburger -- which already
had, as always, plenty of its own.
     Yesterday, dinner at the east-hill apartment of Z's
supervisee Kelly, a true child of the sixties about two
years my junior.  Roughly nine out of every ten books in
her cinder-block-and-wood-plank floor-to-ceiling living-
room bookcase could also be found in one of my bookcases
of the same type at one time or another, including right
now.  She moved to MSM #2 during the Summer of Love just
as I did, "worked social" in Centropolis just when Z
did.  Oddly, they don't click that well, supervisor and
supervisee.  The other supervisee, our longtime lesbian
pal Madge, didn't show -- pleaded bronchitis -- and so I
had to step up strong in conversing.  Enjoyed it.  Even
ate some spicy Mexican food and came out only slightly

the worse for all the heat.  -- But will we be seeing
more of Kelly socially?  Probably not.  Z's awkwardness
with her was a little painful to behold.  Rare too;
before now I've seen this degree of it appear only in
the company of snooty Cawk burban types.
     The war?  High-intensity jockeying continues.  So
desperate is the cabal to come up with a pretext for
their planned invasion, you have to wonder why they
don't just do as many previous administrations have done
(the Gulf of Tonkin hoax certainly comes to mind) and
phony one up.  It almost makes you wonder if they're
just bluffing an attack after all.  But no, this can't
be.  The cost of the buildup in the Mideast has been
stupendous.  The cabal is too macho to be able to back
down now -- they don't have that kind of strength.  "Ha
ha, fooled ya, we were just bluffin'!"  Not a prayer.
     Meanwhile my right knee's throbbing.  I took a
nasty spill on a slick steel sidewalk grate while coming
down the steepest part of east hill after seeing Mama E
off from her doctor's appointment at the usual clinic.
It was a brutal reminder of what I'll face trying to
hang on to my city-walker/flaneur's life into old age.
I needed every bit of my remaining "spryness" to escape
serious injury this time.  If such a spill were to take
place a few years from now I suspect it would put me in
the hospital.
     But Mama E was in fine fettle.  Eyes sparkly, she
told me lots of stories as we awaited the cabulance's
arrival (her ear's healing just fine).  During holidays
when Z was growing up Mama E volunteered to work the
floor at the big downtown Centropolis department store
(where she'd been employed for years) and she'd get so
tired that one time on the way home on the bus when her
street was approaching she called out, "Lamp
Department."  She also confided she doesn't need a radio
or TV anymore because she can hear holiday music playing
in her head and listen to it for hours -- "Silent
Night," "The First Noel" -- and as a patriotic bonus
during these fraught times, "America the Beautiful."
     Pearl Harbor Day this year came and went with

little public notice.  It got some, of course, but
nothing like last year, when it was the sixtieth
anniversary and the 9/11 attacks were fresh in the
public mind, having occurred just under three months
earlier, and the similarities, both real and imagined,
between the two attacks were milked for all they were
worth by the jingoists and reactionaries trying to
impose hard-ass right-wing values on the country.  And
they're still at it today, scheming to do the same, but
this year Pearl Harbor just doesn't have the resonance;
suddenly it's our own country that's about to launch a
"preventive" war against the Iraqis pretty much as the
Japanese did against us -- to expand the empire.
     Ach, ethics!  Politics!  On the 301st day of the
Year of the Water Horse.  "On the edge of a transforming
moment for America in the world" (as a certain pompous
liberal interventionist and globalizer pundit I love to
despise wrote yesterday in his column in the far-coast
paper).


------

53

------


     Darkest day of the year.  Gloomiest too.  So you
pry open the window of the Jean H. Celebratory Advent
Calendar and it's -- the Festival of Light!  St. Lucia's
Day!
     Back in the old country this is a day to be
reckoned with.  Gram and Gramps viewed it the same way
for the new country too, even though the new country
wasn't all that new to them, both having been born here
(although none of their parents were).  Every year on
this date out came the candles and the strange little
Norski cakes.  But it never caught on with their non-

ethnically educated son who became my father.  I'd
pretty much forgotten about those celebrations until Vic
H. reminded me of the Norwegian holiday practices.
Then, wow, Marcelian return!

And today Holly R. left an inspiring voicemail
message.  In the past she's always handed out candles on
this day, but this year she let the practice slide.  And
truly the times are dark this year.  So -- imaginary
candles sent by telephone to reconfirm our quest for
peace and "enhanced sanity."  I like that.  Go, Holly!

What's more it's Friday the 13th.  And I've been
kicked out of the apartment.  Seems unlucky all right.
Amanda, that lean mean cleaning machine, is doing her
thing.  She says she approves of my putting up signs
indicating "No-Clean Zone."  "I like eccentrics.  I'm an
eccentric myself."

So I followed the narrow road to the north.  Black
umbrella.  Feet soaked -- iridescent puddles.  It's the
antifungal time of year for toes.  Backpack soaked
through to the inner stormguard bag.  I thought of
Olwen's haiku club making its annual trek, this time
through the arboretum, and saw lots of good haiku
material myself, including a gull guarding a sopping-wet
discarded jacket on a sidewalk bench outside the J. City
U law school (where June studied) and a big Scottie dog
leaping for snacks held high beneath a bright green
umbrella that for me brought back Japan days.  And all
the way I was treading carefully, dodging not just
puddles and cascades but also gray metal manhole lids.
I'm still sore all over from Monday's spill on the
hillside.  Those slippery lids are everywhere!  I've
come across only one -- and it was on the steep sidewalk
outside the downtown concert hall -- that was coated
with a gritty antislip material, as they all should be.

Up at the six-way corner I walked beneath the Black
Horse sign (logo for an Italian auto dealer) and then --
why didn't I think of doing this before? -- went in to
see if they carry gear bearing that logo.  And they do!
Being flush these days, I bought eighty bucks' worth: a
cup, cap, keychain, fridge magnet, and paste-on decal.

I'm still lusting after a red beach towel and a flag -- but the two together would be another hundred bucks.

Turned west, walked a block up the hill to the pancake place. And here I sit. Breakfast consumed -- it brought back my Yuke era and another franchise belonging to the same chain. The chain's food is still as bad as ever but when you're at peak hunger it can taste pretty good -- and in any event, always more or less the same, which is to say: you know what you'll be getting. And the coffee is also always the same but in this case meaning worse than ever (so it seems); and yet if you're craving caffeine....

And a felicity. My "server" is Lindsay, an occasional fellow rider of the last bus to the hilltop. A sweet short-haired platinum blond from the rural south-central part of our state, probably not much more than eighteen years old -- maybe even less than eighteen -- she finds it "awesome" that the only living jyze grandmaster is doing his thing in her section.

It is gloomy out there, yes it is. Says the other server on duty to a newly arrived customer: "Here's a seat with a view -- the best I can do." Traffic labors by on the back side of the hill, a major thoroughfare that cuts through the area diagonally. Across that road, another angle on the jumbly campus of Jyze City U.

I got hit with a new first-time question last night. Mr. Y at the market that bears his name (on the edge road half a block from the art museum) asked it. I've been buying bananas, fruit juice, and soda from him there -- and at a previous market a few blocks away where he worked for several years before branching out on his own -- for seventeen years, off and on. "When you gonna retire?" he asked. "Ain't!" I cried, suddenly in total denial. (When it gets right down to it, is there any other state to be in? It's all in how, not whether, you deny. -- But of course this doesn't apply to climate-breakdown denials.)

That leaping dog beneath the green umbrella, it wasn't green itself. But this is the cluster of the Green Dog, or Wood Dog.

[ Jyze of the Heavenly Year : White Horse ]

     What I was wondering about last week -- why the
cabal hadn't hoked up a pretext for attacking Iraq --
turned up cherries this week.  They've tried three.  One
blew up in their faces, more or less, canceling the
other two (but I'm sure they'll come up with more --
they're utterly shameless).  The facial came from an
unflagged North Korean vessel stopped by two Spanish
warships acting as U.S. surrogates (hench boats).
Hidden beneath bags of cement they discovered some nasty
chemicals and the makings for twelve Scud missiles.  The
cabal knew these were destined for our bought-off ally
Yemen, but they were sure Yemen would not claim
ownership and bring world condemnation down upon
themselves and therefore the cabal could announce
falsely, and did, that they were destined for Iraq.
Importation of missiles by Iraq would constitute
violation of a U.S.-engineered UN resolution.  But Yemen
tossed a wrench in the works -- claimed ownership.
Shrapnel in U.S. countenance.  No choice but to let the
ship continue on its way.  Cringe cringe -- it's okay,
see, for Arab dictatorships like Yemen's to possess
WMDs.  It's okay for North Korea to make them and sell
them -- an "Axis of Evil" charter member!  (And this
week North Korea let the world know the restart of its
nuclear program is retaliation for the cabal's cutoff of
fuel deliveries and abrogation of the 1994 treaty under
which North Korea agreed to halt that same program.)
     Other uproars too.  Forget forest conservation --
chop down our regional forests and our green regional
out-party politicians with them.  But even bigger: an
in-party senator from the deep south -- the majority
leader in D.C. -- says we'd be better off if our society
were racially segregated.  This too blows up in the
cabal's face.  Their party can't win elections without
support from northern burbs (southern racists alone
aren't enough) and northern burbanites don't like to
think they're supporting open racists.  They want cover.
And the cabal has no choice but to give it to them, and
so the cabal chieftain openly scolds the southern
majority leader who openly favors segregation.

It'll blow over.  But like the Scud ship incident,
this one lays bare the real workings of the system.
     As always, but even more so, much is happening.
Hector on the bus (Mexusan guy who's lately been
absorbed in a highly apt book: "History of the Rise
and Fall of the Roman Empire") -- Hector, I say, is
delighted because it's Feast of Guadelupe Day and he's
talked with his father in Mexico City on the phone.
Stan R., painter and poet, teacher of writing for Lady V
at her MSM #2 college back in the day, husband of
vampire writer Anne R., dies in a southern coastal city:
it's his Heavenly Year.  The Sunday OMP/FAP runs a large
feature on the urgency for boomers of writing last wills
and testaments (and me a pre-boomer, or "silent gen,"
intestate).  Z-wiff's having gum trouble, may need a gum
graft; she thinks it's stress-induced and tells me
she experienced something quite similar during the
crackup of her engagement to Arvin twenty years ago.
     And another fine Tuesday evening with Vic and Jean.
"Glen, are you going to keep coming over," Jean asked,
"after Vic's finished with his book?"  My reply: "No way
you're getting rid of me!"  Vic talked of his worsening
memory problems -- that day he'd blanked out on his own
phone number -- and his latest computer mess-ups.  Jean
filled me in on Ro's burgeoning sex life (he's taken up
with, Jean told me, "a big-boobed Jewish princess from
the burbs").  Jean and Vic squabbled a bit over the
itinerary for their upcoming trip to the megastate to
celebrate Jean's parents' seventieth wedding
anniversary.  Well plied with cheapo bourbon, I
staggered off at eight p.m. for another night of SUI:
scoping under the influence.
     But Elgie?  Not a word from him.  Still!  And
so I've decided the heck with it, I'm not going to worry
anymore.  If his visit happens, it happens.  I'll send
him a Christmas card next week and remind him I'm
holding three hundred bucks in reserve for his round-
trip plane fare and hoping he can make it up for MLK
week or the one immediately thereafter.
     And sister Barb?  Same.  No word from her either.

[ Jyze of the Heavenly Year : White Horse ]

She's never replied to my birthday letter of more than
three months ago.  So I'm letting go.  It's her move and
that's it.

     Christmas cards -- this is the weekend I try to get
mine out.  My plan is to do half a dozen of the
perpetual hand-painted balsawood cards for people I
didn't know or wasn't in communication with last year.
For the rest, year 2003 "tabs," as with license plates,
to cover the "2002" in the upper right-hand corner of
the perpetual cards I sent them last year.

     -- And my own first card came in.  From Ron H. of
the "lost branch."  I never answered his letter sent
after his visit last February.  His message is short and
perfunctory.  But I'm intending to make it up to him.
(And to Z-wiff too.  We're already talking about the
post-Heavenly Year orgies to begin on February 1, the
first day of the Sheep Year.)


                         [+2]


     Just what I didn't want to happen.  I'm losing my
jyze focus!
     It's the Ides of December.  It's Natividad kickoff
day.  It's Bill of Rights Day.  I'm facing a heavy
workweek and all kinds of Christmas-related tasks.
(Why?  Because I want to!  But also because -- I must!
I've got a rep to uphold and will pay a heavy price if I
don't uphold it!)
     So what do I do?  I blow the hours I'd set aside
for tonight's jyze session.  And it was fixing to be a
humdinger!  I was planning to hike up to east hill and
split the session between the primo javahaus (with its
flickering "Darkest Day" candles) and the notorious
east-hill tavern where the Z-woman once did a highly
intoxicated and no doubt intoxicating -- and scantily
attired "to the min of the min," as she's told me --
dance atop the bar (way back before I knew her, sixteen
years before to be exact -- her fortieth birthday).
     Instead I got caught up in reading one of the J-

550

books for the terrible Year of the Blue Pig -- and
that's next cluster's year!  I sat down to check out a
couple of things and suddenly it was four hours later
and I was bathed in sweat.  I'd even neglected to prop
open the hideaway door and turn on the fan!

A big stack of our "joint" Christmas cards awaits
me at home.  Z-wiff's already done her part on them.  We
agreed to get them out by early tomorrow at the latest.

And there's so much that ought not go unmentioned.
Last night the eagerly anticipated Christmas ball put on
by the city workers' union at a club on north hill.
Aida and her new boyfriend couldn't make it but everyone
else did, including June with three Chiusan lady friends
and David with four-months-pregnant Stacy (and just a
day earlier David had won a divisionwide employee award,
a big deal!) and Wei with Gray Sheep Alison -- her
Heavenly Year will start up, as will June's, the very
instant mine ends.  (And so Alison spent much of the
night cadging tips from me on how to wring the most out
of hers.)  And Z wore her new red-silk Heavenly Year
long jacket (actually it's a Great Year coat depicting
the twelve animals but only one elemental variation of
each animal) -- and it was sensational!  But the DJ
wasn't.  The chief organizer quietly complained to Z,
who was already crushed.  What, no funk music?  No
"Popcorn"?  No "Sex Machine"?  We all agreed the dude
was a dud.  I danced twice, and one of those was with
June who doesn't really dance, and especially now.  But
then my sore bones couldn't've taken much more anyway.

National news, lotsa stuff.  Can't go into it much.
Maybe it's just as well.  The former veep for the
previous administration and victim of the cabal's stolen
election (with the reactionary Supreme Court as crucial
accomplices) says he won't run again in 2004.  A
Catholic cardinal resigns in the continuing priestly
pederasty scandal that's rocking dioceses nationwide.  A
rightfully despised former secretary of state, because
he doesn't want to reveal his private clients (like
Saudi Arabia maybe?), resigns from his 9/11 inquiry post
two or three days after accepting appointment to it.

And the uproar over the remark about segregation roars
on.  The senator who made it was once a cheerleader at a
state university just down the road a piece when I was
an exchange student at Tuscaloe College.  A barely
reconstructed pink supremacist, this pathetic man.
Somehow he spaced out the fact that members of his party
aren't supposed to champion segregation before the
national press -- only in private.

Z spent all day working on Christmas cards with the
four D-clan granddaughters (the girl group from our
wedding -- and in my mind they'll go on serenading us
forever); that's why she has so many cards ready to go.
But Grampa D's lymph cancer is resurging (as is Olwen's
brother's colon cancer); and yesterday Mr. D lost his
balance on a ladder while putting up holiday decorations
and took a nasty spill.  Fortunately, though, he
suffered only minor bruises.

Tomorrow Z's hoping to take Mama E on a Christmas
shopping tour.  Fingers crossed.  Yesterday Mama E
wanted us -- delusionally -- to call 911.  Yet even so,
on balance this week was one of her best since coming
out here.

Again no word from Elgie.  Again nothing from Barb.
And I have no hint of an idea what I can do for my Z-
wiff in the way of a Christmas gift or gifts.  Yike yike
yike!


------

54

------


Deep in the bowels of the hideaway building.  Just
where, I won't even try to describe.  But it's the night
of the full moon.  And the pressures of the season are
still pressing hard on me.  Very hard.  Furnace rumbling

and growling.  The big steam pipes are issuing almost,
it would seem, from the core of the earth itself.  A
single wooden chair and lots of bricks, a naked bulb
about five feet up.  Some of the passages back around
the corner must lead down into the underground of the
old city.

And personal news?  Much.  In fact I'm sitting on a
chunk of it.  In a single day letters came in from two
of my sibs.  The one from Barb I haven't even opened
yet; I'm saving it for later.  The one from Rob I
haven't read either -- that too I'll get to when I go
home -- but Z scanned it as I rushed to prepare a batch
of cards for mailing and she told me about a big
surprise: cousin Kar and his wife of five years, Kerani,
have separated.  And Kar's in town or soon will be and
he sounded out Rob on the chances of crashing at his
place over the holidays and Gail vetoed the notion.  We
may be next on Kar's ask list.  I'll wield my own veto
on that, I suspect, if Z doesn't beat me to it with
hers, which she probably will.  But we've already agreed
to invite him over for Christmas dinner, assuming we'll
get the chance to do so, along with Rob and Gail and --
another surprise! -- Mama E (if she's able and willing).

So ratchet up the holiday pressure another notch or
two.  Maybe come up with a goofball gift for Kar so he
won't feel totally left out.

To top it all off, a big rush job swooped in and I
spent most of the evening at the scope office.  When
this happens it's a lot like deadline night at a small
newspaper: Naomi shows up in person and waits to snatch
pages for proofing as fast as I can churn them out.
-- Which is fun in a way, yeah.  And it's a job and the
pay's not half bad and the perks are fabulous.

Naomi said my perennial card from last year is
hanging on her tree at home and she always wonders what
might be coming in next from me -- like this year, for
instance.  Heh heh, I think she'll be pleased with my
"update tab" for that same card.  I've mailed about
twenty of them so far with a dozen still to go,
including Naomi and Larry's.  But for them I think I'd

better drop the "Disclaimer" note that's accompanying all the others.  It refers to certain cards of mine from last year being inspected by the Postal Service for subversive content (which really happened -- and that's all the more reason to drop it, especially for Assistant U.S. Attorney Larry the terrorism specialist).

Every time I hear some rustling back in the shadows by the janitor's shelves I expect a rat to skitter out. "What you doin' on my turf, Jyzer G?"  Hasn't happened yet but it still could.  Or maybe a bat or two.

Also a card came in from Olwen with a haiku she'd written specially for me, and so I wrote her a couple back on the spot (surprising myself, I did, I did).

Out in the larger world things are poppin'.  Aside from the skewering that the in-party's absorbing for letting their bone-deep racism show so openly, it's all bad.  The cabal announces it will deploy an antimissile system ("Son of Star Wars") on our coast out here for the express purpose (purported) of shooting down North Korean missiles.  Since North Korea, furious over the cabal's arrogant treatment (abrogating treaties and including their country in the "Axis of Evil" with Iraq and Iran), is restarting their nuclear program, few folks here are objecting.  The cabal wants to neutralize any North Korean threat to retaliate should we happen to strike them first under our new preemptive strategy announced back in March and reaffirmed in September. Even more, this is a chance for the cabal to advance the right wing's long-term plan to construct a Fortress USA capable of riding out the ecoclysmic mid-twenty-first century upheavals which our own economic and environmental policies have made all but inevitable.

And then there's our Iraq war.  Just today the cabal declared Iraq in "material breach" of the UN resolutions on disarming.  An attack is justified right now -- that's what they're saying.  But they've decided to be "patient" and await the official report from the UN inspectors.  The cabal thinks it has its ducks lined up at the Security Council and thus it won't be obliged to act unilaterally.  It's probably true; the fix appears to be in.  Big-time bribery and threats work.

The next major crunch date, at which point everyone expects the UN to okay an attack, will be January 27th or thereabouts when the inspectors report back to the Security Council.  In the meantime we'll be sending another fifty thousand troops to the camps along Iraq's borders -- right after New Year's -- joining a similar number already there.  We've even announced this.  Later in January a huge call-up of reserves is expected and the size of the invasion force will again double, to two hundred thousand, maybe two fifty.  The soften-em-up bombing campaign will start with the big booms just about the time of Chinese New Year's on February 1st -- booming in the Year of the Gray Sheep and booming out the Heavenly Year of the Black Horse.

So be it.  So it has been ordered and so it will go down.

"Bah-bah-bah humbug, yeah, okay," I'm writing on some of my cards, "but ba-ba-ba BING the Year of the Sheep!"  Z's worked up a snazzy political card around the theme of "regime change at home" and peace on earth.

Elsewise?  (It seems to be heating up down here and that's odd at this time of night -- almost three a.m. Maybe a warm front is rolling in and reactions are sluggish at the steam plant, whose big black brick chimney sticks up like a giant "We're No. 1" finger a couple of blocks north and one west of here -- because El Nino is picking up and we're due for a warm spell while the big storms strike farther down the coast. Then again I heard on the news this afternoon we should expect a storm ourselves tonight, one packing winds of sixty or more miles an hour.)

Elsewise, as I was starting to say, again nothing from Elgie.  I sent off a card to him and tried to keep it both upbeat and laid-back.  Instinct tells me he's having trouble over his matched mother-and-son bankruptcies and maybe his job too and he's too ashamed to tell me.  But I don't think I should pry about it. If I could help out in any significant way I might go ahead and be a buttinski regardless -- but I can't.

That's the policy and I'm holding to it.

Today the Z-spouse attended her long-awaited leadership conference.  On returning home she told me one "actor type" rubbed his leg against hers under the table ("I moved mine back after a suitable pause for giving him the raised-eyebrow look") and another, a woman, told her she, Z, has "more presence in your little finger than most people have in their whole megillah."  And -- it's true!  She does!  I'll testify to that!  (But I'm still planning to look up the precise meaning, if any such exists, of "megillah.")

As for our interpersonal gift situation, the Z-babe and I, she compromised and agreed to -- or rather proposed, and I agreed to -- a limit of "one regular and one small," referring to magnitude of presents.  So the pressure's still on but not to the extent it was.  I'm waiting for ideas to hit.  Inviting them.  And we're now several hours into December 20th.

Christmas Eve we'll be attending an open house at Vic and Jean's loft.  At three o'clock Tuesday afternoon they decided on impulse to do some entertaining this year and by the time I panted in at five-thirty (after the usual four-flight climb from the street, each flight about fifteen feet) they had most of the decorations (which is to say -- lots) up and the tree half festooned with a superb collection of handmade ornaments, many of them one-of-a-kinders hailing from their Italy days. My timing was excellent: I hauled out the balsawood perennial card I'd painted for them and it went right onto the tree.  Twenty minutes later not a single needle of free space remained on that tree.  Because I was present as a Praetorian guard for my ornament they found it circumspect to bump a couple of others, somewhat smaller than mine, to runner-up spots atop a bookcase.

With a twinkle in his eye Vic gave me a copy of the annual Christmas letter he'd just completed for mass mailing to friends and family (some two hundred in all). A paragraph of it went to a "fortunate encounter" with a former editor from MSM #2 who's since been helping him with his book on growing up in Chinatown in the thirties

and forties.  Jean went off after a while to meet a
friend and Vic and I had a good editing talk that kept
digressing to other topics.  As I left he said something
about our friendship being truly extraordinary.  Maybe
we tell ourselves that too much.  But -- it seems true
to me too.  You reach Heavenly age and you realize how
rare and special this kind of friendship is.

Yow -- it's late!  And I have yet to mention this
is a Blue Pig cluster.  "Pig Passing By."  And that a
gorgeous green light shines atop the great white tower
for seasonal reasons and from the south-hill perspective
seems to beckon almost like the one in Gatsby; and with
a full moon shining behind it and just to one side as
seen from a downtown perspective just hours ago --
zowie!  Meanwhile the storm-stripped square plywood pot
for the HQ triangle's live Christmas tree has been
replastered with paper holiday decorations.  For a few
days everything was in tatters -- and this made for a
fine soulful shabbiness at the heart of the 'rangle.


[+2]


Longest night of the year.  Solstice night.  I get
to spend a big hunk of it in an armchair, either the
black one in the living room (as now, with a newly
poured weekly glass of the good bourbon) or the green
one in the bedroom (as Z-wiff tosses about fetchingly
and yet not at all restlessly -- just normally -- before
me).

Iranians celebrate this day with a festival called
Yalda.  It hails from ancient Persian times when
Manicheanism was the prescribed way of seeing the world
-- everything black or white, dark or light, sullied or
pure (a way of seeing that's still highly favored under
other names, including by the neocons running the show
in Washington, D.C.) -- the Iranians stay up all night
partying, feasting, reading aloud poems and stories, the
whole point being to assist the sun and light and
goodness in their struggle to make it through this

longest night.  And of course I'm trying to do something quite similar myself by means of this jyze.

But in truth to me personally, as regards my own life anyway, it doesn't seem a dark night at all.  Far from it.  Light floods in!  The news is good!

If we were still in high Roman times, this would be the peak of the biggest festival of the year. "Saturnalia."  Everything turned upside down: the slave acting as master and the master as slave, wife as husband and husband as wife.  Christianity found such antics heretical and brought in Christmas as a sober and solemn replacement, little realizing the transformative power USAn flacks -- that is, Mad Ave -- would wield some sixteen or seventeen centuries down the pike.  Now we're back to empires and Saturnalia of a sort but we might better call the latter Santanalia (ho ho).

Sun hits its farthest-south point and turns into a Capricornian Goat.  Moon is spectacular: makes the front page in gorgeous photos in both OMP and FAP.  Last night it was stunningly, shockingly beautiful -- Cold Moon, it's called -- presiding in a glowing white palette-shaped setting (moon like a large round illuminated hand hole in the palette) with black wreathes and puffballs and smoke rings racing by in front of it and endlessly shape- and light-shifting.  For a crazed selenophile such as myself this was the night of all nights all-time, the lunarly sublime of the Heavenly Year -- as seen especially from car windows on the way to and from Craig A.'s annual solstice party and out the back window there too.  And from the high bridge as well, enough so nearly to make me drive off the side and tumble us down into the valley and quite possibly demolish a chain of jungle/rez encampments down there.

Earlier that afternoon -- yesterday -- I signed my bucks from Mother's estate over to the city credit union at a measly 2.05 percent interest rate and then re-upped at the WOC (now officially under new ownership but jyze will stick with the old name) -- Z-wiff joining me for both signings -- and then we visited the wooden-toy shop, one of my favorite gift-hunting spots for a couple

of decades now and soon to close its doors forever, and
then hit the ORB on the same block and ran into Betty
and Kat, whom we met again tonight -- but this time by
arrangement -- at the J-town children's theater (Lady U
thespian turf of long ago) to see the D-clan girls
perform in "The Best Christmas Story Ever" (they were
fabulously cute "little angels"), and then at Dak and
Serafina's we gushed over the mini-starlets up close and
in person (they were overexcited and behaving badly --
blew big squirmy iridescent -- and very wet -- bubbles
in my face until dad Dak gently intervened).

But the good news announced earlier. This Heavenly
Year tale will, it now seems almost certain, have its
dramatic ending. Elgie answered Z's e-mail with one of
his own apologizing for not letting us know sooner, but
only this week did he obtain approval to take MLK week
off and so, yes, he'll be coming up then. It's gonna
happen! Already Z and I are scrambling over who'll be
doing what, both during the prepping process and while
he's here. "KILK" is the principle I suggested (though
Z as usual came up with the killer acronym itself): Keep
It Low Key. But...that might not be possible. Aida
even wants to throw a welcoming party for Elgie!
Sheesh. (And I learned Aida now supposedly thinks I'm a
very "humble" fellow and I've "done lots of good work on
[my] white privilege." -- Of course Z would've thrown
me out long ago if I hadn't been laboring away at that
all along, and the same goes for Ladies S, U, and V.)

Also, one of the parcel services has tried to
deliver a package to me with an MSM #1 origin,
presumably sent by Elgie. But otherwise we don't know
much. In fact, nothing. And so I'm planning to call
him at Christmas, the eve or the day of. (He did
suggest we work out the visit details by phone because
his internet computer is "broke." In Z's view this
means he's broke himself -- financially -- and I think
she's probably right. She also wonders if it might mean
his mother has access to his e-mail and she's not too
happy to see it includes a message from my wife, also
known as her son's stepmother. And I'd say that's

another strong possibility.)

   Nor does the good news end there.  Barb's letter is promising too.  True, it explains that her lengthy silence and failure to reply to my birthday letter (which she calls "wonderful"!) is owing to the loss of her ethicist job at the academy at about the same time I sent the letter and also her failure to find another job in the months since, and of course neither of those outcomes is good at all.  But she seems to be doing all right otherwise -- perhaps she's living off her portion of Mother's estate, or maybe Keith's able and willing to carry the full load for a while -- and she sounds ready to bury the hatchet with me.  She doesn't say this in so many words, but she does say she and Keith would like to drive up to see us one of these days.

   So, good news -- if, that is, it holds.  Over and over again Barb and I have managed to mess up our rapprochements.  And in any case an actual meeting is not likely to take place during the Heavenly Year, so what good would it be anyway?  -- No, I don't mean that. It would be good!  Maybe I'll try calling her for Christmas too.  It's the kind of gesture a Heavenly Year geezer might almost be expected to make.  (The actual meeting could even be delayed a bit -- say between twenty-one and thirty-three months -- and thus provide a bit of drama for her own Heavenly Year.)

   And then more good news, almost as shocking: brother Jeff also wrote.  Just a note, it's true, and not as a solo production but as an add-on to wife Angie's annual card, but it's several sentences long and it shows a bit of droll antiwar humor while also mentioning it's possible he and Angie might lose their rental house in Lahontan as a direct result of the post-9/11 cabalian economic downturn.  Just from his tone I tend to think they'll land on their feet.  And I'm more than a little pleased to know the door to Jeff is still open.  So I'm thinking maybe I ought to try to call him on Christmas Day too.

   Z-wiff, meanwhile, in response to my continued pleas, has agreed to a second Christmas compromise.

we'll delay our own gift-opening ceremony until the Sunday following Christmas.  I had to cash in some of my Mama E "enthrallment chips," as Z calls them, to succeed on this, and also I reminded her, Z, I'd agreed to do the same for her last year after her half-sister's death, when we delayed the ceremony until the Olde Christmas of January 6: "the 12th day of Christmas," which is to say: Epiphany.  And I suspect by the time all the scrambling over December 25th has run its course we'll have renegotiated the matter again and settled on January 6th for this year too.  "YOZGOC II," we'll christen it: Year of Z&G's Olde Christmas II.

Today I talked briefly with brother Rob on the phone, inviting him and Gail to drop by Vic and Jean's for the Christmas Eve open house.  They can't make it -- Gail's getting back into town late that same day after her trip to Mentoka during the library's budget-cut closure week -- but I did learn he's known since October about Barb's losing her job -- she mentioned it in her birthday letter to him -- but he'd forgotten to tell me about it.  And he said he would let Kar know he's invited to our Christmas shindig if Kar happens to call him again, but he, Rob, doesn't have a number where Kar can be reached.  Like me, Rob's puzzled about why Kar would want to come to J-town -- Kerani's turf -- for Christmas if they're splitting up.  You'd think he'd go to the far coast or the megastate to see his own family.

Z stopped by A-mart today to buy flowers for the "little angels" of the pageant.  Jean picked them out for her and also threw in a fine curly-leafed poinsettia for us for free; I'm looking at it right now, centered on the window ledge and contrasting so vividly with the black backdrop of the longest night.  (How long does the longest night last in this city?  Fifteen minutes short of sixteen hours, from 4:15 p.m. to 8:00 a.m.)

Jean described herself to Z as an extrovert and said when Vic and I are up in their loft -- we "loners," she called us, and included Ro as one too -- she feels her space is being intruded upon and she just has to get outta there.  But I wonder about this.  I suspect she

has a loner side herself (doesn't everyone?), and it
happens I drop by on her day off, one of the few times
she even has a chance to be alone.  On Christmas Eve
she's scheduled to work until six and yet she and Vic
are still hosting the open house.  Talk about sociable!
(Vic called and left a message for Z just so she'd hear
directly from him he was hoping she could attend -- a
very admirable thing to do, I think.)  -- And Evan W.,
working a few feet away from Jean, told Z he loved my
perennial card "update tab" and hoped he'd be getting a
new one every year.  Can't fail to mention that.

     I should note, too, the openly racist southern U.S.
senator and majority leader has been forced out of
office in record time.  His own party did it because, as
noted before, they wanted to prove to all those northern
white burban voters that they're not supporting a bunch
of ignorant Ku Kluxers.  Far be it from them!  -- And
the deposal probably happened with sufficient dispatch
that it'll be taken to show just that.  Too bad.
Politically this cabal is no slouch.  Again, too bad.
The country, the world will suffer greatly for it.


------

55

------


     Long deep wet Christmas Eve.  Z-wiff all snug in
our bed.  Jazz piano riff on "The First Noel" tinkling
quietly from the radio.  While I in my black armchair --
and also my green Jeep cap, my maroon sweatpants and
badly fraying long-sleeved blue henley, with my ponytail
wildly unlooped -- settle in for a long winter's jyze.
     And the Rat is Red!  Fire Rat!  "Rat in the Field."
As the Heavenly Year rounds the bend into the home
stretch, the second half of the last Great Year: the

back half of the White Horse.

And the three poinsettia are strategically arrayed. The strings of Christmas lights mounted on the big side-by-side bare-lumber bookcases at my back are glowing in a trial run. Z's white platform wedding shoes on their plinth atop the smaller of the bookcases are tapping out a happy imaginary holiday jig. The bag of gifts for Gail and Rob, who'll be arriving at four p.m. (twelve hours and twenty minutes from now), is standing ready on the dining table. The refrigerator is puffed up like a blowfish with the co-op's Christmas dinner to go, turkey being the main dish.

But Mama E probably won't be joining us. She called today and left a message saying she's "too sick." That may well be the case, but in addition she's likely afraid she'll embarrass herself and us with her incontinence, and I think I'd feel that way myself if I were her. But she also wanted to please her daughter, who in turn wanted so badly for her to come. So for a while she, Mama E, said yes, she would come. And now she's saying no.

Nor does it appear Kar will be showing up. As of six hours ago he hadn't called Rob again, and we still have no way to reach him. I'm hoping he might put in a last-minute appearance. And wouldn't that be vintage Kar: a flash of sheepish grin at the door and then he sails on in. "Where's the grub?!" But no, the fact is I'm feeling for him. I'm remembering what that first Christmas was like for me after Lady U and I split up -- not to mention the truly miserable Christmas we went through a year earlier while still in the slow-motion act of splitting up -- and not forgetting Kar is now within a year or two of the age I was then. His marriage to Kerani, in fact, came later in the same year Lady U and I parted. And I even recall his annual Christmas letter from that year trumpeting that he'd found the love of his life. This year, no annual letter from Kar. (Other than my brothers and sister, he's the only Sandefjord or Hutcheson of my generation with whom I've maintained ties, however tenuous at times, for his or her entire life.  Though in truth that's usually been much more his doing than mine.)

News comes on -- I snap it off.  Dead-of-the-night quiet now.  Juddery ticking of three clocks.  I've already heard enough about the Israeli tanks oh so magnanimously withdrawing to the borders of Bethlehem and the new U.S. threats directed at North Korea and North Korea's threats back.  If we attack them, they say, it'll be "uncontrollably catastrophic" for us.  Or more likely for South Korea and maybe Japan and certainly for themselves.  The North Korean regime is not pretty, but when it comes to wreaking catastrophe upon the world, no one holds a candle (not even a Christmas candle!) to the good old USA.

And a merry Christmas to you too!

Z has tried her best but since hearing about her mother's cancellation she's been less than her usual exuberant self.  What a year it's been for her.  It was just at this time last year that Camilla died, her half sister and, other than her mother and Camilla's son Jacob, the only relative with whom she was still close. And seven years ago tonight her longtime friend and onetime housemate Manny, husband of Betty, adoptive father of Kat, died of heart failure on the operating table while undergoing a liver transplant.  Tonight after we opened the gifts from Betty and Kat and talked with them on the phone -- they'll be taking off at noon tomorrow for places southwest -- she broke down and wept as she described for me once again the night of Manny's death, how she and Betty and Kat came home and watched "The Grinch Who Stole Christmas," then went back out to see some other Christmas movie, in the middle of which Betty began wailing loudly.  Two years ago on Christmas Eve the four of us set candles afloat on "Manny Lake" in his memory -- and that was, and is, right behind the children's theater where we saw the pageant the other night.  But it was a blustery, drizzly evening back then and the launchings were not a success.  -- Then again the ongoing familylike relations with Kat and Betty have been highly successful, I'd say, and this is quite an unexpected kind of blessing for all of us -- and most of all, because most unexpected, for me.

Betty gave Z two books as Christmas gifts: "The Vagina Monologues" and "Cunt."  That shows Betty's respect for Z as a person out there on the foaming edge. We gave Betty "The Sopranos Cookbook" and a bubblehead of the sonorous Norusan "A Prairie Home Companion" guy, a longtime favorite of hers (but not of mine or Z's).  I personalized it by adding these Z-dictated words around the hatband of the guy's fedora: "I don't know why I have such a weakness for dames from the Dakotas."

Z's aforementioned nephew Jacob sent a gift package, including a Swiss Army knife for Z and a cube puzzle for me.  This was something he'd never done before for her, much less for me -- but, again, it was his mother, Camilla, who died last Christmas.

And then we opened the package from Elgie.  Z called the parcel service and had them deliver it to her office or it never would've reached us before Christmas. Inside we found a box from a fancy department store containing two scarves, one beige, the other bay (rusty brown).  Gasped Z, "They look like cashmere!"  But no, acrylic.  It's good to know this kid who's grappling with two bankruptcies is not crazy enough to be sending us cashmere scarves!  But we were both touched he would send anything, and especially that he'd make a his-and-her gesture like this.  Z immediately claimed the bay scarf and I bet she'll wear it too.  Me, I'm not a scarf man anymore -- they make no sense for long-distance walkers in J-town since they just soak up the winter rain or mist and make you even colder as well as heavier -- but I used to be a scarf man in cities with other kinds of winters, and maybe Elgie's mother told him that.  Though I doubt it; I don't think he'd ask her and I don't think she'd be happy to know he's sending us his-and-her scarves.  But I'm planning to keep mine right here -- maybe even dangle it from the extender arm of the floor lamp whose shade floats a few inches above my head.  -- Yup; just hung it there and it fits in quite well, draping down onto the chair so that my left shoulder rests against it.  And if a chill should strike, it's right here, closer than the heater.

    Earlier tonight we hit Vic and Jean's open house. For me it was a trip: so many of the names I've been hearing over the past several months took on faces and bodies and started talking in ways I both did and didn't expect.  Among them were the "boring" mathematician Les and his moviemaker wife Kyoko who met the same way Z and I did and at even more advanced ages and who do indeed seem "wildly happy together" just as Jean had said.  Nor was Les "boring" to me -- though Z was surprised at how "aggressive" a conversationalist I was with him (as she stood with her chin pressing into my shoulder blade, a twitch signaling it was time to go).  Ro was up in his loft-within-a-loft for much of the evening bongoing for one of the young female guests.  The loft as a whole looked spectacular with its holiday trimmings but it was chilly; at all times a crowd was gathered around the radiant heater.  Z, as sometimes happens when she's among a large group of strangers, became the mysterious silent one, wandering off to study Vic's paintings up close (the walls are covered with dozens of them) or to sit alone in this or that corner.  Effervescent Jean seemed surprised.  Vic was more than a little red-faced from drinking scotch.  He and I were drawn to each other as always -- Jean kept introducing me as "Vic's editor" -- but we had little chance to do any real talking until the end, with Les, and then just as that started taking off, Z's chin twitch kicked in.  But on the way out I waxed smarmy and said to Vic, "A big part of why the year has truly been Heavenly for me, Mr. Commissioner" -- he was once an arts commissioner for J. City -- "is that I met you," and he said it was the same for him -- and I have no doubt that's true too.

    Out on the HQ streets, though, things were grim. Rainy, cold, blustery, lots of homeless people already stretched out for the night -- Christmas Eve! -- on benches or flattened cardboard boxes in doorways, and others still panhandling.  And there we were -- well no, this was when we arrived -- but carrying wine and a tray

of hors d'oeuvres from the co-op.  As the Christmas
adornments on the plywood box for the evergreen flapped
soggily in the wind, both before and after.

Sixty years ago "White Christmas" was a brand-new
release and I was less than four months old.  And on
this same day in that same year the first surface-to-
surface guided missile was tested in Nazi Germany.  I
know this because I read about it in today's OMP.  And
the tester happened to be the same Nazi rocket scientist
whose path I was to cross a couple of Great Years later
at Mezzu, at which point he was supposedly
rehabilitated: had become a good democrat (oh sure).

Mother and Dad, they'd be pleased to know I'm still
a kid at Christmas.  So blessed and privileged I was as
a youngster -- so many happy Christmases we had.  So
exciting.  So loving -- even then I thought so.  But I'm
much more aware of it now.  I'm also aware of what
mostly eluded me then, and my parents too, I'm sure, and
most Eurusans: how much others had to suffer that we
might be "blessed."  And yes, to our shame -- meaning
that of all Eurusans -- direct causation was involved.

Santa -- the old St. Nicholas, this invention, this
myth, this hoax, a kind of Sasquatch in reverse, he's
gone through a couple of millennia of changes and here
we are -- ho ho ho and a bottle of memory blaster.  And
ain't it fascinating!  The whole dang pageant, and I'm
talking about the putative adult version now.

At my feet the usual coffee table.  On it the same
fabulous cast-iron terra-cotta Black Horse now bedecked
with mistletoe along with the necklace of Z's Heavenly
Month countdown messages from last summer.  Also, a
green African bag, cost five bucks, acquired at the Tree
of Africa festival we attended with Gerry and Leola.
Also the "curled-leaf" poinsettia given to Z by Jean,
whom we didn't know a year ago, and the framed photo of
Elgie, who seemed beyond the edge of the world a year
ago, and a stack of Christmas cards from the likes of my
formerly estranged sister and nearly estranged middle
brother.  So a lot of good things have come down the
chimney this year, yes, and not a single missile among

them -- yet.  And perched atop the makeshift cedar album
chest at the far end of the table, the ever-growing
evergreen Rob and Gail gave us several years ago, now
serving as our Christmas tree.  No lights, no action --
it's just standing there, prime symbol for the day.
     A richness here.  Yes, I'm pleased, almost to the
point of tearing up.  And now I do, check it out!


[+2]


     -- Here it is at last, the old hood.  Yet another
old hood, but this is the hood of the Red Rat Year and
also the upcoming Purple Ox -- last hood before the
present one.  It's been a long process of homing in for
this annal and now I'm almost there.
     Homey doing his J-thing on Boxing Day.  Was living
in the apartment building across the street here at the
time of the ballyhooed Boxing Day storm of '96.  They're
still talking about it six years later -- the city shut
down for several days when a deep freeze hit after a
foot of slushy snow fell -- talking about it in part
because tonight another big storm's supposed to roar in,
not with snow but wind gusts up to, again -- and even a
bit more than last week -- seventy miles an hour.
     In my day our local coffee colossus hadn't yet
claimed this spot.  First floor of an historic building
which at that time was still being restored.  Right here
is where edgeville began.
     Blue and red cop lights are flashing in the street
outside, casting glints on this shiny maple table by the
window.  Farther south, bursts and flows of bright neon
signs with scattered lights of the night skyline
shimmering above.  As I used to do so often back in the
day, tonight I walked straight up the edge road from the
hideaway.  In five years, despite the ongoing yuppifying
and technifying of this area up here, not much has
changed along the way leading to it.  (I couldn't see
inside my old unit B-2 from the alley half a block down
the hill; the blinds were closed and the lights off.)

On the way here I passed right by the three other places where I might've lived, but didn't, during the B-2 era.  They represent the paths not taken.  All three would've led almost certainly to a Z-wiff-less future.  What would've become of me?  Whatever, chances are slim indeed it would've been even a faint shadow of the splendid life I have now.  I totally lucked out!

It's the day after Christmas.  That means it's also the first day of Olde Christmas, as celebrated in that hardy seasonal standby "The Twelve Days of Christmas."  This is relevant again this year because, as predicted, Z-wiff and I have now extended our compromise another week and we'll be celebrating Christmas a second time on Sunday the 5th of January, also known as Twelfth Night, the eve of Epiphany as observed by the church.  This will give both of us more opportunity to come up with gifts and, from a jyze point of view, will also lend a little drama to the middle period between the high holidays of the Solstice Santanalia and the resurrection of the son (no cap!) on January 18th or so.

So in place of unopened Advent windows, which of course ran out on the 25th, we've got a countdown of "Twelve Days" doggerel.  The eye flashes in the wing of the partridge in its pear tree and that's because it's winking.  First day of Kwanzaa!  We light the first candle of our kinara, which occupies the spot on the dining table where the menorah once stood.

And last night on that same spot the Christmas candles held forth.  By coincidence, and for the first time ever, we used the silver candleholders Kar sent us as a wedding present.  It was a lovely feast.  The cost of the catered meal, I learned today, was $99 plus tax, which isn't bad at all.  Thirty bucks a person, say, wouldn't get you half the pig-out in an authentic sit-down restaurant, and the leftovers will be feeding all four of us for several days.

Highlights.  Let's see.  Rob wore the white hemp shirt we gave him for his birthday.  (For some reason Z was amused when I noted after they'd left that Rob's hair is thinning even faster than mine is.)  Gail told

the story of her nightmare mission to Mentoka last week
to wrest her father's ashes from the grasp of her
brilliant but seriously unhinged half-brother (or half
the ashes, actually; her father had directed that they
be split equally between his first wife -- Gail's mother
-- and the second, the brother's mother).

I asked Rob if he wanted to take a crack at carving
the turkey and he wound up doing all of it.  He'd
completely spaced out his long-ago Christmas request for
copies of "Zeno's Conscience" and "Oblomov"; he didn't
even recall hearing about them before.  (I chalk this up
not to aging but to the odd selectivity of memory.)  As
Rob looked through the packet of old photos of Dad I
learned for the first time he thinks the star of "About
Schmidt" (and "Five Easy Pieces," "Easy Rider," etc.) is
the spitting image of our father, especially as he
looked in the seventies.  Myself, I can't see it at all.

And I learned from Barb's Christmas card to Rob
that she's still on unemployment -- it runs out in March
-- and she often attends afternoon services at a nearby
Catholic chapel and loves the live musical performances
there (Lady V and I once had an agonizing run-in on the
steps of that same chapel).  The most impassioned talk
of the evening came over Elgie's applications to law
schools; Rob viewed it as "just plain wrong" that he had
outside help with his essays.  Since Z and I supplied a
large portion of that help, we objected.  It's always
been true Rob's much more the ethical purist and
idealist than I am.  -- We also talked a lot about vites
and supps and the pros and cons of strenuous exercise of
various types.  And during dinner Serafina popped in (a
big surprise!) with a gift for Z, and the two of us
escorted her back to the car to say hello to Dak and the
two little actresses Dalisay and Tala (each holding a
freshly cut red rose in the backseat).  Today -- and
only yesterday did I learn this -- Sera turns fifty.

For this special occasion we brought out Mother's
best china, of which she left me a four-settings portion
(I think Jeff has the other four).  Afterwards I did all
the cleanup, nervously washing the china by hand as

Christmas jazz played and the Christmas lights glowed.
I thought a great deal -- and Rob and I talked a great
deal -- about those marvelous Christmases of our
childhood.  All the work -- the dishes, the cleanup, the
setup, the restraining of excited kids.  And Rob gave me
a stroke or two by saying my own shenanigans back then
were a big part of the excitement of those same
Christmases for him.

*

And meanwhile what news?  Well, North Korea issues
more nuclear taunts but the Empire can't be distracted
right now from its main upcoming war.  Word is antiwar
Germany will be chairing the Security Council in January
so we'll wait to pull the trigger until after February
1st, when a more pliable chair takes over.  A poll says
we J-towners oppose the war by a large margin but the
state as a whole supports it and so does the country as
a whole, as long as it's shown Iraq really does have at
least one of those WMDs of which we have, yes, tens of
thousands.  So far we haven't been able to convince
anyone they do, even though we say we have evidence they
do.  So why don't we send the UN inspectors already
inside Iraq to confirm the existence of the weapons we
say we have evidence of?  Simple -- because we lie.
Everybody assumes that's why.  What other reason could
there be?  Not that it matters a whole lot.  It's
probably not even worth phonying up evidence.  Just go
in there and dominate!  (A marvelous color photo got big
front-page play in the far-coast paper and no doubt many
others.  Santa in a Mideast desert, standing before a
semicircular crowd of thousands of U.S. marines wearing
desert camouflage.  All is dull brown and tan desert
tones except bright red Santa and a few red regimental
flags.  It's the new hyper-imperial Santanalia!)
Meanwhile new studies show the likelihood of
catastrophic abrupt climate change is much greater than
previously supposed.  Abrupt, it turns out, is how
climate change almost always is when the system is
stressed.  And we're stressing it as it's never been
stressed before -- not in the last billion or two years,

571

they say -- except for a few times by the impact of
massive meteors or widespread volcanic eruptions.
     -- This coffee shop's closing early, I just
learned, in fearful homage to the big storm headed our
way.  Twenty minutes to go.  I'm asking myself if I'm
all jyzed out anyway.  Thinking maybe so.
     -- No, I should mention first I did leave a
voicemail for Elgie on Christmas Day.  No call came in
from him or anyone else.  But Z belatedly found a card
from him hidden among the packing slips in the box for
the scarves.  It was just a brief greeting presumably
dashed off in a hurry at the store.  Notably, the card
showed a chorus of yellow happy-faces -- five, no less
-- and Zoelie's name, even though he's seen it spelled
out dozens of times, was written "Zolee."  But I'm not
letting any of this faze me.  I'm still planning to
enjoy getting to know him even if I can't -- and
shouldn't -- patriarchalize him, not even in the sense
of doing some fatherly nudging.  Or maybe I'll try to do
just a tiny bit of that to see how he'll react.
     That's it.  Red Rat entry already all it will ever
be.  Hie on home early before the storm hits.


------

56

------


     The Ox is Purple but today's also Calling Bird Day,
as on the fourth day of Olde Christmas, a/k/a YOZGOC II.
And after calling on Mama E with holiday greetings
earlier this afternoon, I'm now dropping by our original
meet cafe, Z's and mine, to celebrate the prime Purple
Ox anniversary.  Hallowed spot here, right down to the
same table, even the same position at the table (though
the chair I'm pretty sure is a different one).  And on

the bench seat to my left the disembodied spirit of
Zoelie B. disports just as the embodied one did on that
day.  My backpack is holding down the second chair.

Three months short of six years ago that was.  The
actual meet spot, the magazine shop just around the
corner, is still there and the name's still the same,
though the place is up for sale.  And the hood itself
has been technifying at such a rapid clip that we rarely
come out this way anymore, except to celebrate the meet
anniversary.  Soon we won't be able to do that either;
this cafe itself will be closing down.  Permanently.  An
article about it in the OMP says the owner's not
interested in catering to the dot-com techie crowd which
has pretty much taken over the hood.

A ritual nod, that's what's actually happening
here.  (Strings of Christmas lights are glowing along
the tops of the wooden bench backs, green ones, I should
note, and blue ones in the front window and doorway.)

The smoldering look of appraisal, the notorious
recoil when I "innocently" put a hand on her arm.  I a
youngster of just four and a half Great Years.  She
feisty just as advertised but also strikingly blase' and
indifferent -- "passable," she was thinking about me, as
she told me later, but that was only the first
impression.  If it held up for the whole meet scene it
did so just barely -- apparently.  What do I know?
Everything worked out, it was a miracle (therefore),
we're still at it and I expect will continue to be at it
until not just one but both of us are gone, and -- amen.

Last cluster of the solar year.  Before it's over,
the Gregorian calendar flip.  (We're thinking of doing
something on that evening after all.  Maybe we'll hit
the fairgrounds and watch the hyper-hyped New Year's Eve
midnight fireworks ceremony up close.  Just this once,
despite the crowds, because it's the year it is.)

For news?  I'm obliged to report the headlines.
Another 25,000 troops are called up, ordered to pack for
Iraq.  A huge hospital ship sets sail for the Persian
Gulf.  Meanwhile it's leaked that we'll handle that
other acting-up Axis of Evil outfit (N. Korea) by

diplomatic isolation -- make 'em give up their nuke
ambitions or else shred their economy.  Starve 'em out.
Hey, that's the humane route!  Kudos for our cabal!
(It's also the very thing they lambaste the previous
administration for having tried to do with Iraq.)

   Last night we dropped by David and Stacy's for a
little Kwanzaa get-together.  Quentin and Genessa were
there and so was a Eurusan couple from the northern J.
City burbs -- and one of the guy's original growing-up
burbs happened to be the very one that malshaped me for
life (though I liked it fine at the time) -- yes, it was
Gatewood.  In fact the dude lived exactly two blocks
west of our house at 2015 Gatewood, where I resided
from age five through twelve; he was at 2215 Gatewood.
But he's six years my junior and in a number of ways
quite different from me -- politically and arts-wise and
like that.  He must've lived about two houses from the
W. family -- but I didn't think to ask.  He was there
only five years.  He didn't recall brother Jeff at all
though they were just a year apart and attended the same
high school (Gatefield South) for three years.

   And: Elgie finally did return my call.  It was
Saturday afternoon and he was visiting the beach with
some buddies.  They'd planned to rent bikes but it was
too cold for that (wait until he gets to J-town in mid
January!).  I was not very successful in trying to draw
out of him the kind of things he'd like to do during his
visit.  But he said he's excited about the trip, and I
liked him for saying that.  He also said he'd received
rejections from two of the lowest-ranked law schools he
applied to.  Not a good sign, I agreed, but not that bad
either, considering that a school of slightly higher
rank has already accepted him and he has yet to hear
from most of the schools on his list, including a very
good one which specifically asked him to apply.

   It also came out that his mother still does most,
maybe all, of his cooking.  The poor Lady S.  Zoelie's
eyes rolled when I told her this and she asked, "Did she
cook for you too?"  I reminded her that in traditional
Korea men were not even allowed to enter the kitchen --

any such transgression would bring horrible things down
on the whole family.  And Lady S's mother lived with us
when I was in Korea and had some very traditional ideas,
including that one.  Lady S herself had it too, I'd say,
although in largely disguised form.  That's probably why
she ended up cooking for the 'slinger for the year and a
half we lived together in MSM #2, while I was working a
day job so she could stay home and concentrate on her
many arts: dance, calligraphy, painting, fiction,
poetry.  -- But explaining these things isn't easy and
never was, except in a few cases with non-Koreans who'd
actually lived with a traditionally minded Korean.

     Elgie's lining up his flights now.  He's trying to
find one on Friday the 17th with a return on Sunday the
26th.  Almost ten days he'll be up here.  And what he
really wants to do, he says, is "talk, you know, catch
up."  And I'm hoping we'll be able to do just that.  And
for sure I'm aiming to do my part.

     -- The cafe is slowly emptying out.  Music's turned
up louder now, possibly to cover sounds of clanking
dishes hitting the washer in back.  White stucco walls
and ceiling, which is high, fans spinning up there, and
through the window which I glance up at now a city bus
was once visible tumbling maybe a hundred feet through
the air as it fell from the high bridge, its driver
having been attacked by a man with a gun.  Memories!
(I'm not saying I have that memory myself, other than a
makeshift version created from descriptions and photos
in newspaper accounts.)  -- But a new series of
postcards for sale at the magazine shop features the
great old clubs of J-town, a dozen in all, and in
looking through them I realized I'd visited every single
one at least a few times and several many, many times.
"My J-town."  Ephemeral too -- before long the postcards
will be all that remains of those splendid hangouts.

     And I meant to mention: today's Betty's birthday
and she called from the southland.  Loved the Kid Noir
bubblehead.  Kat came on monosyllabically but you could
tell she was in paradise down there -- Nick, Nick's SUV,
Wanda's swimming pool.  They'll be back New Year's Day

and this year they didn't ask us to pick them up -- ever
since Mama E arrived they've held back on that type of
request.   -- And Mama E was not feeling good.  She did
eat a little Christmas pumpkin pie.  Z and I had to
scratch off all the lottery tickets nephew Jacob sent
her, along with a surprisingly affectionate letter which
has caused Z to cancel her plan to chew him out for a
thoughtless diss he laid on her mother on the phone.  At
one point Z broke into tears over Mama E's lack of
responsiveness -- her dismissiveness -- regarding the
gifts and cards Z and I made for her.  It's disease and
age doing it, but sometimes it's hard for Z to hold this
firmly in mind; it doesn't fit well with her need to
keep her hopes up.  Before we left, Mama E put me in
charge of "guarding" the fifty bucks in cash Z gave her.
It's burning a hole in my pocket right now.
        -- So now our meet joint here would like me to move
on.  Loud music stops.  Chairs scrape the floor -- some
are mounting, with help, tables.  (I'm admiring the
daisies in the vase on the next table.  I'm tempted to
extract one for ceremonial presentation later to the Z-
woman.  "Guess where this came from!"  -- Well no, it
won't be happening; the cleanup guy just hauled the vase
away.  My root beer bottle too.  -- "Sure, sure, take it
all, I'm done and that's a fact.")


                        [+2]


        -- Who knew in Gregorian '62 that this place would
become the linchpin?  Symbolic center, sort of.  Pivotal
spinpoint.  Or something like that.
        In the shadow of the giant iconic golf tee.  The
old food arcade, I mean in here we're literally almost
straight down from the slowly turning dish.  The one
with the big electronic Christmas tree up on top and
also lots of explosives bolted down on the roof and the
sides as well.  In about an hour they'll all go kaboom.
        The food arcade is rockin' down below.  We're on
the balcony directly behind the stage where a cover band

is blasting out "Midnight Hour." It's the only place we
had a prayer of grabbing a table. And did! One with a
checkerboard painted on it! The arcade daycare center
behind us provides plenty of jyzin' light. Folks are
lining the rails four or five deep and blocking our view
of the pandemonium down there but that's all right.

Z's off wandering somewhere. She's not in a jyzing
mood. Several thousand people are squirming around in
the huge echoing single room, steppin' out, kickin'
back, jes hangin' and chillin'. Elders such as us truly
are in short supply here tonight. An even bigger crowd
is already gathered around the fountain outside, their
trampling feet releasing a delicious grassy smell so
strong you could almost get high on it (in midwinter!).

Seventies-type music, the ad said. It is that.
Real folks everywhere in view, from urban gangs in
flying formation to brave burban family units in tight
hand-holding self-protective mode.

First time in my two Great Years minus one standard
Gregorian year in J-town that I've made it inside the
fairgrounds for this signature event. It's the one
night in the year J. City is guaranteed to make the
national tube for any reason not related to sports.

Standard year's ending. In some places that
standard is called the Horse Year even though the timing
is Gregorian -- Japan, for one, and Nepal, and probably
a few others -- but of course not here. Nonetheless I'm
feeling some sense of an ending. The next month will be
a kind of bonus, the 25th hour or 19th hole or, indeed,
13th month (though it's actually the 12th moon).

Thirty-one days from now no yearly wrap-ups will be
appearing in the media of the Gregorian domain. No
annual lists of ten best this or that -- books and
albums and movies (we caught a pretty good one earlier
tonight, "About Schmidt," but I didn't see myself or Dad
or anyone I know in it, no, and I did wince at the many
cheap anti-sixties and anti-common-person jokes). The
end-of-year lists I've been coming across this week
contain few works I've viewed myself or that I've wanted
to view. You'd think this might mean I'm nearing my

personal final launch stage.  And I am!  But still, the
annual lists seemed just about as unbeckoning to me ten,
twenty, thirty, forty years back.
    -- Now word's going out on the monstrous echoing
PA, each syllable almost literally a chair lifter, that
the music's ending and everyone should hustle on out to
the ceremonial grounds; and the Z-woman is back just in
time to urge that we get a move on pronto or pay for it
later.  I'm running with you Z-spouse!


[+1]


    So here's 2003.  World Peace Day too (no lie!).
I'm ensconced -- black armchair.  Whose story I now know
better than ever before.
    But before that, this.  The fairgrounds fireworks
were, as expected -- but better than that --
spectacular.  Downright pyrotechnical!  We leaned
against a tree trunk and just about kinked our necks out
peering almost straight up to watch them.  The fireworks
featured so much red white and blue you'd think it was a
leftover Fourth of July display.  Or they were kicking
off the USAn Year or the USAn Century or, as many of
cabalian bent like to say, the Second USAn Century.
Huge crowd, highly diverse, oohing and ahing and often
majorly doped up or openly toking (the fireworks smoke
masked it nicely) or chugging illegal beer or wine (or
all of the above at once and maybe more or much more).
    Almost nine minutes it went on.  The grand finale
knocked our socks off but we quickly slipped them back
on, as it were, and zipped out of there to beat the
crowd.  The trouble was that, as one might expect, many
others in the crowd tried to do the same.  But we ruled
because of our excellent parking spot, like pole
position at a stock-car race.  Dodging squadrons of
drunks staggering in the streets in numerous spots, we
made it home well before one.  Z hit the bed in a flying
dive and I went right to work on her Christmas present
and stayed at it most of the night.

[ Jyze of the Heavenly Year : White Horse ]

    It's Swans A-swimming Day.  Also Kwanzaa Dimming
Day -- that is, last day of.
    Earlier tonight was Adele U.'s annual First Day
shindig.  June and Aida came here around six and we
drove through a "driving" (better, "antidriving") rain
across the lake and through the woods to Adele's burb.
Fine food and good talk, much of both Japan-related
(Adele's a Japusan and just a few weeks short of ending
her reign as JACL president).  No gossip-worthy
incidents to match Aida's bird-dogging of Adele's
Japusan date Colin in a previous year (and then a week
later Emiko's bird-dogging of Colin from Aida at Aida's
annual Twelfth Night blowout, and the Gang of Eight
Asian Women's Caucus founders has never fully recovered
from all this heated Colin-induced action -- though
Emiko was present tonight and making nice with Aida).
    Serafina and family were also present, and it was
from her I heard the story of the black armchair.  This
chair goes all the way back to the days when she and Z
were roommates -- the Manny era.  It led a wild social
life.  Unspeakable things happened in it and around it
-- but Sera couldn't be too specific because Dak was
sitting right there (but the events under discussion
took place close to a decade before he met Sera -- who's
the same age as brother Rob, and she's a quintessential
Dragon if ever there was one, except in size).  I also
learned Z had a cat in those days -- first I've heard of
a cat in her life -- that liked to sharpen its claws on
this chair when it wasn't occupied by a cavorting couple
and at least one ribald occasion when it was.
    In the car coming back I acted up a bit.  Aida was
waxing more pious about religion than I could graciously
put up with.  She solemnly inquired if I had remained a
member of the Gatewood Community Church until I left
home.  "No," I said, "just until I got a mind."  I meant
to say "mind of my own," which would've been bad enough,
but for some reason my tongue froze after "mind."  Hope
she wasn't too insulted.  Guess we'll find out at her
Twelfth Night party on Sunday.  The talk quickly turned
elsewhere and I couldn't tell how she'd reacted to my

gaffe.  Something about Aida consistently brings out the worst in me.

June seemed, as usual, marginally better but still not good.  Her red velvet pantsuit which she filled out so very nicely at previous First Day parties now looked several sizes too large.  She scarcely even reacted when I reminded her that her own Heavenly Year will be starting up the very instant mine ends, just as mine shadowed Z's.  Z was encouraged because June got into a conversation with Kit N., the formidable J-town city-council member, and seemed to hold her own at least for a while, at which point Z stepped in to rescue her.

So, New Year's Day.  I put up the narrow Japanese Sheep Year calendar on the equally narrow column by the refrigerator where the narrow Horse Year calendar had hung.  It starts with January 1, unlike most calendars for the East Asian lunar year, and shows a long narrow herd of goofy Sheep and says "Sheep like to be with Sheep."  And Horses, even though famously carefree and independent, also like to be with Horses.  Funny thing, Aida is a Horse.  (June's staying at her place tonight. Aida herself is staying with Mather, her new main squeeze.  Mather's Heavenly Year will be starting, Aida noted at the party, the instant June's ends.  -- I've got them all talking Heavenly Year lingo just to humor me.  Before I came along few had ever heard of it, including even some descendants of Celestials.)

I wish the Sheep Year calendar showed a Horse for January.  But -- all the other Horses are still in place in unit 203 and they'll carry on until the end.  Just from my spot in the black armchair I can see at least eleven Heavenly steeds.  -- And also see a ferryboat key chain with our housekeys already attached -- Z bought it for Elgie.  Twice tonight I heard her refer to him with great pride as "our son."  I greatly liked that.

So then -- do I have any resolutions?  Just the usual one, I guess:  Keep on keepin' on with the resolutions already in place, until they die a natural death or are pushed aside by newer, stronger, better, or at least different ones.  That could happen at any time

but most likely not in the couple of hours left in today
by NUT count.  January 1 is a notoriously bad day for
resolution formation.

Looking back big-picture style at the Gregorian
year just expired, I'd say it was without a doubt one of
the worst in modern USAn history.  In a way it was even
worse than the Civil War years, because this was the
year we made it clear we'll either rule the world or go
down fighting and take it with us (with our nuclear
threats, our withdrawal from international treaties, our
endorsement of policies that will lead inexorably to
global roasting and numerous other kinds of ecological
calamity).  Were we secretly crossing our fingers when
we did any of these things?  I think not.  Are any of
these statements of mine exaggerations?  Don't I wish!

Can anything be done?  Maybe.  Nothing's certain.
In any case: best to keep trying, yeah.

Try what then?  Don't know.  Work for peace,
consume less, oppose any and all further extensions of
USAn power.  And spread the word.  (I should say oppose
USAn power and corporate power except where the two
clash directly; then, for now anyway, support corporate
power -- and how I do wince to say that.)

Am I anti-USAn?  No!  Anti-hegemonic USAn!


------


57


------


Upstairs at the primo javahaus.  Condensation blurs
the westward downhill view of up-close inner-city
skyline and does it very pleasingly.  Even so I'd still
be able to see the new moon if it hadn't ducked behind a
wide-body tower.  Last moon of the Heavenly Year.  It's
an Ox moon, as the last moon of the year, any lunar year

of the Celestial or Celestial-derived kind, always is.

Around me plenty of seeming moonglow is lighting up
faces, but it's being shed by laptop screens.  Until
about a decade ago in this spot it would've been candles
doing more flickery and romantic (to me anyway) facial
illuminations.  Eight of seventeen tables are occupied
on this triangular black-ceilinged upstairs promontory,
and the faces at five of the eight are digitally
transfixed -- as aptly electronic music plays on the
house sound system, weird bubbly outer-space noises.
Soundtrack of an old Buck Rogers movie, almost, except
for some only-from-Moog riffs (Moog came after Rogers by
a decade or more, I'd say) (and JRX Moog).

But it's good here as always.  Chess players
downstairs, students, scribblers, lovers, bohemians,
even a couple of readers of fat literary books.  The
house coffee takes me way back because it comes from a
caffe (yes, with two Fs) in MSM #2 -- the archetypal
Beat hangout has been branded! -- and I like it, I like
it, it makes me feel even more at home.  It's as if
we're coming together, linking up, keeping the faith, we
people of the moon in a sun-seared, ozone-leaking world.

It's a special night too.  Twelfth Night -- "Or
What You Will" -- but pipers piping and in an hour or so
drummers drumming out the Christmas season in
preparation for tomorrow's Epiphany: the holidays end,
the cabal returns to D.C., the new and even more
reactionary Congress convenes.  As a cabal functionary
is quoted in today's far-coast paper: "Once we get back
to the capital, January's going to be quite a ride."

For us, Z-wiff and me, this was Christmas Day.
It's Olde Christmas, we're olde, so why not?  YOZGOC II.
As usual I was Mr. JIT, Just-in-Time, drenched in sweat
in the overheated living room at seven a.m. as I cut the
last of the cabinet boards after laminating the ninety-
six altered cards before mounting them.  I also came up
with a cover for Z's daytimer, a color-copied collage
made from a dozen of the already framed cards on display
in the living room with "I will not overschedule in
2003" written across them in white script some twenty

times as in student blackboard punishment assignments.
Not too shabby if I do say so myself, except that in a
few places the lamination didn't quite take right and
caused the cover to look a bit gravelly.

Typical husbandly fare, especially the "Do-it-
yourself Cabinet Door Repair Kit."  I couldn't help but
think of Dad and his utilitarian gifts for Mother and
her half-kidding pouts because she'd been hoping for
something a bit more romantic.

For me Z came up with exactly the pair of moosehide
moccasins I'd been pining for.  She also gave me a
bagful of small lovey-dovey items, including three
featuring Black Horses: a blank journal (Horse on the
cover); a jacket patch showing the black bucking bronco
of the Italian sports-car logo (same one I've glued on
the inside front cover of this J-book, but hers is a
cloth version); and a wooden Black Horse on wheels that
couples magnetically onto our Luv Train (June spotted
this rolling equus when they visited the wooden-toy shop
together but it was a zebra then; she envisaged a little
paintwork turning it into a personalized Heavenly Year
emblem).  And all these gifts were gorgeously and
creatively wrapped -- Z's a master at this -- and packed
in a splendid handled bag decorated with Celestial
maidens whose cartoon bubbles, added by Z, offered
oddball commentary on Heavenly Year doings.

Marvelous stuff!  Once again I'm blown away!

-- But the new Ox moon hasn't reappeared.  Has it
ducked down too low?  Most likely.  And last night Elgie
didn't call.  Z predicted this, based on his many blown-
off promises regarding calls and e-mail, and she also
warned me he might well get cold feet and cancel the
whole trip (he's due to arrive in just eleven days).
Not that I needed to be warned; I know his history and
I'm sure he's riddled with "issues" about me that might
cause him to back out.  But I'm still disappointed.  I
ask myself if he'll need to be dissing his father in
bigger ways too; and if so, how big?  What can I do to
help move him past such a need, if he really does have
it, or to help him see the benefits of reliability (if

he has trouble in that area with anyone besides us).
And sadly acknowledge: maybe I can do nothing.
     Meanwhile preparations for the visit are moving
into high gear, just like (in a sense!) the cabal's war
preparations.  And who knows, maybe there won't be a war
just as maybe there won't be a visit.  Washington's
saying diplomacy is the way to handle the North Korean
crisis -- perhaps they'll decide to go that way with
Iraq too.  But I definitely wouldn't count on it.  As
the front cover of today's far-coast paper's Sunday
magazine blares: "The American Empire (Get Used to It)."
But I love that it's Korea calling the cabal's bluff, if
it is a bluff, or forcing them to face the consequences
of their new strategic world-domination policy.  Both
Koreas.  The South too is urging us to negotiate with
the North, suggesting we trade a nonaggression pact for
the North's abandonment of its nuclear program.  We're
again saying no negotiations with "evil" no matter what.
(A little irony here.  I think of my own pleas over the
years that Lady S negotiate with me on the nature of our
relationship with Elgie.  Those pleas essentially went
unanswered.  But then I suppose she'd say I had my own
non-negotiables.  And she'd probably be right.  -- Which
isn't to suggest we couldn't've worked some trade-offs
on them.  But in the end that didn't happen either.)
     USAn pundits seem shocked that the "evil" and
allegedly loony North Korean supreme leader could so
cleverly outmaneuver the imperial USA.  But the survival
of Korea over the centuries has depended on its ability
to diplomatically outsmart far more powerful countries
-- empires, in fact.  And this could be said of many
other relatively small countries.  Our USAn behemoth
will frequently be outwitted and it will flail about in
its wrath and the carnage will be terrible.  Eventually,
as historians never fail to point out, it won't be able
to resist the temptation to overextend itself and will
collapse from its own escalating internal tensions.  But
by then, as USAn Empire supporters can and no doubt do
say behind closed doors, no world worth dominating will
exist.  So why not take the risk now?

          [ Jyze of the Heavenly Year : White Horse ]


     We'll save the world by forcing everyone to live as
we do, except they'll all be our vassals -- that's the
price we demand.  Otherwise say goodbye to the planet.
But of course if they're all living as we do, the
result's the same: goodbye to the planet.  which means
all those others won't be living as we do; they'll be
living as our serfs and slaves.
     Anyone out there in the world got any objections to
that bargain?
     -- In the same issue of the far-coast paper's mag
is a story about a new book: "1421: The Chinese
Discovery of America."  The author is saying he can
prove that the famous fifteenth-century Chinese Treasure
Fleet traveled much farther than anyone now alive
realizes.  It circled the globe, set up colonies on all
the continents.  The Celestials did it first!
     Is it true?  Maybe.  To me the evidence looks less
than solid -- many historians are dismissing the whole
notion as cockamamie, just as you'd expect -- but even
in its spottiness it's still massively suggestive.
Until just forty-one years ago, as the article points
out, the idea that the Vikings explored the northeastern
seaboard of North America was considered equally daffy.
My hunch is the new theory will fly.  If not all, parts
of it.  And for purposes of this jyze project what could
be more delightful?  It was in the Heavenly Year of
Jyzemaster G that the word went out upon the land: the
Celestials were the first to introduce the world as a
whole to itself.
     And then, according to the same book, they
intentionally destroyed all the records of those
voyages.  The Celestial Empire turned inward.  I used to
think this was the historical moment that showed the
inadequacy of Celestial philosophy: its inherent extreme
conservatism.  Now I'm wondering: did it instead show
its farseeing wisdom?  Did the most powerful nation on
earth at that time somehow realize further expansion
would lead to overreach and eventual collapse?  Did it
also envision the chaos and planetary malfunction that
would stem from unbridled scientific "progress"?

Well, maybe.  More power to them if so, if it were possible for them to regain power almost six centuries after giving it up.  The questions today are more difficult.  Mere withdrawal won't do.  Mere conservatism guarantees doom.  Conservatism means doing what we're already doing.  The trend lines would continue on their catastrophic course: population growth, resource depletion, waste production, pollution and all the rest. Extreme or radical conservatism -- reactionary type -- would be even worse: vassals would again become serfs and slaves, just as in the USA-hegemony scenario, and the trend lines would continue anyway.

Celestials, we need new answers.  No delays please. Get right on it!  We have a decade or two at most and that's it; after that there'll be no changing course.

(No news here.  Millions of serious folks are working on this.  Spread the word and join in!)

-- Meanwhile these days in the life.  Holiday life. Live it up, ye Heavenly Year merrymaker!  And I've been trying to.  Going with the seasonal flow, actually. This weekend by itself two highlights.

First, Aida's party.  This was to be the public intro of the aforementioned Mather, Aida's new romantic hope.  Lots of whispering about what he'd be like.  I myself was the object of similar whispering five and a half years ago (as Z-wiff now gleefully confirms) before another such Aida-thrown gala.  Z's and Aida's inner and outer friendship circles overlap about two-thirds, I'd say.  But there's a major difference between then and now: I showed up for the gala.  Mather didn't.  No word yet why.  No one dares to ask -- Aida's putting up an unfazed front.  And another difference between them and us: as a couple they're into low key, go slow.  KILK!

Also a big Scrabble match had been advertised, but Serafina and Dak joined Mather in failing to appear.  A sisterly rift?  No one knows and apparently no one asks. -- But I did have a fine time talking with Rose F., the Afrusan progressive radio talk show host who danced up a storm with me at my wedding.  She's looking to write a book about her peace walk across the country -- no

matter that it took place twenty years ago.  It's
relevant now!  Go for it!  (She's also looking for a
husband.  I immediately thought of Kar.  But -- no.  It
would never fly.  Z emphatically agreed.)

     Then last night, Saturday, we rolled up to a club
just beyond the northern J. City limits for a jazz jam
featuring one of Z's workmates, Ronni G.  Gerry and
Leola met us there but not too many others did.  The
total house was only seventeen, and four of those were
jammers themselves.  But the band was terrific and Ronni
touched me with her soulful interpretations and wowed me
with her powerful pipes.  Best of all, Zoelie and Leola
joined her onstage for a raucous version of "Side by
Side."  (Z misunderstood something I said and thought I
was discouraging her from doing this and I had to work
some to convince her otherwise.  She takes great pride
in her singing and rightfully so.  It was five years ago
next Friday that she put on her legendary one-person
concert for me -- and me alone! -- with her coworker Ted
I. accompanying her on piano.  It remains my single
favorite moment in our entire time together.  A big
altered-card commemoration I did of that occasion hangs
framed on the wall outside her bedroom door.)

     This afternoon we paid what's becoming our regular
Sunday joint visit to Mama E.  I thought she was more
responsive than usual -- she seemed to get a kick out of
answering my questions about Z's old boyfriends -- but Z
thought she was looking "punk" and broke down and wept
in the car afterwards as we drove home and I had to pull
over so she could recover.  But afterwards she seemed
okay, although later she said several times she was
feeling "peculiarly unsettled" today, maybe because of
the stress of Elgie's upcoming visit or because of her
own impending return to work after taking several days
off in addition to the official holidays or maybe
because of her talk with Betty about their mutual friend
Wanda who Betty thinks has less than a year to live (her
cancer's metastasizing) or talking with her friend Terri
in Lahontan about her son Tarik who's going through a
period of depression/tension regarding girlfriend

troubles and unemployment -- and as a pilot with an
Arab-sounding name and Mideast looks (Terri's ancestry
is Lebanese) he's facing bleak employment prospects --
but even more his optimistic apolitical I'm-a-USAn-guy
views are suddenly being seriously undermined (and those
views of Tarik's seem to be a lot like Elgie's, and I
fear Elgie too may soon face a brutal awakening -- and
that will be doubly true if South Korea's policies
become increasingly anti-imperial-USA, as I of course
hope they will -- but the chances of this are not good).
     -- I too had a couple of unexpected long telephone
talks over the weekend, one with Betty and one with Vic,
both reporting on their trips to the southland.  The
seventieth wedding anniversary celebration for Jean's
parents went well despite squabbling among the three
siblings (much like my own siblings and me at the time
of Mother's death, they'd been together as a group only
once in fifteen years) and Vic was able to show Ro his
controversial mural, newly restored, at the historical
society in MSM #2's Chinatown.  Kat made me an origami
bird with some sweet words written on the wings and left
it on the cat-shaped ceramic coffee coaster (which she
also made with Z's help) next to my chair when she and
Betty and Kat's friend Celine came over to pick out what
they wanted (and it turned out to be nearly everything)
from the "purging" Z's been doing while cleaning up her
room in preparation for Elgie's visit.
     And much, much more -- of course.  But this is jyze
and it must come to an end, like all expansive things,
before it overextends itself.  Here at the javahaus a
whole new set of transfixed laptop-lit faces is in place
and the ratio of digital to nondigital has dipped as
some of the empty tables have filled with post-late-
show-movie babblers and romancers.  The condensation on
the windows has deepened -- the streetlight outside has
taken on a fuzzy-edged dull-gold aura that's blocked out
a big chunk of the downtown skyline (call it a moon
surrogate, since the moon never did show -- and this an
ideal moon-viewing spot! -- but the Lake J-town fish
house with its breathtaking view is also ideal and we

did see old luna there earlier tonight along with the
iconic golf-tee-cum-saucer still throbbing in the
afterglow, so it seemed, of its New Year's cosmicgasm).
And right there a good note to pack it in on.


[+2]

    Here it's the day to drag your dried and shedding
Christmas tree and wreath and swag out to the curb for
pickup.  Yet for the Coptics in Egypt and the Orthodox
in Russia and for millions of believers elsewhere it's
Christmas Day.  And for millions of other believers it's
also (since we're past midnight and the fifth day of the
twelfth moon is becoming the sixth day) "the King's"
birthday.  He's sixty-eight including the years of his
resurrection era, which started of course within hours
of his death.  The "Heartbreak Hotel" and "Don't Be
Cruel" and "Hound Dog" guy I'm talking about, just so.
    I'm black-armchair-bound.  That doesn't mean I'm on
my way there; it means I'm there, all but roped in.  My
lips still tingling from the cherry popsicle I just
chomped down.  The transformer on the one streetlight
visible through the window is buzzing loudly again, as
it's been doing on and off for months.  The city still
hasn't responded to our calls about it.  Z's vowing to
knock heads over this at the city offices tomorrow.
    I'm supposed to warn Elgie when he calls that he'll
be subject to lots of street noise in Z's room and he
might want to wear earplugs in bed.  But he hasn't
called yet.  He's five days late and counting.  That is,
Z and I are counting.  Is he?  We're wondering.  Z's
theory is that his mother's raising a stink with him
over this visit.  I don't know what to think.  I'm
trying not to think.  I'm focused on letting it play out
as it will.  I'm hoping to get to know this kid who's
also, still, a man about the same age I was when he was
conceived -- get to know him at least a little bit
anyway.
    In the nation's capital the cabal, as promised,

hits the ground running after the Christmas holidays.
Bingo, they propose massive new tax breaks for the rich.
A few out-party lawmakers squawk feebly, but they're
rich themselves and show no conviction in their
protests.  Same goes for the impending Iraq invasion, of
course, even though the UN inspectors have reported
they've failed to find a "smoking gun" so far.  But a
key politico in England has said he thinks the odds of
our launching a war have fallen from sixty-forty in
favor to sixty-forty against.  This is at least a tiny
bit heartening.  And so is the fact that the cabal is
already backtracking on the nuke showdown with North
Korea and now says (after Japan and probably China
applied some new pressure) we're willing to talk with
the evildoers.  But at the same time we're still
insisting we'll make no concessions to evil.

Meanwhile the far right's makeover of the country
proceeds at warp speed on dozens of tracks.  It's ugly.
But for those who've been paying any attention at all
for the past two, three, many Great Years, or at least
haven't been wearing ideological blinders, it's been
ugly all along.  What's happening now is that the happy-
face masks are coming off.  Now it's all out in the
open: we are the people we warned everyone about -- and
we're proud of it.  And everyone's supposed to cheer.
It's not enough to do what the cover of the far-coast
paper's Sunday mag counsels -- "Get used to it."
Instead we've gotta pull for the home team, the white
hats, the good guys, the pinkskins.  Otherwise we're --
unpatriotic!  Even traitorous!  Treasonous!  Seditious!

Who says so?  It's everywhere!  It's everyone!
(Except for an enclave of sanity here and there -- the
Soviets of J. City and Lahontan and MSM #2 and a few
others.)

I've gotten myself started.  Now I'll try to get
myself stopped.  Shouldn't be too hard to do: just shift
back to the merely personal and then be selective.  But
first this reminder: war tensions continue to build.
The real crunch time is still twenty days off.  In the
meantime we're doing everything we can to provoke Iraq

into starting the war on its own, thus sparing us the crunch and the bad press (overseas only, to be sure) of our starting it. We're already bombing, we're running massive war "exercises" on the Iraq border, we're conducting so-called psyops missions, threatening and bribing and economically strong-arming everyone in sight -- what a spectacle! And it'll only be getting better! Buckle up!

So then the shift to the personal. For me on this level it's been a fine day. On my way to Vic and Jean's I stopped at the ORB and bought (using Betty and Kat's Christmas gift certificate to pay for most of it) the new book about the Celestial Empire's alleged discovery of the Americas. (Yes, all three: North, Central, South.) Then Vic and Jean and I had a great old time rapping about it, Vic and I meanwhile getting snockered on the usual hooch. And why not? It's Tuesday night! And his computer's still down. It's been down so long now he's actually (as he likes to joke) gone back to painting again just to have something to do.

He was telling me that even in his student days in Norway he was hearing versions of this same "1421" theory. The architecture of Norski stave churches, the coins with the holes in them -- he didn't have to be told, he could see it himself in so many places and ways: clear Celestial influence. He was a little displeased with what he called the "tongue-in-cheek" tone of the article about the "1421" book; he figures it won't be long now before the evidence the book presents is verified and the theory is nailed down as fact and all the world histories of the past millennium must be radically rewritten. I hope he's right and I think there's at least a chance he is. But even if he's not, the histories should still be rewritten. The Celestial Empire gets nothing close to its due -- even without the "discovery of the Americas" as one of its achievements. Its greatest achievement of all was to halt its own expansion. Now we face the daunting task of figuring out a way to do that ourselves with our own marauding empire.

      But I said that already.  Possibly more than once.
      -- Maybe best to stop right here for tonight.  I
was thinking of laying out a list of minor incidents and
dishing some dish -- about tonight's talk with Hector on
the bus (which went roaring past the turn leading to the
high bridge, the bus did, and the driver had to
improvise a detour through narrow back streets) and what
jazz warbler Ronni G. said about loving Z's and my
"interaction as a couple" and suchlike -- but a little
extra sleep tonight might do me some good.  And I'm
trying to accustom myself to hitting the rack earlier so
I'll not be made too groggy by rising early when Elgie's
here, if he really does show.  And even if he doesn't, I
have no choice but to go on assuming he will and start
getting serious about readying the apartment -- and I'd
have more time for that tomorrow afternoon (when I can
make cleaning noises, as I can't now) if I were to crash
in the next few minutes.  -- Today, by the way, I did
successfully replace the "mixet" knob on the bathtub
tap, an important early step in visit prepping.
      So the Yellow Tiger roars out just as it roared in.
Bounds out.  Last of the Tigers, gone.  I too bound out
-- of being chairbound -- and am bound for bed and hope
to be bedbound for eight hours plus, whooee!


                       ------


                        58


                       ------



      Rainy Saturday night in the HQ triangle.  Tonight
they're not out in droves, the partiers.  But I had to
come here.  My last Heavenly chance.  That's how it
looks.
      So here's the firehouse saloon.  Its rows of old
fire helmets and various other types of fire gear ride

the century-old brick walls high up, sort of like trophy animal heads.  City fire-department headquarters are a block to the south.  And on the far side of the headquarters (where Aida's brother Ray works in one of the engine companies) the lucky Heavenly Year composite Brown Horse stands proud atop its sky platform.  I stopped under it to pay the usual obeisance and then passed several other live-music clubs before coming here.  No way could I set up anywhere else.  Here's the best spot.  Main reason: it's not part of the joint-cover circuit.  No live music.  Cost of a drink, I'm in. I stretched before sitting down in the booth; "Long day?" queried the bartender with a familiar smile, as if I were a regular.  But I'm not.  Far from it.  Even the cost of a drink is usually too much for me.

Special night.  Feels like it anyway -- and that's because it actually isn't.  After this, see, they all will be, unless maybe Elgie backs out on his visit.  And he might do that.  Still no call.  But Z and I have been prepping all day anyway.  I cleaned out my closet for the first time in years.  Discovered I can no longer fit into many of my old shirts.  That's how much the WOC's bulked me up over a four-year period.  So I made up a hand-me-down bag.  Elgie will get first crack, then Rob. I figure Elgie will go for a few of the slicker items (which came to me as gifts that I've never worn at all) and Rob will wind up with what he likes anyway.

Well, no, this night is special in a different way as well.  It's Popeye's birthday.  He was born 111 years ago today, the same year the hideaway building went up. And I hadn't thought of this before yesterday: he was fifty when I was born (and for a few hours bore his first name) -- the same age, again, Rob is now.

Sad news too -- Jean's father died Thursday night at age eighty-seven (Mama E's age).  He survived the big clan gathering to honor his and his wife's seventieth wedding anniversary by only ten days.  And Vic lost a good friend the night before that.  "We felt strange all day," he said in his phone message.  "Now we're just waiting for number three."  I called him right away upon

getting the message but felt I didn't do very well at
the condolence task.  Z came up with a wake gift --
champagne and stout -- and I'm planning to try my luck
at making a card for V&J when I arrive home tonight.
        -- Bar's slowly filling up.  Cleavage and bare
midriffs parading by.  Across the street they're lining
up outside the kinky old quasi-S&M club, with only a few
wusses wearing jackets despite the cold and windblown
rain.  Sound system in here is amping up -- tired grungy
stuff from a decade ago -- s'all right though.
        If I'm in luck an enerjyzer bunny will go hopping
by on one or more of the five TV screens in action and
its color will be gold.  The Earth Rabbit.  Presiding
cluster beast.  The calendrically astute will know this
means we're into 4697.  (And "1421," I'll say, is a
fascinating read.  I'm a third of the way in and I'm
persuaded by the case for kicking most of the famous
Western so-called explorers off the "discovery" list --
and maybe even the whole sorry lot of 'em.)
        Real world?  Twin crises continue.  The Hermit
Kingdom (several times I've come across newspaper
accounts bestowing that ancient term for all of Korea on
North Korea alone) -- the northern part of the Hermit
Kingdom, I'll say, withdraws from the Nuke Non-
Proliferation Treaty and the whole "developed" world
goes bonkers.  But our cabal still insists it's not a
crisis.  And nobody bothers to point out that under the
terms of that same treaty a nation has a right to
withdraw if it's been threatened with attack by a nuke-
bearing nation -- and our cabal has explicitly done just
that several times to North Korea and is still doing it.
North Korea is also correct in observing that the
cabal's policy is leading toward -- inciting -- world
war.  But our homegrown media all agree: North Korea,
they're the crazy ones, the dangerous ones.  We with our
tens of thousands of nukes and long-range missiles and
bombers and nuke-bearing submarine fleet, our many
hundreds of overseas bases, our long list of aggressions
over the past two centuries, our genocide of millions of
Natives, our current brazenly upfront first-strike

nuclear policy -- we're the sane ones, aggrieved, seeing ourselves as being pushed around by an impoverished nation with a population one fifteenth the size of ours and an economy a thousandth the size of ours.

Other crisis? Mixed signals. Yesterday's big banner headline says (exhibiting unusual headline prolixity even for the far-coast paper): "WITH 'NO SMOKING GUN' IN IRAQ, FEBRUARY ATTACK IS LESS LIKELY." But today's OMP reports another thirty-five thousand U.S. marines have been ordered to the Mideast. The U.K. calls up its reserves. Our secretary of state observes there's "nothing magical about January 27 as a decision point." Elsewhere new Al Qaeda "spectaculars" are predicted for the opening days of our Iraq invasion (and are openly called for by desperate Palestinian groups).

Conclusion? Odds are increasing that the Heavenly Year of Jyzeslinger G will come to an end with both crises still hanging fire. For the internal dynamics of this annal -- beginning, middle, climax, end -- not so good, but for a sense of how things are looking for the next Heavenly Year cycle -- meaning the sixty years to come -- an accurate lead-in. Sets the stage fairly well -- but only hints at the perils to come. And is way light on the eco/climate angle.

"World's on fire!" I'm mouthing the words to the assembled up-high fire gear in here. Sound system's overwhelmingly loud right now anyway -- everything everyone in the room is saying is just mouthing as far as I can tell. And some of that gear seems to be moving in time with the beat. Big, big fire a-comin', folks!

-- And I have no ice cubes left to suck. Not only that, I'm wasted from the effort to turn back my sleep schedule by a couple of hours. And my booth is being eyed. Some of these guys doing the eyeing look like they're awaiting orders for Iraq themselves or wish they were. You could scrub floors with their brush haircuts. I feel -- supererogatory. On my forehead it's stamped: "Surplus." Or: "Old School." Or: "Shelf life expired."

Gangway for New Gen!

[ Jyze of the Heavenly Year : White Horse ]


(Nah, I could hang on awhile.  Jes the usual punks
here.  Dinosaur jyzeslinger scares 'em, awes 'em, I can
see it in the way they peer back over here again and
again.  "Never mess with a man pushing a J-stick.")


[+2]


East-depot saloon.  The Heavenly Yearling's here to
bid it goodbye.  Out on the streets of the AQ, posters
are already up for the Year of the Sheep.  In today's
mail we received our tickets for the New Year's Eve bash
at the best of our hilltop Chinese restaurants (for its
owners, though, the Sheep Year will not be good: their
building will be coming down in a few weeks to make way
for the new light-rail station's staging area -- another
prime example, I'd say, and I'm far from the only one,
of arrogant dominant-culture decision-making).
I've grabbed the high table next to the south
entrance.  A high stool too, and with it comes a fine
view of a rainy early-evening street scene, the AQ bus
terminal, the east depot itself, the campanile at the
west depot, and -- as a centerpiece -- the pyramidal
steeple of the great white tower with its green light at
the top aglow, building lights shining, mist softening
everything -- all this seen through complex interior
window reflections and the blue and red neons of beer
signs as traffic rolls by outside with windshield wipers
laboring and walkers slog by beneath umbrellas -- within
arm's reach but through wavy distorting glass.  All of
it at the price of the occasional cold blast as the door
opens a few feet away -- roughly about once a minute.
Could be an oddball icy dragon breath blowing on it --
one of the beasts is curled around the light pole just
outside the door to the south, its head about ten feet
up but facing directly toward us down here.
Two blocks east at the pavilion park a rally's
underway.  Against the war, against the roundups of
immigrants and visaholders from Mideast and "Axis of
Evil" and other alleged "terrorist-harboring" nations.


596

[ Jyze of the Heavenly Year : White Horse ]

A few hundred people braving the elements -- candles
flickering beneath umbrellas (a tiny hunk of white wax
from one of those candles is still stuck to the ring
finger -- which is ringless as always -- of my jyzin'
hand).  Two of our more leftward local elected
officials, Guy S. and Willis E., spoke rousingly while I
was there, with several more yet to appear.  TV
camerapeople, cops, and no doubt a posse of plainclothes
agents for Homeland Security were snatching our images.
A right-wing drunk a few steps from me kept bellowing
"Who are you to say that?" to the speakers until he
crumpled down into a puddle and went silent (befuddled
and bepuddled).  Z arrived shortly after I did, her
wheeled bag thundering along behind her on the bricks.
We hit all the stalls and wound up with a pocketful of
political buttons.  I'm wearing two now: "War on the
World?  Not in our Name!" and a blue triangle on a black
background to express solidarity with those being
rounded up (the Nazis issued blue triangles to gypsies
before hauling them off to the gas chambers) (the main
INS jail for this region, as it happens, is just a few
blocks south of here and, as I know from grand-jury
scoping, it's packed full these days).

    What else is new?  Not a heckuva lot -- except that
the cabal's turnaround on North Korea is now nearly
complete: they're saying we'll supply energy to North
Korea if the country will give up its nuke program.  But
this isn't negotiating with evil, see.  How can anyone
take these cabal bozos seriously?  -- Oh yeah, I forgot:
they wield overwhelming military power.  As the joint
chief of staff boasted in an interview that ran in
today's OMP, "If we want to fight, we win."

    And as Guy S. said in his speech: "We're a great
nation only as a democracy, not as an empire."  Talking
truth to power.  Trouble is, power can usually trump
truth, at least in the short run.  And usually in the
long run as well, because power can almost always
control what passes for truth.  But power can't always
control events, and events are frequently creating new
conditions for which old truths are a bad fit, making

power scramble to reshape truth; and sometimes power
slips up on this.  Then too, power can be challenged by
other forms of power, lesser centers, groups,
individuals -- voices, even of the animal and the
inanimate.  "Power to the planet!"  (Lotsa luck though.)
     -- Any other news?  Still no word from Elgie.  I've
decided I'll call him tomorrow (after discussing this
with Z) and my aim will be twofold: to confirm we'll be
picking him up at the airport Friday night and also to
set up a "fog plan" in case his flight's delayed or
diverted elsewhere, as often happens in the nasty kind
of weather we've been seeing in recent weeks.
     Also tomorrow I take the Z-mobile in for servicing.
Wednesday and Thursday I do the laundry and clean the
bathrooms and kitchen -- and also present my bunch of
Heavenly Year balloons for reinflation at the party
store.  One last gallop around the track for the grand
Water Horse balloon and the rest of the hideaway herd.
     That's it.  Gotta get to work.  A last nod first,
though, to the Golden Rabbit: appreciating its
settling for a quick entry here.  Kwikjyze for the
Golden Rabbit.  It limps off affectingly through the
frozen grass of Heavenly fields.


                      ------


                       59


                      ------



     The full moon is the eye of the White Dragon.  It
watched over me as I walked down here, first to A-mart
and then to the teahouse, where I now sit by the glass
window in the floor looking down into history, Heavenly
and not so Heavenly.  Sixty years and nine months ago,
Year of the Black Horse, those items were stored there
at the time of the Japusan roundup.  That occurred as I

was riding around Lahontan and various other cities in
my mother's special in-body carrying chamber.  Now I
wear a blue triangle protesting another kind of roundup
based on race and national background.

But I was shopping for champagne at A-mart.  Yes,
the visit's still on.  Tonight it starts.  I'm on my way
in to work -- it's around quarter to seven now, later
than I'd like -- and in four hours Z will pick me up
downtown and we'll head out to the airport.  Elgie's due
in at midnight.  These days you need something like an
act of Congress to get out to the disembarking area, so
we'll meet him at the baggage carousel.

Will we recognize each other?  Quite possibly not.
More likely, since photos have been exchanged, just an
edge of doubt will arise on both sides.  Z predicts
he'll be wearing a nice brand-name dress shirt, pressed
trousers, a tweed jacket.  Or did she say tweed
trousers?  Whichever, the description sounded about
right to me.  MSM #2 kid but strongly influenced by MSM
#1 and heading for law school.  Meanwhile his father, an
aging sixties kind of guy who also happens to be in his
sixties (very early sixties!) wearing a currently
scorned ponytail and a "No Iraq War" button in addition
to the one with the blue triangle on it, will be spiffed
down, as it were, in his usual work outfit.

It just might be a bit awkward at first.  Good
thing Z'll be along to keep things hopping, at which
she's always a wowzer if she wants to be -- and in this
case I'm sure she'll want to be.  We'll open the
champagne at unit 203 and not long after that I'll have
to go back down to work.  If I'm lucky, I'll also be
able to do some jyzing there.

Only last night did Elgie finally confirm he'd be
coming.  Very offhandedly too: he'd changed flights and
told us the new airline and new approximate arrival time
but he'd neglected to jot down the new flight number.
Z's taken aback by his overall blase' approach.  Is it a
thirty-something thing (slightly premature)?  Is it an
intentional or semi-intentional dissing of "Pops"?
What's going on?  Certainly I don't know.  I'm plenty

nervous, though.  Pups and I gonna be able to "bond"?
Sure hope so.  I'll be trying my best to nudge things in
that direction.  Could be our one and only chance.

I bumped into Z's work colleague David M. while
picking up the champagne at A-mart.  "Gettin' excited?"
were his first words.  Z's been talking up this big
reunion for weeks with her friends and coworkers.

(Shortly after that I ran into Chun, my janitor pal
from the scope office.  She's been laid off and is now
working part-time in the kitchen at the largest of the
restaurants in the A-mart food court.)

Meanwhile the world political crisis keeps
building.  Yesterday the UN inspectors in Iraq found a
dozen warheads that could be used to carry chemicals.
They hail from the eighties, everyone agrees, and Iraq
says they're just forgotten artillery shells or rockets
left over from the Gulf War -- that's certainly what
they look like in the photos -- but the U.S. may pounce
on them as the "smoking gun."  At the same time North
Korea's deft maneuvering has flipped the cabal
completely: now we're offering them energy, talks,
future pacts, just about anything to calm the media
circus and keep the focus on Iraq where the imperial
prize is so much greater.  North Korea rightly calls the
offers stalling and "pie in the sky."  They could easily
keep the U.S. spinning in place for months by shooting
off a test rocket every week or two.

Most of the world is still talking about granting
the UN inspectors more time to do their job in Iraq --
up to as much as a year.  The U.S. wants action soon and
is trying to keep the focus on the inspectors' report
scheduled to be delivered to the Security Council by
January 27th, ten days from now.  Clearly the cabal
wants to launch its attack shortly after that date.  Big
protests are slated for tomorrow in D.C. and elsewhere,
in this country and overseas.  Even the strong-arming
and bribing the cabal's been doing might not ensure a
Security Council vote in its favor, so the talk now is
that a vote isn't needed; Resolution 1441 permits the
U.S. to choose on its own.

Showdown at the OK Corral.
Oh these are riveting times.
-- And I must rush on.  Will return later, I hope,
with the human-interest portion of tonight's newscast:
the first eyewitness report on the GPS father/son
reunion.

*          *

-- And so it came to pass.  And it was good!  And
it will be good!
This going down in the scope-office conference
room, a bit past three a.m., the giant framed memorial
photo of the unfallen twin towers looking on, the fridge
out in the hall humming loudly and spasmodically
(something's wrong with it: a post-it says so).
But ooh, the nerves!  We arrived at the airport
forty minutes early -- decided we'd go out to meet the
prodigal son at the plane.  Stripped ourselves,
accordingly, of all metal: knives, automatic weapons,
granades, all that.  But it turns out you simply can't
meet people at the plane anymore.  Post-9/11 security.
Lots of steely-eyed tough guys hanging about and for
want of more subversive-looking targets an unhealthy
number seemed to be fastening on the throwback sixties
guy with the ponytail.  Or was I flattering myself?
All arrivees from all gates on concourses C, D, and
N were coming in at the same entrance -- a near-constant
flow even at midnight.  Then just minutes after the
arrivals screen said Elgie's plane had landed, the PA
told us belatedly our "checkpoint" was closing and now
all arrivees would be passing through "Checkpoint
Charlie," a good hundred yards to the south.  Off in the
distance we could see people already emerging from the
gate there and heading down the escalator to the baggage
carousels.  Had we missed him?  Z and I split up, she to
search at the carousels while I watched at Charlie.
Lots of faces to wonder about.  Here's one on a guy
about the right height, right hair color -- but in jeans
cutoffs and flip-flops?  Didn't want to look away from
any prime candidates too soon -- but meanwhile more
primes were rounding the bend and fanning out into the

lobby, many moving fast.  Flights from half a dozen
western U.S. and Pacific Rim cities.  Lots of Asian and
semi-Asian or "hapa" faces.  -- And here's Z back (she's
in her tight jeans, white running shoes, casual brown
top -- by appearance a fit mate and then some for one of
my ilk, no question, and every bit as excitedly into the
drama) -- she's looking mystified, shrugging, hands
lifted, eyebrows raised -- no Elgie.

    And just then the kid strides into view.  Tall, all
in black, lean -- recognizes us almost instantly as Z
spots him first and waves, with me a second or two
behind -- he comes loping over and I head out to embrace
him, Z letting me go first.  Kid's a little taller than
I am.  More angular face than I'd been expecting from
the photos.  I say -- what?  "One of the great moments
of my life," something like that.  He: "It is, it is."
I'm thinking maybe I'm about to break into tears.  But
here's Z to be introduced and then we're swept along --
his only luggage is a large carry-on bag.  Right away it
seems we're relating well -- arms around each other like
old buddies as we ride up the escalator toward the
parking garage.  Jovial small talk.

    His demeanor from the start: an Asian male's
eagerness to please, alert smiling deference, prolonged
pauses that show a concern not to offend (often with
eyes flitting searchingly from Z to me and back, or away
from both of us), but also a quickness to reply if he
feels sure about what's expected.  Almost hyper-polite
-- but very likable.  Deferring to the elders!  Love it!
(Well no, not really.  But I think we'll get past it.
Early on he said, "I think I'm still feeling a little
shy.")

    So then the drive back, just ten or twelve minutes,
including that glorious moment cresting the rise at the
north end of the S-curve when J. City pops into view
startlingly close and colorful and huge and all lit up
in the night -- my first view of it back in the world's
Fair summer and it's now, in a version much enhanced
over the years, his first.  Well, his second, but he has
no memory of the actual first, which came fourteen or

fifteen years ago, though he does recall the visit
itself (it lasted only three or four hours between
flights on his way with his mother to Seoul -- the last
time I saw either of them before tonight).

A quick stop at the south-hill overlook for a truly
up-close view of the downtown skyline for orientation
purposes -- the orange-brick DC castle standing floodlit
at our backs -- "What the heck is that?" he asked -- and
then to 1511, up, a quick tour of 203 (Z's added some
decorations to the chalked-in "Welcome Son Glen to Your
Jyze City Home" sign on the entryway lightbox).  Then we
break out the champagne and do a standing toast in the
living-room chair cluster.  Chitchat for a while.  Z's
good at asking the kind of questions he likes to answer.
I'm noticing we both got it right on his clothes.  She
predicted the pressed slacks, I the muscle T (both
black, along with his snug down jacket) -- the shoes
being sort of slick (I'd say) brown loafers, pointy,
Italianate.  I could almost hear Z thinking, ooh, nice
arms on the boy!  Looked like he might've put in an hour
or two at the gym shortly before leaving.  The lad is
hot, yeah -- chip off the old Pops block, right, just as
Z said with a chuckle (but surely she meant it!).

Looks a bit like cousin Kar -- height, build,
angularity of facial bones.  Also I could see his uncle
Hyu around his eyes and mouth -- less of Lady S herself
except in the set of his mouth during certain intensely
polite smiles (recalling her dance stage smiles).

I asked him point-blank if his mother's still okay
with the trip.  He said yes.  He should feel free, I
said, to call right away to let her know he'd arrived
safely.  He gave a polite assent but said he wanted to
call his friends first.

Not much new we learned.  He did receive a couple
more rejection letters from law schools, both of them
"middle tier."  Still only the one acceptance.  U of
Texas hasn't responded yet but is currently looking good
to him because of the low tuition and Austin being the
"music capital of the world" (and an ex-military Korusan
friend of his is a law student there).  The prospect of

facing Texas-style racism and militant frontier
conservatism doesn't seem to trouble him.  Nor had he
even heard about our supreme USAn leader coming out
against affirmative action this week in a case involving
the University of Michigan, including the law school
there, which is the one that asked him to apply.
(Buncha JRXes up there.)
     -- And then I had to go.  Came here, finished up my
scoping in one hour, now this jyze.  It's well past my
bedtime already!  -- The new one, that is, for the
duration of Elgie's visit: half past three.  In the
morning Z will be taking him out to her co-op and the
big south-end discount mart so he can pick out some grub
he likes.  He's still a "fruitarian," he says, but "with
exceptions."  Drinks coffee, tea, wine, a little beer.
-- For the ten days of his stay I'll be getting up at
half past eleven and hopefully by one I'll be ready to
roll.  Sez he loves to walk: I'm planning to put him
to the test on that (and have been thinking for months
about what some of those hikes might be).  Tomorrow,
though, a south-hill "peace potluck" is on tap (it's
part of the nationwide antiwar demos) followed by dinner
out; then I'll introduce him to my hideaway office and
the walkable downtown, waterfront, public market, HQ,
AQ, maybe a quick sample of the nightlife scene since
he's already asked several questions about it.
     -- So it's happening.  Heavenly Year climax.  This
is it!


[+2]


     Why not simply describe what the kid and the J-
slinger have been up to for the past two days.  Not that
there's any other realistic choice.  Keep it simple.
"KISS."  Because we're under tough time constraints
again.  -- Which is also jyze's excuse for arriving here
a day late.
     And what a day we missed.  Birthday of the woman
who would've been the mother of Elgie's oldest sibling

(half-sibling actually) had not a highly necessary
family-planning move intervened.  Lady K I'm talking
about.  Also it was the official kickoff date for the
Lewis & Clark (JRX) bicentennial celebration, and if
those two with their motley crew hadn't opened the way
for Eurusans in big numbers to colonize and ethnically
"cleanse" our region there might never have been a
literary breakthrough into the jyze era, nor, one
suspects, would those Horse balloons be spinning
overhead in Jyzer Ink World Headquarters in the historic
quarter where Jyze City itself began.  And it was the
official last full-moon day of the Heavenly Year.  And
in the nation's capital the largest antiwar gathering
since the Vietnam era -- half a million or more -- took
place to protest the coming U.S. invasion of Iraq.
     White Dragon cluster!
     Things are happening on a lot of levels with the
visit of the prodigal son (and only legal heir, most
likely, "of blood," after Z-wiff and I are both gone,
though his quasi-sister Kat ought to count too, and
will).  I'm digesting, I'm absorbing, I'm puzzling, I'm
enjoying, I'm gawking, I'm balking, I'm bonding, I'm
falling apart, I'm reassembling myself -- and all these
would probably apply to him too and maybe to Z as well.
     On the level of "Hey, how's the visit going?" I'd
still say it's going great.
     Real quick (because I ought to be in bed right now
so as to be able to rise in time for the noon start of
tomorrow's MLK Day protest march here in J-town, and I'm
not even home yet), Saturday opened with a cameo at the
south-hill "peace potluck," followed by a crosstown trip
to the Yuke to buy an urgently needed textbook for
Elgie's biology course, followed by a dash to an east-
hill theater to see the marvelous "Talk to Her."  Then
came dinner at a nearby restaurant as a lounge singer
serenaded table to table, and then after dropping off Z
at home (it was her bedtime already) the son and I did a
quick tour of the HQ on foot and then hit the hideaway.
There I showed him, among other things, the huge photo
album going back to 1964 in which he and I and his

mother are pretty much the only subjects and watched
with watery eyes myself as the tears rolled down his
cheeks while he paged through it.  And then a long
impromptu talk in the Z-mobile (parked on the middle
road in the HQ) about his school and career choices.
Then after returning home, an almost equally long talk
with Z in bed (this is just me now, mind) about what it
all might mean and portend.

Today coffee at the AQ teahouse, the New Year's
festival at the Japanese theater (in which calligraphers
performed live on stage and dancers and a koto player
evoked, for me anyway, both Lady U and Lady S, who
herself is a superb calligrapher -- and this was the
"First Writing" festival, a traditional part of the
Japanese New Year celebration); then a trip up to the
north end to introduce Elgie to Mama E (who seemed to be
wowed by the young man -- "You could go into the
movies!"), with a brief stop along the way so that
Serafina and family could meet him; and then dinner at
the north-end arcade as something called a "conversation
cafe" took place at the next table and we got our own
jaw-down going pretty good too, followed by some serious
book browsing; and then back home for dessert (chocolate
pie with a healthy twist) and Z's off to bed, Elgie's
off to the internet, I'm off to work (where this is
going down -- again in the conference room).

If I can just stop driving the wrong way up one-way
streets (I've done it no fewer than three times) I think
the chances are good this visit will keep being terrific
for all concerned.  That's what I think.  But there must
be a catch somewhere, a down period, a realization of
limits, maybe a facedown with buried conflicts and pain.
Mustn't there?  Maybe not.  Who knows.  -- But it sure
does feel good so far.

(I've learned a few new things about Elgie but not
much.  Tomorrow night for noting those, and maybe some
details to fill in today's quick outline.  Or maybe not.
The pace of events may continue to be overwhelming.
It'll be no bad thing if that's so, jyze needs or no
jyze needs.)

[+1]

-- Caught a break tonight.  Scope work expected to take four hours took only a little over two.  So now I have a couple of hours to jyze to my heart's content before meeting Elgie at eleven down in the HQ triangle. Right now he's working out at the WOC -- my own club! Wearing my own swim shorts!  -- Well, no, he took one look at them and decided maybe he'd rather not try out the jacuzzi after all.  And they're not really swimming trunks either; they're running shorts I've pressed into service for whirlpool use.  A bit ragged in spots, yeah.

Our numbers at the march were estimated at fifteen thousand.  Good weather; dry, not too cold.  The three of us along with Kat and her boyfriend, Avery, hooked up with Aida and Sera and Dak and the two adorables, Tala and Dalisay, both of whom were whizzing about on small scooters.  Shortly after the start Elgie informed me it was the first protest march of any kind he'd ever taken part in.  Avery's a bright Cawk kid and from the knowing look he gave me at one point I suspect Kat's told him an embarrassing story or two about old Subunk G.

It was much bigger and also much Cawkier than your average MLK Day march of the past few years.  The route was the usual spectacular one up and over east hill and then down to the federal building (I'd heard it would be ending up at the downtown plaza this year -- but no). The PA system at the federal building was not good and our sight lines were even worse, so I led the other four -- Z, Elgie, Kat, Avery -- on a brief downtown tour on foot as we made our way to the central plaza and then to the fairgrounds via monorail.

First stop was a new downtown hotel which Elgie wanted to see because he'd recently stayed in one belonging to the same chain in FCM #1 and liked it.

Second stop was the old J. City Tower to show them the site of my first scope office but even more to see the notorious mural in the gilded lobby featuring the "pioneers" and early railroaders, its infamous quotation from the railroad mogul reminding us that "Westward the course of empire ever takes its way."

Third stop, the new symphony hall and the quotation inscribed in stone above the garden of remembrance with its wall of names of our state's war dead (since my year of birth as it happens: 1942).  Same quotation I've mentioned in these pages several times before: "We leave you our deaths.  Give them their meaning."  As I told Elgie in front of the others, he wouldn't be here today had it not been for the man who wrote those words.  It was that same man who told me about the writing program at Mezzu and dashed off a letter to the director essentially assuring I'd get a fellowship.  Before then I'd never even heard of the Mezzu writers' workshop and I wouldn't've gone there if not for the recommendation and encouragement from him.  "And that's about it," I said.  "Well," piped up Z-wiff, "don't forget the part about meeting Elgie's mother there."  "Oh yeah.  That's sort of crucial too."  "And don't forget it wasn't really any one person who made all this happen; it was the cosmos."  "And that's crucial as well," I agreed.

Then onward to the current scope building, just so Elgie could know where it is I perform my nighttime day job (but "scoping out" the actual office would've been far too complicated and disruptive for the people laboring away up there at that hour).

Then "gliding above the edgetown rooftops" -- except that many of the buildings there now tower over the monorail -- to the fairgrounds.  Eats at the food arcade first as an MLK Day gospel choir worked a large crowd into a frenzy, and then, after Avery departed to meet his parents, we did the quintessential tourist thing and rode up to the iconic golf tee's observation deck (where you could still see burn marks left by the New Year's fireworks display on the metal supports outside).  Yeah, quite a view up there.  Photos with Elgie's fancy digital camera, which he'd been wielding from time to time ever since arriving.  It was a first, visiting the spinning saucer at the top, not just for him but for me too, as far as I can recall -- and I was

present for its opening, almost.  Within a few months.
     Then by monorail and bus back to the car parked
near where the march originated (with a stop at a
downtown shop to pick up a radio with special headphones
which we hope might ease Mama E's tinnitus problems).
And crosstown to Betty and Kat's, where Elgie and I
spent twenty amusing minutes up in Kat's room as she
showed us photos and mementos and otherwise strutted her
stuff.  Then when the local news came on we watched to
see if we could catch ourselves on TV.  We didn't, but
it was close; our group had passed by a guy Z knew being
interviewed by a TV crew and a few seconds of that
interview made it.  (The world news led off with new
warnings from the cabal to other nations: join us in the
attack on Iraq or suffer the consequences.  Or if Iraq's
supreme leader would agree to go into exile and meet
various other humiliating conditions, we would call off
our attack dogs.  That is, we would just go in and take
over and remake the country in our image -- though the
cabal left that part implicit.)
     Then home, Z's tank now being close to empty.  Just
as Elgie and I were leaving again, landlord Raphael
showed up to check out some plumbing damaged by do-it-
yourself repairs in the kitchen above ours; the
resulting leak had caused water to pour into our kitchen
while I slept this past morning.  (It had happened once
before so no one panicked.)  And then the hideaway and
the club and, for me, the scope office.
     Fine moments all day long.  Best of the lot, Elgie
threw an arm around me and I reciprocated -- this in the
central plaza after the march -- and we walked along
that way for half a block before he suddenly twisted
away, giggling raucously: "You're tickling me!"
Unintentionally to be sure -- but in the ribs, he said.
     Coffee shop's closing now.  I've done no catchup on
details from yesterday and also I've been able to
provide only a few from today.  Will I have a chance to
add some later? Could, I suppose.  Probably won't.  If
not, this last word, or these last ten:  All's still
well with the kid and me (and Z)!

------

60

------


A surprise start for the last cluster of the fifth
Great Year and the penultimate cluster of them all --
Silver Snake!  Table with a wobble at a chain coffee
shop overlooking "Manny Lake."  Scion and only known
blood heir Elgie S. is out there at this moment jogging
around the lake, the famous two-point-eight-mile loop.
Bikers, roller-bladers, strollers, power walkers, dog
walkers -- and handsome DJ Glen from MSM #1.
   The wobble's not that bad.  Just enough to jolt my
train of thought at the right margin of each line, as if
a switch engine's banged into the left margin.
   All's still going well with the visit.  I'm on what
Z calls "natural Exhilarin."  But on our way up here --
it's midafternoon Thursday -- I got a bit of a wobble-
inducing jolt.  Suddenly the lad wants to move his
return flight back from Sunday evening to early Saturday
morning -- day after tomorrow!  Seems he learned a
couple of days ago that a surprise party will take place
Saturday night down in MSM #1 for his best friend,
Wilson, and Wilson's been "sort of depressed" lately and
needs a boost.  Of course I'm not about to raise any
objections to Elgie's doing such a good deed.  I approve
of it!  But I'm disappointed too, there's no denying.
   In another surprise he suggested out of the blue
that we attend a women's basketball game at the U
tonight.  He learned about it on the web.  He has this
odd attraction to very tall women -- a fetish almost.  I
can understand it a little better now seeing he's fairly
tall himself and no doubt is made highly conscious of it
in the Asiusan community where he spends most of his

time.  But still -- a whiff of the eugenic about it as
well.  We've talked about this, albeit gingerly.
     So we'll go to the game.  Sounds like fun actually.
Yesterday we did a good deal of campus strolling and
today we'll be doing some more.  Z must attend an
important meeting tonight, so it'll be just Pops and
Pups.
     Right before our drive out here, lunch with June
and Z at the Italian joint in the HQ triangle.  -- Or
no, first, on our way down from the hill, Elgie and I
stopped at the A-mart flower shop.  Jean stepped back,
appraised the two of us for a long moment with tilted
head, index finger rubbing chin, eyes scrunched and
flicking between us, and finally observed to me, "He has
more hair."  And it's true!  Though we haven't counted.
But Vic won't be getting back in from the megastate
until Friday night, so he won't be able to meet Elgie
this time.  ("Won't be able to do X this time" is
getting to be a stock refrain -- but will there really
be a next time?  Given the bogglingly ambitious academic
program the lad's laid out for himself over the next
eight to ten years he'll be one very busy aspiring
biotech inventor who's also in training to become an
M.D. and, at the same time, his own lawyer.)  -- Jean
saying she ad-libbed a lengthy speech at her father's
funeral and drank a lot and more than a hundred people
showed up and she "had a wonderful, wonderful time --
really!"
     More on June Q. later.  And on brother Rob, the
campus visit, the rest.  The jogger should be rounding
the bend any second now.  (He also proposed biking, the
two of us.  But in my Heavenly Year I'm finally wising
up enough not to ask my body to work too strenuously
without careful preparation and gradual ratcheting.)
-- And I see him loping this way and waving.

*          *

     -- Some seven hours later.  Twists and turns and
now I find myself upstairs at the primo javahaus.  All
tables occupied, mostly showing serious student action
-- books, flying fingers, glowing screens.  Also chess.

611

Also romance (both gay and hetero).  -- And now my
favorite table by the window rail is opening up ---
*

     Slight delay there while the departing threesome
and I searched for a missing scarf.  Couldn't find it.
I've promised to turn it in at the counter if I should
happen to come across it somewhere.
     The iconic-saucer view, it's sparklingly clear.  No
vapor on the javahaus windows tonight even though it's
drizzly out there.
     Where's the kid at this moment?  I dropped him off
at the WOC at nine but that's closed by now.  On two
other nights while I was working he wound up hitting the
bar at that same sleek hotel he had checked out earlier
(on the high road just two blocks from the scope
office).  Last night, while he was catching a movie on
the downtown glitz strip, Aiyana, his current flame
(they met in early November but I hadn't heard about her
until this week) -- Aiyana, I say, rang him up from
Tokyo, where she's visiting a friend, and he had her
call him back in twenty minutes so he could get over to
the same hotel bar.  Then they talked for over two hours
and he wound up taking a cab to south hill.  As he says:
this Aiyana thing is developing fast -- "maybe too
fast."  But he can't help himself; he goes into things
wholeheartedly.  A chip off the aforementioned old
block, or in Z's acronym, a COOB.  (Aiyana tells him
he's the nicest guy in MSM #1.  She's already said she'd
be willing to follow him wherever he goes to law school.
But he's determined to meet other women -- maybe even to
"add some more Norski blood to the family line" --
saying this only half jokingly, I think, or maybe less
than half.  Yet he's lonely and his hormones are raging
and so are Aiyana's -- she's twenty-eight and has had
only one other man in her life, "an older guy," a ten-
year affair which she's still caught up in but would
like to break away from -- and her parents are pressing
her to marry that same guy.  And they're loaded -- her
father, perhaps not just coincidentally, manufactures
biotech equipment -- and Elgie's deep in the hole

financially and about to go much deeper.  So --
interesting times ahead for them both.)
     This day by the calendar: I must peg it.  Lunarly
it's a beaut, the fourth anniversary of the wedding of
Z&G before the gathered personal deities.  They in turn
advised us to make it official before the community and
with the blessing of the state, which we of course did
do some nine moons later, on the 15th day (full moon) of
the eighth lunar month.  And pretty much ever since I've
had one or another copper band turning my left-hand ring
finger green, including right now, and am proud of them
all -- flash that copper for the multitude to gape at in
awe and stunnedness!
     By coincidence this is also the sesquicentennial
anniversary of the first Eurusan-style wedding performed
in our city back in 1853 and the sesquicentennial minus
three years of the infamous first Battle of J-town,
which followed by one day the signing of the even more
infamous treaty under which the local tribes were
stripped of their lands for a song and a sheaf of solemn
promises, only a few of which were kept -- and the
litigation regarding that shameful treaty still goes on
today to little effect and occasionally this jyzer right
here scopes a deposition of some sort related to it.
(The first Battle of J-town's only Cawk casualty,
perhaps not noted in these pages before now, was the
fifteen-year-old son of the aforementioned first Cawk
claimant of property atop south hill, including the land
on which Z and I now reside.)
     Fathers and sons!  My son also disappeared from my
life when he was fifteen.  And then in my Heavenly Year
came the reunion.  The ceremonial passing of the baton.
In this instance I've given him, among a few other
things, my best jacket, the vintage brown leather one.
It fits him quite well.  On me it's now a little tight.
     -- Meanwhile, to shift for a moment to contemporary
world affairs, war tensions just keep torquing up.  The
cabal is "steaming" over France and Germany's refusal to
support an immediate U.S. attack on Iraq.  The cabal is
applying all the pressure it can to gain Security

Council blessing but either way, yea or nay, it's a near
certainty an attack is imminent.  More and more troops
are leaving for the Middle East.  The public opposes the
war virtually everywhere, including now even in the U.S.
-- so says at least one poll -- but the cabal plunges
ahead regardless and many other governments fall in line
because of (A) our bribes or (B) fear of consequences to
their own status and longevity in office if they don't.
If the cabal can do "regime change" in Iraq, it can do
it anywhere.  And it's threatening to do just that, if
necessary, by repeating its idiot credo in an ever
louder voice:  If you're not with us, you're against us!
    UN report coming up Monday, our supreme leader's
State of the Union address Tuesday.  The week ahead
should tell the story.  -- And a good thing, because the
Heavenly Year concludes at week's end.  Wouldn't want to
leave any strings that big dangling that loose.  -- But
maybe I'll have to.  Final decisions may still be
postponed.  For me it'll likely all be a matter of
probabilities.  And those I can state right now.  Absent
a last-minute coup or resignation and flight into exile
by the supreme Iraqi leader, it's ninety-eight percent
certain the cabal will attack, and then it's only
slightly less likely the consequences for the world will
be calamitous.  The only remaining question of interest
is whether the attack will be sanctioned by the Security
Council.  I'd say it's less than fifty/fifty it will, in
which case the U.S. will be in contravention of
international law (as the president of France, among
other grandees, has publicly stated) and we can at least
hope for a Security Council resolution calling for an
invasion of the U.S. unless regime change happens here
within thirty days.  (Ha.  That's a joke.)
    So much for the fate of the planet from the war
angle.  Returning to the return of the prodigal son, I
must say even a minimalist jyze account of significant
events and developments related to his stay here is far
beyond my reach.  And all the marvelous, touching,
humorous, perplexing, heartening and heartrending
moments -- a meager random sampling of these is the best

I can offer.  And I'm not even sure I can come up with
the goods on that.  Have I mentioned it?  I'm running on
adrenaline, I'm emotionally exhausted, I'm spacy and
exhilarated and my memory banks, what few remain, are
massively overloaded.  -- And now a voice calls out from
below, "Ten minutes!"  Oh such exquisite timing!
     I'll stop for the night.  Get some rest.  Tomorrow
will be Elgie's last full day here.  Very early Saturday
morning I'll be taking him to the airport.  After
returning home from that I should have a chance to do
some catching up on the basics.  As for the rest -- or
no, rather as for the whole durn thing -- it'll be
reverbing for months or years.  And the meaning of all
this?  Only first assessments will be possible.  But I
can say this much: they'll be the opposite of the war
assessments.  Things with Elgie are looking very good!
Splendid!  It's true!


                       [+2]


     So the kid's gone home.  The whirlwind's passed,
setting me down ever so gently right here, still
stupefied, befuddled, delighted.  Amazed!
     Just the way a Heavenly Year ought to be at the far
end of its very late dramatic peak.
     Perched in and atop the big corner plant is the
"It's a boy!" stork.  Only now does it occur to me it's
served an auspicious purpose for the five or so months
it's been around (there or on the balcony).  Wish I'd
had my wits about me enough to point this out to Elgie.
A little late but the big stork arrives bearing the son
in a bundle suspended from its beak.  Never mind the
overt male-genitalia shape of the bundle.  Never mind
that the name written in the space provided on that
bundle is "Jyzeslinger G."  See -- I myself served as
the surrogate son until the real one could get up here.
The father is the surrogate child of the man (who is the
jyzeslinger!).  (Or does that make even cockeyed sense?)
     A fast trip to the airport at five a.m. after Z-

wiff stumbled out from our bedroom in her robe to say
goodbye.  Dark, few cars, those on the freeway going
very fast.  I'm pleased to be making no more spacy
driving blunders.  And at the drop-off a fine quick
embrace after the offspring unloads his luggage.  Then,
as he turns to go -- and I really like this -- he says,
"Hey, let's do that again!" and steps around to the
driver's-side door where I'm about to slide in and we do
it again.  "No tickling this time!" he warned.  Very
fine.  I'm digging it.  I'm still reeling.

Earlier I teared up a bit as we talked in the
living room.  It was only the third time, and it came as
I was mentioning the second time (the first was when we
were looking at the photo album at the hideaway).  That
second time happened in the car as I backed into the
garage stall with Z seated next to me and Elgie in the
backseat.  We'd been talking about when he'd had his big
growth spurt.  It had come at about the same age mine
did, he said, about twelve.  I said I didn't think I'd
heard about it at the time it occurred, probably because
I'd asked my own mother to spare me such details as she
might've gleaned from her talks with Lady S for fear I'd
go insane or my heart would break.

I've told him before: my separation from him wasn't
what I wanted.  I cared and loved always.  Now he's
seeing it and believing it.  Or at least starting to.
"So does this mean you approve of me?" he asked with an
impish smile at one point in that last talk.  "Well, I
approve of you too, Pops.  You make the grade with me."

A three-hour marathon this time (he sipping from a
bizarre drink only an MSM #1 fast-laner could tolerate:
aronia juice with a splash of scotch).  A couple of our
other talks were that long, and several more were an
hour or two.  By the end he seemed much more at ease.
No doubt I pontificated or avunculated a bit here and
there.  All this impacted wisdom thrashing to get out!

The last day was a laugher.  The three of us drove
up to the northeast burbs shortly after noon so Elgie
could take a look at one of the prime alternative-
medicine schools in the country.  (This is at the same

university where Z received her leadership master's, and
an old friend (female) now teaching there spotted her in
the lobby shortly after we arrived and came over for a
chat and then was visibly nonplussed by Elgie's saying
he was interested in biotech.  Could the inhabitants of
any campus in the country be less disposed to look
favorably upon such ambitions as his?  It was a good
idea of Z's to introduce him to the place.  The sight of
lots of serious, appealing alternative-world students
made a stronger statement than either of us ever could
manage about the benefits of a different approach than
his current one to matters of health and nutrition.

Then, because he wanted to see it, to the campus of
the software behemoth a tier of burbs farther out from
the city.  Building 11, Building 29, Building 50, on and
on and on.  Security is so tight post-9/11 that the
company declined to provide directions over the phone on
how to find the place; we had to rely on a call to
friend Wes P. from Z's book group (he used to work
there).  At one point I drove around and around a
traffic circle outside Building 17, I think it was, just
to show I could do it.  Z and I kept up an antiburban,
anti-Big Tech patter the whole time, amusing to us
anyway and seemingly to him too.  But we all know which
way the world's currently going and likely to keep going
-- until, that is, the final flameout/floodout.

Then to our region's "premier mall" in the
satellite city across the lake -- another Z idea, this
one maybe not so inspired.  But perhaps Elgie needed to
see our area can do malls too even if J. City itself
generally prefers not to.  Coffee, then book-buying at a
sterile chain bookstore at the mall (he'd expressed
interest in reading something on sibling theory, which
he'd never heard of before Z and I mentioned it).

Then back to J-town, a brief layover at 1511 for
freshening up, and onward to the west side for dinner
with Betty and Kat.  Stops along the way to admire the
spectacular downtown skyline view across the bay,
especially fine on this night of roaming clouds and
patches of clingy mist here and there, and then to walk

the beach along the northern shore (reminiscent to Elgie
of one he likes near MSM #1) and pose for pix atop the
base of the celebrated one-twentieth-scale Statue of
Liberty (only lately restored from its most recent
vandalizing).  Then dinner at the homestead restaurant,
an oversize history-drenched log cabin a block or so
from the 1852 landing site of the original Cawk invasion
party.  Another bit of inspired planning by Z.  Kat,
just back from a day of snowboarding, was starry-eyed
over Elgie.  Conversation was humorously enlivened by
yesterday's schoolyard incident: Kat and Avery nabbed in
flagrante French-kissing.  An embarrassing call home for
both followed, orchestrated by -- who else? -- the vice-
principal.  Betty said he couldn't stop laughing as he
described the kids' "vice."  But regs are regs.  And
tomorrow, no longer willing to trust Kat's good sense,
Betty will be taking her to Planned Parenthood.  This
happening one month to the day short of Kat's entry into
teenhood -- her thirteenth birthday, solar kind.

All the above, and also Betty's nonstop questions
put to Elgie and Z's annoyance with an overly brisk and
brusque waitperson, made for what Elgie later called an
"intriguing and very enjoyable" dinner.  I think he
really meant it.  Presumably it was the "family" part
that made it so.  (But would he rather have been in MSM
#1 with his buddies?  Earlier that morning another
friend called from down there to suggest he come back
that very afternoon -- Friday -- and Elgie replied, and
quite resolutely, as I stood next to him: "It's not
possible, we're going out to dinner!")

-- Vic called from MSM #2 and again from the J-town
airport last night trying to arrange a get-together with
me and Elgie but it wasn't to be.  Sadly.  Still I was
touched by the effort he made.

Today Z was away at a conference on race and social
justice.  After dropping off Elgie at the airport I was
too wasted to take up the J-book and so planned to get
back to it this past afternoon at the Tet Festival at
the fairgrounds -- as welcomings gear up for the Year of
the Sheep, or Year of the Ram as A-mart styles it, or

[ Jyze of the Heavenly Year : White Horse ]


Year of the Goat as Tet does, or Year of the Lamb as I
used to call it with Lady U -- a Lamb herself -- but I
wound up sleeping in until almost four p.m., and Z
arrived home shortly after that.  Later we dropped by a
new Asian "fusion" spot in the AQ for dinner -- it's
doing well at drawing a new and much younger crowd to
the area -- and while there we did the "post-visitems,"
as she dubbed them: lots of wistful talk, what this
might've meant and what that might've meant.  It's just
the start for those -- of course!
     Rain patter.  It's now ten past five in the a.m.
Already I'm back to my normal schedule.  But usually at
ten after five I don't feel anywhere near this tired.
     And about those gaps I wanted to fill in.  Haven't
gotten very far, no.  Will try again tomorrow.  And
then, denouement duly nodded to and telegraphed, it'll
be time for the grand Heavenly Year finale.


                        [+1]


     -- Jyze set up here once before.  A chair pulled
close to the atrium railing on the top floor of the
hideaway building.  Above, a large skylight fracturing
the upper portions of nearby skyscrapers in a blurry
kaleidoscopic effect across most of the ceiling.  Below
-- four stories down -- the two lit-up but venetian-
blinded windows of the Jyzer Ink office.  For sounds,
just the blowers of the heating system.  -- And now some
familiar loud voices from three stories below: the
Filipino transgender escort service (I jest not -- in
fact they're often whooping it up at this hour).
     Another day of recovery.  Super Bowl Sunday, as it
happens.  Earlier when I walked into the east-depot
saloon I caught the last two seconds (no more, no less)
of the game on the big-screen TV.  The saloon patrons
were not happy: the Raiders had their hooks handed to
them by the Buccaneers.  Or in a nod to the upcoming
rollover to the Sheep year we'll say they got fleeced.
     It was in the office a dozen feet to my left that

the toxic mold was first discovered two years ago.  Most
of the tenants up here landed in the hospital.  Another
lingering consequence is that far fewer plants dangle
from the atrium railings -- as noted before, they make
the air more hospitable to mold.  Smells fine to me up
here now though.  But if this entry stops abruptly,
well...guess I'll have been less lucky this time around.

     Sitting at my office desk I was realizing how the
hours Elgie and I spent down there passed in a daze.
That was true of the whole visit, yes, but especially
those hours.  I thought we'd have time to come back
there at least once more, maybe twice or three times
more, so I didn't try to show him everything at once.
Among the items he didn't see were three other photo
albums, several scrapbooks, Mentoka postcards, letters I
wrote to him or about him when he was an infant, a two-
binder collection of family letters going back three
generations.  Next visit for all those, I guess.  Or I
could start sending some of them down to him piecemeal.

     Another thought: it's a good thing we haven't yet
kept our vow, Z and I, and gone in to do our wills.  It
would've just been a big waste of time and money -- for
me anyway.  With Elgie in the picture now everything
needs rethinking.  -- True, he was in the picture before
as well, but then he was a remote mystery figure and I
was trying not to think about him too much.  Now's
different.  Just how, though, remains, like so much
else, to be seen.  Will he want item X or won't he?  If
he does, it's his, either directly or through Z.  His or
Kat's, I suppose.  And what's "it"?  Everything.  Which
isn't much, no, except for the huge collection of my own
words stored in that office down there.

     Today's also, to repeat, the anniversary of the
infamous Battle of J-town, the first one.  Tonight after
paying my usual respects to my lucky composite Brown
Horse I visited the site of the south blockhouse (where
a century-old stone building now stands) and then walked
the course of the stockade wall and two blocks farther
north to the hideaway-building door.  Imagined the
shells from the black U.S. warship, anchored just

offshore in the bay, whistling over my head.  The scores
of homeless drifters thronging the park tonight stood in
for the ghostly spirits warned of by the great eponymous
chief.  And war was in the air anyway, with the major
decision points coming up tomorrow at the UN and then
Tuesday with the State of the Union address.  Same kind
of decision faced by the invaders right here back in
1856, but involving different tribes and different
orders of magnitude in terms of population and distance
and firepower.  But still: will they go peacefully to
their backwater reservations we'll set aside for them in
the general vicinity where they've lived for eons or
will we have to disarm them by wiping them out?  Back
then it was the leader among the local chiefs who chose
to fight our orders who was regime-changed (and hanged
on trumped-up evidence later that same year -- and the
Natusan center I often walk by now is named after him).

An eight-page special section arrived with today's
Sunday OMP/FAP: "The Brink of War."  The latest rumor is
that the U.S. has caved to the opposition of four other
Security Council permanent members (France, Germany,
Russia, China) and will let the inspectors work for a
few more weeks.  The cabal is furious and mud is flying
over what they call the "European double-cross."  Our
supreme leader's ratings are sinking, opposition to the
war is increasing everywhere.  Even the mainstream
pundits are becoming aware this is an historic moment
for world power arrangements, quite possibly setting the
tone and the basic ground rules for decades to come.

I try to keep a sense of perspective.  If the U.S.
goes unilateral here, as it's saying it has every right
to do, that's very bad.  But if the U.S. and Europe join
forces to attack Iraq, that's also very bad -- and in
the long run, maybe even worse.  Rich against poor,
white against color, Christian against Muslim, West
against the rest.

And then there's Elgie's other country, Korea.  It
appears the global South and East are finally developing
the will to defy the United States, possibly even to
cast their lot with the successor state to the old

Celestial Empire.  If we attack Iraq unilaterally and win in a cakewalk, as the cabal's certain we will, few doubt North Korea will be next.  If we attack Iraq multilaterally and win in a cakewalk, the same.  Or maybe we'll take down Iran first, after Iraq, since they're right next door, and then go after North Korea. And then the big kahuna, the ultimate challenger, the successor state itself: China.

If an attack on Iraq can be averted, at least a faint long-term hope would remain alive that the world's focus could shift to avoiding the looming eco/climate catastrophe.  If that attack can't be averted, the hope would be much, much fainter.  It would be War of the World (if it isn't already) with everyone the loser.

Haven't I been saying this all year?  Well sure! It bears lots of repeating!

-- I promised myself to try to do some catchup on Elgie's visit.  It won't be as much as I'd like, but here goes.

Tuesday at brother Rob's -- Uncle Rob's to Elgie -- a look at the stairway family gallery and an extended talk in Rob's garret study, including an examination of some new genealogical material from Norway via Ron H. and the "lost branch."  It's written in Norwegian but contains a number of fascinating pictures, including one of the Perry S. clan taken about 1949 in Lahontan with wives and children present, myself among them -- I make my first entry into the genealogical annals into which I'll soon entirely disappear!  We also paged through parts of Rob's photo albums where the infant Elgie shows up several times.  And something I never knew before came to light: during a visit to MSM #1 in the mid eighties Rob took Elgie out to buy his very first turntable (thus in a sense launching his career as "DJ Glen").  -- And for its Heavenly Year relevance I'll note here that Rob has set up a new garret "Water Dragon Shrine" featuring various items Z and I have given him over his past few birthdays and Christmases.

Then the three of us drove to the railcar diner for a classic old-time Jyze City dinner out with drinks,

clearly an eye-opener for Elgie.  Vintage gum-snapping
waitress -- "You boys ready for another round?"  Rob and
Elgie appeared to enjoy each other's company quite a
lot.  I was especially pleased when Rob talked about how
much he'd admired Elgie's mother, Lady S, and how they'd
always gotten along well.  (But did Elgie hear the
unspoken part about others in the family who didn't get
along so well with her?  I think probably not.
Certainly Rob didn't mean to suggest it.)
     Next day, lunch with June at the Italian restaurant
right across the street from Vic and Jean's building,
preceded by an office visit at the utility (where a
dozen of Z's friends and coworkers gathered to meet her
"new stepson").  For June this luncheon was supposed to
be therapeutic, and I think it probably was.  She perked
right up at her first sight of Elgie.  Sat across from
us in the booth gazing at the two of us with shining
eyes and saying, "This is amazing.  This is
unbelievable."  Also: "If I saw him with his mother,
probably I'd think he looks like her too -- but still,
this is incredible."  Elgie was also impressed with
June, less by her law-school efforts, it seemed, or her
Confucian pedigree, than by the fact that her brother's
a widely admired professor in computer science at one of
the top-ranked tech universities in the country.  I was
personally touched when the three of us were walking up
to the high road (Z had already peeled off to her
office) that June made a point of telling Elgie I'm her
"very, very good friend" and "he and I have talked many,
many hours about you -- even all night sometimes."  And
then an aside to me: "Call me next week because I want
to hear everything!  This is really amazing!"  -- So it
seemed she'd been lifted out of her doldrums at least
temporarily.  And Z agreed: she thinks now I should see
June more often to bolster the healing process.  Which
I'll gladly do after the Heavenly Year ends (and June's
begins).
     And a raft of isolated details.  Several rafts.
The raft of Elgie's love-life alone could take up a few
dozen jyze pages.  Another raft for tales of his mother.

One for his childhood and youth history, one for his
adult history, one for his projected career.  A couple
of large miscellaneous rafts.  Imagine them all right
here -- because who has time now to launch such a
flotilla?  The last bus is due soon.

As the building blowers keep blowing.  The moon has
entered its last quarter of the last month of the
Heavenly Year -- in fact it put in a dramatic appearance
directly ahead of us as we drove to the airport, Elgie
and I, as if delivering its blessing -- or maybe just
grabbing a best-angle view on this astonishing sight.
(I too say it was astonishing, yes I do.  I see this
whole reunion just about the way June does.)

All week, meanwhile, Mama E's been in a heightened,
but not severe or alarming, delusional state.  She's
been leaving us dozens of voicemails, most of them on
the theme of "I didn't do it."  Just what "it" is we
haven't been able to figure out, but she's afraid
someone will tell us about "it" and she says we mustn't
believe that person.  Z's theory, which sounds plausible
to me, is that Mama E was shook up to learn Elgie was
staying with us and she now believes she could be
staying with us herself.  Somehow, that's Mama E's "it."

-- And so penultimate comes to ultimate and climax
to denouement and endgame to grand finale.  Celebrations
are already in progress.  This being Tet weekend, Little
Saigon at the eastern end of the AQ is at peak bustle.
Evan W.'s annual Chinese New Year's card came in -- a
little substandard this year, Z thinks, with its cross-
eyed Sheep.  Vic and Jean may throw another party, this
one for Chinese year's-end.  We're cleaning up the
apartment and appeasing the Kitchen God and following
all protocol.  We're ready.  I'm ready.  I'm exhausted.
But I can bring it for one last cluster, oh yes.

This cluster right here, Silver Snake, it's Z-
wiff's -- the year in which she was born -- and the last
words are for her.  She was fabulous this week.  Bent
over backwards, spent a bundle, helped guide me through
the hard parts.  I'm grateful to her beyond words --
even beyond all these words.

# SHORT BOOK F

# [ Jyze of the Black Horse ]

------

61

------

Not just another day.  But it's starting out in familiar fashion.  At the moment I'm holing up at Z-geist for an hour or two after walking down from the hill.  Drizzly afternoon.  Right outside the window here something unusual: a herd of the new upright single-axle scooters called Segways (JRX).  I didn't know that while standing in place with motors idling they fidget almost like horses.  Two utility meter readers are tending them out there as the others buy coffee in here.

Around the corner, the lucky Brown Horse which is all five Horses in one.  The day's too wet to sit outside where that Horse could deliver direct-line-of-sight blessings.  (And there they go, the Segway posse. Reminds me of a squadron of forklifts starting up after break at a factory -- the Crest Electronics factory of four decades ago, for instance, my summer job there -- in fact for two summers.)

Moment of truth on the war?  It's come and gone and we're all still hanging.  One of the UN's chief nuclear inspectors says Iraq appears to have no nuclear program, but the other one faults that country for failing to cooperate as fully as he'd've liked.  This gives new leverage to the cabal in its attempt to gain Security Council support for the invasion.  And then in his long-awaited State of the Union address last night our supreme leader leveled another threat, and a very familiar one: if the doubters on the Security Council don't come around, we'll invade Iraq without the council's sanction.  Snarled this cowboy-like right in their faces -- and ours.

What to say?  A miracle could happen?  Things look
very bad, both short and long term.  But I'm within a
few days of being a post-Heavenly elder.  It's well
known "things" often look just this way to fossils like
me.  Nonetheless I'll put my faith in the trend-buckers
of upcoming generations.  In my remaining viable time on
this shriekin' orb I'll be doing what I can to help them
out.
        Sounds straight-arrow?  Sounds less than enthused?
Sounds drab?  I dunno.  But this is how it is.
        As the old "Common Sense" guy once observed: "These
are the times that try" -- yeah, that.  Souls of soon-
to-be-body-shuckin' pale pink males especially, or at
least a few such specimens here and there.  But also a
few billion other souls of various politically decreed
categories.  It's common sense!  Such sense just needs a
few high-powered campaign donors, that's all.  Alas, to
the high-powered this sense makes no sense at all.
(Today is the "Common Sense" man's birthday.  Were he
around in our era he'd be lucky to find a columnist gig
with an alternative rag.  He'd be a blogger or a
zinester, most likely.  Wilderness voice.  Maybe holing
up right here in maximally remote Jyze City.)
        Trouble is, it's in the immediate interest of a
large majority of USAns to support the power structure
as it is, because they benefit from it and they're well
aware of this.  That this structure and the arrangements
it's based on are leading to catastrophe -- and not just
for others -- is something not so easily grokked by
those who depend on mainstream or far-right USAn media
for their information.  That's the rub right now.
-- And maybe that particular rub will dissolve when the
catastrophes start occurring.  9/11 is just the start of
the start.  A few more days like that along with a few
crises of the eco/climate kind and people might call for
a different approach vis-a-vis power structures.
        But scribbling all this over and over is no fun.
It's just more polemic.  Let's liven things up here!
        I'm on my way out to the Scandi quarter to pick up
the Z-mobile.  On the way back in I'm planning to drive

by the funeral home that'll be handling our ashes.
Maybe even stop and check it out.  Feel the vibes.
     All week it's been wind-down time regarding the
Elgie visit.  Moving things back into Z's room.
Noticing what went uneaten (both bags of tiny carrots
untouched -- he's just like Z on tiny carrots!).
Discovering he didn't return our extra set of house keys
(needed for Amanda's visits).  Discussing the meaning of
this, this, and this.  Announcing new aha!s.  Receiving
impressions from many who met the lad.  ("Really a cool
guy" -- trainer T.J. at the club.  "So handsome!" --
most of the women and all the gay men at Z's office.
"He's so -- what's the opposite of corrupted?" -- June.)
     For me I notice life now seems a little different.
I worry more.  I'm caught up in being a dad, however
delayed.  I ask others for advice on what I should do to
help Elgie grow, deepen, realize more about the various
things I think important for him (and for me too).  It's
not a bad feeling at all -- certainly not! -- but it's
puzzling.  Frustrating too, at least at times.  What can
I do that will have some real impact, with the young
fellow arriving at the exact halfway point of his own
lifetime Heavenly Year -- lunisolar birthday number
thirty -- just three weeks from today?
     No contacts from him yet.  Z-wiff wonders: will he
send a thank-you note?  Well, I hope he will, but I'm
not sure he'll feel obliged.  After all, he thanked me
at the airport (as I did him).  So should I suggest he
send one to her?  We've already set aside a big sheaf of
printed material to mail him (all of it bearing on his
interests, his career, sibling theory, his obsession
with tall female basketball players and having ten kids
and various other fascinomas).  And: what to get him for
his epochal birthday?  It'll be the first birthday
present I've ever given him -- or maybe there was one
when he turned a year old by the solar calendar, in
which case this will be the first he can consciously
appreciate, that is, if it's merited.  So what kind of
gift can I come up with that he'd really go for?
     Thoughts like these.  Issues.  How to approach.

will take time for sure to figure it all out or even a
small part of it.  Meanwhile just be a genial old Pops.
Be grateful for this startling change in our lives.
-- Yeah, but be engaged too.  Listen closely.  Show you
care.  "Caring is the only daring."  Keep daring in a
caring way.  Even if the going gets tough as it almost
certainly will now and then or possibly more often than
that or maybe much more often.

     -- As mentioned earlier, after I finish up here
I'll be heading out to the Scandi quarter.  It's a good
place to be visiting today.  That back-to-my-roots
feeling.  Did they burn a Viking ship out there
yesterday?  Norwegian Yule officially ended and it's a
Shetland Island custom to do such a torching -- I read
about it in yesterday's OMP -- and so why not do it
here?  A lot more Norskis here than in the Shetlands.

     Also today?  "Today in history" -- something highly
apt for a closing cluster.  The eponymous chief's famous
speech took place on this date in 1854.  Today the
ghosts are everywhere.  Across the street, hiding behind
the girders still propping up the old redbrick hotel (as
a woman walking by outside startles me by flipping up
her unfurled umbrella and, after it does a full twirl,
catching it quite stylishly, same as I frequently try to
do but rarely succeed).  -- And laptops stand atop the
window counter in here at all four seats, I see, in a
preternaturally neat little row, and all four diligently
attended to, painted fingertips tickling tiny keyboards.

     -- Last night a fine evening with Vic and Jean.  We
watched the State of the Union speech until we couldn't
stand it anymore and then turned the sound off.  When I
look at our supreme leader I see Alfred E. Neuman; Jean
sees Howdy Doody; Vic sees Hitler (JRX).  It was
touching to be with V&J when our own state governor, a
Chiusan, came on to offer the out-party response -- the
first descendant of Celestials ever to do that.  For him
we turned the sound back on.  Given his extreme middle-
of-the-road moderation -- old Master Kung himself
would've been proud of that -- he wasn't half bad.
     Even more touching, Jean's tales of her father's

funeral.  As noted before, she spoke to the mourners for
a lengthy period -- "It went by so fast but it had to be
at least, I don't know, half an hour?" -- at the
mountain cemetery outside her hometown before a crowd of
well over a hundred.  Afterwards her mother surprised
everyone when, after tottering up to the coffin with the
aid of her walker, she threw her arms around it -- the
coffin, this is -- as best she could and kissed it again
and again.  Among those present -- many quite wealthy,
including Jean's sister -- V&J were the bohemians.  Jean
no longer lets the hometown folks intimidate her: she
wears short skirts, beats her drums.  "Finally I can be
myself with them!"  We sat around talking for several
hours -- very good for her, Vic thought, because she's
feeling the pain now.  (Her big high-school Cawk-boy/
banker's-son "Splendor in the Grass" love didn't show up
for the funeral, though he still lives in the area.  She
wishes he had: "Somehow it would've completed the
circle."  -- The families on both sides having adamantly
opposed that relationship.  -- Oh: and she passed along
the news that Evan W., while opening a box of bananas at
A-mart, was bitten by a spider or scorpion and had to be
rushed to the hospital and that explained the shakiness
of the brushwork on his Year of the Sheep cards -- but
he went ahead with them anyway.  He sends out hundreds
every year and has done so for decades.)
        -- Yipe, cryeth the jyzer.  Yipe again!  It's time
to get moving here!  Long bus trip ahead and the garage
closes at 5:30.  -- And by the way, not only is this a
heavy grand-jury week but also a big back order came in
today.  The next couple of days will be a hard squeeze.
But -- and of course -- jyze must go on.  (Until Friday
night, that is, day after tomorrow, and then it stops --
maybe for good.  Which is to say: forever.  Literally
for good, not so much; forever, maybe.)


[+1]


And now real quick this question: how the heck did

I do it?  From zero to sixty-one in a mere 354 days!
From Water Horse to Water Horse, looping the loop -- 780
lifetime loops of the luna.
     So one last visit with the balloons.  They're
sagging again -- need yet another shot of laughing gas.
The supreme lightness of being a Heavenly Year balloon!
-- And these three will have been no other kind, known
no other life, because with the end of the year they
come down.  Poof!  Ssssss!  It was a very fine year!
     -- But was it?  For me personally, yes.  Never a
better.  Jyzing can all by itself make it so, after all,
and seems to have done just that once again.  But even
if not it would've been so anyway.  Deepening love with
Z, reconnecting with Elgie, meeting Vic -- that's one
terrific year right there.  Carrying on at a good level
with brother Rob, reopening possibilities with sister
Barb (though I still haven't called her), doing the
subunk bit with Kat and Betty -- also excellent.  And
I'm pleased about the array of friendships sustained
(certainly an abundance beyond any I've known before)
with Wei and Alison, Gerry and Leola, Jay and Melanie,
Jess and Gwen, Paz and Tobey, the D-clan young and old,
and especially with June (through good and bad -- and
just tonight was another of those goods, on which more
later).  And not to be forgotten, a major presence
throughout the year, lovable and exasperating, comical
and tragic: Mama E.  (Letting the credits roll here.)
     Take a bow, all of you -- current permanent cast of
the real life, jyze and nonjyze.  You've all been
fabulous!  (And Jean and Ro ought to be in there too.
And David and Stacy.  And Rob's Gail.  And Olwen and
Trent!  Sheez -- I can't even keep track of them all!)
     -- Big fat dictionary atop its spinning wooden Jyze
Central bookstand: I'll give it a couple of twirls
before I leave (in six minutes).  The Horse balloon is
spinning too right now, slowly, entirely on its own.
The many volumes of typed-up urjyze and protojyze
patiently await their long-promised careful loving
attention.  The family photos, the paintings, the
letters -- they'll all be staying on here.  As will I --

[ Jyze of the Heavenly Year : Black Horse ]

I've got work to do in this room and plenty of it, and
it's all the kind of work I relish.  But for now I've
gotta go.  -- And will continue this later at home,
because I've touched on only the personal aspect of the
year, and even left out a key part of that.  If not more
than one.

*          *

     -- And home later it is.  Mid fifth watch.  Double
hour of the Tiger.  Black armchair.  Clocks ticking in
triplicate.  Wind whoooing and wires bumping against the
house.  A Black Horse galloping atop the couch, framed
mola version, and it's saying (in an appended cartoon
bubble emerging from its muzzle, yellow writing on
orange backdrop), "Z-wiff tired, but da origami zebra
will be like our marital heaven...a work in progress."
     See?  Luck.  Wotta spouse.  She tried to make me an
origami zebra -- after coming in late and exhausted from
a twelve-hour day -- so I could celebrate my last
Heavenly day just right.  I have the mangled piece of
black-and-white-striped paper right here.  And when that
got all tangled up in her tired fingers, she thought of
the clever talking-horse-mola substitution.  You ask me,
that's one heckuva wiff.  And we'll soon be heading into
our seventh year together!
     So enough with the blissed-out uxoria.  Onward with
the review of year 4700.
     I'm one of those for whom the personal is to a high
degree political and vice versa.  So when I say it's
been a marvelous year personally, I'm leaving out a big
chunk of myself for which it's been a horrifying year.
It's been so bad!  Fascinating, yes, but also terrible.
Every trend line going in the wrong direction.  Reaction
on the rise everywhere with my own country leading the
backwards charge.  (Well, no, not everywhere.  We've
become so frightening that a few other countries seem to
be waking up to the dangers of the neocon/neolibs' USAn
world order -- Brazil, for example, and maybe even South
Korea.  And the descendants of the Celestials also seem
to be moving in a positive direction.)
     My Heavenly Year -- the extended sixty-year period

633

I'm talking about now -- began with Pearl Harbor.  The
enemy there was one of the few nations the West hadn't
succeeded in colonizing; now that nation was fighting
back by adopting the worst of the principles and tactics
of the colonizers.  The long arc follows: the West beats
back its challengers and extends its hegemony in the
Cold War era -- with the U.S. emerging as the victor in
the internal battle to rule the West itself (first over
Germany, then over the Soviet Union) -- the world of
European pink folks and their diaspora.  Now at the end
of the arc another colonized nation or bloc of nations
(this time neocolonized) has its own angry warriors
starting to fight back, with some adopting fascist
social structures and ways of fighting every bit as
cruel as our own.  Again we've declared war and are
lashing out with messianic fury to maintain and expand
our hegemony -- but this time, again, it's at a higher,
much more dangerous level and the planet itself and all
of human life are at risk.  It's pretty simple: we win,
humanity loses.  Period.  Except there's more: all but
the simplest forms of life lose.

Step by step this year we've watched the cabal in
Washington march us all down the plank.  We're now
poised to jump.  We'll be plunging into endless war.  We
can't win it and neither can anyone else.  At home USAns
will be living in a permanently militarized national-
security state.  The rest of the world will have it much
worse.

-- Go through the drill on this again?  No.  Once
more wheel out slim hopes.  Hope I'm wrong here!  Hope
tens or hundreds of millions won't have to die so the
U.S. can mindlessly preserve the "free enterprise"
(i.e., cappie) world order.  Hope most of the remaining
billions won't be forced to live in extreme poverty and
under severe repression in an environmentally stripped
and perilous world with sea levels rapidly rising and
nature in furious revolt against the ever-greater
insults we're hurling at it.

At five to five a.m. on a night suddenly no longer
stormy.  Blew itself out, it did!  (Always a sucker for

the pathetic fallacy, I grab for one more here -- maybe
the last.)  And it's almost dawn of the final day of the
Heavenly Year.  Or -- what time is dawn arriving these
days?  It's probably still an hour or so away.

That doesn't mean I won't stop now for the night.
Need to make a few last pleas to the Kitchen God before
that domestic deity flies off with a full report on me
and the rest of us -- to the Jade Emperor.  Who will
decide what we deserve for the coming year.  All of us.
Tell the Jade one not to be too harsh on us, O Kitchen
God.  But also tell the Jade one not to be too easy on
us -- and especially on the warlike tribe of USAns whose
hubris and arrogance and greed have surged out of
control.  Let it be known we deserve a severe
chastising, O Kitchen God, or whatever it might take to
bring on radical USAn behavior change.


[+1]


-- It's not so much the cold and the rain as the
wind as amplifier of the cold and the rain.  But here's
the shelter with a view at the hilltop strip park,
northeast corner of the wall-less structure, a soggy
picnic table.  Had to deploy several pieces of notebook
paper to wipe away half a dozen little bonbons of pigeon
droppings before I could sit down and I'm just hoping I
got them all.

Laid out before me to the northwest, the usual
spectacular city view in its winter mode: gray-wreathed
and streaked, many shades, near-white to near-black,
with dark diagonal crosshatchings of rainy areas,
and the water of the bay and the sound reflecting all
this.  Wide curving tongue of freeway emerging from the
downtown maw and seeming to sass us up here -- it's
clogged and all vehicle lights are shining at two p.m.

For many living on south hill or nearby it's the
last day of the year.  Grand finale getting underway.
Down below the firecrackers will soon be starting up
again in the AQ.  They've been building for the past

several nights -- including a brief skyrocket shoot-'em-
up about twelve hours ago (two a.m.) at the house across
the street from 1511 and one lot to the south -- and so
it appears tonight's rollover will be a noisy one.

    I mentioned "us."  Sassing us up here in the
shelter.  Three homeless guys and me, each of us holding
down a personal table.  No more free tables at the inn.
We're all porcinely layered up against the weather.  Two
of us have our gear in shopping carts, one has a
humongous aluminum-frame backpack, one a beat-up brown
backpack held together with duct tape (me).  Nobody's
talking.  We're all staring out at the view.  I'm the
only one who has a bed of winter pansies within plucking
distance.  And a big flock of unhappy pigeons is milling
around outside, likely hoping to return before too much
longer to these sheltered tables.

    News today?  War councils.  "Weeks, not months."
Our secretary of state -- former four-star (or was it
five?) army general of Afrusan provenance -- said to be
scrambling to gather believable evidence of Iraqi
"cheating" to present to the UN next week.  The cabal's
had months to hoke something up.  Will the war-resisting
nations buy the "evidence"?  Go for the preposterous
claim that it, whatever it is, justifies war?

    -- As always I liked walking over here from 1511.
Every house but one on the street behind ours, both
sides, is plastered with antiwar signs and banners.  And
several fruit trees, I'm not sure what kind, are already
in full bloom -- a form of natural tribute, as it
appears, to the block's political consciousness as well
as the power of climate change.  We're in late January!

    And now a word about June.  I met her at the chain
coffee shop at the base of the city's tallest building
-- the big black finger sticking up right now at north-
northwest on my compass here in the park, framed by bare
tree branches -- and presented her with her Heavenly
Year of the Water Sheep totem (personalized by Z and me
and made in Taiwan where she was born) and we took it up
to her office in the honeycomb cubicles on the 38th
floor of the municipal tower, the second-biggest upright

finger out there.  She promised she'll keep it next to
the plant atop her filing cabinet for her entire
Heavenly Year -- which starts later tonight.

It was another kind of baton-passing ceremony.  One
kind with Elgie, now this.  (And I reminded her that, as
she told me herself long ago, Horses and Sheep are
highly compatible and so we understand each other and
therefore must listen carefully to each other's counsel
and help each other through the hard times.  Her reply:
"Yes, of course.")

Then up to the central plaza with June, to the
interior food court.  As promised last week, lots of
talk about Elgie.  Many aspects of his story -- and so
mine with his mother -- are comprehensible only to
someone familiar with both USAn and traditional
Confucian culture, and June is deeply familiar with
both.  She catches on immediately.  Having raised two
sons mostly on her own, she has even more insights to
offer.  I listen.  I'll be listening in the future.
This learning process is only beginning.

A fine moment when I took both her hands and looked
deep into her eyes up close -- "recharging" her as best
I could and with Z-wiff's encouragement.  She's still
struggling to emerge from her depression.  She said she
thought it helped -- she felt more relaxed after our
talk.  And then she hopped on her bus and went back to
her big empty house in the northern burbs and I walked
three blocks south to the scope office.

Work up the wazoo.  On the first day of the coming
post-Heavenly (for me) Year I'll be needing to make an
extra trip in to try to catch up -- on a Saturday night!
Z-wiff will be disappointed.  We've been looking forward
to this return to normalcy for weeks.  Well, and so it's
starting out with a dose of fairly uncommon normalcy,
that's all -- uncommon but scarcely unheard of.

The guy at the far table's coughing a lot now.
I've been reading that TB's on the rise among the street
population here.  On the last bus of the night it's
prime hacking season and sometimes it gets pretty grim.

The Filipino independence hero and novelist

presiding all this time.  His bust, a dozen paces up the hill, looking right at us.  Wonder what he'd think of being an icon in a park of the imperial successors to the imperialists who murdered him.  He might enjoy the irony but would he let it undermine his indignation?  I don't think so!  And surely he'd be pleased to witness our little scene of supplication down here.  -- As a big working-type dude in a Jyze City baseball cap marches through dragging a very large black poodle who seems to find our shelter's bouquet of sniffs quite fascinating.

-- And several more guys just popped up from the hobo camp in the greenbelt "jungle/rez" down below. Workers from the DC castle at my back are sprinting for their SUVs illegally parked in the strip-park lot.  My feet are shivering.  The pigeons continue to be annoyed. It's time to go.  A hot shower and then I dress for the big hilltop New Year's Eve blowout.  And after that, sometime but I'm not sure when, a few last words.

*        *

Three a.m. and I'm on my way home from work. "Brain fried."  But here I am.  Sitting in the Z-mobile, however.  Passenger seat.  Only vehicle parked on this side of the street on the whole three-block stretch between A-mart and the AQ's main east-west drag.

Twelve full orbits of the moon ago I was sitting on the steps twenty feet to my right.  Gazing to the east in search of a moon I knew wouldn't be visibly rising, though rising it still was.  Tonight I'm gazing in that same direction, in tribute, in closure mode, in celebration, and this time moonrise is still about five hours away.  But I know I wouldn't be able to get up in the middle of my upside-down night to do what I'm doing now.  This is close enough.  Just about splits the difference between the official midnight solar start or eleven p.m. (Rat hour) lunar start of the new day and the 8:14 a.m. technical start of the new lunar year.

Ghost rider in the sky -- that's my nag, Water Horse, galloping off, Black, blending in, invisible, but still unquestionably up there, in motion.  Yee-ha!

Plutocrat #2's building behind me, A-mart across to

the left (with restaurant lights on, New Year's red-and-
white lights still blazing, big stone lantern floodlit
too), service station to the right (it's a different
brand of gas now), big empty A-mart parking lot straight
ahead and the orange-brick DC castle hovering above that
half a mile away and four or five hundred feet up in the
usual spot on the northern prow of the hill, still
floodlit at night but not as brightly as it was a year
ago (owing to a municipal cost-saving measure).  And
then the big expanse of eastern sky.  Cloudy.  Not rainy
at this moment but the streets and just about everything
else in sight are wet.  Glittery.  A city trash-pickup
truck scoots by, odd little possumlike vehicle, the kind
that -- like me! -- comes out mainly at night.
     What am I doing here?  Ending it.  Offering up this
jyze to the gods of our own human imagining, which is to
say: all of them (to my knowledge).  Practicing
obeisance.  Noting once again that, as always, just
about everything here in the earthly realm will have to
be left hanging.  The political stuff, the personal
stuff.  How will it all come out?  World fate?  Well of
course we just don't know.  Art and religion and
rationality may pretend otherwise; believe in what one
or two or even all three of those grand abstractions
have to tell us and you can also believe you know.  But
you don't know.  Jyze has no illusions on this score.
     Tonight we feasted at the hilltop Chinese
restaurant and then listened to a Celestial trio play
marvelously on antique instruments -- zitherlike and
fiddlelike -- whose names no one at our table could
pronounce.  It was a neighborhood gathering of seventy
or eighty folks beneath a gorgeous mural as long as the
room itself -- mountains, a lake, a pavilion, cavorting
maidens.  It was a lovely way to end the year.  Later as
I held the car door open for Z-wiff while dropping her
off at home on my way to work I told her to take a good
look -- "It's the last time you'll see me in a Heavenly
upright state."  And then she to me in our driveway
after hopping out: "Time for one last Heavenly kiss?"
     Now like Cinderella after the ball (oh so

platitudinously!) we repledge our ultimate loyalty to the Emperor Quotidian in its delightful full uncapped manifestation.

Dead ahead, I should mention, a set of alternately blinking "Do Not Enter" signs in pink. Down below a freight train is rumbling by, horn trumpeting. Every now and then a string of firecrackers goes off somewhere not too far away. And if I lean forward, I can see -- already! -- part of a rippling Year of the Ram flag where the Year of the Horse flag used to be.

A thought that snuck up on me a few days ago: jyze is now entering its tenth year of existence. It's had close to a full decade's run! More than I ever dreamed possible. Jyze has brought me new life. -- And I'm saying it continues to do so, yes. But will jyze itself continue? Well, I don't know. For me, maybe it will and maybe it won't. I need some time off, but I could come back in a year, or at age 64, say, or at 70 or 72 (the next Horse year) or 75 or at any time if the circumstances were compelling. Or I could devote myself to something else -- typing up all this jyze, as one possibility, and trying to make it at least passably readable. Or -- focus on the ur and the proto. Or -- on painting. Or -- on loving. Or -- on trying to help wrench the world off the horrific course my own country has done far more than any other to set it on. Or -- on all of the above. Or -- on any combination, as long as it includes the two last-named and the first-named.

For others? Any other jyzers out there? I hope so. I recommend the practice highly. You can learn a lot from it and have a fine time doing it and feel afterwards you've accomplished something. And you'll be convinced you see everything around you much better than you ever did before, and quite possibly that will be the actual case. Hard to beat that.

I'm holding out the baton, ready to pass it on.

-- And I just wanna say it once more: it's been Heavenly!


END